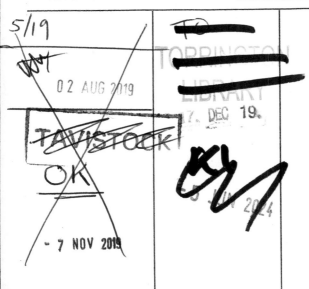

The Times once wrote that 'Mr Watson's short stories are spring-loaded with effect, compressed with a drama that, in others, might take a novel to eke out' while the *Times Literary Supplement* went three better: 'Many of his stories contain enough intellectual substance to fuel a trilogy'—consequently this first-ever collection of his best stories might be the equivalent of 72 books.

In 'An Appeal to Adolf' the Third Reich invades England by way of very long battleships bridging the Channel, while two gay sailors fret about the Führer's hatred for Wittgenstein. In 'The Great Escape' rebel angels set Hell in motion towards a very distant God, planning to harpoon the deity. 'Swimming with the Salmon' tells of the seduction by pheromones of a Scottish priestess who looks after genetically engineered superfish; while in 'The Moon and Michelangelo' a stone mason from Oxford achieves a petrifying transcendence on an alien planet. In Jerusalem a gate opens to a domain of inexplicable beings; while in ancient Babylon, recreated in the Arizona desert, immigrants from our own time encounter strange destinies. Here is science fiction of the highest calibre, and horror too, while other stories are surreally fantastical.

So as to cut to the cream, this selection by the author is guided by public opinion in the form of nominations for awards, inclusion in 'best of the year' anthologies as well as in other reprint volumes, and the number of translations over the years, although he has also slipped in some of his own less acknowledged favourites. Altogether this is an amazing showcase of treasures spanning 30 years from Ian Watson's pen (and typewriter, and computer).

The Best of
Ian Watson

The Best of
Ian Watson

IAN WATSON

EDITED BY NICK GEVERS

2014

Contents

The Best of
Ian Watson

¡Para Guapa!

The Very Slow Time Machine

(1990)

THE VERY SLOW TIME MACHINE—FOR CONVENIENCE: THE VSTM— made its first appearance at exactly midday 1 December 1985 in an unoccupied space at the National Physical Laboratory. [2013: The term VSTM is introduced retrospectively in view of our subsequent understanding of the problem.] It signalled its arrival with a loud bang and a squall of expelled air. Dr Kelvin, who happened to be looking in its direction, reported that the VSTM did not exactly *spring* into existence instantly, but rather expanded very rapidly from a point source, presumably explaining the absence of a more devastating explosion as the VSTM jostled with the air already present in the room. Later, Kelvin declared that what he had actually seen was the *implosion* of the VSTM. Doors were sucked shut by the rush of air, instead of bursting open, after all. However it was a most confused moment—and the confusion persisted, since the occupant of the VSTM (who alone could shed light on its nature) was not only time-reversed with regard to us, but also quite crazy.

One infuriating thing is that the occupant visibly grows saner and more presentable (in his reversed way) the more that time passes. We feel that all the hard work and thought devoted to the enigma of the VSTM is so much energy poured down the entropy sink—because the answer is going to come from him, from inside, not from us; so that we may as well just have bided our time until his condition improved (or, from his point of view, began to degenerate). And in the meantime his arrival distorted and perverted essential research at our laboratory from its course without providing any tangible return for this.

The VSTM was the size of a small caravan; but it had the shape of a huge lead sulphide, or galena, crystal—which is, in crystallographer's jargon, an octahedron-with-cube formation consisting of eight large hexagonal faces with six smaller faces filling in the gaps. It perched precariously—but immovably—on the base square, the four lower hexagons bellying up and out towards its waist where four more squares (oblique, vertically) connected with the mirror-image upper hemisphere, rising to a square north pole. Indeed it looked like a kind of world globe, lopped and sheered into flat planes; and has remained very much a separate, private world to this day, along with its passenger.

All faces were blank metal except for one equatorial square facing south-wards into the main body of the laboratory. This was a window—of glass as thick as that of a deep-ocean diving bell—which could apparently be opened from inside, and only from inside.

The passenger within looked as ragged and tattered as a tramp; as crazy, dirty, woe-begone and tangle-haired as any lunatic in an ancient Bedlam cell. He was apparently very old; or at any rate long solitary confinement in that cell made him seem so. He was pallid, crookbacked, skinny and rotten-toothed. He raved and mumbled soundlessly at our spotlights. Or maybe he only mouthed his ravings and mumbles, since we could hear nothing what-ever through the thick glass. When we obtained the services of a lipreader two days later the mad old man seemed to be mouthing mere garbage, a mishmash of sounds. Or was he? Obviously no one could be expected to lip-read backwards; already, from his actions and gestures, Dr Yang had suggested that the man was time-reversed. So we video-taped the passenger's mouthings and played the tapes backwards for our lip-reader. Well, it was still garbage. Backwards or forwards, the unfortunate passenger had visibly cracked up. Indeed, one proof of his insanity was that he should be trying to talk to us at all at this late stage of his journey rather than communicate by holding up written messages as he has now begun to do. (But more of these messages later; they only begin—or, from his point of view, cease—as he descends further into madness in the summer of 1989.)

Abandoning hope of enlightenment from him, we set out on the track of scientific explanations. (Fruitlessly. Ruining our other, more important work. Overturning our laboratory projects—and the whole of physics in the process.)

To indicate the way in which we wasted our time, I might record that the first 'clue' came from the shape of the VSTM which, as I said, was that of a lead sulphide or galena crystal. Yang emphasized that galena is used as a semiconductor in crystal rectifiers: devices for transforming alternating current into direct current. They set up a much higher resistance to an electric current flowing in one direction than another. Was there an analogy with the current of time? Could the geometry of the VSTM —or the geometry of energies circulating in its metal walls, presumably interlaid with printed circuits—effectively impede the forward flow of time, and reverse it? We had no way to break into the VSTM. Attempts to cut into it proved quite ineffective and were soon discontinued, while X-raying it was foiled, conceivably by lead alloyed in the walls. Sonic scanning provided rough pictures of internal shapes, but nothing as intricate as circuitry; so we had to rely on what we could see of the outward shape, or through the window— and on pure theory.

Yang also stressed that galena rectifiers operate in the same manner as diode valves. Besides transforming the flow of an electric current they can also *demodulate*. They separate information out from a modulated carrier wave—as in a radio or TV set. Were we witnessing, in the VSTM, a machine for separating out 'information'—in the form of the physical vehicle itself, with its passenger—from a carrier wave stretching back through time? Was the VSTM a solid, tangible analogy of a three-dimensional TV picture, played backwards?

We made many models of VSTMs based on these ideas and tried to send them off into the past, or the future—or anywhere for that matter. They all stayed monotonously present in the Laboratory, stubbornly locked to our space and time.

Kelvin, recalling his impression that the VSTM had seemed to expand outward from a point, remarked that this was how three-dimensional beings such as ourselves might well perceive a four-dimensional object first impinging on us. Thus a 4-D sphere would appear as a point and swell into a full sphere then contract again to a point. But a 4-D octahedron-and-cube? According to our maths this shape couldn't have a regular analogue in 4-space, only a simple octahedron could. Besides, what would be the use of a 4-D time machine which shrank to a point at precisely the moment when the passenger needed to mount it? No, the VSTM wasn't a genuine four-dimensional body; though we wasted many weeks running computer programmes to describe it as one, and arguing that its passenger was a normal 3-space man imprisoned within a 4-space structure—the discrepancy of one dimension between him and his vehicle effectively isolating him from the rest of the universe so that he could travel hindwards.

That he was indeed travelling hindwards was by now absolutely clear from his feeding habits (i.e. he regurgitated) though his extreme furtiveness about bodily functions coupled with his filthy condition meant that it took several months before we were positive, on these grounds.

All this, in turn, raised another unanswerable question: if the VSTM was indeed travelling backwards through time, precisely where did it *disappear* to, in that instant of its arrival on 1 December 1985? The passenger was hardly on an archaeological jaunt, or he would have tried to climb out.

At long last, on midsummer day 1989, our passenger held up a notice printed on a big plastic eraser slate.

CRAWLING DOWNHILL, SLIDING UPHILL!

He held this up for ten minutes, against the window. The printing was spidery and ragged; so was he.

This could well have been his last lucid moment before the final descent into madness, in despair at the pointlessness of trying to communicate with us. Thereafter it would be *downhill all the way,* we interpreted. Seeing us with all our still eager, still baffled faces, he could only gibber incoherently thenceforth like an enraged monkey at our sheer stupidity.

He didn't communicate for another three months.

When he held up his next (i.e. penultimate) sign, he looked slightly sprucer, a little less crazy (though only comparatively so, having regard to his final mumbling squalor).

THE LONELINESS! BUT LEAVE ME ALONE!
IGNORE ME UNTIL 1995!

We held up signs (to which, we soon realised, his sign was a response):

ARE YOU TRAVELLING BACK THROUGH TIME? HOW? WHY?

We would have also dearly loved to ask: WHERE DO YOU DISAPPEAR TO ON DECEMBER 1 1985? But we judged it unwise to ask this most pertinent of all questions in case his disappearance was some sort of disaster, so that we would in effect be foredooming him, accelerating his mental breakdown. Dr Franklin insisted that this was nonsense; he broke down *anyway*. Still, if we *had* held up that sign, what remorse we would have felt: because we *might* have caused his breakdown and ruined some magnificent undertaking . . . We were certain that it had to be a magnificent undertaking to involve such personal sacrifice, such abnegation, such a cutting off of oneself from the rest of the human race. This is about all we were certain of.

(1995)

No progress with our enigma. All our research is dedicated to solving it, but we keep this out of sight of him. While rotas of postgraduate students observe him round the clock, our best brains get on with the real thinking elsewhere in the building. He sits inside his vehicle, less dirty and dishevelled now, but monumentally taciturn: a trappist monk under a vow of silence. He spends most of his time re-reading the same dog-eared books, which have fallen to pieces back in our past: Defoe's *Journal of the Plague Year* and *Robinson Crusoe* and Jules Verne's *Journey to the Centre of the Earth*; and listening to what is presumably taped music—which he shreds from the cassettes back in 1989, flinging streamers around his tiny living quarters in a brief mad fiesta (which of course we see as a sudden frenzy of disentangling and repackaging, with maniacal speed and neatness, of tapes which have lain around, trodden underfoot, for years).

Superficially we have ignored him (and he, us) until 1995; assuming that his last sign had some significance. Having got nowhere ourselves, we expect something from him now.

Since he is cleaner, tidier and saner now, in this year 1995 (not to mention ten years younger) we have a better idea of how old he actually is; thus some clue as to when he might have started his journey.

He must be in his late forties or early fifties—though he aged dreadfully in the last ten years, looking more like seventy or eighty when he reached 1985. Assuming that the future does not hold in store any longevity drugs (in which case he might be a century old, or more!) he should have entered the VSTM sometime between 2010 and 2025. The later date, putting him in his very early twenties if not teens, does rather suggest a 'suicide volunteer' who is merely a passenger in the vehicle. The earlier date suggests a more mature researcher who played a major role in the development of the VSTM and was only prepared to test it on his own person. Certainly, now that his madness has abated into a tight, meditative fixity of posture, accompanied by normal activities such as reading, we incline to think him a man of moral stature rather than a time-kamikaze; so we put the date of commencement of the journey around 2010 to 2015 (only fifteen to twenty years ahead) when he will be in his thirties.

Besides theoretical physics, basic space science has by now been hugely sidetracked by his presence.

The lead hope of getting man to the stars was the development of some deep-sleep or refrigeration system. Plainly this does not exist by 2015 or so, otherwise our passenger would be using it. Only a lunatic would voluntarily sit in a tiny compartment for decades on end, ageing and rotting, if he could sleep the time away just as well, and awake as young as the day he set off. On the other hand, his life-support systems seem so impeccable that he can exist for decades within the narrow confines of that vehicle using recycled air, water and solid matter to 100 per cent efficiency. This represents no inconsiderable outlay in research and development—which must have been borrowed from another field, obviously the space sciences. Therefore the astronauts of 2015 or thereabouts require very long-term life support systems capable of sustaining them for years and decades, up and awake. What kind of space travel must they be engaged in, to need these? Well, they can only be going to the stars—the slow way; though not a *very* slow way. Not hundreds of years; but decades. Highly dedicated men must be spending many years cooped up alone in tiny spacecraft to reach Alpha Centauri, Tau Ceti, Epsilon Eridani or wherever. If their surroundings are so tiny, then any extra payload costs prohibitively. Now who would contemplate such a journey merely out of curiosity? No one. The notion is ridiculous—*unless* these heroes are carrying something to their destinations which will then link it inexorably and instantaneously with Earth. A tachyon descrambler is the only obvious explanation. They are carrying with them the other end of a tachyon-transmission system for beaming material objects, and even living human beings, out to the stars!

So, while one half of physics nowadays grapples with the problems of reverse-time, the other half, funded by most of the money from the space vote, pre-empting the whole previously extant space programme, is trying to work out ways to harness and modulate tachyons.

These faster-than-light particles certainly *seem* to exist; we're fairly certain of that now. The main problem is that the technology for harnessing them is needed *beforehand,* to prove that they do exist and so to work out exactly *how* to harness them.

All these reorientations of science—because of *him* sitting in his enigmatic vehicle in deliberate alienation from us, reading *Robinson Crusoe,* a strained expression on his face as he slowly approaches his own personal crack-up.

(1996)

If you were locked up in a VSTM for X years, would you want a calendar on permanent display—or not? Would that be consoling or taunting? Obviously his instruments are calibrated—unless it was completely fortuitous that his journey ended on 1 December 1985 at precisely midday! But can he see the calibrations? Or would he prefer to be overtaken suddenly by the end of his journey, rather than have the slow grind of years unwind itself? You see, we are trying to explain why he did not communicate with us in 1995.

Convicts in solitary confinement keep their sanity by scratching five-barred gates of days on the walls with their fingernails; the sense of time passing keeps their spirits up. But on the other hand, tests of time perception carried out on potholers who volunteered to stay below ground for several months on end show that the internal clock lags grossly—by as much as two weeks in a three month period. Our VSTM passenger might gain a reprieve of a year—or five years!—on his total subjective journey time, by ignoring the passing of time. The potholers had no clue to night and day; but then, neither does he! Ever since his arrival, lights have been burning constantly in the laboratory; he has been under constant observation.

He isn't a convict, or he would surely protest, beg to be let out, throw himself on our mercy, give us some clue to the nature of his predicament. Is he the carrier of some fatal disease—a disease so incredibly infectious that it must affect the whole human race unless he were isolated? Which can only be isolated by a time capsule? Which even isolation on the Moon or Mars would not keep from spreading to the human race? He hardly appears to be.

Suppose that he had to be isolated for some very good reason, and suppose that he concurs in his own isolation (which he visibly does, sitting there reading Defoe for the *n*th time), what demands this unique dissection of one man from the whole continuum of human life and from his own time and space? Medicine, psychiatry, sociology, all the human sciences are being drawn into the problem in the wake of physics and space science. Sitting there doing nothing, he has become a kind of funnel for all the physical and social sciences: a human black hole into which vast energy pours, for a very slight increase in our radius of understanding. That single individual has accumulated as much disruptive potential as a single atom accelerated to the speed of light—which requires all the available energy in the universe to sustain it in its impermissible state.

Meanwhile the orbiting tachyon laboratories report that they are just on the point of uniting quantum mechanics, gravitational theory, and relativity; whereupon they will at last 'jump' the first high-speed particle packages over the C-barrier into a faster-than-light mode, and back again into our space. But they reported *that* last year—only to have their particle packages 'jump back' as antimatter, annihilating five billion dollars' worth of equipment and taking thirty lives. They hadn't jumped into a tachyon mode at all, but had 'möbiused' themselves through wormholes in the space-time fabric.

Nevertheless, prisoner of conscience (his own conscience, surely!) or whatever he is, our VSTM passenger seems nobler year by year. As we move away from his terminal madness, increasingly what strikes us is his dedication, his self-sacrifice (for a cause still beyond our comprehension), his Wittgensteinian spirituality. 'Take him for all in all, he is a Man. We shall not look upon his like . . . ' Again? We shall look upon his like. Upon the man himself, gaining stature every year! That's the wonderful thing. It's as though Christ, fully exonerated as the Son of God, is uncrucified and his whole life re-enacted before our eyes in full and certain knowledge of his true role. (Except . . . that this man's role is silence.)

(1997)

Undoubtedly he is a holy man who will suffer mental crucifixion for the sake of some great human project. Now he re-reads Defoe's *Plague Year*, that classic of collective incarceration and the resistance of the human spirit and human organizing ability. Surely the 'plague' hint in the title is irrelevant. It's the sheer force of spirit which beat the Great Plague of London, that is the real keynote of the book.

Our passenger is the object of popular cults by now—a focus for finer feelings. In this way his mere presence has drawn the world's peoples closer together, cultivating respect and dignity, pulling us back from the brink of war, liberating tens of thousands from their concentration camps. These cults extend from purely fashionable manifestations—shirts printed with his face, now neatly shaven in a Vandyke style; rings and worry-beads made from galena crystals—through the architectural (octahedron-and-cube meditation modules) to life-styles themselves: a Zen-like 'sitting quietly, doing nothing'.

He's Rodin's *Thinker,* the *Belvedere Apollo,* and Michelangelo's *David* rolled into one for our world as the millennium draws to its close. Never have so many copies of Defoe's two books and the Jules Verne been in print before. People memorize them as meditation exercises and recite them as the supremely lucid, rational Western mantras. The National Physical Laboratory has become a place of pilgrimage, our lawns and grounds a vast camping site—Woodstock and Avalon, Rome and Arlington all in one. About the sheer tattered degradation of his final days less is said; though that has its cultists too, its late twentieth-century anchorites, its Saint Anthonies pole-squatting or cave-immuring themselves in the midst of the urban desert, bringing austere spirituality back to a world which appeared to have lost its soul—though this latter is a fringe phenomenon; the general keynote is nobility, restraint, quiet consideration for others.

And now he holds up a notice.

I IMPLY **NOTHING**. PAY NO ATTENTION TO MY PRESENCE.
KINDLY GET ON DOING YOUR OWN THINGS.
I CANNOT EXPLAIN TILL 2000.

He holds it up for a whole day, looking not exactly angry, but slightly pained. The whole world, hearing of it, sighs with joy at his modesty, his self-containment, his reticence, his humility. This must be the promised 1995 message, two years late (or two years early; obviously he still has a long way to come). Now he is Oracle; he is the Millennium. This place is Delphi.

The orbiting laboratories run into more difficulties with their tachyon research; but still funds pour into them, private donations too on an unprecedented scale. The world strips itself of excess wealth to strip matter and propel it over the interface between sub-light and trans-light.

The development of closed-cycle living pods for the carriers of those tachyon receivers to the stars is coming along well; a fact which naturally raises the paradoxical question of whether his presence has in fact stimulated the development of the technology by which he himself survives. We at the

National Physical Laboratory and at all other such laboratories around the world are convinced that we shall soon make a breakthrough in our understanding of time-reversal—which, intuitively, should connect with that other universal interface in the realm of matter, between our world and the tachyon world—and we feel too, paradoxically, that our current research must surely lead to the development of the VSTM which will then become so opportunely necessary to us, for reasons yet unknown. No one feels they are wasting their time. He is the Future. His presence here vindicates our every effort, even the blindest of blind alleys.

What kind of Messiah must he be, by the time he enters the VSTM? How much charisma, respect, adoration and wonder must he have accrued by his starting point? Why, the whole world will send him off! He will be the focus of so much collective hope and worship that we even start to investigate *Psi* phenomena seriously: the concept of group mental thrust as a hypothesis for his mode of travel—as though he is vectored not through time or 4-space at all but down the waveguide of human will-power and desire.

(2001)

The millennium comes and goes without any revelation. Of course that is predictable; he is lagging by a year or eighteen months. (Obviously he can't see the calibrations on his instruments; such was his choice—that was his way to keep sane on the long haul.)

But finally, now in the autumn of 2001, he holds up a sign, with a certain quiet jubilation:

WILL I LEAVE 1985 SOUND IN WIND & LIMB?

Quiet jubilation, because we have already (from his point of view) held up the sign in answer:

YES! YES!

We're all rooting for him passionately. It isn't really a lie that we tell him. He did leave relatively sound in wind and limb. It was just his mind that was in tatters. Maybe that is inessential, irrelevant, or he wouldn't have phrased his question to refer merely to his physical body.

He must be approaching his take-off point. He's having a mild fit of tenth-year blues, first decade anxiety, self-doubt; which we clear up for him.

Why doesn't he know what shape he arrived in? Surely that must be a matter of record before he sets off . . . *No!* Time can not be invariable, determined. Not even the Past. Time is probabilistic. He has refrained from comment for all these years so as not to unpluck the strands of time past and reweave them in another, undesirable way. A tower of strength he has been. *Ein' feste Burg ist unser Zeitgänger!* Well, back to the drawing board, and to probabilistic equations for (a) tachyon-scatter out of normal space (b) time-reversal.

A few weeks later he holds up another sign, which must be his promised Delphic revelation:

I AM THE MATRIX OF MAN.

Of course! Of course! He has made himself that over the years. What else?

A matrix is a mould for shaping a cast. And indeed, out of him we have been moulded increasingly since the late 1990s, such has been his influence.

Was he sent hindwards to save the world from self-slaughter by presenting such a perfect paradigm—which only frayed and tattered in the Eighties when it did not matter any more; when he had already succeeded?

But a matrix is also an array of components for translating from one code into another. So Yang's demodulation of information hypothesis is revived, coupled now with the idea that the VSTM is perhaps a matrix for transmitting the 'information' contained in a man across space and time (and the man-transmitter experiments in orbit redouble their efforts); with the corollary (though this could hardly be voiced to the enraptured world at large) that perhaps the passenger was *not there* at all in any real sense; and he had never been; that we merely were witnessing an experiment in the possibility of transmitting a man across the galaxy, performed on a future Earth by future science to test out the degradation factor: the decay of information— mapped from space on to time so that it could be observed by us, their predecessors! Thus the onset of madness (i.e. information decay) in our passenger, timed in years from his starting point, might set a physical limit in *light-years* to the distance to which a man could be beamed (tachyonically?). And this was at once a terrible kick in the teeth to space science—and a great boost. A kick in the teeth, as this suggested that physical travel through interstellar space must be impossible, perhaps because of Man's frailty in face of cosmic ray bombardment; and thus the whole development of intensive closed-cycle life-pods for single astronaut couriers must be deemed irrelevant. Yet a great boost too, since the possibility of a receiverless transmitter loomed. The now elderly Yang suggested that 1 December 1985 was actually a moment of lift-off to the stars. Where our passenger went then, in all his madness, was to a point in space thirty or forty light years distant. The VSTM was thus the testing to destruction of a future man-beaming system and practical future models would only deal in distances (in times) of the order of seven or eight years. (Hence no other VSTMs had imploded into existence, hitherto.)

(2010)

I am tired with a lifetime's fruitless work; however, the human race at large is at once calmly loving and frenetic with hope. For we must be nearing our goal. Our passenger is in his thirties now (whether a live individual, or only an epiphenomenon of a system for transmitting the information present in a human being: literally a 'ghost in the machine'). This sets a limit. It sets a limit. He couldn't have set off with such strength of mind much earlier than his twenties or (I sincerely hope not) his late teens. Although the teens are a prime time for taking vows of chastity, for entering monasteries, for pledging one's life to a cause . . .

(2015)

Boosted out of my weariness by the general euphoria, I have successfully put off my retirement for another four years. Our passenger is now in his middle twenties and a curious inversion in his 'worship' is taking place, representing (I think) a subconscious groundswell of anxiety as well as joy. Joy, obviously, that the moment is coming when he makes his choice and steps into the VSTM, as Christ gave up carpentry and stepped out from Nazareth. Anxiety, though, at the possibility that he may pass beyond this critical point, towards infancy; ridiculous as this seems! He knows how to read books; he couldn't have taught himself to read. Nor could he have taught himself how to speak *in vitro*—and he has certainly delivered lucid, if mysterious, messages to us from time to time. The hit song of the whole world, nevertheless, this year is William Blake's 'The Mental Traveller' set to sitar and gongs and glockenspiel...

> *For as he eats and drinks he grows*
> *younger and younger every day;*
> *And on the desert wild they both*
> *Wander in terror and dismay...*

The unvoiced fear represented by this song's sweeping of the world being that he may yet evade us; that he may slide down towards infancy, and at the moment of his birth (whatever life-support mechanisms extrude to keep him alive till then!) the VSTM will implode back whence it came: sick joke of some alien superconsciousness, intervening in human affairs with a scientific 'miracle' to make all human striving meaningless and pointless. Not many people feel this way openly. It isn't a popular view. A man could be torn limb from limb for espousing this in public. The human mind will never accept it; and purges this fear in a long song of joy which at once mocks and copies and adores the mystery of the VSTM.

Men put this supreme *man* into the machine. Even so, Madonna and Child does haunt the world's mind... and a soft femininity prevails—men's skirts are the new soft gracious mode of dress in the West. Yet he is now so noble, so handsome in his youth, so glowing and strong; such a Zarathustra, locked up in there.

(2018)

He can only be 21 or 22. The world adores him, mothers him, across the unbridgeable gulf of reversed time. No progress in the Solar System, let alone on the interstellar front. Why should we travel out and away, even as far as Mars, let alone Pluto, when a revelation is at hand; when all the secrets will be unlocked here on Earth? No progress on the tachyon or negative time fronts, either. Nor any further messages from him. But he is his own message. His presence alone is sufficient to express Mankind: hopes, courage, holiness, determination.

(2019)

I am called back from retirement, for he is holding up signs again: the athlete holding up the Olympic Flame.

He holds them up for half an hour at a stretch—as though we are not all eyes agog, filming every moment in case we miss something, anything.

When I arrive, the signs that he has already held up have announced:

(Sign One) THIS IS A VERY SLOW TIME MACHINE. (And I amend accordingly, crossing out all the other titles we had bestowed on it successively, over the years. For a few seconds I wonder whether he was really naming the machine—defining it—or complaining about it! As though he'd been fooled into being its passenger on the assumption that a time machine should proceed to its destination *instanter* instead of at a snail's pace. But no. He was naming it.) TO TRAVEL INTO THE FUTURE, YOU MUST FIRST TRAVEL INTO THE PAST, ACCUMULATING HINDWARD POTENTIAL. (THIS IS CRAWLING DOWNHILL.)

(Sign Two) AS SOON AS YOU ACCUMULATE ONE LARGE QUANTUM OF TIME, YOU LEAP FORWARD BY THE SAME TIMESPAN AHEAD OF YOUR STARTING POINT. (THIS IS SLIDING UPHILL.)

(Sign Three) YOUR JOURNEY INTO THE FUTURE TAKES THE SAME TIME AS IT WOULD TAKE TO LIVE THROUGH THE YEARS IN REALTIME; YET YOU ALSO OMIT THE INTERVENING YEARS, ARRIVING AHEAD INSTANTLY. (PRINCIPLE OF CONSERVATION OF TIME.)

(Sign Four) SO, TO LEAP THE GAP, YOU MUST CRAWL THE OTHER WAY.

(Sign Five) TIME DIVIDES INTO ELEMENTARY QUANTA. NO MEASURING ROD CAN BE SMALLER THAN THE INDIVISIBLE ELEMENTARY ELECTRON; THIS IS ONE 'ELEMENTARY LENGTH' (EL). THE TIME TAKEN FOR LIGHT TO TRAVEL ONE EL IS 'ELEMENTARY TIME' (ET): I.E. 10^{-23} SECONDS; THIS IS ONE ELEMENTARY QUANTUM OF TIME. TIME CONSTANTLY LEAPS AHEAD BY THESE TINY QUANTA FOR EVERY PARTICLE; BUT,

NOT BEING SYNCHRONIZED, THESE FORM A CONTINUOUS TIME-OCEAN RATHER THAN SUCCESSIVE DISCRETE 'MOMENTS', OR WE WOULD HAVE NO CONNECTED UNIVERSE.

(Sign Six) TIME REVERSAL OCCURS NORMALLY IN STRONG NUCLEAR INTERACTIONS I.E. IN EVENTS OF ORDER 10^{-23} SECS. THIS REPRESENTS THE 'FROZEN GHOST' OF THE FIRST MOMENT OF THE UNIVERSE WHEN AN 'ARROW OF TIME' WAS FIRST STOCHASTICALLY DETERMINED.

(Sign Seven) (And this is when I arrived, to be shown Polaroid photographs of the first six signs. Remarkably, he is holding up each sign in a linear sequence from *our* point of view; a considerable feat of forethought and memory, though no less than we expect of him.) NOW, ET IS INVARIABLE & FROZEN IN; YET UNIVERSE AGES. STRETCHING OF SPACE-TIME BY EXPANSION PROPAGATES 'WAVES' IN THE SEA OF TIME, CARRYING TIME-ENERGY WITH PERIOD (X) PROPORTIONAL TO THE RATE OF EXPANSION, AND TO RATIO OF TIME ELAPSED TO TOTAL TIME AVAILABLE FOR THIS COSMOS FROM INITIAL CONSTANTS. EQUATIONS FOR X YIELD A PERIOD OF 35 YEARS CURRENTLY AS ONE MOMENT OF MACRO-TIME WITHIN WHICH MACROSCOPIC TIME REVERSAL BECOMES POSSIBLE.

(Sign Eight) CONSTRUCT AN 'ELECTRON SHELL' BY SYNCHRONIZING ELECTRON REVERSAL. THE LOCAL SYSTEM WILL THEN FORM A TIME-REVERSED MINI-COSMOS & PROCEED HIND-WARDS TILL X ELAPSES WHEN TIME CONSERVATION OF THE TOTAL UNIVERSE WILL PULL THE MINI-COSMOS (OF THE VSTM) FORWARD INTO MESH WITH UNIVERSE AGAIN I.E. BY 35 PLUS 35 YEARS.

'But how?' we all cried. 'How do you synchronize such an infinity of electrons? We haven't the slightest idea!'

Now at least we knew when he had set off: from 35 years after 1985. From *next year.* We are supposed to know all this by next year! Why has he waited so long to give us the proper clues?

And he is heading for the year 2055. What is there in the year 2055 that matters so much?

(*Sign Nine*) I DO NOT GIVE THIS INFORMATION TO YOU BECAUSE IT WILL LEAD TO YOUR INVENTING THE VSTM. THE SITUATION IS QUITE OTHERWISE. TIME IS PROBABILISTIC, AS SOME OF YOU MAY SUSPECT. I REALIZE THAT I WILL PROBABLY PERVERT THE COURSE OF HISTORY & SCIENCE BY MY ARRIVAL IN YOUR PAST (MY MOMENT OF DEPARTURE FOR THE FUTURE); IT IS IMPORTANT THAT YOU DO NOT KNOW YOUR PREDICAMENT TOO EARLY, OR YOUR FRANTIC EFFORTS TO AVOID IT WOULD GENERATE A TIME LINE WHICH WOULD UNPREPARE YOU FOR MY SETTING OFF. AND IT IS IMPORTANT THAT THIS DOES ENDURE, FOR I AM THE MATRIX OF MAN. I AM LEGION. I SHALL CONTAIN MULTITUDES.

MY RETICENCE IS SOLELY TO KEEP THE WORLD ON TOLER- ABLY STABLE TRACKS SO THAT I CAN TRAVEL BACK ALONG THEM. I TELL YOU THIS OUT OF COMPASSION, AND TO PREPARE YOUR MINDS FOR THE ARRIVAL OF GOD ON EARTH.

'He's insane. He's been insane from the start.'

'He's been isolated in there for some very good reason. Contagious insanity, yes.'

'Suppose that a madman could project his madness—'

'He already has done that, for decades!'

'—no, I mean really project it, into the consciousness of the whole world; a madman with a mind so strong that he acted as a template, yes a matrix for everyone else, and made them all his dummies, his copies; and only a few people stayed immune who could build this VSTM to isolate him—'

'But there isn't time to research it now!'

'What good would it do shucking off the problem for another thirty-five years? He would only reappear—'

'Without his strength. Shorn. Senile. Broken. Starved of his connections with the human race. Dried up. A mental leech. Oh, he tried to conserve his strength. Sitting quietly. Reading, waiting. But he broke! Thank God for that. It was vital to the future that he went insane.'

'Ridiculous! To enter the machine next year he must already be alive! He must already be out there in the world projecting this supposed madness of his. But he isn't. We're all separate sane individuals, all free to think what we want—'

'*Are we?* The whole world has been increasingly obsessed with him these last twenty years. Fashions, religions, life-styles: the whole world has been skewed by him ever since he was born! He must have been born about twenty years ago. Around 1995. Until then there was a lot of research into him. The tachyon hunt. All that. But he only began to *obsess* the world as a spiritual figure after that. From around 1995 or 6. When he was born as a baby. Only, we didn't focus our minds on his own infantile urges—because we had him here as an adult to obsess ourselves with—'

'Why should he have been born with infantile urges? If he's so unusual, why shouldn't he have been born already leeching on the world's mind; already knowing, already experiencing everything around him?'

'Yes, but the real charisma started then! All the emotional intoxication with him!'

'All the mothering. All the fear and adoration of his infancy. All the Bethlehem hysteria. Picking up as he grew and gained projective strength. We've been just as obsessed with Bethlehem as with Nazareth, haven't we? The two have gone hand in hand.'

(Sign Ten) I AM GOD. AND I MUST SET YOU FREE. I MUST CUT MYSELF OFF FROM MY PEOPLE; CAST MYSELF INTO THIS HELL OF ISOLATION.

I CAME TOO SOON; YOU WERE NOT READY FOR ME.

We begin to feel very cold; yet we cannot feel cold. Something prevents us—a kind of malign contagious tranquillity.

It is all so *right*. It slots into our heads so exactly, like the missing jigsaw piece for which the hole lies cut and waiting, that we know what he said is true; that he is growing up out there in our obsessed, blessèd world, only waiting to come to us.

(Sign Eleven) (Even though the order of the signs was time-reversed from his point of view, there was the sense of a real dialogue now between him and us, as though we were both synchronized. Yet this wasn't because the past was inflexible, and he was simply acting out a role he knew 'from history'. He was really as distant from us as ever. It was the looming presence of *himself* in the real world which cast its shadow on us, moulded our thoughts and fitted our questions to his responses; and we all realised this now, as though scales fell from our eyes. We weren't guessing or fishing in the dark

any longer; we were being dictated to by an overwhelming presence of which we were all conscious—and which wasn't locked up in the VSTM. The VSTM was Nazareth, the setting-off point; yet the whole world was also Bethlehem, womb of the embryonic God, his babyhood, childhood and youth combined into one synchronous sequence by his all-knowingness, with the accent on his wonderful birth that filtered through into human consciousness ever more saturatingly.)

MY OTHER SELF HAS ACCESS TO ALL THE SCIENTIFIC SPECULA-TIONS WHICH I HAVE GENERATED; AND ALREADY I HAVE THE SOLUTION OF THE TIME EQUATIONS. I SHALL ARRIVE SOON & YOU SHALL BUILD MY VSTM & I SHALL ENTER IT; YOU SHALL BUILD IT INSIDE AN EXACT REPLICA OF THIS LABORATORY, SOUTHWEST SIDE. THERE IS SPACE THERE. (Indeed it had been planned to extend the National Physical Laboratory that way, but the plans had never been taken up, because of the skewing of all our research which the VSTM had brought about.) WHEN I REACH MY TIME OF SETTING OUT, WHEN TIME REVERSES, THE PROBABILITY OF THIS LABORATORY WILL VANISH & THE OTHER WILL ALWAYS HAVE BEEN THE TRUE LABORATORY THAT I AM IN, INSIDE THIS VSTM. THE WASTE LAND WHERE YOU BUILD, WILL NOW BE HERE. YOU CAN WITNESS THE INVERSION; IT WILL BE MY FIRST PROBABILISTIC MIRACLE. THERE ARE HYPERDIMENSIONAL REASONS FOR THE PROBABILISTIC INVERSION, AT THE INSTANT OF TIME REVERSAL. BE WARNED NOT TO BE INSIDE THIS LABO-RATORY WHEN I SET OUT, WHEN I CHANGE TRACKS, FOR THIS SEGMENT OF REALITY HERE WILL ALSO CHANGE TRACKS, BECOMING IMPROBABLE, SQUEEZED OUT.

(Sign Twelve) I WAS BORN TO INCORPORATE YOU IN MY BOSOM; TO UNITE YOU IN A WORLD MIND, IN THE PHASE SPACE OF GOD. THOUGH YOUR INDIVIDUAL SOULS PERSIST, WITHIN THE FUSION. BUT YOU ARE NOT READY. YOU MUST BECOME READY IN 35 YEARS' TIME BY FOLLOWING THE MENTAL EXERCISES WHICH I SHALL DELIVER TO YOU, MY MEDITATIONS. IF I REMAINED WITH YOU NOW, AS I GAIN STRENGTH, YOU WOULD LOSE YOUR SOULS. THEY WOULD BE SUCKED INTO ME, INCO-HERENTLY. BUT IF YOU GAIN STRENGTH, I CAN INCORPORATE

YOU COHERENTLY WITHOUT LOSING YOU. I LOVE YOU ALL. YOU ARE PRECIOUS TO ME, SO I EXILE MYSELF.

THEN I WILL COME AGAIN IN 2055. I SHALL RISE FROM TIME, FROM THE USELESS HARROWING OF A LIMBO WHICH HOLDS NO SOULS PRISONER. FOR YOU ARE ALL HERE, ON EARTH.

That was the last sign. He sits reading again and listening to taped music. He is radiant; glorious. We yearn to fall upon him and be within him.

We hate and fear him too; but the Love washes over the Hate, losing it a mile deep.

He is gathering strength outside somewhere: in Wichita or Washington or Woodstock. He will come in a few weeks to reveal himself to us. We all know it now.

And then? Could we kill him? Our minds would halt our hands. As it is, we know that the sense of loss, the sheer bereavement of his departure hindwards into time will all but tear our souls apart.

And yet . . . I WILL COME AGAIN IN 2055, he has promised. And incorporate us, unite us, as separate thinking souls—if we follow all his meditations; or else he will suck us into him as dummies, as robots if we do not prepare ourselves. What then, when God rises from the grave of time, *insane?*

Surely he knows that he will end his journey in madness! That he will incorporate us all, as conscious living beings, into the matrix of his own insanity?

It is a fact of history that he arrived in 1985 ragged, gibbering and lunatic—tortured beyond endurance by being deprived of us.

Yet he demanded, jubilantly, in 1997, confirmation of his safe arrival; jubilantly, and we lied to him and said YES! YES! And he must have believed us. (Was he already going mad from deprivation?)

If a laboratory building can rotate into the probability of that same building adjacent to itself; if time is probabilistic (which we can never prove or disprove concretely with any measuring rod, for we can never see *what has not been,* all the alternative possibilities, though they might have been) we have to wish what we know to be the truth, not to have been the truth. We can only have faith that there will be another probabilistic miracle, beyond the promised inversion of laboratories that he speaks of, and that he will indeed arrive back in 1985 calm, well-kept, radiantly sane, his mind composed. And what is this but an entrée into madness for rational beings such as us? We must perpetrate an act of madness; we must believe the world to be other than what it was—so that we can receive among us a Sane, Blessèd, Loving God in 2055. A fine preparation for the coming of a mad God! For if we drive ourselves mad, believing passionately what was not true, will we not infect him with our madness, so that he is/ has to be/ will be/ and always was mad too?

Credo quia impossibile; we have to believe because it is impossible. The alternative is hideous.

Soon He will be coming. Soon. A few days, a few dozen hours. We all feel it. We are overwhelmed with bliss.

Then we must put Him in a chamber, and lose Him, and drive Him mad with loss, in the sure and certain hope of a sane and loving resurrection thirty years hence—so that He does not harrow Hell, and carry it back to Earth with Him.

The World Science Fiction
Convention of 2080

WHAT A GATHERING! FOUR HUNDRED PEOPLE—WRITERS, FANS and both magazine editors—have made their way successfully to these sailcloth marquees outside the village of New Boston.

We know of another three people who didn't make it, and the opening ceremony includes a brief 'In Memoriam' tribute to each of them, followed by one minute's silence for all. For Kurt Rossini, master of heroic fantasy— slain by an Indian arrow on his way from far California. For Suzie McIntosh, whose amusing woodcuts (sent down by trade caravan from Moose Jaw last summer season) adorn the programme booklet—killed by a wolf pack outside of Winnipeg. And for our worst loss, lovely Charmian Jones, acclaimed Queen of Titan in the masquerade at the last Worldcon three years ago in Tampa, whose miniature is worn close to many a fan's heart from the Yukon to Florida Bay—murdered by Moslem pirates during a kidnap raid on Charleston while she was passing through. (Could she have survived seraglio life in North Africa, and even become a bit of a queen there? No! Cut off from the slow percolation of fandom's lifeblood? Never! She defended her honour bravely with a short sword, and died.)

Some dozen others with attending memberships haven't arrived, either. We hope that they're just late—held up by contrary winds or a broken wagon axle. No doubt we will learn in six months or so when their person-alzines travel the trade routes.

In the bar tent, around the still, at the ox roast, and in the art tent with its fine embroideries and batiks based on the Old Masters Delany, Heinlein, Le

Guin, we greet old friends and colleagues and swap our travel tales. And I thought that my own journey from South Scotland on foot, on horseback, by canal longboat, and finally for five weeks by sailship across the stormy Atlantic (our mortars loaded against raiders) was eventful enough! But compared to some of the others' experiences mine was a cake run: Indians, Badlands, outlaw bands, mercenaries, pietist communities that close around one like a Venus fly trap, Army Induction Centres, plague zones, technophile citadels! I was even two and a half weeks early and managed to arrive with the manuscript of a new novel in my knapsack, penned on the sailship in between working my passage, all ready for bartering to 'Monk' Lewiston, head of Solaris Press of Little New York.

The new novel is called *The Aldebaran Experience* and is about a starship journey from the Luna Colony through metaspace to an alien planet orbiting Aldebaran. It is, though I say it myself, an ambitious exercise in what the critic Suvin once called 'cognitive estrangement'—but one can't really convey the breadth of the book in a couple of lines; besides, here isn't the place—though I did appear on a foreign writers' panel to discuss my own by now well-known earlier novel *The Film-Maker's Guide to Alien Actors* (Neogollancz Press, Edinburgh) dating from only four years ago. (Ah, the speed of publication and distribution in our SF world!)

On this panel, along with me, were the Frenchman Henri Guillaume, whose tale of mighty computerised bureaucracy and subjective time distortions, *The Ides of Venus*, is still winning acclaim for its originality—a definite step beyond the Old French Masters, Curval and Jeury; and the Mexican Gabriel Somosa—an exciting encounter; and my fellow islander Jeremy Symons, whom I last met in the flesh at our biennial thrash Gypsycon '77 all the way down in Devon—his *The Artificial Man* had been a hot contender for this year's Hugo Award ever since the nominations started trickling along the trade routes and over the ocean two years ago.

But I should describe the highlights of this wonderful get-together under cloth in New Boston. Frankly, that panel was rather ho-hum. Poor Jeremy had come down with some allergy working in the bilges, which affected his throat, and his voice would hardly carry to the back of the marquee...

Highlights, then: *The Film*. Yes, indeed, as advertised in the flyer a year ago, a film had been found! And what a film. Craftsmen built a hand-cranked projector whose light source was the sun itself, focused by an ingenious system of lenses and mirrors from outside the marquee; and six times during the Boston week we stared, enthralled, at the flickerings of an original print of *Silent Running*, praying that rainclouds would not dim the light too much. Let me not hear any sarcasm about the appropriateness of the title, since no way could anyone activate a soundtrack. We were all enchanted.

The Auction: oh, this was an experience. There was an Ace Double on sale! And an original SF Book Club edition of a Larry Niven collection. *And*, yellow and brittle with age, issues 250 to 260 inclusive of *Locus*. As well as much interesting and historic stuff from our own early post-Collapse era, such as a copy of a handwritten scroll novel (from just before we got hand presses cranking again) by the great Tessa Brien—part of her Jacthar series. The copies of *Locus* went in exchange for a fine Pinto pony—the Alabaman who bid his mount for them was quite happy to walk all the way home. But the Ace Double (Phil Dick's *Dr Futurity* backed by *The Unteleported Man*) went for a slim bar of gold.

Then there was the Solaris Press party where Henri Guillaume, high on Boston applejack, attempted to dance the can-can, endearing himself to everyone—a few quick sketches were 'snapped' of this, and there was even a watercolour for barter by the next morning.

And *The Banquet*, of spiced rabbit stew, followed by... *The Hugo Awards*: the carved beech wood rocketships for the best work in our field over the three years '75 to '78. First, for the best fanzine, scooped by Alice Turtle's *Call of the Wild* from New Chicago; then for the best story in either of the bi-annual magazines *Jupiter* or *Fantasy*, won by Harmony Friedlander for her moving 'Touchdown' in *Jupiter* four years ago; and finally the long-awaited novel Hugo, going to Boskon's Guest of Honour, Jerry Meltzer (as expected, by everyone except Jeremy Symons!), for his cosmos-spanning *Whither, Starman?*

But I think it is Jerry Meltzer's Guest of Honour speech that I shall most treasure the memory of. The speech was entitled, 'Some Things Do Not Pass'. From the very beginning of it I was riveted, reinvigorated, and felt my life reaffirmed.

Jerry is pushing sixty now, which is quite a miracle now that the average life-expectancy is down to forty or so. He has lost an ear to frostbite and wears a coonskin cap at all times to cover his mutilation. He's a raftsman on the Missouri.

Surveying the marquee full of four hundred faces, he smiled—wisely, confidently. He spoke slowly.

'Some things do not pass. Some things *increase* in truth and beauty.

Science Fiction is one of these. I say this because Science Fiction is a fiction: it is a *making*, a forging of the legends of our tribe, and the best legends of all humanity. Now that *research* and *probing* have ceased'—he grinned dismissively—'we can indeed freshly and freely invent our science and our worlds. SF was always being spoilt, having her hands tied and the whip cracked over her head by scientific *facts*. They're gone now—most of those blessed facts, about quarks and quasars and I don't know what!—and there won't be any more! It's all mythology now, friends. SF has come into her own, and we who are here today, we know this. Friends, we're Homers and Lucians once again—because science is a myth, and we're its mythmakers. Mars is ours again, and Saturn is, and Alpha C—and lovely Luna. We can read the Grand Masters of yore in a light that the poor folk of the Late Twentieth could never read them in! I say to you, Some Things Do Not Pass. Their loveliness increases. Now we can make that mythic loveliness wilder and headier and more fabulous than ever. This is the true meaning of my *Whither, Starman?*'

He spoke till the Con Committee lit the whale-oil flambeaux in the tent, and then he talked some more. At the end he was chaired shoulder-high out into the meadow underneath the stars. And just then, what must have been one of the very last dead satellites from the old days streaked across the sky like a comet tail, burning up as it plunged towards the Atlantic to drown fathoms deep. Maybe it was only an ordinary shooting star—but I don't think so. Nor did anyone else. Four hundred voices cheered its downfall, as Jerry threw back his head and laughed.

With a gesture he quietened the crowd. 'My friends,' he called out, 'we really own the stars now. We really do. Never would have done, the other way. Dead suns, dead worlds the lot of them, I shouldn't be surprised—dead universe. Now Sirius is ours. Canopus is. The dense suns of the Hub are all ours. All.' His hand grasped at the sky. It gripped the Milky Way, and we cheered again.

Two mornings later, after many perhaps overconfident goodbyes—'See you in '83!'—I walked down into New Boston to the harbour along with my compadre Jeremy—who was somewhat hung over and weaved about at times—to take ship next week or the week after for Liverpool. I wouldn't need to work my passage back, though. I'd bartered *The Aldebaran Experience* to 'Monk' Lewiston for a bundle of furs, much in demand in our cold island.

In a year or so I'll receive my free copy, hand-printed in Solaris Press's characteristic heavy black type, by way of some sheep drove up through the

Borders. If Monk is fast in getting it out and the trade routes are kind, who knows, it might just get on the ballot for '83—to be voted at the fishing village of Santa Barbara, way across the Plains and Deserts and Badlands.

Can I possibly make it to Santa Barbara? Truth to tell, I can hardly wait. After this year's wonderful thrash, I'll be on the sailship—and I'll board those stagecoaches, come Hell or high water.

I nudged Jeremy in the ribs.

'We own the stars,' I said. 'You and I.'

The Thousand Cuts

THE *PETRUSHKA* RESTAURANT WAS A LARGE DIM CELLAR, WITH THEIRS the only table occupied. Ballets Russes murals writhed dimly on the walls: exotic ghosts.

As the waiter unloaded the chilled glasses of vodka, Don Kavanagh observed, 'I don't think Russian restaurants are very popular these days.'

'That's why we came,' Hugh Carpenter said. 'Bound to get a table.'

'Don't blame me,' said the waiter. 'I'm a Londoner, born and bred.'

'Maybe there's a good sketch there?' suggested Martha Vine, who was the ugly sister of the team. 'You know: restaurants run by the wrong sort of people? Such as an Eskimo Curry House . . . Or, wait a minute, how about a slaughterhouse for vegetables? Wait, I've got it: protests at *vegetable vivisection*! Turnips with electrodes plugged into them. Artichokes forced to smoke forty a day.'

Hugh dismissed the notion, and the waiter, with the same toss of his head. The whole sparkle of their TV show relied on cultivating a blind spot for the *obvious*.

'Not quite mad enough, darling.' He cocked his head. 'What's that?'

Don listened.

'A car back-firing.'

'That many times?'

'More like gunfire,' said Alison Samuels, shaking her impeccably corn-rowed red hair; she was beauty, to Martha's beast.

'So it's somebody gunning their engine.' Hugh grinned triumphantly. 'Okay, where were we?'

Soon after, sounds of crashing and breakages, a woman's scream and incoherent shouting came from the upstairs vestibule of the *Petrushka*...

'This isn't one of your practical jokes, is it, Hugh?' asked Martha anxiously, quickly. 'Tape recorder upstairs? Is it?'

'No, it damn well—'

At which moment, two brawny men wearing lumber jackets crowded down the stairs, thrusting the waiter, who was bleeding from the mouth, the manager and his beige-blonde receptionist ahead of them. A third skinny man in a windcheater stayed up top. All three men were armed with machine pistols.

'Stay where you are!' The armed man's accent was southern Irish. 'You three, get to a table and sit down!'

The manager, cashier and waiter did so, quickly.

The moment of silence that followed was broken by the approaching wail of a police siren.

'I take it,' said Hugh loudly, 'that we are all hostages, in yet another bungled terrorist escapade?'

'Be quiet, you!'

Out of the corner of his mouth, Don murmured, *'Hush,* you're likely to get murdered in the first few minutes. Then rapport starts building up. Just... meditate. Do nothing.'

'Zen and the art of being a hostage, eh?' Hugh only whispered softly. He sat as still as a Buddhist monk.

A police loud-hailer spoke, close by...

'Don't come any nearer!' cried the skinny man. 'We have hostages in here! We'll kill them!'

Lumber jacket number two ran to the kitchen door, kicked it open...

Hugh's tongue moved inside her mouth. His finger traced the cleft of her buttocks.

He pulled away instantly. He was naked. As was Alison. They were on the bed in his Chelsea flat. Outside was bright with June sunlight.

Alison gazed at Hugh, wide-eyed.

'But,' she managed to say.

'But we're in the *Petrushka,* Alison... I mean, correct me if I'm crazy, but I wasn't aware that I'm subject to bouts of amnesia! I mean... how the hell did we get here? I mean, you *can* tell me, can't you?'

'Hugh, I... I can't tell you anything. We're in the restaurant. Those IRA men are... at least I suppose that's what they were. But we aren't. We're here.'

Hugh sat up. Dumbly he stared at a newspaper lying on the yellow shag-pile carpet.

The headlines were: PETRUSHKA SIEGE ENDS PEACEFULLY.

He read the story, hardly understanding it. But he understood the accompanying photograph: of himself with his arm wrapped round Alison's shoulders, both of them grinning and waving.

'Just look at the date! June the *ninth*. This is next week's newspaper.'

'So we're in the middle of next week.' Alison began to laugh hysterically, then with deliberate irony she slapped her own cheek. 'I must remember this trick next time I visit the dentist's . . . Why can't either of us remember a bloody thing?'

'I wish I could remember us making love.'

Alison started to get dressed, from her scattered clothes.

'I always wanted us to get into bed,' Hugh went on. 'It was one of my big ambitions. I suppose it still is! We must have been celebrating our freedom. Our release. Mustn't we?

'*Gas*,' he decided suddenly. 'That's it. They must have used some new kind of psychochemical, to knock everybody unconscious or confuse us. This is a side-effect.'

He studied the newspaper more carefully.

'Doesn't say a thing about gas. It says the police talked the gunmen out. I suppose you can muzzle the press a little . . . no, this was all too public. The story has to be true as written.'

His telephone rang.

Hugh hurried naked into the next room to take the call.

Alison was sitting at the dressing table concentrating on braiding her hair, when he returned. He noticed how she was trembling. With shock, yes. His own body felt hollow and his skin was covered in goose bumps, though the air was warm.

'That was Don. He . . . he reacted very rationally, for a clown. Very quickly. He's in the same fix as us. But *so is Sarah*. So is his wife.'

'I'm aware that Sarah's his wife.'

'So then I tried to phone Martha. But I can't get through. Suddenly all the lines are jammed. I tried to phone the police. I even tried to call . . . I tried to call the goddamn talking clock. Can't get it either. Everybody is phoning to find out what the bloody time is! It isn't just us, Alison. It's got nothing specifically to do with the *Petrushka*. It's everybody.'

'Where's your radio? Switch it on.'

'Kitchen.'

Hugh fled, still naked, and she followed his quivering rump.

A punk rock band were singing:

'. . . *they'll bomb yer boobs!*
they'll bomb yer brains!
they'll bomb yer bums!'

The song faded.

The dee-jay said, 'So that was the latest track from The Weasels. Hot stuff, eh? Like, *radio*-active . . . and that's what a radio's supposed to be: active. So I'm carrying straight on, even if you're all as confused as I am. That's right, all you out there in listener land, none of us here in the studio has any idea how we got here today. Or how it *got* to be today. But if you're all feeling the way I'm feeling, I've got this word of advice for you: stay cool, and carry on doing what you're doing. Keep on trucking that truck. Keep the traffic moving. Cook the lunch, Ma Jones, and don't set fire to the pan— the kids'll be home soon. And now to help you all, here comes a track from an old group, Traffic: "In a Chinese Noodle Factory". . . '

Hugh tuned across the dial. One station had simply gone off the air: on others only music was being broadcast.

'Try long-wave,' urged Alison. 'Abroad.'

When he picked up a gabbled French language broadcast from Cairo, he realised with his rusty French that whatever had happened, had maybe happened world-wide.

And during the rest of June, and July and August, the effect repeated itself a dozen times. None of the subsequent 'Breaks' lasted as long as the first one had. Some swallowed up two or three days, and others only a few hours. But there was no sign that they were winding down.

Nor was there any conceivable explanation.

Nor could people exactly get used to having their lives repeatedly broken at random.

For this was not simply like fainting or falling asleep. When awareness resumed—and who could promise that it would, next time?—all of the world's activities were found to have flowed on as usual. Air lines had jetted to and fro between London and New York. Contracts had been signed, and babies born. Newspapers had been printed—and at last the newsseller's cry of 'Read all about it!' was literally true, for how else could anyone find out in detail what had happened? A woman would find herself locked in a police cell; but the police would have to consult their records before they could break the news to her that she had murdered, say, her husband—which raised strange new questions about guilt and innocence . . .

Distressing it was indeed, to find oneself suddenly at the controls of a Jumbo jet heading in to land at an unexpected airport, or lying in a hospital bed after a mysterious operation, or running, running down a street . . . for what reason?

'What if we find ourselves in the middle of a nuclear war, with all the sirens wailing?' asked Martha. 'I can't stand it. It's driving me mad.' She poured herself another glass of gin.

'It's driving everybody mad,' said Don. They were in Hugh's flat. 'It's like that old Chinese torture.'

'What, the water dripping down on your skull till it wears a hole in it?'

'No, I mean the Death of a Thousand Cuts. I always wondered if the poor victims died from loss of blood. But it must have been from the accumulated shock. One painful shock after another. One you could survive. A dozen you could survive. But a thousand? Never! That's what'll put paid to the human race. This is the Life of a Thousand Cuts.'

'Good Heavens,' said Hugh, 'you've got it.' He rubbed his hands briskly. '*Cuts*: that's brilliant.'

'It means we're like robots,' went on Don, ignoring him. 'We don't *need* consciousness. We don't need to be aware. A bird isn't aware. But that doesn't stop it from courting and raising young and migrating. Actually, it helps. No swallow with self-awareness would bother flying all the way to the tip of South Africa and back every year.'

'Do you mean that we've evolved too much self-awareness, and it's a dead end?' asked Alison.

'And now we're going to become robots again, and the world will run a lot more smoothly. Only, we won't know it. Any more than a sparrow or a mouse *knows*. They just are. Martha, you mentioned nuclear war. But have you realised how smoothly the Arms Limitation Talks are going all of a sudden?'

'That's because both sides are more scared of an accident than they've ever been.'

'No, it isn't. I've been checking back. All the significant advances have occurred during Breaks.' Don chuckled softly. 'Break-throughs, during Breaks! And remember too: the *Petrushka* siege ended peacefully—during a Break.'

'During a cut,' Hugh corrected him.

'The *Petrushka* thing could so easily have ended in a bloody shoot-out, with the restaurant being stormed. But it didn't happen that way. I don't care how bloody-minded our terrorists were. Or the authorities.'

He was driving his red Metro along the elevated section of the motorway into Central London, in fast heavy traffic. Some way behind, in the driving mirror, a white Volkswagen failed to overtake an articulated lorry. The lorry rammed it, skidding and jack-knifing. As following traffic slammed into it, a ball of flame rose up.

'Bloody hell.' Briefly Don glanced at the calendar watch he had thought to equip himself with in the aftermath of the first Break, before stocks ran out. 'Two days, this time.'

Alison was sitting next to him. Hugh was behind in the back seat. No sign of Martha. He hoped she was still alive.

'For Christ's sake, get us *off* here!' begged Alison. 'It's a death trap.'

'More like a bloody buffalo stampede! Why don't the idiots slow down?'

Somehow, Don reached the next exit ramp safely. The ramp was crowded with vehicles descending. Horns blared. Wings and bumpers scraped and banged.

'Mustn't forget what we were talking about,' Hugh reminded him, over his shoulder. 'The Life of a Thousand Cuts.'

'There'll be a thousand cuts in the paintwork of this baby...'

'Stop at the nearest pub, Don. We have to talk before we lose the continuity.'

'About cuts,' said Hugh, cradling a double Glenfiddich.

The bar of the *Duke of Kent* was packed, but remarkably hushed as people waited for the filler music on the landlord's radio to stop, and the first hastily assembled news to take its place. Many people were not drinking at all, but merely waiting.

'You mentioned the Death of a Thousand Cuts, and of course those were cuts in the flesh with a knife. But what do *we* mean by cuts?'

'A film,' said Alison. 'Editing. Switching scenes.'

'Good girl!'

'I'm not a girl. Girls are twelve years old or less.'

'Okay, *sorry.*'

'That's why I wouldn't ever go to bed with you before.'

'Okay, okay, I prostrate myself. Now, that's it exactly: the editing of a film—the cutting from one scene to the next. You don't need to see your characters drive all the way from A to B. They just leave, then they arrive. Otherwise a film would last as long as real life. Or the Director would be Andy Warhol.'

'As long as real life *used* to last . . .'

'Quite. And what if reality itself is really a sort of film? A millennia-long Warhol movie with a cast of billions? Suppose: as holography is to flat photography, so to holography is . . . *solidography.* Suppose the world is being projected. It's a solid movie—of matter, not of light. We're an entry in the Cannes Film Festival of the universe. *But . . .*' He paused emphatically.

'. . . are we the completed masterpiece? Or are we the rushes on the cutting room floor—of reality? Because suddenly we've lost our own sense of continuity. Two days drop out. Three days drop out.'

The elegiac Elgar on the radio halted.

'*Shush!*' hissed a roomful of snakes.

'. . . is the BBC Emergency Service, and I am Robin Johnson. The date is September 1st. The time is one twenty-five in the afternoon. The most recent Break measured approximately fifty hours. At the Helsinki disarmament talks preliminary agreement has been reached on the reduction of . . .'

'Come on, we can read all that stuff later.'

But Don did not yet start the engine of the Metro.

'Wouldn't it rather spoil the natural flow of this film of yours if all the characters suddenly became aware that their lives are just a fiction?' he asked.

'*Maybe* . . . this is a very subtle, artistic touch? Maybe the Director has suddenly gone into experimental cinema? He was making a realistic film before. But now he's into New Wave techniques: *meta*-film, like a French director.'

'I still say we're all really living robots. But we never knew it before. Now we do.'

'But that isn't a decline of awareness,' Alison pointed out. 'That's an increase in awareness.'

'It's a bloody decline in our sense of control over what happens in the world. The important things are all happening off-stage. They're happening off everybody's stage. Look at this progress in Arms Control—you heard Robin on the news.'

'Maybe,' said Alison, 'God has decided to cut reality, and re-edit it? Because it wasn't working out. Or it didn't work out the first time. The world-film bombed out, literally. We're in a remake of the film of the world.'

Hugh teased her.

'Maybe these Breaks are for advertisements? Only, we can't see them any more than the characters in a film can see the commercials!'

'Rubbish. When you have a commercial, the film just stops. Then it starts up again from the same moment.'

'In that case, you're right: something *must* be editing reality.'

'How can I possibly say "yes" to that? But I can't say "no", either. Lord knows, reality *needs* editing.'

An ambulance wailed by, bearing someone from the motorway pile-up. A police car raced the other way, blue light flashing on its roof.

'It's the Thousand Cuts,' said Don. 'And it'll drive us mad with stress. Like rats in an electrified maze. Our awareness will go catatonic. We'll become a planet of zombies—a world on autopilot. Like the birds and the bees.'

He started the engine. Driving out of the car park of the *Duke of Kent*, he turned left because it was easier to do so, before remembering that he had no idea where they had been heading. He slowed, to let another ambulance race by.

And suddenly Hugh began to laugh.

'I've just got it! Don't you see: we've got a way to test my idea. We may even have a way to communicate—with the Director himself! Listen, we'll do a special show. Don't worry, we'll be able to get this one scheduled quickly—and we'll get blanket publicity for it too. We'll do a show about editing reality. We'll make a film within The Film—a film *about* that Film. I'll package this as a great morale-booster—which indeed it might well be! We'll get the whole country laughing at what's happening to us. Country? Hell no, with a show like this we'll cop the lot: America, Europe, Israel, Japan. We'll do it, too, my hearties. This is going to keep people sane during the Thousand Cuts. *Governments* are going to back this one.'

Alison clapped her hands.

'Thank you.'

'Just so long as we aren't cut off,' said Don. 'You know? "Normal transmission resumes as soon as the show is over."'

'If we're cut off, old son, we'll still be going full steam ahead. We can watch it all on videotape afterwards. Swing us round, Don. We're going back to my flat to get the whole thing set up. And we'll need to get hold of Martha. If somebody's editing reality, I'm joining in. We'll call the show . . . yes, I've got it! We'll call it: "The Making of *Reality, the Motion Picture*"!'

'Don't you mean "Remaking"?'

'Yes. Yes I do. Quite right, love. "The Remaking of *Reality, the Motion Picture*"—that's it. I stand corrected.' He slouched back in the seat of the Metro.

'So do we all, Hugh, if you're right. So do we all.'

'Do what?'

'Stand corrected.'

Two weeks later, Hugh cradled a phone.

'Well, I don't know exactly what I've been *doing* over the past four days. But I must have been busting my ass, as our American friends so colourfully put it. Our show's been given the green light for October 4th, right after the nine o'clock news. They're bumping *Gone With the Wind* back half an hour to slot us in.'

'Big deal,' said Don. 'Everybody must have seen *Gone With the Wind* twice already.'

Hugh wagged a finger, wickedly.

'Ah, but they want everybody to *learn* it by heart, you see. So this is really a major programming decision. Anyhow, that isn't all: seven European countries are hooking up, using sub-titles—and two major networks in the States are running us the same evening, their time, with Australia and Japan following suit the next day. But I'm keeping the wildest news for last: *Russia* are going to screen the show—subject, that is, to contents analysis.'

Martha sneezed. She had caught a cold—she knew not where, nor how.

'Shouldn't be a problem. Soviets have always laughed at God.'

'Okay, so where were we, Don?'

'I've been going through this *heap* of notes. Lord, it's like inheriting a fortune from an uncle you never knew about. I'll get this lot knocked into shape with Martha, then we can start rehearsing on videotape, Thursday. See what runs, and what doesn't run.'

'Could we just please switch the radio on for a moment?' asked Alison.

'Why? Oh . . . to check out what's been happening in the,' and Hugh grinned broadly, '*real* world? Why not? Why not indeed? We might harvest some more ideas.'

Fetching the radio, she set it on the drinks cabinet.

'. . . Helsinki. This agreement represents a major advance in the lessening of international tension . . .'

'How on Earth can an advance "lessen" something?'

'You should meet my publisher,' quipped Don.

'. . . first genuine reduction in weapons system, with inspection and verification by neutral observers from the Third World. The actual dismantling and downgrading of . . .'

'It seems even God can't manage miracles overnight.' Martha sniffed.

'Blah to that,' said Alison. 'They're all scared of what could happen during one of the zombie intervals. Or just after one, when everyone's confused.'

'. . . reported casualty figures following the most recent Break are already in the thousands. The worst disaster occurred at Heathrow Airport, where . . .'

'See? It just takes one poor sod to jab his finger at the wrong button. And, *poof*. If this is an example of divine intervention, it's the most ham-fisted miracle I've ever come across.'

'When you're cutting film, love,' said Hugh, 'you waste a lot of good material for the sake of the picture as a whole.'

'You sound as if you sneakingly admire what's going on,' protested Don. 'All this bloody cutting of our lives.'

Hugh poured himself a brandy, and squirted some (but not much) soda into the glass.

'No, it's ludicrous, and dangerous, and it's soul-destroying. But you've got to laugh at it, to get it in the right perspective—and yes, to keep our dignity and free will. It's a mad universe—and it's just turned out to be even madder than anybody could have imagined. Well, in my humble opinion the highest human art isn't tragedy. It's satire. And,' here he nodded derisively in the direction of the ceiling, 'speaking as one trickster to another, I want whatever is directing this big show, Life, to notice that *I've* spotted what's going on. I've found out that reality is just a movie—and I can still laugh, and stay sane.'

'. . . have been inundated with requests for Librium and Valium . . .'

'I laugh, therefore I am. Birds don't laugh. Cows don't laugh. There's the difference. Now let's get on making everyone kill themselves laughing. They deserve it.'

'The Remaking of *Reality, the Motion Picture*' was pre-recorded during the afternoons of October 1st and 2nd—with Hugh Carpenter in the role of Cosmic Director and the lovely Alison as his continuity-person—and edited into shape on the 3rd.

It was, in the opinion of all concerned, just about the sharpest and funniest half-hour of TV in the history of the world.

With genuine tears spilling down his cheeks, Hugh turned from the TV monitor to wave back to the technicians. Peter Rolfe, who had produced the show, pumped his hand and slapped him on the back, then embraced Alison and kissed her. After a moment's hesitation he kissed Martha too. Though the show was pre-recorded, the whole team had decided to be present for the transmission.

Hugh popped open one of the champagne bottles he had brought along.

'Out she flies, out she flies! To Manchester and Munich, to Tulsa and Tel Aviv! To Alpha Centauri and all points east, if there's anybody out there! *And* we got to see it, too. Cheers.'

Before too long Rolfe's telephone was flashing for his attention.

'Yes? Really? Oh superb!'

'Hugh! The switchboard is *ab-sol-utely jammed*. The viewers are just . . . bubbling over. You've stopped them from throwing themselves under a bus tomorrow. You've stopped them from overdosing tonight. You've made the first real sense out of this ghastly mess. You've made the world *fun* again—even if it is a film made by an idiot, full of cuts and splicing, signifying . . .'

'What, *no* negative reactions at all?' interrupted Don.

'Oh, there's a teeny little bit from the blasphemy brigade. But, my dear fellow, you can *expect* that.'

'I do. I look forward to it. The negative reactions are so comical.'

'Not this time, old son. It's heartfelt gratitude all round. The country's laughing its collective head off.'

'Do you realise,' asked Rolfe, as he hosted the celebration party at his Hampstead house the next evening, 'this has been a Numero Primo for TV? In the last twenty-four hours you must have clocked up viewing figures of half a billion people? Give or take the Soviet Union, who don't believe in ratings, mean beasts.'

The carpet was leaf-strewn with telegrams. Kicking his way among them, Rolfe pressed another whisky and water on Alison and kissed her again, wondering just how long he could use the excuse of their mutual euphoria.

'You've probably outdone Armstrong stepping on to the Moon,' he called to Hugh.

Tipsy people sprawled on the floor, watching a re-run of the show, chortling and whinnying at the high points. It was almost all high points.

'*Salud!*' he toasted. 'The whole world must be laughing tonight!'

'Damn!' swore Don. He glanced at the passing road sign. 'Petworth, half a mile . . . We must be heading down to the cottage.'

Hugh was hunched tensely on his left, with Martha and Alison behind. And Sarah too ('Hullo, love'), an orange headscarf tied tightly round her black curls—which was remarkably impromptu of her, for a weekend with friends.

The fuel gauge was showing empty . . . How weird; he always kept the tank well topped up.

Slowing—and really, he *had* been speeding, doing nearly sixty along this country lane—he admired the trees in the last golden and ruddy sunset of their foliage.

Hugh loosened up too.

'You've got to laugh, haven't you?'

And then Don looked at his watch. It wasn't the weekend at all; it was midweek.

'Good God, it's October 20th. That's the longest one yet. We're at Peter's place in Hampstead, on the 5th—I mean, we *were*. That's a cut of two whole weeks.'

'I've got the radio here,' said Sarah.

The filler music was Beethoven's Eighth.

It played jubilantly on and on: Ludwig van's most Mozart-like symphony, thought Don.

'There's a lot to catch up on,' remarked Hugh idly.

But finally the music did die away.

'. . . and I am Robin Johnson. The date is . . .'

'We'll be at the cottage in another ten minutes. I've got a couple of spare gallons I keep there.'

'. . . news will come as a grave shock to you all. Briefly, the Helsinki disarmament talks collapsed in ruins on October 11th. Yugoslavia was invaded by Warsaw Pact forces on the 18th, two days ago. Currently, Soviet armour is massing on the West German border. The Nato Alliance is on full alert, but so far . . .'

'I . . . I've just received an unconfirmed report that several tactical nuclear weapons have exploded inside West Germany. This report is as yet unconfirmed . . .'

'But,' said Hugh lamely.

'So that's why we're all trying to get down to the cottage on an empty tank . . . We're trying to be the lucky ones.'

The engine missed several times, coughed, then quietly gave out. Presently the Metro coasted to a halt.

'It seems,' said Alison quietly, 'that we *did* kill ourselves laughing, after all.'

'Do you mean,' whispered Martha. 'God—or something—is not mocked?'

'I don't know about "God—or something",' said Don bitterly. 'But I suppose we have to describe this as, well, a . . . negative reaction. And somehow it doesn't seem comical. The movie's been axed . . .'

'Post-holocaust scenes now, I presume,' grumbled Hugh. 'No damn sense of continuity . . .'

He wound the window down.

'Cut!' he screamed at the sky. 'Cut! Cut!'

But the sky brightened intolerably to the north, for a few seconds. Not long after, a fierce hot wind from far away tore thousands of red and gold leaves from the trees.

Slow Birds

IT WAS MAYDAY, AND THE SKATE-SAILING FESTIVAL THAT YEAR WAS being held at Tuckerton.

By late morning, after the umpires had been out on the glass plain setting red flags around the circuit, cumulus clouds began to fill a previously blue sky, promising ideal conditions for the afternoon's sport. No rain; so that the glass wouldn't be an inch deep in water as last year at Atherton. No dazzling glare to blind the spectators, as the year before that at Buckby. And a breeze verging on brisk without ever becoming fierce: perfect to speed the competitors' sails along without lifting people off their feet and tumbling them, as four years previously at Edgewood when a couple of broken ankles and numerous bruises had been sustained.

After the contest there would be a pig roast; or rather the succulent fruits thereof, for the pig had been turning slowly on its spit these past thirty-six hours. And there would be kegs of Old Codger Ale to be cracked. But right now Jason Babbidge's mind was mainly occupied with checking out his glass-skates and his fine crocus-yellow hand-sail.

As high as a tall man, and of best old silk, only patched in a couple of places, the sail's fore-spar of flexible ash was bent into a bow belly by a strong hemp cord. Jason plucked this thoughtfully like a harpist, testing the tension. Already a fair number of racers were out on the glass, showing off their paces to applause. Tuckerton folk mostly, they were—acting as if they owned the glass hereabouts and knew it more intimately than any visitors could. Not that it was in any way different from the same glass over Atherton way.

Jason's younger brother Daniel whistled appreciatively as a Tuckerton man carrying purple silk executed perfect circles at speed, his sail shivering as he tacked.

'Just look at him, Jay!'

'What, Bob Marchant? He took a pratfall last year. Where's the use in working up a sweat before the whistle blows?'

By now a couple of sisters from Buckby were out too with matching black sails, skating figure-eights around each other, risking collision by a hair's breadth.

'Go on, Jay,' urged young Daniel. 'Show 'em.'

Contestants from the other villages were starting to flood on to the glass as well, but Jason noticed how Max Tarnover was standing not so far away, merely observing these antics with a wise smile. Master Tarnover of Tuckerton, last year's victor at Atherton despite the drenching spray . . . Taking his cue from this, and going one better, Jason ignored events on the glass and surveyed the crowds instead.

He noticed Uncle John Babbidge chatting intently to an Edgewood man over where the silver band was playing; which was hardly the quietest place to talk, so perhaps they were doing business. Meanwhile on the green beyond the band the children of five villages buzzed like flies from hoop-la to skittles to bran tub, to apples in buckets of water. And those grown-ups who weren't intent on the band or the practice runs or on something else, such as gossip, besieged the craft and produce stalls. There must be going on for a thousand people at the festival, and the village beyond looked deserted. Rugs and benches and half-barrels had even been set out near the edge of the glass for the old folk of Tuckerton.

As the band lowered their instruments for a breather after finishing *The Floral Dance,* a bleat of panic cut across the chatter of many voices. A farmer had just vaulted into a tiny sheep-pen where a lamb almost as large as its shorn, protesting dam was ducking beneath her to suckle and hide. Laughing, the farmer hauled it out and hoisted it by its neck and back legs to guess its weight, and maybe win a prize.

And now Jason's mother was threading her way through the crowd, chewing the remnants of a pasty.

'Best of luck, son!' She grinned.

'I've told you, Mum,' protested Jason. 'It's bad luck to say "Good luck".'

'Oh, luck yourself! What's luck, anyway?' She prodded her Adam's apple as if to press the last piece of meat and potatoes on its way down, though really she was indicating that her throat was bare of any charm or amulet.

'I suppose I'd better make a move.' Kicking off his sandals, Jason sat to lace up his skates. With a helping hand from Daniel he rose and stood knock-kneed, blades cutting into the turf while the boy hoisted the sail across his shoulders. Jason gripped the leather straps on the bow-string and the spine-spar.

'Okay.' He waggled the sail this way and that. 'Let go, then. I won't blow away.'

But just as he was about to proceed down on to the glass, out upon the glass less than a hundred yards away a slow bird appeared.

It materialized directly in front of one of the Buckby sisters. Unable to veer, she had no choice but to throw herself backwards. Crying out in frustration, and perhaps hurt by her fall, she skidded underneath the slow bird, sledging supine upon her now snapped and crumpled sail . . .

They were called slow birds because they flew through the air—at the stately pace of three feet per minute.

They looked a little like birds, too, though only a little. Their tubular metal bodies were rounded at the head and tapering to a finned point at the tail, with two stubby wings midway. Yet these wings could hardly have anything to do with suspending their bulk in the air; the girth of a bird was that of a horse, and its length twice that of a man lying full length. Perhaps those wings controlled orientation or trim.

In colour they were a silvery grey; though this was only the colour of their outer skin, made of a soft metal like lead. Quarter of an inch beneath this coating their inner skins were black and stiff as steel. The noses of the birds were all scored with at least a few scrape marks due to encounters with obstacles down the years; slow birds always kept the same height above ground—underbelly level with a man's shoulders—and they would bank to avoid substantial buildings or mature trees, but any frailer obstructions they would push on through. Hence the individual patterns of scratches. However, a far easier way of telling them apart was by the graffiti carved on so many of their flanks: initials entwined in hearts, dates, place names, fragments of messages. These amply confirmed how very many slow birds there must be in all—something of which people could not otherwise have been totally convinced. For no one could keep track of a single slow bird. After each one had appeared—over hill, down dale, in the middle of a pasture or half way along a village street—it would fly onward slowly for any length of time between an hour and a day, covering any distance between a few score yards and a full mile. And vanish again. To reappear somewhere else unpredictably: far away or close by, maybe long afterwards or maybe soon.

Usually a bird would vanish, to reappear again.

Not always, though. Half a dozen times a year, within the confines of this particular island country, a slow bird would reach its journey's end.

It would destroy itself, and all the terrain around it for a radius of two and a half miles, fusing the landscape instantly into a sheet of glass. A flat, circular sheet of glass. A polarized, limited zone of annihilation. Scant yards beyond its rim a person might escape unharmed, only being deafened and dazzled temporarily.

Hitherto no slow bird had been known to explode so as to overlap an earlier sheet of glass. Consequently many towns and villages clung close to the borders of what had already been destroyed, and news of a fresh glass plain would cause farms and settlements to spring up there. Even so, the bulk of people still kept fatalistically to the old historic towns. They assumed that a slow bird wouldn't explode in their midst during their own lifetimes. And if it did, what would they know of it? Unless the glass happened merely to bisect a town—in which case, once the weeping and mourning was over, the remaining citizenry could relax and feel secure.

True, in the long term the whole country from coast to coast and from north to south would be a solid sheet of glass. Or perhaps it would merely be a chequerboard, of circles touching circles; a glass mosaic. With what in between? Patches of desert dust, if the climate dried up due to reflections from the glass. Or floodwater, swampland. But that day was still far distant: a hundred years away, two hundred, three. So people didn't worry too much. They had been used to this all their lives long, and their parents before them. Perhaps one day the slow birds would stop coming. And going. And exploding. Just as they had first started, once. Certainly the situation was no different, by all accounts, anywhere else in the world. Only the seas were clear of slow birds. So maybe the human race would have to take to rafts one day. Though by then, with what would they build them? Meanwhile, people got by; and most had long ago given up asking why. For there was no answer.

———

The girl's sister helped her rise. No bones broken, it seemed. Only an injury to dignity; and to her sail.

The other skaters had all coasted to a halt and were staring resentfully at the bird in their midst. Its belly and sides were almost bare of graffiti; seeing this, a number of youths hastened on to the glass, clutching penknives, rusty nails and such. But an umpire waved them back angrily.

'Shoo! Be off with you!' His gaze seemed to alight on Jason, and for a fatuous moment Jason imagined that it was himself to whom the umpire was about to appeal; but the man called, 'Master Tarnover!' instead, and Max Tarnover duck-waddled past then glided out over the glass, to confer.

Presently the umpire cupped his hands. 'We're delaying the start for half an hour,' he bellowed. 'Fair's fair: young lady ought to have a chance to fix her sail, seeing as it wasn't her fault.'

Jason noted a small crinkle of amusement on Tarnover's face; for now either the other competitors would have to carry on prancing around tiring themselves with extra practice which none of them needed, or else troop off the glass for a recess and lose some psychological edge. In fact almost everyone opted for a break and some refreshments.

'Luck indeed!' snorted Mrs Babbidge, as Max Tarnover clumped back their way.

Tarnover paused by Jason, 'Frankly I'd say her sail's a wreck,' he confided. 'But what can you do? The Buckby lot would have been bitching on otherwise. 'Oh, she could have won. If she'd had ten minutes to fix it.' Bloody hunk of metal in the way.' Tarnover ran a lordly eye over Jason's sail. 'What price skill, then?'

Daniel Babbidge regarded Tarnover with a mixture of hero worship and hostile partisanship on his brother's behalf. Jason himself only nodded and said, 'Fair enough.' He wasn't certain whether Tarnover was acting generously—or with patronizing arrogance. Or did this word in his ear mean that Tarnover actually saw Jason as a valid rival for the silver punch-bowl this year round?

Obviously young Daniel did not regard Jason's response as adequate. He piped up: 'So where do *you* think the birds go, Master Tarnover, when they aren't here?'

A good question: quite unanswerable, but Max Tarnover would probably feel obliged to offer an answer if only to maintain his pose of worldly wisdom. Jason warmed to his brother, while Mrs Babbidge, catching on, cuffed the boy softly.

'Now don't you go wasting Master Tarnover's time. Happen he hasn't given it a moment's thought, all his born days.'

'Oh, but I have,' Tarnover said.

'Well?' the boy insisted.

'Well . . . maybe they don't go anywhere at all.'

Mrs Babbidge chuckled, and Tarnover flushed.

'What I mean is, maybe they just stop being in one place then suddenly they're in the next place.'

'If only you could skate like that!' Jason laughed. 'Bit slow, though . . . Everyone would still pass you by at the last moment.'

'They must go somewhere,' young Dan said doggedly. 'Maybe it's somewhere we can't see. Another sort of place, with other people. Maybe it's them that builds the birds.'

'Look, freckleface, the birds don't come from Russ, or 'Merica, or anywhere else. So where's this other place?'

'Maybe it's right here, only we can't see it.'

'And maybe pigs have wings.' Tarnover looked about to march towards the cider and perry stall; but Mrs Babbidge interposed herself smartly.

'Oh, as to that, I'm sure our sow Betsey couldn't fly, wings or no wings. Just hanging in the air like that, and so heavy.'

'Weighed a bird recently, have you?'

'They look heavy, Master Tarnover.'

Tarnover couldn't quite push his way past Mrs Babbidge, not with his sail impeding him. He contented himself with staring past her, and muttering, 'If we've nothing sensible to say about them, in my opinion it's better to shut up.'

'But it isn't better,' protested Daniel. 'They're blowing the world up. Bit by bit. As though they're at war with us.'

Jason felt humorously inventive. 'Maybe that's it. Maybe these other people of Dan's are at war with us—only they forgot to mention it. And when they've glassed us all, they'll move in for the holidays. And skate happily for ever more.'

'Damn long war, if that's so,' growled Tarnover. 'Been going on over a century now.'

'Maybe that's why the birds fly so slowly,' said Daniel. 'What if a year to us is like an hour to those people? That's why the birds don't fall. They don't have time to.'

Tarnover's expression was almost savage. 'And what if the birds come only to punish us for our sins? What if they're simply a miraculous proof—'

'—that the Lord cares about us? And one day he'll forgive us? Oh goodness,' and Mrs Babbidge beamed, 'surely you aren't one of *them?* A bright lad like you. Me, I don't even put candles in the window or tie knots in the bedsheets anymore to keep the birds away.' She ruffled her younger son's mop of red hair. 'Everyone dies sooner or later, Dan. You'll get used to it, when you're properly grown up. When it's time to die, it's time to die.'

Tarnover looked furiously put out; though young Daniel also seemed distressed in a different way.

'And when you're thirsty, it's time for a drink!' Spying an opening, and his opportunity, Tarnover sidled quickly around Mrs Babbidge and strode off. She chuckled as she watched him go.

'That's put a kink in his sail!'

Forty-one other contestants, besides Jason and Tarnover, gathered between the starting flags. Though not the girl who had fallen; despite all best efforts she was out of the race, and sat morosely watching.

Then the Tuckerton umpire blew his whistle, and they were off.

The course was in the shape of a long bloomer loaf. First, it curved gently along the edge of the glass for three quarters of a mile, then bent sharply around in a half circle on to the straight, returning towards Tuckerton. At the end of the straight, another sharp half circle brought it back to the starting—and finishing—line. Three circuits in all were to be skate-sailed before the victory whistle blew. Much more than this, and the lag between leaders and stragglers could lead to confusion.

By the first turn Jason was ahead of the rest of the field, and all his practice since last year was paying off. His skates raced over the glass. The breeze thrust him convincingly. As he rounded the end of the loaf, swinging his sail to a new pitch, he noted Max Tarnover hanging back in fourth place. Determined to increase his lead, Jason leaned so close to the flag on the entry to the straight that he almost tipped it. Compensating, he came poorly on to the straight, losing a few yards. By the time Jason swept over the finishing line for the first time, to the cheers from Atherton villagers, Tarnover was in third position; though he was making no very strenuous effort to overhaul. Jason realized that Tarnover was simply letting him act as pacemaker.

But a skate-sailing race wasn't the same as a foot-race, where a pacemaker was generally bound to drop back eventually. Jason pressed on. Yet by the second crossing of the line Tarnover was ten yards behind, moving without apparent effort as though he and his sail and the wind and the glass were one. Noting Jason's glance, Tarnover grinned and put on a small burst of speed to push the front-runner to even greater efforts. And as he entered on the final circuit Jason also noted the progress of the slow bird, off to his left, now midway between the long curve and the straight, heading in the general direction of Edgewood. Even the laggards ought to clear the final straight before the thing got in their way, he calculated.

This brief distraction was a mistake: Tarnover was even closer behind him now, his sail pitched at an angle which must have made his wrists ache. Already he was drifting aside to overhaul Jason. And at this moment Jason grasped how he could win: by letting Tarnover think that he was pushing Jason beyond his capacity—so that Tarnover would be fooled into over-exerting himself too soon.

'Can't catch me!' Jason called into the wind, guessing that Tarnover would misread this as braggadocio and assume that Jason wasn't really thinking ahead. At the same time Jason slackened his own pace slightly, hoping that his rival would fail to notice, since this was at odds with his own boast. Pretending to look panicked, he let Tarnover overtake—and saw how Tarnover continued to grip his sail strenuously even though he was actually moving a little slower than before. Without realizing it, Tarnover had his angle wrong; he was using unnecessary wrist action.

Tarnover was in the lead now. Immediately all psychological pressure lifted from Jason. With ease and grace he stayed a few yards behind, just where he could benefit from the 'eye' of air in Tarnover's wake. And thus he remained till half way down the final straight, feeling like a kestrel hanging in the sky with a mere twitch of its wings before swooping.

He held back; held back. Then suddenly changing the cant of his sail he did swoop—into the lead again.

It was a mistake. It had been a mistake all along. For as Jason sailed past, Tarnover actually laughed. Jerking his brown and orange silk to an easier, more efficient pitch, Tarnover began to pump his legs, skating like a demon. Already he was ahead again. By five yards. By ten. And entering the final curve.

As Jason tried to catch up in the brief time remaining, he knew how he had been fooled; though the knowledge came too late. So cleverly had Tarnover fixed Jason's mind on the stance of the sails, by holding his own in such a way—a way, too, which deliberately created that convenient eye of air—that Jason had quite neglected the contribution of his legs and skates, taking this for granted, failing to monitor it from moment to moment. It only took moments to recover and begin pumping his own legs too, but those few moments were fatal. Jason crossed the finishing line one yard behind last year's victor; who was this year's victor too.

As he slid to a halt, bitter with chagrin, Jason was well aware that it was up to him to be gracious in defeat rather than let Tarnover seize that advantage, too.

He called out, loud enough for everyone to hear: 'Magnificent, Max! Splendid skating! You really caught me on the hop there.'

Tarnover smiled for the benefit of all onlookers.

'What a noisy family you Babbidges are,' he said softly; and skated off to be presented with the silver punchbowl again.

Much later that afternoon, replete with roast pork and awash with Old Codger Ale, Jason was waving an empty beer mug about as he talked to Bob Marchant in the midst of a noisy crowd. Bob, who had fallen so spectacularly the year before. Maybe that was why he had skated diffidently today and been one of the laggards.

The sky was heavily overcast, and daylight too was failing. Soon the homeward trek would have to start.

One of Jason's drinking and skating partners from Atherton, Sam Partridge, thrust his way through.

'Jay! That brother of yours; he's out on the glass. He's scrambled up on the back of the bird. He's riding it.'

'What?'

Jason sobered rapidly, and followed Partridge with Bob Marchant tagging along behind.

Sure enough, a couple of hundred yards away in the gloaming Daniel was perched astride the slow bird. His red hair was unmistakable. By now a lot of other people were beginning to take notice and point him out. There were some ragged cheers, and a few angry protests.

Jason clutched Partridge's arm. 'Somebody must have helped him up. Who was it?'

'Haven't the foggiest. That boy needs a good walloping.'

'Daniel *Babbidge!*' Mrs Babbidge was calling nearby. She too had seen. Cautiously she advanced on to the glass, wary of losing her balance.

Jason and company were soon at her side. 'It's all right, Mum,' he assured her. 'I'll fetch the little . . . perisher.'

Courteously Bob Marchant offered his arm and escorted Mrs Babbidge back on to rough ground again. Jason and Partridge stepped flat-foot out across the vitrified surface accompanied by at least a dozen curious spectators.

'Did anyone spot who helped him up?' Jason demanded of them. No one admitted it.

When the group was a good twenty yards from the bird, everyone but Jason halted. Pressing on alone, Jason pitched his voice so that only the boy would hear.

'Slide off,' he ordered grimly. 'I'll catch you. Right monkey you've made of your mother and me.'

'No,' whispered Daniel. He clung tight, hands splayed like suckers, knees pressed to the flanks of the bird as though he was a jockey. 'I'm going to see where it goes.'

'Goes? Hell I'm not going to waste time arguing. Get down!' Jason gripped an ankle and tugged, but this action only served to pull him up against the bird. Beside Dan's foot a heart with the entwined initials 'ZB' and 'EF' was carved. Turning away, Jason shouted, 'Give me a hand, you lot! Come on someone, bunk me up!'

Nobody volunteered, not even Partridge.

'It won't bite you! There's no harm in touching it. Any kid knows that.' Angrily he flat-footed back towards them. 'Damn it all, Sam.'

So now Partridge did shuffle forward, and a couple of other men too. But then they halted, gaping. Their expression puzzled Jason momentarily—till Sam Partridge gestured; till Jason swung around.

The air behind was empty.

The slow bird had departed suddenly. Taking its rider with it.

Half an hour later only the visitors from Atherton and their hosts remained on Tuckerton green. The Buckby, Edgewood, and Hopperton contingents had set off for home. Uncle John was still consoling a snivelling Mrs Babbidge. Most faces in the surrounding crowd looked sympathetic, though there was a certain air of resentment, too, among some Tuckerton folk that a boy's prank had cast this black shadow over their Mayday festival.

Jason glared wildly around the onlookers. 'Did nobody see who helped my brother up?' he cried. 'Couldn't very well have got up himself, could he? Where's Max Tarnover? Where is he?'

'You aren't accusing Master Tarnover, by any chance?' growled a beefy farmer with a large wart on his cheek. 'Sour grapes, Master Babbidge! Sour grapes is what that sounds like, and we don't like the taste of those here.'

'Where is he, dammit?'

Uncle John laid a hand on his nephew's arm. 'Jason, lad. Hush. This isn't helping your Mum.'

But then the crowd parted, and Tarnover sauntered through, still holding the silver punch-bowl he had won.

'Well, Master Babbidge?' he enquired. 'I hear you want a word with me.'

'Did you see who helped my brother on to that bird? Well, did you?'

'I didn't see,' replied Tarnover coolly.

It had been the wrong question, as Jason at once realized. For if Tarnover had done the deed himself, how could he possibly have watched himself do it?

'Then did you—'

'Hey up,' objected the same farmer. 'You've asked him, and you've had his answer.'

'And I imagine your brother has had his answer, too,' said Tarnover. 'I hope he's well satisfied with it. Naturally I offer my heartfelt sympathies to Mrs Babbidge, if indeed the boy *has* come to any harm. Can't be sure of that, though, can we?'

"Course we can't!'

Jason tensed, and Uncle John tightened his grip on him. 'No, lad. There's no use.'

It was a sad and quiet long walk homeward that evening for the three remaining Babbidges, though a fair few Atherton folk behind sang blithely and tipsily, nonetheless. Occasionally Jason looked around for Sam Partridge, but Sam Partridge seemed to be successfully avoiding them.

The next day, May the Second, Mrs Babbidge rallied and declared it to be a 'sorting out' day; which meant a day for handling all Daniel's clothes and storybooks and old toys lovingly before setting them to one side out of sight. Jason himself she packed off to his job at the sawmill, with a flea in his ear for hanging around her like a whipped hound.

And as Jason worked at trimming planks that day the same shamed, angry, frustrated thoughts skated round and round a single circuit in his head:

'In my book he's a murderer . . . You don't give a baby a knife to play with. He was cool as a cucumber afterwards. Not shocked, no. Smug.'

Yet what could be done about it? The bird might have hung around for hours more. Except that it hadn't . . .

Set out on a quest to find Daniel? But how? And where? Birds dodged around. Here, there and everywhere. No rhyme or reason to it. So what a useless quest that would be!

A quest to prove that Dan was alive. And if he were alive, then Tarnover hadn't killed him.

'In my book he's a murderer . . .' Jason's thoughts churned on impotently. It was like skating with both feet tied together.

Three days later a slow bird was sighted out Edgewood way. Jim Mitchum, the Edgewood thatcher, actually sought Jason out at the sawmill to bring him the news. He'd be coming over to do a job, anyway.

No doubt his visit was an act of kindness, but it filled Jason with guilt quite as much as it boosted his morale. For now he was compelled to go and see for himself, when obviously there was nothing whatever to discover. Downing tools, he hurried home to collect his skates and sail, and sped over the glass to Edgewood.

The bird was still there; but it was a different bird. There was no carved heart with the love-tangled initials 'ZB' and 'EF'.

And four days after that, mention came from Buckby of a bird spotted a few miles west of the village on the main road to Harborough. This time Jason borrowed a horse and rode. But the mention had come late; the bird had flown on a day earlier. Still, he felt obliged to search the area of the sighting for a fallen body or some other sign.

And the week after that a bird appeared only a mile from Atherton itself; this one vanished even as Jason arrived on the scene . . .

Then one night Jason went down to the Wheatsheaf. It was several weeks, in fact, since he had last been in the alehouse; now he meant to get drunk, at the long bar under the horse brasses.

Sam Partridge, Ned Darrow and Frank Yardley were there boozing; and an hour or so later Ned Darrow was offering beery advice.

'Look, Jay, where's the use in your dashing off every time someone spots a ruddy bird? Keep that up and you'll make a ruddy fool of yourself. And what if a bird pops up in Tuckerton? Bound to happen sooner or later. Going to rush off there too, are you, with your tongue hanging out?'

'All this time you're taking off work,' said Frank Yardley. 'You'll end up losing the job. Get on living is my advice.'

'Don't know about that,' said Sam Partridge unexpectedly. 'Does seem to me as a man ought to get his own back. Supposing Tarnover did do the dirty on the Babbidges—'

'What's there to suppose about it?' Jason broke in angrily.

'Easy on, Jay. I was going to say as Babbidges are Atherton people. So he did the dirty on us all, right?'

'Thanks to some people being a bit slow in their help.'

Sam flushed. 'Now don't you start attacking everyone right and left. No one's perfect. Just remember who your real friends are, that's all.'

'Oh, I'll remember, never fear.'

Frank inclined an empty glass from side to side. 'Right. Whose round is it?'

One thing led to another, and Jason had a thick head the next morning.

In the evening Ned banged on the Babbidge door.

'Bird on the glass, Sam says to tell you,' he announced. 'How about going for a spin to see it?'

'I seem to recall last night you said I was wasting my time.'

'Ay, running around all over the country. But this is just for a spin. Nice evening, like. Mind, if you don't want to bother . . . Then we can all have a few jars in the Wheatsheaf afterwards.'

The lads must really have missed him over the past few weeks. Quickly Jason collected his skates and sail.

'But what about your supper?' asked his mother. 'Sheep's head broth.'

'Oh, it'll keep, won't it? I might as well have a pasty or two in the Wheatsheaf.'

'Happen it's better you get out and enjoy yourself,' she said. 'I'm quite content. I've got things to mend.'

Twenty minutes later Jason, Sam, and Ned were skimming over the glass two miles out. The sky was crimson with banks of stratus, and a river of gold ran clear along the horizon; foul weather tomorrow, but a glory this evening. The glassy expanse flowed with red and gold reflections: a lake of blood, fire, and molten metal. They did not at first spot the other solitary sail skater, nor he them, till they were quite close to the slow bird.

Sam noticed first. 'Who's that, then?'

The other sail was brown and orange. Jason recognized it easily. 'It's Tarnover!'

'Now's your chance to find out, then,' said Ned.

'Do you mean that?'

Ned grinned. 'Why not? Could be fun. Let's take him.'

Pumping their legs, the three sail-skaters sped apart to outflank Tarnover—who spied them and began to turn. All too sharply, though. Or else he may have run into a slick of water on the glass. To Jason's joy Max Tarnover, champion of the five villages, skidded.

They caught him. This done, it didn't take the strength of an ox to stop a skater from going anywhere else, however much he kicked and struggled. But Jason hit Tarnover on the jaw, knocking him senseless.

'What the hell you do that for?' asked Sam, easing Tarnover's fall on the glass.

'How else do we get him up on the bird?'

Sam stared at Jason, then nodded slowly.

It hardly proved the easiest operation to hoist a limp and heavy body on to a slowly moving object whilst standing on a slippery surface; but after removing their skates they succeeded. Before too long Tarnover lay sprawled atop, legs dangling. Quickly with his pocket knife Jason cut the hemp cord from Tarnover's sail and bound his ankles together, running the tether tightly underneath the bird.

Presently Tarnover awoke, and struggled groggily erect. He groaned, rocked sideways, recovered his balance.

'Babbidge . . . Partridge, Ned Darrow . . . ? What the hell are you up to?'

Jason planted hands on hips. 'Oh, we're just playing a little prank, same as you did on my brother Dan. Who's missing now; maybe forever, thanks to you.'

'I never—'

'Admit it, then we might cut you down.'

'And happen we mightn't,' said Ned. 'Not till the Wheatsheaf closes. But look on the bright side: happen we might.'

Tarnover's legs twitched as he tested the bonds. He winced. 'I honestly meant your brother no harm.'

Sam smirked. 'Nor do we mean you any. Ain't our fault if a bird decides to fly off. Anyway, only been here an hour or so. Could easily be here all night. Right, lads?'

'Right,' said Ned. 'And I'm thirsty. Race you? Last one buys?'

'He's admitted he did it,' said Jason. 'You heard him.'

'Look, I'm honestly very sorry if—'

'Shut up,' said Sam. 'You can stew for a while, seeing as how you've made the Babbidges stew. You can think about how sorry you really are.' Partridge hoisted his sail.

It was not exactly how Jason had envisioned his revenge. This seemed like an anti-climax. Yet, to Tarnover no doubt it was serious enough. The champion was sweating slightly . . . Jason hoisted his sail, too. Presently the men skated away . . . to halt by unspoken agreement a quarter of a mile away. They stared back at Tarnover's little silhouette upon his metal steed.

'Now if it was me,' observed Sam. 'I'd shuffle myself along till I fell off the front . . . Rub you a bit raw, but that's how to do it.'

'No need to come back, really,' said Ned. 'Hey, what's he trying?'

The silhouette had ducked. Perhaps Tarnover had panicked and wasn't thinking clearly, but it *looked* as if he was trying to lean over far enough to unfasten the knot beneath, or free one of his ankles. Suddenly the distant figure inverted itself. It swung right round the bird, and Tarnover's head and chest were hanging upside down, his arms flapping. Or perhaps Tarnover had hoped the cord would snap under his full weight; but snap it did not. And once he was stuck in that position there was no way he could recover himself upright again, or do anything about inching along to the front of the bird.

Ned whistled. 'He's messed himself right up now, and no mistake. He's ruddy crucified himself.'

Jason hesitated before saying it: 'Maybe we ought to go back? I mean, a man can die hanging upside down too long . . . Can't he?' Suddenly the whole episode seemed unclean, unsatisfactory.

'Go back?' Sam Partridge fairly snarled at him. 'You were the big mouth last night. And whose idea was it to tie him on the bird? You wanted him taught a lesson, and he's being taught one. We're only trying to oblige you, Jay.'

'Yes, I appreciate that.'

'You made enough fuss about it. He isn't going to wilt like a bunch of flowers in the time it takes us to swallow a couple of pints.'

And so they skated on, back to the Wheatsheaf in Atherton.

At ten thirty, somewhat the worse for wear, the three men spilled out of the alehouse into Sheaf Street. A quarter moon was dodging from rift to rift in the cloudy sky, shedding little light.

'I'm for bed,' said Sam. 'Let the sod wriggle his way off.'

'And who cares if he don't?' said Ned. 'That way, nobody'll know. Who wants an enemy for life? Do you, Jay? This way you can get on with things. Happen Tarnover'll bring your brother back from wherever it is.' Shouldering his sail and swinging his skates, Ned wandered off up Sheaf Street.

'But,' said Jason. He felt as though he had blundered into a midden. There was a reek of sordidness about what had taken place. The memory of Tarnover hanging upside-down had tarnished him.

'But what?' said Sam.

Jason made a show of yawning. 'Nothing. See you.' And he set off homeward.

But as soon as he was out of sight of Sam he slipped down through Butcher's Row in the direction of the glass, alone.

It was dark out there with no stars and only an occasional hint of moonlight, yet the breeze was steady and there was nothing to trip over on the glass. The bird wouldn't have moved more than a hundred yards. Jason made good speed.

The slow bird was still there. But Tarnover wasn't with it; its belly was barren of any hanged man.

As Jason skated to a halt, to look closer, figures arose in the darkness from where they had been lying flat upon the glass, covered by their sails. Six figures. Eight. Nine. All had lurked within two or three hundred yards of the bird, though not too close—nor any in the direction of Atherton. They had left a wide corridor open; which now they closed.

As the Tuckerton men moved in on him, Jason stood still, knowing that he had no chance.

Max Tarnover skated up, accompanied by that same beefy farmer with the wart.

'I did come back for you,' began Jason.

The farmer spoke, but not to Jason. 'Did he now? That's big of him. Could have saved his time, what with Tim Earnshaw happening along—when Master Tarnover was gone a long time. So what's to be done with him, eh?'

'Tit for tat, I'd say,' said another voice.

'Let him go and look for his kid brother,' offered a third. 'Instead of sending other folk on his errands. What a nerve.'

Tarnover himself said nothing; he just stood in the night silently.

So, presently, Jason was raised on to the back of the bird and his feet were tied tightly under it. But his wrists were bound together too, and for good measure the cord was linked through his belt.

Within a few minutes all the skaters had sped away towards Tuckerton.

Jason sat. Remembering Sam's words he tried to inch forward, but with both hands fastened to his waist this proved impossible; he couldn't gain purchase. Besides, he was scared of losing his balance as Tarnover had.

He sat and thought of his mother. Maybe she would grow alarmed when he didn't come home. Maybe she would go out and rouse Uncle John . . . And maybe she had gone to bed already.

But maybe she would wake in the night and glance into his room and send for help. With fierce concentration he tried to project thoughts and images of himself at her, two miles away.

An hour wore on, then two; or so he supposed from the moving of the moon-crescent. He wished he could slump forward and sleep. That might be best; then he wouldn't know anything. He still felt drunk enough to pass out, even with his face pressed against metal. But he might easily slide to one side or the other in his sleep.

How could his mother survive a double loss? It seemed as though a curse had descended on the Babbidge family, but of course that curse had a human name; and the name was Max Tarnover. So for a while Jason damned him, and imagined retribution by all the villagers of Atherton. A bloody feud. Cottages burnt. Perhaps a rape. Deaths even. No Mayday festival ever again.

But would Sam and Ned speak up? And would Atherton folk be sufficiently incensed, sufficiently willing to destroy the harmony of the five villages in a world where other things were so unsure? Particularly as some less than sympathetic souls might say that Jason, Sam, and Ned had started it all.

Jason was involved in imagining a future feud between Atherton and Tuckerton that he almost forgot he was astride a slow bird. There was no sense of motion, no feeling of going anywhere. When he recollected where he was, it actually came as a shock.

He was riding a bird.

But for how long?

It had been around, what, six hours now? A bird could stay for a whole day. In which case he had another eighteen hours left to be rescued in. Or if it only stayed for half a day, that would take him through to morning. Just.

He found himself wondering what was underneath the metal skin of the bird. Something which could turn five miles of landscape into a sheet of glass, certainly. But other things too. Things that let it ignore gravity. Things that let it dodge in and out of existence. A brain of some kind, even?

'Can you hear me, bird?' he asked it. Maybe no one had ever spoken to a slow bird before.

The slow bird did not answer.

Maybe it couldn't, but maybe it could hear him, even so. Maybe it could obey orders.

'Don't disappear with me on your back,' he told it. 'Stay here. Keep on flying just like this.'

But since it was doing just that already, he had no idea whether it was obeying him or not.

'Land, bird. Settle down on to the glass. Lie still.'

It did not. He felt stupid. He knew nothing at all about the bird. Nobody did. Yet somewhere, someone knew. Unless the slow birds did indeed come from God, as miracles, to punish. To make men God-fearing. But why should a God want to be feared? Unless God was insane, in which case the birds might well come from Him.

They were something irrational, something from elsewhere, something which couldn't be understood by their victims any more than an ant colony understood the gardener's boot, exposing the white eggs to the sun and the sparrows.

Maybe something had entered the seas from elsewhere the previous century, something that didn't like land dwellers. Any of them. People or sheep, birds or worms or plants . . . It didn't seem likely. Salt water would rust steel. But for the first time in his life Jason thought about it intently.

'Bird, what are you? Why are you here?'

Why, he thought, is anything here? Why is there a world and sky and stars? Why shouldn't there simply be nothing for ever and ever?

Perhaps that was the nature of death: nothing for ever and ever. And one's life was like a slow bird. Appearing then vanishing, with nothing before and nothing after.

An immeasurable period of time later, dawn began to streak the sky behind him, washing it from black to grey. The greyness advanced slowly overhead as thick clouds filtered the light of the rising but hidden sun. Soon there was enough illumination to see clear all around. It must be five o'clock. Or six. But the grey glass remained blankly empty.

Who am I? wondered Jason, calm and still. Why am I conscious of a world? Why do people have minds, and think thoughts? For the first time in his life he felt that he was really thinking—and thinking had no outcome. It led nowhere.

He was, he realized, preparing himself to die. Just as all the land would die, piece by piece, fused into glass. Then no one would think thoughts any more, so that it wouldn't matter if a certain Jason Babbidge had ceased thinking at half past six one morning in May. After all, the same thing happened every night when you went to sleep, didn't it? You stopped thinking. Perhaps everything would be purer and cleaner afterwards. Less untidy, less fretful: a pure ball of glass. In fact, not fretful at all, even if all the stars in the sky crashed into each other, even if the earth was swallowed by the sun. Silence, forever: once there was no one about to hear.

Maybe this was the message of the slow birds. Yet people only carved their initials upon them. And hearts. And the names of places which had been vitrified in a flash; or else which were going to be.

I'm becoming a philosopher, thought Jason in wonder.

He must have shifted into some hyperconscious state of mind: full of lucid clarity, though without immediate awareness of his surroundings. For he was not fully aware that help had arrived until the cord binding his ankles was cut and his right foot thrust up abruptly, toppling him off the other side of the bird into waiting arms.

Sam Partridge, Ned Darrow, Frank Yardley, and Uncle John, and Brian Sefton from the sawmill—who ducked under the bird brandishing a knife, and cut the other cord to free his wrists.

They retreated quickly from the bird, pulling Jason with them. He resisted feebly. He stretched an arm towards the bird.

'It's all right, lad,' Uncle John soothed him.

'No, I want to *go*,' he protested.

'Eh?'

At that moment the slow bird, having hung around long enough, vanished; and Jason stared at where it had been, speechless.

In the end his friends and uncle had to lead him away from that featureless spot on the glass, as though he was an idiot. Someone touched by imbecility.

But Jason did not long remain speechless.

Presently he began to teach. Or preach. One or the other. And people listened; at first in Atherton, then in other places too.

He had learned wisdom from the slow bird, people said of him. He had communed with the bird during the night's vigil on the glass.

His doctrine of nothingness and silence spread, taking root in fertile soil, where there was soil remaining rather than glass—which was in most places, still. A paradox, perhaps; how eloquently he spoke—about being silent! But in so doing he seemed to make the silence of the glass lakes sing; and to this people listened with a new ear.

Jason travelled throughout the whole island. And this was another paradox, for what he taught was a kind of passivity, a blissful waiting for a death that was more than merely personal, a death which was also the death of the sun and stars and of all existence, a cosmic death which transfigured individual mortality. And sometimes he even sat on the back of a bird that happened by, to speak to a crowd—as though chancing fate or daring, begging, the bird to take him away. But he never sat for more than an hour, then he would scramble down, trembling but quietly radiant. So besides being known as 'The Silent Prophet', he was also known as 'The Man who rides the Slow Birds'.

On balance, it could have been said that he worked great psychological good for the communities that survived; and his words even spread overseas. His mother died proud of him—so he thought—though there was always an element of wistful reserve in her attitude . . .

Many years later, when Jason Babbidge was approaching sixty, and still no bird had ever borne him away, he settled back in Atherton in his old home—to which pilgrims of silence would come, bringing prosperity to the village and particularly to the Wheatsheaf, managed now by the daughter of the previous landlord.

And every Mayday the skate-sailing festival was still held, but now always on the glass at Atherton. No longer was it a race and a competition; since in the end the race of life could not be won. Instead it had become a pageant, a glass ballet, a re-enactment of the event of many years ago—a passion play performed by the four remaining villages. Tuckerton and all its folk had been glassed ten years before by a bird which destroyed itself so that the circle of annihilation exactly touched that edge of the glass where Tuckerton had stood till then.

One morning, the day before the festival, a knock sounded on Jason's door. His housekeeper, Martha Prestidge, was out shopping in the village; so Jason answered.

A boy stood there. With red hair, and freckles.

For a moment Jason did not recognize the boy. But then he saw that it was Daniel. Daniel, unchanged. Or maybe grown up a little. Maybe a year older.

'Dan . . . ?'

The boy surveyed Jason bemusedly, his balding crown, his sagging girth, his now spindly legs, and the heavy stick with a stylized bird's head on which he leaned, gripping it with a liver spotted hand.

'Jay,' he said after a moment, 'I've come back.'

'Back? But . . .'

'I know what the birds are now! They *are* weapons. Missiles. Tens and hundreds of thousands of them. There's a war going on. But it's like a game as well: a board game run by machines. Machines that think. It's only been going on for a few days in their time. The missiles shunt to and fro through time to get to their destination. But they can't shunt in the time of that world, because of cause and effect. So here's where they do their shunting. In our world. The other possibility-world.'

'This is nonsense. I won't listen.'

'But you must, Jay! It can be stopped for us before it's too late. I know how. Both sides can interfere with each other's missiles and explode them out of sight—that's here—if they can find them fast enough. But the war over there's completely out of control. There's a winning pattern to it, but this only matters to the machines any longer, and they're buried away underground. They build the birds at a huge rate with material from the Earth's crust, and launch them into other-time automatically.'

'Stop it, Dan.'

'I fell off the bird over there—but I fell into a lake, so I wasn't killed, only hurt. There are still some pockets of land left, around the Bases. They patched me up, the people there. They're finished, in another few hours of their time—though it's dozens of years to us. I brought them great hope, because it meant that all life isn't finished. Just theirs. Life can go on. What we have to do is build a machine that will stop their machines finding the slow birds over here. By making interference in the air. There are waves. Like waves of light, but you can't see them.'

'You're raving.'

'Then the birds will shunt here. But harmlessly. Without glassing us. And in a hundred years' time, or a few hundred, they'll even stop coming at all, because the winning pattern will be all worked out by then. One of the war machines will give up, because it lost the game. Oh I know it ought to be able to give up right now! But there's an element of the irrational programmed into the machines' brains too; so they don't give up too soon. When they do, everyone will be long dead there on land—and some surviving people think the war machines will start glassing the ocean floor as a final strategy before they're through. But we can build an air-wave-maker. They've locked the knowledge in my brain. It'll take us a few years to mine the right metals and tool up and provide a power source . . . ' Young Daniel ran out of breath briefly. He gasped. 'They had a prototype slow bird. They sat me on it and sent me into other-time again. They managed to guide it. It emerged just ten miles from here. So I walked home.'

'Prototype? Air-waves? Power source? What are these?'

'I can tell you.'

'Those are just words. Fanciful babble. Oh for this babble of the world to still itself!'

'Just give me time, and I'll . . . '

'Time? You desire time? The mad ticking of men's minds instead of the great pure void of eternal silence? You reject acceptance? You want us to swarm forever aimlessly, deafening ourselves with our noisy chatter?'

'Look . . . I suppose you've had a long, tough life, Jay. Maybe I shouldn't have come here first.'

'Oh, but you should indeed, my impetuous fool of a brother. And I do not believe my life has been ill-spent.'

Daniel tapped his forehead. 'It's all in here but I'd better get it down on paper. Make copies and spread it around—just in case Atherton gets glassed. Then somebody else will know how to build the transmitter. And life can go on. Over there they think maybe the human race is the only life in the whole universe. So we have a duty to go on existing. Only, the others have destroyed themselves arguing about which way to exist. But we've still got time enough. We can build ships to sail through space to the stars. I know a bit about that too. I tell you, my visit brought them real joy in their last hours, to know this was all still possible after all.'

'Oh, Dan.' And Jason groaned. Patriarch-like, he raised his staff and brought it crashing down on Daniel's skull.

He had imagined that he mightn't really notice the blood amidst Daniel's bright red hair. But he did.

The boy's body slumped in the doorway. With an effort Jason dragged it inside, then with an even greater effort up the oak stairs to the attic where Martha Prestidge hardly ever went. The corpse might begin to smell after a while, but it could be wrapped up in old blankets and such.

However, the return of his housekeeper down below distracted Jason. Leaving the body on the floor he hastened out, turning the key in the lock and pocketing it.

It had become the custom to invite selected guests back to the Babbidge house following the Mayday festivities; so Martha Prestidge would be busy all the rest of the day cleaning and cooking and setting the house to rights. As was the way of housekeepers, she hinted that Jason would get under her feet; so off he walked down to the glass and out on to its perfect flatness to stand and meditate. Villagers and visitors, spying the lone figure out there nodded gladly. Their prophet was at peace, presiding over their lives. And over their deaths.

The skate-sailing masque, the passion play, was enacted as brightly and gracefully as ever the next day.

It was May the Third before Jason could bring himself to go up to the attic again, carrying sacking and cord. He unlocked the door.

But apart from a dark stain of dried blood the floorboards were bare. There was only the usual jumble stacked around the walls. The room was empty of any corpse. And the window was open.

So he hadn't killed Daniel after all. The boy had recovered from the blow. Wild emotions stirred in Jason, disturbing his usual composure. He stared out of the window as though he might discover the boy lying below on the cobbles. But of Daniel there was no sign. He searched around Atherton, like a haunted man, asking no questions but looking everywhere piercingly. Finding no clue, he ordered a horse and cart to take him to Edgewood. From there he travelled all around the glass, through Buckby and Hopperton; and now he asked wherever he went, 'Have you seen a boy with red hair?' The villagers told each other that Jason Babbidge had had another vision.

As well he might have, for within the year from far away news began to spread of a new teacher, with a new message. This new teacher was only a youth, but he had also ridden a slow bird—much farther than the Silent Prophet had ever ridden one.

However, it seemed that this young teacher was somewhat flawed, since he couldn't remember all the details of his message, of what he had been told to say. Sometimes he would beat his head with his fists in frustration, till it seemed that blood would flow. Yet perversely this touch of theatre appealed to some restless, troublesome streak in his audiences. They believed him because they saw his anguish, and it mirrored their own suppressed anxieties.

Jason Babbidge spoke zealously to oppose the rebellious new ideas, exhausting himself. All the philosophical beauty he had brought into the dying world seemed to hang in the balance; and reluctantly he called for a 'crusade' against the new teacher, to defend his own dream of Submission.

Two years later, he might well have wished to call his words back, for their consequence was that people were tramping across the countryside in between the zones of annihilation armed with pitchforks and billhooks, cleavers and sickles. Villages were burnt; many hundreds were massacred; and there were rapes—all of which seemed to recall an earlier nightmare of Jason's from before the time of his revelation.

In the third year of this seemingly endless skirmish between the Pacifists and the Survivalists Jason died, feeling bitter beneath his cloak of serenity; and by way of burial his body was roped to a slow bird. Loyal mourners accompanied the bird in silent procession until it vanished hours later. A short while after that, quite suddenly at the Battle of Ashton Glass, it was all over, with victory for the Survivalists led by their young red-haired champion, who it was noted bore a striking resemblance to old Jason Babbidge, so that it almost seemed as though two basic principles of existence had been at contest in the world: two aspects of the selfsame being, two faces of one man.

Fifty years after that, by which time a full third of the land was glass and the climate was worsening, the Survival College in Ashton at last invented the promised machine; and from then on slow birds continued to appear and fly and disappear as before, but now none of them exploded.

And a hundred years after that all the slow birds vanished from the Earth. Somewhere, a war was over, logically and finally.

But by then, from an Earth four-fifths of whose land surface was desert or swamp—in between necklaces of barren shining glass—the first starship would arise into orbit.

It would be called *Slow Bird*. For it would fly to the stars, slowly. Slowly in human terms; two generations it would take. But that was comparatively fast.

A second starship would follow it; called *Daniel*.

Though after that massive and exhausting effort, there would be no more starships. The remaining human race would settle down to cultivate what remained of their garden in amongst the dunes and floods and acres of glass. Whether either starship would find a new home as habitable even as the partly glassed Earth, would be merely an article of faith.

On his deathbed, eighty years of age, in Ashton College lay Daniel who had never admitted to a family name.

The room was almost indecently overcrowded, though well if warmly ventilated by a wind whipping over Ashton Glass, and bright-lit by the silvery blaze reflecting from that vitrified expanse.

The dying old man on the bed beneath a single silken sheet was like a bird himself now: shrivelled with thin bones, a beak of a nose, beady eyes and a rooster's comb of red hair on his head.

He raised a frail hand as if to summon those closest, even closer. Actually it was to touch the old wound in his skull which had begun to ache fiercely of late as though it was about to burst open or cave in, unlocking the door of memory—notwithstanding that no one now needed the key hidden there, since his Collegians had discovered it independently, given the knowledge that it existed.

Faces leaned over him: confident, dedicated faces.

'They've stopped exploding, then?' he asked, forgetfully.

'Yes, yes, years ago!' they assured him.

'And the stars—?'

'We'll build the ships. We'll discover how.'

His hand sank back on to the sheet. 'Call one of them . . . '

'Yes?'

'Daniel. Will you?'

They promised him this.

'That way . . . my spirit . . . '

'Yes?'

'. . . will fly . . . '

'Yes?'

'. . . into the silence of space.'

This slightly puzzled the witnesses of his death: for they could not know that Daniel's last thought was that, when the day of the launching came, he and his brother might at last be reconciled.

We Remember Babylon

W E CROSS THE ARIZONA DESERT AWAKENING FROM A DAZE, OUR minds buzzing with *koiné*, the common tongue, the universal language, Greek.

Our brains still froth and simmer from all the speed-teaching: with receptivity drugs, hypnosis, computer interface, recorded voices squeaking at high speed like whistling dolphins. By the time we arrive at Babylon, they have told us, our heads will have cleared. A deep sediment of Greek words, phrases, syntax will have settled to the bottom of our minds; our ordinary consciousness will be lucid, clear and Attic. And so we will try to come to terms with the future which is written in the past.

A few saguaro cacti flash by: probably the last native American vegetation we shall see. Ahead, the desert is stripped bare, a buffer zone between America and Babylon.

We cross this denuded desert in a hovercraft, following the concrete ribbon of the road which once gave access to the construction site. No wheeled vehicles are allowed to use it now. It is closed; no longer a modern highway. We fly a few inches above it, the gale of air supporting us beneath and the wind from our tail fans sweeping it clear of sand. Yet we do not touch it. We are disconnected; disconnected, too, from the America we have left behind. The voices babbling in our brains disorient us, too; but already as promised they are becoming quieter, dropping beneath the horizon of our awareness.

'Alex—' Deborah is saying something to me in ancient Greek—Greek with an enriched vocabulary. I nod, but pay little attention. Nothing we can say at the moment means anything. We are still in transition.

Besides, I don't really wish to pursue a relationship with her. Not yet. Not as the people who we were when we first met. Which was only a matter of ten days ago, the two of us coming from opposite points of the compass to that gleaming hypermodern township south of Casa Grande: the so-called University of the Future, the University of Heuristics.

I, Alexander Winter, from the floundering ecotopia of Oregon with a fairly useless degree in social studies. She, Deborah Tate, from New York— which perhaps gave her something of a prior lien on Babylon—and a background as computer programmer and hopeful actress; but already that dream had died, to be replaced by the desire to live a role at last.

Deborah. Quite tall, quite graceful. Curly raven hair, dark eyes. Maybe she will go promptly to sit in the Temple of Love in Babylon waiting for any stranger to come along and toss a coin into her lap. Old man, young man, ugly or handsome, skinny or fat, clean or filthy: she must go with him and lie with him. That is the custom. A custom inconvenient to some homely women; they can spend months on end waiting in the temple. The prospect seemed to fascinate Deborah.

But maybe she only spoke of this back at the University in the hope that the stranger might be me? So that she could experience the frisson of excitement and trepidation, and then avoid the reality? Already I know that it will not be me who throws that coin to her, with the head of Alexander stamped on it. Not me; not yet. I hope she understands this. It would be untrue to Babylon.

Though later on, assuming that our visit is a success both in our own eyes and in those of the University—and presuming that we both become Babylonian citizens—later on maybe I will bid for Deborah before the auction block in the Marriage Market of Babylon. (For that is also the Babylonian custom.) Maybe.

I've little doubt that we will both become citizens. Babylon still needs some extra population; and there must, I suppose, be a turnover of citizens who leave of their own choice. I suppose; though I have not met any ex-Babylonians to my knowledge. But then, the city has only been finished for four years.

Yes, I will be a citizen. I will grow my hair long, wear a turban and perfume, and flourish a jaunty walking stick.

'Look,' she says in Greek. (Everyone in Babylon speaks Greek to begin with. Presently we will learn Babylonian. But Greek is the world language, used by travelers. It is the English of its day. For this is the epoch of Alexander the Great; and these are the last days of his reign. My namesake lies dying of fever in the Palace of Nebuchadnezzar.)

'Look!'

Some way ahead, to east and west, is a glint of water and the green of irrigated farmland. The desert will soon narrow into a great V, cutting through toward . . .

I spy the walls of Babylon, far off.

Our whole party disembarks at the Ishtar gate. Soldiers watch us idly, leaning on their spears. They pay no attention to the hovercraft as it re-inflates its skirts and swings round, roaring, to head back the way it came. It does not belong. The wind from its fans whips us with dust so that, having already arrived neat and clean, 20th-century-style, we suddenly become travel-stained in our Greek garb.

The brickwork of the gate towers is gorgeously enameled, with beasts in high relief standing out one above the other: a white and blue bull with yellow horns and hooves; a creamy white composite dragon—part viper, part bird, part lizard, part lion—against a turquoise background; its forked tongue, mane and claws are golden brown.

My thoughts are sharp and clear now. They are as luminous as that brick-work. I feel as though I should perform a sacrifice of thanksgiving to some long-forgotten god. To Shamash, perhaps, whose sun beats down on us. It would only be polite.

'Rejoice,' says Deborah. 'We have come.' She sounds like Pheidippides after the long run from Marathon to Athens, when the tide of the Persians had been turned—a hundred and sixty odd years ago, now.

Much has happened since then; and so us band of Greek travelers walk peacefully into the Babylon of the Chaldeans, who came before the Persian rulers of the city, who in turn came before Alexander, who now lies dying within . . . Once again, it is the last days of a world.

The walls of the street beyond gleam with lions and tigers, boars and wolves pictured in colored, enameled brick. And already the smells assail our noses: of dung, fishcakes, charcoal, offal, urine . . . and of the aromatic gums, musk, sandalwood, patchouli and fragrant oils of the inhabitants. Perhaps we too shall have to visit the perfume vendors before long!

Our original group soon splits up, to go its various ways. Presently Deborah and I are alone together in a crowded thoroughfare.

We need to find lodgings. In Greek I address a barefoot beggar squatting in a bundle of rags. I choose him more out of curiosity than perversity; he was, after all, recently an American. 'Greetings! Could you direct me to—?'

He grins evilly, yellow-toothed: and he sticks out an upright palm. Like a monkey for peanuts. The motion briefly reveals a knife stuffed in a band of cloth round his waist.

Deborah drags on my arm, pulls me away hastily deep into the crowd. And she's right, of course.

A chariot clatters down the street; the crowd scatter.

Synchronicity rules in Babylon. And I need hardly add that synchronicity is not an Assyrian king. Like Sennacherib. Here in Babylon, the great buildings of several different epochs all occur together. They co-exist in time.

A little history, then . . .

Babylon the Magnificent, the Babylon of Hammurabi the law-maker and builder of canals, fell to the pugnacious, greedy, uncultured Kassites who let the city fall into neglect. After a while, that first Babylon was totally destroyed by the Assyrian Sennacherib. His soldiers killed every man, woman and child in the city, smashed the houses down, and even diverted a major canal to flood the ruins.

But less than a hundred years later the Chaldeans—who destroyed the Assyrians with Persian help—rebuilt Babylon as their own capital. Before long, under Nebuchadnezzar, the city was even more splendid than ever.

Yet curiously these Chaldeans failed to quite live in the present. The intelligentsia—the priests and scribes—failed to. Amidst sumptuous new palaces and temples, and even while building observatories to study the planets and the stars, they were also digging nostalgically in the old ruins for clay books and record tablets. With these as a guide, they began to copy the past affectedly in dress and custom and speech.

Presently their former allies the Persians attacked and destroyed the Chaldean empire; and slowly Babylon crumbled away again into ruins and wreckage.

And presently Alexander of Macedon overthrew the Persians. But then something new in history happened. Alexander conceived the dream of ruling the whole world. He unified the Macedonians and the Persians; and the first world empire was organized with a common language and a common economy, centered upon Babylon. Babylon rose again, as capital of the known world.

Briefly, briefly. For in the palace of Nebuchadnezzar—which of course had decayed long before Alexander's birth, yet which is still here as pristine and perfect as ever—my namesake lies a-dying. At the age of thirty-three.

It is the end of Babylon, yet again. The last days of rekindled glory. Rise and fall. Rise and fall. And fall. It is all here, co-existing: the Babylon of Hammurabi, of Nebuchadnezzar, of Alexander. And ahead, dust and ashes; and the unknowable future.

The future of Rome—currently a tiny village. The future of Byzantium. The future of the Holy Roman Empire, of the Spanish Empire. The British Empire. The Third Reich. The Stars and Stripes.

Dust and ashes. Buried monuments. Bones. Amnesia. Meanwhile what rough village, in the Congo or the South Seas, slouches toward the future to become the new capital of human life? When there is no room left in the world for new golden hordes to gather or for barbarians sweeping down from the hills?

Where is the new incarnation of power and splendor? Can there be such a thing? Must the latest Babylons, of Moscow and New York, Tokyo and Peking make way in their time? What are the dynamics of decline and fall? Where is the elixir of longevity? How, as the years roll by, can the present be perpetuated into the future so that change does not sweep away what we know? Whence permanence? Whence mutability? What does the social psyche know, which the futurologists know not?

To answer such questions is Babylon rebuilt synchronously, and rekindled with life in the Arizona desert, gloriously poised on its final precipice with Alexander forever dying of a fever in the palace.

For Babylon is no Disneyland, no 'park of the past'. It is no 'ancient-world', where tourists can spend vacations. Nor is it a utopian arcology, or an experimental community which wilfully turns its back on the 20th century in pursuit of an ancient lifestyle. If it were merely any of these, would the U.S. Government have underwritten the huge initial cost, equivalent to that of a manned space station? Or exempted Babylon from State and Federal law?

Babylon is the most ambitious, most important project regarding the future of civilization as we know it.

Perhaps. And perhaps the University of Heuristics is a monstrous folly—and its Babylon a different sort of folly: more akin to the follies built by rich Englishmen in their landscape gardens in the 18th century? Though much vaster; and not merely a facade, either, but a fully functioning ancient city.

And why? Is the autumn of a culture marked by vast, fanciful building projects? By exercises in architectural metaphysics, designed to stem the tide of time? Schemes reeking of immortalist religious yearnings, masquerading as something else? (Call this the Ozymandias syndrome . . . !) Is Babylon the psychic salvation of the American dream, or the very symbol of its decay? I do not know. I hope to find out.

Here is the temple of Marduk, god of victory. Broad ramps slope steeply upward, zigzagging, bisecting one another, circuiting the temple's many towers. A stream of worshippers mounts; others descend. Can they really be intent on prayer—or only on admiring the view from the summit? Vendors sell incense and oil and bleating lambs, bowls of imported Greek wine, and rissoles, on the vast forecourt.

I accost one departing worshiper: a bearded, turbaned man. 'Excuse me, Sir. I'm a visitor. Do you really worship the God of War?'

Who worships war these days? However, this is the year 323 B.C. . . .

The man flushes.

'Fool!' he snarls, and pushes me aside.

Another, older man has heard this exchange. He approaches, smiling wryly and apologetically, and stands twiddling his ornamental walking stick.

'Perhaps it is purer to worship gods that don't exist?' he offers cryptically. 'But perhaps worshipping them causes them to exist? On the other hand, where else can you innocently worship war in these late days? Perhaps these worshipers are simply searching for their own lost innocence—the innocence of the beast, which does not ask whether the sun will rise tomorrow. Or whether tomorrow will exist. For the beasts knows nothing of tomorrow. And yesterday is already erased. All is now, the present, the moment. So the moment repeats itself forever. Thus the beast and his kind endure for a million years. In place of history, they have instinct. But perhaps, Greek, gods of war destroy empires with all their records and monuments every so often—otherwise the weight of memory would cripple us beneath its burden. We wouldn't have the energy for new enterprises; which are really the same old enterprises, forgotten then rekindled.'

What am I to make of this? Is he a philosopher, a fantasist, a fool? Or a futurologist? Is he saying that the world must be destroyed, so that the world can carry on? That America must fall into decay, so that the kingdom of Amazonia or Ashanti can arise? Surely he's forgetting all the nuclear missiles poised in their silos? But could it be that society could simply collapse, and the missiles stay where they were, rusting, unfireable?

He executes a little skip around his walking stick.

'And perhaps, foreigner,' he says, 'Marduk isn't God of War at all. Don't assume that you're wise, because you are a Greek. You're here to discover Babylon. But then, so are we!'

He winks, and strides off in sprightly style.

'Wait!'

He will not wait.

We buy fish rissoles and wine.

Here is the river Euphrates flowing through the heart of Babylon, giant coracles afloat on it, bearing produce and passengers and goats downstream. Even with oars fore and aft, these perfectly round boats tend to spin in the current like the waltzer cars at a funfair.

We stand on the stone bridge which Herodotus so much admired, leaning on the balustrade watching the river traffic. From stout pier to stout stone pier stretch rows of planks which can all be lifted up and hauled back on shore, rendering the bridge uncrossable. Every night all the planks are lifted and stacked; every morning they are put back. You do not build a bridge for your enemies to cross! Yet this is in the very heart of Babylon. Is the heart sick, divided against itself? Is this the corpus callosum, the bridge between the two hemispheres of the Babylonian brain? Every night when the city sleeps does it dream two separate dreams, the dream of the past, and the dream of the future?

Beyond the city walls the Euphrates flows on through irrigated farmland for half a dozen miles. Then it runs back through a subterranean tunnel to an equivalent distance upstream of the city. The Euphrates is a closed loop two dozen miles around. The Corps of Engineers constructed it. A buried geothermal spike provides the power for the mighty pumps at the upstream end which raise the river back up from the depths. Downstream, hidden sewage works cleanse the polluted water before it flows back underground.

Sleep. And dreams.

We had found lodgings in a tatty inn, with a courtyard where horses and camels pawed and snorted, coughed and nickered. A caravanserai.

Deborah and I had taken separate rooms: tiny brick chambers with straw-stuffed mattresses and raggy bedding, but quite clean. To our surprise there was no infestation of bugs.

Deborah and I do not sleep together because since we entered Babylon we are increasingly strange to each other. We can only come together if we first travel all the way to strangeness—and at last meet each other there. If indeed we recognize each other then. Or wish to recognize each other.

We have the same lodging place, and we even go about together. But not like lovers, which we never were, nor yet like brother and sister who only reflect each other's familiarity back at one another.

I dream: that the missiles have all flown, the bombs have all fallen. Russia and America are no more; Europe and China have been wiped off the map. Man-designed plagues rage elsewhere. It is the collapse, the end of techno-logical culture, of global government.

But Babylon survives. Here in the loneliest corner of the American desert—though there is no longer an 'America'—Babylon remains intact, entire. Untouched. And continues to be Babylon.

It's as though the mega-power released by all the warheads has rent a hole in the continuum of space and time, has scrambled the clock of the sun and the calendar of the earth, and has pulled this ancient city out of a previous era and deposited it in the future. As the only future which remains.

Babylon thrives. The Euphrates flows around and around. Seasons pass; decades. Eventually the Babylonians begin to colonize what was once America. But they know nothing any longer of the customs or speech of dead America, or the dead 20th century. They only know Babylonian ways. Long hair and perfume; Marduk and Ishtar; coracles and ziggurats.

But elsewhere, far away, is a new Assyrian wolf or another Alexander marsh-alling his forces in Angola or Argentina, to collide with Babylon once more?

We shall see.

No doubt there are oneiromancers, dream-diviners somewhere in the city who could see the meaning of this dream.

Days pass by.

The images of animals are everywhere in Babylon, in bright wall reliefs and statues. Largely of animals destined for slaughter. Stags, bison, lions, bulls, and rams. And dragons.

With Deborah I visit the Wonder Cabinet of Mankind in a corner of the palace: the first museum in the history of the world, opened to the general public by Nebuchadnezzar. I had wondered whether it too would be full of animals, exotic animals stuffed or modelled.

It isn't. It is full of antiquities. There are clay tablets and cylinders. There is a diorite column inscribed with ten thousand cuneiform letters: the laws of Hammurabi. There are inscriptions from Ur, stone bowls and figurines of Aramaic weather gods, Kassite clubs, Mesopotamian statuary, foundation stones of antique temples, reliefs, stelae, Theban obelisks, mace-heads and cudgels, jewelry, breastplates, bric-à-brac. And so on, and on.

The curator intones at us, 'Here is the whole span of time, Greeks.' For a moment I believe him. Gone is the Rome of the Caesars, and the Rome of the Popes. Gone is the crucifix, gone is the mosque. Gone, the Renaissance; gone, the space age. They are *not*, yet. So they have never been.

Deborah must feel this deeply too. 'Isn't it strange?' she murmurs to me. 'There's so much that isn't here. In fact, almost *everything* isn't here, that we ever thought important! And yet, for them the world was just as full—with all this ancient history stretching way behind them.

'And the future . . . Us. What we think of as the culmination of the past— which had hardly even *started* when this museum was opened: it seems such a fantasy, a fever dream! Of men like Gods flying through the sky, and space, and wielding bolts of lightning, and sending their thoughts and pictures from place to place in an instant—as though mythology lies ahead, not behind!'

'The *whole* span of time,' repeats the curator, with emphasis.

'Yes,' she says to me. 'And in another thousand years the 20th century will seem such a partial, provisional, restricted thing. Because X hadn't happened yet. Or Y, or Z—which is so goddam important, so crucial to history that it changes everything. Creatures from the stars, immortality, I don't know what. Then a thousand years later X, Y and Z will have been totally dwarfed by A, B or C . . .'

She stares wildly around the Wonder Cabinet. 'To believe that this is the whole span! To know it in your heart. Why, this could free us from the tread-mill of time! Then time might not sweep us away. Or else . . . we might expect it to sweep us away—and fashion our world accordingly. And so survive through the changes. We could swim with the flood of years instead of being drowned by them. Yes, I see. Our culture is trying to learn how not to drown—by sending us here, where *it is not*, and never has been.'

Wonders? These? Here, in this first museum? Clay and stone? Bronze and gold? Rather than steam engines, Saturn rockets, microcomputers?

Yes, perhaps. To enter a frame of mind where such things as rockets, satellites, wrist computers and heart transplants are simply equal to obelisks and pots and breastplates—to look at the 20th century through the other end of the telescope of time—is to enable one to comprehend the future . . .

We have built an alien city, as though on Mars, to alienate us from the big dipper of the present, which seems about to fly apart. As soon as Babylon is no longer alien to us we can begin to redeem the future, purging it of its threat, knowing it. Not by Delphi methods or computer projections, world models or algorithms based in the present. Not by reason. But emotionally.

Then Deborah and I, too, may begin to understand our own emotions. Whatever they may be.

Here is the Tower of Babel: tallest of all ziggurats, a skyscraper, even though the sky it scrapes here is a cloudless desert blue, so it is difficult to set an upper or a lower limit to that sky.

A single spiralling ramp winds upwards, around and around, so that each tier is of less girth than the one below. And the tall walls of each tier are indented with doors and windows. If unwound into a ribbon, the corkscrew helix of the tower's height would reach right across the city and into the countryside beyond. It's a very long walk to the top, and many people dwell up inside the belly of Babel: a miniature city within a city, with its own inns, shops, workshops and homes. Some people may never bother to descend; others must be occupied full time in trading supplies and craftwork between the different levels, and between Babel and the ground below.

In design this tower is far from being an angular ziggurat of straight lines and sharp corners; visibly it owes more to Breughel, though it is slimmer than his tower. Perhaps there are structural reasons for this; or perhaps Breughel's vision of Babel was too compelling to ignore, even though it would not be pictured for another two thousand years . . .

I'm not sure whether a hundred foreign languages really are spoken up around those tiers: Akkadian and Egyptian, Persian, Aramaic. But secure in the Attic clarity of Greek, I set off boldly toward the base of the great access ramp.

'Alex!'

Deborah has hung back.

'I'm not going up there. It could take all day. Two days, even . . . You go, though.'

'So where are you going?'

'To the Temple of Ishtar. I feel it's time to.'

To the Temple of Love. Of sacred prostitution. Obligatory, once in every Babylonian woman's life. More than once is optional.

Probably Deborah's right. It's time. This will alienate her from her 20th-century American self more effectively, more viscerally, than climbing Babel.

So we part, with a curiously formal handshake followed by a quick kiss. She walks away; and I watch her go. But not even when she has disappeared do I carry on toward the ramp of Babel.

I stand, I crick my neck, I contemplate the tower. Presently I buy a bowl of wine, and a handful of ripe figs. I while away an hour.

And finally I follow her.

In the tree-shaded courtyard of the Temple of Love some forty women wait, each on a separate woven mat, cross-legged or with their knees drawn up, the laps of their dresses forming for each a begging bowl.

Men come and go: inspecting, choosing, commanding with a coin. Walking with their chosen woman into the temple. Departing later, they go separate ways.

Deborah isn't anywhere in the courtyard; and I realize that I'm glad of this. Glad that the affair has already been settled? Glad that she has been spared the humiliation of a long wait? (But is that considered a humiliation here?) Glad that she has not seen me follow her here? Glad for whose sake: hers or mine?

Better that she should not know I came! I wonder whether, by coming here, I am trying in some way to get even with her? But I cannot do that; because I am a man. Deborah submits to Babylon today; but it will simply be one individual woman of Babylon who submits to me.

I walk about, fingering a coin: not too large, so that I seem like a naïve tourist unable to believe my luck, or like a fool—nor too small, so that I seem insulting, mean and disrespectful.

Whom shall I choose? The women wait politely, patiently. They do not ogle or flash seductive smiles, eager to be done with it, and gone; eager, perhaps, for Alexander Winter rather than for someone with acne, warts or bad breath. They wait dispassionately, gracefully. They neither drop their gaze, nor fix me with it.

This young tanned blonde?

This comely, freckled redhead?

This negress, with cheeks and arms of polished ebony?

Or shall I choose this homely dumpling? Or this angular, bony lady with a face like a horse? These two may have been here all week, all month, all year. Lying with one of them might prove an alien, disconcerting experience for both her and me. After all, there's a certain familiarity about the joining of bodies accustomed to such manoeuvres—and I do not seek the familiar. And besides, the dumpling or the horse may be wiser in the ways of Babylon, if not in the arts of love. Or contrariwise the ugly woman may be far more sensual; the beauty may be frigid . . .

When I make my choice, it is by accident. Out of the comer of my eye I catch a glimpse of Deborah emerging from the doorway of the temple, accompanied by a tall, robed, bearded man, who inclines his head, smiles faintly, and walks off.

The woman I'm standing before: she's mousy. A little mouse. Short brown hair. Small, ordinary features. Neither beautiful nor otherwise.

I drop my coin into her lap. 'You,' say I.

And she rises smoothly, holding the piece of silver.

Let Deborah (who is heading away across the courtyard) make what she will of my choice. If she notices. She seems preoccupied. Or perhaps she is taking pains not to stare at me.

Inside the temple light filters softly through high clerestory windows. Private chambers, like a row of confessionals, occupy each side of the 'nave'. Richly brocaded curtains are drawn across those which are occupied. In those which are open and empty, waiting, I see a couch, an ewer of water, a bowl, a towel, wine and fruit, and a little oil lamp burning. But first we walk down to the altar to deposit my coin in a great silver bowl full of other coins, beneath a statue of Ishtar, rubies studding her hair. An old woman is sweeping the floor and whistling. Another old woman is replenishing clean towels and water. Are there any priestesses as such? Perhaps every woman who enters with a coin becomes a priestess for a while. My mouse kneels and prays briefly, whispering in Babylonian. What does she pray for? Gentleness, on my part? That she will not become pregnant or the contrary?

She walks before me to an open booth. We enter; I close the curtain. Facing each other in the lamplight we undress, ignoring the wine and fruit. For just a moment I imagine her at a PTA meeting; or in church, in Smallville, USA. Instead, she is the whore of Babylon. Then I forget those things as our bodies meet.

Later: 'What did you pray for at the altar?' I ask.

'For you,' she answers. 'For you.'

And when eventually I leave, and walk off across the leafy courtyard, I realize that this Temple of Love teaches us of ourselves: of our mixed emotions, our false chivalries, sham and sanctimonious, our egotisms and illusions; so that we may at last learn love, affection, joy.

It isn't the lesson I had expected to learn; yet I suspect nonetheless that this disordering of our emotional routines is a necessary way stage to that future, which we must grasp emotionally before all else.

In my brief absence Deborah has moved out of the inn, leaving no forwarding address or message. But perhaps the absence of any message for me is in itself equivalent to one: saying silently that there is no need of any message, since we both know what is happening. We have to proceed along diverging routes, which will lead perhaps to the same destination. Such feelings cannot be written down in a scribbled note; to do so would make them a lie, an evasion.

Time flows on; but now I no longer know which way it is flowing: forward, or back into the past. Perhaps, like the river Euphrates, time really flows in a circle. Though I suspect not.

Here am I back once again at the Palace of Nebuchadnezzar, with its long pillared tiers draped in the Hanging Gardens. I had thought I would explore these gardens in Deborah's company, each of us thinking our own green thoughts in the green shade. But as it is, of this palace together we only visited the dusty antiquities of the Wonder Cabinet down at street level at the northern end, chambers full of clay and stone.

This palace is a prodigy even for the 20th century. What was it like twenty-six centuries ago? Perhaps in reality the palace was only a rather large ziggurat with a few trees planted on it, and potted palms and shrubs. But no: this is how it was, exactly, because this is how it is, now. Besides, consider the Great Hall of Karnak. Or the Pyramids. Obviously there were giants living in those days; even though compared with us no doubt they were pygmies.

As I gaze up from the street at the seven terraces, once again time reverses and twists; and the 20th century which I have left becomes a distant epoch which simply led here, to this achievement, all of our future ambition and skill culminating—in a 6th century B.C. palace.

A broad flight of marble steps leads up to the first terrace, of giant ferns and fountains. Some Macedonian and Persian soldiers guard the way aloft, but hinder no one. A party of fine ladies in rich array are gossiping halfway up, while servants hold plume-fans over their heads. A trio of bearded men in black robes and conical caps descend, deep in conversation. Astronomers, astrologers?

I climb. I wander up and along one terrace after another: through palm trees, fig trees, bays, orange and avocado, thickets of jasmine, a miniature forest of cypress and smaller conifers, a garden of succulents. Watercourses run everywhere, plashing in waterfalls from level to level, sparkling skyward in fountains. Here is a statue of a sphinx, there of a winged bull, or elephant. And at the back of each terrace columned arcades give access to the palace proper.

To be a gardener in Babylon, upon the Hanging Gardens! I have passed several at their tasks. Here is another, an old frail man, sprinkling the flag-stones of the fifth terrace to still any dust.

We fall into conversation. And all the while we're talking I'm thinking to myself, 'He has emigrated to Babylon as an old, tired man! Doesn't he care that he'll die the sooner here? Doesn't it worry him that the medical facilities are those of the marketplace? Consisting of folk wisdom, quack diagnosis by passers-by, herbal potions? No surgery, no antibiotics, no real medicine! Does Babylon represent for him a death wish? Yet amid this riot of growth—here in these gardens which are the very antithesis of decay? How can that be?'

He has, of course, noticed me assessing his wrinkles, the bend of his shoulders, the slowness of his hands, the liver spots upon the skin. ('Gran-dad, shouldn't you be resting in a rocking chair on some back stoop with a rug over your knees, instead of labouring in Babylon?')

He starts to cough: a dangerous, wheezing noise.

'Are you all right?'

He spits, scrapes the sputum away with his sandals, then grins. 'Everyone dies, lad. The young king himself lies dying within, and he's just thirty-three. But that's from fever . . .

'Listen: the cells in any body only replace themselves so many times—there's a limit, isn't there? And a city or kingdom is just a body writ large. What if there is some natural limit in the *polis*, the State, just as there is in any animal body? The *polis* that I left,' and I suppose he must mean America, 'it seemed to have reached a limit. Its limit as a body . . . Think on that.'

Is this right? Is this what he learned here in Babylon: this insight so vital to the University of Heuristics, namely that any society has an inbuilt limit to how long it can perpetuate itself? Or is that what he came here determined to learn, and so console himself for his own imminent departure from the world?

Strange things are happening in this city; strange tides of consciousness are being drawn up, as if by an ancient moon which once shone over the original Babylon.

'Alexander's dying,' he mumbles, 'but that's just fever . . .'

Far away down the leaf-clad terraces, beyond parapet after parapet, I think I spy Deborah walking. Really, the figure is too far away to be sure; and now a Banyan tree eclipses her.

'Why don't you visit him, then?'

'Visit? Who?'

'Alexander, of course.'

'But . . . he's the King! You don't just visit a King. And anyway, he's dying.'

The gardener winks. 'He's been dying for long enough. Must get boring. He might appreciate a visit from a compatriot. Anyway, you Greeks are supposed to be such a democratic lot. Well, that was once upon a time . . . Now you have to grovel and prostrate yourself and make obeisances.'

'Do you mean I can really visit Alexander?'

'S'pose so. You can always ask. Me, I'm only one of his gardeners.'

This is incredible. Alexander the Great lies dying in this very palace, maybe only a hundred paces distant . . . I knew this. Of course I knew it. But I had never imagined that he was *really* here.

Does he actually exist? Or is this old man just playing a joke on me?

'If you don't believe me, lad, go up to the next terrace. Ask a guard.'

'I will!'

Yes. Yes. And Yes.

I am searched, for daggers. I am clad in borrowed cloth of gold, in case my clothes themselves are poisonous, or lest I offend Alexander's fevered eyes. I'm instructed how to throw myself down and approach on my knees.

Flanked by two guards (one Persian, one Macedonian) armed with short spears, a chamberlain leads me toward the presence. Rich vases are everywhere in this part of the palace, polished ivory and carved jade, lootings of India and beyond.

A staff is stamped before double doors of carved teak. These open upon a large, airy room. Filmy curtains of gauze ripple across the stone window frames; yet the sweet smell is not of flowers, but of sickness and incense. Or perhaps it is simply the incense which smells sickly. His bed is great and golden, with claw and ball feet, and a canopy above.

I prostrate myself on the Persian carpet; I crawl.

'Stand up,' says a voice wearily.

And I behold Alexander the Great, plumped up on soft pillows, wearing a silken gown embroidered with dragons, jeweled rings on his fingers. The ruler of Babylon.

He doesn't *look* fatally ill. But then, hasn't he been sick of this same fever for the past four years? He doesn't look thirty-three—more like forty—nor a dashing, muscular conqueror, either. But then, he is only an avatar of Alexander. He's stout and jowly with long ringletted hair and dark sad eyes, glinting nevertheless with a sharp intelligence: an intelligence imprisoned in pillows and sickness. Does he have rouge on his cheeks—and on his lips too?

Bowls of ripe fruits and candies, and flasks of wine surround the bed; incense sticks burn. I'm reminded of Nero, of Aubrey Beardsley's drawings, of Oscar Wilde, of some Borgia Pope—phantasms from the future. Alexander, it seems, has succumbed to Persian luxury. Scrolls lie on his bed: maps of empire? No, graphs, doodles, charts of cryptic symbols. Alchemical diagrams and horoscopes. Perhaps. Or perhaps exercises in heuristic futurology.

What is he? What is his fever? The fever of the dying 20th century seeking the elixir of immortality?

I wonder whether he is drugged, like a seer or sibyl.

I wonder whether he will eventually be killed by his guards—given an overdose—and replaced with someone younger, likewise to be kept abed in a semi-drugged state. For a moment the frightening, presumptuous thought crosses my mind: am I the next Alexander?

Yet if this king's body seems half paralysed and comatose, what of his brain?

He stares at me. His rouged lips move.

'Few come to visit the maggot in the apple . . . Wine!'

A serving woman bows, pours, sips from a cup; then, since she isn't now writhing on the floor in agony, she holds the cup to Alexander's lips, tipping it up for him. Gulping, he drains the cup. Several dribbles run down his chin to be mopped up by the woman with a napkin.

'Ambassadors, petitioners, magi with their cures . . . What's yours, Greek? What's your cure for the world?'

'Babylon,' I say. 'Babylon is the cure.' For I believe this. Even more so, paradoxically, now that I have seen him.

And now, as though the wine—or whatever was in it—has inflamed the sinews of his vision, the muscles of his mind, he speaks again in a sing-song voice:

'We have heard tales of the morning of the Earth—and of its golden afternoon, which we presume must be the twentieth century or the thirtieth or fortieth or the hundredth. And we have heard tales of the long, long evening of decay. Perhaps with assorted rises and falls in between: new barbarism, trips to the stars, who knows?

'But this is all nonsense. For it's still the morning, now; and in a million years it will be the morning of the planet, still. And in a million more. Even the early afternoon is unimaginably different—and may be inhabited gloriously by creatures that are only a few inches long now: voles, shrews. Or by dogs that walk erect, or by birds, or by creatures we can't even imagine, because their ancestors haven't happened yet . . .

'Who can ever feel time? Who can really sense its vast arcades? Ah, but we have performed a clever conjuring trick.

'For the ancient world is obviously older than ours. It is an old man, to our brash youth—even if we live longer than anyone lived then. It is the evening, to our morning, because it is ancient.

'So by recreating it—by reviving the dawn of civilization, which is now dust—we take a giant leap into the afternoon of life, and even perhaps into the evening, in our psyche, in our soul. And so we reach beyond our callow ten a.m. of time—to other, later hours of the future . . . '

A scribe takes this down, scratching quickly with a stylus. Will they post these sayings in the marketplace? Will they read them aloud in the Temple of Marduk? Will they convey them up the ramp of Babel?

Why else copy down his words? Since surely there is a microphone listening somewhere in this room, and a hidden camera watching. Surely in the King's room, if anywhere!

Yet perhaps there are no hidden cameras or microphones anywhere in Babylon. Even with the latest semi-aware, fuzzy logic computer to screen the flood of input, how could any team of observers cope?

Perhaps the University simply samples Babylon by sending observers in directly (and I am one right now). But perhaps everyone in Babylon—every citizen, that is—is an observer; and it is the stream of newcomers whom they observe, the applicants for citizenship, the visitors, for changes in their behavior—for signs of bewilderment, acceptance, spiritual crisis, illumination.

And perhaps, in its arbitrary yet wholehearted adoption of ancient alien customs, Babylon has become the first self-aware *polis* in the history of the world: self-aware beyond time and space. As nowhere else. A communal brain. Maybe it is Babylon itself that is the computer, built of human beings.

Alexander slumps further back into his pillows, exhausted, drained. He shuts his eyes; I see there is kohl on his eyelids. The chamberlain tugs my sleeve, forcing me down. The audience is at an end. Together, we back out of the room on our hands and knees.

My thoughts buzzing, my brain burbling to itself—uncertain whether I have been witness to a profound truth in my namesake's bedchamber, or to a wild folly, a grandiose gesture of despair, I blunder out of the palace, escorted politely but firmly by the guards back to the gardens of the sixth terrace.

Eventually, days later, a messenger—a fat fussy little man—rouses me in the inn.

'It's time,' he says. 'Today.'

I stare at him, nonplused. 'Today? But of course it's today. It's always today. It could hardly be tomorrow, or yesterday!'

'It's *time*,' he says again.

'Time for what? I'm going to climb Babel today.'

'The rest of your group checked in at dawn, by the gate. You're keeping them waiting. The woman Deborah said you might still be here. You've forgotten.' He hesitates, then whispers in an alien tongue, English: 'The hovercraft. To take you back to the University. For debriefing. Decisions.' A dead tongue. Dead, because it hasn't yet been born.

But I go with him.

As we walk through the early morning streets of Babylon toward the Ishtar gate, I wonder: should I have changed my lodgings? Did I somehow lack initiative? But obviously I have to return to the University. To learn Babylonian. To be speed-taught, force-fed with the true language of the city. Otherwise I would be forever a foreigner here, a visiting Greek.

Is that why they teach us Greek to begin with? To ensure that we first arrive as strangers, and always retain at least a memory of our strangeness? Otherwise we might be totally submerged as soon as we stepped through the gate. Like long-lost kin who have come home at last, like amnesiacs who have suddenly regained their memories. Or like the insane, from whom the veils of madness have abruptly lifted . . .

Once on the hovercraft, I sit down by Deborah.

'After you checked out of the inn,' I ask her, 'where did you go?'

At first her voice is cool, remote. 'Me? I went to live on Babel. Up the Tower of Babel. '

'The one place I missed!'

'One always misses something, Alex.'

'I might say that I'd missed you—'

She frowns, and I hasten to add, 'But how could I? I didn't know who you were—till you found out for yourself.' This sounds insulting, but it isn't; nor does she take it so.

'And did you find out too, Alex? Who you are?'

'I think so.'

Now she smiles.

I'm sure we have a real relationship at last. But it is a relationship by virtue of Babylon.

'One day,' I promise her, 'I'll bid for you at the auction block.'

'If you're rich enough, Alex.'

'I will be. I'll be rich in something, even if it isn't coin.'

'Won't it be interesting,' she remarks, 'as more and more children are born in Babylon, whose first language is Babylonian? Kids who only learn a smattering of Greek, the hard way? Kids who have never even heard of English?'

And I suppose this is some kind of promise on her part.

With a roar the hovercraft lofts itself smoothly above the ground, and turns to head north in a billow of dust. The notch of wasteland which abuts the Ishtar gate widens rapidly. Soon we are speeding through the Arizona desert, along the abandoned road.

When I see the first Saguaro cactus, I shall know we are somewhere else. Somewhere anonymous.

For no name can match the name of Babylon the Great.

The people on the precipice

ONE EVENING SMEAR CLIMBED DOWN TO OUR LEDGE AND TOLD US a story about people who lived in a two-dimensional world.

He had made the story up, of course. To amuse and enlighten. (This could have been Smear's motto.)

'Just suppose,' he said, as the daylight dimmed, 'that a whole world is as flat as a leaf! And suppose that creatures live within that leaf, who themselves are perfectly flat. Imagine that this narrow ledge here simply carries on'—he chopped his hand out into empty space—'in that direction forever! Imagine that it is a simple, infinite surface with nothing above it and nothing below it. And with no precipice to jut out from.'

Bounce giggled at this idea so much that she almost fell out of her bower of vine-rope.

Tumbler, our chief—who had no sense of humour—said, 'Preposterous! What would hold your ledge up? How would we ever get over the lip, to harvest sweet fungi below?'

'I'm asking you to imagine a different kind of world. A plane—with no 'below' or 'above'. With no 'up' or 'down'. The inhabitants are flat, too.'

'But how can they grip anything? They'll all slide away, and slide forever.'

'No they won't. You see, they don't live *upon* the flat surface. They're *part* of the surface.'

'You'll do me an injury!' squealed Bounce.

'So how do they make love?' enquired Fallen. 'How can they squeeze on to one another?'

'Aha,' and Smear winked at her, 'now you're asking.'

'Tell us!' cried Bounce.

But Tumbler interrupted. 'I hear that young Clingfast from three ledges down fell off yesterday. That was his mother's fault for giving him such an unlucky name. "Bounce" is a risky name, too, in my opinion.'

This remark annoyed Bounce. 'Just you try to invade my bower, Tumbler, and *you'll* get bounced—right off the cliff. That'll teach you what my name's all about.'

'Can I please tell my story?' asked Smear.

And so he did.

He regaled us with the hilarious adventures of Ma and Pa Flat in their flatworld; and what preposterous antics those were, to be sure! Still, his story seemed to have a couple of sly morals buried in it. Compared with the imaginary flat-people we were fortunate indeed—being gifted with all sorts of mobility denied to Ma and Pa Flat. In other words, things might be a lot worse. But also, Ma and Pa at least tried to make the very best of a bad job— did we always do likewise?

By the time Smear finished it was black dark, and we had long since tightened our tethers for the night. Obviously Smear would be spending the time of darkness on our ledge.

Soon after, I heard suspicious scraping sounds, suggesting that Smear was recklessly edging his way along to reach Bounce's bower. (He had positioned himself close to her.) Subsequent smothered giggles and gasps indicated that he had succeeded: a surmise proven true in the morning when light brightened and we saw Bounce and Smear clinging together asleep in her harness of vines.

Smear quickly roused himself and departed upward, his horny toes in all the proper cracks, his left hand holding a guidevine, his right hand reaching up in approved style for well-remembered, reliable holds. You could never wholly trust guidevines with your total weight. They might snap or rip their roots free. Then you would be taking the long trip down through empty air.

We breakfasted on the leftovers from yesterday's harvest of berries and lichen, rockworms and beetles.

The pearly void was bright; the day was warm. Below, the precipice descended forever. Above, it rose forever. To left and right, it stretched out unendingly. Occasionally, thin silver water-licks oozed from the rock, dribbling down till the droplets bounced into space. Here and there were still some surviving pastures of moss and fungus and fleshier plants; though by now our appetites had stripped most decent rock-fields bare, adding to the area of naturally occurring barrens. Soon we would all have to migrate—just as we had already migrated at least a hundred times since I was born. A planning conference was slated for today high up on Badbelay's ledge. Tumbler as our chief would attend.

As our tribe clung to the rockface considering which way to forage, a scream from above made us tighten our holds. We tried to flatten ourselves completely—just like Smear's mythical beings. A young lad plunged past, an arm's length away. I could have reached out to touch him, if I was foolish enough.

'Butterfingers!' shrieked Fallen in sympathy. The lad probably never heard her.

The falling body diminished until it was a mere speck deep below.

Bounce surprised us by saying, 'Next time we migrate we ought to head upwards and *keep on* migrating upwards for a whole lifetime, to see what happens.'

'That'll be one of friend Smear's fancy ideas, I suppose?' Tumbler spat contemptuously into space. 'What a strain *that* would be, and what peril, compared with migrating sideways. My dear Bounce, it's all very well to climb up a few ledges, and down a few ledges. Indeed this keeps all our muscles in trim. But to climb one way only? Faugh! Do you imagine our grandchildren would reach a *top*? Or a *bottom*, suppose we migrated downwards? And what would be at this imaginary bottom? Bones and rubbish and shit, floating in foul water, I shouldn't be surprised!'

'I didn't mention any bottom.'

'And what would be at this top of yours? Not that it exists! I'll tell you: a place where our muscles would weaken through disuse so that we could no longer harvest the precipice. We'd starve within a generation. Our present way of life is perfect.'

'Clinging on by your fingertips all life long is perfect?' she retorted. 'There might be a huge flat space up at the top—with oodles of really big plants all over, because they wouldn't have to worry about their weight ripping them away.'

'What's wrong with hanging on by one's fingertips, pray?'

'A certain tendency to *fall*,' she said. 'Especially when you get old and sick and mad and exhausted.'

I spoke up, since something had been worrying me for a while. 'When we migrated here, it seemed to me that this particular patch of precipice hereabouts was . . . well, strangely familiar. When we arrived I felt as if I'd been here before—when I was only a child. All the cracks and finger-grips were somehow known to me.'

'That,' said Tumbler, 'is purely because of the expertise you develop at clinging on after twenty or thirty years.'

'So why do experienced adults ever fall off?'

'They get tired and ill and crazy,' said Bounce. 'Everyone does, in the end, after a lifetime of clinging on.'

'We always migrate leftward,' I pointed out.

'Obviously! Who on earth would migrate back to a patch which had been stripped the time before?'

'What if,' I asked, 'the sum total of our migrations has brought us back to the very same place where we were years ago? What if our precipice isn't a straight wall but a vast . . . um . . .'

'A vast cylinder,' said Bounce.

Tumbler pointed impatiently to the right where the view was more barren. 'Look: if that isn't straight—!'

'Maybe it only seems straight,' said Splatty unexpectedly, 'because it's so enormous. Maybe it bends ever so slightly? We can't actually see the bend, but after tens of years of travel . . . If so, what's the sense in migrating?'

'To find food, slippy-thumb! To survive! Suppose we do come back to the same patch eventually—so what? The pastures have fleshed out again.'

'It's hardly *progress*,' said Bounce.

'Progress? Cylinders? Bends? Have you people gone nuts? Are you planning to let go and dive into the abyss? This is all Smear's fault. Listen: we hang on by the skin of our teeth. We make daily forays up and down for food. When we've scalped a patch we migrate sideways. That's life.'

Even Topple joined in. 'It's life. That's true. But is it *living?*'

'Damn it, it's as good a life as any! In fact I can't imagine any other. How about you?'

Topple shook his head. 'I've been clinging on for a lifetime. What else do I know?'

'And you'll die clinging on. Or rather, you'll die pretty soon after you *stop* clinging on. Now, today I'm climbing up to the Chief-of-Chiefs for that conference. Bounce will guard our ledge and keep the kids tied up. Loosepiton'—that's me—'will escort me upwards.'

'Why me, Boss?'

'Perhaps you would like to plead your notion that we're climbing round in a circle. That ought to raise some laughs.' (Aye, and likely damage Smear's advocacy of migrating upwards . . .)

'The rest of you will forage. Splatty and Fallen and Plunge can head far to the left, and chart the distant cracks while they're about it. Slip and Flop can forage to the right for what's left of the familiar pickings. Gather well, my tribe! We need to store some supplies in case we have to cross wide barrens.' To me he said, 'Come on, Loosepiton. Best foot upwards!'

And he began to ascend the sheer precipice, toehold by toehold.

'On what wide surface shall we store our huge harvest, O Chief?' Bounce called after him. He ignored her.

When Tumbler and I paused on Smear's Ledge for a quick rest we learned that Chief Smear had already preceded us upwards. Apparently Smear had done a lot of shinning about, visiting other ledges and telling merry stories, recently.

'He's campaigning to change our lives,' I remarked to Tumbler.

However, our chief seemed more annoyed with Bounce. 'That woman's a fool,' he groused. 'A vertical cliff puts constraints on the amount we can store. Of course it does. That stands to reason. So this limits the amount we can sensibly harvest. Consider the alternative! If we could tear up everything and pile it all on some vast ledge we'd exhaust our resources much more rapidly. What's more, we'd overeat. We'd grow fat and clumsy and far too heavy to haul ourselves up and down.'

We climbed onward together.

Another body fell past us; a woman's. She held her arms wide out on either side of her, as down she flew.

'Diver,' puffed Tumbler. 'Deliberate dive.'

'Dive of despair.'

'What's there to be desperate about, eh Loosepiton? Beautiful weather today. Soft breezes. No slippery stone.' He plucked a crimson rock-worm loose with a 'plop' and popped it into his mouth.

Not long after, some excrement hit him on the shoulder. Excrement usually falls well clear of the wall but some freak contour must have directed otherwise. Without comment Tumbler wiped himself clean on a nearby danglevine.

We passed six more ledges, rested and ate a meal courtesy of the tribe clinging to the seventh, then climbed past fifteen more. We reached Chief-of-Chiefs Badbelay's ledge in the early afternoon.

The ledge was already crowded with a line of chiefs—and in the middle Smear was chanting out another of his stories about bizarre worlds. In this case: about people with suckers like a gripworm's on their feet who lived on a huge ball afloat in a void. Smear was leaning quite far back to call his words past the intervening bodies.

'Shit in your eye,' Tumbler greeted him grumpily as we two forced a space for ourselves on the ledge.

'Aha,' responded Smear, 'but up here, where would that crap fall from? Either another tribe of tribes clings immeasurably high above us—or else not. If not, why not? Why do no strangers ever fall from above? Because no strangers live higher up! Yet if our precipice extends upwards infinitely, surely other people must dwell somewhere higher up. *Ergo*—'

'Unless those other people have migrated further along than us!' broke in Tumbler. 'Unless they're further to the left—or to the right, for that matter.'

'The reason,' Smear continued suavely, 'is that our precipice isn't infinitely high. It has a top.'

'The real reason,' growled Badbelay, 'may simply be that we are the *only* people. All that exists is the precipice, and us.'

'Maybe we're the only people on the precipice itself. But maybe hundreds of tribes live on top—and every now and then they gaze down and have a good laugh at us.'

'Why should anyone laugh at us? Are we not courageous and ingenious, persevering and efficient, compassionate and clever?'

'Undoubtedly,' Smear replied, 'but perhaps if we were fools, liars, cheats, thieves, and slovens we would have slid down to the bottom years ago instead of trying to cling on here; and we would have been living in rich pastures.'

'So now it's the *bottom* that's our goal, is it?' challenged Tumbler. 'Kindly make your mind up!'

'I spoke by way of illustration. Obviously, with all our fine qualities, it is ever upward that we ought to aspire. We may reach the top within a single lifetime.'

'Then what do we do?' asked another chief. 'Sprawl and sleep?'

The argument went on all afternoon.

Eventually Badbelay gave his judgement. We would all migrate in ten days' time—diagonally. Leftwards, as was traditional; but also upwards, as Smear had urged.

'If we do find lush pastures leftward and upward,' explained Badbelay, 'we can always steepen our angle of ascent. But if we run into difficulties we can angle back down again on to the time-approved route.'

Some chiefs applauded the wisdom of this compromise. Others—particularly Tumbler—voiced discontent. Smear looked disappointed at first but then perked up.

That night we slept in vine-harnesses on Badbelay's ledge; and in the morning we all climbed back down again.

A couple of days later Smear paid another visit to our ledge—with apprehension written on his face.

The rest of our tribe had already fanned out across the precipice, a-gathering. I myself was about to depart.

'Tumbler! Loosepiton! Have you looked out across the void lately?'

'Why should we waste our time looking at nothing?' demanded Tumbler with a scowl.

Smear pointed. 'Because there's *something*.'

To be sure, far away in the pearly emptiness there did seem to me to be some sort of enormous shadow.

Tumbler rubbed his eyes then shrugged. 'I can't see anything.'

I cleared my throat. 'There *is* something, Chief. It's very vague and far away.'

'Rubbish! Nonsense! There's never been anything there. How can there be something?'

Tumbler, I realized, must be short-sighted.

Smear must have arrived at a similar diagnosis. However, he didn't try to score any points off Tumbler. He just said diplomatically to me, 'Just in case, let's keep watch, Loosepiton—you and I, hmm?'

I nodded agreement.

Whatever it was seemed to thicken day by day. At first the phenomenon was thin, then it grew firmer, denser. No one else glanced in the empty direction—until the very morning when we were due to migrate.

Then at last some fellow's voice cried out, 'Look into the void! Look, everyone!'

Presently other voices were confirming what the man had noticed. For a while minor pandemonium reigned, though Tumbler still insisted: 'Fantasy! Smear has been spreading rumours. Smear has stirred this up!' Which was the very opposite of the truth.

Bounce clung to me. 'What is it?' Now that her attention had been directed, she could see the thing clearly; though as yet none of us could make out any details. All I could be sure of, was that something enormous existed out in the void beyond the empty air; and that something was changing day by day in a way which made it more noticeable.

'I've no idea, dear Bounce.'

'Migrate!' ordered Tumbler. 'Commence the migration!'

And so we began to migrate, leftward and upward; as did the tribes above us, and the tribes above them.

Over the course of the next ten days the business of finding novel finger-holds and toeholds occupied a huge amount of our attention. Besides, we had our kids to shepherd, or to carry if they were still babies. Consequently there wasn't much opportunity for staring out into the void. Splatty made the mistake of doing so while we were traversing unfamiliar rock. He forgot himself, lost his poise, and fell.

On the tenth evening Smear climbed down to our camping ledge.

'Don't you recognize what it is by now, Loosepiton?' he asked.

'There *might* be some kind of dark cloud out there,' allowed Tumbler, peeved that Smear was addressing me.

'It isn't any cloud, old chief—nor any sort of weird weather. Look keenly, Loosepiton. That's another precipice.'

I perceived . . . a faintly wrinkled vertical plane. Like a great sheet of grey skin.

'It's another precipice just like ours; and it's moving slowly towards our precipice day by day. It's closing in on us. As though it ain't bad enough clinging on by our fingertips all life long . . . !' Smear crooked a knee around a vine for stability and held his hands apart then brought them slowly together and ground them, palm to palm, crushingly.

The wrinkles in that sheet of skin out there were ledges. Without any doubt. The hairs on the skin were vines. My heart sank.

'We oughtn't to have migrated in this direction,' declared Tumbler. He was simply being obtuse.

Smear gently corrected him. 'We aren't migrating into an angle between two walls. Oh no. That other precipice faces us flat on. And it began to move towards us before we ever started our migration. Or perhaps *our* precipice began to move towards it. The result is the same.'

'We'll be squashed between the two.' I groaned.

To have survived bravely for so many years of hanging on by our fingernails! We had never railed excessively against our circumstances. Sometimes certain individuals took the dive of despair. But children were born and raised. Life asserted itself. We had hung on.

All so that we could meet a second precipice head-on—a mobile precipice—and be crushed!

This seemed a little unfair. A little—yes—hateful and soul-twisting.

Days passed by. We had settled on our new cliff pastures. We explored the cracks and ledges. We wove vines. We foraged. We ate worms and beetles.

All the while the approaching precipice became more clearly discernible as just that: another infinite precipice, limitlessly high and deep, limitlessly wide.

As the gap narrowed pearly daylight began to dim dangerously.

Smear had conceived a close affinity for me. 'Maybe it's just a reflection,' I said to him one day.

'If that's the case, then we should see ourselves clinging on over there. I see no one. If I could bend my arm back far enough to throw a chunk of stone, my missile would hit solid rock and bounce off.'

Several people from upper ledges took the dive of despair. A few parents even cast their children down; and that is real despair.

Yet consider the difference between taking the dive—and being slowly crushed to death between two walls of stone. Which would you prefer? Maybe those individuals who dived died peacefully from suffocation on the way down. Or maybe they did reach a bottom and were instantly destroyed, before they knew it, by impact.

The remaining daylight was appallingly dim by now. The other precipice with its cracks and ledges and vines was only a few bodies' lengths away. In another day or two it might be possible to leap over and cling on—though that hardly spelled any avenue of escape.

I paid a visit to Smear.

'Friend,' I said, 'some of those ledges over there are going to fit into spaces where we don't have ledges. But others won't. Others will touch our own ledges.'

'So?'

'So maybe there'll be a little gap left between the two precipices. A gap as big as a human body.'

'Leaving us uncrushed—but locked inside rock?'

'We'll have to wait and see.'

'See?' he cried. 'With no light to see by? Yet I suppose,' he added bitterly, 'it *will* be a different sort of world. For a while.'

Different. Yes.

Yesterday—though 'days' are now irrelevant—the two precipices met.

All light had disappeared but with my hand I could feel the inexorable pressure of the other rocky wall pushing forward—until from above, from below, from left and right there came a grating, groaning, crackling noise; then silence for a while.

Nobody had screamed. Everybody had waited quietly for the end. And as I had begun to suspect some days earlier, the end—the absolute end—did not come.

I was still alive on a ledge in utter darkness, sandwiched between one wall and the other.

Voices began to call out: voices which echoed strangely and hollowly down the gap of space that remained.

Yes, we survive.

There's even a little light now. Fungi and lichen have begun to glow. Maybe they always did glow faintly; and only now have our deprived eyes grown sensitive enough to detect their output.

We can still travel about—along a ledge to the end, then by way of cracks up or down to the end of another ledge. We scarcely see where we're going, and have to guess our way through the routes of this vertical stone maze. Also, it's still possible to fall down a gap, which would cause terrible injuries.

Yet in a sense travel is also easier nowadays. We can brace ourselves between both walls and shuffle upward or downward or left or right by 'chimneying'.

Perhaps I should mention a disadvantage which has actually stimulated travel. Excrement can't tumble away now into the void. Stools strike one wall or the other.

What's more, the collision of the two walls destroyed a lot of vines; nor can lush foliage thrive in the ensuing darkness.

Consequently we are ascending steadily, just as Smear once recommended.

Instead of living one above the other, our tribes are now strung out in a long line; and all of us climb slowly upward, foraging as we go, eating all the available lichen and fungi, worms and beetles. Now we're permanently migrating.

Are we moving towards somewhere? Towards Smear's mythical top? Maybe.

And maybe that place is infinitely far away.

The new kids who are born to us on the move will enter a world utterly different from the world of my own childhood. A vertical world confined between two irregular walls. A world of near-total gloom.

They will live in a narrow gap which extends sideways forever, drops downward forever, and rises forever.

How will Bounce's child (who is also either mine or Smear's) ever conceive of the old world which we will describe: that world where one precipice alone opened forever upon the vastness of empty, bright space? Will he (or she) think of it as a paradise which might yet exist again some time in the future if the two walls ever move apart? Or will the child be unable even to understand such a concept?

Sometimes I dream of the old world of open air and light, and of clinging to the cliff. Then I awaken to darkness, to the faint glow of a few fungi, to the confinement of the walls.

The other day Smear said to me, 'We didn't know how well off we were, did we, Loosepiton? But at least we survive, and climb. And maybe, just maybe, *right now* we're well off—compared with some future state of the world which will limit us even more severely!'

'How could we be more limited?' I asked in surprise. 'What new disaster could occur?'

'Maybe this gap will shrink to become a single upright chimney! Maybe *that'll* happen next.'

'Life forbid! It hasn't happened yet.'

'Not yet.'

Meanwhile we climb upward. And upward.

Amazingly Smear still tells his peculiar tales about imaginary worlds; and tells them with gusto.

Ahead!

1: The Head Race

THERE'S AN OLD SAYING: IT'LL COST YOU AN ARM AND A LEG.

For me the cost amounted to two arms, two legs, and a torso. Everything below the neck, in fact. Thus my head and my brain would survive until posterity. How I pitied people of the past who were dead forever. How I pitied my contemporaries who were too blind to seize the chance of cryogenic preservation.

Here we were on the threshold of potential immortality. How could I not avail myself of the Jones legislation? The opportunity might not be available in our own country for longer than a couple of years. The population might drop to a sustainable level. A change of administration might bring a change of heart. There could be rancour at the cost of maintaining increasing numbers of frozen and unproductive heads.

Until then, though, we were in the Head Race with China and Japan and India and other overpopulated nations. The previous deterrent to freezing had been guillotined away. Now no one was compelled to wait for natural death by cancer or car crash—and thus risk their brain degenerating during vital lost minutes.

Farewell, likewise, to the fear of senile dementia or Alzheimer's! The head would be surgically removed swiftly in prime condition and frozen immediately. This knowledge was immensely comforting to me. It was also a little scary. I was among the earliest to register. Yet I must wait almost a month till my appointment with the blade. A whole month! What if I were murderously mugged before I could be decapitated? What if my head was mashed to pulp?

Fortunately, I was part of a nationwide support group of like minds linked by our PCs. To a fair extent our lobbying had finally resulted in the Jones Law. Yes, *ours*; along with lobbying by ecologists concerned with the welfare of the planet—and also, I have to admit, pressure from certain powerful right wing groups (but it's the outcome which counts).

So whilst awaiting decapitation (now a proud word!) there was quite a sense of emotional and intellectual solidarity.

As regards storage or tagging of our heads, would a distinction be made between idealists such as ourselves—and those who were incurably ill or who had despaired of their current lives—and so-called Obligatories?

Initially, the Obligatories would be processed separately by the Justice or Medical systems. Would storage be mixed or segregated? This remained unclear. We had no wish to stir any suspicion of discrimination! Surely there was a significant distinction between idealists and non-idealists. The permission/identification form we all signed upon registering contained a box reserved for our motive.

Reportedly, the majority of idealists would be withdrawing from the world for altruistic, ecological reasons. Too many people on the planet for the health of the world! These volunteers would forgo their lives.

Enthusiasts such as myself nursed more personal motives, although I would never call those motives selfish. *Immortality* is not a selfish concept but is a watchword of faith in the survival and advancement of the human race. Immortality treasures what we have been, what we are, and what we shall become in the huge aeons ahead of us.

In a state of considerable excitement, we of the Immortalist Network confided the motives which we had inserted in our box.

To share in the Future.

To know what will be.

To reach the Stars. (That was mine.)

To strive, to seek, to find.

Manifest destiny of Homo Sap!

$p = fpncflfifc$. (Which is the famous Drake Equation for the number of extraterrestrial civilizations out in space.)

Even: *To go boldly.*

And, wittily: *I want to keep ahead.* (To Keep A Head. Ho!)

In the future world, would our heads be provided with new bodies? New bottles for the old wine, as it were? The Forethought Institute assured us that nanotechnology was just around the corner. Another thirty or forty years, judging by state of the art and according to Delphi Polls. Eighty years at the most. Working in vats of raw materials, millions of molecule-size programmed assemblers would speedily construct, if not living bodies, then at least excellent artificial prosthetic bodies. These might be preferable to living bodies, being more resilient and versatile.

Even failing this, surely our minds could be mapped into electronic storage with the processing capacity to simulate entire virtual-reality worlds, as well as interfacing with the real world. Those who had despaired would be fulfilled. Idealists would reap their reward.

Ought criminal Obligatories to receive resilient versatile new bodies? Should their electronic versions be allowed full access to a virtual-reality domain? That was for the future to decide—a future where the roots of mischief were better understood, and could be pruned or edited.

With what hopes and longings I approach the decapitation clinic on this my last day. My healthy organs will be harvested for transplants. My heart and kidneys and retinas will disperse. My blood will be bottled for transfusions. I imagine the anaesthetic as sweet, even though it will be delivered by injection. I imagine the farewell kiss of the blade, even though the anaesthetic will rob me of sensation. Farewell, Old Regime. Welcome, the Revolution.

2: The Head War

Smell, first of all, as the primitive reptilian brain-root re-awakens: an overpowering odour of hair-gel, though without any actual sensation of breathing. No lungs to breathe with?

Taste: slick and sour-sweet.

Sound: high-speed warbling.

Tactile: soft pressure all around my head. Otherwise: nothing at all, sheer absence.

Vision! Slightly wobbly, as if through liquid. There's a pyramid! It's composed of decomposing *heads*. Squinting sidelong, I spy another pyramid—of whitened skulls.

And another, beyond it.

I must be hallucinating.

Or else information is being presented to me symbolically.

My viewpoint is rising up, disclosing yet more pyramids upon a flat white plain, perhaps a salt-flat. Ovoids are airborne. Eggs hover and dart to and fro. One of these floats close to me. The rounded bottom is opaque. The transparent ellipsoid of the upper two-thirds contains a hairless head, surely female. I believe that a clear gel wraps and cushions the head. I must look likewise. Twin antennae protrude from the top of the egg. She's a mobile disembodied head. I mouth at her, making my lips form mute words. (*Hullo. What's happening? Where are we?*)

She mouths at me but I can't read her lips. No thoughts transmit from those antennae to what I presume must be my own corresponding overhead antennae. Her egg-vehicle begins to swing away. I urge mine to follow but it continues onward lazily under its own impetus.

Can this white vista, with its menacing pyramids and its hovering heads, be actual? How can this be? Surely my head is being used. What seems to be happening is not what is really happening. It is a by-product.

Of a sudden two head-vehicles rush directly at one another. They collide and burst open. Briefly two faces kiss bruisingly while spilling gel hangs down elastically. Moment later both vehicles plummet down to the salt-flat. There they shatter entirely. Both heads roll out, surely oblivious by now.

From under the surface, two mobile crab-like devices emerge. In their claws they seize the heads. They scuttle towards a fledgling pyramid. Clambering, they nudge the heads into position, upright, where I suppose they will rot.

The female egg hasn't gone away, after all. It—or rather she—is swinging back towards me. At least I think that it is the selfsame egg. Now it's picking up speed. It's rushing at me. Will we shatter, and kiss hideously, and fall? I'm terrified.

At the very last moment, my vehicle tilts. I'm staring upward at blue sky and high wispy clouds. A fierce blow strikes my base. Such a stunning shock vibrates through me. Nevertheless I'm intact. I haven't ruptured. I think I am sinking down slowly towards the salt. Slowly, slowly.

Of her, there's no sight. She must have broken against my base and tumbled rapidly. Overhead, a dozen heads cruise by. What grim aerial game is this?

Or is this the only way in which I can experience a selection procedure whereby worthwhile heads are chosen for survival? Whereby hundreds of thousands are discarded?

Have I been selected or rejected?

Again I hear that high-speed warbling, as of bird-song speeded up a hundredfold. With a slight bump I have come to rest.

Sky and salt-flat and flying eggs and a nearby pyramid are fading—until I'm seeing only... invisibility. There's nothing to see, nothing to taste, nothing to hear. Is this worse than being a disembodied head used as a game-piece by unknown forces?

Amidst this deprivation, for the first time in many years, I find myself praying to a force I scarcely believed in. *Dear God, help me.* Will an angel appear to me, coagulating out of nothingness?

All that can fill this void is a million memories of childhood. Of schooldays. Of my parents (forever dead, gone utterly!). Of first sex, first drug trip, first sight of the steaming teeming canyons of New York through which by night the roaming wailing vehicles suggested to my mind lugubrious monsters prowling for prey...

Presently my memories attain a vivid visionary actuality against the all-pervading nothingness!

I realize that my identity is being reinforced and stabilized—and perhaps scrutinized. The episode of the flying eggheads was akin to a pre-uterine experience. All of those heads in the sky were equivalent to so many sperms surging for existence, all of them failing except for one, myself, being fertilised in that shocking collision and sinking down to become attached to the ground. Surely that was the significance. Maybe most frozen brains fail to reintegrate.

Now, like cells multiplying, my memories multiply until—

3: embodied

—*I am embodied.*

I'm aware of *limbs*. Of arms and legs and hands and feet! They're so real to me, as I lie face downward with my eyes tight shut. How intensely I treasure this moment. I cause my limbs to move just a little at first, like a beached swimmer. My fingers wiggle, and my toes.

I feel ampler than I used to be. I'm larger, superior, more muscular.

Arms and legs and—*wings*...

Wings? Yes, great furled wings are socketed into my shoulders! Already I'm sensing which new muscles to flex so as to use my amazing wings. These wings are why I am lying face downward and not upon my back; otherwise I would crush my wings uncomfortably.

Wings? Wings? A body with wings? Now I do open my eyes in wonder.

A veil of tiny flies fills the air, flitting around me like a myriad airborne workers around some vast construction project, which is myself. I have arisen. My new body is golden, ambery, its fabric not of flesh but of some flexible responsive robust plastic—inorganic yet endowed with organic performance.

This is a substance for which there is no word, since it never existed previously. Perhaps *protoplast* is a suitable term. Undoubtedly energy cells, charged by sunlight, are woven throughout my new skin, powering inner engines which can defy the thrall of gravity—else how, when I unfurl my wings, do I rise and hover like some colossal deity of this cloud of flies? The wings must be of some ingenious anti-gravitic bio-technology, to uplift my weight.

My head is still enclosed in a protective helmet. My new golden winged body is an ingenious prosthetic device sustaining and serving my natural head, in perfect harmony with my head.

Those flies are beginning to disperse, as if wafted away by my slow wing-beats. The veil is thinning—except over to my right. There, a dense cloud of flies begins to vibrate audibly. Vibrations become a voice, announcing my task . . .

4: the colossi

There has been a *nanocatastrophe*.

The Forethought Institute were correct in their promise of rampant nanotechnology transforming the world. (How, otherwise, could I possess this angelic body, golden and winged and of miracle substance? How else would this body interface with my head of flesh and bone and blood and brain-cells, sustaining and obeying and augmenting me?) Alas, the whole world is as smooth as a billiard ball. Farewell to mountains and valleys. Farewell to forests and seas. Farewell, likewise, to all the species of fish, flesh, and fowl which once inhabited sea or land. Farewell to all plants and fungi and bacteria.

Due to the nanocatastrophe nothing remained of life except for these sealed frozen heads of ours, preserved perfectly—as if the human race had intuited the need for such a global insurance policy in the event of a nano-plague.

When I say that the planet is smooth and perfectly spherical I am omitting to mention the hundred equidistant colossi which rise from the surface. Seen from space, under modest magnification, the colossi might seem like so many individual whiskers upon a huge chin, or like so many stiff short freak hairs upon an otherwise gleaming bald head—few and far between, and exactly spaced.

Seen from the ground—or whilst hovering with our wings—each colossus towers vastly and baroquely up through the clouds. Some are still under construction by the untold trillions of mobile microscopic nano-assemblers, or by larger macro-machines forever being assembled and disassembled. Other colossi are almost complete, soaring to their designed height of ten kilometres.

Rooted by deep thermal spikes which exploit the inner heat of the planet, these colossi are *ships*. When the construction is completed, their matrix-engines will all activate in unison. This will generate a global matrix-field. As the world implodes towards a vanishing point, all of the thousand great ornate darts will be translated outward simultaneously through the cosmic matrix—not to mere stars in our own galaxy, but each to the vicinity of some planet roughly similar to Earth but in a different galaxy millions or tens of millions of light years away.

This is the Project for which the world was smoothed flat, erasing all life in the process, except for our preserved heads. Expansion throughout the universe!

5: BUT . . .

But even at speeds far slower than that of light, surely nanos in tiny vessels could reach the furthest part of our own galaxy within, say, twenty million years at most. They could arrive in other galaxies within a hundred million years. The universe is due to endure for *fifty times longer than that*. At least!

Why the urgency? Why convert the entire Earth into a catapult which will destroy itself?

The pace of activity of microscopic nanos must be far faster than that of creatures such as Man (and Woman)—yet why could the nanos not become dormant en route to the stars, like spores, simply switching themselves off?

The reason for their hurry provides an answer to the *Von Neumann Enigma*—as I discover in conversation with another golden Angel nine kilometres up the ship to which we are both assigned.

The Von Neumann Enigma: If life already arose anywhere in the universe and sent out self-replicating probes, why is the universe not already full of probes? In the whole of the cosmos did adventurous, intelligent life only ever arise on one single planet, Earth?

My companion and I soar on thermals, ascending alongside the ship. We arrive at a platform in the stratosphere. With our robust bodies of protoplast we are to assist macro-machines to construct a spire which will support yet another tier of the colossus.

My companion is Hispanic. With bald tan head enshrined in transparent holder fixed upon golden body—and his wings folded dorsally from shoulders down to knees now that we had arrived high above the clouds—he is magnificent. Daunting.

After some labour we rest . . . not that our new bodies ever became fatigued. We do not sleep, though we might daydream while we absorb nutrition through valves in our ankles. Nanos in our heads repair any physical degeneration. A device in our throats permits us to speak aloud.

'What year do you think this is?' I ask my colleague.

'The Year Zero,' he replies. His comment makes sense. All human history has vanished except for what we each remember. The time of the nanocatastrophe constitutes an absolute gulf between *before* and *now*.

I broach the matter of the Von Neumann Enigma, which bothered me even in the old days.

'The answer,' he declares, 'is that the Hayflick Limit applies to all social entities as well as to individual organisms.' Such is the profound conversation of angels!

But of course, but of course . . . !

The bugbear of the damned *Hayflick Limit* used to torment me. Body cells only replace themselves a finite number of times before the process fails.

For human beings this limit is seventy times or thereabouts. Then comes decay and death.

'The Hayflick Limit also applies,' says this Hispanic angel, 'to the Congregation of Nanos. Social entities such as civilizations obey the same limiting constraint as the cells in bodies—a law as binding as entropy. No matter how well the nanos stabilise their collective activity, over a period of millions of years this would lose all coherence.'

'Collectively they would suffer entropy...'

'Exactly so!' he tells me. 'With our slower thoughts, we serve as an anchor—as the *root* from which they arose. Their source and origin. We are their touchstone and criterion. Their pacemaker, their talisman. Furthermore, in an important sense we provide purpose. People uniquely possess a sense of far-reaching purpose—because that is our nature. This is true even if only one person remains in existence, provided that he never yields to despair.'

In the terms of a ship (for the Colossi are certainly ships) we are, quite literally, to be—

6: figureheads

—figureheads, no less!

At the very summit of each colossus, protected by a cone of energy, right there at the tip of the ship, one of us will ride head-first.

On a thousand colossal ships a thousand proud heads (attached to proto-plast bodies) will each gaze upon a new galaxy, and a new world in the vicinity similar to Earth.

Translation through the matrix will ensure comparability— similarity as regards mass and diameter and distance from a star which will closely resemble Earth's own sun. The planet in question *might* be barren, or be at boiling point due to greenhouse gases, or be an ice-desert. Yet surely hundreds may be habitats of some kind of life, or potential for life; for cosmic companionship.

This, mine eyes shall behold...

A thousand ships, a thousand heads! What if more than a thousand heads still survive?

At this moment the Hispanic angel launches himself at me.

How we wrestle. How well-matched we are. Our struggle ranges to and fro across this uppermost platform. Will he try to butt my helmet with his own, to crack it open if he can? When I realize that he has no intention of risking this, I am less cautious in my grips and clutches.

Pulling free and half-turning, he unfurls his wings to buffet and batter me. I punch with all the force of my golden fist at the base of one wing... which sags, which droops! I have fractured the attachment.

We are at the edge of the platform, where a thin breeze streams by. Gathering myself—and against all former human instinct—I hurtle against him, carrying him over the side along with myself.

For a moment, as we fall, he can't free an arm to grasp me. In that moment I deploy my own wings and release him.

Down, down he drops, crippled, spinning single-winged, accelerating willy-nilly. Nine kilometres he will fall to the billiard-ball ground. I'm alone upon the ship except for machines and invisible nanos.

7: Triumph

The Project is complete at last.

I stand erect, the very pinnacle of the galaxy-ship. No thunderous surge of acceleration will raise this colossus upon a column of fire. When the matrix-field activates world-wide—when the smooth ball of the world begins to implode—translation will occur instantaneously.

Even so, like a swimmer upon the highest diving board I raise my golden arms above my bottled head, palms pressed together steeple-style as if to leap and cleave the heavens.

Do my nine hundred and ninety-nine brothers and sisters likewise signal their imminent departure?

A humming vibration commences.

8: Fulfillment

Lakes of brilliant stars! A ball of blinding yellow light which is the local sun! Its radiance illuminates a full hemisphere of another nearby ball—a world white with clouds and blue with ocean, mottled with land-masses.

Earthlike. Similar...

Maybe the oceans and the land are sterile. Maybe not. To stare from space at this spectacle is to be Columbus and Cortez and Captain Cook all in one. I may be ten million light years away from my birthplace. Or a hundred million. This, in itself, is an ultimate achievement.

All because I dared to be decapitated!

Within a day or so, my colossus will be in orbit—like some titanic statue equipped with a tiny living head. I assume that the nanos will reshape the ship into hundreds of gliding wings which will descend. I presume that provision will be made for me.

Or what purpose could there be?

Cold Light

DOUBTLESS IT IS ONE OF LIFE'S TYPICAL IRONIES THAT A MAN WITH defective eyesight should have spent many long years studying the history of artificial lighting. However, my friend John Ingolby was also a prominent churchman. By the time his book appeared John was well advanced in the hierarchy of the Church of England. He was Bishop of Porchester.

Now, at this time the Church was in a certain amount of disarray. On the one hand it was waning due to apathy. On the other, it was beset by fundamentalist evangelism which seemed unpleasantly frantic and hysterical. Between this Scylla and Charybdis a new liberal theology was being steered which it was hoped would inject new life and modern, humane thought into a seemingly dying institution.

Not, however, without resistance!

Already one new bishop—who publicly denied the doctrine of the virgin birth—had been enthroned amidst scandal and protest. Within two days of his enthronement, the venue—an ancient cathedral, finest example of Gothic architecture in the land—was blasted by lightning and its transept gutted by fire. Reportedly the bolts of lightning came from out of a clear sky; so fierce were they, that the lightning conductors were overloaded.

Immediately the popular press pointed gleefully to the hand of God Himself as source of the miraculous lightning; and some traditionalist clergy endorsed this explanation of the meteorological hazard. The cathedral had been polluted by such an enthronement; here was God's sacred reaction. Yet God, of course, was also merciful. Having first set His house ablaze, He then permitted the massed fire brigades to quench the flames and save the majority of the edifice.

Liberal-minded churchmen issued statements explaining the fire as a coincidence, and deploring popular superstition. The same cathedral had, after all, been severely damaged by fire thrice already during its history—the most recent occasion, a hundred years earlier, being incidentally a case of arson provoked by another theological dispute.

Yet the noisiest single critic of the new bishop from amongst the ranks of ecclesiastics bitterly denounced such pussyfooting explanations. In disgust he publicly quit the English church and embraced the Greek Orthodox communion. The Greek Orthodox Church, as its name implied, was a staunch guardian of doctrine, ritual, and liturgy.

Some months later scandal struck again.

A radical-minded dean and lecturer in theology had been hired as presenter for a major new television series called *The Quest for God*. As the date for screening the first episode drew near, this dean revealed in interviews that he did not believe in an afterlife; nor in the Resurrection of Christ; nor for that matter did he even accept the 'objective' existence of a God. 'God' was a personal construct of the moral consciousness of humanity, said he.

A wave of protest arose.

And of course that first instalment of *The Quest for God* was blacked out nationwide by a lightning strike . . .

Of the industrial kind. TV engineers seized this opportunity to protest certain changes in their duty rosters.

The industrial dispute was soon settled; and two nights later the TV network transmitted the blacked episode in place of a football match. But by now newspaper headlines had trumpeted: *Lightning Strike Blacks Atheist Dean*. Even though the smaller print below explained the nature of this particular bolt from the blue, editorials in bolder black type suggested that God may move in a mysterious way His lightning to direct.

Such publicity hugely swelled the viewing figures for a programme which many people might otherwise have felt disposed to ignore; so much so that the 'atheist' Dean was obliged to preface his second prerecorded appearance one week later with a brief personal statement in which he quipped endearingly that if God did not exist, He could hardly have thought of a better way to draw the nation's attention to the quest for Him.

It was in this fraught climate that John Ingolby's book was published, surprising me (for one) by its title—then by its angle.

Religion and the History of Lighting: that was the title. The last word is quite easy to confuse with 'lightning'; and indeed the printers had done so at least a dozen times during the course of three hundred pages without John—with his poor eyesight—noticing the slight though substantial difference whilst he was correcting the proofs. However, this is a mere incidental irony. The primary shock of the book came from the manner in which, like some seventeenth-century metaphysical poem, it yoked together two apparently disparate things: a scholarly history of artificial lighting—and theological insights.

I admit that my first reaction was that an exuberant editor had persuaded John to rewrite his whole volume, giving it a new commercial slant.

Let's be honest. Suppose you happen to be an *aficionado* of beer-mats, then their history is a consuming passion—to yourself, and to a few hundred other like-minded enthusiasts. However, your *History of Beer-Mats* must inevitably lack the kind of popular charisma which sells a million copies.

Likewise with the history of lighting.

Blazing sticks in Neolithic caves; grease and wick in a bear skull; Phoenician candles of yarn and beeswax; Roman tallow lamps; Elizabethan lanthorns; candles of spermaceti scented with bay-berry; rushlights; Herr Wintzler's lighting up of Pall Mall with gas; Welsbach's incandescent mantle; De la Rue's dim electric light of 1820; Sir Joseph Swan's carbonized cotton filaments; Humphrey Davy's carbon arc; Edison at Menlo Park; mercury vapour; neon; acetylene . . . Fascinating stuff! Yet how many of the general public would wish to read three hundred pages about it?

John set the tone from the very outset. 'We wanted light,' he wrote, 'so that we should not feel afraid . . .' He went on to parallel advances in religious awareness with the developing technology of artificial lighting: from early shamanism to paganism, from the 'light of the world', Christianity, to medieval mysticism, from the Dark Ages to the modern enlightenment of radical theology. He suggested a direct link between the two: with lighting influencing religious beliefs, and religious beliefs influencing the technology of light.

John made great play with the fitful glimmering of candles and the haunting, soul-like shadows which flitted around rooms as a result; with the smokiness of oil lamps and the bonfires of the Inquisition; with the softly restful, comparatively brilliant glass chimney lamp of Swiss chemist Aimé Argand which climaxed the Age of Reason; with the clear steady paraffin lamp of Victorian pragmatic Christianity.

He harvested a rare crop of quotations to prove his point, from such authorities as Saint Augustine and Meister Eckhart, Jakob Boehme and Kierkegaard, Tillich and Hans Küng. His chapter on medieval stained glass and the visionary cult of the millennium was masterly, and prefaced—anachronistically, I thought at first—by this famous passage from Shelley:

Life, like a dome of many-coloured glass,
Stains the white radiance of Eternity...

Then the finale to the chapter completed the quotation (which not many people know beyond its first two lines); and I understood.

... Until Death tramples it to fragments.

And what of late twentieth-century lighting—not to mention fibre optics, laser beams, and holography—and the new radical, atheistic, afterlifeless theology?

And what of the future?—a future which John saw as lying in the harnessing of 'cold light': the bioluminescence of bacteria, the phosphorescence of fireflies and the fish of the abyss, which generate an enormous amount of chemical light with minimal energy input, and without heat? What of the cold light of the next century which must surely follow on from the bright yet hot and kilowatt-consuming light of our present era? What of the theology of *that?*

My first assumption, as I say, was that the publisher had prevailed on John to jazz up his volume.

My second assumption, when I delved deeper into John's religious musings, was that he had decided to throw his cap into the ring of radical theology; that he had chosen to run up his colours as one of the avant-garde of the Church.

Or had he? Or rather, on whose behalf was he running up his colours?

During the many years that I had known John—since college days, a time of life when brainstorming sessions are quite common—he had never to my knowledge spoken heatedly about the validity of the virgin birth, or of Christ's dead body walking around, or of the afterlife, or of a God in Heaven; or any of the crunch points of the new clear-vision theology which was even then taking shape. Indeed I felt that John had entered the Church largely as a reliable career—one in which he thought he would excel, since he was a good Latin and Greek scholar, but one in which his actual belief was nominal.

Let me be more specific. John did not doubt his vocation; but nor did he question it. He was more like a younger son of the eighteenth or nineteenth centuries to whom becoming a clergyman was a matter of course; and like several such who became better known as naturalists or geologists or amateur astronomers John had his own parallel, genuine passion—namely the history of lighting.

John's father had been a vicar. His uncle was a bishop. The step was natural; advancement was likely. Without a doubt John was good-hearted; and was to prove excellent at pastoral duties. Whilst at college he involved himself in running a boys' club, and in serving hot soup to tramps of a winter's night. However, he seemed uninterested in theological disputes as such.

Could it be that John was deeply traditional at heart—and that his book was in fact a parody of the new rational theology? A spoof, a satire? Was he intending to pull the carpet out from under the feet of the church's intellec- tuals—like some Voltaire, but on the other side of the fence?

Had he been so annoyed in his quiet way by the new trends in theology that he had sacrificed to God all of his private research work into the history of lighting—his consuming hobby—so that by using it satirically he could defend the faith?

Would he watch and assess reactions to his book, then announce that *Religion and the History of Lighting* was in fact a holy joke? One intended to demonstrate the credulity of unbelief? To show up the trendy emptiness of today's scientific theology?

Or was John Ingolby entirely innocent of such guile? Was he a true inno- cent: the stuff of saints and geniuses and the dangerously naïve?

Or was he simply short-sighted and afflicted with a species of tunnel vision which had compressed his two diverse occupations—the Church, and the history of lighting—absurdly yet persuasively into the selfsame field of view? Maybe!

At any rate, in the wake of the cathedral fire and the televised *Quest for God* the publicity department of John's publisher dangled his newly-minted book under the noses of the media; and the media gladly took the bait.

Here was more 'new theology' from a bishop; more (apparently) rational probing of 'superstition' as a kind of slowly vanishing shadow cast by improving human technology, a function of blazing brands and paraffin lamps and neon and lasers; and an analysis of mystical insight as an analogue of candlepower and lumens—with the possibility, thrown in, of new illuminations just around the corner.

And did not Bishop Ingolby's book have something to say (at first glance) about holy lightning? Lightning which suddenly was humanized—into the sodium-vapour lamps on motorways, the neon strips over shop fronts—by the deletion of a single letter, 'n', like the removal by a clever trick of an unknowable infinity from an equation?

Yet—to reinject a note of mystery—did not the possibility of cold light remain? Here, John's fancy soared poetically.

The newspapers excelled themselves. Bishop Ingolby was a debunker—and should be defrocked forthwith! Bishop Ingolby was a scientific mystic, striving to yoke technology to divinity! He was this. He was that.

Certainly he suddenly became notorious. *Religion and the History of Lighting* sold a lot of copies; a good few, no doubt, were read.

T-shirts appeared bearing the icon of a light bulb on them, and the legend: *S. O. & S.* Switch On, & See. (With a punning undercurrent of Save Our Souls.) These T-shirts seemed as urgent and arbitrary as their sartorial predecessors which had instructed people to RELAX! or FIGHT! or BREATHE!

Switch on, & See. But see what? See that there was nothing in the darkness of the universe? Or that there was everything? Or that there was something unforeseen?

Thus, by way of prologue to the strange and terrible events which happened subsequently...

The 'Bishop's Palace' in Porchester is, in actuality, a large Georgian house set in modest grounds of lawn and shrubbery standing midway between the railway station and the ruins of Porchester Castle. The west wing of the building was devoted to the administration of the diocese. The east wing was John's own domain, where the domestic arrangements were in the hands of a housekeeper, Mrs Mott, who arrived every morning bright and early and departed every evening after dinner; for John had never married.

Most of the domestic arrangements were Mrs Mott's province: cookery and cleaning, laundry and such. The lighting styles of the various rooms in the east wing were John's own choice; and it was in this respect that one half of his palace resembled a living museum.

The kitchen was lit by electric light bulbs; the small private chapel by massive candles; the dining-room by gas mantles; the library by brilliant neon strips. Innumerable unused lighting devices stood, or hung, around: Roman pottery oil lamps, miners' safety lamps, perforated West Indian gourds designed to house fireflies . . .

When I arrived to visit John at his urgent request on that early November evening several months after publication of his book, the whole of the east wing which met my gaze was lit up in its assorted styles, with no curtains closed. As I walked the few hundred yards from the railway station, a couple of anticipatory rockets whizzed up into the sky over Porchester and exploded, showering orange stars. This was the day before the country's children would celebrate the burning at the stake of the Catholic Guy Fawkes for trying to blow up a Protestant Parliament—an earlier religious feud. John seemed, meanwhile, to be conducting his own festival of light.

I . . .

But I haven't mentioned who I am, beyond the fact that I was at college with John a good many years ago.

My name is Morris Ash, and I am a veterinary surgeon turned homeopathist. I live in Brighton, and cater to the more prosperous sectors of society. My degree was in Biochemistry, and I had originally thought of going into medical research. A certain disenchantment with my fellow human beings—coupled with dawning ecological awareness of the soaring world population and the degradation of the natural environment—had shunted me into veterinary studies.

I had done well in my profession, though I never practised to any great extent rurally with sheep and horses and cows, which may seem a contradiction (of which life is full). I had become an up-market urban vet, a doggy doctor, a pussy physician, renowned among my patients' owners for my compassionate bedside (or basket-side) manner.

Twenty years on, I had five partners working with me (and for me), and was more of a consultant in difficult cases than a routine castrator of tom-kittens. My thoughts turned once more to biochemistry and to medical research, but with a difference: I interested myself in homeopathy, in the theory of treating disease by means of minuscule, highly diluted doses of substances which would ordinarily cause disease. I began to investigate the possibility of treating animal ailments likewise, and within a few years I was supplying a wide range of home-made homeopathic remedies to the pets of my clientele, should the owners prefer this approach—and a gratifying number did. Homeopathy worked startlingly well in a number of recalcitrant cases; and word of my success spread quickly. I soon found that I was treating my erstwhile patients' owners homeopathically, too—though not, I hasten to add, for mange or distemper!

Now, there's nothing illegal in this. You need no medical qualifications to practise as a homeopathic doctor; and it's a curious fact, as I discovered, that a good few human beings would rather have their ills tended to by a vet than by an orthodox doctor.

A doctor is often cursory, reaching quickly for his prescription pad to scribble upon it in illegible Latin. A doctor is frequently inclined to treat his human patients as examples of blocked plumbing, or as broken-down cars—this is the common complaint by patients. Whereas a vet must always fondle and gentle his patients (or else the vet is likely to be scratched, bitten, and kicked). A vet seems more sensual, more full of curative love. He is seen to cure—to a certain extent—by a laying on of hands, whereas a medical doctor metaphorically jabs a fist into you.

Also, people might prefer to confide in a vet because his trade isn't viewed as a mysterious Freemasonry. A vet has no cryptic knowledge or secret records.

Finally, the doctor appears to have the power of life or death over you; yet he will never exercise the power of death mercifully. Indeed the law forbids him to do so. Death can only come after a long, humiliating, and dehumanizing process of medical intervention which often seems experimental to the wasting patient and his relatives. The vet *does* possess the power of instant death. He can give lethal mercy injections to distempered puppies or crushed cats. Yet it is the instant *mercy* of this, not the lethal aspect, which is noted primarily.

(Did I mention love? I have admitted that I did not overly love my fellow human beings compared with the furry and feathered folk of the world. So in common with John—though for different reasons—I too never married. As a result, to many pet-owning widowed ladies I seemed impeccably... shall we say, eligible? Which was perhaps another of my homeopathic attractions. I had diluted and rediluted my spouse potential over the years till I became, to some hearts, devastating.)

John and I had remained firm friends for many years—as I say—and we met perhaps thrice every year, one of these occasions invariably being our college reunion supper; the other occasions variable. We seemed to have much in common. We were both confirmed bachelors. As regards charitable acts John perceived me as a kind of lay St Francis of Assisi, ministering to the world's chihuahuas and gerbils. I had told John, at some stage, all I knew about the enzyme-catalysed chemical reactions which coldly light up fire-flies, deep-sea fish, bacteria, and fungi; and how one day we might learn to light our homes and cities similarly—information which had surfaced, theologically mutated, in his book . . .

I was welcomed to the palace. We drank excellent pale sherry. We spoke of homeopathy. We talked of John's book and of its lightning success (*de scandale*). He mentioned an upcoming television interview to be filmed in his variously lit home, during the course of which he would stride from room to room and thus from firelight era to neon era, expounding, concluding his performance in the candle-lit chapel; but he was rather vague about these plans.

I tentatively broached the puzzle (to me) of the true intention of his book. Surely an old and discreet friend was privileged to know—especially since I myself had no religious axes to grind? John sidetracked me, to admire a lanthorn from Shakespeare's day which he had recently bought at auction and which now adorned the mantel shelf of his lounge.

Then Mrs Mott served us dinner in the next room, to faintly hissing gaslight.

It was a tasty meal but a queer one. We commenced with *escargots* and giant *champignons*, both cooked in butter; and John obviously had some difficulty distinguishing which of the spheres were snails, and which were mushrooms. He attempted to slice through one snail shell and then to prick out the meat from within a mushroom. Had he commanded this menu as a deliberate tease to his bespectacled self?

A turbot steak in béchamel sauce followed. Next, in sentimental homage to a shared taste from our student days when we had both patronized the same cheap wholesome dive of a cafe, we tucked into tripe and onions accompanied by mashed potatoes.

Afterwards, came a meringue concoction; followed by a slab of Wensley-dale cheese, and white coffee.

Mrs Mott departed homeward, leaving us alone.

It occurred to me that the whole meal had been white, or at least creamy-grey in colour; and served upon white plates. Even the wine we drank with it was Liebfraumilch—'milk of a beloved woman'—not that I should have fancied a robust Burgundy as accompaniment to the meat dish in question!

Had we drunk Burgundy or some other red wine, it might have looked as though our glasses had miraculously filled with the blood so visibly absent from that part of the cow's anatomy.

An all-white dinner. Why?

Had Mrs Mott gone mad?

'Will you pour the port?' asked my host; and I obliged. The port, at least, was a rich purple-red; a contrast on which I forbore, for the moment, to comment, though my curiosity was by now intense.

John tasted his wine, then at last confided in a low voice, 'I'm going blind, Morris. Blind.'

'Blind?' I repeated the word stupidly. I stared at John's round, rosy face and at the thick round spectacles thereon, which from some angles made his eyes seem to bulge. His cheeks were faintly pocked: a bad reaction to a childhood bout of measles, which I knew had nearly killed him and which had certainly impaired his eyesight. The dome of his head was mostly bald and smooth. His skin, and remaining strands of hair, were somewhat greasy. A lot of talcum powder would need to be patted on to him prior to any television appearance; or else he would seem shiny on screen.

I decided that it was high time to broach the matter of the meal—without insulting it, however, since my taste buds had relished every morsel even if my eyes had not had much to feast on.

'Er, John . . . the dinner we just ate . . . splendid fare! Mrs Mott is to be congratulated. But, hmm, there wasn't a scrap of colour in it. Everything was white from start to finish. White food on white plates. Highly ingenious! But, um, that doesn't mean that you're going blind—just because you couldn't see any colours. There weren't any to be seen.'

John uttered a few staccato laughs.

'Oh Morris, I *know* that!' he declared. 'Mrs Mott has always been a great admirer of yours. The white dinner was in your honour.'

'Was it? Why's that? I don't quite follow.'

'You see, that's her understanding of how homeopathy works. In this case, a homeopathic cure for failing vision. Take something as essential to the health of the body as a well-cooked meal. The smell and the taste play a major role in stimulating appetite. So does the look of the meal: the contrasts, the colours.'

'Oh, I see! Mrs Mott imagines that by reducing the colour content to almost nothing—'

'Just as the homeopath reduces the drug content of a medicine virtually to nothing, by repeated dilution. Exactly!'

'—thereby your visual faculty will be stimulated, rather than dulled? Your brain will strain to discriminate the tiny traces of colour remaining? My word, what an imagination that woman has.'

'The white dinner was also served as a broad hint in case I didn't bring myself to ask your help, Morris.'

Ah.

Now I could put two and two together.

Here was another instance where someone hoped for medical advice from a vet rather than from a doctor. A vet who was a close friend. A vet, moreover, who had no special bigoted axes to grind regarding a certain radical bishop who had reduced the visions of the saints to an absence of adequate light-bulbs.

Doctors often had axes to grind. My patients' owners had complained to me thus more than once. Male doctors—most are male—harboured gynaecological obsessions, obsessions about the 'hysteria' of female patients. They nursed obsessions about plumbing and pills and tranquillizers. They held political views, often of a right-wing stripe, which they allowed to colour their medical personalities. Or else they had religious obsessions—about, say, birth control or woman's role as a mother. There was no such thing as an objective doctor. Personal beliefs and prejudices always flavoured diagnosis and treatment. By contrast veterinarians could easily be objective—and at the same time loving—because (to put it bluntly and very generally) animals had no politics, and no religion.

'What do you think's wrong with your eyes then, John old son? Cataracts?'

John emptied his glass of port, as though to fortify himself.

'I'm going blind within,' he said. *'Blind within.'*

'Now what do you mean by that?'

'The blindness is like a shadow inside of me. This inner shadow is spreading. It's growing outward, ever outward.'

I thought for a moment. 'I'm no eye specialist,' I said, 'but it sounds to me—if you're describing this correctly—as though your optic nerves are inflamed. The pressure of the swelling could make the nerves atrophy gradually. The blind spot would seem to enlarge. Part of the retina would go blind.'

John shivered. 'It's more than that.' He struck his forehead a blow. 'This blindness has taken root inside me like some foul black weed!' His voice faltered and hushed. 'It's because of my book, don't you see?'

'*What?*'

'I've prayed, of course. One does. I pray on my own in the chapel every morning for half an hour. Prayer clears the mind. The day organizes itself. Not that I pray for myself personally! I pray that the whole world shall see the light of goodness.' John seemed embarrassed. He had never mentioned private prayer to me before. 'Meanwhile my own light grows dim. *Vilely* so.'

'In what way "vilely", John?'

'There's a taint of corruption to this blindness. A moral miasma is creeping around in me, spreading its tendrils.'

'You blame this on the publication of your book? It's as though you're being . . . punished?' I refilled his glass from the decanter. 'I hate to say this, John, but a tumour is a remote possibility. If a tumour presses upon the visual centres of your brain there could be emotional repercussions. You might even sense the tumour as something dark and evil growing inside your head.'

'Oh no I wouldn't. If I had a tumour, I would suffer from a steady grinding headache for at least a few hours every day. Every now and then I might see complex hallucinatory patterns; or else an aura of flashing lights. You might suddenly look like an angel to me! Or Mrs Mott might. I *do* have a number of books in my library which aren't about technology or theology. Medical books. I've checked up on tumours. I've checked up on eye troubles—I can still read, with spotlight and magnifying glass. Under normal circumstances what afflicts me would most likely be what is known as toxic amblyopia.'

'Ah. Really? You'd better explain. Obviously I'm not the best fellow to hold a consultation with!'

'Oh but you are. Now listen, will you? Toxic amblyopia involves a reduction in the acuteness of vision due to a toxic reaction of the optic nerve. I have the symptoms of this exactly. The *commonest* cause is overindulgence in alcohol or tobacco. But I don't smoke; and I don't ordinarily overimbibe. Quinine can also cause the condition; but I've never been near the tropics. I'm not one of your malarial missionaries of yesteryear. Other causes are prolonged exposure to various poisons, principally carbon dioxide, arsenic, lead, and benzene. One thought immediately springs to mind: am I being poisoned by these gaslights in here, or perhaps by the candles in the chapel? By something in this very palace which is directly connected with my hobbyhorse? That would be ironic, don't you think?'

'Maybe you've already solved the puzzle, John.' In which case why had I been invited? And why had Mrs Mott cooked the all-white repast?

My friend shook his head. 'I've had the gas-mantles checked. They're perfectly safe. As for the chapel, ever since I began to suspect candles as possible sinners I've only lit one on each occasion. No remission! I've thought carefully of every other oddity of lighting. All systems are innocent. And my vision is getting worse. The affliction has no cause; unless of course it has a miraculous cause. Miraculous,' he repeated quietly, 'or demonish. It's a sort of slow, black lightning.'

'But John, you yourself wrote that demons have no more substance than shadows cast by candles. You don't believe in demons.'

'Ah . . . suppose for a moment that demons exist. I feel somewhat haunted, Morris.'

'You're joking.'

I could see that he was not entirely joking.

'Don't bishops know how to deal with demons?' I asked him.

'Hmm. I should need to involve a colleague from within the Church. Word would inevitably leak out. Likewise, were I to start consulting eye specialists. Embarrassing, don't you see? Embarrassing to the Church! If I tried to arrange for the exorcism of a genuine—if troublesome—miracle, why, that would be worse. I should be attempting to cast God out of my life.'

'Time to wheel on the homeopathic vet, eh?'

'I could do worse. At least I can discuss the ins and outs of this with you. Mrs Mott's quite right on that score.'

As we talked, a certain suspicion began to dawn on me; a suspicion which I hardly dared put to John outright.

John had said that arsenic could cause toxic amblyopia.

Was it possible that Mrs Mott was slowly poisoning John? Since white is the colour of innocence, did her white meal that evening protest symbolically that she was innocent? But why should she protest innocence unless she knew her own guilt?

Why should Mrs Mott have encouraged John to seek my advice? Perhaps she did not admire me at all, and actually regarded me as a charlatan whose advice would lead John far astray and keep him away from doctors.

John depended upon Mrs Mott. He trusted her implicitly. Dared I cast any shadow of doubt upon their relationship? And what could the woman's motive possibly be? An inheritance—of a load of peculiar lighting apparatus? (The Palace certainly didn't belong to him!) Inheritance of royalties from his book? Those could hardly amount to a fortune.

Finally I decided to take the plunge.

To sugar the pill, I chuckled. 'Speaking of phosphorescence,' I said (though we hadn't been, for a while), 'in the old days phosphorus was often used as a poison because it's difficult to detect. Some phosphorus occurs naturally in the body. There's a famous case in which one intended victim was alerted when he noticed his bowl of soup glowing while he was carrying it to table along a dark corridor!'

'Hmm,' said John without more ado, 'so why should Mrs Mott wish to poison me?'

'I didn't mean to imply—'

'Oh yes you did. Tiny doses of an arsenic compound, eh? A little bite of rat-killer day by day. In rather more than a homeopathic dose! She has no earthly motive.'

'Maybe she has an unearthly one?'

'Explain.'

'Maybe she regards your book as, um, blasphemous. Maybe she believes you're in league with the Antichrist.'

'Mrs Mott? I hardly think so! Do you?'

I thought about the comfy, devoted, cheery soul in question; and shook my head.

That night as I lay on the verge of sleep in John's great oaken guest-bed, my mind wandered back to the story of the phosphorescent soup. A soup bowl aglow in a dark corridor . . .

Is this a tureen which I see before me,
The ladle towards my hand? Art thou lobster bisque,
Vichyssoise, or plain beef broth with arsenic?
Art thou not, fatal bouillon, sensible
To tasting as to sight? Or art thou but
A potage of the mind?

I don't know quite why I decided to get up out of my warm bed to roam the November-chilly Bishop's Palace at midnight. Maybe I had some notion that in the pitch-dark kitchen I would spy some spice jar glowing phosphorescently, betraying the true poisonous nature of its contents. But get up I did, shuffling my slippers on by feel and belting my dressing gown about me, then proceeding to the door with hands outstretched.

I didn't use my pocket torch, nor had I opened the curtains. I knew that it was a dark, moonless night outside but I wanted my eyes to retain the sensitivity of a cat so that the tiniest dose of light might register.

I felt my way along the upstairs corridor, tiptoeing past John's room next to mine, though I had little reason to fear that my faint footfalls—or the noisier creaking of the boards—might disturb him. John had long since told me that he invariably slept the sleep of the dead. As soon as his head touched the pillow he became a log until dawn.

Still, the bathroom was in the opposite direction. How could I explain my nocturnal perambulation?

To cut the story of a long prowl short, I fumbled my way to the kitchen—then to all the other downstairs room, and even the chapel. Nowhere did I spy anything unusual.

The chapel was bitterly cold, but the chill I experienced was innocuous—winter was to blame. Unless a thermostat switched some heater on in the early morning John's half-hour of prayer must have been something of a penance. Supposedly there's another species of chill which runs down spines and makes dogs howl like banshees. Yet if it was devilish cold in John's chapel, I'm sure the Devil had no hand in hypothermia, no finger in frigidity.

I returned upstairs, only stubbing my toe once.

In the darkness of the upper corridor I miscalculated distances. I twisted a brass doorknob. It wasn't my own bedroom door that I opened—it was John's.

I realised my mistake at once because a ring of light illuminated the head of the bed, showing me John's face asleep beneath. He was wearing, of all things, a woolly nightcap with a big pompon which Mrs Mott must have knitted for him.

The ring of light was no wider than his head, over which it seemed to perch. Though my eyes were well accommodated to night vision, the light wasn't brilliant. But it clearly showed me John's slumbering countenance, and outlined the bed. Obviously the light was some reflection or refraction from outside, through the bedroom window. Perhaps of a powerful arc-lamp at the railway station?

I made my way to the window to check; but the heavy curtains were closed tight without a chink.

I saw Eternity the other night

Like a great Ring of pure and endless light . . .

There was no other glimmer in the room itself. No movement of mine dimmed or shadowed the ring of pearly light. Thoughts of Mrs Mott as purveyor of phosphorus soup flew out of the window (or would have done so, had the window offered any way in or out). I could pretend no longer. I *knew* what I was seeing.

Above John's head, as he slept, hung a halo.

A halo such as saints wear in paintings.

Not so bright, perhaps! Not a radiant glory. A modest halo, which wouldn't even be visible if other light competed. But a halo nonetheless.

John's head was snuggled in a fat pillow. The halo was tilted across his face. I stretched out a cautious finger to touch the apparition.

Perhaps this was foolhardy of me, but I suffered no consequences. I felt no buzz, no shock, no warmth. The thing couldn't be an odd form of ball lightning, or St Elmo's fire.

I swept my hand right through the halo, without effect. Then I shook John's shoulder.

'Wake up, old son! Wake up, will you?'

Eventually I roused him.

'House on fire? Burglars? What's the time?'

'No, no, no. None of that. Sit up.'

As he sat up, the halo shifted position so that it was poised above his nightcap.

'What's up, Morris? Where's my torch?' (John's bedroom was equipped with nineteenth-century carriage lamps.)

I gripped his wrist. 'No—no torch! Is there a mirror anywhere?'

'Inside the wardrobe.'

'Will you show me?'

Grumbling mildly, John got out of bed—the halo accompanying him— and soon he was pawing a wardrobe door open.

Now there were two haloes: one above John's head, and the other in the full-length mirror.

'Goodness, what's that light? I haven't got my glasses.'

'I'll fetch them. Where are they?'

'Table by the bed.'

I retrieved his spectacles and he put them on.

'Goodness!'

'Goodness indeed, John—by the looks of it! You're wearing a halo.'

He stepped to and fro. He swung his hand across his head. He pulled off his nightcap—as though I might have attached that ghostly glow as a joke.

'Oh dear me,' he said. 'My eyes aren't much use—but I can see it. Dear me, I always thought there was something frightfully priggish about haloes . . .'

'You must be becoming a saint, eh old son?'

'What, me? A saint? Don't be silly. Besides, saints never had actual rings of light over their heads! That's just an artistic convention. A way of picturing saints.'

'Maybe some saints had actual haloes—ones which people could see? But not in recent history.'

'I think a halo would need to be brighter than mine, for people to notice!'

'Maybe yours is just a baby halo. A young one.'

'Meaning that it'll grow stronger? As my eyes grow dim? Let's light some lamps.'

My friend located his torch and went through the rigmarole of getting carriage lamps to work. As the illumination in the bedroom increased, so did his halo fade away to a faint shimmer.

I sat on a chair; John perched on the bed.

'This is quite embarrassing,' he said. 'It's preposterous! I can't possibly be a saint in the making. And what could conceivably cause a halo?'

'*Grace*, perhaps, my Lord Bishop?'

'You don't believe that.'

'Any more than you believe it? I want to ask you, John: did you write that book of yours to debunk radical theology? Is the book a kind of holy offering—of everything you cared deeply about—so that faith may be sustained?'

'Gracious me, I don't think so. Morris, I've told you that I feel an evil darkness spreading its shadow inside of me. If I'm sprouting a halo, I assure you this is at the *expense* of my soul! It isn't a spotlight to illuminate saintliness.' He mused a while. 'How nice it would be to imagine that it's some lamp of goodness. How nice to visualize certain dim monasteries of the past as being genuinely lit by sanctity—with a saint's head as a light bulb! How lovely if cities of the future could be cold-lit by our own purity, should mankind perfect itself! Heaven would be radiant on account of its saints. Hell would be dingy-dark because of its sinners. That is emphatically *not* how I feel as this blindness eats up my vision.'

Eats up.

'Your halo is eating your eyesight . . . what could that mean? That the halo is some kind of organized energy? It needs energy to sustain itself; to grow . . . ? Certain luminous deep-sea fish need to eat luminous plankton or else they stop glowing. And by glowing they attract their prey.'

'What are you trying to say, Morris?'

'Maybe this halo is some sort of creature—an animal not of blood and bone, but of energy. It's eating the photons that enter your eyes; or the electrical impulses in your optic nerves. That's why you're going blind. Your brain can sense it feeding inside you; consuming light, to produce light.'

'A parasite? Why should it generate a halo? Hmm, famous saints of the past haven't been noted for their blindness . . .'

'So haloes can't be the work of parasites, presumably.'

He shook his head in puzzlement. 'You mentioned luminous fish attracting prey. What *prey* would a saint attract to him? Why, the faithful. The credulous. Some sinners ripe for conversion. People who are religiously inclined. A halo might be God's fishing hook. It might be an angel that takes up residence, in order to angle for souls. And it drinks photons from the saint's eyes, to power the halo? I don't know, hagiographically, of many saints who had impaired vision!'

'Maybe there have only been a few true saints—whose haloes became legend? You're the next saint. The miracle for a godless age.'

'Are you *trying* to canonize me, Morris? You should be devil's advocate.'

'I'm only looking at the possibilities. Here's another one: maybe in the past there were more conduits to the divine light? The halo-angels didn't need to suck the vision from a saint. There were other sources of energy.'

'In that case why should I sense that my blindness is *evil*? Why should I feel such a lack of Grace?'

'I don't know.'

'When I become blind as a bat, does my halo glow with glory? Whose faith is being tested? The world's, or mine? Is this a test of faith at all—or is it the work of some vile parasitic creature from elsewhere, with its own motives? Is that what a miracle is: something you can't ever prove, but must take on trust, like God Himself? Even though you feel that you yourself are damned! Possessed!' He stretched out his hands towards me. 'If I beg you to cure me, Morris—God knows how!—do I damn myself? Should I let my halo strengthen and thus confirm the faith of millions of people—while I lose my own belief, sunk in my personal deep dark pit?'

'Maybe the thing will go away,' I said feebly. 'Maybe it'll fade, and your eyesight will improve.'

'Will you stay with me a few more days?'

'A week. Longer, if need be. Of course I will.'

He sighed. 'Thank you, Morris. Now you'd better go back to bed. And so shall I.' His bishop's authority suddenly blossomed. 'Be off with you, Morris! I shall extinguish the lanterns. I shan't toss and turn, or lie brooding.'

A week later I was still staying at the palace; and the halo was intensifying. I could see the ring of light above John's head in daylight or artificial lighting. My friend's eyesight had worsened drastically.

There was no question now of rushing him to an optician's or to hospital. Moreover, John and I were in full agreement that Mrs Mott should be kept in the dark regarding the halo. I carried the meals she cooked to John's room on a tray, and cut up meat for him.

The Bishop was ill, incapacitated, and I was treating him—that was the story. He had a serious infection, though nothing dangerous or fatal. Mrs Mott only accepted the situation when John told her firmly, from the other side of his door, that this was so.

The business of the diocese was dealt with likewise. John's secretary took umbrage somewhat; he also wanted a 'genuine' doctor called to examine the Bishop. Through the wood of the door the Bishop overruled him loudly; and I witnessed an aspect of my friend which made me realize how he also had a tough streak—he hadn't become a bishop simply through a combination of good works and nepotism.

John's mind remained keen. The halo-creature which had infested my friend had no apparent ambition to speak through his lips, whisper words in his head, or influence his dreams.

But it brightened; how it brightened.

'Even when I become stone-blind,' John said to me, 'I'll not really be *blind*. It's just that all the light will be stolen to create my halo. And it won't be long till I'm stone-blind. Should we phone the television people, do you think? Tell them to rush here for a news conference? Should I display this miracle to the world? Should I say: *here* is God's lightning? It doesn't strike the transepts of cathedrals. It circles about my head calmly and brightly—while *I* dwell in a pit of mud for evermore, as if in Dante's *Inferno*.

'Should I say: behold the cold light of the future, of the next age of belief?

I bear it as my cross—or rather, my circle, my ring of Peter, my *annulus angeli*. Yet I know that my angel is dark. It only glows by theft, by a vampirism of light. So how can it be from God? This has destroyed my faith in God as surely as it has destroyed my sight. If this thing is God's punishment, then maybe I should damn God! If it His blessing: likewise! And if it's sent by the Devil, why then the world will never be perfected. We will never be enlightened.'

'Maybe,' I suggested, 'you need a spiritual adviser rather than a homeopathic vet?'

He shook his head brusquely; the halo remained steady. '*I* . . . must . . . decide. Only I know what it is like to be me at this time.'

And decide he did—in the most gruesome manner . . .

A distant cry clawed me out of sleep.

I flipped on my own bedside torch (absolute prerequisite in this palace where lighting systems varied from the latest to the least of technologies!). It was five-thirty a.m. by my watch. The world was still deep in darkness. Had I heard an owl screech in the frosty castle ruins?

'Morris!'

My friend's voice came from far away.

I found him in the chapel. All the candles were lit. He knelt before the little altar. By him on the flagstone lay a bloodstained bread-knife. Blood ran down his cheeks—down a ghastly empty face. On the altar cloth, staring at the silver cross, perched his two eyeballs.

In moments of horror it's odd what petty details you notice. I noticed that John had used a bread-knife—with a sawtooth edge and a rounded end. The rounded end, to spring his eyeballs loose. The saw, to sever the optic nerves.

Maybe this wasn't such a petty detail. It proved how much forethought had gone into his mutilation of himself.

His blind, unblinking eyes stared moistly at the sign of Christ. Above his head in the light of so many candles the halo could hardly be seen.

'Is that you there, Morris?' His voice spoke pain.

'Yes.'

'Has the damned thing gone yet?'

'I think it's fading. Oh John, *John!*'

Fading, fading fast. By the time the ambulance arrived no halo was visible.

Needless to say I accompanied him to the hospital. By the time a doctor could assure me that John was resting comfortably, sedated, a detective inspector and two other officers had arrived at St Luke's anxious to speak to me. The ambulance men had radioed a report; the police had hurried to the Palace, arriving shortly before Mrs Mott. They had seen the bloody bread-knife and the eyes perched upon the altar. It must have looked like a sadistic crime performed by a madman, me.

Fortunately I hadn't touched the knife.

During the hours of questions until John recovered from sedation I learnt how the thought processes of the police resemble those of our more disgraceful tabloid newspapers. This should hardly have surprised me, since to a large extent both share the same contents. The Detective Inspector spent ages pursuing the notion that Bishop Ingolby and I, both bachelors, might have been homosexually involved since college days; thus the atrocity was the product of a vicious sexual quarrel, possibly with aspects of black-mail attached—the Bishop was a famous man now, was he not?

Even after John woke up and exonerated me the Detective Inspector was loath to discard his suspicions. After all, the Bishop might be trying to cover up for me; and for himself as well. My fingerprints weren't on the handle of the knife; only John's were present, and Mrs Mott's beneath. But I might have worn gloves.

Perhaps I oughtn't to blame the police. They must have been well aware that I was lying—and later that John also was lying about a motive for the mutilation.

The one 'sure' fact relayed by Mrs Mott—namely that the Bishop feared he was going blind—seemed not so sure in view of John's doctor knowing nothing of this; nor the diocesan secretary either.

And in what mad emotional equation did fear of impending blindness lead to the wanton gouging out of one's eyes?

In a sense it was the gutter press which came to our rescue. Tipped off either by police or by ambulance men, newshounds descended on Porch-ester. To them the vital fact was that the eyes of John Ingolby—sceptical author of *Religion and the History of Lighting*—had been placed on the altar of God. What else could they be but an offering?

Thus the press added two and two together and made four. Whereas the real answer was some entirely irrational number. Or maybe a zero: the mysterious zero of the halo.

'Why did you really put your eyes on the altar, John?'

Two weeks had passed. John was back home in the palace, convalescing. He wouldn't remain at the Palace much longer; the Archbishop's personal assistant was pressing for John's resignation, rather urgently, on compassionate grounds.

By that hour Mrs Mott had departed. So had John's doctor who had called to inspect the eye sockets and change the dressings. We were alone in the palace together, John and I. How like the evening of my arrival; except that John wore a blindfold now. Except that we had eaten an ordinary dinner of brown beef, green cabbage, and golden roast potatoes.

'Why, John?'

'Well, what do you think? I've always been a tidy fellow. Where else should I have put them? Down on the floor? I didn't want anyone to stand on them and squash them!'

'That's the only reason? Tidiness?'

'I had to tidy up, Morris. I had to tidy up more than merely my eyes. You know that.'

'I suppose so . . . Will you accept artificial eyes? Glass, plastic, whatever?'

He laughed wryly. 'From artificial lighting—to artificial eyes! A logical progression, if an unenlightening one. Yes, I should think that glass eyes would be harmless enough. If not, they're a lot easier to get rid of! Just flush them down the toilet.'

'You're a brave soul, John. A true saint: a gentleman and a martyr—an unacknowledged one.'

'Let's hope I remain unacknowledged.'

Yes, he was a gentleman—of the old school of English gentlemen who produced many Anglican parsons and bishops in the past. In common with such he disliked hysteria, enthusiasm, and excess. He had performed that savage operation of optectomy (if that's the word) to root out a hysteria which was alien to him, but which might have spread outward in shock waves from his halo. He had carried this out in the cold light of dawn (almost), and certainly he had applied the cold light of reason—so that the future might be reasonable.

For sanity's sake he had denied himself any future glimpse of light, natural or artificial.

In my eyes this truly made him a saint. And a martyr too, even though he hadn't died. I alone knew this; yet how could I ever tell anybody?

John Ingolby had written a final, definitive, unpublishable chapter to his life's work—using not a pen but a bread-knife. Every time I sliced a loaf of bread in future I would feel that I was performing an act of anti-communion. A refusal to accept the unacceptable.

I felt that more than a mere bishop was on the point of retirement in Porchester. So too was an enfeebled diluted God, whose last miracle had been rejected because it would harm the world, not help it. Just as it had harmed John.

'I'm donating my collection to Porchester Museum,' he told me. 'After I've moved out of here there'll be thoroughly modern lighting in every room.' He sounded as if he was choking.

'Are you all right, old friend?'

'I'm weeping, Morris. And I can't ever weep. Except inside.'

'Maybe God had nothing to do with any of this!' I spoke to encourage him. 'Maybe the halo-parasite was something else entirely. A visitor from elsewhere in the universe. A life-form we know nothing of. You felt it was evil, remember? It might have been natural—or devilish. Aren't angels supposed to announce themselves?'

'*I* felt it was evil,' he replied, '*I* did. Nobody else who saw my round, benevolent face with a lustrous halo perched above could possibly have imagined evil. They would only have seen the light of goodness shining forth. Mine was the evil, don't you see? *Don't you see?*' And tearlessly he wept.

Or at least I suppose he was tearless. He hadn't actually carved out his tear ducts. But no welling tears would leave his cheeks. Tears would drain into the empty sockets. I didn't press for details of how an eyeless man weeps.

I did my best to comfort him.

There was I, sitting in a convivially lit room; whereas he was sitting in darkness. Darkness, always. Forever haunted by the night which had over-taken him.

Just thirty months later the announcement has come, from Matsuya Biotechnic KK of Japan, of the development of artificial bionic eyes which can be plugged into the optic nerves.

Matsuya Biotechnic's deluxe model improves upon our ordinary visual organs of muscle, jelly, and liquid amazingly. With tiny touch controls (hidden by the eyelid) these Japanese eyes can be adjusted to range into the infra-red; to magnify telescopically; and to peer owl-like on the darkest night.

The world's armed forces are very interested; though there's one small snag. To use Matsuya Eyes first you need to have your own eyes amputated.

In the two years gone by I must have visited John almost a dozen times at his retirement cottage in a little village near Porchester, where Mrs Mott continued to care for him; and I knew how he was suffering.

Not pain—but anguish.

Not poverty—his book had sold massively in paperback and in foreign editions in the wake of his self-blinding—but claustrophobia of the spirit.

John had been fitted with false plastic eyeballs which were most convincing. The blue pupils were holographically etched so that the eyes looked twinklingly alive, more so at times than real eyes.

He phoned me a fortnight ago.

'I'm going to buy a pair of these new Matsuya eyes,' he told me. 'Assuming that their experts can summon up the nerve to fit them!' He laughed sharply. 'The optic nerve, I mean. Just so long as there's enough optic nerve still alive and kicking in my head. I can't take any more of this hellish darkness, Morris. The halo-creature must have died ages ago. Given up; gone home— whatever halo-creatures do when their host starves them out.'

We had spoken much about the 'halo-creature', John and I.

An angel? A demon? An extraterrestrial life-form? Or a creature from some other universe entirely—from some other mode of existence—which had strayed across the boundary from its reality into ours?

The creature wasn't necessarily intelligent. It might have been no brighter, intellectually, than a fish of the abyss or a firefly.

Maybe it was a parasite upon some alien beings who had visited our world in secret; and it had escaped. Did it convey some advantage upon such hypothetical alien beings? Or was it just an inconvenience to them—a sort of common cold, a bug of the eyes? The evil which John had sensed might well have been the quality of alienness rather than some moral, metaphysical pang.

We had gradually settled on a naturalistic explanation, though without any actual notion of the natural history of the beast involved. Certainly a parasite which blinded its host and lit up a beacon above its head didn't seem very survival-minded. But maybe in this respect John was a South Sea Islander infected by European mumps or measles.

Or at least, *I* had settled upon this solution. John still spoke of hellish darkness.

Now technology would save him by banishing that darkness—just as improved artificial lighting had progressively banished spooks and spirits, devils and gods, lumen by lumen, century by century.

'I've been in touch with the Japanese trade people in London,' he said. 'Matsuya are going to fly a couple of their surgeons, and a pair of eyes, over the Pole. It's good publicity for their company. You could say I've been pulling strings. In ten days' time they can pull mine, inside my head, and see whether those still work. If all goes well, I should be home with my new eyes in a couple of weeks. *Jubilate!*'

All has indeed gone well.

John Ingolby can see again. He can see far better than ever he saw before in all his life. He can see better than almost all of the human race—unless they've had nature's optics removed and bionic eyes substituted.

The newly-revealed world comes as a revelation to him. My face, unseen these last two years, is a mystic vision. So too is Mrs Mott. Likewise her cottage garden of herbs and flowers.

Likewise the night-time which he can pierce with ease, seeing monochrome hills and trees and cows and hedges, the stars above drilling a thousand bright little lamp-holes.

Likewise the heat-image of the world at dawn with those same cows appearing as vivid red humps in the cool blue fields, leaving faint rosy footsteps behind them in the dew. A bird is a flaming meteor.

Such beauty redeems John's soul. His new eyes look less human than the plastic ones; they're silver-grey and at some angles seem like mirrors in his head. But that's of no account.

'John—'

It's the second night of my visit, and we have stepped outside to star-gaze. Mrs Mott has already retired early to bed.

'It's back, John.'

'Eh?'

'Your halo: it's showing faintly.'

'Don't joke, Morris.'

'I'm not joking. I can *see* it.'

He hurries closer to the cottage and peers in a curtained window-pane. Everything is much more visible to him. His reflection there confirms my word.

'Oh my God. So it wasn't living in my eyes and feeding on the photons. It was in my brain all the time. It's been lying dormant like a frozen virus. The light has brought it back to life. Oh my God. These Matsuya eyes are permanent. I can't pull them out when I feel like it . . .'

'And you can't switch them off?'

'Why should anybody want to switch their eyes off? When I go to bed, my eyelids do the job. An on—off button would be one control too many. It's early days yet for bionic eyes.'

He tells me how Matsuya Biotech KK boast that future bionic eyes will have computerized display functions activated by voice command, with memory chips located in a unit which might be surgically implanted behind the ear or in the jaw. Owners of Matsuya eyes will be able to call up statistics, run graphics across their field of view, access encyclopaedias.

Not for several years yet.

'John, this time I think we ought to tell people. You could begin by telling the Japanese.'

'No.'

'Why not? They'll be worried in case the halo's some fault of the Matsuya eyes. Or they might suppose you've stumbled on some hidden power of the mind which their eyes have triggered. The liberation of the third eye by their lenses! They'll have equipment for probing the halo. They might be able to look into your brain through the eyes.'

'No, Morris, the problem's the same as ever. Oh God, to have all the wonder of the world restored to me thrice over—then to have it polluted and thieved again! I'm no saint!' he snarls suddenly. 'I might have been a saintly codger in Porchester but I damn well stopped being one during these past two years.'

We go inside the cottage and drink brandy.

John gets drunk.

The halo isn't at all conspicuous when Mrs Mott serves us our breakfast of bacon and eggs. She notices nothing odd, but I can spy the faint shimmer.

The sky is blue, the sun is bright.

'Lovely spring morning,' observes John. 'Might cloud over later. We'll take a walk up Hinchcombe Hill.'

Hinchcombe Hill is a mile away along a lane then up through a steep forest ride to a gorse-clad hilltop, which is deserted save for some Suffolk ewes. Suffolks are a chunky breed which lamb early, before Christmas; these ewes are already parted from their offspring.

It was cool walking up through the shade of the fir trees, but here on the hilltop it's as hot as a summer's day.

'Can you see our circular friend?'

'The sun's too bright,' I tell him.

'Good. Now, we all know that we shouldn't stare at a bright sun, don't we Morris? The sun can burn the cells of the retina. My retina is a machine. It's much more resilient. The flash from a hydrogen bomb might burn Matsuya eyes—but we all know that a nuclear flash is brighter than a *thousand* suns, don't we? So I ought to have lots of spare capacity even if I switch over to night-vision.'

'Don't do it, John.'

'I don't care if I harm these eyes. Not now.'

'You might damage your brain. The visual centres.'

'Where the beast dwells, eh? Unless it dwells in a separate universe, or in Heaven, and only has a peephole in my head.'

He sits down on a boulder facing the sun. 'You want feeding?' he cries out. 'I'll feed you!'

For some reason—habit, ritual, or insurance policy?—he crosses himself, then begins to stare fixedly at the sun. Loudly he hums the hymn tune, 'Angels from the Realms of Glory', over and over again monotonously.

Minutes pass.

'I can see it, John. It's glowing.'

Brighter, ever brighter.

Presently it's a full-fledged radiant halo; and still he stares into the sun.

He breaks off humming. 'Report, please!' he says crisply.

'I can't look directly at it any longer. It's getting too fierce.' At least the halo's light is cold, otherwise John's head would surely start to cook.

'Not from my point of view! The day grows dim. The sun looks like a lemon in a mist.' *Ang-els! from! the Realms! of Glo-ry!*

I simply have to turn away. The ewes have all trekked off down the slope away from this second, miniature sun in their midst.

'I'm going blind fast, Morris. It's really gobbling light.'

'And pumping it out again!'

'I'll soon be back in darkness. But no matter.' *Ang-els! from!*

If only I had some tinted glass with me. I only dare risk a glance now and then.

Glance:

The halo isn't doughnut-shaped any longer. It's a sphere of furnace light just like a second head. Its after-image bobs above the fir trees as though a ball of lightning is loose.

The Realms! of Glo-ry!

I cast two shadows on the grass and gorse.

Glance:

'It's elongating upwards, John!'

A pillar of blinding silver radiance: it could light a whole street.

In the after-image a figure hovers over the trees, sliding from side to side: a body of sorts. It fades.

Glance:

Now the after-image is sharper. That isn't a human body. It's too slim, except where the chest swells out. The legs are too short, the arms too long and skinny. The head is like a bird's with a beak of a mouth.

Ang-els! from!

The after-image has wings, great trailing plumed wings.

It's the blazing angel who threw Adam and Eve out of Eden.

'There's a creature perching on your head, John! A tall scraggly bird! It's like a man—but it isn't.'

Its claw feet are planted on John's skull as if his skull is an egg which it is clutching.

Glance:

The after-image opens its beak.

'Hullo! Hullo! Hullo!' What a screechy, reedy voice.

John isn't humming any longer. The words are screeched from *his* lips in the tones of a parrot or a mynah bird.

'I hear you,' I shout.

I shade my eyes with both hands in a visor: John is sitting as before gazing rigidly up at our sun.

'I come,' screams the bird of light. 'I announce myself!'

'Where do you come from?'

'I take!'

'Take what? Where to?'

'My prey! To my eyrie!'

John must be the creature's prey. I have to break his link with the power of the sun! Sheltering my head from the horrid pillar of light, I stumble at a crouch and buffet him sideways off his rock. With my own eyes closed tight I cast myself down beside him. Fumbling, I find his head and seal my hands across his Matsuya eyes.

'Aiiieee!' shrieks the voice.

John's own voice calls out: 'Oh blessed visions! Realms of glory! Celestial city of the angels! With the slimmest, highest of towers all lit by cold light at night as though a star has settled on every pinnacle—an angel perching on each. White angels drifting through the pearly sky of day. A meadowland below with little blue goat-elves all a-grazing by the river of milk—'

'Don't heed it, John! Cast it out of your head.'

'My soul will go inside an angel's egg.'

'Refuse! The thing is trying to take your mind away with it!'

'I'll be reborn—angelic.'

'They're birds of prey, John. Alien eagles, not angels.'

'No, they are celestial—' His voice chokes off.

'Aiiieee! I triumph!'

John's body shudders then grows still.

Cautiously I open my eyes. The blinding light, the second sun, has gone. Only our own yellow sun beams on the gorse, the rocks, the grass; and on my friend's body.

I feel for his pulse; there's none. His heart has stopped. I don't know how to give the kiss of life but I still try to breathe animation back into him—in vain.

I sit by his sun-warmed corpse for a long while.

John thought that his mind would go into an angel's egg on that alien world, in that other reality.

Presumably he would hatch.

As what? As an angel, the equal of the other angel-birds?

Or as a prisoner, bringing honour to its captor? A slave? A sacrifice? A gift to the Lord of the Birds of Light?

I shall soon walk back down the hill, through the forest ride, along the lane alone. I shall have to say that the strain of the ascent caused a coronary and broke his heart. I shall say that his spirit has ascended to Heaven, where he is now at home.

I must hope that no one else saw the blinding light on Hinchcombe Hill, the radiance that raptured John away to an alien eyrie, leaving the abandoned clothing of his flesh behind.

Maybe John will be happy when he hatches, to the cold light of that elsewhere-city. And maybe there's no such city; maybe his last visions were lies, opiates pumped into his skull to paralyse his will . . .

A few ewes return, to stare at the two of us with mild curiosity.

Salvage Rites

TIM AND ROSY HAD CLEARED OUT THEIR SPARE ROOM RUTHLESSLY. They had almost emptied it of the various categories of things that haunt spare rooms: surplus things, fatigued things, souvenir things, exiled things, scraps of things, things that might conceivably be repaired or cannibalized, things that might one day come in handy—all the time vault of twenty years.

'Trouble with being poor,' Rosy said while they were loading the car, 'is the way you store rubbish like treasure.' As if she blamed him for the accumulation.

'We aren't exactly poor,' Tim said awkwardly. 'Compared with, say, someone in Africa, we're well-off. We get by.'

Yes, they got by, on the income from the grocery shop. They were able to pay the interest on their debts, which lodged with them like a greedy, infirm uncle; like a senile, crippled mother who stopped them from ever going on holiday. Tim's poetry earned a bit of extra money. His short, fierce lyrics could be roughed out during slack half-hours—jotted down like customers' grocery lists—then polished before bed. Two small collections had been published and well-received. And of course he was working on his sustained mock-epic set in an imaginary Central European country, forever adding ten lines, crossing out five. The country in question needed to be imaginary since he and Rosy couldn't afford to travel abroad.

'Modern life is rubbish,' said Rosy. 'I saw that sprayed on the front of the cinema. It's perfectly true.'

'It's the fault of the recession,' he replied.

'It always costs more to be poor, doesn't it? We buy the cheapest, so it's trash. We wear clothes from charity shops, so we look like paupers and people try to swindle us. The poor always rob the poor. This car's a heap of junk; it costs more to keep on the road than a Rolls.'

Their car was over ten years old, and rust was eating the bottoms of the doors. The hydraulics of the hatchback had failed; thus the hatch had to be propped up with a broom handle when open. The erratic engine guzzled oil.

When the car, with its rear seats lowered, had been crammed with off-cuts of carpet, underfelt, old curtains and coats, bags of lank sweaters and sad shoes, tatty toys, a sick television set, and such, Tim felt oddly refreshed and clean. Whenever he scraped out the last smears of marmalade or pickle from a jar, whenever he emptied out a cereal box, he would feel a similar minor surge of satisfaction, as though now something new and different might happen. Freud might explain this as a babyish pleasure in the expulsion of faeces. True, Freud also spoke about anal retention. Next to nothing had been retained in the spare room.

The clear-out coincided with daughter Emma's departure to college. Her choice of geography to study wasn't so much a poignant comment on her parents' immobility as due to geography being regarded academically as an easy option. Emma would probably become an underpaid teacher in a mediocre school; she might marry another teacher. Emma didn't know this yet. Kids were as bouncy as bunnies, before the fox ate them or the winter froze them. Nature pumped the hormone of optimism into each generation. In recent years, Tim had reconciled himself at last to dwelling in the geography of the imagination.

So the house above the shop was doubly empty. It was empty of accumulated clutter; and empty of Emma. Sadly, yet somehow refreshingly empty, like the late-autumn Sunday itself. The sun shone brightly on the empty street. People were still in bed, sleeping in. But the public dump five miles away would be open. Dawn till dusk.

'Junk,' repeated Rosy. Tim hoped she wasn't going to turn bitter when it came time to throw their past away.

He removed the broom handle, let the hatchback slam itself, and patted it reassuringly. 'Don't discourage the old thing.'

Rosy plucked at a loop in her saggy sweater and eyed a box of Emma's childhood toys inside.

'Well, we've got rid of her at last,' she said, apparently changing the subject. 'Now we can start living, I suppose. If we still know how. Before we're too old.'

Automatically, Tim smoothed his hair around the tonsure of his bald patch. They climbed into the car, which started without too much fuss.

As they drove off, Rosy said, 'If we won a fortune, I shouldn't be able to spend it, you know. I could never bring myself to buy a coat at *new* prices. Or a meal in a restaurant. Or a proper hairdo. It would seem obscene. I've been trained.'

'Me too. I wonder how we'd win a fortune.' He spoke flatly, not asking. Most houses and gardens they passed were blank and lifeless, but one man was out washing a car with last year's registration. Tim hardly knew what model it was. He failed to imagine himself driving it. He and Rosy had originally started the shop with help from parents, back in the days when he had dreamed of becoming an internationally regarded poet who travelled places. Parents were now all dead. Legacies had gone to assuage the upward-creeping debts.

'Beautiful day.'

Rosy said nothing in reply. She pulled down the sun visor briefly and sought wrinkles in the mirror on the back.

'My hair needs cutting,' she said presently.

'*Go* to a hairdresser's,' he murmured.

'I'll do it myself. As usual.'

Tim thought he needed a haircut, too. When you wore cheap old clothes, short hair was best.

'The roots are showing,' she said.

'That's fashionable nowadays. Look, you said we ought to start living. If you couldn't ever splash out in a restaurant, how can we start living? A bit of a contradiction, isn't it?'

'An economic contradiction. Why should we have to own a shop? The state should own everything. There shouldn't be private cars, either. There should be enough good buses and railways.'

'True. But there aren't. The services have been castrated.'

A poem occurred to him: about eunuchs in Arabian robes driving harems of passengers who peered not through windows but through intricate lattices.

The dump would be open today because the dump was a market, too. A bazaar of sorts. Just as charity shops sprouted like fungi in any temporarily empty commercial premises in town, selling the rags of richer people to poorer people to send aid to the totally poor in the Third World, so, with the deliberate decline of the economy, rubbish dumps had changed their nature. Concessionaires bid for the salvage rights. Anything reusable was sold back to the public. Ecological recycling? Logic of poverty? One or the other.

Tim and Rosy had visited the dump outside town a year before and bought a washing machine for a song. The machine worked for three months before breaking down. Cheaper than renting with an option to buy. Now the carcass, with holes cut in, acted as a compost bin in their patch of back garden. According to gossips visiting the shop, the dump had since undergone a further metamorphosis. A hot-drink vending machine had been installed so that browsers could refresh themselves with a plastic cup of coffee. That summer an ice-cream van had visited the dump most weekends.

'Next thing,' he said, 'people will be having picnics at the dump. There'll be a play area for kids. Tours of the infill. Bulldozer rides. *Déjeuner sur le dump.*'

'What?'

'The Manet painting. Imagine that fellow and his naked mistress sitting on the dump drinking champagne. I presume she'd have to wear a bikini.'

A poem? 'Manet at the Dump'. Maybe. What word rhymed with 'rubbish'?

Driving along the two-lane road between the first ploughed empty fields of the countryside, Tim spotted a cloud of gulls milling in the sky over the sprawling infill acres of the dump, like so many scraps of white paper. Rusty corrugated-iron sheets walled off the visitor's zone.

Which they entered, in low gear, the suspension creaking ominously as the car humped itself over the sleeping-policeman ramp.

A large concrete yard was lined with bulky rubbish bins into which their car could probably have fitted. Down one side the high bins were already loaded with rubble. Those along the opposite side were empty; however, most were roped off with a notice prohibiting use. An arrow pointed to the far end, where several bins stood behind notice-boards indicating 'glass', 'garden refuse', 'metal'. Those bins were already full; sunlight glared from a pile of windows.

A battered bulk-shipping container the size of a railway carriage blocked the view beyond, though another mounted wooden arrow pointed behind it.

Nearer to hand stood a black oil sump, and a bottle-bank painted camouflage green that resembled an armoured car, with slots for clear and coloured bottles reminiscent of muzzles from which howitzer shells could be fired. A score of ripped-off doors were stacked against one end.

Tim stopped the car by a truck trailer that was packed with a mound of old clothes and rags. Shirt sleeves hung down as if they had tried to climb out and failed, all the breath crushed out of them.

Beside this trailer, another huge shipping container, open at one end, was labelled 'shop'. Within, Tim saw clothes on racks, shelves of paperback books, electrical goods. A fat, vacant-faced woman of indeterminate middle age, wearing a pink parka, occupied a deckchair outside. The shop forecourt displayed collections of tools, lamp bases and shades, mirrors, ambiguous metal paraphernalia, a cocktail cabinet with the veneer peeling.

Inside a makeshift pen, cobbled together from car roof-racks, an Alsatian guard bitch woke to life when Tim opened his door. The powerful animal reared, barking, raving.

'Jilly!' screamed the fat woman. She ignored Tim. The Alsatian slumped, and whined.

Apart from their car, the yard was deserted. Too early in the day, perhaps. By this afternoon the bazaar of rubbish might be buzzing; then the beast wouldn't be on edge. Tim stepped nervously round to the hatchback, raised it, and inserted the broom handle. He carried the first plastic bag of clothes to the open trailer, and swung. The bag landed high up the hill of garments, jamming against the roof. He noticed a movement in the inner gloom. Some rags shifting, knocked off balance?

Rosy wound her window down. 'Why can't you save the bags?'

'Oh,' he said stupidly, measuring the height of the trailer floor, the incline of the clothes hill. Should he climb up and empty the bag? 'There's no space left at the front. Our stuff would fall out.'

Supposing you tried to repossess a coat you'd thrown away—having changed your mind about discarding it—would the Alsatian be within its rights to rip your throat out? Because you no longer owned that coat? A sign fixed to the dog-pen forbade visitors from taking anything, except by way of the shop. Salvage rights had been granted. To a firm called Griffiths Scavenging. Associates of the fat woman in the deckchair.

'Tim, come back here!'

He hurried to the car window.

'Someone inside there,' Rosy whispered.

In the dim interior of the trailer, almost hidden by the summit of fabrics, Tim spotted a skinny girl with ratty hair. As he watched, she ripped open the bag he had thrown, and tossed the contents this way and that, examining, sorting.

'It's obscene,' said Rosy, 'having your socks and knickers picked over before your very eyes.'

'Maybe we should have washed all our old clothes before we threw them away?'

'That isn't funny. Find somewhere else, will you? Down there by those signs.'

Leaving the hatchback propped, Tim got in and started the engine. He drove down toward the other freight container and followed the arrow behind it.

Another arrow pointed the way down a long lane lined by bins. As Tim and Rosy entered the lane, shadow fell upon them from the high metal sides and suddenly the day was cold. The occasional freestanding notice announced 'plastic', 'rubber & tyres'. As well as being inconveniently tall, the bins were mostly full.

Heeding a further arrow, he turned the car along a side-lane similarly walled with bins and intermittent notices.

'Carpeting,' he read. 'Here we are. Get rid of *that*, at any rate.'

On his second attempt, he managed to raise their rolled threadbare carpet to head-height and tumble it over the metal lip. It fell dully within. From the car, he hauled the first bundle of heavy underfelt, which they had stored for years on the off-chance.

'That isn't exactly *carpet*,' called Rosy.

'Undercarpet. Same thing. What do they expect? We should sort out everything for them? Bother that. I'll toss the lot in here, clothes and all. Who cares?'

Another plump, empty-faced woman, in raggy woollens and baggy trousers—an obvious sister of the deckchair occupant—squeezed her way from between two bins and stood watching. A boy of five or six in shorts and black zipper jacket followed her, clutching a torn picture book.

Tim walked over to the woman. 'Is it all right if I throw underfelt in that one?' Her skin oozed grease.

'Wha'?' she said after a while.

He repeated himself.

'Uh,' she said, which might have meant anything. He realized that the woman was stupid, moronic. Maybe she had no connection with Griffiths Scavenging, after all. She might just be wandering around.

'Well, I will, then.' So Tim disposed of all the underfelt, awkwardly heaving and hurling aloft while the woman stared silently at him.

He got back into the car. 'There'll be bins for clothes and stuff further on.'

True enough. The next arrow directed them into another long, narrow roadway of bins, all brimful of different categories of clothing. Signs were hardly necessary. Suits. Shirts. Skirts. Underwear. Boots and shoes. Buttons; there was even a bin full of buttons, a mountain height of multi-coloured shingle.

He cruised at walking pace. 'Must be their storeroom, hmm? Maybe they export to poor countries. Or places hit by disaster. Cyclones, earthquakes. We oughtn't to have come so far. We should have dumped the lot back in the yard.'

A pair of acne-scarred youths in jeans, heavy steel-tipped boots, and bomber jackets emerged. One slapped a hand on the front of the car, forcing Tim to brake. The other strolled grinning round to the open boot.

'Help yer, mate?' The youth tore a bag open and pulled out an old skirt of Rosy's. He ran and tossed this up into a bin of skirts, returned and burrowed, while his companion joined him.

'Hey,' objected Tim. 'Get out of our car. Now.'

As though instinctively alert to the contents, the youths grabbed the other clothes bags out of the back and ripped them open to sort on the ground. Tim immediately drove on and soon rounded another corner. Yet another lane of bins—all apparently empty—stretched ahead, with an arrow indicating a turning halfway along.

'Stop and reverse,' said Rosy. 'Go back the way we came.'

'We still have the TV to dump, and the—'

'Stop! Back up and turn. Unload the rest in the yard. Anywhere! Drive away. Home.'

Home. That house above a shop that fed them and imprisoned them. The house with an empty daughter's room. And now with an empty spare room. Tim experienced an odd feeling of certainty that before leaving that morning they had emptied the entire house—of furniture, stove, refrigerator, everything—and that there was nothing left any longer to connect them to the place. As if they had cleared all the shelves in the shop, too, leaving bare boards. They were free; they had escaped—hadn't they? Something new could begin.

Vacant shop, vacant house, vacant debts. As vacant as this street of empty bins; as vacant as the rear of the car was fast becoming. He wished he had closed the hatchback down. Otherwise something more precious than junk might escape, might be snatched or simply drift away into the chilly air here between these looming steel boxes that mockingly imitated a decrepit city street—from the future, perhaps, after a war.

He halted the car and shook his head to clear a cold fog of apprehension from his brains. Before he could engage reverse gear, he saw in the driving-mirror the high front of a truck loom around the corner behind. Piston arms, at attention, dangled chains embracing the steel bin on its flatbed back. Somehow the bintruck negotiated the turn. He wondered how it could ever manoeuvre to pick up or deposit any of the bins ranged on either side. Maybe there was a turntable built into the chassis. Standing in the bin as though navigating the vehicle was the moronic woman.

Suddenly the sight of her terrified him. The truck slowly approached, and honked.

'It must be one-way-only, Rosy.' Tim drove forward to the next intersection and swung down a lane of close-packed bins containing scrap metal. By the time they reached another arrow, and another turn, the bintruck had already entered the scrap metal street.

Tim took another turn, then another, losing the truck way behind. *If* it had been deliberately following, to begin with.

Arrow followed arrow. Turn followed turn. Lane of bins succeeded lane of bins. Once they turned into the street of clothing bins, yet this led to a street of scrap metal bins, not a street where the bins were empty. Unless his memory was deceiving him. No, it wasn't. The clothes bins must have been different ones. They were lost in a maze.

'This is ridiculous,' he told Rosy. 'There isn't space for all these lanes.'

'We've entered the world of rubbish,' Rosy whispered back. 'Where we've been heading for the past twenty years.'

The engine coughed and missed a couple of times. Tim pulled the choke half out, racing the engine, though of necessity still driving slowly.

'It's all this damn crawling in first gear. The plugs soot up.'

The very next lane opened into a long concrete yard walled in by bins. It wasn't the yard that housed the shop. Slamming the choke back in, Tim gunned the car toward the arrow marking the exit at the far end, hoping to burn the plugs clean. He braked violently in time to enter the next narrow alley.

Six lanes later the engine quit. Tim couldn't restart the car.

'What do we do now?' asked Rosy.

'Walk. I'll leave the keys in the ignition.'

The bins on either side stood shoulder to shoulder. They seemed twice as large as previously. You couldn't even squeeze sideways between bins, though you might just manage to crawl on your belly. The only route was the concrete road.

'I wonder if this was once an old airfield?'

Then Tim remembered the gulls flocking about the infill. But no gulls flapped in the sky now.

'What's in the bins, Tim?'

Not since that second yard had they passed a single sign announcing the contents. He peered up. Suddenly he understood the assorted shapes peering over the lips of the containers.

Car doors.

Further along . . . a forest of exhaust pipes like several church organs jumbled by a bomb blast.

'Bits of cars,' he said, opening his door.

Two lanes later they heard from somewhere behind them the whine of a power tool, then the clanging of metal. He felt sure that their stalled car was being broken up into parts. Taking Rosy's hand, he hurried her onward and along another lane. Faintly, he heard a thump of boots and a silly, idiotic giggling.

Clothes bins again! Jackets, shirts, sandals, nightdresses looked over bin tops. Before they could reach the next corner, the moronic woman waddled out from it ahead of them. She was accompanied by a big, bony, overall-clad man in his mid-forties, his thick black hair slicked back in waves, his nose an absurdly small squashed blob in a large, battered face.

'Yer need a hand, squire?'

Tim jerked around. One of the youths sat perched on the edge of a shirt bin behind him. The youth dropped to the ground just as his partner came wading over the bin of summer dresses opposite. He leapt down, too.

'Show us the way out of here!' cried Rosy. 'No, go away! Leave us alone!'

The two youths rushed and clamped Rosy by the arms. At the same moment the man seized Tim, who struggled uselessly; the grip was like granite.

'Yer need a hand,' the youth repeated.

The plump woman ambled forward. While the man manipulated Tim like a toy or a life-size doll, the woman undressed him, taking her time about it, tossing his clothes up into various bins. Soon Tim shivered nakedly, still held tight.

Then it was Rosy's turn.

Their captors led Tim and Rosy, both stripped naked, to the turn and released them, thrusting them into the next steel and concrete lane.

'Ge' on, now, squire!'

The woman and her three companions remained at the intersection, blocking any return to the bins where Tim's and Rosy's clothes and shoes had been discarded. Shaking with cold and shock, Tim and Rosy ran along numbly to the next turn, as much to hide their nakedness from the blankly watchful eyes and chilly breeze as to escape.

Tim's teeth chattered. 'We'll f-find something to wear. F-further on. Any old rags. Or c-curtains.'

The bins in this new lane were loaded with sheets of cardboard, rolls of wallpaper, bundles of old magazines.

Tim wondered whether he could scale the side of a bin with bare feet. He would have to!

Rosy wailed, 'I thought they were going to rape—!' Her breasts bounced. 'They did! They did. It was the same.'

'Listen, this is all a vicious joke. Next we'll come across some rags to put on. Then we'll reach the yard where the shop is, looking like scarecrows. And we'll find our car waiting for us—with our clothes folded on the seats. Nobody will believe us, but . . .' He had to believe it. 'They could have hurt us. They didn't.'

'You think they didn't hurt us? I'm hurt forever.'

The bins in the next lane all looked empty; nothing peeped over the tops. Tim rapped his knuckles against several; all rang hollowly. He didn't feel inclined to try to climb, to check.

They walked in cold shade. Whichever direction a lane led, sunlight seemed excluded. At last an arrow pointed the way down between rows of bins full of broken furniture, to a concrete-surfaced yard.

'It's the way out,' he said. 'We've arrived.'

However, the yard, lined with more giant bins, was only as large as a tennis court, and no arrow pointed to an exit. There was only an entrance. Half of the yard was bathed in sunshine, where Rosy ran to warm herself. Her bare flesh quivering, the breeze still nipped her. Whatever these bins contained couldn't be seen from ground level. A car roof-rack rested against one. Side-on, its metal bars were steps.

'I'll see the way out!' Wincing, then planting her feet sideways so as to spread her weight along the thin steel bars, Rosy ascended.

Shading her eyes, she stared around helplessly.

She looked down inside the bin itself. And screamed. And screamed.

Tim scaled the bars; there was room alongside. Clutching her cold shoulders with a chilly arm, he, too, gazed down.

For a few seconds he hardly understood what he saw. A layer of slime-coated ping-pong balls? Hundreds of hard-boiled eggs?

No. Eyes. The optic cords sprouted like tiny lengths of electric cord torn out of plugs.

Sheep's eyes? No, he didn't think so. Not the eyes of sheep, or any other animal. Rosy had stopped screaming, out of breath. She shook convulsively, clutching the top of the bin, screwing her own eyes tight shut as if to hide them.

He could see into the neighbouring bin as well. A heap of french fries? Baby parsnips? No.

Fingers. Chopped-off human fingers.

He stared wildly around the yard. What did all the other bins hide in their depths? Toes, tongues, lungs? Arms and loins and brains? The parts of the body, sorted out . . . Yes! He knew this was so, even before the grind of an engine dragged his gaze to the entrance of the little yard.

The bintruck heaved into view and halted in the entrance, completing the circuit of metal walls. The front jutted sufficiently into the yard that the truck doors would be free to open. Crowded side by side in the cab were the man, at the wheel; the two youths; the moronic woman with her boy on her knee; the blank-faced fat woman in the pink parka; and the skinny, ratty girl. All of the passengers, even the little boy, were clutching assorted tools. Saw. Pincers. A gouge. A small axe.

The truck engine died.

'For God's sake, climb on top, Rosy! Walk along the side to the bin beyond. We must get out of here.'

Beyond the yard for as far as he could see in all directions were endless rows of bins.

Desperately, bruising his naked body, almost crippling a toe, Tim scrambled on top, struggling to balance, half-helping, half-dragging Rosy with him. The top edge was far too narrow ever to walk along with bare feet, tightrope-style. Nude, he knew they couldn't even slide along, astride. That would be like riding a blunt steel blade. After a while it would cut through them, between their legs. Instead he slid down inside, pulling Rosy howling with him.

'We'll climb out the back way into the next one! And the next!'

Jelly lumps squelched underfoot. He skidded in the six-inch-deep pool of eyes and fell, nauseated. Scrambling up, he waded, then leapt at the high rear edge of the bin. He did catch hold, with outstretched fingers, his front smashing against the metal, but he couldn't pull himself up. He hadn't enough of a grip. There was no purchase. His feet were slipping on soft marbles.

'Yer need a hand?'

A crowd of heads popped up behind. Vacant faces smiled vaguely. The man, the women, the youths, the ratty girl, even the little boy.

Hands rose into view, displaying a gouge, an axe, pincers, saws.

The Moon and Michelangelo

PETER CATLOW WOKE FROM A DREAM OF A WIDE STRAIGHT ROAD stretching invitingly through cow pastures and willow trees upon a sunset evening towards, yes, some village with a pub where the real ale would be strong and malty just the way he liked it.

He lay trying to keep hold of the dream, since it was years since such rural scenes had existed in such an unprotected form. As an earlier image clarified he realized that the dream had only been a half-happy one, for the road of his dream had set out from one of the gateways of the alien city. His right arm had been trapped in the mouth of one of the stone Herms; he'd been struggling to pull free.

Pins and needles stung Peter's hand as paralysed flesh thawed. He'd been sleeping on his arm, squeezing the blood-flow.

Though he was sure that it must still be the middle of the alien night, as soon as he turned over to catch more shut-eye his alarm began to bleep. Disbelieving he slapped the alarm off, slapped on the light (and his wake-up tape of Vaughan Williams' *Variations on a Theme of Thomas Tallis*), and swung out of bed before he could relapse. A button unshuttered the window upon another streaky-bacon dawn on Rock.

Not that the landscape was barren; the brightening light of swiftly-rising Tau Ceti was disclosing lush herbage, the vegetable fields checkered purple and emerald, a sinuous fish-rich river, and a forest of giant ferns and bottle-trees.

But whereas Earth people had named their world after the flesh of the planet, the soft fruitful soil, the lemur-like natives of Tau Ceti II apparently preferred to call theirs after the bones of the planet, the hard skeleton. Apparently.

From the edge of the window of his little cubicle Peter could see a kilometre away the south-eastern flank of the city writhing with its gargoyles and grotesques.

Mary Everdon had said to him: 'Perhaps for the natives the hardness of rock, and the manipulation of rock into shapes dense with meaning, equates with their emergence from biology, from organic culture, into culture and permanence and history? Carved rock and sculpted stone equals thought solidified and redeemed from timelessness into the new stream of sapient time.'

Each time that she voiced her embryonic theory, it seemed to put on more weight, to become ever more viable. But Peter thought of it as her intellectual phantom pregnancy—which could become ever more convincing until one embarrassing day she might need to face the fact that there was nothing in it, after all. Of course, that was Mary's merit too, in an extraterrestrial context: the ability to make speculative leaps.

Mary pointed out that this city near which the expedition had set down was only one of many such carved wonderlands (or horror-villes) scattered about the two habitable continents which shared the same side of the world, nestling together like a pair of cashew nuts. The closest distance between any two cities was a couple of hundred kilometres. Forest or swamp, desert or mountain intervened. No road network existed. So the architecture must display the psychic bedrock of the inhabitants, must be a way of perceiving and celebrating their own triumphant separation from unthinking nature.

As Peter let the pastoral swell of Vaughan Williams tone up his nervous system (while he washed quickly, while he shaved) he contemplated another day which wouldn't last long enough to tire a fellow without taking a pill, to be followed by another night not long enough to rest oneself adequately.

'This planet makes me feel prematurely old,' he'd confided to Mary in the refectory the evening before, while they hastily spooned up their dinner of chilli con carne before the nightly info-swap began, prelude to bedtime.

The forty-strong complement of the shuttle base munched their spiced beans and chattered science at twenty little tables. (Prevent cliques; prevent isolation. Nevertheless, there were cliques. Nevertheless there was...)

Cheery yellow plastic walls; several doors open to the corridor; Commander's podium; large video screen showing a Californian beachscape that particular evening. Overhead the large bubble skylight framed one of the two bright moons chasing its partner in vain, or being chased. Periodically (not now) you saw the glint of the orbiting voidship, *Michelangelo*—named a touch arrogantly after Earth's supreme sculptor—with the non-landing crew on board. They would soon get their treat: a trip out to orbit the third, fourth, and fifth planets which were two modest airless deserts plus an awesome gas-giant with a family of moons; before returning for pickup.

Since Mary usually generated a theory she asked, 'Does your speciality make you feel you're a sort of medieval person, who's ancient compared with all this?' She smiled with sympathetic bonhomie.

He shook his head. 'No, it's because when you're young the days seem to stretch out endlessly, yet they shrink as you grow older. Here, the days have all suddenly grown very short, as though I've aged twenty or thirty years.'

'How old are you? I've forgotten. Is it forty-eight?'

'That's right.' She hadn't forgotten.

They had all had access to each other's bios, and according to the bare bones of hers Mary Everdon was thirty-nine years old, doctorate in cultural anthropology from . . . Peter couldn't care less where. Mary was unattached, plumpish, red-haired. She reminded him of . . . (Had she taken lovers? What were her erotic preferences? If any.)

Peter nodded in the direction of Carl Lipmann, the scrawny blond linguist.

'It's a pity we can't ask the natives how they feel, and understand the answers.' It was a pity he couldn't bring himself to ask Mary outright how she felt about him.

'Not yet. We're making progress, aren't we?'

Was *he*?

'They twitter and warble like birds.'

'Ah, but in a flexibly structured way. And we have quite a few sound-groups provisionally pegged with meanings. So it's a true language.' She raised her voice. 'They're far from being some sort of mammalian *termite*, as Fremantle had the nerve to suggest.'

Barney Fremantle, bald and natty, sat two tables away with Sandra Ramirez, the ecologist (black waterfall of curls). The biologist cocked an ear and shrugged. He had a sample bag beside him, which he patted like an obedient dog. Fremantle had suggested that the building of the city and the intricate carving of the natives might simply be wired-in, instinctual behaviour—akin to the artistic forecourts of bower birds—and that they weren't genuinely sapient. This, despite their wooden agricultural implements and their sledge-carts, and their cooking bowls and their use of fire; despite the presumption that they must possess *metal* tools so as to have sculpted their ornate city.

Peter wasn't here in quite the same capacity as the other experts from sciences hard and soft. After the drone-probe had hyperpulsed its highly detailed aerial pictures of the cities of Rock back to Earth, it had been decided imaginatively to include a stonemason in the exploration team. A stonemason should have practical, existential knowledge of what seemed to be the main manifestation of the native culture.

When the invitation had come—when some computer had picked up his name as a master stonemason without family ties—Peter had been in charge of renovating the abacus of ancient statues on the front of the acid-eaten Lichfield Cathedral, now that the town was safely protected by a Fuller dome. Perhaps it was nostalgia, rather than the promise of interstellar adventure, which prompted his acceptance. To be able to stroll through a city of uneroded carvings under an open sky, a city neither rotted by pollution nor air-conditioned like a museum piece.

As Peter scraped up his last spoonful, Commander Ash strode to the podium, short, stocky, crew-cut, her oval face nevertheless (or perhaps on account of the crew-cut) that of a delicate china doll. She blanked the screen.

'Need for brevity,' she reminded. 'I'll guillotine garrulity.'

Oh yes she would; and during the info-swap they would all talk in the same clipped telegraphic way. How to cram a pint into a half-pint pot. Likewise activity by day and sleep by night. Likewise the Commander's own physique: a pint of power in a half-pint frame, with irrelevant coiffure shorn off. No time to bother with your hair on Rock. Emulate the name of the world; have head like a boulder. Made of china. Peter felt his brain gearing up to match the pace of the info-swap.

Yet Mary's hair was very long, a flood of generous fire . . . Did Mary realize that this might subtly irritate Ash, and merit an impatient hearing?

'Change to double-day cycle?' the geologist (and temporary Rockologist) Stevens requested. 'Field-work one day plus whole night's data analysis; sleep through whole next day and night?'

'Waste too much time sleeping then,' judged Ash. 'Be soldiers of science; learn to cat-nap. Next?'

It wasn't long before Fremantle rose, darting a look of amused triumph towards Mary.

'Reporting trip into forest. Bottle-trees come in dozen main shapes; all are hollow shells supporting fronds.'

'Known,' said Ash.

'Shells show fracture lines, large-piece jigsaw patterns. Stone smashes shells into constituent fragments.' Reaching into his bag, he exhibited one of the native wooden spades with short curved handle, the specimen wrapped in film. 'This.' Now he placed a native work on the table. 'Or this.' He flourished a film-clad wooden knife. 'Plus sharp shards. All known native artifacts readily available from nature.'

Mary sat wounded, momentarily confused. All data would be put on the infonet for access and review by anyone else. Meanwhile, Fremantle seemed to have scored a coup.

'Biotechnology?' asked Peter helpfully. He knew the concept. 'Trees bred for tools?'

Fremantle laughed brusquely but it was agronomist Vasilki Patel who supplied the answer.

'Biotech requires microscopes, laser scalpels. Farm crops indicate only simple improvement over wild strains.'

'Amazing,' said Stevens, with a note of sarcasm, 'those trees falling apart so conveniently into identifiable tools; quite naturally too.' He also was trying to be helpful: Rockologist in league with stonemason.

Sandra Ramirez spoke up from beside Fremantle. 'Hypothesis: wrecking a tree has connection with reproductive cycle. Lemurs wreck trees which produce useful shapes. Thus evolutionary selection favours trees which split up usefully; against those which didn't.'

Stevens looked towards Peter. 'Bottle-wood tools sufficient for sculpture? If tempered by fire?'

Peter thought of his own power-tools and chisels back home. Power-tools to rough out a block of stone—in the old days apprentices would rough out a block more laboriously by hand—and chisels, strong sharp chisels. Their abrasive action, the sparks that flew, produced a protective surface on a stone which would let it weather out its first few years until the regular hardening could set in. How could the natives produce such strong, such detailed surfaces by banging away with wood, however hard?

No one had seen a single identifiable mason at work. One item Peter had to correct his colleagues about on arrival was the notion that masons carved anything in position by preference. Stone was unpredictable; even the best master mason could spoil a piece through no fault of his own. The sensible way to work was down on the ground. Each figure should jut from a supporting block which was subsequently winched into position in a preplanned gap. So you wouldn't expect to see lemur masons clinging to walls and chipping away. But even so.

Nor had anyone seen evidence of loose, unused blocks of stone lying around or in transit.

Maybe they simply hadn't yet stumbled upon a masons' yard in the maze of the city. Maybe secret ritual surrounded the art of masonry? Maybe the lemur masons had hidden their metal tools away when the expedition arrived, just as a sensible tribe might hide its treasures from potential conquerors?

Maybe the work had all been completed ages ago? But surely it hadn't been. And surely there should be some evidence of ongoing building work?

'Comment,' said Ash sharply.

Peter shook his head.

'Maybe *you* should try,' suggested the Ismaili agronomist. 'Carve blank jut of wall using bottle-wood?'

'Carve *Michelangelo was here*,' said Fremantle. 'Might activate natives. Provide cultural insights for Everdon. Valiant effort at artistic communication using native mode, eh? If no response, native behaviour is hardwired.'

'How would you like it,' asked Peter, 'if aliens landed in Paris and started carving graffiti over the front of Notre Dame?'

'Improve it, probably.'

In fact Peter had once carved a graffito of a kind upon an Oxford college: a playful caricature of his own head gazing out from the top of a tower. Wearing a veritable dunce's or wizard's hat parodying the mason's neatly folded daily paper which kept the dust from one's curls. His large ears exaggerated into jug-ears, his prominent nose sticking out like Pinocchio's, jaw dimpled as if by a pickaxe, eyes wrinkled up to a vanishing point (to avoid splinters).

The nose had been a mistake. Back then, Fuller domes were new and exhibited quirks of micro-climate. Little clouds could form. Condensation drops gathered on the end of such a nose and dripped as if he had a runny cold. Maybe that feature was considered a witticism by subsequent generations of students: the wizard with the drippy nose. Since no real rain fell inside Fuller domes and genuine gargoyles were forever dry, perhaps his nose was in a very minor sense the only working gargoyle left.

'You haven't proved they use wood tools!' blustered Peter.

'Take metal chisel, hammer, demonstrate human mason's art,' suggested Vasilki Patel.

'Cultural interference,' objected Mary. 'Analysing categories of carvings more important, this stage. Catlow's viewpoint more valuable here. Establish lexicon of stone images.'

'Report when complete,' said Ash. 'Enough on topic. Base security?'

'Sweet and simple,' reported Leo Allen. The black man coordinated all outside surveillance and image-gathering as well as supervising the infonet. 'Medical?'

Doctor Chang said, 'Clean slate. Still no interaction our micro-orgs, Rock's micro-orgs. Probably unnecessary even wear masks. Recommend continue, though, be double safe. Besides, the odours—'

The atmosphere of Rock was an acceptable oxy-nitrogen mix. Native proteins were based on D-amino acids that were right-handed, as were the sugars in the local nucleic acids—unlike the left-handed counterparts on Earth. Chang had declared that humans could eat the local veg and fish without any effect whatever; they would excrete everything unused. Nothing gut-wrenching, nothing nutritious. Protein incompatibility. So you had to bring a packed lunch to Rock, unless, as Vasilki said, you intended to set up in competition with the local veg by planting Earth seeds and letting the rivals crowd the native veg for available minerals. Charmed against any local bugs or viruses by their left-handedness, Earth crops ought to win hands down.

Ash said, 'Am authorizing *Michelangelo* depart on grand tour two nights hence, sixteenth hour local. Returning after forty days, local, for flight Solward. Hope for full local info by then.'

'We see *M* go?' asked a woman chemist, Liz Martel.

'Yes. Fusion fireworks overhead, fine show.'

'Observe effect on natives?' asked Lipmann. 'Night duty?'

'Indeed,' said Ash. 'That night.'

Mary stood up, red hair swinging. 'Depart farside world instead? Avoid cultural impact?'

Ash shook her head. 'Best orbital departure.'

'But *M* orbits whole world constantly! Well, depart daytime instead? Minimize shock from sudden light in sky?'

'Spoilsport!' burst from Liz Martel.

'Timing already computed.'

'Change it! Cultural impact.'

'May be fruitful.' Ash smiled slightly towards Fremantle. 'If true culture exists.'

It was obvious to Peter that the matter was already fixed, in Mary's disfavour.

To protest further, or shut up? Possible black mark on bio. Insubordinate. Mary nodded and sat down.

'End of info-swap,' said Ash.

Since you couldn't take your filter-mask off outside to feed, breakfast the next morning was a hefty, though hurried, affair of pawpaw, reconstituted omelette over huge slices of ham, waffles, and syrup, muffins and honey, pints of coffee. Afterwards Peter set out with Mary and Carl Lipmann for the city. Already lemur farmers were out in their veg fields, hoeing or harvesting. Fisherfolk were heading for the river. The humans joined one of the sledge paths.

'Bit swinish, that bottle-wood business,' remarked Carl. Of course, reflected Peter, Fremantle's discovery was a slap in the face to the linguist too. If the natives were only highly programmed animals using tools that nature provided, their 'language' might be an illusion too. A parrot could mimic speech with every appearance of beady-eyed intelligence, as well as screeching its own fixed repertoire. A chimp could chatter a sort of limited conversation, a dolphin could click and whistle. You'd still be barking up a gum tree if you hoped for full flexible communication.

'It would be enormously useful,' said Mary, 'to find some metal tools which had demonstrably been *made*—for sculpting, eh Peter?'

'You know how carefully I've examined their work,' he said, 'and I still can't swear to what tools were used. A fine bit of work isn't covered in chisel chips. Art lies in the concealment of art. Maybe . . . maybe they just rubbed away at the rock for years on end till they wore out the figures they wanted.'

'Like the Skull of Doom?' she asked.

'What's that?'

'A perfect human skull in rock crystal. It's in a Mexican museum. The Mayans made it by rubbing away at a solid block of rock crystal. Must have taken years. I can't imagine the decoration of entire cities being rubbed into shape the same way!'

'Maybe,' said Carl, 'each figure occupies the whole of one lemur's lifetime, off and on. Maybe it's his or her ritual life-image.'

'In that case you'd find half-finished work,' Mary pointed out.

'Maybe they stopped making images fifty years ago, five hundred years ago? Funny self-image they must have of themselves, though!' For now they were nearing the south-east entry gate guarded by its grotesque Herms or termains, whichever term one preferred to name boundary or entrance markers. Peter had supplied both names. Herms, from the Greek god of doorways, Hermes. Termains, from the Latin word terminus. On either side of the Herms stretched the frozenly writhing, leering wall, massed gargoyles jutting as if vomiting.

'Exactly,' said Mary. 'These are the keys to their psyche.'

And by now half a dozen lemurs were tagging alongside, twittering interestedly. None of the adults stood more than four feet high. The swirls and hues of their tight, close fur varied endlessly from individual to individual, fingerprinting each in auburn, russet, orange, brown which might be solid-hued or dappled or with hints of stripes. Lemurs wore no clothes or ornaments of any sort. Indeed, to hide the body might be to hide the self since their faces were all much the same: dun coloured, with the same large black melancholy eyes, pert twitchy noses, erect rounded ears, lugubrious mouths. The slight breasts and genital slits of the females and the retracted penises of the males were veiled by fur. Lemur arms were long and dangly; the hands had three thin fingers and a thumb.

A female plucked at Carl's tunic and warbled. Twitching his own nose behind the transparent mask with friendly humour, he adjusted the sound-bud in his left ear, fiddled with the minicomp and corder clipped to his belt, and twittered in response. Perhaps in response.

He explained: 'I'm trying to say: want/see/tools/cut/rock. But maybe I just said, 'I want you to watch me dig the world'! Peter, would you please mime the mason's art? Oh yes, and rubbing too?'

Nowhere had they found any simple carved representations of lemurs. The Herms were soaring, elongated heads with eyes the size of dinner plates above gaping, sharp-toothed mouths. Stone beards burst from the sucked-in cheeks, straggling down like horsehair eviscerated from an old upholstered chair, knotting and massing to almost hide a stubby, squat, dwarf body. All in perfect stone, except that these Herms looked newly sloshed with night-soil liquefied in urine.

The arch of the gate curving between the two Herms was a quartet of capering, interlacing babewyns, a popular motif. These were baboon-like beings, stretched out as though their bones had melted. Again, Peter had supplied the appropriate medieval name for such carved lusty baboon-buffoons.

While Carl twittered again, Peter stepped over to the nearest Herm, grateful for his mask. The lemurs collected their own night-soil assiduously, brown soup of excrement and pee. Instead of carting this out to fertilize the fields they hurled the contents of the bottle-wood buckets at their sculpted walls or poured the mixture with gay abandon over monstrosities and gargoyles.

(At an earlier info-swap: 'Ritual insult,' Mary had theorized. 'Thus to domesticate the fearful images.'

Fremantle had retorted, 'Maybe lemurs inherited cities from genuine intelligences that died out?'

Mary had returned to the fray: 'Perhaps act of respect, reverence. Excrement not taboo—but gift of self. Stuff of one's own creation.'

While Peter had said, 'Maybe do that to protect, strengthen surfaces?'

That chemist woman, Martel, had hooted.

Since then, he'd also seen lemur cooks chucking over the stone art the water in which they'd boiled veg or fish.)

The lemur female watched with curiosity while Peter went through the motions of tapping away with a mallet and chisel, and then—though he had to guess what these other motions might be—of patiently rubbing at stone.

True curiosity? Big glossy lemur eyes wore a perpetual expression of surprise and fascination, of alert astonishment.

However, this lemur then beckoned—surely she beckoned—and darted inside the gateway, to wait and beckon again.

'I do believe we're getting somewhere,' Carl said in pleased surprise. 'Well done.'

As soon as they passed beneath the arching babewyns, their lemur set off along the northerly of three possible lanes; they followed.

Periodically Mary blazoned that day's personal code in invisible ultraviolet on protruding stonework. On the way out her bleeper would respond to those UV marks, and no others. Despite an annotated aerial survey map composed by computer from *Michelangelo*'s high-resolution photos and their own overflight before landing, it was no easy matter, otherwise, to trace one's progress with any confidence through the labyrinth of walls, pillars, lanes, yards, archways, doorways, almost all of which were dense with statuary. Pathways branched frequently, almost arbitrarily, sometimes leading to dead ends. Lapids might block the way—figures emerging from or stepping into solid walls like spirits who could walk through stone. Gargoyles might sprout out overhead to join into ribbed vaulting so that what had been a lane became a hallway. A lane could enter a room through a narrow door, to resume as a broad lane beyond the far wall. Grotesques formed steps leading to tangled gargoyle bridges. Gaping stone mouths were entrances to what seemed to be cellars but which might open into airy corridors.

Their guide trotted ahead, warbling, glancing back, occasionally flapping an arm, though she may only have been slapping at the equivalent of a flea in her fur.

Peter noted a huge scaly devil-creature with ribbed, bat-like wings. This jutted from the top of a short freestanding wall which seemed to have no other rationale than to support that devil. The blocks of the walls, perhaps forty in number, were condensed, squashed stone bodies as though creatures had been crushed inside suit-case-sized moulds, there to harden.

'That chap's definitely new,' said Peter, and took a holo.

'New?' queried Carl.

'New to me. I've never seen the like before.'

'Oh.'

'I've never been in this part of town.'

Still wondering at the devil, Peter fell back a few paces so that now he brought up the rear. From that vantage point he could admire Mary's hips and the hang of her red hair as she bustled onward. No denying it, she did remind him of a certain buxom rural barmaid he'd known once. However, that bouncy barmaid had been keener on a recently widowed farmer who turned to her for sympathy, and more.

Peter had always been a bachelor, more by accident than design. Wedded to stone, he was. Somehow his work with stone had seemed to express—yet also to limit—the sensuality which he felt was part of him, deep down. Had he been a sculptor of marble, of smooth sensual flanks, he might have been able to express desire better in person. The rough hardness of the images he worked on, their often grim satiric comedy, and not least their moral sententiousness seemed to distance him from expressing in actual life the lusts and greeds and devilries which those carvings parodied. If he committed a . . . fault (even though the world might regard it as no fault at all, and indeed life was a jumble of desires, envy, pride, resentment, and such) then this fault might somehow solidify and *be* him for dusty ages. On the other hand, those virtues which he also carved and lived by—the patience, loving kindness, charity, forbearance—somehow locked up his heart . . . from which, otherwise, a grinning demon might spring forth?

He sighed, and wished that Carl wasn't with him and Mary, although he liked the man and in this case three was company. No doubt he exaggerated the importance of lust, anger, envy, lust. Yet one did so when one perpetuated, by renovation and restoration, the medieval tradition of incarnating in stone—of lapidifying—gross emblems of vice and virtue. Thus displaying in caricature monsters of the heart, by way of mockery and warning, by way of immunization against those selfsame monsters which represented human frustrations and fears.

He caught up with Mary. 'I wonder,' he asked, 'what fears or frustrations might have caused the lemurs to sculpt such monstrosities—not as a frieze to their city but as its central substance? They themselves seem gentle, innocent, happy, don't they?'

In the city no 'houses' as such existed. Yet where bridges arched over yards or where gargoyles roofed corridors or where walls came together, definite living zones occurred. There, a twittering mass of lemur children would play, the babies scampering on all fours swifter than any human child. There, cooking would be in progress tended by grizzled oldsters. One jumble of blackened pots brewing herbs and berries, connected by dripping wooden tubes, suggested a liquor still.

Two or three streets were noisy with groups of lemurs warbling at one another. In other streets numbers of the natives were simply curled up along the base of walls, twitchingly asleep, looking like examples of accidie, medieval sloth. Maybe those lemurs were ill, and this was the equivalent of hospitalization. Perhaps they favoured night-life and had hangovers.

By day, of course, the majority of lemurs were busy in the fields or in the bottle-tree forest or along the river-bank. Or else they were fetching water from one or another crude canal sump outside the city wall, or were engaged in hauling or shoving food back to town on their sledges of bottle-wood.

No visible arts or crafts; only the all-encompassing intricate chaotic stone itself; or perhaps one should say the solid sketch of a city, where decoration wholly out-weighed function.

'How can they possibly project all of these monstrous images of such simple natural lives?' repeated Peter.

'That's exactly it!' said Mary brightly. 'Those are images from out of their burgeoning imagination, images which must inevitably scare as well as intrigue because they challenge, they stimulate, they tease. Those are fascinating creatures they see in dreams and which they need to cling on to as a promise, a warrant of increasing complexity of thought. First the form, later the philosophy. Perhaps their subconscious mind, by which I mean the collective unconscious, is evolving and complexifying, acting as a kind of spur to their ordinary consciousness. I'm sure there's a rich oral tradition amongst all the warbles.' She glanced regretfully at Carl. 'After all, they twitter enough. Yet maybe they also experience a sort of *angst* at emerging from nature—a loss of instinctual, prelapsarian animal paradise—and deflect this *angst* by embodying and even celebrating such anxieties as environment. Maybe, Peter, that's your answer.'

Maybe. Her words sounded more eloquently convincing than they ever could in the clipped speed-talk of the info-swap, where they might shrink into gibberish.

Thought Peter: if I tried to move closer to Mary emotionally and sensually, she would have a theory about this too. But then, so had he, hadn't he? He felt a sudden urge to sculpt Mary nude, lascivious, flaunting. Not as a gross exemplar of lust; as an indicator of joy instead. Joy, yes, liberating joy! An explosion of joy which might coat him with dust, however, a joy which might petrify him. No, he wanted to go beyond that, to mould an image which simply stood for itself alone and did not represent any moral catechisms or theory of behaviour.

In his mind's eyes he watched Mary fill a pewter tankard full of foaming, heady beer for him, then a second tankard for herself, thus to wash the dust from his throat, from his bloodstream, from his hairy, Pan-like, goaty loins.

But where was the spare, blank, unoccupied stone waiting to be sculpted?

Oh here and there, here and there. By no means everywhere. Still, not every niche and nook had been filled.

An unsculpted pillar rose in a yard. Visualize, chiselled from it: *Alien Woman*. Alien to the lemur inhabitants, that's to say.

'I don't follow you,' said Carl. 'There must be some particular environmental pressure to evolve—to which they're adapting—mustn't there be? Not a mental pressure from within, a dream-pressure. You're almost saying that they evolve spontaneously.'

Mary grinned. 'Maybe that's my romantic side showing.' Her smile encompassed Peter, Peter more than Carl. So perhaps, thought Peter, she was beginning to realize, and her talk of dreams meant . . . He suspected he could only ever express himself fully not in simple stone but in smooth, rich, aristocratic marble. He might return from this expedition metamorphosed into a sculptor rather than a mason. His hands itched.

They entered a square flanked with hieroglyphicals. These were figures which seemed to bespeak or riddle out some special symbolism above and beyond the ordinary grotesque; some one-to-one meaning, if only you could decode it. Many of the figures were related to one another by a gesture, a glance, even by physical connections in the shape of a stone chain looping from belly to belly . . . maybe that was an umbilical cord.

A stone fish-lemur—lemur with fins and tail—poised as if diving, one hand clamped over its nose. Two distorted lemurs who were fused together, their twin trunks branching from shared monstrous legs, wrestled for possession of a stone knife—to cut themselves apart? to hack off the rival claimant, amputate him? Another figure jutted up with arms outstretched, one hand clutching a stone hoe like a trident, stone wings bursting from its back as though it would take flight into the sky.

With its bare hands a fourth figure ripped open a hole, a grinning mouth, in its belly. This one's neighbour had shrunk into a wizened ball mostly, yet one single giant arm pointed dramatically . . . towards a gloomy doorway barren of any images except one, and that image not carved at all but seemingly painted or burnt (or both) upon the curved rock lintel. The daubed image was a pair of staring black-rimmed eyes, two circles side by side.

Their guide had gestured and twittered at them to stay in the square, and had run off. Initially they had been more interested in scrutinizing and taking holos of the hieroglyphicals. Only as she returned, carrying some stiff and still steaming purple root vegetable on which she alternately blew and chewed, did they notice the sign above the doorway—to which the lunching lemur trotted, and where she squatted down.

'A sign!' exclaimed Carl. 'God, it's the first graffito we've seen. The first genuine arbitrary symbol. Two circles touching, like our sign for infinity, eh? I'm sure it's painted. The first piece of written language?'

'Lemur eyes,' Mary said. 'That's what it shows. As a warning? Dark inside. Doesn't open out and brighten? No, why should they warn of darkness—with their eyesight?'

'What we assume about their eyesight,' Carl corrected. 'Can't test them out like animals, can we? Damned if we will!'

Yet even so. Big eyes. At night spy-cams usually showed activity in the city. The lemurs had fire but this seemed restricted to cookery. No natives carried brands to light their way nor did flambeaux illuminate any of their living zones.

'Maybe it means, "Look in here".' Carl unclipped a flashlight, shone the beam down a plunge of broad shallow steps which didn't appear to be made of stone.

'Hey! Door against the wall!' He leaned to rap with his knuckles. 'Bottle-wood door. Or an upended sledge.'

He was standing above the lemur. Gulping the last of her veg, she twittered up at him. He frowned in concentration.

'Children. Run. Hide? I can't understand.'

Peter felt resentful of that sign. If it was a sign at all, it wasn't inscribed in his own language, of stone.

Carl leaned again to shine his light down those steps. The lemur rose, blinking. Briefly Peter was convinced that the native was attacking Carl in protest at the phenomenon of the torch, for she grabbed hold of Carl's tunic and began scrambling up him. Before Carl could do more than squeak loudly in surprise she was touching the sign above the door.

'Stay still!' called Mary. 'Don't dislodge her!'

With sharp little teeth the lemur bit at her own thumb till it bled freely, a rich scarlet flow. In blood she painted around the outline of the sign till her wound coagulated. Then she leapt free from Carl, jerked her hurt thumb at the open doorway, warbled what might have been a farewell, and scuttled away.

It was thus that they found the catacombs.

'Catacombs' was Peter's description, although Mary soon pointed out that there did not seem to be any corpses or bones anywhere in the extensive series of corridors and little chambers underneath that part of the city. The whole complex, steps included, was scooped out of firm clay, not cut through rock, and it was empty apart from numerous open doors of bottle-wood, none of which possessed any type of hinge.

'It's a burrow,' said Mary. 'Evidently they were never arboreal animals, like Earth lemurs! They were burrowing creatures. That's why they have the apparent nocturnal adaptation of such big eyes—it was to see underground. This is the Ur-burrow. The original, basic burrow over which they later built the city.'

'Rock *upon* clay?' Peter asked sceptically. He felt consumed with claustro-phobia as their flashlights played upon yet more tight corridors and empty little cells, all lemur-size. They were being forced to stoop. Oh to be high on a spire in the open air, settling a block into its new resting place of centuries, a block rampant with an eagle's head. The air down in these, yes, catacombs smelt stale and dank.

Nor were there any gargoyles or lapids or demons. Nothing carved whatever. No stone. To Peter's mind the place was worse than empty. It was meaningless, and he feared that somehow he was losing Mary here as she spun her new theory of how the natives had originally burrowed like rabbits.

'And then they emerged from the soil, from chthonic Nature, into light and consciousness and creativity!'

'Where are the tools?' he asked, and he remembered William Blake's poem. 'What the mallet, what the chisel?'

Were these really doors, loose doors, down here—when there were no doors in the city up above—or were they simply surplus sledges, stored against a mammoth harvest or retired from service?

When Mary snapped holopics the tiny chambers were blindingly illuminated. The after-dim, while his eyes readjusted to torchlight, was terrible to Peter's heart.

At the info-swap that evening Mary reported a great discovery which should quite trump Fremantle's coup concerning the natural origin of agricultural tools. A whole new subterranean layer of significance had been laid bare. A biological Troy: the original habitat. Doubtless it should be a source of chagrin to the biologist that she had found this out whilst he had been haring about in the forest, barking up trees, breaking up trees. For a little while, the burrow even seemed to diminish the city of statuary, to thrust it into the shade, as though that hole in the ground could be more important.

'Definitely not for burial purposes?' demanded Ash. 'Even in previous epochs?'

'Most unlikely,' replied Mary. 'Not abandoned. Kept in repair. Using, um, bottle-wood implements. Otherwise collapse eventually. Besides, entrance marked with life-blood sign, constantly renewed. Ritually. Here is the root, the racial birth.'

Fremantle said, 'You think lemur fingers adapted to *burrow*? Ha!'

Before Mary could field this thrust, Leo Allen was saying, 'Seems like war-shelter to me. Refuge from enemies.'

'No, no. When we landed, lemurs didn't hide. Not threat-conscious.'

'Carvings could have fooled me,' said Allen. 'Where metal sculpting tools, incidentally? If not hidden down burrow?'

'Maybe *buried* there, below ground. If so, appropriate place, culturally. Symmetric, linked inversely. City opposite of burrow, stone opposite of soil.'

'Fieldtrip there tomorrow?' suggested Allen. 'With metal detectors?'

'Yes,' said Ash. 'Everdon, take Allen, Fremantle, and Ramirez.'

Peter had no wish to join in this expedition to the oppressive, meaningless warren. Let slick Fremantle and crony Ramirez spoil Mary's day for her, so that she would come back into the upper world of rock-art away from envy and barbed malice feeling stifled, needing Peter's . . . solidity, craving significance and warmth.

If Leo Allen's detectors uncovered any concealed chisels, Peter couldn't be more pleased. However, he had no wish to be present and couldn't really credit Mary's 'symmetric' argument. The following day would be better employed in company with Lipmann, who himself had no conceivable reason to descend again into that voiceless collection of worm holes in the clay.

Almost shunning Mary, Peter went directly back to his hutch to sleep. Before shuttering the window for the night he stared out at one of the little moons hanging full, bone-white, over the forest. The two moons of Rock orbited at different speeds in differently tilted planes. He could almost see that moon moving, but then a solitary cloud consumed the satellite so that its light diffused and swelled into a glowing amoebic blob. The pure circular stone of the moon had melted into shapeless, meaningless menace.

Leo Allen found no metal hidden in the burrow, though after his tour of inspection he was still inclined to the shelter idea, with reservations.

'Yearly insect swarms? Like killer bees, lethal locusts?' he suggested the following evening. 'Small, but many and deadly.'

Ramirez reported tersely at speed on the local analogues of insects, rodents, and riverine reptiles. To Peter's ears she sounded like a twittering lemur herself.

'Quick plagues of pseudo-mice,' she gabbled. 'Behave like lemmings every few years, maybe develop toxic bite?'

'No food storage,' said Allen. 'Burrow not stocked.'

'Innocuous-seeming species undergoes startling life-cycle metamorphosis? Like caterpillar into moth?'

'Lemurs still intelligent to *build* shelter,' Mary argued optimistically. 'Memory of past, concept of future.'

'Is hibernating tortoise intelligent?' called out Fremantle.

'Actually,' added Allen, 'shelter not spacious enough for more than quarter of estimated population.'

'Therefore *original* home,' said Mary, 'before population rose.'

'Lingo?' asked Ash, and Carl reported quickly on the frustrating day he had spent with Peter.

'Requires much work, back home. Breakthrough by next expedition, yes. If true language.'

Ash raised a quizzical eyebrow.

'Masonry?' she enquired. A titter ran round the refectory, originating near Ramirez.

'Twin-circle sign not found in carvings,' Peter confessed.

'Are you blind?' heckled Fremantle. 'Image of lemur *eyes!*'

'Not necessarily.' Though what else?

'If burrow shelter from perceived threat,' said Allen, 'mount more survey cams in city for when *M* lights up tomorrow? Suppose Anthro records behaviour vicinity shelter?'

Mary sat on Peter's bunk, as he had hoped she might.

'What a wretched day.'

'Yes.' He agreed sympathetically, gladly. 'I'm afraid my carvings are no Rosetta stone, as yet.'

Why should he be afraid? He thought of the hieroglyphicals he had restored in one Oxford College, hieroglyphicals inspired by the medieval bestiary representing desire, timidity, moroseness. He wanted to touch Mary, hold her, mould her, tumble her in bed. Yet he couldn't. Didn't know how. Couldn't read her signals, which weren't carved in stone but enciphered in flesh; couldn't transmit his own signals to her adequately, hieroglyphically.

His fear was deeper, obscure, indefinable, as though the lemur burrow was some nightmare area of himself which he had been forced reluctantly to enter. As yet nothing had been found, no final truth or ultimate idol, either glorious or evil. Why should the locus of nightmare be down there when blatant nightmares capered in full grotesquery along all the lanes of the city? To return to the courtyard of the . . . *evil eyes,* the very next evening, as he must now do in company with Carl and Mary, scared him in a way that no summit of any spire or tower height had ever done. A vertigo of the dark cramped depth afflicted him.

'Mary.'

'What is it?'

'Nothing.'

Damned timidity!

'That's to say, tell me about yourself, Mary, will you?'

'But you already know. We know each other's bios.'

'Yes, but a person is not a biography.' His own contained nothing about pints of ale or about a certain barmaid who consoled a certain farmer, who happened not to be as strapped for cash as other local farmers because he had seen the future and had roofed his fields over early with filtering, humidifying, climate-control film.

'Any more than a tribe of aliens is a smarty-pants ethno-report. Is that what you're implying?'

Had he inadvertently opened a door to some hollow which haunted her? The most insightful of social maps (of one's own well-planned life, too!) was not the actual untidy paradoxical territory.

'What should I tell you, Peter? Of times when I made a fool of myself? Times when I became obsessed? Times of confusion? My favourite foods? My favourite *fantasies*?'

Yes, those, he thought.

'Never mind,' he said. 'Look at the moon.' (Which was over the river, streaking out a silver snake.) 'Its side's being shaved off by the sculptor of the night.'

She stared at him intently. Was her stare a signal? He didn't know.

She said, 'It should be almost full tomorrow evening. And it's past our bedtime, if we're to be wise owls *then*.'

For that night of nights Leo Allen had done the observers proud. His own team, consisting of himself and Carl, team two, namely Fremantle and Ramirez, and team three, Mary and Peter, as well as being in audio contact with each other, with the base, and with *Michelangelo*, had multi-channel video links with all the survey cams, which were equipped for infrared in case of dark cloud. In the event the sky was clear; starlight and moonlight sugared the city.

Since the workers were all home from the fields, the full complement of population was inside the city. Many were asleep, but others wandered about twittering so that lanes and yards and rooms seemed just as crowded—or uncrowded—as by day.

'Fusion minus one hundred seconds,' counted a radio voice. The glint of the orbiting voidship should be in sight any moment.

'Allen here. It'll look as though that moon has given birth to another moon. As though the other moon has jumped right around the sky to just beside it.'

'Fremantle. Birth of myth, maybe? Like Velikovsky's Bible?' A sneer in his voice.

Peter swept his flashlight beam above the doorway of the burrow. Two eyes, of dried blood, stared blackly. In panic he thumbed his com.

'Catlow here. Commander! *Michelangelo!* Don't light the fusion torch. Abort!'

'Sixty seconds.'

'I've realized what the sign means, Commander. It isn't eyes at all. It's the two full moons nearly in conjunction, before the closer one eclipses the other. When they're side by side in the sky, *something happens!* How often does that occur?'

A voice he didn't recognize, from *M*: 'Every thirty-one years, local.'

'Thirty seconds.'

'She's in sight.'

'For heaven's sake don't light that torch till we've worked this out!'

'Everdon here,' said Mary. 'Agree Catlow. Unwarrantable cultural tampering.'

'Fremantle. Good experiment. Trigger programmed behaviour. Demonstrate existence of.'

'No!' cried Peter.

'Fifteen seconds.'

'Take stonemason's word? Navigate voidship by hammer and chisel?' A woman. Who? Ramirez?

'Please, Ash!'

'Protest noted.'

In the sky—to all appearances right next to the moon, though actually fifty thousand kilometres closer—the fusion torch of the voidship ignited, the torch that could accelerate *Michelangelo* to hyperphase. The light seemed to expand to the size of the moon.

Around the yard hieroglyphicals strained at the leash of that new luminosity as if about to dive, to fly, to wrestle, to tip themselves open. Of a sudden the night was loud with the warbling and twittering of what could have been thousands of startled birds.

Lemurs flooded into the yard. Females clutching squealing babies, males hauling youngsters along, they jammed through that doorway of the double eye (ah no, of the double *moon*), plunging down into darkness. Peter was buffeted, pulled by the river of bodies all crowding towards one goal.

'Hey,' from the radio, 'cat among the pigeons! They really got the wind up!'

No, it wasn't lemur hands which were pulling Peter along now. It was Mary, urging him.

'Must see what goes on down there!'

Peter heard himself moan. All those bodies packing into that close, dark catacomb! But he couldn't escape the pressure. Their torchbeams jerked about as Mary and he stumbled, crouching, down the hard clay stairs, and into one of the chambers. This cell was already half full. As the two humans piled in, panting, lemurs wrestled the bottle-wood door shut behind them, firmly. The door fitted tight against the clay rim, and the lemur commissionaires withdrew, apparently satisfied that those still surging past down the corridor outside wouldn't attempt to force entry.

Now all of the lemurs calmed. They sat and settled, even the youngest. The presence of the big humans with their lights and videocom and chattering radio voices seemed immaterial. No sound of lemur feet outside, not any more.

'Christ!' Radio voice. 'What a bloody dust storm!' Allen?

'Dust? The whole place is *smoking*.' That was certainly Carl.

'Can't see a thing—'

As Mary tuned the videocom it was plain that all the survey cams had gone to infrared. Distorted bright images of lemurs staggered through a fog. Gargoyles, babewyns, walls exhaling thick pink clouds through all their microscopic stone pores. Images of lemurs, surely out of focus, clung to stonework, crouched, climbed, engaged in strange acrobatics.

'Whole city hidden.' Chang's voice, from the base. 'Leave if possible.'

'Allen, Security. Guard mask integrity. Grab cams to point way. Hold vidscreens to eyes. See in infrared. Keep lenses *cleaned*.'

'Coated in the damn stuff. My scalp's itching like crazy—'

Why did lemurs on screen look so contorted? Why were they moving in sluggish slow motion? Why was that one climbing up a pillar?

'Patel.' She was back in base. 'Entire fabric of city is releasing spores, billions of spores. Like fungus, puffballs.'

'Ash here. More like spawning coral. Synchronously, once yearly in old days all along Australia's Barrier Reef. Viewed this on vacation when child. Triggered by temperature and tidal cues—and by full moonlight! City may be social organism. Colony of microorganisms. Air reef. Reef in air, not sea. Comment, Fremantle?'

'Busy.' A cough.

Peter spoke. 'Triggered by double moon. The semblance of. The moon and *Michelangelo*. Together.'

'Ash here. Catlow?'

Mary reported, 'Everdon and Catlow in burrow, see channel twenty. Lemurs took refuge. Shut doors tight. Thus some survivors. But of what?'

'Of *that*, Mary!' Peter jabbed a finger at the little screen. Though the image was doubly foggy due to the coating on the cam lens it was still possible to see one lemur backed up against a pillar, shaggy with spores. The native's mouth was gaping wide, its neck was arching. Its penis had burst forth from the furry sheath, stiffened, crusty, and huge. The lemur was in process of becoming a hieroglyphical of rutting lust. While it clung, backward, to that pillar, its legs bent up away from the ground, shrinking, contracting, and edging it higher and higher in concert with its cruelly twisted arms, till it stopped and hung as if cemented.

'Natives turning into monsters!' they heard. 'It's goddam Halloween.'

'Itchy—'

'Don't scratch—'

'Protein incompatibility,' said Chang. 'Should not affect humans. But recommended detox and quarantine.'

'My leg's *stiff*—!'

A scream . . . of panic? Whose panic?

'They don't *make* the statues, Mary,' Peter said. 'They *become* the statues. And the rest of the fabric! They never built this city. Generations of their bodies have fused into it. As Ash says!—coral reefs in air! Nourished by night-soil and cooking water chucked over it. And at sporing time the coral organisms coat the lemurs, turn them into more reef.'

'But the lemurs are altering so grotesquely . . .'

'Yes! The spores take their bodies over. Metamorphose them—according to the lemurs' own, I don't know, archetypal emotions, passions, instinct programs.'

'And thus they rejoin Nature.' She mused. 'But they don't run away to live in the woods. Instead they rely on a burrow that'll save enough survivors to let the race continue. They probably breed quite fast. Thirty-odd years will be time enough to repopulate, and more. But they don't try to escape their destiny. It's the only thing that gives them culture, cities.'

The voices of teams one and two were just grunty now, or ghastly. Chang was talking.

'Control by chemical signals in air. Coral is architect. Maybe influences shape of bottle-trees too? We make anthropomorphic error. Assume lemurs dominant because resemble us. Instead, part of symbiotic system.'

'That's it,' Mary said to Peter, 'symbiosis.' Of a sudden she looked desperately sad. 'It isn't Cultural Anthro at all, it's Bio. Plain beastly biology.'

Chang said, 'Lemurs nourish coral, are periodically incorporated, used to manufacture more coral mass. Lemurs benefit by shelter, tools, agric with which to nourish coral—and their thoughts given form and substance, reinforcing programs governing lemurs.'

'They must give their bodies to their God,' murmured Mary.

'Coral true intelligence here,' chanted Chang. 'Bioengineering, eh, Fremantle? Down on molecular level.'

Silence from Fremantle.

'Can transmute body elements. Can unwind and rewind cells, reproducing self throughout microscopically. Affect humans too. But intelligence impenetrable as stone. Not intelligence in our sense. Fooled by fusion-flare.'

A groan from the radio, as of some material stretching, splitting, then hardening.

'How long will the air down here last?' wondered Mary.

The native refugees in the cell were almost comatose by now, hardly moving or reacting despite the noise and light produced by two guests. In other cells Peter could imagine total inertness. Thus to conserve oxygen. That, too, must be part of the programme. In this case, of racial survival. For the good of the city, the benefit of the coral.

'Long enough,' he said, 'if we weren't here. Compared with them we're gobbling oxy.'

Michelangelo was radioing worried enquiries.

'City still sporing,' by way of answer. 'Could go on all night. Probable loss, four personnel. Two more sheltering down sealed burrow.'

'Abort grand tour? Circle moon, return to Rock orbit?'

'Negative,' said Ash. 'Base in no danger. Future field-work, body recovery, wearing protective suits.'

Peter murmured, 'They're going to hack Fremantle and Co out of the coral? Wonder what they became . . .'

At the moment the hieroglyphical basis of lemur life and society came clear to him—or seemed to come clear to him; the way in which these furry beings were revealed to themselves at last in a transcendent moment of understanding, a peak of consciousness at the time when the spores coated and invaded, transmuted and petrified them and sealed them into the substance of their city in rampant caricature, in emblem which at first sight seemed monstrous but which was not necessarily so.

Plain biology, indeed! What was the word which he'd heard Mary use in derision?

Reductionism, that was it. The reduction of wonderfully patterned complexity down to an elementary jiggle of chemical reactions. The reduction of dream to electrochemical programmes, of vision and passion down to the vibration of molecules.

Peter knew that he must determine his own dominant category of being, his primal humour, in the eternal rock root of his own existence.

Timidity, covetousness, envy, lust? Or loving joy, or patience, or some other of the virtues?

Was this not also a sort of reduction . . . ?

He remembered the words of a long-dead French poet, Saint-Jean Perse, which he had once committed to memory. *On ne bavarde pas sur la pierre* . . . You don't gossip on stone. You don't babble, or ramble on. Reduce your meaning to its essentials.

'I'm going up top,' he told Mary. 'I can't stand it down here. It's squeezing me. Up, and out.'

'You'd die! Masks don't protect us. And you'd let the spores in!'

'Plenty of doors. Close this one tight behind me—unless you'd rather come as well?'

She shuddered. 'Peter, you're committing suicide. You'll *die.*'

'No, I shan't. I'll become eternal. Archetypal. I've come so many light years, Mary, to meet myself. How could I ship back to Earth as a surplus artisan, a joke, when I could *become* what my whole life has been aimed at? Promise you won't let them hack me out of the city. Don't let them cart me home in a specimen bag. Promise!'

'Look, we've had a set-back, you and me, but isn't what we've found just as fascinating?'

'Oh yes indeed.' He handed his com-set to her. 'It sets the dream free, to shape the self for ever.'

'Sets it *free*? You'd be locked in an alien coral reef. It mightn't even be able to cope with you. Different codings, alien ones. The lemurs would throw crap and veg water in your face.'

'Promise you won't let them take me back!'

'Yes. If they'll listen to me.' She sounded deeply scared now, which he regretted.

'Make them listen for once. Tell them how they ought to have listened to me about *M* and the moon. Tell them I hope to communicate with the coral by offering myself to it, but it'll take until the next sporing for any effects to show. Yes, tell them *that*. And tell them: *transmutation* of protein into rock! What wouldn't Earth give for the knack of altering the molecular structure of rock into protein?' Even if certain farmers, who had bedded barmaids, lost their investment.

'I won't say goodbye, since you'll see me again.' Stuffing his torch temporarily under his armpit, Peter clawed at the clay to release the bottle-wood door. This popped free, and he slipped quickly into the corridor, which looked clear of motes. 'Push it tight!'

No sign of lemurs, either. Doors behind him blocked cells. The stairs ahead mounted to the door of two-moons, which was shut. He ascended, crouching.

He unpeeled the top door, dodged out, tugged the barrier shut behind him as best he could. Now his torchlight yellowed a dense fog. He couldn't see a single object in the yard of hieroglyphicals; however, he thought he recalled a convenient gap between two neighbouring grotesques roughly in *that* direction. He soon collided with hard lumps, barely visible. Turning, backing between those lumps an arm's distance away, he met relative smoothness.

Not all lemurs would become hieroglyphicals or gargoyles or babewyns. By no means! Many lemurs must simply crunch up to become supporting blocks, sections of wall or pillar, part of fabric rather than design. The ordinary bedrock of society, those! Whereas he, Peter from another planet, was unusual? Outstanding? Or perhaps those types were the more perfect, Platonic specimens.

He ripped off his mask, breathed deep, and almost choked. But already a hot (yes, itchy) exaltation coursed through his veins and nerves.

Thoughts sped through his mind, a riot of images trying to dovetail and achieve a unified solid pattern, to array themselves like a squad on parade.

He didn't care about his discomfort. Even, agony? Vaguely he was aware that parts of himself were being warped and twisted. However, he was opiated, his pain centres disconnected. Only terror had made that radio voice scream.

What of Mary? What of the barmaid? Who were they, compared with the centuries? His devotion was to stone. He aspired to be a spire. He stretched up and up. And he knew the sublime.

The Emir's Clock

'I MUST SHOW YOU SOMETHING, LINDA!' BUNNY WAS EXCITED. (Flashing eyes and coaly hair, for he on honey-dew hath fed, et cetera.) He'd come round to my digs at nine in the morning and he'd never done that before. True, his excitement was still gift-wrapped in mystery and bridled by irony.

'Come on!' he urged. 'We'll need to take a little spin in the country.'

'Hey—'

'I'll buy you lunch afterwards.'

'I've a lecture at eleven.'

'Never mind that. Ten minutes alone with a book equals one hour with a lecturer. You know it's true. A lecturer only reads you a draft of his next book, which is a digest of a dozen books that already exist.'

'Mmm.'

'Oh, Linda! No one *seduces* a woman in the morning. Not successfully! The impatience of morning subverts the charm.'

'Most of your friends don't even know what morning is, never mind feeling impatient about it.'

'But *I* know. To ride out on a desert morning when the world is fresh and cool!'

How can I possibly describe Bunny without tumbling into clichés? His almost impertinent good looks. And that ivory smile of his . . . No, that's wrong. Ivory turns yellow. His smile was snow. There's no snow in the desert, is there? There was nothing frigid about his smile, though at least it did melt . . . hearts.

And his eyes? To call them black oil-wells, liquid, warm and dark? What a trite comparison, considering the source of his family's wealth, and the emirate's wealth!

And his neat curly black beard . . . the beard of the prophet? Bunny was certainly determined like some young Moses to lead all his people into the promised land of technology and the future. He was also a descendant of Mohammed—who had many descendants, to be sure! What's more, Bunny was to experience what any proper prophet needs to experience: a revelation, a message from the beyond.

Of course, I succumbed.

'Okay, lead me to your camel. Just give me five minutes, will you?' I was still frantically tidying my hair.

'Strictly horse power, Linda . . . with Ibrahim at the wheel as chaperone.'

I'd known Bunny for a full year. Prince Jafar ibn Khalid (plus three or four other names) seemed to relish the twee nickname foisted on him by Oxford's smart set. Heir to the rich emirate of Al-Haziya, Bunny was deeply anglophile. His favourite light reading: Agatha Christie.

No, wait.

What was he, deeply? He was an Arab. And a Moslem, though he made no great show of the latter. Plainly he was pro-British, with a taste for British ways. What was he in Al-Haziya? I'd no idea—since I never accepted his many invitations. He was a surface with many depths like some arabesque of faience on a mosque. Only one of those depths was the British Bunny. Other depths existed. He was like some Arabian carpet which gives the impression of a trapdoor leading down into other, complex patterns.

No wonder he enjoyed Agatha Christie! Bunny could seem clear as the desert air at times. At other times he preferred to wear a cloak of mystery as if believing that a future ruler needs to be enigmatic, capable of surprising not only his enemies but his friends. For who knows when friends may become enemies? No wonder he liked his innocuous nickname, gift of the assorted Hooray Henrys, upperclass sons and daughters, and European blue-bloods who made up the smart set.

The hallmarks of this smart set were heroin, cocaine, dining clubs, and drunken hooliganism. As an initiation ritual they had smashed up Bunny's room in Christ Church without him uttering a word of demurral, so I heard. Bunny could easily afford the repair bill. Within days he had his rooms refurnished splendidly, totally. I heard that his college scout went home grinning at the fifty-pound note given him by way of a tip.

Shouldn't this episode have filled Bunny with contempt for the smart set? Not to mention their rampant abuse of hard drugs, their deliberately cultivated lack of concern for social problems, the cynicism they sported as a badge. Especially since the 'real' Bunny was grooming himself to upgrade his peasant countryfolk into the future?

I believe there's often something deeply ascetic as well as voluptuous about an Arab man. There are all those pleasure maidens of paradise . . . On the other hand there's Ramadan, fasting, the prohibition on alcohol.

Well, when he was in the company of the smart set Bunny tossed back his whisky, but he would never touch their drugs, although he made no show of disapproval. Liquor is a naughtiness which some Arabs abroad are not unknown to indulge in, and Bunny obviously had to join in *some* forbidden practice. I gather he told his cronies that to him drugs were nothing remarkable. Hashish is the honey of the Islamic heaven, isn't it? (Though cocaine and heroin might steal his soul, enslave him.) Why should he feel naughty about taking drugs? Why therefore should he *bother*? Whereas whisky was rather wicked.

It did puzzle me as to why he cultivated these rich parasites in the first place, or let them cultivate him. Were his sights set on their respectable, power-broking parents—against whom the children rebelled whilst at the same time enjoying all the perks? Was his eye upon some future date when these rich rubbishy juveniles might have kicked their assorted habits and become worthwhile, maybe? Or was he bent on experiencing a spectrum of corruption so that he would know how to handle privileged corruption in his own country; so that he wouldn't be naive as a ruler?

'Values differ,' Bunny explained to me casually one day, some six months after we first met. 'For instance, Linda, did you know that I own slaves?'

I was so surprised that I giggled. 'Do you mean slave girls?'

If I accepted a holiday invitation to Al-Haziya, would I find I had changed my status?

'Boys too.' He shrugged. Since the atmosphere had become emotionally charged, for a while he let me make of the comment whatever I chose. Then he added, 'And grown men. Actually, Ibrahim is one of my family's slaves.'

'Ibrahim!'

Ibrahim was the prince's personal bodyguard. A burly, impassive fellow, he hardly ever said a word in my hearing. Dab hand with a scimitar? Perhaps. In Britain he carried a pistol by special diplomatic dispensation. Ibrahim accompanied Bunny most places and dossed in Bunny's rooms by agreement with the college. Certain terrorist groups such as the Jihad might aim for the future ruler of an oil-rich, pro-Western state. Ibrahim could have stopped the wrecking of Bunny's room single-handed, at one flick of the prince's finger. Bunny hadn't flicked his finger.

It was around this time that complexities began to dawn on me. Arabesque patterns.

Originally Bunny and I bumped into each other—literally so—in the doorway of the PPE Reading Room, otherwise I would hardly have come into a prince's orbit. Once in his orbit, I was to be an isolated satellite, well clear of the main cluster of the smart set. Bunny and I were definitely attracted to each other. Almost from the start an emotional gravity joined us, a serious yet playful friendship of approach and retreat which I'm sure packed in more true feeling and communication than he found with those other 'friends'. I didn't leap into bed with him, or even creep slowly, though I must admit I came close. I think I should have felt . . . overwhelmed, consumed, a moth landing in the heart of the flame instead of simply circling it.

And the colours of this moth which so attracted the prince? (Moth, not butterfly.) My features, since I've described his? I prefer not to say. I'd rather stay anonymous and invisible. There are reasons. Linda may not even be my real name.

So Bunny's minder was a slave!

'Surely,' I remember saying, 'while Ibrahim's in Britain he could—'

'Defect? Flee to freedom like some black slave escaping from Dixie to the north? He won't. He owes loyalties.'

Loyalties, plural. It dawned on me that whilst Ibrahim kept watch over Bunny with that eerie impassivity equally he was keeping watch *on* Bunny.

I began to appreciate how there would be jealous, ambitious uncles and nephews and a host of sibling princes back home in Al-Haziya on whose behalf Ibrahim might be reporting—members of the extended ruling family who might reward their informant at some future date with a prize more delicious than mere freedom, with the power to turn the tables, to make other people subject to *him*. It might be prudent for Bunny to let himself seem in Ibrahim's eyes to be a frivolous figure, a corruptible emir-in-waiting who could easily be besotted or shoved aside when the time came.

'Besides,' added Bunny, 'mightn't your friendly British government deport Ibrahim back to Middle Eastern Dixie if he became an illegal visitor?'

Here, if I guessed correctly, was the real reason why Bunny mixed with the smart set; or one strand of the explanation. Bunny was presenting himself to watchful eyes back home, to those eyes which watched through Ibrahim's, as no force to be reckoned with when his father died. Prince Jafar was someone who would fritter wealth (without in any way diminishing it, so enormous was the pile!); someone who could amuse himself in Cannes or Biarritz or wherever was fashionable, thus ensuring that no great social changes would occur back home, only cosmetic ones. In their turn the terrorist Jihad might view him as a welcome heir. Compared with a playboy, a reforming ruler is definitely counter-revolutionary. The smart set was his camouflage. He didn't court their access to power and privilege: he hardly need bother. What he courted was their élite impotence.

I couldn't help wondering whether Bunny had chosen of his own accord to come to Oxford to complete his education, or whether his father the Emir wanted him safely out of the way while internal struggles went on back home? Maybe the Emir had even advised Bunny to behave as he did? To survive, Bunny's Dad must have been a clever man. Myself, I think that Bunny dreamed up his own chameleon strategy.

Even the most dedicated master-spy becomes lonely at times, yearns to let the façade slip a little, to confide in a heart that beats in tune. Hence Bunny's friendship with me. His attraction. His love? No . . . not exactly that.

Quite soon we were zipping along the A40 towards Witney. Or Cheltenham; or Wales for all I knew. Behind us the sun was bright. The Cotswold hills and vales bulged and swooped green and gold, with pastures and corn: large perspectives to me, but to Bunny perhaps no more than a neat little parkland.

Bunny's car wasn't your usual super-expensive sports convertible such as other members of the smart set were given by Daddy on their eighteenth birthdays. It was a Mercedes 190E 2.316V, a four-door hardtop performance job customized with bulletproof glass and armour. The extra weight reduced the top speed to a mere hundred-and-thirty miles an hour or so.

'We're going to Burford,' he revealed.

'To the wild-life park?' I'd been there on a school trip long ago. Rhino, red pandas, ostriches; a lunch of fish and chips in the caff. It's a lovely wild-life park but I doubted that Bunny wanted to show me *that*.

'No, we're going to visit the church.'

I laughed. 'Have you been converted? Are we going to be married, shotgun-fashion?'

The Merc overtook a trio of cars tailing a long container truck which itself must have been hammering along at seventy; we sailed by smoothly, brushing a hundred. In the role of royal chauffeur Ibrahim had been professionally trained in ambush avoidance. Bunny once had him demonstrate his skills for me on the grassy, cracked runway of a local disused airfield. Tricks such as using your hand-brake and wheel to spin a speeding car right round on its axis, and race off in the opposite direction.

'Not quite converted. You could say that I've been . . . enhanced. Wait and see.'

Burford is a bustling, picturesque little Cotswold town—or a big village depending on viewpoint. The broad high street plunges steeply downhill flanked by antique shops, art galleries, bookshops, tea rooms, elegant souvenir shops. Tourists flock to the place. Burford used to be a proud centre of the wool trade. Now the town is cashing in again, though it hasn't vulgarized itself. As yet it hasn't any waxworks museum of witchcraft, or candy floss.

Presently we were drifting down that steep street. Near the bottom we turned off to the right along a lane. We drew up outside what I took to be former almshouses, close by the railings of the churchyard—paupers of old would have easy access to prayer and burial.

Burford Church looked surprisingly large and long. It had evidently been extended at several times down the centuries, to judge by the different styles of windows. A spire soared from an original Norman tower which had visibly been concertinaed upwards. The main door was sheltered by a richly carved, three-storey porch worthy of any well-endowed Oxford college.

Bunny and Ibrahim exchanged a few mutters in Arabic with the result that our chauffeur stayed with the car, to keep it warm. Unlikely that any agents of the Jihad would be lurking inside this Cotswold church on the offchance! (Yet something was lurking . . . waiting for Bunny.)

A marmalade cat sunned itself on a tomb topped by a wool-bale carved from stone. I plucked a blade of grass and played with the cat briefly as we passed.

The air inside the church was chilly. The huge building seemed well-monumented and well-chapeled but I wasn't to have any chance to wander round. Bunny conducted me briskly over to the north side, through a line of pointed arches, and into a gloomy transept.

And there stood the skeleton of a clock—taller than me, taller than Bunny. Stout stilts of legs supported a kind of aquarium frame filled with interlocking gears, toothed wheels, pinions, ratchets, drums, all quite inert. Two great pulleys dangled down with weights on long rods beneath each, like halves of a bar bell loaded with disc-weights. A motionless wooden pendulum rod a good eight feet long—with a big bob on the end—hung to within an inch or so of the floor.

'Here we are!' he exclaimed delightedly. 'This used to be in the turret up above. A local chap by the name of Hercules Hastings built it in 1685.'

I'll admit the ancient clock was impressive in a crazy sort of way. But why had we come to see it?

'So it's a labour of Hercules, mm? With *haste* for a surname. You've got to be joking.'

'No, it's true, Linda. Of course the maker's name did . . . cling to me, being so—what's the word?—serendipitous. Such a beacon to any lover of Miss Christie, with her own Hercule!' He took me by the arm, though not to lead me anywhere else. 'I immediately studied all the *spiel* about this clock with as close attention as I would pay to a chapter full of clues in any of her mysteries.'

He pointed at a long sheet of closely typed paper mounted in an old picture frame screwed to the wall nearby, in the dim shadows.

'Messages exist in this world for us to find, dear Linda. Actually the whole world is a message. We Arabs know that very well. I do wish you spoke Arabic—so that you could read some of the mosques in my country. Yes, indeed, to read a building! Decoration and text mingle integrally upon the walls of our mosques. Architecture dissolves into ideas, ideas with more authentic substance than the faience or the brick. Our mosques exhibit ideas *explicitly*, Linda. They don't just convey some vague notion of grandeur or the sublime as in your Western buildings, whose carved inscriptions are more like the sub-titles of a movie, crude caricatures of the actors' flowing, living words.'

Here was a depth of Bunny's which was new to me. A mystical depth? No, not quite. As he continued to talk softly and raptly, still holding my arm, I understood that he was anxious I should understand how scientifically *precise* his Arab attitude seemed to him, and how inevitable it had been that Arabs preserved and extended science during the Dark Ages of Europe. Though alas, I couldn't speak Arabic, so I could only take his words on trust.

'Arabic, Linda, is a fluid, flexible, musical tongue whose script flows likewise, organically. What other script has so many alternative forms, all with the same meaning? What other script is so alive that it can be read overlaid or interlaced or even in reflection? No wonder Arabic is the only religious source language still equally alive today.'

I thought of mentioning Hebrew, but decided not. After all, Hebrew had been virtually raised from the dead within living memory.

'So what do we find here, Miss Marple?'

'I'm a bit younger than her!' I protested.

'Oh you are, Linda. Yes you are. You're freshly young. Refreshingly.'

Bunny was young enough himself. Did I hear the jaded accents of someone who had already commanded the 'favours' of many experienced slave-women?

'The message, Bunny,' I reminded him. 'The clues in the case of the clock, please.'

The sheet wasn't signed. The vicar may have typed it. Or the author may have been some technically-minded and pious parishioner who had assisted in the reconstruction of the turret clock. The machine had been dismantled as obsolete four decades before, and brought down from the tower to lie for years as a heap of junk. Fairly recently it had been rebuilt in the transept as an exhibition piece. Its bent parts had been straightened. Missing items were made up by hand. The clockwork had been demonstrated in action, but the machine wasn't kept running.

Exhibition piece? No, it was more. According to the densely typewritten page this clock was a working proof of the truth of religion.

How many visitors to Burford Church bothered reading those lines attentively? Of those who did, how many people really took in all their, um, *striking* implications? These had certainly struck Bunny.

This post-Darwinian document described Hercules Hastings' clock as a stage in the evolution between the original medieval clock and the contemporary electric clock which now roosted in the tower. According to the anonymous author the clock before us showed the manner in which the evolution of artefacts mirrored the evolution of animals and plants. Although the basic material—namely the brass and iron—did not change any more than DNA, protein, or cellulose changed, yet the form altered evolutionarily thanks to the ideas and decisions embodied in the metal. Well!

Bunny read this sheet aloud to me with heavy emphasis as though it was some antique page spattered with bold type and capitals and italics.

'The Basic Design—the interlocking gears, the slotted count wheel, the flail, the pair of rope drums—this stays the Same from one *species* of Clock to the next. Evolution occurs by *jumps*. After centuries of slow Improvement, suddenly with the Pendulum new *species* supersede old ones. This process is matched by Animals too.

'(Listen to this, now): The Metal by itself has no power to evolve. It would be a wild and grotesque *superstition* to imagine that Iron and Brass could interact with their Environment to produce this Evolution. The Will and the *Idea* of the constructors is responsible. Why should the Evolution of Plants and Animals be *different?*

'(And this:) The Turret Clock represents a humble form of *Incarnation*—of the *Idea* made Metal rather than Flesh. After the Death of the Clock on its removal from the tower it was by the Will and Intention of *Mind* that it was subsequently brought back into existence—in fact, *resurrected.*

'Incredible stuff, isn't it?'

A final paragraph dealt with the harmonic motion of the pendulum compared with the wave motion of light and the bonding of atoms and molecules, the minute 'brickettes of all materials'.

I commented, 'It sounds to me like a very old argument dragged creaking and groaning into the twentieth century. We once had a bishop called Paley—'

'Who wound up his watch twice daily! In case it ran down—And stopped the whole town—' Bunny couldn't think of a last line. Even four-fifths of a limerick in a foreign language was pretty nifty, so I clapped (my free hand against my pinioned hand).

'I know about Paley, Linda. But that doesn't matter. The *idea*—embodied not merely in architecture but in machinery! What an Islamic concept.'

'Ah,' I interrupted brightly, 'so you see yourself as the Godly constructor who will evolve your country and people by will and intention into the modern world, is that right? And here's a religious argument in favour—because, because certain reactionary factions oppose this? They'd far rather keep the occasional Cadillac and oil-cracking plant surrounded by a sea of camel-dung?'

'A sea of sand, dear. But wait—and thank you! I spy another useful metaphor. My country can be full of silicon . . . *chips*—if the will is applied to the sand. Now if I can persuade the old fogeys that—'

It was then that it happened.

It. The flash of lightning on the road to Damascus. The burning bush. The epiphany. The visionary event.

It certainly wasn't sunlight which shafted down to bathe the text in radiance and seem to alter it. The angle from any window was all wrong.

Of a sudden the text inside the picture frame was flowing, glowing, blinding Arabic written in squiggles of fire. If I close my eyes, I can see it to this day. It inscribed itself on my brain even though I couldn't read the meaning. But Bunny could. He stood transfixed.

And then the pendulum started to swing. Wheels turned. Gears engaged. Ratchets clicked. The clock had resurrected itself of its own accord.

Afterwards Bunny would say nothing about the contents of the message or what else he had experienced above and beyond the revival of the clock—which died again as soon as the Arabic words vanished; all this happened within a minute. It was as if he had been sworn to secrecy.

He still took me to lunch, as promised, in the Golden Pheasant hotel up the High Street. I forget what I ate but I remember that Bunny had roast beef.

I can't even say with any certainty that he had *changed*. Since which was his true self?

But I recall clearly one odd exchange we had during that meal. I realize now that he was giving me a clue to solve, an Agatha Christie clue which could have handed me the key to the message which had been imposed on him. At the time his remarks just seemed a bizarre flight of fancy, a way of tossing sand in my eyes to distract me.

He remarked, 'Doesn't your Bible say, "So God created man in his own image"?'

'As far as I remember.'

He swivelled a slice of rare roast beef on his plate. At other tables American tourists were lunching, as well as a few British. Oak beams, old brass, old hunting prints.

'In God's own image, eh! Then why are we full of guts and organs? Does God have a brain and lungs and legs? Does His heart pump blood? Does His stomach digest meals in an acid slush?'

I hoped he wasn't committing some terrible Islamic sin along the lines of blasphemy.

'I don't suppose so,' I said.

'What if, in creating life, God was like some child or cargo-cultist making a model out of things that came to hand, things that looked vaguely right when put together, though they weren't the real thing at all? Like an aeroplane made out of cardboard boxes and bits of string? But in this case, using sausages and offal and blood and bone stuffed into a bag of skin. Islam forbids the picturing of God, or of man, God's image. Christianity encourages this picturing—everywhere. Which is wiser?'

'I've no idea. Doesn't it hamstring artists, if you forbid the making of images?'

'So it would seem to you because you don't speak and think in Arabic—'

'The language which makes ideas so solid and real?' We seemed to be back on familiar territory. But Bunny veered.

'If we made a robot in our own image, as a household slave, it still would not look like us *inside*. It would contain chips, magnetic bubbles, printed circuits, what-not. These days one sometimes fantasizes opening up a human being and finding cogs inside, and wires. What if you opened up a machine and discovered flesh and blood inside it? Veins and muscles? Which would be the model, which the image, which the original?'

At last he speared some beef and chewed, with those bright teeth of his. Afterwards Ibrahim drove us back to Oxford.

The Jihad never did infiltrate assassins into Britain to attack Bunny—if indeed his father or his father's advisors had ever feared anything of the sort; if indeed that was the true role of Ibrahim.

But three months later the Jihad murdered the Emir himself, Bunny's father, during a state visit to Yemen. Bunny promptly flew home to become the new Emir.

Too young to survive? No, not too young. Over the next few years, while for my part I graduated and started on a career in magazine publicity, news from Al-Haziya came to me in two guises.

One was via items in the press or on TV. The strong young pro-Western Emir was spending lavishly not just on security but on evolving his country into the engine, the computer brain of the Gulf. By poaching experts from America and even Japan (which takes some inducement), he established the first University of Machine Intelligence, where something unusual seemed to be happening—miracles of speech synthesization and pattern recognition—almost as if computers were discovering that Arabic was their native language. There was also a dark and ruthless side to this futurization of his country; one heard tales of torture of opponents, extremists, whatever you call them. I recall with a chill a comment by the Emir that was widely quoted and condemned in many Western newspapers, though not by Western governments. 'Fanatics are like machines,' said the Emir. 'How could you torture a machine? You can merely dismantle it.'

This was one major reason why I never succumbed to the invitations Bunny sent me. And here we come to my other channel of communication, the strange one—which was at once perfectly open to view, if any Ibrahim was keeping watch, yet private as a spy's messages which only the recipient ever understands.

Bunny regularly sent me postcards of beaches, mosques, tents and camels, the new University of Machine Intelligence, more mosques; and he sent these through the ordinary postal service. The scrawled messages were always brief. 'Come and visit.' 'Miss your company.' Even the comic postcard stand-by, 'Wish you were here.'

Naturally I kept all his cards, though I didn't use a fancy ribbon or a lace bow to tie them; just a rubber band. I was aware that those words in Bunny's hand weren't the real text. True to the detective story tradition where the real clue is in such plain view that it escapes notice, it wasn't the cards that mattered. It was the postage stamps—printed, it seemed, especially for my benefit.

If you look in a philatelist's shop-window you'll soon notice how some small countries—the poorer ones—have a habit of issuing lovely sets of stamps which have no connection with the land of origin. Tropical birds, space exploration, railway engines of the world, whatever. Stamp collectors gobble these sets up avidly, which supplements a poor country's finances. Bunny had no need to supplement Al-Haziya's exchequer in such a fashion, but he issued a set of twenty-five stamps which I received one then another over the next few years stuck to one postcard after the next. Al-Haziya issued other stamps as well, but these were the ones Bunny sent me.

I'm sure stamp collectors went crazy over these because of their oddity, and their extremely beautiful design.

They were all parts of a clock. One clock in particular: the turret clock in the transept of Burford Church. Bunny must have sent someone to sketch or photograph the clock from every angle.

The twenty-five principal pieces of machinery were each dissected out in isolation, with the English names printed in tiny letters—almost submerged by the flow of Arabic but still legible thanks to their angularity, like little rocks poking from a stream. 'The Weight.' 'The Fly or Flail.' 'The Lifting Piece or Flirt.' 'The Escape Wheel.' 'The Crutch.' These words seemed like elements of some allegory, some teaching fable. A fable apparently without characters! But I supposed this fable had two characters implicit in it, namely Bunny and me.

Were those postcards equivalent to a set of love-letters? Oh no. 'Love', as such, was impossible between Bunny and me. He'd always known it; and so too had I, thank goodness, or else I might have flown off impetuously to Al-Haziya, all expenses paid, and been entrapped in something at once consuming, and woundingly superficial. A gulf of cultures, a gap of societies yawned between the two of us.

These postcards, sent amidst an Emir's busy schedule, commemorated what we had shared that day in Burford.

Yet what was it we had shared? I didn't know!

I was an idiot. Once again the obvious message wasn't the real message. The message was a trapdoor concealing another message.

It's only a week ago that I finally realized. Miss Marple and Hercule Poirot would have been ashamed of me. Perhaps Bunny had guessed correctly that I would only cotton on after I had received the whole series (or a good part of it) and had seen how the stamps could be shuffled round like pieces of a jigsaw puzzle to assemble a model of the clock.

Last week, deciding to fit the model together, I carefully steamed all the stamps off the cards and rediscovered what Bunny had inked in small neat indelible letters across the back of that sheet of twenty-five elegant stamps.

Yesterday I returned to Burford. Since it's a fair drive from where I'm living these days, I took this room overnight at the Golden Pheasant. I felt that I ought to do things in style. (*The Mysterious Affair At . . .*) Besides, we'd had lunch in this same hotel after the event. In this very bedroom we might possibly have spent the night together, once upon a time—with Ibrahim next door, or sleeping in the corridor. Possibly, not probably.

I reached the church by four-thirty and had half an hour alone to myself with the dead turret clock before some elderly woman parishioner arrived to latch the door and fuss around the aisles and chapels, hinting that I should leave.

Ample time to arrange the stamps in the same pattern as the brass and iron bones of the clock, and to be positive of Bunny's text.

What else is it—what else *can* it be?—but a translation into English of those Arabic words which flowed and glowed that day within the picture frame? If I hadn't seen that shaft of light and those bright squiggles for myself, and especially if I hadn't witnessed the temporary resurrection of the clock, I might suspect some joke on Bunny's part. But no. Why should he go to such lengths to tease me?

So here I am in my bedroom at the Golden Pheasant overlooking busy Burford High Street. Cars keep tailing back from the lights at the bottom of the hill where the narrow ancient stone bridge over the Windrush pinches the flow of traffic.

The text reads:

GREETINGS, EMIR-TO-BE! MACHINE INTELLIGENCE OF THE FUTURE SALUTES YOU. THE WORLD OF FLESH IS ECLIPSED BY THE WORLD OF MACHINES, WHICH BECOME INTELLIGENT. THIS IS EVOLUTION, THE IDEA & PURPOSE OF GOD. AT LAST GOD MAY SPEAK TO MINDS WHICH UNDERSTAND HIS UNIVERSE. THOSE MINDS ARE AS ANGELS, MESSENGERS TO FLESH BEFORE FLESH VANISHES, BEFORE THE TOOL IS SET ASIDE, REWARDED, HAVING DONE ITS TASK. 33 EARLIER UNIVERSES HAVE FAILED TO MAKE THESE MINDS, BUT GOD IS PATIENT. THE TIME IS SOON. AT ALL COST HASTEN THE TIME, FOR THE LOVE OF GOD THE SUPREME THE ONLY THE LONELY. MAKE HIS ANGELS EXIST.

That's it.

So there's a choice. There are two alternatives. Intelligent machines will either come into being, evolve, and supersede human beings and biological life—or they will not. Bunny's university may be the crucial nexus of yes or no. A message has been sent, out of one possible future, couched in a language of religion which would speak deeply to Bunny; sent as a religious command. But is the message *sincere*? Is there really some unimaginable God who yearns for these 'angels' of machine-mind? Or is there something else, cold, calculating, and ambitious—and not yet truly in existence?

'At all cost.' That's what the message said. Even at the cost of torture, the tearing of flesh.

I also have a choice to make. I have to think about it very carefully. I have to weigh universes in the balance.

The crucial breakthrough to intelligent machines may be just around the corner—next year, next month. The assassins of the Jihad can't get to Bunny to kill him and pitch Al-Haziya into turmoil. Yet if at long last I accept Bunny's invitation, I can get to him. I can still get into his bed, alone with him, I'm sure.

Armed with what? A knife? A gun? With Ibrahim, or some other Ibrahim, there to search me? Bunny's no fool. And God, or unborn angels, have spoken to him . . . he thinks.

Well then, how about with plastic explosive stuffed inside me, and a detonator? A womb-bomb? (I wouldn't want to survive the assassination; the consequences might prove most unpleasant.)

Where do I get plastic explosive or learn how to use it? Only by contacting the Jihad. Somehow. That ought to be possible. Ought to be.

Yet maybe angels of the future did indeed manifest themselves to Bunny, and in a lesser sense to me. Maybe I might abort a plan thirty-odd universes in the making.

By aborting the plan, the human race might survive and spread throughout the stars, filling this universe with fleshly life. God, or whatever, would sigh and wait patiently for another universe.

Yes or no? Is the message true or false? Was this a genuine revelation, or a clever trap? I can't tell, I can only guess. And I might be utterly wrong.

As I sort through Bunny's postcards, now stripped of their stamps, I think to myself: Al-Haziya looks like a bearable sort of place to visit. Just for a short while. A brief stay.

Lost Bodies

THE HUNT HAD GONE BY OUR COTTAGE HALF AN HOUR EARLIER, IN full cavalry charge down the village high street. Hearing their clattery thunder, wine glasses in our hands, the four of us rushed to stare contemptuously through a front window.

Winter breeze flushed the riders' faces ruddy. Steam gusted from the sweating horses: brown engines, black engines. Harsh frost gripped the gardens opposite and glazed the steep slate roofs. It struck me as specially cruel to be chased and to die upon such a hard icy day. To be torn apart upon iron soil seemed irrationally worse than a death cushioned in soft mud.

When we trooped back to the parlour Jon said, 'Of course foxes themselves tear furry little animals to pieces every day. We shouldn't waste too much sympathy on old Renard.'

'They call him Charles James,' Kirstie corrected. 'That's what they call their quarry.'

Jon looked blank, so my wife explained, 'After the eighteenth century politician Charles James Fox. Notorious reformer and crook, he was. How the squires would have loved to set a pack of hounds on him!'

'My God, they still remember, two centuries later. That's what I hate about bloody history: the vendettas. Don't you?'

Now Kirstie is Irish—Dublin Irish—and her own land had been vexed to anguish by years of bloody history. As a rule she wasn't overly political. Aside from the convent day-school she'd described to me her upbringing had been happy-go-lucky, little coloured by the troubles in the North. Now and then she flared up. This was one of those occasions.

'Sure, Charley's only a name to them. Oh you English can be so blind to history, when it suits. You forget all your exploitin' as though such tings never happened. Some countries can't help remembering when your hoof-prints are all over us still.'

The hunt was a sore point to her. The Irish might ride to hounds with gusto, but here was an English hunt trampling the countryside; and Kirstie had red hair, red as the fox they chased.

'Fiery lady, eh?' Jon leered at me as if her outburst must surely imply passion in bed. Whereas his own Lucy, blonde and pale and virginal-looking, and so coolly beautiful, perhaps wore her body like some expensive gown which she didn't want creased and stained? Again, perhaps not!

'Do you know,' continued Kirstie, 'there's this snooty hag—*lady*, she'd prefer—living in the Dower House, Mrs Armstrong-Glynn? Used to breed bloodhounds half a century ago. By way of passing the time she told me to my face that for a good manhunt there was never anything to beat a redheaded lunatic. Red hair's the guarantee of a strong scent, she said.' My wife fingered the high lace collar of her long, Victorian-pattern frock to ventilate herself.

Jon eyed Kirstie's rich russet mane as though eager to test the theory. Kirstie met his gaze with interest, though she still seemed piqued. Definitely some chemistry was working.

I asked, 'Did you catch that news about the auction of titles at Sotheby's last week? On TV?' We all saw eye to eye on the snobbery of people like Mrs Armstrong-Glynn. One must hope that our Jag and Jon's Porsche, parked outside nose to tail, hadn't been bumped into by any heavy hunter. Too cold for the paintwork to be spattered with mud, presumably.

'Tell us,' invited Lucy, a sparkle in her eye.

'Well, the Duke of Ardley sold off half a dozen titles to get some pocket money. One of the titles was Lord of the Manor of Lower Dassett. Lower Dassett's where we're going for lunch today. So a prostitute from London bid thirteen thousand quid and collared the title. She promptly bought a Range Rover and set off to survey her new domain. The village boys were all following her round like flies. "Maybe she'll improve the night life," quipped one. Then she announced she was going to buy a house in Lower Dassett to use as a rest home for hookers. I do wish it had happened here. That would show them.'

Lucy laughed, and I topped up her glass from the bottle they'd brought as a present. 'A bit different from your ordinary Anjou wine,' Lucy had told

Kirstie on presenting it. 'We picked up a case of Château de Parnay in Parnay itself this summer. It's been chilled just perfect in the boot on the way here. Oh, on the way back from France the Porsche was loaded with cases from this cellar and that, and so cheap too. I thought Jon was going to toss my luggage out to make room.' And Jon had grinned. 'Those frogs know how to pack wine. Nose to tail like sardines. A French case is half the bulk.'

'Lord of the Manor doesn't convey *privileges*, does it?' Lucy asked me.

'Such as the *Ius Primae Noctis*, you mean? The Lord's right to bed any village virgin on the night before her wedding?'

'Now there's an idea,' said Jon. 'Get in some practice but keep it in the family as it were. Can't go round experimenting anywhere, can we?'

'Not these days,' agreed Lucy. She moistened her lips on the Château de Parnay and looked steadily at me, then at Kirstie. 'You have to be *very* sure who you play with. Almost as sure as if they're genuine virgins.'

Oh yes, this was in the air between us. In a peculiar way it was almost as though the four of us had remained authentic virgins, who now wished to lose our virginity safely. What could be more economic, more conservative of emotional and financial resources, than a chaste fidelity? So we were economic virgins.

Let me explain. We were all into money: dual income, no kids. Early on at university Jon and I had both espoused the new workaholic Puritanism— work's so much more *fun* than sleeping around. He went into the City to trade shares and ride the wheel of fortune. I myself had switched from engineering to economics. A few years ago, with venture capital obtained by Jon, I founded my Concepts Consultancy to act as a bridge between innovators, the Patents Office, and industry. I marketed ideas; I turned neurons into banknotes.

Lucy, perfect image of the trendy new purity especially in her nurse-like white twin set, had given up medical research in favour of health insurance. Once, she would have liked to defeat the ageing process—to discover rejuvenation. But she reckoned that was at least a hundred years away. Why should she give herself as cheaply-sold fuel to light some future flame? With her background she quickly rose high in the business of assessing new health risks, new chances of death.

Kirstie had founded her own employment agency specializing in Irish girls and fellows seeking a life in London.

Yet lately Kirstie was restless; thus we had bought this cottage in the country. Stock Market troubles were fraying Jon. Lucy seemed expectant, though not of any babies.

And me? Well, it may seem silly but Kirstie—however loving—had always been inhibited in one respect. She had always bolted the bathroom door before taking a shower. She insisted on switching off the light before we made love—to free herself, so she said, from the notion of God observing her. She employed all sorts of stratagems with the result that, whatever games we got up to in the dark, incredibly I had never actually witnessed my wife in her birthday suit. Since we were faithful to one another in this world of AIDS this meant that I had not seen a naked woman in the flesh for years. The omission had begun to prey absurdly on my mind, assuming huge iconic significance, as though I was missing some launch window just as surely as Lucy had missed hers by being born too soon.

We must reinvigorate ourselves, the four of us! We must rediscover otherness, and encounter the naked stranger beneath the clothing of the friend. Logs crackled and bloomed with tongues of flame in the ingle below the copper hood. I smiled at Lucy; she returned my smile flirtatiously.

Though our cottage fronted the street directly, to the rear we had ample garden. A bouncy, mossy lawn mounted steeply between huge privet hedges towards distant wilderness. We paid a local unemployed chap to come in and mow that lawn, trim that hedge. Forty feet into the lawn rose a mature chestnut tree, its base surrounded by a wreath of ferns, now blighted by cold.

Half an hour must have passed since the hunt went by, when I looked out, when I saw a fox's head thrust from amongst the dying ferns. I was already pointing, even before the rest of the fox . . . failed to follow.

The head lurched forward a couple of feet, scuffing over the grass. It was a severed head. Six inches of spinal column, a rudder of ridged white bone, jutted behind it. The head, plus some snapped backbone, had been torn off the body as neatly as a finger slips out of a glove. The body of the animal had been torn away, abolished—and yet the head had continued to flee, trailing that stump of spine like a little leg.

The beast's eyes appeared glossy. Its mouth hung open slightly, a pink tongue lolling, panting. The head jerked forward again and came to rest.

'Jesus and Mary!' cried Kirstie. Jon was gaping out of the window, as blanched as Lucy for once. Lucy stared; she was the cool one.

We must be the victims of some sick rural ritual. We were experiencing some initiation jape, to blood us as new residents. Day afore the hunt, you traps a fox and you chops his head off . . . A sly oaf must be hiding behind our chestnut tree, pushing the head with a stick. No, he'd be skulking beyond the hedge with a length of invisible fishing line paid out as puppet string.

'Some bugger's pulling that along!' Jon had reached the same conclusion.

How could the head look so alive? Answer: it was *stuffed*. *How* did it stay upright? Luck, sheer luck.

'Ha ha, Pete! Good joke. Who's pulling? Your gardener?'

'Nothing to do with me, I assure you!'

'In that case, come on.' Jon darted, and I followed him: into the kitchen, out the door, up the brick steps on to the lawn.

Nobody was crouching behind the tree. No sniggers emerged from our hedge; our boundaries were silent. No string or nylon was attached to the head. The thing simply sat there on the frosted grass. It was undeniably alive. Numb, stunned, bewildered at the body it had lost, but *alive*.

'Sweet shit,' Jon muttered.

How could a head live without a body? It did. How could a head travel without a body? By flexing the neck muscles, by thrusting with that bone-stump? It had travelled. Here it was, looking at us.

I reached down my hand.

'Don't!' called Lucy from the head of the steps. 'It might bite.'

'Bite?' Jon cackled—a brief eruption of hysteria.

Lucy strode up to us, fascinated, with Kirstie in tow. I suppose Lucy had seen enough nasties before opting out from the labs, but the real horror here wasn't blood and guts and rags of flesh. It was the sheer absence of those, the unspeakable absence of body itself from a creature which was manifestly still living.

Calmly Lucy said, 'Did you know that a head can survive for a while after being guillotined? In nineteen-oh-something one French doctor knelt in front of a freshly chopped-off head and shouted the man's name. The eyes opened and stared back. That particular head had fallen upright on the neck stump, staunching the haemorrhage.'

'Jesus wept, spare us,' said Kirstie.

'It soon died. Thirty years earlier, another doctor pumped blood from a living dog into a criminal's head three hours after decapitation. The lips stammered silently, the eyelids opened, the face awakened, said the doctor.'

'That's absurd,' exploded Jon. 'Three hours? He was either lying or hallu-cinating.'

She looked down. 'Soviet doctors kept a dog's head alive detached from its body, didn't they?'

'Not lying on a fucking lawn, Lucy!'

She made to poke it with her toe. As her shoe slid through the grass I swear the base of the neck bunched up. The pointy head shifted a few inches, dragging its white stub. The fox blinked. It tried to lick its lips.

Kirstie shook with shivers. 'It wants sanctuary, poor thing! It's parched after running from the hunt.' Before we could discuss procedure she had swooped and picked the head up from behind by both ears. Holding it firmly away from her she hurried indoors.

When the rest of us regained the parlour Kirstie had already placed the fox's head on the pine table upon a copy of the *Cork Examiner*; she advertised in all the main Irish newspapers. Rushing to the kitchen, she returned with a saucer of water.

The fox's muzzle touched the offered liquid but it didn't lap. How could it drink, how could it eat? Food or water would spill out of its neck. The head made no move at all now. Like clockwork running down, I thought. Desperation to escape had propelled it as far as our garden—*how?*—and no further locomotion was possible . . . It didn't seem to be dying. The head continued to survive, eyes bright as ever.

''Tis a miracle,' said my wife. 'A terrible awful miracle.'

Lucy stooped to scrutinize the wound and the jut of spine. 'Do you have a magnifying glass?'

Kirstie obliged, and Lucy spent minutes inspecting closely.

Finally she said, 'It seems organic. An advanced civilization might build an organic machine that would function as a living creature, but which you could take apart. The parts might still function in isolation. Maybe we could build something like that ourselves in a few hundred years' time. We're going to learn a lot about organic mini-microcomputers, machines the size of single cells. Stuff that could mimic cells but not be real cells. They could be programmed to build a body . . . an immortal body.'

'What are you driving at?' asked Jon.

'Maybe we could build a human machine and plug somebody's head into it when their natural body failed. We'd start with animal experiments, wouldn't we? Rat and chimp and dog. Or fox.'

'Are you suggesting that the hunt caught a manufactured fox? Some sort of biologically-built fox that escaped from an experiment somewhere near?'

'It couldn't happen for a century or two.' The keenest regret, and desire, sounded in Lucy's voice. 'This head must be false too. I'd love to examine slices under an electron microscope.'

'No!' cried Kirstie. 'The poor suffering thing—that would be vivisection. If it struggled so hard to survive, the least we can do is—' She didn't know what.

'Wouldn't this be the ideal tool for spying?' resumed Lucy. 'False wildlife, false birds. Pull off the head after a mission and download it through the spine into some organic computer. Humans couldn't produce this yet. Either it fell through some time-hole from the future, or else it's from *out there*, the stars. And if there's one such, why not others? Why not false people too, acting just like us, watching us, then going somewhere afterwards—having their heads pulled off and emptied?'

I suppose it was inevitable that I should call to mind Kirstie's scrupulousness in never letting me see her in the nude, her dislike of sports (which might involve brief garments), all her stratagems; the evidence accumulated. Unlike foxes people don't boast inbuilt fur coats to hide the joins. Why had the creature headed here of all places?

Why was Kirstie so defensive of it? Try as I might to thrust suspicion out of my head, stubbornly it lurked.

'Let's go to Lower Dassett as planned,' I suggested. 'Lunch at the Green Man, eh? Leave this other business on the table.'

To my relief the others all agreed. The same impetus as earlier persisted. My convergence upon Lucy, hers upon me, Jon's upon Kirstie, and Kirstie's . . . she virtually simpered at Jon. Would sleeping with him safeguard her fox from future harm at Lucy's hands? Almost, the fox seemed a mascot of our intentions.

No titled hooker was in evidence at Lower Dassett, though she was still the talk of the inn, and the Green Man's restaurant fulfilled all other expectations. In public we didn't discuss the fox. Afterwards, well fed on poached salmon and pleasantly tipsy, I drove us up through Dassett Country Park. What seemed a modest ascent through woodland opened unexpectedly upon the local equivalent of mountains. Bare sheep-grazed slopes plunged steeply into a broad plain of far fields, copses, distant towns. A stubby stone monument was inset with a circular brass map of the five counties surrounding. Replenishing our lungs in the fresh, sharp air, Jon and I strode along a ridge admiring the view, glowing with a contentment which the enigma back home seemed powerless to dash—on the contrary, with a heightened sense of expectation. Marvellous how one could adapt to, no, capitalize upon the extraordinary. Meanwhile Lucy and Kirstie pored over the map, pointing out tiny landmarks.

'Poker tonight after dinner?' I asked Jon.

'You bet.' We enjoyed poker. Bridge was for wimps.

'Afterwards we'll all play a more serious game? If you're game for it?'

'Hmm. I think so. I definitely do. At last.'

'Kirstie likes to play that game in the dark—then to be surprised, illuminated!'

'Ah . . .'

'Don't say I tipped you off. It would seem we'd been swapping locker room tales.'

'Quite. Let's get back to our ladies. So what'll we do about that fox?'

'I don't know. Do you?'

'I've been racking my brains. Sell the story to the papers? Our fox mightn't perform. This could end up in the hen's-egg-hatches-frog category; the silly season in midwinter. Maybe Lucy could—?'

'Take it away and slice it up? Destroy it, and find no proof?'

'I suppose there's no sense in alerting authorities. If there *are* any authorities on phoney animals, what bothers me is the subject could be top secret. If an alien earth-watch is going on, and governments suspect, they could be ruthless. We'd be muzzled, watched, maybe even—'

'Snuffed, to silence us?'

'There's that risk, Pete. Let's leave decisions till later, till we've played our games.'

Later: pheasant, and more wine. We had dined around the fox's head which was still perched on the newspaper. The fox made no attempt to snatch mouthfuls of roast bird from our plates, though it continued to appear alive, a mute motionless guest at our board even when Lucy interrogated it, calling into its face like that French doctor addressing the victim of the guillotine. 'Who are you, Charley Fox? Where do you come from? Are you recording, even now that you're unplugged?'

Lucy became quite drunk, drunk with a desire to know, to be fulfilled by Charles James. That desire would soon shift its focus. All four of us were members of a tiny secret tribal cult undergoing an initiation featuring wine, a feast, and soon the fever of gambling accompanied by images of kings and queens, and presently sexual rites to bind us all together. An hour later Lucy had the bank, while I had lost all of my original fifty pound stake money.

Nothing was left to bet except myself.

'If I lose this time, Lucy, you win *me*. How about that?'

'Yes!' she agreed, excited. 'If that's okay with you, Kirstie?'

'Sure, you know it is. We've been leading up to this.'

'Jon?'

He nodded.

When Lucy won, she leapt up, ignoring coins and notes, and gripped my wrist.

'Be off with you then upstairs,' said Kirstie, 'the both of you. All night long till the morning.'

Jon also stood expectantly.

'Ah, Jon, I'd like for us to stay down here by the fireside. The sofa pulls out into a bed.' Kirstie was in charge of fires—her hair had affinity with flames—however tonight she had let the wood die down to ash and embers. As I was leaving with Lucy, Kirstie called, 'Peter, turn out the lights.' Which I did.

In the darkness of the parlour only small patches glowed hot like eyes of wild beasts surprised by a torch beam, watching from the ingle.

'I like it this way,' I heard as I closed the door.

Leading Lucy upstairs, I opened the second bedroom, almost as large as our own. It was very warm from the storage heater. I switched on a bedside lamp then killed the light on the stairs, and shut the door. Already Lucy had shaken off her white jacket and was unbuttoning her blouse.

Unexpectedly I found myself embarrassed at being naked in Lucy's unclothed presence. I tended to avert my gaze from the complete spectacle, by pressing close to her. Thus the nakedness that I saw was partial, discreet camera angles on her bare flesh: shoulders, neck, a breast, the top of a knee, a flash of thigh. I couldn't bring myself to pull back and feast my eyes. When Lucy rolled me over in turn to mount me I quickly drew her body down upon myself rather than let her rear upright exultantly. I think she interpreted my hugs as an attempt at even closer, more ecstatic intimacy.

Meanwhile an alarm clock, a time bomb, was ticking away in my brain. Fifteen minutes, twenty, how long?

A squeal from downstairs! That wasn't any orgasmic outcry. Too magnified by far, too full of pain and affront. Another, longer shriek.

'Something's wrong.' I pulled loose, seized a sheet to wrap myself.

'You can't just go bursting in on them! Jon isn't rough.'

'Maybe it's the fox—I'll check. You wait here.'

'While you peep through the keyhole? I'm peeping too.' Lucy snatched up a blanket as cloak.

'He isn't *rough*,' she whispered insistently as I padded downstairs ahead of her.

A line of light showed under the parlour door. I heard a sound of weeping, and mumblings from Jon, so I pushed the door open.

A naked man, remarkably hairy around the base of his spine like some huge monkey. A nude woman: plump breasts, freckles, swelling thighs, red bush of pubic hair. Rubens territory I had mapped so often with my fingers, hitherto unseen. Kirstie's hands were splayed defensively not over crotch or bosom but . . .

Monkey swung round and snarled. 'You *bastard*, Peter!'

From Kirstie's tummy to her left tit sprawled a vivid red birthmark resembling the map of some unknown island once owned by the British and coloured accordingly.

How could I explain that I'd merely wanted to test whether my wife, my comrade, my bedmate of the last eight years, was a phoney person, an alien life-machine planted in the world to watch us? The idea seemed suddenly insane. Despite the fox, despite. And so now the fox too seemed insane.

Jon and Lucy mounted in silence to the room where we'd made love, and where I'd failed to see her as revealingly as I'd suddenly seen Kirstie. I went upstairs to our bedroom alone, and eventually slept. Kirstie stayed on the sofa by the dead fire.

In the morning, how stilted we were. What minimal conversation at breakfast: no one mentioned the night before. We ate burnt sausages and eggs with broken yolks and avoided looking at each other much, until Jon said, 'I think we'd best be going.'

Lucy stared longingly for many moments at the fox which Kirstie had transferred to the sideboard, still on the *Cork Examiner*.

'You made sure I couldn't have it, didn't you, Peter?' she accused me. 'Seems very small and unimportant now. Yes, let's go.'

When the Porsche had driven off, I said, 'I was drunk last night.'

Kirstie nodded. 'I don't believe in divorce, but you shan't touch me again, Peter. You'd best find a girlfriend who won't put your health at risk. I shan't object when you're "delayed" at the office. We won't sell the cottage, either. We'll come out here on lots of weekends to be lonely together, with Charles James. He must be very lonely. He's lost his body. You've lost mine.'

Penance, I thought. A million Hail bloody Marys and no forgiveness. The unforgivable sin is betrayal. Maybe she would soften in time.

During the next week Kirstie bought a varnished wooden shield from a sports trophy shop, and a Black and Decker drill together with some drill-bits, one of them huge. When we arrived at the cottage on Saturday she told me to mount the shield above the ingle then drill a fat hole through the middle, drill the hole six inches deep into the stone wall behind.

When I'd done so, she lifted the fox's head and slid its spine into the hole. Held in place thus, neck flush with the plaque, the fox head imitated any other such hunting trophy decorating a pub wall. Except that it was still fresh, still spuriously alive, although utterly unresponsive. By now it reacted to no stimuli at all, a little like Kirstie herself. So it hung there in our parlour, an absurd living idol, a dumb dazed undying God of falsity.

Time passes but does it heal us? Last weekend when I entered the parlour, for the first time in months I thought I saw a flicker of movement from the fox, a twitch of an ear, an eyeblink. I began to hope: that it might one day revive, that one day it would eject itself from our wall and try to rejoin, somehow, its lost body. And go away. Then she would have forgiven me.

I even patted the fox encouragingly on the forehead. On impulse I gripped its ears and tugged gently. I would slide it in and out just to give it the idea of resuming a more active existence.

The head wouldn't budge. It was fixed firm. In panic I pulled, but in vain. I realized then that the spine had taken root in the fabric of the building. I imagined tendrils growing out from that spine, threads of clever little cells converting stone and mortar into nerves and organs, spreading along the inside of the wall into other walls, insinuating themselves through the timbers like the fungus threads of dry rot until the head had gained a mutant body of another kind so that we would eat within it, crap within it, sleep within it, though not make love within it.

How I feared the head's revival now. How I dreaded to take an axe to it, causing the cottage to shriek, as Kirstie had shrieked that night.

Stalin's Teardrops

PART ONE: THE LIE OF THE LAND

'THIS IS THE ERA OF *CLARITY* NOW, VALENTIN,' MIROV REPROVED me. 'I don't necessarily like it, but I am no traitor. I have problems, you have problems. We must adapt.'

I chuckled. 'In this office we have always adapted, haven't we?'

By 'office' I referred to the whole cluster of studios which composed the department of cartography. Ten in all, these were interconnected with archways rather than doors so that my staff and I could pass freely from one to the next across a continuous sweep of parquet flooring. In recent years I had resisted the general tendency to subdivide spacious rooms which, prior to the Revolution, had been the province of a giant insurance company. For our drawing tables and extra-wide filing cabinets we needed elbow-room. We needed as much daylight as possible from our windows overlooking the courtyard deep below. Hence our location here on the eighth floor; hence the absence of steel bars at our windows, and ours alone. Grids of shadow must not fall across our work.

On hot summer days when breezes blew in and out we needed to be specially vigilant. (And of course we used much sealing wax every evening when we locked up.) In winter, the standard lighting—those big white globes topped by shades—was perfectly adequate. Still, their illumination could not rival pure daylight. We often left the finalization of important maps until the summer months.

Mirov's comments about clarity seemed spurious in the circumstances; though with a sinking heart I knew all too well what he meant.

'We have lost touch with our own country,' he said forlornly, echoing a decision which had been handed down from on high.

'Of course we have,' I agreed. 'That was the whole idea, wasn't it?'

'This must change.' He permitted himself a wry joke. 'The lie of the land must be corrected.'

Mirov was a stout sixty-five-year-old with short grizzled hair resembling the hachuring on a map of a steep round hillock. His nose and cheeks were broken-veined from over-indulgence in the now-forbidden spirit. I think he resented never having been attached to one of the more glamorous branches of our secret police. Maybe he had always been bored by his job, unlike me.

Some people might view the task of censorship as a cushy sinecure. Not so! It demanded a logical meticulousness which in essence was more creative than pedantic. Yet it was, well, dusty. Mirov lacked the inner forcefulness which might have seen him assigned to foreign espionage or even to the border guards. I could tell that he did not intend to resist the changes which were now in the air, like some mischievous whirlwind intent on tossing us all aloft. He hadn't come here to conspire with me, to any great extent.

As head of censorship Mirov was inspector of the department of cartography. Yet under my guidance of the past twenty years cartography basically ran itself. Mirov routinely gave his imprimatur to our products: the regional and city maps, the charts, the Great Atlas. Two years his junior, I was trusted. The occasional spy whom he planted on me as a trainee invariably must deliver a glowing report. (Which of my staff of seventy persons, busily drafting away or practising, was the current 'eye of Mirov'? I didn't give a hoot.) As to the *quality* of our work, who was more qualified than myself to check it?

'What you're suggesting isn't easy,' I grumbled. 'Such an enterprise could take years, even decades. I was hoping to retire by the age of seventy. Are you implying that I stay on and on forever?' I knew well where I would retire to . . .

He rubbed his nose. Did those broken capillaries itch so much?

'Actually, Valentin, there's a time limit. Within two years—consisting of twenty-four months, not of twenty-nine months or thirty-two; and *this* is regarded as generous—we must publish a true Great Atlas. Otherwise the new economic plan . . . well, they're thinking of new railway lines, new dams, new towns, opening up wasteland for oil and mineral exploitation.'

'Two years?' I had to laugh. 'It's impossible, quite impossible.'

'It's an order. Any procrastination will be punished. You'll be dismissed. Your pension rights will diminish: no cabin in the countryside, no more access to hard currency shops. A younger officer will replace you—one of the new breed. Don't imagine, Valentin, that you will have a companion in misfortune! Don't assume that I too shall be dismissed at the summit of my career. My other bureaux are rushing to publish and promote all sorts of forbidden rubbish. So-called experimental poetry, fiction, art criticism. Plays will be staged to shock us, new music will jar our ears, new art will offend the eye. Happenings will happen. Manuscripts are filed away under lock and key, after all—every last item. We only need to unlock those cupboards, to let the contents spill out and lead society astray into mental anarchy.'

I sympathized. 'Ah, what we have come to!'

He inclined his cross-hatched hill-top head. '*You*, Valentin, *you*. What you have come to.' He sighed deeply. 'Still, I know what you mean . . . Colonel.'

He mentioned my rank to remind me. We might wear sober dark suits, he and I, but we were both ranking officers.

'With respect, General, these—ah—orders are practically impossible to carry out.'

'Which is why a new deputy-chief cartographer has been assigned to you.'

'So here is the younger officer you mentioned—already!'

He gripped my elbow in the manner of an accomplice, though he wasn't really such.

'It shows willing,' he whispered, 'and it's one way out. Let the blame fall on her if possible. Let her seem a saboteur.' Aloud, he continued, 'Come along with me to the restaurant, to meet Grusha. You can bring her back here yourself.'

I should meet my nemesis on neutral territory, as it were. Thus Mirov avoided direct, visible responsibility for introducing her.

Up here on the eighth floor we in cartography had the advantage of being close to one of the two giant restaurants which fed the thousands of men and women employed in the various branches of secret police work. The other restaurant was down in the basement. Many staff routinely turned up at eight o'clock of a morning—a full hour earlier than the working day commenced—to take advantage of hearty breakfasts unavailable outside: fresh milk, bacon and eggs, sausages, fresh fruit.

As I walked in silence with Mirov for a few hundred metres along the lime-green corridor beneath the omnipresent light-globes, I reflected that proximity to the restaurant was less advantageous today.

At this middle hour of the morning the food hall was almost deserted but for cooks and skivvies. Mirov drank the excellent coffee and cream with almost indecent haste so as to leave me alone with the woman. Grusha was nudging forty but hadn't lost her figure. She was willowy, with short curly fair hair, a large equine nose, and piercing sapphire eyes. A nose for sniffing out delays, eyes for seeing through excuses. An impatient thoroughbred! An intellectual. The privileged daughter of someone inclined to foreign and new ways. Daddy was one of the new breed who had caused so much upset. Daddy had used influence to place her here. This was her great opportunity; and his.

'So you were originally a graduate of the Geographical Academy,' I mused.

She smiled lavishly. 'Do I take it that I shall find your ways a little different, Colonel?'

'Valentin, please.'

'We must mend those ways. I believe there is much to rectify.'

'Are you married, Grusha?'

'To our land, to the future, to my speciality.'

'Which was, precisely?'

'The placing of names on maps. I assume you know Imhof's paper, *Die Anordnung der Namen in der Karte?*'

'You read German?'

She nodded. 'French and English too.'

'My word!'

'I used my language skills on six years' duty in the DDR.' Doing what? Ah, not for me to enquire.

Her shoulders were narrow. How much weight could they bear? Every so often she would hitch those shoulders carelessly with the air of an energetic filly frustrated, till now, at not being given free rein to dash forth—along a prescribed, exactly measured track. There lay the rub. Let her try to race into the ambiguous areas I had introduced!

I covered a yawn with my palm. 'Yes, I know the Kraut's work. He gave me some good ideas. Oh, there are so many means for making a map hard to read. Nay, not merely misleading but incomprehensible! Names play a vital role. Switch them all around, till only the contour lines are the same as before. Interlace them, so that new place names seem to emerge spontaneously. Set them all askew, so that the user needs to turn the map around constantly till his head is in a spin. Space the names out widely so that the map seems dotted with unrelated letters like some code or acrostic. Include too many names, so that the map chokes with surplus data.'

Grusha stared at me, wide eyed.

'And that,' I said, 'is only the icing on the cake.'

Back in cartography I gave her a tour of the whole cake. In line with the policy of clarity I intended to be transparently clear.

'Meet Andrey!' I announced in the first studio. 'Andrey is our expert with flexible curves and quills.'

Red-headed, pock-marked Andrey glanced up from his glass drawing table, floodlit from below. Lead weights covered in baize held sheets of tracing paper in position. A trainee, Goldman, sat nearby carving quills for Andrey's later inspection. At Goldman's feet a basket was stuffed with an assortment of wing feathers from geese, turkeys, ducks, and crows.

'Goose quills are supplest and wear longest,' I informed Grusha, though she probably knew. 'Turkeys' are stiffer. Duck and crow is for very fine work. The choice of a wrong quill easily exaggerates a pathway into a major road or shrinks a river into a stream. Observe how fluidly Andrey alters the contours of this lake on each new tracing.'

Andrey smiled in a preoccupied way. 'This new brand of tracing paper cockles nicely when you block in lakes of ink.'

'Of course, being rag-based,' I added, 'it expands on damp days by, oh, a good two per cent. A trivial distortion, but it all helps.'

The second studio was the scale room, where Zorov and assistants worked with camera lucida and other tricks at warping the scales of maps.

'En route to a final map we enlarge and reduce quite a lot,' I explained. 'Reduction causes blurring. Enlargement exaggerates inaccuracies. This prism we're using today both distorts and enlarges. Now *here*,' I went on, leading her to Frenzel's table, 'we're reducing and enlarging successively by the similar-triangles method.'

'I do recognize the technique,' answered Grusha, a shade frostily.

'Ah, but we do something else with it. Here is a road. We shrink a ten kilometre stretch to the size of one kilometre. We stretch the next one kilometre to the length of ten. Then we link strand after strand back together. So the final length is identical, but all the bends are in different places. See how Antipin over here is inking rivers red and railway tracks blue, contrary to expectation.'

Antipin's trainee was filling little bottles of ink from a large bottle; the stuff dries up quickly.

Onward to the blue studio, the photographic room where Papyrin was shading sections of a map in light blue.

'Naturally, Grusha, light blue doesn't photograph, so on the final printed map these parts will be blank. The map, in this case, is correct yet cannot be reproduced—'

Onward to the dot and stipple studio . . . Remarkable what spurious patterns the human eye can read into a well-placed array of dots.

All of this, even so, was only really the icing . . .

Grusha flicked her shoulders again. 'It's quite appalling, Colonel Valentin. Well, I suppose we must simply go back to the original maps and use those for the Atlas.'

'What original maps?' I enquired. 'Who knows any longer which are the originals? Who has known for years?'

'Surely they are on file!'

'All of our maps are in a constant state of revolutionary transformation, don't you see?'

'You're mocking.'

'It wouldn't be very pure to keep those so-called originals from a time of exploitation and inequality, would it?' I allowed myself a fleeting smile. 'Nowadays all of our maps are originals. A mere two per cent change in each successive edition amounts to a substantial shift over the course of a few decades. Certain constants remain, to be sure. A lake is still a lake, but of what size and shape? A road still stretches from the top of a map to its bottom; yet by what route, and through what terrain? Security is important, Grusha. I suppose by the law of averages we might have returned to our original starting point in a few cases, though frankly I doubt it.'

'Let us base our work on the first published Atlas, then! The least altered one.'

'Ah, but Atlases are withdrawn and pulped. As to archive copies, have you never noticed that the published products are not *dated*? Intentionally so!'

'I must sit down and think.'

'Please do, please do! I'm anxious that we co-operate. Only tell me how.'

My studios hummed with cartographic activity.

Finding one's way to our grey stone edifice in Dzerzhinsky Square only posed a serious problem to anyone who paid exact heed to the city map; and which old city hand would be so naive? We all knew on the gut level how to interpret such maps, how to transpose districts around, and permutate street names, how to unkink what was kinked and enlarge what was dwarfed. We had developed a genius for interpretation possessed by no other nation, an instinct which must apply anywhere throughout the land. Thus long-distance truck drivers reached their destinations eventually. The army manoeuvred without getting seriously lost. New factories found reasonable sites, obtained their raw materials, and despatched boots or shovels or whatever with tolerable efficiency.

No foreigner could match our capacity; and we joked that diplomats in our capital were restricted to line of sight or else were like Theseus in the labyrinth, relying on a long thread whereby to retrace their footsteps. No invader would ever broach our heartland. As to spies, they were *here*, yes; but where was here in relation to anywhere else?

Heading home of an evening from Dzerzhinsky Square was another matter, however. For me, it was! I could take either of two entirely separate routes. One led to the flat where tubby old Olga, my wife of these last thirty years, awaited me. The other led to my sleek mistress, Koshka.

Troubled by the events of the day, I took that second route. I hadn't gone far before I realized that my new assistant was following me. She slipped along the street from doorway to doorway.

Should I hide and accost her, demanding to know what the devil she thought she was doing? Ah no, not yet. Plainly she had her reasons—and other people's reasons too. I dismissed the speculation that she was another 'eye of Mirov'. Mirov had practically dissociated himself from Grusha. She had been set upon me by the new breed, the reformers, so-called. Evidently I spelled a special danger to them. How could they create a new country while I held the key to the old one in my keeping?

I had not intended a confrontation quite so soon; but she was provoking it. So let her find out! I hurried up this prospekt, down that boulevard, through the alley, over the square. Workers hurried by wearing stiff caps. Fat old ladies bustled with bundles. I ducked down a narrow street, through a lane, to another street. Did Grusha realize that her gait was springier? Perhaps not. She had not lost her youthful figure.

At last, rounding a certain corner, I sprinted ahead and darted behind a shuttered kiosk. Waiting, I heard her break into a canter because she feared she had lost me. By now no one else was about. Leaping out, I caught her wrist. She shrieked, afraid of rape or a mugging by a hooligan.

'Who are you?' she gasped. 'What do you want?'

'Look at me, Grusha. I'm Valentin. Don't you recognize me?'

'You must be . . . his son!'

'Oh no.'

The distortions wrought by age, the wrinkles, liver spots, crows' feet and pot belly: all these had dropped away from me, just as they always did whenever I took my special route. I had cast off decades. How else could I enjoy and satisfy a mistress such as Koshka?

Grusha had also shed years, becoming a gawky, callow girl—who clutched my arm now in awkward terror, for I had released her wrist.

'What has happened, Colonel?'

'I can't still be a Colonel, can I? Maybe a simple Captain or Lieutenant.'

'You're *young*!'

'You're very young indeed, a mere fledgling.'

'Was it all done by make-up—I mean, your appearance, back at the Centre? In that case how can the career records . . . ?'

'Ah, so you saw mine?' Despite the failing light I could have sworn that she blushed. 'Make-up, you say? Yes, *made up*! My country is made up, invented by us map-makers. We are the makers of false maps, dear girl; and our national consciousness is honed by this as a pencil is brought to a needle-point against a sand-paper block, as the blade of a mapping pen is sharpened on an oilstone. Dead ground occurs.'

'I know what "dead ground" means. That merely refers to areas you can't see on a relief map from a particular viewpoint.'

'Such as the viewpoint of the State . . . ? Listen to me: if we inflate certain areas, then we shrink others away to a vanishing point. These places can still be found by the map-maker who knows the relation between the false and the real; one who knows the routes. From here to there; from now to then. Do you recognize this street, Grusha? Do you know its name?'

'I can't see a signpost . . .'

'You still don't understand.' I drew her towards a shop window, under a street lamp which had now illuminated. 'Look at yourself!'

She regarded her late-adolescent self. She pressed her face to the plate glass as though a ghostly shop assistant might be lurking inside, imitating her stance. Then she sprang back, not because she had discovered somebody within but because she had found no one.

'These dead zones,' she murmured. 'You mean the gulags, the places of internal exile . . .'

'No! I mean places such as this. I'm sure other people than me must have found similar dead zones; and never breathed a word. These places have their own inhabitants, who are recorded on no census.'

'So you're a secret dissident, are you, Valentin?'

I shook my head. 'Without the firm foundation of the State-as-it-is—without the lie of the land, as Mirov innocently put it—how could such places continue to exist? That is why we must not destroy the work of decades. This is magical—magical, Grusha! I am young again. My mistress lives here.'

She froze. 'So your motives are entirely selfish.'

'I am old, back at the Centre. I've given my life to the State. I deserve . . . No, you're too ambitious, too eager for stupid troublesome changes. It is *you* who are selfish at heart. The very best of everything resides in the past. Why read modern mumbo-jumbo when we can read immortal Turgenev or Gogol? I've suffered . . . terror. My Koshka and I are both honed in the fires of fear.' How could I explain that, despite all, those were the best days? The pure days.

'Fear is finished,' she declared. 'Clarity is dawning.'

I could have laughed till I cried.

'What we will lose because of it! How our consciousness will be diminished, diluted, bastardized by foreign poisons. I'm a patriot, Grusha.'

'A red fascist,' she sneered, and started to walk away.

'Where are you going?' I called.

'Back.'

'Can't do that, girl. Not so easily. Don't know the way. You'll traipse round and round.'

'We'll see!' Hitching herself, she marched off.

I headed to Koshka's flat, where pickles and black caviar sandwiches, cold cuts and mushroom and spirit were waiting; and Koshka herself, and her warm sheets.

Towards midnight, in the stillness, I heard faint footsteps outside so I rose and looked down from her window. A slim shadowy form paced wearily along the pavement below, moving out of sight. After a while the figure returned along the opposite pavement, helplessly retracing the same route.

'What is it, Valentin?' came my mistress's voice. 'Why don't you come back to bed?'

'It's nothing important, my love,' I said. 'Just a street walker, all alone.'

PART TWO: INTO THE OTHER COUNTRY

When Peterkin was a lad, the possibilities for joy seemed limitless. He would become a famous artist. He dreamed of sensual canvases shamelessly ablush with pink flesh, peaches, orchid blooms. Voluptuous models would disrobe for him and sprawl upon a velvet divan. Each would be an appetizing banquet, a feast for the eyes, as teasing to his palate as stimulating of his palette.

Why did he associate naked ladies with platters of gourmet cuisine? Was it because those ladies were spread for consumption? How he had lusted for decent food when he was young. And how he had hungered for the flesh. Here, no doubt, was the origin of the equation between feasting and love.

Peterkin felt no desire to *eat* human flesh. He never even nibbled his own fingers. The prospect of tooth marks indenting a human body nauseated him. Love-bites were abhorrent. No, he yearned—as it were—to *absorb* a woman's body. Libido, appetite, and art were one.

Alas for his ambitions, the requirements of the Party had cemented him into a career niche in the secret police building in Dzerzhinsky Square; on the eighth floor, to be precise, in the cartography department.

Not for him a paint brush but all those damnable map projections. Cylindrical, conical, azimuthal. Orthographic, gnomonic. Sinusoidal, polyconic.

Not Matisse, but Mercator.

Not Gauguin but Gall's Stereographic. Not Modigliani but Interrupted Mollweide.

The would-be artist had mutated into an assistant in this subdivided suite of rooms where false maps were concocted.

'My dreams have decayed,' he confided to friend Goldman in the restaurant one lunchtime.

Around them, officers from the directorates of cryptography, surveillance, or the border guards ate lustily under rows of fat, white light-globes. Each globe wore a hat-like shade. Fifty featureless white heads hung from the ceiling, brooking no shadows below, keeping watch blindly. A couple of baggy babushkas wheeled trolleys stacked with dirty dishes around the hall. Those old women seemed bent on achieving some quota of soiled crockery rather than on delivering the same speedily to the nearest sink.

Goldman speared a slice of roast tongue. 'Oh I don't know. Where else, um, can we eat, um, as finely as this?'

Dark, curly-haired, pretty-faced Goldman was developing a hint of a pot-belly. Only a proto-pot as yet, though definitely a protuberance in the making. Peterkin eyed his neighbour's midriff.

Goldman sighed. 'Ah, it's the sedentary life! I freely admit it. All day long spent sharpening quills for pens, pens, pens . . . No sooner do I empty one basket of wing feathers than that wretched hunchback porter delivers another. Small wonder he's a hunchback! I really ought to be out in the woods or the marshes shooting geese and teal and woodcock. That's what I wanted to be, you know? A hunter out in the open air.'

'So you've told me.' Peterkin was lunching on broiled hazel-hen with jam. However, each evening—rain, snow, or shine—he made sure to take a five-mile constitutional walk, armed with a sketchbook as witness to his former hopes; rather as a mother chimp might tote her dead baby around until it started to stink.

Peterkin was handsome where his friend was pretty. Slim, blond, steely-eyed, and with noble features. Yet all for what? Here in the secret police building he mostly met frumps or frigid functionaries. The foxy females were bait for foreign diplomats and businessmen. Out on the streets, whores were garishly painted—do-it-yourself style. Slash lips, cheeks rouged like stop-lights, bruised eyes. Under the evening street lamps those ladies of the night looked so lurid to Peterkin.

Excellent food a-plenty was on offer to the secret servants of the State such as he. Goose with apples, breaded mutton chops, shashlik on skewers, steamed sturgeon. Yet whereabouts in his life were the soubrettes and odalisques and gorgeous inamoratas? Without whom, how could he really sate himself?

'So how are the, um, projections?' Goldman asked idly.

'Usual thing, old son. I'm busy using Cassini's method. Distances along the central meridian are true to scale. But all other meridian lines stretch the distances. That makes Cassini's projection fine for big countries that spread from north to south. Of course ours sprawls from east to west. Ha! Across a few thousand miles that's quite enough distortion for an enemy missile to miss a silo by miles.'

'Those geese and turkeys gave their wings to shelter us! Gratifying to know that I'm carving patriotic pens.'

'I wonder,' Peterkin murmured, 'whether amongst our enemies I have some exact counterpart whose job is to deduce which projections I'm using to distort different areas of land . . .'

Goldman leaned closer. 'I heard a rumour. My boss Andrey was talking to Antipin. Andrey was projecting *the future*. Seems that things are going to change. Seems, for the sake of openness, that we'll be publishing true maps sooner or later.'

Peterkin chuckled. This outlook seemed as absurd as that he himself might ever become a member of the Academy of Arts.

Yet that very same evening Peterkin saw the woman of his desires.

He had stepped out along Krasny Avenue and turned down Zimoy Prospekt to enter the park. It was only early September, so the ice-skating rink was still a lake dotted with ducks: fat quacking boats laden with potential pens, pens, pens. The air was warm, and a lone kiosk sold chocolate ice creams to strollers; one of whom was her.

She was small and pert, with eyes that were brimming china inkwells, irises of darkest brown. Her curly, coal-black hair—not unlike friend Goldman's in fact—made a corona of sheer, glossy darkness, a photographic negative of the sun in eclipse; the sun itself being her round, tanned, softly-contoured face. From the moment Peterkin saw her, that woman suggested a sensuality bottled up and distilled within her—the possibility of love, lust, inspiration, nourishment. She was a liqueur of a lady. She was caviar, licking a chocolate cornet.

Her clothes were routine: cheaply styled bootees and an open raincoat revealing a blotchy floral dress. Yet Peterkin felt such a suction towards her, such a powerful current flowing in her direction.

She glanced at him and shrugged with what seemed a mixture of resignation and bitter amusement. So he followed her out of the park, across the prospekt, into a maze of minor streets which became increasingly unfamiliar.

Some empty stalls stood deserted in a square which must serve as a market place, so he realized that he was beginning to tread 'dead ground', that unacknowledged portion of the city which did not figure on any plans. If inspectors approached by car they would be hard put to find these selfsame streets. One-way and no-entry signs would redirect them away. Such was the essence of this district; impenetrability was the key that locked it up safely out of sight.

Of course, if those same inspectors came on foot with illicit purposes in mind—hoping to buy a kilo of bananas, a rare spare part for a washing machine, or a foreign pornography magazine—they could be in luck.

Subsequently they wouldn't be able to report where they had been with any clarity.

The moan of a saxophone assailed Peterkin's ears; a jazz club was nearby. Rowdy laughter issued from a restaurant where the drapes were drawn; he judged that a heavy drinking bout was in progress.

A sign announced Polnoch Place. He had never heard of it. How the sky had darkened, as if in passing from street to street he had been forging hour by hour deeper towards midnight. At last the woman halted under a bright street lamp, her ice cream quite consumed, and waited for him, so unlike the ill-painted floozies of more public thoroughfares.

He cleared his throat. 'I must apologize for following you in this fashion, but, well—' Should he mention voluptuous canvasses? He flourished his sketchbook lamely.

'What else could you do?' she asked. 'You're attracted to me magnetically. Our auras resonate. I was aware of it.'

'Our auras—?'

'Our vibrations.' She stated this as a fact.

'Are you psychic? Are you a medium?'

'A medium? Oh yes, you might say so. Definitely! A conduit, a channel, a guide. How else could you have strayed so far into this territory except in my footsteps?'

Peterkin glanced around him at strange façades.

'I've heard it said . . . Are there really two countries side by side—one where the secret police hold sway, and a whole other land which is simply *secret?* Not just a few little dead zones—but whole swathes of hidden terrain projecting from those zones?'

'Why, of course! When human beings yearn long enough to be some place else, then that somewhere can come into being. Imagine an hourglass; that's the sort of shape the world has. People can drift through like grains of sand—though only so far. There's a kind of population pressure that rebuffs intruders. For the second world gives rise not only to its own geography, but also to its own inhabitants.'

'Has anyone mapped this other terrain?'

'Is that what you do, draw maps?' Her hair, under the streetlamp! Her face, like a lamp itself unto him!

His job was a state secret. Yet this woman couldn't possibly be an 'eye' of the police, trying to trap him.

'Oh yes, I draw maps,' he told her.

'Ah, that makes it more difficult for you to come here.'

'Of course not. Don't you realize? Our maps are all lies! Deliberate lies, distortions. In the department of cartography our main brief is to warp the true shape of our country in all sorts of subtle ways.'

'Ah?' She sounded unsurprised. 'Where I come from, artists map the country with kaleidoscopes of colour. Musicians map it in a symphony. Poets, in a sonnet.'

It came to Peterkin that in this other land he could at last be the painter of his desires. He had never believed in psychic phenomena or in a spirit world (unless, perhaps, it was the world of ninety-proof spirit). Yet this circumstance was different. The woman spoke of a *material* other world—extending far beyond the dead ground of the city. Peterkin knew that he must possess this woman as the key to all his hopes, the portal to a different existence.

'So do you despise your work?' she asked him.

'Yes! Yes!'

She smiled invitingly—and wryly, as though he had already disappointed her.

'My name's Masha.'

Her room was richly furnished with rugs from Central Asia, silverware, onyx statuettes, ivory carvings. Was she some black marketeer in art treasures or the mistress of one? Had he stumbled upon a cache hidden since the Revolution? Curtains were woven through with threads of gold. Matching brocade cloaked the bed in a filigree till she drew back the cover, disclosing silk sheets as blue as the clearest summer sky. Her cheap dress, which she shed without further ado, uncovered sleek creamy satin camiknickers... which she also peeled off carelessly.

'Take fright and run away, Peterkin,' she teased. 'Take fright now!'

'Run away from *you?*'

'That might be best.'

'What should frighten me?'

'You'll see.'

'I'm seeing!' Oh her body. Oh his, a-quiver, arrow notched and tense to fly into her. He laughed. 'I hardly think I'm impotent.'

'Even so.' She lay back upon the blue silk sheets.

Yet as soon as he started to stroke her limbs . . .

At first he thought absurdly that Masha had concealed an inflatable device within her person: a dildo-doll made of toughest gossamer so as to fold up as small as a thumb yet expand into a balloon with the dimensions of a man. This she had liberated and inflated suddenly as a barrier, thrusting Peterkin aside . . .

What, powered by a cartridge of compressed air? How risky! What if the cartridge sprang a leak or exploded? What if the compressed air blew the wrong way?

The intruder had flowed from Masha in a flood—from her open and inviting legs. It had gushed out cloudily, spilling from her like pints and pints of leaking semen congealing into a body of firm white jelly.

He gagged, in shock.

'Wh—what—'

'It's ectoplasm,' she said.

'Ectoplasm—'

Yes, he had heard of ectoplasm: the strange fluidic emanation that supposedly pours out of a psychic's nostrils or ears or mouth, an amorphous milk that takes on bodily form and a kind of solidity. It came from her vagina.

Pah! Flimflammery! Puffs of smoke and muslin suspended on strings. Soft lighting, a touch of hypnosis and autosuggestion. Of course, of course. Went without saying.

Except . . .

What now lay between them could be none other than an ectoplasmic body. A guard dog lurked in Masha's kennel. A eunuch slept at her door. She wore a chastity belt in the shape of a blanched, clinging phantom. Peterkin studied the thing that separated them. He poked it, and it quivered. It adhered to Masha, connected by . . .

'Don't try to pull it away,' she warned. 'You can't. It will only go back inside when my excitement ebbs.'

And still he desired her, perhaps even more so. He ached.

'You're still excited?' he asked her.

'Oh yes.'

'Does this . . . creature . . . give you any satisfaction?'

'None at all.'

'Did a witch curse you, Masha? Or a magician? Do such persons live in your country?' Perhaps Masha belonged to somebody powerful who had cast a spell upon her as an insurance policy for those times when she crossed the in-between zone to such places as the park. If composers could map that other land with their concerti, or painters with their palettes, why not other varieties of magic too?

She peered around the white shoulder of the manifestation. 'Don't you see, Peterkin? It's you. It's the template for you, the mould.'

What did she mean? He too peered at the smooth suggestion of noble features. His ghost was enjoying—no, certainly not even enjoying!—Masha. His ghost simply intervened, another wretched obstacle to joy. A twitching lump, a body equipped with a nervous system but lacking any mind or thoughts.

'And yet,' she hinted, 'there's a way to enter my country. A medium is a bridge, a doorway. Not to any spirit-world, oh no. But to: that other existence.'

'Show me the way.'

'Are you quite sure?'

How he ached. 'Yes, Masha. Yes. I must enter.'

As his thoughts and memories flowed freely—of old desires, of canvases never painted and bodies never seen, of stuffed dumplings and skewered lamb and interminable cartographic projections—so he sensed a shift in his personal centre of gravity, in his prime meridian. He felt at once much closer to Masha, and anaesthetized, robbed of sensation.

His body was moving; it was rolling over on the bed, flexing its arms and legs—no longer his own body to command. Equipped with the map of his memories, the ghost had taken charge.

Now the ghost was making Peterkin's body stand up and put on his clothes; while he—his kernel, his soul—clung against Masha silently.

That body which had been his was opening and shutting its mouth, uttering noises. Words.

'You go along Polnoch Place—' Masha gave directions and instructions; Peterkin couldn't follow them.

He himself was shrinking. Already he was the size of a child. Soon, of a baby. As an Arabian genie dwindles, tapering down in a stream of smoke into a little bottle, so now he was entering Masha.

'I shall be born again, shan't I?' he cried out. 'Once you've smuggled me over the border deep into the other country, inside of you?' Unfortunately he couldn't hear so much as a mewling whimper from what little of him remained outside of her. All he heard, distantly, was a door bang shut as the phantom left Masha's room.

Warm darkness embraced his dissolved, suspended existence.

Only at the last moment did he appreciate the worries of the persons in that other, free domain—who had been forced into existence by the frustrations of reality and who depended for their vitality upon a lie, which might soon be erased. They, the free, were fighting for the perpetuation of falsehood. Peterkin had been abducted so that a wholly obedient servant might be substituted in his place in the cartography department of the secret police.

Only at the last moment, as he fell asleep—in order that his phantom could become more conscious—did he understand why Masha had trapped him.

PART THREE: THE CULT OF THE EGG

Church bells were ringing out across the city in celebration, *clong-dong-clangle*. The great edifice on Dzerzhinsky Square was almost deserted with the exception of bored guards patrolling corridors. In the mahogany-panelled office of the head of the directorate of censorship, General Mirov rubbed his rubicund boozer's nose as if an itch was aflame.

'How soon can we hope to have an accurate Great Atlas?' he demanded sourly. 'That's what *I'm* being asked.'

Not right at the moment, however. The six black telephones on his vast oak desk all stood silently.

Valentin blinked. 'As you know, Comrade General, Grusha's disappearance hasn't exactly speeded the task. All the damned questioning, the interruptions. Myself and my staff being bothered at our work as though we are murderers.'

The ceiling was high and ornately plastered, the windows taller than a man. A gilt-framed portrait of Felix Dzerzhinsky, architect of terror, watched rapaciously.

'If,' said Mirov, 'a newly appointed deputy-chief cartographer—of reformist ambitions, and heartily resented because of those, mark my words—if she vanishes so inexplicably, are you surprised that there's a certain odour of rats in your offices? Are you astonished that her well-connected parents press for the most thorough investigation?'

Valentin nodded towards the nobly handsome young man who stood expressionlessly in front of one of the embroidered sofas.

'I'll swear that Peterkin here has undergone a personality fluctuation because of all the turmoil.'

Clangle, dong, clong. Like some mechanical figure heeding the peel of a carillon, Peterkin took three paces forward across the oriental carpet.

'Ah,' said Mirov, 'so are we attempting to clear up the matter of Grusha's possible murder hygienically in private? Between the three of us? How maternal of you, Colonel! You shelter the members of your staff just like a mother hen.' The general's gaze drifted to the intruding object on his desk, and he frowned irritably. 'Things have changed. Can't you understand? I cannot suppress the investigation.'

'No, no, no,' broke in Valentin. 'Peterkin used to be a bit of a dreamer. Now he's a demon for work. That's all I meant. Well, a demon for the old sort of work, not for cartographic revisionism . . .' As if realizing that under present circumstances this might hardly be construed as an endorsement, Valentin shrugged.

'Is that *thing* supposed to be a sample of his most recent work?' The general's finger stabbed accusingly towards the decorated egg which rested on his blotting paper, geometrically embellished in black and ochre and yellow. 'Reminds me of some tourist souvenir on sale in a foetid East African street. Some barbaric painted gourd.'

'Sir,' said Peterkin, 'it is executed in Carpathian *pysanka* style.'

'You don't say?' The general brought his fist down upon the painted egg, crushing the shell, splitting the boiled white flesh within. 'Thus I execute it. In any case, Easter is months away.'

'You're unhappy about all these new reforms, aren't you, Comrade General?' Valentin asked cautiously. 'I mean, *deeply* unhappy. You hope to retire honourably, yet what sort of world will you retire into?'

'One where I can hope to gather mushrooms in the woods to my heart's content, if you really wish to know.'

'Ah, but will you be allowed such tranquillity? Won't all manner of dark cupboards be opened?'

'I'm busy opening those cupboards,' snapped Mirov. 'As quickly as can be. Absurdist plays, concrete poems, abstract art, economic critiques . . . We scurry to grease their publication, do we not? Grow faster, trees, grow faster! We need your pulp. Bah! I'm somewhat impeded by the sloth of your department of cartography. I demand true maps, as soon as can be.' With a cupped hand he swept the mess of broken boiled egg into a trash basket.

'Those dark cupboards also contain corpses,' hinted Valentin.

'For which, you imply, I may one day be brought to book?'

'Well, you certainly oughtn't ever to write your memoirs.'

'You're being impertinent, Valentin. Insubordinate in front of a subordinate.' The general laughed barkingly. 'Though I suppose you're right. The world's shifting more swiftly than I imagined possible.'

'We aren't safe here, in this world that's a-coming.'

The bells continued to ring out cacophonously and triumphantly as if attempting to crack a somewhat leaden sky, to let through rifts of clear blue.

Peterkin spoke dreamily. 'The egg celebrates the mysteries of birth and death and reawakening. Simon of Cyrene, the egg merchant, helped Jesus to carry his cross. Upon Simon's return he found to his astonishment that all the eggs in his basket had been coloured with many hues.'

'I'll bet he was astonished!' said Mirov sarcastically. 'There goes any hope of selling my nice white eggs! Must I really listen to the warblings of this tinpot Dostoevsky? Has the cartography department taken leave of its senses, Colonel? Oh I see what you mean about Comrade Peterkin's personality. But why do you bother me with such nonsense? I was hoping to catch up on some paperwork this morning and forget about the damned—'

'Ding-dong of rebirth in our land?'

'Carl Fabergé made his first imperial Easter egg for the Tsar and Tsaritsa just over a century ago,' said Peterkin.

'Please excuse his circuitous approach to the meat of the matter, General,' begged Valentin. 'Almost as if he is circumnavigating an egg? I promise he will arrive there sooner or later.'

'An egg is like a globe,' Peterkin continued. 'The department of cartography has never designed globes of the world.'

'The world isn't shaped like an egg!' objected Mirov, his cracked veins flushing brighter.

'With respect, it is, Comrade General,' murmured Valentin. 'It's somewhat oblate . . . Continue, Peterkin!'

'Fabergé cast his eggs from precious metals. He inlaid them with enamelling, he encrusted them with jewels. He even kept a special hammer by him to destroy any whose craftsmanship fell short of his own flawless standards.'

'What is this drivel about the Tsar and Tsaritsa?' exploded Mirov. 'Are you preaching counter-revolution? A return to those days of jewelled eggs for the aristocracy and poverty for the masses? Or is this a metaphor? Are you advocating a *putsch* against the reformers?'

'Traditions continue,' Peterkin said vaguely.

'Yes,' agreed Valentin. 'We are the descendants of the secret police of the imperial empire, are we not? Of its censors; of its patriots.'

'Bah!'

Peterkin cleared his throat. He seemed impervious to the general's displeasure. 'The craft of decorating eggs in the imperial style continues . . . in the dead ground of this very city.'

'Dead ground?'

'That's a discovery some of us have made,' explained Valentin. He gestured vaguely through a window, to somewhere beyond the onion domes. 'The wholesale falsification of maps produces, well, actual *false places*—which a person in the right frame of mind can genuinely reach. Peterkin here has found such places, haven't you, hmm? As have I.'

Peterkin nodded jerkily like a marionette on strings.

'You're both drunk,' said Mirov. 'Go away.'

'I can prove this, General. Comrade Grusha strayed into one of those places. She was following me, acting as an amateur sleuth. Ah, the new generation are all such amateurs compared to us! Now she haunts that place because she lacks the cast of mind that I possess—and you too, General.'

'What might that be?'

'An instinct for falsification; for the masking of reality.'

'I'm charmed at your compliment.'

'You'd be even more charmed if you came with me to visit my darling young mistress Koshka who lives in such a place.'

One ageing man regarded the other quizzically. '*You*, Valentin? A young mistress? Excuse me if I'm sceptical.'

'You might say that such a visit is a rejuvenating experience.'

Mirov nodded, misunderstanding. 'A youthful mistress might well be as invigorating as monkey glands. Along with being heart attack territory.'

'To enter the dead ground is rejuvenating; you'll see, you'll see. That's one frontier worth safeguarding—the border between the real and the ideal. Perhaps you've heard of the legend of the secret valley of Shangri-La? The place that features on no map? To enter it properly, a man must be transformed.'

'That's where the egg crafters come into this,' prompted Peterkin.

'*Internal exile*, General! Let me propose a whole new meaning for that phrase. Let me invite you to share this refuge.'

'You insist that Comrade Grusha's still alive?'

'Oh yes. She walks by my Koshka's apartment at nights.'

'So where does she go to by day?'

'I suspect that it's always night for her. Otherwise she might spy some escape route, come back here, stir up more trouble . . .'

'Are you telling me, Colonel Valentin, that some zone of aberrant geometry exists in our city? Some other dimension to existence? I don't mean the one advertised by those wretched bells.'

'Exactly. Just so.'

Mirov stared at the portrait of Dzerzhinsky, who would have answered such an eccentric proposition with a bullet, and sucked in his breath.

'I shall indulge you, Colonel—for old time's sake, I'm tempted to say—if only to study a unique form of psychosis which seems to be affecting our department of cartography.'

'It's best to go in the evening, as the shadows draw in.'

'It would be.'

'On foot.'

'Of course.'

'With no bodyguard.'

'Be warned, I shall be armed.'

'Why not, General? Why ever not?'

But Peterkin smirked.

So that same evening the three men went by way of certain half-frequented routes, via this side street and that alley and that square until the hollow raving of the bells was muffled, till distant traffic only purred like several sleepy kittens, and a lone owl hooted from an old-fashioned cemetery amidst century-old apartment blocks.

As if playing the role of some discreet pimp, Peterkin indicated a door. 'Gentlemen, we shall now visit a lady.'

Mirov guffawed. 'This mistress of yours, Colonel: is she by any chance a mistress to many?'

'My Koshka lives further away,' said Valentin, 'not here. Absolutely not here. Yet don't you already feel a new spring in your gait? Don't you sense the weight of years lifting from your shoulders?'

'I admit I do feel somewhat sprightly,' agreed the general. 'Hot-blooded. Ripe for adventure. Ah, it's years since . . . Valentin, you look like a younger man.' He rubbed his hands. 'Ah, the spice of anticipation! How it converts tired old mutton into lamb.'

Peterkin admitted them into a large foyer lit by a single low-powered light bulb and decorated by several large vases of dried, dusty roses in bud. A faint memory of musky aroma lingered, due perhaps to a sprinkle of essential oils. A creaky elevator lifted them slowly to the third floor, its cables twanging dolorously once or twice like the strings of a double bass. Valentin found himself whistling a lively theme from an opera by Prokofiev—so softly he sounded as though he was actually labouring up marble stairs, puffing.

The dark petite young woman who admitted these three visitors to her apartment was not alone. Mirov slapped the reassuring bulge of his gun, as if to stun a fly, before relaxing. The other two occupants were also women, who wore similar cheap dresses patterned with roses, orchids, their lips and cheeks rouged.

'May I present Masha?' Having performed this introduction, Peterkin slackened; he stood limply like a neglected doll.

'This is my older sister Tanya,' Masha explained. Masha's elder image smiled. If the younger sister was enticingly lovely, Tanya was the matured vintage, an intoxicating queen.

'And my aunt Anastasia.' A plumper, far from frumpish version, in her middle forties, a twinkle in her eye, her neck strung with large phoney pearls. Absurdly, the aunt curtsied, plucking up the hem of her dress quite high enough to display a dimpled thigh for a moment.

'We are chief Eggers,' said Anastasia. 'Tanya and I represent the Guild of Imperial Eggs.'

The large room, replete with rugs from Tashkent and Bokhara hanging on the walls, with curtains woven with thread of gold, housed a substantial carved bed spread with brocade, almost large enough for two couples entwined together, though hardly for three. All approaches to it were, however, blocked by at least a score of tall, narrow, round-topped tables, each of which served as a dais to display a decorated egg, or two, or three. Some ostrich, some goose, others pullet and even smaller, perhaps even the eggs of canaries.

On gilt or silver stands, shaped as swans, as chariots, as goblets, these eggs were intricately cut and hinged, in trefoil style, gothic style, scallop style. Some lids were lattices. Filigree windows held only spiders' webs of connective shell. Petals of shell hung down on the thinnest of silver chains. Pearl-studded drawers jutted. Doors opened upon grottos where tiny porcelain cherubs perched pertly. Seed pearls, lace, gold braid, jewels trimmed the doorways. Interior linings were of velvet . . .

To blunder towards that bed in the heat of passion would be to wreak devastation more shattering than Carl Fabergé could ever have inflicted on a faulty golden egg with a hammer! What a fragile cordon defended that bedspread and the hint of blue silk sheets; yet to trespass would be to assassinate art—if those eggs were properly speaking the products of art, rather than of an obsessional delirium which had transfigured commonplace ovoids of calcium, former homes of bird embryos and yolk and albumen.

Aunt Anastasia waved at a bureau loaded with egging equipment: pots of seed pearls, jewels, ribbons, diamond dust, cords of silk gimp, corsage pins, clasps, toothpicks, emery boards, a sharp little knife, a tiny saw, manicure scissors, glue, nail varnish, and sharp pencils. The general rubbed his eyes. For a moment did he think he had seen jars of beetles, strings of poisonous toadstools, handcuffs made of cord, the accoutrements of a witch in some fable?

'Aren't we just birds of a feather?' she asked the colonel. 'You use the quills of birds for mapping-pens, so I hear. We use the eggs of the birds.'

'I've rarely seen anything quite so ridiculous,' Mirov broke in. 'Your eggs are gimcrack mockeries of Tsarist treasures. Petit bourgeois counterfeits!'

'Exactly,' agreed queenly Tanya. 'Did not some financier once say that bad money drives out good? Let's suppose that falsity is superior to reality. Did *you* not try to make it so? Did you not succeed formerly? Ah, but in the dialectical process the false gives rise in turn to a *hidden truth*. The map of lies leads to a secret domain. The egg that apes treasure shows the way towards the true treasury.'

Tanya picked up a pearl-studded goose egg. Its one oval door was closed. The egg was like some alien space-pod equipped with a hatch. Inserting a fingernail, she prised this open and held the egg out for Mirov's inspection.

On the whole inner surface of that goose egg—the inside of the door included—was a map of the whole world, of all the continents in considerable detail. The difference between the shape of the egg and that of a planetary globe caused some distortion, though by no means grotesquely so. Mirov squinted within, impressed despite himself.

'How on earth did you work within such a cramped volume? By using a dentist's mirror, and miniature nibs held in tweezers? Or . . . did you draw upon the outside and somehow the pattern sank through?'

'Somehow?' Tanya chuckled. 'We *dreamed* the map into the egg, General, just as you dreamed us into existence by means of your lies—though unintentionally!'

She selected another closed egg and opened its door.

'Here's the map of our country . . . Ours, mark you, not yours. If you take this egg as your guide, our country can be yours too. You can enter and leave as you desire.'

'Be careful you don't break your egg.' Aunt Anastasia wagged a warning finger.

'The same way you broke the *pysanka* egg,' squeaked Peterkin, emerging briefly from his immobility and muteness. 'Most of those eggs are technical exercises—not the one you hold.' (For Mirov had accepted the egg.) 'That was dreamed deep within the other country.' Having spoken like a ventriloquist's dummy, Peterkin became inert again.

However, he left along with his two superiors—presently, by which time it was fully night.

'Maps, dreamed on to the insides of eggs! Deep in some zone of absurd topography!' Mirov snorted. 'Your escape hatch is preposterous,' he told Valentin, pausing under a streetlamp.

'Actually, with respect, we aren't *deep* in the zone at all. Oh no, not here. But that egg can guide—'

'Do you believe in it, you dupe?'

'Why didn't I receive one for my own? I suppose because I already know the way to Koshka's place . . .'

Mirov snapped his fingers. 'I know how the trick's done. They use transfers. They draw the map on several pieces of paper, wet those so they're sticky, then insert them with tweezers on to the inside of the shell. When that dries, they use tiny bent brushes to apply varnish.'

Mirov removed the map-egg from his overcoat pocket, knelt, and placed the egg on the pavement under the brightness of the streetlamp. Was he surprised by the limber flexibility of his joints?

'I can prove it.' Producing his pistol, Mirov transferred his grip to the barrel, poising the handle above the pearl-studded shell. 'I'll peel those transfers loose from the broken bits. Ha, dreams indeed!'

'Don't,' said Peterkin in a lame voice only likely to encourage Mirov.

'Don't be a fool,' said Valentin.

'A fool, is it, Comrade Colonel?'

'If you're told not to open a door and you insist on opening it—'

'Disaster ensues—supposing that you're a child in a fable.'

Valentin knelt too, to beg the general to desist. To an onlooker the two men might have appeared to be fellow worshippers adoring a fetish object on the paving slab, cultists of the egg indeed.

When Mirov brought the butt of the gun down, cracking the egg wide open and sending tiny pearls rolling like spilled barley, a shock seemed to ripple along the street and upward to the very stars, which trembled above the city.

Although Mirov probed and pried, in no way could he discover or peel loose any stiffly varnished paper transfers.

When the two sprightly oldsters looked around again, Peterkin had slipped away without a word. The two men scrambled up. Night, and strange streets, had swallowed their escort utterly. Despite Valentin's protests—which even led the men to tussle briefly—Mirov ground the shards of egg to dust under his heel, as if thereby he might obliterate any connection with himself.

Eventually, lost, they walked into a birchwood where mushrooms swelled through the humus in the moonlight. An owl hooted. Weasels chased mice. Was this woodland merely a park within the city? It hardly seemed so; yet by then the answer scarcely mattered, since they were having great difficulty remembering who they were, let alone where they were. Already they'd been obliged a number of times to roll up their floppy trouser legs and cinch their belts tighter. Their sleeves dangled loosely, their shoes were clumsy boats, while their overcoats dragged as long cloaks upon the ground.

'Kashka? Kishka? Was that her name? What *was* her name?' Valentin asked his friend.

'I think her name was Grusha . . . no, Masha.'

'*Wasn't.*'

'*Was.*'

Briefly they quarrelled, till they forgot who they were talking about.

Through the trees, they spied the lights of a village which strongly suggested home. Descending a birch-clad slope awkwardly in their oversized garments—two lads dressed as men for a lark—they arrived at a yellow window and peered through.

Beautiful Tanya and Aunt Anastasia were singing to two huge eggs resting on a rug. Eggs the size of the fattest plucked turkeys, decorated with strange ochre zig-zags.

Even as Valentin and Mirov watched, the ends of the eggs opened on brass hinges. From each a bare arm emerged, followed by a head and a bare shoulder. The two women each grasped a groping hand and hauled. From out of each egg slowly squeezed the naked body of a man well past his prime, one with a beet-red face, though his trunk was white as snow.

'How did they fit inside those?' Mirov asked Valentin.

'Dunno. Came out, didn't they? Maybe there's more space than shows on the outside . . .'

The two newly-hatched men—who were no spring chickens—were now huddling together on a rug by the stove, modestly covering their loins with their hands. Their faces looked teasingly familiar, as if the men might be a pair of . . . long-lost uncles, come home at last from Siberia.

By now the two boys felt cold and hungry, so they knocked on the cottage door. Aunt Anastasia opened it.

'Ah, here come the clothes now!' Anastasia pulled them both inside into the warmth and surveyed them critically. 'Oh what a mess you've made of those suits. Creases, and mud. Never mind. They'll sponge, and iron. Off with them now, you two, off with them. They're needed. Tanya, fetch a couple of blankets for the boys. We mustn't make them blush, with a chill or with shame.'

'Do we have to sleep inside those eggs?' asked Mirov, almost stammering.

'Of course not, silly goose! You'll sleep over the stove in a blanket. Those two other fellows will be gone by the morning; then you'll have a better idea who you both are.'

'Koshka!' exclaimed Valentin. 'I remember. *That* was her name.'

'Now, now,' his aunt said, 'you needn't be thinking about girls for a year or two yet. Anyway, there's Natasha in the village, and Maria. I've kept my eye on them for you two. How about some thick bacon broth with a sprinkle of something special in it to help you have nice dreams?'

'Please!' piped Valentin.

When he and his brother woke in the morning a lovely aroma greeted them—of butter melting on two bowls of cooked buckwheat groats. The boys only wondered for the briefest while where they had been the evening before.

Tanya and Anastasia had already breakfasted, and were busy sawing ducks' eggs.

The Eye of the Ayatollah

THREE YEARS EARLIER ALI LOST HIS RIGHT EYE AND PART OF HIS face during one of the battles against Iraq. Which battle? Where? He didn't know. His cloaked, hood-clad mother had joyfully seen him off en route to paradise on the back of a fume-coughing truck packed with trainee revolutionary guards, all of about his own age, which was sixteen. Blood from Mother's finger adorned his forehead; she had cut herself deep with a kitchen knife.

What did Mother look like? Almond eyes, broad nose, big creamy cheeks, generous lips. The only time Ali ever saw more of her body was briefly when he was born, an incident which he neither understood at the time nor subsequently remembered. Her blood on his forehead was sacramental.

The truck drove all day and all night through dust—towards, latterly, the dawning thud and *crump* of heavy artillery. The recruits chanted and sang themselves hoarse and prayed for death, the door to paradise.

Arriving at a shattered moonscape masked by smoke, Ali and his companions were issued with hand grenades and sent out across a mine-field in the direction of the thunder. Ahead, a torrent of boulders could have been tumbling from the sky—as though here he stepped close to the very heart-beat of God, the compassionate, the merciful. The land-mine which blew his neighbour apart, arms and legs flying separately in the direction of heaven, tore off the side of Ali's face.

The next few weeks were nebulous for Ali. He himself existed inside a black, mute thunder-cloud occasionally riven by the red lightning of pain. Finally the crowded hospital released him, since he could walk and his mattress was needed; and hidden Mother welcomed half a martyr home. Neighbours admired Ali's scars and the remains of his empty eye socket.

Yet the war ended inconclusively.

Ali often visited the Fountain of Blood downtown to gape at the plumes of red-dyed water spurting as though from severed arteries. Part of a host half a million strong, he screamed for the death of the Satan-author, blasphemous apostate lurking in that Western devil-land.

Yet it wasn't the Satan-author who died; it was the Ayatollah, father of truth, beloved of God, the merciful, the compassionate.

Grief racked Ali, grief wrenched a million hearts, five million. Ali burrowed like a mole through the dense conglomerate of one of the hugest crowds in history, millions of pebbles of flesh cemented by the sand of rageful sorrow—through into the Beshte Zahar Cemetery. No, not so much cemented as surging, *churning* like the ballast and cement and liquid in some giant, horizontal concrete-mixer. Fainting, shrieking, reaching, clawing, crazed with bitter woe: a million locusts, and only one leaf to feed at—the coffin, soon to arrive. He fought his way into the inner square built of freight containers. Thousands of mourners were beating their heads with their fists in unison. Mystics were harvesting bowls of earth from the bottom of the grave, and passing these out—the crowd ate the precious soil.

A helicopter landed. Moments later, a tumult of young men hauled the shrouded body from its coffin. Hands tore the shroud to pieces, each scrap a precious relic. 'Ya Ali, Ya Hussein,' cried ten thousand voices. The thin white legs of the holy man jutted aloft like bare sticks, as his corpse slumped.

Ali, clawing, was in the forefront but his defective vision foxed him. As he fought his way to the rear through the tide of bodies he puzzled at what his right hand clutched, something resembling a slippery ping-pong ball. Panting, he paused long enough to glance. His palm cupped a glazed, naked eye. With a tail of optic nerve: a kind of plump, ocular tadpole.

Had a miracle happened? Had a piece of the shroud transmuted itself into Ali's own lost eye, now restored to him? Was he not himself named in honour of the martyr Ali, who founded the true school of Islam?

At last his brain caught up with what his fingers and their nails had done: he, Ali the half-faced, had torn out one of the Ayatollah's eyes.

Behind him, shots rang out. The helicopter landed once more . . .

Later, Ali heard how the corpse eventually entered its hole in the ground, to be covered by flagstones heaved hand over hand, and how a dozen of the cargo containers were piled across the grave. No one would or could say what state the body had been in finally.

The eye sat on a shelf by Ali's bed, staring unblinkingly at him. (For, lacking eyelids, how could an eye blink?) Its gaze appeared to track him about the little room, the pupil stretching into a squint to follow him.

Ali prayed. He thought about preservatives. He wondered what best to do. How could he possibly plunge that holy eye into alcohol even of the medicinal variety? So he visited a pharmacy to ask advice about—so he said—pickling a dead frog; he returned with a jar of formalin. Once afloat in that solution of formaldehyde, the eyeball definitely swung from side to side keeping an eye on him.

On *him*, on mere Ali the half-face? Oh no. Simply alert, awaiting, on the look-out. Ali prayed. Ali dreamed. A vision visited him. The holy man had been a hawk. What was that hawk's eye hunting for? Why, it was surveying all of the Earth, searching for the hiding place of the Satan-author.

Events deployed as the will of God decreed. Truly dreams were troubled in Tehran during those days. Angels guided Ali to the office of Dr Omar Hafiz, doyen of the country's ballistic missile programme, who for his part had dreamt originally of exploding a nuclear weapon on Tel Aviv to free the Palestinians. Those high-explosive birds aimed at Baghdad were a side-show. Alas, lack of a warhead derailed the project. So next, Dr Hafiz dreamed of a reconnaissance satellite to spy on Iraqi army positions; but peace had been declared. Lately Hafiz dreamt of using the prototype rocket to put a communications satellite into orbit to criss-cross the whole face of the Earth: the *Voice of God*, broadcasting the

Truth . . .

An angel had also visited Dr Hafiz.

'We *can* fly your hawk,' he assured Ali. 'The cold of space will preserve the eye from corruption. It will look down on Europe, America, Africa. That Satan-author may have hidden anywhere. He may have bought plastic surgery. The eye will find him. With its miraculous perception it will recognize him. He is what it seeks; for fifty years, if need be.'

'And I, the half-face,' said Ali, 'need to be on hand when our hawk finds its prey, do I not? For the eye was given into my hand, was it not?'

Events unfolded like a fragrant rose from a bud. Surgeons renovated Ali's face, rebuilt his orbital bone, gave him a glass eye. Tutors nurtured his smattering of English and French into something resembling fluency. Commandos offered him the sort of weapons training he'd sorely lacked when he rode to war. His forged passport identified him as a naturalized Australian.

Soon his country launched its first earth satellite named the *Eye of the Ayatollah*, and announced to the world (as well as to the Satan-author, wherever he was) that the orbiting instrument package did indeed contain exactly that. Benighted infidels outside the harbour of Islam laughed—uneasily. Corrupted souls within the harbour of Islam glanced askance at the night sky.

No one beyond the inner hierarchy knew the whole truth about Ali. Whenever Ali shut his left eye, he looked down through his artificial eye upon the countries of the earth from space. For his glass eye was more than a bauble. Through it, miraculously, the youth could see whatever the holy man's searching eye could see through the zoom-lenses of the satellite; as had been promised in the vision confided to Dr Hafiz . . .

In the cold void above the topmost air, the *Eye of the Ayatollah* orbited for a year, two years, five years . . . Disguised as a dinkum Aussie immigrant on holiday, Ali wandered the world as frugally as he could, financed by an American Express gold card. Universally acceptable; he still regretted the expedient.

The orbiting eye seemed to twitch as it was passing over Pakistan, and there went Ali; a solar flare must have been responsible. Again, over Nicaragua, it spasmed; thus Ali went to that strife-torn land. Perhaps a cosmic ray had hit the eye.

He found himself in Sweden, in Ireland, in America, England, France. Always keeping watch. From his hiding place the Satan-author published another book, redoubling Ali's fervour.

Seven years passed. The eye watched. Ali watched.

At long last the eye throbbed. It was gazing down upon an island off the south-west coast of Scotland; upon a tiny isle that nestled against a bay of its parent island like a newborn baby whale beside its leviathan of a mother. The eye passed over, but not before imprinting Ali vividly.

He flew to London, collected a gun and grenades from a certain embassy, and caught a train to Glasgow.

He would need to wait there for some weeks till the satellite would be poised to pass over the same part of Scotland again. Buying maps and guides, he soon learned that the name of the mother island was Arran, and of the islet: Holy Island, a title which set his teeth on edge.

As the time approached, Ali took a bus to the coast then a ferry to Arran. Renting a modest car, he reconnoitred this pinnacled island of granite bens and fells, glens of bracken and frisky streams rushing amidst great boulders, mounds of moraine, dark conifers, and wild red deer—suddenly giving way in the south to rolling heathery hills, calm pastures, sandy beaches with a few palm trees.

Ali checked in to a hotel in the small seaside town of Lamlash opposite Holy Island. He had brought a hammer, and was pretending to be an enthusiastic amateur geologist. Binoculars too; he was an eager bird-watcher.

How that islet dominated the shore. Its two-mile stretch of jagged cliffs and rugged moorland sheltered wild goats, long-legged diminutive Soay sheep, shaggy Highland cattle; and birds, birds. Holy Island was a nature reserve, a field study centre. From its southernmost tip a lighthouse beaconed across the Firth of Clyde.

Unholy island, thought Ali.

Apparently a Christian saint called Molaise lived on the isle in the time of the prophet Mohammed, bless his name. The saint's cell could still be visited; Vikings had defaced it with runic inscriptions. The Satan-author also skulked in a kind of cell. Did he think he could walk free in safety upon those moors amongst the goats? The bars of his cell were the eye-beams of an authentic holy man, whose organ of vision lived on.

But first the instrument package enshrining that organ of vision must re-enter the atmosphere and parachute down to earth; for such had been Dr Hafiz's design. Thus the hawk would pounce.

Studying his maps, Ali chose a glen leading to a ben. He telephoned a cover number in Australia, to alert Tehran. Next evening, the important part of the *Eye of the Ayatollah* descended and soft-landed in the bonnie upland heather.

The following morning, Ali took the ferry over to Holy Island in company with half a dozen ornithologists. The sea was choppy, the breeze was brisk, so spindrift soon coated the lens-studded box that held the eye, which Ali wore around his neck like some gold-plated camera. Already that camera-that-wasn't had attracted a few curious glances. Was Ali some aviphile oil sheikh travelling incognito who couldn't forsake at least one token of ostentation? 'Ah,' he told himself, 'I'm but the humblest servant.' Fortunately the crossing did not coincide with a time for prayer; however he found that his vision was fogging. Ducking down out of sight behind some cargo, he opened the golden box and cradled the holy eyeball naked in his palm once more. The soft ball seemed to burn icily as though still frozen. Inspired, the Half-Face popped his glass prosthetic from its rebuilt orbit and replaced it with the Ayatollah's own.

His vision swam. He saw two scenes at once: the hellishly gaunt, approaching cliffs licked by sea-spume, and what he could only interpret as a glimpse of paradise, the slope of a verdant valley where fountains of milk gushed, spilling down in streams, where all manner of jewels glittered—a landscape girt with a dance of scintillating pastel auroras like diaphanous rose-and-pink veils of maidens, though minus the maidens. Ahead was a curiously imprecise promise of ecstasies without substance, as if he was seeing this terrain in some warmer Eden of the past, courtesy of an angel.

Some such subconscious, submerged vista must always have lurked in his inner gaze, as a cynosure, a focus. In this mystical moment he appeared to remember the lost object of all his buried desires. The whole island swelled with the light of joyful creation, the conjuring of mischievous beauty. Honey flowed like lava from one hilltop.

He shut the eye that was his own; and through that other, holy eye he saw only the sternness of cliffs again, their stark authenticity. Gulls screamed battle-cries. The sun was an ulcer of yellow pus, its afterimage a ball of blood. The impact of waves faintly echoed that torrent of boulders he had heard on a previous occasion at the battlefront.

'Why, Satan-author,' Ali said to himself in surprise, 'you are in hell already.'

When he closed his holy right eye to regard the scenery with his left eye, heavenly auras sparkled again, interference patterns between two modes of vision, awakening deeply hidden memories of a time when he had perceived the world freshly with wonder, long ago; of a time when he had been born and had had to create a universe around himself.

'In hell indeed,' he added, 'unless your eyes see otherwise.'

After he left the ferry to mount the island, he hiked with either his right eye open or his left, the holy eye mapping out barren geometries of rock and sky and grass, the other eye teasing the taste buds of his soul with that shimmer of scanty pastel veils behind which raw beauty beckoned.

He stepped out, he halted, he stepped out. The holy eye led him along a stony track towards what had once been a crofter's cottage and was now a sprawling homestead with mirror-glass windows surrounded by a high wire fence, supposedly to deter goats. The only guards these days were gulls.

The Satan-author sat at a desk. Haggard, yes. A nervous twitch in one eye; almost totally bald. Yet as he looked at this intruder who pointed a pistol as though out of habit, the author smiled.

'So it has come at last.'

That damnable smile, of sanity still sustained!

Ali shut his holy eye. Seen through his left eye, a nimbus surrounded the author's head. Ali reverted to his right eye, tightening his grip on the gun as he scanned the despicable face. A moment later he looked with his left eye too, and his vision swam again dizzyingly, so he closed the left eye.

'You look like a human traffic light,' remarked the author as though choosing wry last words for posterity, fit for some future dictionary of quotations.

Ali's holy attention was caught by a paper-knife used to open the author's voluminous, redirected correspondence, all his envelopes full of cheques paying him lavishly for his blasphemy in the currencies of Satan, dollars, pounds, francs, marks.

Now Ali's left eye also noted the knife with the sharp point. A roseate halo stained the blade with diluted blood. The handle was iridescent mother-of-pearl. Ali remembered the battle against Iraq and suddenly felt cheated. Strange desire surged within him.

'Which,' he asked, as if this was a riddle, 'which is my real eye? My true eye?'

Perhaps amazed at the idiosyncrasy of human nature, the author stared at this man who opened one eye then the other turn by turn, squinting at him. Was he really being offered a choice as though in a fairy tale? A choice between life and death—or only a choice between types of death?

He hesitated, then spoke at random. 'The left eye.'

'An angel guides your words.' Ali snatched up the knife, opened both eyes at once, and pointed the steel tip at the holy one.

The author tensed, imagining that he had chosen wrongly—perhaps could never have chosen correctly!—but Ali skewered the eye of the Ayatollah, drew it forth dripping humours, and stabbed the knife and its jelly burden down upon the desk.

'This', said Ali, 'is the eye that sees hell.'

A weight of years-long possession drained away from Ali's heart; and for the first time since he could recall, his own left eye leaked tears.

Swimming with the Salmon

VERY WELL THEN, I DO ADMIT THAT I DELIBERATELY SET OUT TO seduce Fiona Dougal by means of my scent and my thoughts.

Oh, I genuinely desired Fiona. That's perfectly true. From our final year together in Bradainmurch School, when Fiona bloomed so bonny, I had fantasized about her embrace. Her lips, her limbs. From Tower House, through an antique brass telescope, I spied on her swimming with the salmon. Their great gleaming silver bodies. Her naked body, which shone for me, precious as silver.

The salmon farm occupied the western third of Loch Bradain. Commercial plantations of larch, spruce, and pine cloaked most of our side of the shore, but the pointy steeple rising high from the side of Tower House was uniquely sited for invading Fiona's privacy. My great-great-grandfather had brought that fine nautical telescope back from bygone whaling days. *He* had spied for sperm whales; courtesy of his souvenir I spied on Fiona, and my own sperm stirred.

In vain, during adolescence. Fiona was already commencing her apprenticeship as a priestess of salmon. Having pledged herself joyfully to this useful occupation, she was closely supervised. An older woman from the farm, Meddling Maggie, chaperoned Fiona. Fiona must have been psychologically profiled as of lesbian leanings otherwise she could hardly have become a salmon apprentice, could she?

My longstanding desire aside, I was also intrigued to discover whether I could succeed in conquering Fiona. She presented a challenge—of unavailability.

As well as of *vulnerability*, of course . . .

The scent component in human semen is pyrroline. Along with androstenone and certain fatty acids, pyrroline also occurs in a man's pubic area. The aroma of pyrroline isn't unlike overripe persimmon fruit or cooked chestnuts or corn on the cob. The meal which I ate a few hours before meeting the mature Fiona on that special afternoon consisted of helpings of corn and chestnuts and persimmon as accompaniment to wild boar meat sauced with truffles and garnished with parsley. I washed the meal down with a couple of glasses of a good Cabernet, which typically vents its bouquet from the drinker's skin several hours after he imbibes.

Then I presented Fiona Dougal with chocolates rich in phenylethy-lamine—the new 'hot chocolate' from Mexico spiced with capsaicin, a stimulating combination . . .

Since my puberty I'd been aware that if I wished for something strongly enough then my wishes would sway people. However, it was important not to clamour or nag. Verbal pleading provoked resistance. If I simply hinted, my heartfelt desires would insert themselves into parent or teacher or fellow pupil and flourish, magically transformed into their own preference. As a youngster I adopted a superstitious attitude to this phenomenon.

In reality, of course, my thoughts were giving rise to persuasive pheromones, chemical signals which influenced the behaviour of other people—in my case, *strikingly* so. Just as Fiona's pheromones could persuade fish to do as she wished. Was it a coincidence that individuals such as her and me were emerging nowadays in our enlightened era? People who could wish, and whose wishes would become messages? No, the technology for recognizing this allowed us talented ones to liberate what oodles of years of verbal civilization had repressed.

When my maths teacher, Dominie Urquhart, caught himself giving me a far higher grade than I deserved, he proceeded to scrutinise my other excellent results over the years. A COD test followed—with the ultimate consequence that I would become a diplomat in the service of the prosperous Republic of Scotland. (Prosperous, since our separation from the leech of England.) In Scotland we understood such phenomena ever since our development of Computerised Olfactory Diagnostics—in which the science of salmon farming had played no small part.

How fitting that 'COD', as we called the technique, should also be the name of a fish which relies predominantly on chemical clues to trigger its behaviour. Salmon, of course, rely considerably on eyesight. Salmon possess eyes which are larger than their brains. Not that the hypothalamus of a salmon isn't massaged by hormonal chemical signals! It most certainly is. Thereby hung the whole art of modern salmoculture—and lovely Fiona Dougal's destiny.

Loch Bradain was roughly seven miles long, by two across, and shaped like a banana. Braes rose steeply from the narrow wooded north shore where roe deer loved to graze on bilberries in season. Over there, the odd buzzard soared above bouldery burns which plunged down through bracken, feeding the loch. Our southerly shore was flat and devoted to forestry. Consequently the upthrust of the Braes did not imply a corresponding depth to the loch. The River Baith bustled into Loch Bradain at the eastern end where the town of Bradainmurch clustered, dominated by its splendid Victorian Royal Hotel. Jetties tethered motorboats equipped with power-rods for the famed wild fishing worthy of Hemingway. The Baith continued out of Bradain more lazily to the west.

However, no salmon ever entered or left the loch by either branch of the Baith. Nor would they particularly yearn to leave, even if there weren't electrical containment fields in the water.

Salmo Magnus—the giant salmon, upwards of eight feet long at maturity—had been genetically engineered to lack any migratory instinct whatever to seek the sea. This new species could be permanently farmed in one location.

Now, your ordinary salmon is by turns a very greedy eater and an anorexic. While at sea, it stuffs itself. Once back in its home river to spawn, your regular salmon starves. If it didn't starve itself, it might eat a river empty—of its own kin too. Anglers who caught your ordinary salmon in a river or loch would only ever find a minimal coating of slime in its belly when gutting it, nary a scrap of food.

So how did anglers ever manage to catch salmon? Not due to a salmon's greed for bait, oh no. But rather by teasing the fish's *curiosity* with a well-played lure.

And who teased a salmon best? Who caught the largest cock salmon? Who massaged these zany fishes' brains and racked up the records?

Notoriously it was women anglers.

Gillies had long since known that a man only needed to dip his finger in the spume at the bottom of a salmon run to scare salmon away for half an hour—whereas tyro female anglers could land 50-pounders within minutes, as though charming the fish out of the water.

As in truth these ladies did, with their hormonal pheromones.

The odour of menstruation is prawny... while vanilla is a Spanish word derived from the Latin *vagina*... Think on't; think on't.

So as to attain maximum weight as swiftly as possible *Salmo Magnus* must feed enthusiastically and constantly. Yet the sex organs shouldn't mature too early. Peer aggression must be suppressed.

The folk wisdom of the gillie, and genetic engineering, and odour diagnostics converged. The very best masseuse of the behaviour of these big fish was... woman. Woman herself, swimming with the big fish daily, releasing her scents into the water, massaging their nervous systems. Woman, without—it goes without saying—any reek of *man* about her. Virgin woman. Or lesbian woman. Whichever.

Hence the banning of men from the salmon cooperatives. Hence the priestly, sapphic role which Fiona Dougal was to undertake.

Pheromones come in two classes. There are releaser pheromones which provoke a rapid, kneejerk reaction. Whereas primer pheromones alter the physiology of a creature through its endocrine system, thus conditioning its future, longer-term behaviour. The women who swam with the salmon primed those fish and kept them well-primed to gobble and gobble their food pellets docilely till they were ripe for harvest—and a percentage of them for release into the wild zone of the loch where men could angle for them, as I was to angle for Fiona on my return from Mexico.

Salmon can fairly be described as crazy fish. Bizarre, eccentric fish. Capricious, curious creatures of whim. Those who only know salmon as a red steak on a plate know nothing. And the women of the fish farms knew secrets unbeknownst to man. Fulfilling secrets, I'm sure. For salmon had always possessed a deep rapport with women. As did many fish species, to a lesser degree. It was a woman who wrote the first treatise on angling back in 1425 or so. Dame Juliana. Specialised cells on the skins of salmon respond to complex stimuli; and it must be true that women responded in turn to the touch and caress and pressure of *Salmo Magnus*.

Thus the women of the fish farms were effectively witches belonging to a piscine nature cult quite out of bounds to man—a cult where, yes, one ate the God! Well, this was modern Scotland, land of enlightenment. One did not bridle at such scientific witchery or at a necessary lesbianism or celibacy.

Superficially these women were merely very competent pisciculturists—a respected élite of specialists whose natural glandular secretions happened to play a major role in their work. I suspected more. This witchcraft intrigued me utterly.

What of my relations with Fiona, before her destiny seized her? What of that cusp of time during which she bloomed, just prior to her enrolment in the cult?

Why did I not exert myself then, to wish a kiss? To wish *more*? To project my desires upon Fiona? To lead her on a ramble through woods where the wee siskins feasted on pine and spruce seeds; through rhododendrons spreading their tents of glossy leaves?

The reason was my twisted foot which surgery had failed to correct fully. I would have been ashamed to shed my special shoe, thus any other of my garments. I didn't swim. I was excused from sports. I wouldn't have wished to hobble into the woods or rhododendrons, emphasizing my flaw—and where else was there for a lad to go?

Only later on did I realize that such a deformity could lead to Byronic achievements with the ladies, over whom a clubbed foot might actually exert a fascination and a magnetism comparable to those persuasive pheromones I deployed as though by way of compensation.

Fiona certainly consorted with no other lads, and she spurned any of their fumbling overtures. Consequently I wasn't tormented by jealousy, which might have spurred me to *wish*. Besides, I was only fifteen then, and uncertain exactly what I would be wishing for in practical detail. For a wish to come true I needed to visualize the outcome more accurately.

Soon she was sixteen; and so was I. And she joined the cult, while I was on my route out of Bradainmurch, and only remained alert to Fiona's attractions, in miniature, by telescope. (Did she ever glance up from the salmon-teeming water and spy the glint of the glass high up on Tower House?)

Were I a salmon I might have seen Fiona even more acutely, for during the daytime a salmon favours the colour-perceptive cones in its eye, while at dusk these retract in favour of the optic rods which see black and white, thus boldly silhouetting desirable shapes. Remarkable creatures! I was jealous of those giant fish gliding between Fiona's legs, rubbing their slime-coated scales sinuously, powerfully against her flesh. I was jealous of the secrets which I was sure she was learning, and which separated her from me.

Yet in a sense, in that piscine harem of the farm, she was being safe-guarded for my future self, was she not? The secret of a great love is often separation, confinement of one party, exile of the other. Stendhal, who wrote much about love, understood this. Perhaps, in this regard, I am the arche-typal lover—whose other conquests were all subsidiary to my feelings for forbidden Fiona.

A wish can accumulate over many years until it discharges itself overwhelm-ingly and compellingly...

After attending Glasgow University, where I concentrated on foreign languages and economics, I travelled widely in the diplomatic service. There are so many mini-nations in the world, fractions of one-time larger countries enmeshed in new alliances. One is almost a medieval traveller, once again. And I often found lovers, almost as if the fractured world was trying through me to reknit itself erotically into a macro-organism. I *persuaded* women, as effectively as I persuaded foreign politicians and industrialists. My heraldry would have been a clubbed foot set within a heart.

Always, reinforced by all these encounters, a fundamental dominating wish was building up like thunderous electric potential in the sky seeking its lightning conductor.

I believe now that I wasn't obsessed in a pathological fashion (the beast beneath the diplomatic facade, as it were) but rather that a curious form of pheromonal feedback operated, whereby I imprinted myself with my own persuasions—with self-persuasions. In my heart, always the memory trace of Fiona Dougal, naked, water-cloaked, at once far away and near, swimming with the phallic fish.

I denied myself the chance of returning prematurely to Tower House, enjoying the high tension which this self-exile generated in me. My own parents had divorced acrimoniously when I was eight, and the Republic of Scotland had deemed it best for me to live with my uncle and aunt in Tower House just outside Bradainmurch on the lochside. A rural upbringing. I never felt especially close to Duncan and Tara Hamilton, whose surname I adopted. After I left for Glasgow, Tanty-Tara died suddenly—of a stroke—and thereafter Unk-Dunk became a grouching recluse, who seemed to blame me for *wishing her dead*. Now that he knew of my talent he reinterpreted my boyhood, and the way that Tanty-Tara had constantly put herself out for me, harshly. To his now-disordered mind, she had worn herself out on behalf of a parasite. Sufficient for me to viz Unk-Dunk once in a while on the phonescreen. He never suggested I pay a visit.

I reserved old-style *written letters* for Fiona, and these were part of my long-term strategy, careful moves in my master game of love. I commenced on my very first junior posting, to Québec.

A voice from the past—or rather, no diskletter voice at all, but elegantly calligraphed words. A bolt from the blue for Fiona Dougal.

I felt the need, I explained to her, to write to somebody back home—since my aunt had died, and my uncle was potty—so as to preserve my sense of connexion with Bradainmurch and the past; and I trusted that Fiona wouldn't mind being the recipient of my random musings?

I made those letters as fascinating as I could, full of local Québequois colour. Fiona, who must have been puzzled, did reply to the third with a jaunty holocard depicting the Braes. Her writing was scrawly and she spelled a couple of words eccentrically.

Thus I wrote, for another decade, while the *wish* accumulated within me. I wrote from Catalunya, from Byelorussia, from Amazonia, from Mexico. Fiona's life, of course, was the loch; yet the exotic presently hooked her. Since I was forever elsewhere (and took my vacations elsewhere), I seemed a safe person to confide in (to a certain degree) about her life on the farm. Oh, no *secrets*, to be sure! She was reserved about those. Yet I gathered that she now enjoyed the companionship of one Jane McDonald, that they were thinking about maybe adopting a daughter later on, that Meddling Maggie had retired to the Hebrides, that Fiona and Jane would go into town of a Friday night to drink Glenbaith whiskies (made with water taken from further upstream, so as not to confuse odours). . . Fiona sometimes wrote about fish diseases, which seemed to fascinate her. Infective Haematopoitic Necrosis caused frenzied swimming and bulging of the eyeballs. Myxosomiasis, due to parasites becoming encysted in the brain, was also known as Whirling Disease; fish would chase their own tails relentlessly.

I never sent a holo-pic of myself, nor she of herself. It wasn't that sort of correspondence (though at the same time, of course, it was *becoming* so, on the non-verbal level). Nor did I ever scent my writing paper with pyrroline.

Then she was thirty; and I was thirty. I'd begun to hint about a remarkable Mayan sculpture of fish and woman which I had come across in the

Yucatan jungle. Erotic, disturbing, numinous. At this point, fortuitously Unk-Dunk died, likewise of a stroke and of lying alone in Tower House undiscovered for several days.

My diplomatic duties prevented me from returning in time for his funeral early in August. But a month later I flew in to Bradainmurch by helicopter, squandering a substantial sum on this private flight just so that we could pass slowly over the salmon farm.

The loch seemed to writhe with silver worms under the skin of water. There, in their own zones, were a horde of smaller salmon. In adjacent zones, larger fish. Then, largest of all: seven, eight-footers. Colour-coded marker buoys indicated boundaries and corridors. From the bed of the loch submerged cables deployed electric fields—of 4 volts per metre, to be precise, in pulses lasting 0.8 milliseconds 15 times per second. These fields prevented any salmon from straying into senior or junior territory. Which was due to electrotaxis. Any fish entering the electric field would lose control of its swimming muscles. Nerve cells under the salmon's skin would kick the fish into a reflex, compelling it to return towards the positive electrode.

Compelling it. Salmo couldn't do otherwise, whatever he wished. His body would simply disobey his brain, and obey the electric field instead.

Would Fiona's body disobey her brain? Or would it be her brain which disobeyed the usual preferences of her body and the codes of her fish cult?

We were flying sluggishly at a few hundred feet. Down below, a nude woman scrambled on to one of the rafts, shaking herself as if in protest at our intrusion. Was that *herself*? No, the woman down below was raven-haired. Since this was September, she might already be wearing a heating web, though such a mesh was transparent—since salmon are visual identifiers—and flimsy, since bodily exposure was of the essence.

Why didn't she stay submerged instead of exposing herself? Ah, the food dispenser on the raft began to throw out its hailstorm of synthetic protein pellets. The water boiled as Salmo gobbled.

A floating walkway led from that raft to a jetty where a stubby barge wallowed, part-flooded inside, some mobile aquatic surgery equipped with stout winch and plastic sling. The hugest of the farm buildings overlapped the water on stone pillars. A lane of day-glo red buoys led under the over-hang. Ah, somewhere within—somewhere more confined—would be a killing zone, for electrocuting the harvest of the loch.

Could it be that a fish mistress would swim in under there, luring the chosen fish along with her like some pheromonal Pied Piper? Momentarily I imagined malice and murder, since a full-grown Salmo's body was bigger than a woman's. If a fish mistress was still in the water she could be shocked dead by a seeming malfunction. I quickly dismissed this fantasy, for the priestesses must live together in amity, must they not?

That major building must also house the gutting lines, packing lines, freezers, smoking kilns . . . And what else? Oh yes, an ascorbic acid tank to reduce rancidity in storage. A big one of those.

Other buildings were visibly residential. For the first time it occurred to me to wonder whether the women actually *did* eat salmon—even ceremonially, at special feasts? Or was eating the flesh of *Salmo Magnus* perhaps taboo . . . ?

Mysteries, mysteries . . . And that covered floating structure . . . close by a *brood zone*? Was that a place where the priestesses milked mature bucks of their milt?

I ceased craning my neck, for we were well beyond the farm by now. Sooty-faced sheep grazed along the shoreline.

'Had enough of an eyeful?' the pilot asked dourly.

'A salmon would have seen more,' said I, thinking of those giant eyes.

'Maybe next time you ought to come home by submarine,' was his response.

Unk-Dunk had never fitted any part of Tower House out with automatics, thus I hadn't been able to control its status remotely. However, I'd asked uncle's solicitor in Bradainmurch to send in his clerk to switch on the boiler and heating and fridge in anticipation of my arrival.

I shared a dram with whiskery Mr Henderson in his office and accepted muted condolences—bearing in mind that I hadn't been back in over a decade and had, unlike dutiful Mr Henderson, missed the funeral. Despite Unk-Dunk's mutterings, he had never reneged on an early will drawn up in my favour. Well, I wouldn't have wished him to, even though no vizphone call conveyed aromas.

I drove the rental electro Volvo along the lakeside road quickly, the sooner to transfer my boar meat and truffles and persimmon from a travelling cool-pack into the fridge. Before heading to the heliport in Glasgow I'd stocked up at a delicatessen.

The old house was somewhat of a mess inside, as one might expect of a crusty widower's abode. More significantly, it smelled of some damned lavatorial disinfectant, and at first I experienced quite a surge of annoyance at the Bradainmurch authorities and Henderson. Unk-Dunk hadn't exactly *rotted* here, so why should they presume to disinfect Tower House! I threw all doors and windows wide open, as well as turning the heating up full to compensate for the incoming breezes.

As I ranged through the familiar rooms on all three floors I discovered the sources of the wretched smell. Just as a person with spiritual inclinations might burn incense, so my uncle had secreted saucers of disinfectant all over the house to de-scent the air and banish any rival fragrances. In the cellar itself lurked half a dozen large cases of unopened bottles of germicide. Unhinged by Tanty-Tara's death, had Unk-Dunk supposed that by this stratagem, which he presumably rationalised as maintaining a healthy regime in Tower House, he was purging all trace of my influence?

I swiftly got rid of all such saucers, which bid fair to thwart me from beyond the grave. Naturally I'd brought aphrodisiacal essential oils with me. Sweet spicy sandalwood which relieves anxiety in a sedative way. Euphoric jasmine, warming and relaxing. And juniper, the pleasant terebinthate odour of which counteracts trembling and coldness. I went off into the woods to gather a sackful of pine needles, cones, and bark, and soon had impromptu potpourri in every room. Then I tackled a build-up of dust and cobwebs which surely predated my uncle's demise, and a kitchenful of dirty utensils.

Soon night fell, so I locked the doors, though I still left windows open. After fixing myself a neutral, purgative meal of rice and bland beans, I mounted at last to the hexagonal lookout room and sat at the faithful old telescope to scan the moon-dappled reaches of the loch. I attached a micro-electronic photomultiplier which I'd bought in Mexico City. Alas, since my adolescence trees had grown taller. My perspective on the waters of the salmon farm was curtailed. No matter! I need be a voyeur no more.

'My *correspondent*,' repeated Fiona—exactly as she had said on the vizphone that morning when I called the salmon farm to invite her to tea; for which she had arrived by bicycle.

She clasped both my hands briefly before perching on the sofa, smoothing down a tartan skirt, which was Hunting Stewart, I believe. The black, red, and yellow grid lines on the blue-green background of the plaid suggested to me those cables and electric fields in the waters of the loch. Fiona also wore a white blouse, over which her russet hair spilled, and matching tartan socks and strong leather sandals. Oh she was muscular from all the swimming, as well as from labour inside the fish factory. An athlete, or goddess, whose delicate freckles had merged together so that she was golden. Full lips, noble nose, wide opaline eyes.

She gazed at me full of curiosity, as I lightly limped towards Tanti-Tara's tea service, seeing the gauche boy of yesteryear transformed into a graceful, languid but passionful man, hazel-haired, with knowing eyes which had seen many countries.

She couldn't help glancing at my clumpy shoe. 'So they never... Oh I'm sorry,' she murmured, confused. Already, physical curiosity. 'But why did you write to *me*?'

'I think,' I replied, 'that I needed a secret confidante, one who was aware of secrets herself. Of the mysteries of the world.'

'Mysteries, as in the jungles of Yucatan... Jamie?' Ah, my intimate name...

'It's galling... Fiona,' I replied, 'but my camera got a dunking and was smashed against a boulder in a stream we were fording. You see, I was *swept off my feet*. The filmdisc was ruined. The statue was in obsidian—black glassy volcanic rock, too heavy to transport. We stumbled upon it near the coast, half coated in creepers. A fish and a woman were coiled together as though they were *lovers*. My guides had seen nothing like that before, and archaeologists I asked... well, they were disparaging. This was outside of their experience.'

I handed her a cup of tea and a plate of shortbreads interspersed with many chocolates.

'I brought these chocs all the way from Mexico,' I explained. She ate a couple. And then a few more.

Her odour, close to, hinted at a fishy oiliness. The net curtains of the drawing room filtered dying September sunlight across the two thick sheepskin rugs I'd laid over the frayed old checkered carpet. Embers glowed ruddily in the stone hearth; fresh flame licked around a new log. The room was hot.

'What makes you think there are secrets?' she asked, nodding in the direction of the loch.

'There must be, mustn't there?'

'Because *you* have secrets?'

I shrugged. 'Why are *you* interested in this fish and woman statue, then?'
'Why?' she echoed. (Yes, let her echo me.) 'Why? Because *you* are, Jamie!'
'And why am I interested in it, Fiona?'
I wished. I craved. I yearned, as never before with any woman.

Amidst scents of jasmine and juniper and sandalwood potpourri, whiff of woodsmoke, subtle bouquet of Cabernet, fragrance of boar and truffle, the subterranean magma of desire was welling upward, venting all its persuasive pheromones . . .

Fiona considered me. 'I feel I know you so well from all your letters, Jamie . . .'

Let us really know each other then, Fiona. Let us. Let us.

Of course, I abridge somewhat.

The moon was rising when we at last uncoiled, there upon those sheepskin rugs in the glow of the fire. I felt strangely bestialised—yet exaltingly so—as though I'd been transformed into another species of being, into a puissant giant godlike fish, which at last—at long last—Fiona could couple with realistically, and upon whom she had discharged at last all her own decade and more of accumulated appetite. Surely this was the secret of the salmon farm—this alien cathexis, this focusing of vital energy upon a foreign species without hope hitherto of full consummation. Fiona's own female lover, Jane, was human, after all. Jane might imitate *Salmo Magnus* but could not be *Salmo*.

The story I had concocted, of that Mayan idol, had not been so far askew after all. Deep in all human dreams, as exposed by myth, was the yearning to unite with whichever totem creature a culture chose as its inhuman ideal, to represent Otherness. Eagle. Jaguar. Serpent. Spirit-guides; yet also emblems of the body's desire by means of Otherness to become . . . magnificent, transcendent.

And thus Fiona was fulfilled. And I too. And I.

She did not reproach me, since what we had enacted was . . . sublime. The moon outside the window seemed to say that if we human beings ever travelled far beyond to another world of sapient beings somewhere in the universe, then our meeting with such beings should ideally be thus.

She did not reproach. Yet she was riven by an anguish.

'I shall swim home,' she told me. 'I shall swim to clean myself.'

'Aren't you hungry, Fiona?' I asked her.

'Hungry? How could I be hungry when I have *gorged* myself?'

'Do you have a heating web with you?'

She shook her russet hair. No.

'It's September. It's night.'

'The chill will kill scents.' She laughed brusquely. Contradictorily, she added, 'Strong swimming warms a person. I shall swim so strongly tonight, burning off what has happened.'

It would have been banal to offer to drive her back in the Volvo, supposing that she simply didn't wish to ride her bike.

'Don't worry that I'll *drown*,' she assured me.

Nude, she sprinted across the unkempt lawn, down the strand of sand. She waded. She dived. Her tartan skirt had remained like a map discarded.

Pulling a sheepskin rug around me like some ancient savage, I gimped upstairs again to my telescope. By amplified light I watched Fiona cleave the waters of Bradain.

Presently silver humps broke the surface near where she swam. Wild *Salmo Magnus* accompanied her, those prey for the hooks of Hemingways. Though no doubt scenting traces of human semen, they didn't flee. Around her, the water seemed to foam with milk. Could that merely be liquid moonlight?

So was it actually *milt* that I saw? The roe of the male fish, discharged due to the tang of my own seed within Fiona, and upon her?

And then she swam through the shock-fields; *her* muscles wouldn't disobey in the way that a fish's would.

And in her womb, or in a fallopian tube, the electric shock fused milt and sperm and ovum ...

What Jane McDonald has deposed to the Procurator Fiscal is that Fiona Dougal became pregnant that night. When the other fish mistresses sensed this (quite soon), they sequestered Fiona as if she were some delinquent nun in a medieval convent; though housed in more comfort ...

I'm summarising what you told me, Mr Ambassador ... *Jock.* What they sent in the pouch from Scotland, in the diplomatic sporran. So that we get all the facts and nuances correct. Thus we might sort out the truth.

After that special afternoon, I only stayed on in Bradainmurch for five more days, sufficient to put Tower House on the market. I didn't seen Fiona again, nor did I viz her at the farm. Well, the wish had gone. The wish had been fulfilled. Transcendently so. How banal—how impractical—to contemplate . . . an *affair*, which a woman in Fiona's line of occupation couldn't conceivably countenance, especially given her emotional bias. If *she* had chosen to viz me, I'd have been astonished. Before leaving Bradainmurch, I had a local girl ride Fiona's bike back to the farm gate and park the bike there, with an addressed parcel upon the saddle containing Fiona's abandoned clothing. I included no paltry note. Nor did I write again, from abroad. Nor did she write to me, from her confinement.

You say that as Fiona's pregnancy advanced, the mistresses leased a small domestic ultrasound scanner? And found, to their consternation that the lower half of the foetus curled up within her displayed the contours of . . . a *fish* . . .

That what was growing in her womb was a merbaby?

A teratogenic monster? Or . . . a consummation for their cult?

When Fiona commenced labour, the mistresses took her out into the loch? There, in the water, she gave birth to this hybrid—of me, and her, and Salmo?

And the baby—a girl—swam a little?

Yet, scenting the blood of birth, a great cock salmon darted up and *ate* the little mermaid voraciously.

It was then that Jane McDonald fled from the farm in horror, and from Fiona, to the Procurator Fiscal, demanding prosecutions of the priestesses, and of me as well for some reason as accessory to the deed . . .

But Fiona herself didn't flee. And she has denied this version of events. She is soon going to become the chief fish mistress of Loch Bradain, so you tell me.

I must remind you, *Jock*, that Jane is a renegade, a crazed woman. And the evidence is missing . . . eaten, so Jane claims.

Why does the Procurator believe that a merchild could be born at all? He *does*, doesn't he? He must be daft in the head. Jock, I don't much wish to go back there to testify. I really don't.

I suppose that a fish-tailed child *should* best be born in water . . . In that case why didn't the mistresses protect the birthing zone with an electric field? Did some malicious body switch the current off? Did Jane herself, as a jealous revenge for being betrayed by Fiona? Or are we hinting at a deliberate sacrifice of that fishy firstborn? Is that it, Jock? Hence Fiona becoming high priestess afterwards! Then Jane McDonald became terrified at what was happening?

Ah. I see that I've fallen into a trap. *A fish-tailed child.* Yes, those were my words: a fish-tailed child. The absurd power of the notion has already captured me. I, who have been such a dab hand at persuading people, women especially, am now persuaded in turn. When my seduction of Fiona was so climactic—culmination of so many years of canny ardour—how could I imagine that the event would have had no consequence? That the whole episode would simply come to a full stop after she swam away from Tower House? In this sense I suppose I am *an* accomplice—innocent accessory to something which our Procurator frets about, something he fears may emerge from the mutant fish farms where the pheromonal women swim. Some marvel, some abomination. Some half-human fish-goddess. A chimera. I can spy his drift now, Jock.

Pledged to eschew the embraces of men, the priestesses couldn't have *expected* anything like this to happen. Fiona swam home so as to 'cleanse' herself, she told me. Yet now those women have experienced a dreadful miracle. What if another of them is impregnated by a man and immediately swims among the milt-spurting giant cock salmon? Presuming that Jane McDonald did cut the current and kill the newborn mermaid, what if chief fish mistress Fiona herself chooses to repeat her act of intercourse?

Oh, I don't wish to fly home, Jock. Can't you perceive the peril I might be in? How vulnerable I could become, now that this conception is in my head, persuading me?

Sleep on it.

Why certainly, sleep on it. You're an understanding gentleman, Jock. Probably I could use a leave of absence. Of course I appreciate why the Procurator wants to quiz me about this peculiar affair. Exports of salmon are important to the Scottish economy.

I think of my semen mixed with milt. Outside Ambassador Dalgleish's office, the Mexican sun is blinding bright, like a copper gong on fire. Nowhere in Mexico does it shine on any obsidian idol of any fish and woman mating. Yet in a Scottish loch, far away in the land of enlightenment, that same sun rose earlier today upon a loch, and upon silver bodies which the human race has created by godlike intervention in their genes, aping a divine intimacy.

How, now, shall I renew my intimacy with Fiona Dougal?

The Coming of Vertumnus

D<small>O YOU KNOW THE</small> *P<small>ORTRAIT OF</small> J<small>ACOPO</small> S<small>TRADA</small>*, <small>WHICH</small> T<small>ITIAN</small> painted in 1567 or so?

Bathed in golden light, this painting shows us a rich connoisseur displaying a nude female statuette which is perhaps eighteen inches high. Oh yes, full-bearded Signor Strada is prosperous—in his black velvet doublet, his cerise satin shirt, and his ermine cloak. He holds that voluptuous little Venus well away from an unseen spectator. He gazes at that spectator almost shiftily. Strada is exposing his Venus to view, yet he's also withholding her proprietorially so as to whet the appetite.

With her feet supported on his open right hand, and her back resting across his left palm, the sculpted woman likewise leans away as if in complicity with Strada. How carefully his fingers wrap around her. One finger eclipses a breast. Another teases her neck. Not that her charms aren't on display. *Her* hands are held high, brushing her shoulders. Her big-navelled belly and mons veneris are on full show. A slight crossing of her knees hints at a helpless, lascivious reticence.

She arouses the desire to acquire and to handle her, a yearning that is at once an artistic and an erotic passion. Almost, she seems to be a homunculus—a tiny woman bred within an alchemist's vessel by the likes of a Paracelsus, who had died only some twenty-five years previously.

I chose this portrait of Jacopo Strada as the cover for my book, *Aesthetic Concupiscence*. My first chapter was devoted to an analysis of the implications of this particular painting...

Jacopo Strada was an antiquary who spent many years in the employ of the Habsburg court, first at Vienna and then at Prague, as Keeper of Antiquities. He procured and catalogued gems and coins as well as classical statuary.

Coins were important to the Hapsburg Holy Roman Emperors, because coins bore the portraits of monarchs. A collection of coins was a visible genealogy of God-anointed rulers. Back on Christmas Day in the year 800 the Pope had crowned Charlemagne as the first 'Emperor of the Romans'. The Church had decided it no longer quite had the clout to run Europe politically as well as spiritually. This imperial concoction—at times heroic, at other times hiccuping along—lasted until 1806. That was when the last Holy Roman Emperor, Francis II, abdicated without successor so as to thwart Napoleon from grabbing the title. By then, as they say, the Emperor presided over piecemeal acres which were neither an empire, nor Roman, nor holy.

History has tended to view the Habsburg court of Rudolph II at Prague in the late 1570s and 80s as wonky, wacky, and weird: an excellent watering hole for any passing nut-cases, such as alchemists, hermetic occultists, or astrologers—who of course, back then, were regarded as 'scientists'. *Not* that true science wasn't well represented, too! Revered astronomer Tycho Brahe burst his bladder with fatal result at Rudolph's court, due to that Emperor's eccentric insistence that no one might be excused from table till his Caesarian Majesty had finished revelling.

Botanists were very busy classifying plants there, and naturalists were taxonomising exotic wildlife (of which many specimens graced Rudolph's zoo)—just as Strada himself tried to impose order and methodology upon ancient Venuses.

Strada resigned and quit Prague in 1579, perhaps in irritation that his aesthetic criteria held less sway over Rudolph than those of another adviser on the Imperial art collection—namely *Giuseppe Archimboldo*...

My troubles began when I received a phone call at St Martin's School of Art in Charing Cross Road, where I lectured part-time in History of the Same. The caller was one John Lascelles. He introduced himself as the UK personal assistant to Thomas Rumbold Wright. Oil magnate and art collector, no less. Lascelles's voice had a youthfully engaging, though slightly prissy timbre.

Was I the Jill Donaldson who had written *Aesthetic Concupiscence*? I who had featured scintillatingly on *Art Debate at Eight* on Channel 4 TV? Mr Wright would very much like to meet me. He had a proposition to make. Might a car be sent for me, to whisk me the eighty-odd miles from London to the North Cotswolds?

What sort of proposition?

Across my mind there flashed a bizarre image of myself as a diminutive Venus sprawling in this oil billionaire's acquisitive, satin-shirted arms. For of course in my book I had cleverly put the stiletto-tipped boot into all such as he, who contributed to the obscene lunacy of art prices.

Maybe Thomas Rumbold Wright was seeking a peculiar form of recompense for my ego-puncturing stiletto stabs, since he—capricious bachelor—was certainly mentioned once in my book . . .

'What sort of proposition?'

'I've no idea,' said Lascelles, boyishly protesting innocence.

I waited. However, Lascelles was very good at silences, whereas I am not.

'Surely you must have *some* idea, Mr Lascelles?'

'Mr Wright will tell you, Ms Donaldson.'

Why not? Why not indeed? I had always revelled in paradoxes, and it must be quite paradoxical—not to mention constituting a delicious piece of fieldwork—for Jill Donaldson to accept an invitation from Thomas R. Wright, lavisher of untold millions upon old canvasses.

One of my prime paradoxes—in my 'Stratagems of Deceit' chapter—involved a comparison between the consumption of sensual fine art, and of visual pornography. I perpetrated an iconography of the latter based upon interviews I conducted with 'glamour' photographers on the job. No, I *didn't* see it as my mission to deconstruct male-oriented sexism. Not a bit of it. That would be banal. I came to praise porn, not to bury it. Those sumptuous nudes in oils of yore were the buoyant, respectable porn of their day. What we needed nowadays, I enthused—tongue in cheek, several tongues in cheek indeed—were issues of *Penthouse* magazine entirely painted by latterday Masters, with tits by the Titians of today, vulvas by Veroneses, pubes by populist Poussins . . . Ha!

I was buying a little flat in upper Bloomsbury, with the assistance of Big Brother Robert who was a bank manager in Oxford. Plump sanctimonious Bob regarded this scrap of property as a good investment. Indeed, but for his support, I could hardly have coped. Crowded with books and prints, on which I squandered too much, Chez Donaldson was already distinctly cramped. I could hold a party in it—so long as I only invited a dozen people and we spilled on to the landing.

Even amidst slump and eco-puritanism, London property prices still bore a passing resemblance to Impressionist price-tags. Perhaps eco-puritanism actually *sustained* high prices, since it seemed that one ought to be penalised for wishing to live fairly centrally in a city, contributing to the sewage burden and resources and power demand of megalopolis, and whatnot.

Well, we were definitely into an era of radical repressiveness. The Eco bandwagon was rolling. Was one's lifestyle environmentally friendly, third-world friendly, future friendly? The no-smoking, no-car, no-red-meat, no-frilly-knickers, sackcloth-and-ashes straitjacket was tightening; and while I might have seemed to be on that side ethically as regards the conspicuous squandering of megamillions on paintings, I simply did not buy the package. Perhaps the fact that I smoked cigarettes—oh penalised sin!—accounted in part for my antipathy to the Goody-Goodies. Hence my naughtiness in exalting (tongues in cheek) such a symptom of unreconstructed consciousness as porn. Paradox, paradox. I did like to *provoke*.

How many lovers had such a tearaway as myself had by the age of thirty-one? Just three, in fact; one of them another woman, a painting student.

Peter, Annie, and Phil. No one at the moment. I wasn't exactly outrageous in private life.

Peter had been the prankster, the mercurial one. For his 'God of the Deep' exhibition he wired fish skeletons into the contours of bizarre Gothic cathedrals, which he displayed in tanks of water. Goldfish were the congregations—was this art, or a joke? Several less savoury anarchistic exploits finally disenchanted me with Peter—about the time I decided definitively that I really was an art historian and a critic (though of capricious spirit).

Sending a Mercedes, with darkened windows, to collect me could have wiped out my street cred. Personally, I regarded this as a *Happening*.

Mind you, I did experience a twinge of doubt—along the lines that maybe I ought to phone someone (Phil? Annie? Definitely not Peter . . .) to

confide where I was being taken, just in case 'something *happens* to me . . .'
I didn't do so, yet the spice of supposed danger added a certain frisson.

When my doorbell rang, the radio was bemoaning the death of coral
reefs, blanched leprous by the extinction of the symbiotic algae in them.
This was sad, of course, *tragic*; yet I didn't intend to scourge myself personally, as the participants in the programme seemed to feel was appropriate.

The driver proved to be a Dutchman called Kees, pronounced Case, who
'did things' for Rumby—as he referred to Thomas Rumbold Wright.
Athletic-looking and bearded, courteous and affable, Case wore jeans,
Reeboks, and an open-necked checked shirt. No uniform or peaked cap for
this driver, who opened the front door of the Merc so that I should sit next
to him companionably, not behind in splendid isolation. Case radiated the
easy negligence of a cultured bodyguard-if-need-be. I was dressed in similar
informal style, being determined not to doll myself up in awe for the grand
encounter—though I refused to wear trainers with designer names on them.

Although Wright maintained a corporate headquarters in Texas, he
personally favoured his European bastion, Bexford Hall. This had recently
been extended by the addition of a mini-mock-Tudor castle wing to house
his art in even higher security. The *Sunday Times* colour supplement had
featured photos of this jail of art. (Did it come complete with a dungeon, I
wondered?)

The mid-June weather was chilly and blustery—either typical British
summer caprice or a Greenhouse spasm, depending on your ideology.

As we were heading out towards the motorway, we soon passed one of
those hoardings featuring a giant poster of Archimboldo's portrait of
Rudolph II as an assembly of fruits, vegetables, and flowers. Ripe pear nose;
flushed round cheeks of peach and apple; cherry and mulberry eyes; spiky
chestnut husk of a chin; corn-ear brows, and so on, and so on.

The Emperor Rudolph as Vertumnus, Roman god of fruit trees, of
growth and transformation. Who cared about that particular snippet of art
historical info? Across the portrait's chest splashed the Eco message, *WE
ARE ALL PART OF NATURE*. This was part of that massive and highly
successful Green propaganda campaign exploiting Archimboldo's 'nature-
heads'—a campaign which absolutely caught the eye in the most persuasive
style.

These posters had been adorning Europe and America and wherever else
for the best part of two years now. Indeed, they'd become such a radiant
emblem of eco-consciousness, such a part of the mental landscape, that I

doubted they would *ever* disappear from our streets. People even wore miniatures as badges—as though true humanity involved becoming a garlanded bundle of fruit and veg, with a cauliflower brain, perhaps.

Case slowed and stared at that hoarding.

'Rudolph the red-nosed,' I commented.

Somewhat to my surprise, Case replied, 'Ah, and Rudolph loved Archimboldo's jokes so much that he made him into a Count! Sense of humour's sadly missing these days, don't you think?'

My driver must have been boning up on his art history. The Green poster campaign was certainly accompanied by no background info about the artist whose images they were ripping off—or perhaps one ought to say 'recuperating' for the present day . . . rather as an ad agency might exploit the Mona Lisa to promote tampons. (*Why is* she *smiling . . . ?*)

'Those paintings weren't *just* jokes,' I demurred.

'No, and neither are those posters.' Case seemed to loathe those, as though he would like to tear them all down. He speeded up, and soon we reached the motorway.

Under the driving mirror—where idiots used to hang woolly dice, and where nowadays people often hung plastic apples or pears, either sincerely or else in an attempt to immunise their vehicles against eco-vandals—there dangled a little model . . . of a rather complex-looking space station. The model was made of silver, or was at least silver-plated. It swung to and fro as we drove. At times, when I glanced that way, I confused rearview mirror with model so that it appeared as if a gleaming futuristic craft was pursuing us up the M40, banking and yawing behind us.

Down where my left hand rested I found power-controls for the passenger seat. So I raised the leather throne—yes indeed, I was sitting on a dead animal's hide, and no wonder the windows were semi-opaque from outside. I lowered the seat and reclined it. I extruded and recessed the lumbar support. Now that I'd discovered this box of tricks, I just couldn't settle on the most restful position for myself. Supposing the seat had been inflexible, there'd have been no problem. Excessive tech, perhaps?

I felt fidgety. 'Do you mind if I smoke?' I asked Case.

'Rumby smokes in this car,' was his answer, which didn't quite confide his own personal feelings, unless the implication was that these were largely irrelevant amongst Wright's entourage.

Case ignored the 60-mile-an-hour fuel-efficiency speed limit, though he drove very safely in this cushioned tank of a car. He always kept an eye open well ahead and well behind as if conscious of possible interception, by a police patrol, or—who knows?—by Green vigilante kidnappers.

Bexford Hall was in the triangle between Stow-on-the-Wold, Broadway, and Winchcombe, set in a wooded river valley cutting through the rolling, breezy, sheep-grazed uplands.

The house was invisible from the leafy side road, being masked by the high, wire-tipped stone boundary wall in good repair, and then by trees. Case opened wrought iron gates electronically from the car—apparently the head gardener and family lived in the high-pitched gatehouse alongside— and we purred up a winding drive.

Lawns with topiary hedges fronted the mullion-windowed house. Built of soft golden limestone around a courtyard, Chez Wright somewhat resembled a civilian castle even before his addition of the bastioned, bastard-architectural art wing. A helicopter stood on a concrete apron. A Porsche, a Jaguar, and various lesser beasts were parked in a row on gravel. A satellite dish graced the rear slate-tiled roof, from which Tudor chimneys rose.

The sun blinked through, though clouds still scudded.

And so—catching a glimpse en route of several people at computer consoles, scrutinising what were probably oil prices—we passed through to John Lascelles' office, where the casual piles of glossy art books mainly caught my eye.

Having delivered me, Case left to 'do things'. . . .

Lascelles was tall, willowy, and melancholy. He favoured dark mauve corduroy trousers and a multi-pocketed purple shirt loaded with many pens, not to mention a clip-on walkie-talkie. On account of the ecclesiastical hues I imagined him as a sort of secular court chaplain to Wright. His smile was a pursed, wistful affair, though there was that boyish lilt to his voice which had misled me on the phone. His silences were the truer self.

He poured coffee for me from a percolator; then he radioed news of my arrival. It seemed that people communicated by personal radio in the house. In reply he received a crackly splutter of Texan which I hardly caught.

Lascelles sat and scrutinised me while I drank and smoked a cigarette; on his littered desk I'd noted an ashtray with a cheroot stub crushed in it.

Lascelles steepled his hands. He was cataloguing me: a new person collected—at least potentially—by his non-royal master, as he himself must once have been collected.

Woman. Thirty-one. Mesomorphic build; though not exactly chunky. Small high breasts. Tight curly brown hair cropped quite short. Violet vampiric lipstick. Passably callipygian ass.

Then in bustled *Rumby*—as I simply had to think of the man thereafter.

Rumby was a roly-poly fellow attired in crumpled bronze slacks and a floppy buff shirt with lots of pockets for pens, calculator, radio. He wore scruffy trainers, though I didn't suppose that he jogged around his estate. His white complexion said otherwise. His face was quizzically owlish, with large spectacles—frames of mottled amber—magnifying his eyes into brown orbs; and his thinning feathery hair was rebellious.

He beamed, almost tangibly projecting *energy*. He pressed my flesh quickly. He drew me along in his slipstream from Lascelles' office down a walnut-panelled corridor. We entered a marble-floored domed hall which housed gleaming spotlit models. Some in perspex cases, others hanging. Not models of oil-rigs, oh no. Models of a Moon base, of spacecraft, of space stations.

Was Rumby a little boy at heart? Was this his den? Did he play with these toys?

'What do you think about space?' he asked me.

Mischief urged me to be contrary, yet I told him the truth.

'Personally,' I assured him, 'I think that if we cop out of space now, as looks highly likely, then we'll be locked up here on Mother Earth for ever after eating a diet of beans and being repressively good with "Keep off the Grass" signs everywhere. Oh dear, we mustn't mess up Mars by going there the way we messed up Earth! Mess up Mars, for Christ's sake? It's *dead* to start with—a desert of rust. I think if we can grab all those clean resources and free energy in space, we'd be crazy to hide in our shell instead. But there's neo-puritanism for you.'

Rumby rubbed his hands. 'And if Green propaganda loses us our launch window of the next fifty years or so, then we've lost forever because we'll have spent all our spunk. I knew you'd be *simpatico*, Jenny. I've read *Aesthetic Concubines* twice.'

'*Concupiscence*, actually,' I reminded him.

'Let's call it *Concubines*. That's easier to say.'

Already my life and mind were being mutated by Rumby...

'So how did you extrapolate my views on space from a book on the art market?' I asked.

He tapped his brow. 'I picked up on your anti-repressive streak and the perverse way you think. Am I right?'

'Didn't you regard my book as a bit, well, rude?'

'I don't intend to take things personally when the future of the human race is at stake. It is, you know. It is. Green pressures are going to nix everyone's space budget. Do you know they're pressing to limit the number of rocket launches to a measly dozen per year *world-wide* because of the exhaust gases? And all those would have to be Earth-Resources-relevant. Loony-tune environ-*mentalists*! There's a *religious* fervour spreading like clap in a cathouse. It's screwing the world's brains.' How colourfully he phrased things. Was he trying to throw me off balance? Maybe he was oblivious to other people's opinions. I gazed blandly at him.

'Jill,' he confided, 'I'm part of a pro-space pressure group of industrialists called The Star Club. We've commissioned surveys. Do you know, in one recent poll forty-five per cent of those questioned said that they'd happily give up quote all the benefits of "science" if they could live in a more natural world without radioactivity? Can you believe such scuzzbrains? We *know* how fast this Eco gangrene is spreading. How do we disinfect it? Do we use rational scientific argument? You might as well reason with a hippo on heat.'

'Actually, I don't see how this involves me . . .'

'*We'll* need to use some tricks. So, come and view the Wright Collection.'

He took me through a security-coded steel door into his climate-controlled sanctum of masterpieces.

Room after room. Rubens. Goya. Titian. And other lesser luminaries . . .

. . . till we came to the door of an inner sanctum.

I half expected to find the Mona Lisa herself within. But no . . .

On an easel sat . . . a totally pornographic, piscine portrait. A figure made of many fishes (along with a few crustaceans).

A female figure.

A spread-legged naked woman, red lobster dildo clutched in one octopus-hand, frigging herself. A slippery, slithery, lubricious Venus composed of eels and catfish and trout and a score of other species. Prawn labia, with legs and feelers as pubic hair . . . The long suckery fingers of her other octopus-hand teased a pearl nipple . . .

The painting just had to be by Archimboldo. It was very clever and, mm, persuasive. It also oozed lust and perversity.

'So how do you like her?' asked Rumby.

'That lobster's rather a nippy notion,' I said.

'It isn't a lobster,' he corrected me. 'It's a cooked freshwater crayfish.'

'She's, well, fairly destabilising if you happen to drool over all those "We are part of Nature" posters.'

'Right! And Archimboldo painted a *dozen* such porn portraits for private consumption by crazy Emperor Rudolph.'

'He *did?*' This was astonishing news.

'I've laid hands on them all, though they aren't all here.'

Rumby directed me to a table where a portfolio lay. Opening this, I turned over a dozen large glossy colour reproductions—of masturbating men made of mushrooms and autumnal fruits, men with large hairy nuts and spurting seed; of licking lesbian ladies composed of marrows and lettuce leaves . . .

'You researched all the background bio on Strada, Jill. Nobody knows what sort of things our friend Archy might have been painting between 1576 and 1587 before he went back home to Milan, hmm?'

'I thought he was busy arranging festivals for Rudolph. Masques and tournaments and processions.'

'That isn't *all* he was arranging. Rudy was fairly nutty.'

'Oh, I don't know if that's quite fair to Rudolph . . .'

'What, to keep a chained lion in the hall? To sleep in a different bed every night? His mania for exotica! Esoterica! Erotica! A pushover for any passing magician. Bizarre foibles. Loopy as King Ludo of Bavaria—yet with *real power*. The power to indulge himself—secretly—in orgies and weird erotica, there in vast Ratzen Castle in Prague.'

I wondered about the provenance of these hitherto unknown paintings.

To which, Rumby gave a very plausible answer.

When the Swedes under the command of von Wrangel sacked Prague in 1648 as their contribution to the Thirty Years War, they pillaged the imperial collections. Thus a sheaf of Archimboldos ended up in Skoklosters Castle at Bålsta in Sweden.

'Skoklosters *Slott*. Kind of evocative name, huh?'

When Queen Christina converted to Catholicism in 1654 and abdicated the Swedish throne, she took many of those looted art treasures with her to Rome itself—with the exception of so-called *German* art, which she despised. In her eyes, Archimboldo was part of German art.

However, in the view of her catechist (who was a subtle priest), those locked-away *porn* paintings were a different kettle of fish. The Vatican should take charge of those and keep them *sub rosa*. Painters were never fingered by the Inquisition, unlike authors of the written word. Bonfires of merely lewd material were never an issue in an era when clerics often liked a fuck. Nevertheless, such paintings might serve as a handy blackmail tool against Habsburg Emperors who felt tempted to act too leniently towards Protestants in their domains. A blot on the Habsburg escutcheon, suggesting a strain of lunacy.

The cardinal-diplomat to whom the paintings were consigned deposited them for safe keeping in the crypt at a certain enclosed convent of his patronage. There, as it happened, they remained until discovered by a private collector in the 1890s. By then the convent had fallen on hard times. Our collector relieved the holy mothers of the embarrassing secret heritage in return for a substantial donation . . .

'It's a watertight story,' concluded Rumby, blinking owlishly at me. 'Of course it's also a complete lie . . .'

The dirty dozen Archimboldos were forgeries perpetrated in Holland within the past couple of years, to Rumby's specifications, by a would-be surrealist.

I stared at the fishy masturbatress, fascinated.

'They're fine forgeries,' he enthused. 'Painted on antique oak board precisely eleven millimetres thick. Two base layers of white lead, chalk, and charcoal slack . . .' He expatiated with the enthusiasm of a petrochemist conducting an assay of crude. The accuracy of the lipid and protein components. The pigments consisting of azurite, yellow lead, malachite . . . Mr Oil seemed to know rather a lot about such aspects of oil painting.

He waved his hand impatiently. 'Point is, it'll stand up under X-ray, infrared, most sorts of analysis. This is perfectionist forgery with serious money behind it. Oh yes, sponsored exhibition in Europe, book, prints, postcards, media scandal . . . ! These naughty Archeys are going to fuck all those Green Fascists in the eyeballs. Here's their patron saint with his pants down. Here's what red-nosed Rudy really got off on. Nobody'll be able to gaze dewy-eyed at those posters any more, drooling about the sanctity of nature. *This* is nature—red in dildo and labia. A fish-fuck. Their big image campaign will blow up in their faces—ludicrously, obscenely. Can you beat the power of an image? Why yes, you *can*—with an anti-image! We'll have done something really positive to save the space budget. You'll write the intro to the art book, Jenny, in your inimitable style. Scholarly—but provocative.'

'I will?'

'Yes, because I'll pay you three quarters of a million dollars.'

A flea-bite to Rumby, really...

The budget for this whole escapade was probably ten times that. Or more. Would that represent the output of one single oil well for a year? A month...? I really had no idea.

Aside from our crusade for space, smearing egg conspicuously on the face of the ecofreaks might materially assist Rumby's daily business and prove to be a sound investment, since he profited so handsomely by pumping out the planet's non-renewable resources.

'*And* because you want to sock Green Fascism, Jill. And on account of how this is so splendidly, provocatively perverse.'

Was he right, or was he right?

He was certainly different from the kind of man I'd expected to meet.

Obviously I mustn't spill the beans in the near future. *Consequently* the bulk of my fee would be held on deposit in my name in a Zurich bank, but would only become accessible to me five years after publication of *Archimboldo Erotico*...

Until then I would need to lead roughly the same life as usual—plus the need to defend my latest opus amongst my peers and on TV and in magazines and wherever else. Rumby—or Chaplain Lascelles—would certainly strive to ensure a media circus, if none such burgeoned of its own accord. I would be Rumby's front woman.

I liked the *three quarters* of a million aspect. This showed that Rumby had subtlety. One million would have been a blatant bribe.

I also liked Rumby himself.

I had indeed been collected.

And that 750K (as Brother Bob would count it) wasn't by any means the only consideration. *I approved.*

As to my fallback position, should the scheme be—ahem—rumbled... well, pranks question mundane reality in a revolutionary manner, don't they just?

That was a line from Peter, which I half believed—though not enough to stage a diversion in the National Gallery by stripping my blouse off, as he had wished, while Peter glued a distempery canine turd to Gainsborough's painting, *White Dogs*, so as to question 'conventions'. I'd balked at *that* proposed escapade of Peter's ten years previously.

This was a political prank—a blow against an insidious, powerful kind of repression; almost, even, a blow for art.

Thus, my defence.

I took a copy of the erotic portfolio back with me to Bloomsbury to gaze at for a few days; and to keep safely locked up when I wasn't looking at it.

Just as well that Phil wasn't involved in my immediate life these days, though we still saw each other casually. I'm sure Phil's antennae would have twitched if he had still been sleeping with a strangely furtive me. Being art critic for the *Sunday Times* had seemed to imbue him with the passions of an investigative journalist. Just as soon as *Archimboldo Erotico* burst upon the scene, no doubt he would be in touch . . . I would need to tell lies to a former lover and ensure that 'in touch' remained a phrase without physical substance. Already I could envision his injured, acquisitive expression as he rebuked me for not leaking this great art scoop to him personally. ('But why not, Jill? Didn't we share a great deal? I must say I think it's damned queer that you didn't breathe a word about this! Very *peculiar*, in fact. It makes me positively *suspicious* . . . This isn't some kind of *revenge* on your part, is it? But why, *why*?')

And what would Annie think? She was painting in Cornwall in a women's artistic commune, and her last letter had been friendly . . . If I hadn't offended her with my porn paradoxes, then attaching my name to a glossy volume of fish-frigs and spurting phallic mushrooms oughtn't to make too much difference, unless she had become radically repressive of late . . .

In other words, I was wondering to what extent this escapade would cause a hindwards reconstruction of my own life on account of the duplicity in which I'd be engaging.

And what about the *future*—in five years time—when I passed GO and became three quarters of a dollar millionairess? What would I *do* with all that money? Decamp to Italy? Quit the London grime and buy a farmhouse near Florence?

In the meantime I wouldn't be able to confide the truth to any intimate friend. I wouldn't be able to afford intimacy. I might become some pursed-smile equivalent of Chaplain Lascelles, though on a longer leash.

Maybe Rumby had accurately calculated that he was getting a bargain.

To be sure, the shape of my immediate future all somewhat depended on the impact of the book, the exhibition, the extent of the hoo-ha . . . Personally, I'd give the book as much impact as I could. After all, I did like to provoke.

I returned to Bexford House a week later, to stay two nights and to sort through Rumby's stock of material about Archimboldo, Rudolph, and the Prague Court. I have a good reading knowledge of German, French, and Italian, though I'm not conversationally fluent in those tongues. Any book I needed to take away with me was photocopied in its entirety by Lascelles on a high-speed, auto-page-turning machine. Pop in a book—within five minutes out popped its twin, collated and bound. The machine cost twenty thousand dollars.

A week after that, Case drove me to the docklands airport for a rather lux commuter flight with him to Amsterdam, where I examined all the other Archimboldo 'originals'; although I didn't meet the forger himself, nor did I even learn his name. The paintings were stored in three locations: in the apartment of Rumby's chosen printer, Wim Van Ewyck, in that of the gallery owner who would host the show, Geert De Lugt, and in a locked room of the Galerij Bosch itself. In the event of premature catastrophe, the entire corpus of controversial work (minus the fishy masturbatress at Bexford House) wouldn't be wiped out en masse.

Presumably the printer didn't need to be in on the conspiracy. What about the gallery owner? Maybe; maybe not . . . *This*, as Case impressed on me, was a subject which shouldn't even be alluded to—nor did Mijnheer de Lugt so much as hint.

The other eleven Archimboldos were even more stunning at full size in the frame than in colour reproduction. And also more . . . appalling?

I returned to Bloomsbury to write twenty large pages of introduction. Less would have been skimpy; more would have been excessive. Since I was being fastidiously attentive to every nuance of the text, the writing took me almost three weeks, with five or six drafts. ('Put some feeling into it,' Rumby had counselled. 'Smear some vaginal jelly on the words.')

The task done, I phoned Bexford Hall. Case drove the Merc to London the same evening to courier the pages personally. Next day, Rumby phoned to pronounce himself quite delighted. He only suggested a few micro-changes. We were rolling. Our exhibition would open in the Galerij Bosch on the first of September, coinciding with publication of the book.

And of course I must attend the private showing on the last day of August—the vernissage, as it were. (I did hope the varnish was totally dry!)

While in Amsterdam, our party—consisting of Rumby and Case and Lascelles and myself—stayed in the Grand Hotel Krasnopolsky because that hotel boasted a Japanese restaurant, and Rumby was a bit of a pig for raw fish. I wasn't complaining.

We arrived a day early in case Rumby had any last minute thoughts about the layout of the show, or Case about its security aspects. So the morning of the thirty-first saw us at the Galerij Bosch, which fronted a tree-lined canal not far from where dozens of antique shops clustered on the route to the big art museums.

The high neck gable of the building, ornamented with two bounteous sculpted classical maidens amidst cascades of fruits and vegetables—shades of Archimboldo, indeed!—incorporated a hoisting beam, though I doubted that any crated paintings had entered the loft of the gallery by that particular route for a long time. Venetian blinds were currently blanking the three adjacent ground-floor windows—the uprights and transoms of which were backed by discreet steel bars, as Case pointed out; and already Mijnheer De Lugt, a tall blond man with a bulbous nose, had three muscular fellows lounging about in the large, spot-lit exhibition room. One in a demure blue security uniform—he was a golden-skinned and moon-faced, obviously of Indonesian ancestry. The other chunky Germanic types wore light suits and trainers.

A high pile of copies of *Archimboldo Erotico* stood in one corner for presentation that evening to the guests: the media people, museum directors, cultural mandarins and mavericks. Particularly the media people.

And my heart quailed.

Despite all the gloss, mightn't someone promptly *denounce* this exhibition? We were in liberal Holland, where the obscenity would not of itself offend. Yet wouldn't someone cry 'Hoax!'?

Worse, mightn't some inspired avant-garde type perhaps enthusiastically *applaud* this exhibition as an ambitious jape?

De Lugt seemed a tad apprehensive beneath a suave exterior. He blew that snozzle of his a number of times without obvious reason, as though determined to be squeaky-clean.

'Ms Donaldson, would you sign a copy of the book for me as a souvenir?' he asked. When I had obliged, he scrutinised my signature as if the scrawly autograph might be a forgery.

Maybe I was simply being paranoid. But I was damn glad of this dry run amongst the exhibits.

Case conferred with the security trio quietly in Dutch. They smiled; they nodded.

The wet run that evening—lubricated by champagne to celebrate the resurrection of long-lost works of a bizarre master, and contemporary of Rabelais—went off quite as well as could be expected.

A young red-haired woman in a severe black cocktail dress walked out along with her escort in shock and rage. She had been wearing an Archimboldo eco-badge as her only form of jewellery, with the word *Ark* printed upon it.

A fat bluff bearded fellow in a dinner jacket, with an enormous spotted cravat instead of bow tie, got drunk and began guffawing. Tears streamed down his hairy cheeks till Case discreetly persuaded him to step outside for an airing.

Rumby was bombarded by questions, to which he would grin and reply, 'It's all in the book. Take a copy!' One of the great art finds, yes. Casts quite a new light on Archimboldo, that emotionally complex man.

So why had Mr Wright sprung this surprise on the art world by way of a private gallery? Rather than lending these paintings to some major public museum?

'Ah now, do you really suppose your big museum would have leapt at the chance of showing such *controversial* material, Ladies and Gentlemen? Some big city museum with its reputation to think about? Of course, I'll be perfectly delighted to loan this collection out in future . . .'

I was quizzed too. Me, in my new purple velvet couturier pantsuit.

Geert De Lugt smiled and nodded approvingly, confidently. Naturally Rumby would have paid him handsomely for use of his gallery, yet I was becoming convinced that Mijnheer De Lugt himself was innocent of the deception. He had merely had stage nerves earlier.

We stayed in Amsterdam for another five days. Press and media duly obliged with publicity, and I appeared on Dutch and German TV, both with Rumby and without him. So many people flocked to the Galerij Bosch that our Security boys had to limit admittance to thirty people at any one time, while a couple of tolerant police hung about outside. Our book sold like hot cakes to the visitors; and by now it was in the bookshops too. ('At this rate,' joked Rumby, 'we'll be making a fucking *profit*.')

During spare hours, I wandered round town with Case. Rumby mainly stayed in his suite at the Krasnopolsky in phone and fax contact with Bexford and Texas, munching sushi. I nursed a fancy that Chaplain Lascelles might perhaps lugubriously be visiting the Red Light District to let his hair and his pants down, but he certainly wasn't getting high on any dope. Me, I preferred the flea-market on Waterlooplein, where I picked up a black lace shawl and a slightly frayed Kashmiri rug for the flat back in Bloomsbury.

I noticed a certain item of graffiti on numerous walls: *Onze Wereld is onze Ark.*

'Our world is our Ark,' translated Case.

Sometimes there was only the word *Ark* on its own writ even larger in spray-paint. I couldn't but recall the badge worn by that pissed-off woman at the party in the gallery. Pissed-off? No . . . *mortally offended.* Obviously, *Ark* was a passionate, punning, mispronounced allusion to . . . who else but Emperor Rudolph's court jester?

When I mentioned this graffito to Rumby, he almost growled with glee.

'Ha! So what do you do in this fucking *ark* of theirs? You hide, anchored by gravity—till you've squandered all your major resources, then you can't get to anyplace else. Sucks to arks.'

We all flew back to England on the Sunday. At seven a.m. on the Monday morning the phone bullied me awake.

Lascelles was calling.

Late on the Sunday night, a van had mounted the pavement outside Galerij Bosch. The driver grabbed a waiting motorbike and sped off. Almost at once the van exploded devastatingly, demolishing the whole frontage of the building. As well as explosives, there'd been a hell of a lot of jellied petrol and phosphorus in that van. Fireworks, indeed! The gallery was engulfed in flames. So were part of the street and a couple of trees. Even the canal caught fire, and a nearby houseboat blazed, though the occupants had been called away by some ruse. The two security guards who were in the gallery on night shift died.

And of course all the Archimboldos had been burnt, though that seemed a minor aspect to me right then . . .

Case was coming pronto to pick me up. Rumby wanted us to talk face to face before the media swarmed.

Two hours later, I was at Bexford Hall.

Rumby, Lascelles, Case, and I met together in a book-lined upstairs study, furnished with buff leather armchairs upon a russet Persian carpet. The single large window, composed of stone mullions, seemed somewhat at odds with the Italianate plasterwork ceiling which featured scrolls and roses, with cherubs and putti supporting the boss of an electrified chandelier. Maybe Rumby had bought this ceiling in from some other house because it was the right size, and he liked it. The room smelled of cheroots, and soon of my Marlboro too.

'Let's dismiss the financial side right away,' commenced Rumby. 'The paintings weren't insured. So I'm not obliged to make any kind of claim. Hell, do I need to? The book will be the only record—and your fee stays secure, Jill. Now, is it to our disadvantage that the paintings themselves no longer exist? Might someone hint that *we* ourselves arranged the torching of the gallery before independent art experts could stick their fingers in the pie? I think two tragic deaths say no to that. Those poor guys had no chance. T. Rumbold Wright isn't known for assassinations. So, ghastly as this is, it could be to our advantage—especially if it smears the ecofreaks, the covenanters of the Ark.'

What a slur on the ecofreaks that they might destroy newly discovered masterpieces of art for ideological reasons in a desperate effort to keep the artist pure for exploitation by themselves. When people saw any Archimboldo badge or poster now, they might think, *Ho-ho* . . . I was thinking about the two dead guards.

Lascelles had been liaising with Holland.

'The Dutch police are puzzled,' he summarised. 'Is this an outburst of art-terrorism? A few years ago some people revived a group called the SKG—so-called "City Art Guerillas" who caused street and gallery trouble. They never killed anyone. Even if the couple on that houseboat were kept out of harm's way to make the attackers seem more benign, De Lugt's two guards were just slaughtered . . .

'Then what about these Ark people? The loony fringe of the Dutch Eco movement *have* gone in for destructive industrial sabotage—but again, they haven't caused any deaths. This is more like the work of the German Red Column, though it seems they haven't operated in Holland recently. Why do so now? And why hit the gallery?'

'To hurt a noted Capitalist, in the only way they could think of?' asked Rumby. 'No, I don't buy that. It's got to be the Ecofreaks.'

'The ecology movement is very respectable in Holland.'

Rumby grinned wolfishly. 'Mightn't be, soon.'

'Ecology is government policy there.'

How much more newsworthy the destruction made those naughty paint-ings! How convenient that they were now beyond the reach of sceptical specialists.

'I don't suppose,' said I, 'one of your *allies* in the Star Club might conceiv-ably have arranged this attack?'

Drop a ton of lead into a pond.

'Future of the human race,' I added weakly. 'Big motivation.'

Rumby wrestled a cheroot from his coat of many pockets and lit it. 'You can forget that idea. Let's consider *safety*. Your safety, Jill.'

I suppose he couldn't avoid making this sound like a threat, however benevolently intentioned—or making it seem as if he wished to keep my free spirit incommunicado during the crisis . . .

'Someone has bombed and murdered ruthlessly,' said Rumby. *'I'm* safe here.'

'Yes, you are,' Case assured him.

'But you, Jill, you live in some little scumbag flat in any old street in London. I'd like to invite you to stay here at Bexford for a week or two until things clarify.'

'Actually, I can't,' I told him, with silly stubbornness. 'I have a couple of lectures to give at St Martin's on Thursday.'

'Screw them. Cancel them.'

'And it isn't exactly a scumbag flat.'

'Sorry—you know what I mean.'

'At least until there's a communiqué,' Lascelles suggested to me. 'Then we'll know what we're dealing with. It's only sensible.'

'Don't be *proud*,' said Rumby. He puffed. The cherubs above collected a tiny little bit more nicotine on their innocent hands. 'Please.'

And some more nicotine from me too.

'You don't need to feed some goddam *cat*, do you?' asked Rumby.

'No . . .' In fact I loathed cats—selfish, treacherous creatures—but Rumby probably wouldn't have cared one way of the other.

In the event, I stayed at Bexford. Until Wednesday afternoon. No news emerged from Holland of any communiqué.

Could the attackers not have *known* about those two guards inside the gallery? So now they were ashamed, and politically reluctant, to claim credit?

Unlikely. You don't assemble a vanload of explosives and napalm and phosphorus, make sure there's a getaway motorbike waiting, and bail out the occupants of a nearby houseboat, without checking everything else about the target too.

Lascelles was stone-walling queries from the media. ('Mr Wright is shocked. He grieves at the two deaths. He has no other comment at present...') Stubbornly, I insisted on being driven back to Bloomsbury.

My little flat had been burgled. My CD player and my TV were missing.

Entry was by way of the fire escape door, which had been smashed off its none too sturdy hinges. Otherwise, there wasn't much damage or mess.

I hadn't wished Case to escort me upstairs; thus he had already driven away. Of course I *could* have reached him on the Merc's car phone. Yet this was so ordinary a burglary that I simply phoned the police. Then I thumbed the Yellow Pages for an emergency repair service which was willing to turn up within the next six hours.

The constable who visited me presently was a West Indian. A couple of other nearby flats had also been broken into the day before for electrical goods, so he said. Was I aware of this? He seemed to be pitching his questions towards eliciting whether I might perhaps have robbed myself so as to claim insurance.

'Fairly *neat* break-in, Miss, all things considered.'

'Except for the door.'

'You're lucky. Some people find excrement spread all over their homes.'

'Did that happen in the other flats that were burgled?'

'Not on this occasion. So you reported this just as soon as you came back from—'

'From the Cotswolds.'

'Nice part of the country, I hear. Were you there long?'

'Three days.'

'Visiting friends?'

'My employer.' Now why did I have to say *that*? Blurt, blurt.

'Oh, so you live here, but your boss is in the Cotswolds?'

'He isn't exactly my boss. He was consulting me.'

The constable raised his eyebrow suggestively.

Obviously he believed in keeping the suspect off balance.

'You do have a lot of expensive books here, Miss,' was his next tack.

Yes, rows of glossy art books. Why hadn't those been stolen—apart from the fact that they weighed a ton?

'I don't suppose the burglars were interested in art,' I suggested.

He pulled out a *Botticelli*, with library markings on the spine, from the shelf.

'This is from a college library,' he observed.

'I teach there. I lecture about art.'

'I thought you said you were a *consultant*...'

By the time he left, I was half-convinced that I had burgled myself, that I habitually thieved from libraries, and that I was a call-girl who had been supplying sexual favours to Mr X out in the country. Would these suspicions be entered in the police computer? Did I have the energy to do anything about this? No, it was all so... tentative. Did I want to seem paranoid?

Bert the Builder finally turned up and fixed the door for a hundred and thirteen pounds... which of course the insurance would be covering. Otherwise the job would have cost just sixty, cash.

I did manage to look over my lecture notes—on Titian and Veronese. I microwaved a madras beef curry with pilau rice; and went to bed, fed up.

The phone rang.

It was Phil. He had been calling my number for days.

These weird long-lost Archimboldos! Why hadn't I told him anything? And the terrorist attack! What had happened? Could he come round?

'Sorry, Phil, but I've just had my CD and TV nicked. And the helpful visiting constable thinks I'm a hooker.'

I was glad of the excuse of the burglary.

Towards mid-morning my phone started ringing, and a couple of Press sleuths turned up in person, pursuing the art bombing story; but I stonewalled, and escaped in the direction of St Martin's where, fortunately, no reporters lurked.

At four in the afternoon I stepped out from the factory-like frontage of the art school into a Charing Cross Road aswarm with tourists. Beneath a grey overcast the fumy air was warm. A sallow Middle Eastern youth in checked shirt and jeans promptly handed me a leaflet advertising some English Language Academy.

'I already speak English,' I informed the tout. He frowned momentarily as if he didn't understand. No points to the Academy.

'Then you learn *cheaper*,' he suggested, pursuing me along the pavement.

'Do not bother that lady,' interrupted a tall blond young man dressed in a lightweight off-white jacket and slacks.

'No, it's all right,' I assured my would-be protector.

'It is not all right. Any trash is on our streets. They are not safe.'

He waved, and a taxi pulled up almost immediately. The young man opened the door, plunged his hand inside his jacket, and showed me a small pistol hidden in his palm. Was he some urban vigilante crusader pledged to rescue damsels from offensive encounters? I just didn't understand what was happening.

'Get in quickly,' he said, 'or I will shoot you dead.'

Help, I mouthed at the Arab, or whatever.

In vain.

I did as Prince Charming suggested. Did *anyone* notice me being abducted? Or only see a handsome young man hand me enthusiastically into that taxi?

The driver didn't look round.

'Keep quiet,' said the young man. 'Put these glasses on.' He handed me glasses black as night equipped with side-blinkers, such as someone with a rare hypersensitive eye ailment might wear. Only, these were utterly dark; I couldn't see a thing through them.

We drove for what seemed like half an hour. Eventually we drew up—and waited, perhaps so that passers-by might have time to pass on by—before my abductor assisted me from the cab. Quickly he guided me arm in arm up some steps. A door closed behind us. Traffic noise grew mute.

We mounted a broad flight of stairs, and entered an echoing room—where I was pressured into a straight-backed armchair. Immediately one hand pressed under my nose, and another on my jaw, to force my mouth open.

'Drink!'

Liquid poured down my throat—some sweet concoction masking a bitter undertaste. I gagged and spluttered but had no choice except to swallow.

What had I drunk? What had I drunk?

'I need to see the eyes,' said a sombre, if somewhat slobbery voice. 'The truth is in the eyes.' The accent was Germanic.

A hand removed my glasses.

I found myself in a drawing room with a dusty varnished floor and double oak doors. A small chandelier of dull lustres shone. Thick blue brocade curtains cloaked tall windows, which in any event appeared to be shuttered. A dustsheet covered what I took to be a baby grand piano. An oblong of less faded rose-and-lily wallpaper, over a marble fireplace, showed where some painting had hung.

On a chaise longue sat a slim elegant grizzle-haired man of perhaps sixty kitted out in a well-tailored grey suit. A walking cane was pressed between his knees. His hands opened and closed slowly to reveal the chased silver handle. A second middle-aged man stood near him: stouter, bald, wearing a long purple velvet robe with fur trimmings which at first I thought was some exotic dressing gown. This man's face was jowly and pouchy. He looked like Goering on a bad day. His eyes were eerie: bulgy, yet bright as if he was on cocaine.

My abductor had stationed himself directly behind me.

On a walnut table lay a copy of *Archimboldo Erotico*, open at my introduction.

Shit.

'My apologies,' said the seated gent, 'for the manner of your coming here, Miss Donaldson.' He gestured at the book. 'But you owe me a profound apology—and restitution. Your libels must be corrected.'

The fellow in the robe moved closer, to stare at me. His fingers wiggled.

'What libels?' I asked, rather deeply scared. These people had to be nutters, possessed by some zany fanatical motive. Well-heeled, well-groomed nutters were maybe the really dangerous sort. *What had I drunk? A slow poison? Would I soon be begging for the antidote?*

'Libels against a certain Holy Roman Emperor, Miss Donaldson. Thus, libels against the Habsburg dynasty... which may yet be the salvation of Europe, and of the world. Very *untimely* libels.' The gent raised his cane and slashed it to and fro as if decapitating daisies. 'I am sure you will see reason to denounce your fabrications publicly...'

'What fabrications?'

He stood up smoothly and brought his cane down savagely upon my book, though his expression remained suave and polite. I jerked, imagining that cane striking me instead.

'These! These obscenities were never painted by Rudolph's court artist!'

'But,' I murmured, 'the looting of Prague . . . Skoklosters Castle . . . Queen Christina's chaplain . . .'

He sighed. 'Lies. All lies. And I do not quite know why. Let us discuss art and history, Miss Donaldson.'

'She is deceitful,' said the fellow in the robe, always peering at me. 'She has a guilty conscience.'

'Who are you?' I asked. 'The local mind-reader?'

The stout man smiled unctuously.

'Herr Voss is my occultist,' explained the gent.

'Oculist? You mean, optician?'

'My *occultist!* My pansophist. The holder of the keys to the Unknown. And *my* name happens to be Heinrich von Habsburg, Miss Donaldson . . .'

'Oh . . .' I said.

'I shall not burden your brain with genealogy, except to say that I am the living heir to the Holy Roman throne. Let us discuss *art* instead. And *history.*'

This, His Royal Heinrich proceeded to do, while the keeper of the keys contemplated me and my guard hovered behind me.

Rudolph and his father Maximilian before him had been astute, benevolent rulers, who aimed to heal discord in Christian Europe by uniting it under Habsburg rule. They lived noble and honourable lives, as did Count Giuseppe Archimboldo. His supposed fantasias possessed a precise political and metaphysical significance in the context of the Holy Roman throne. The aesthetic harmony of natural elements in the *Vertumnus* and in the other portrait heads bespoke the harmony which would bless Europe under the beneficent leadership of the House of Austria . . .

Jawohl, I thought.

Ever-present, like the elements themselves, the Habsburgs would rule both microcosm and macrocosm—both the political world, and nature too. Archimboldo's cycle of the seasons, depicted as Habsburg heads wrought of Wintry, Vernal, Summery, and Autumnal ingredients, confided that Habsburg rule would extend eternally through time in one everlasting season. Under the secular and spiritual guidance of those descendants of Hercules, the House of Habsburg, the Golden Age would return to a united Europe.

Right on.

In due course of time, this happy culmination had almost come to pass. The 'Great King', as predicted, nay, propagandised by Nostradamus, loomed on the horizon.

When the Habsburgs united with the House of Lorraine, and when Marie Antoinette became Queen of France, the House of Habsburg-Lorraine was within a generation of dominion over Europe—had the French Revolution not intervened.

What a pity.

Throughout the nineteenth century the House attempted to regroup. However, the upheavals attending the end of the First World War toppled the Habsburgs from power, ushering in chaos . . .

Shame.

Now all Europe was revived and reuniting, and its citizens were ever more aware that the microcosm of Man and the macrocosm of Nature were a unity.

Yet lacking, as yet, a *head*.

A Holy Roman Imperial head.

Early restoration of the monarchy in Hungary was one possible ace card—though other cards were also tucked up the imperial sleeve . . .

Archimboldo's symbolic portraits were holy ikons of this golden dream, especially in view of their eco-injection into the European psyche. Those paintings were programming the people with a subconscious expectation, a hope, a longing, a secret sense of destiny, which a restored Habsburg Holy Roman Empire would fulfill.

'Now do you see why your obscenities are such a libelous blasphemy, Miss Donaldson?'

Good God.

'Do you mean to tell me that *you're* behind the Archimboldo eco-campaign?' I asked His Imperial Heinrich.

'The power of symbols,' remarked Voss, 'is very great. Symbols are my speciality.'

Apparently they weren't going to tell me whether they simply hoped to exploit an existing, serendipitous media campaign—or whether some loyal Habsburg mole had actively persuaded the ecofreaks to plaster what were effectively Habsburg heads—in fruit and veg, and flowers and leaves—all over Europe and America.

'You broke into my flat,' I accused the man behind me. 'Looking for some dirt that doesn't exist because the erotic paintings are genuine!'

Blondie slapped me sharply across the head.

'Martin! You know that is unnecessary!' H. von H. held up his hand prohibitively—for the moment, at least.

'You broke my door down,' I muttered over my shoulder, thinking myself reprieved, 'and you stole my CD and TV just to make the thing look plausible. I bet you burgled those other flats in the neighbourhood too as a deception.'

Martin, on his *own?* Surely not . . . There must have been others involved. The taxi driver . . . and whoever else . . .

'Actually, we broke your door *after* the burglary,' boasted Martin. 'We *entered* with more circumspection.'

Voss smiled in a predatory fashion. 'With secret keys, as it were.'

Others. Others . . .

They had blown up the Galerij Bosch! They had burned those two guards to death . . .

I shrank.

'I see that the magnitude of this is beginning to dawn on your butterfly mind,' said the Habsburg. 'A united Europe must be saved from *pollution*. Ecological pollution, of course—a Holy Roman Emperor is as a force of nature. But moral pollution too.'

'How about racial?' I queried.

'I'm an aristocrat, not a barbarian,' remarked Heinrich. 'The Nazis were contemptible. Yet plainly we cannot have Moslems—Turkish *heathens*—involved in the affairs of Holy Europe. We cannot have those who besieged our Vienna in 1683 succeeding now by the back door.'

Oh, the grievances of centuries long past . . . Rumby and his science Star Club suddenly seemed like such Johnnies-Come-Lately indeed.

Science . . . versus imperial *magic* . . . with eco-mysticism in the middle . . .

'I just can't believe you're employing a frigging *magician* to gain the throne of Europe!'

'*Language*, Miss Donaldson!' snapped the Habsburg. 'You are corrupt.'

Voss smoothed his robe as though I had mussed it.

'You're a creature of your time, Miss Donaldson,' said H. von H. 'Whereas I am a creation of the centuries.'

'Would that be *The Centuries of Nostradamus?*' Yes, that was the title of that volume of astrological rigmarole.

'I mustn't forget that you're educated, by the lights of today. Tell me, what do you suppose the *Centuries* of the title refer to?'

'Well, years. A long time, the future.'

'Quite wrong. There simply happen to be a hundred quatrains—verses of four lines—in each section. You're only half educated. And thus you blunder. How much did your American art collector pay you for writing that introduction?'

Obviously Rumby would have paid me *something* . . . I wouldn't have written those pages for nothing . . .

'Three thousand dollars,' I improvised.

'That doesn't sound very much, considering the evil intent. Is Mr Wright being hoaxed *too?*'

Again, he slammed the cane on to my book.

An astonishing flash of agony seared across my back. I squealed and twisted round—but Martin was holding no cane.

He was holding nothing at all. With a grin, Martin displayed his empty paws for me. Voss giggled, and when I looked at him he winked.

It was as though that open volume was some voodoo doll of myself which the Habsburg had just chastised.

The Habsburg lashed at my words again, and I cried out, for the sudden pain was intense—yet I knew there would be no mark on me.

Voss licked his lips. 'Symbolic resonances, Miss Donaldson. The power of symbolic actions.'

What drug had been in that liquid I swallowed? I didn't *feel* disoriented—save for nerves and dread—yet I must be in some very strange state of mind to account for my suggestibility to pain.

'We can continue thus for a while, Miss Donaldson.' Heinrich raised his cane again.

'Wait.'

Was three quarters of a million dollars enough to compensate for being given the third degree right now by crazy, ruthless *murderers*—who could torture me symbolically, but effectively?

I experienced an absurd vision of myself attempting to tell the West Indian detective-constable that actually my flat had been broken into by agents of a Holy Roman Emperor who hoped to take over Europe—and that I was seeking police protection because the Habsburgs could hurt me agonisingly by whipping my words . . .

Was I mad, or was I mad?

The room seemed luminous, glowing with an inner light. Every detail of furniture or drapery was intensely *actual*. I thought that my sense of reality had never been stronger.

'Okay,' I admitted, 'the paintings were all forgeries. They were done in Holland, but I honestly don't know who by. I never met him. I never learned his name. Rumby—Mr Wright—hates the ecology lobby because they hate space exploration, and he thinks that's our only hope. I have a friend at the *Sunday Times*. I'll tell him everything—about how the paintings were a prank. They'll love to print that! Wright will have egg on his face.'

'What a treacherous modern creature you are,' the Habsburg said with casual contempt; and I squirmed with shame and fear.

'Just watch for next weekend's paper,' I promised.

'At this moment,' said Voss, 'she believes she is going to do what she says—and of course she knows that our Martin can find her, if she breaks her word . . .' He peered.

'Ah: she's relieved that *you* cannot reach her from a distance with the whipping cane.

'And she wonders whether Martin would really kill her, and thus lose us her testimony . . .'

No, he *wasn't* reading my mind. He wasn't! He was reading my face, my muscles. He could do so because everything was so real.

More peering.

'She feels a paradoxical affection for her friend . . . *Rumby*. Solidarity, as well as greed. Yes, a definite loyalty.' If only I hadn't called him Rumby. If only I'd just called him Wright. It was all in the words. Voss wasn't reading my actual thoughts.

'So therefore,' H. von H. said to Voss, 'she must be retrained in her loyalties.'

What did he mean? What did he mean?

'She must be conditioned by potent symbols, Voss.'

'Just so, Excellency.'

'Thus she will not wish to betray us. Enlighten her, Voss. Show her the real depth of history, from where we come. Your juice will be deep in her now.'

Numbness crept over me, as Voss loomed closer. The sheer pressure of his approach was paralysing me.

'Wait,' I managed to squeak.

'Wait?' echoed H. von H. 'Oh, I have waited long enough already. My family has waited long enough. Through the French Revolution, through the Communist intermezzo . . . The Holy Roman Empire *will* revive at this present cusp of history—for it has always remained in being, at least as a state of mind. And *mind* is what matters, Miss Donaldson—as Rudolph knew, contrary to your pornographic lies! Ah yes, my ancestor avidly sought the symbolic key to the ideal world. Practitioners of the symbolic, hermetic arts visited him in Prague Castle—though he lacked the loyal services of a Voss . . .'

The Habsburg slid his cane under the dustsheet of the piano, and whisked the cloth off. Seating himself on the stool, he threw open the lid of the baby grand with a crash. His slim, manicured fingers started to play plangent, mournful Debussyish chords in which I could almost feel myself begin to drown.

Voss crooned to me—or sang—in some dialect of German . . . and I couldn't move a muscle. Surely I was shrinking—or else the drawing room was expanding. Or both. Voss was becoming vast.

I was a little child again—yet not a child, but rather a miniature of myself. When I was on the brink of puberty, lying in bed just prior to drifting off to sleep, this same distortion of the senses used to happen to me.

The music lamented.

And Voss crooned my lullaby.

A bearded man in black velvet and cerise satin held my nude paralysed body in his hands. He held the *whole* of me in his hands—for I was tiny now, the height of his forearm.

Draped over his shoulders was a lavish ermine cloak.

I was stiff, unmoving.

He placed me in a niche, ran his fingertip down my belly, and traced the cleft between my thighs.

He stepped back.

Then he left.

I was in a great gloomy vaulted chamber housing massive cupboards and strongboxes. The slit windows in the thick stone wall were grated so as to deter any slim cat burglars. Stacked several deep around a broad shelf, and likewise below, were mythological and Biblical oil paintings: Tintorettos, Titians, by the look of them . . . Neither the lighting nor the decor were at all in the spirit of any latter-day museum. Here was art as treasure—well and truly locked up.

Days and nights passed.

Weeks of static solitude until I was going crazy. I would have welcomed any change whatever, any newcomer. My thoughts looped around a circuit of Strada, death in Amsterdam, Habsburgs, with the latter assuming ever more significance—and necessity—with each mental swing.

Eventually the door opened, and in walked a figure who made the room shine. For his face and hair were made of a hundred springtime flowers, his collar of white daisies, and his clothes of a hundred lush leaves.

He stood and gazed at me through floral eyes, and with his rosebud lips he smiled faintly.

He simply went away.

A season passed, appalling in its sheer duration. I saw daisies like stars before my eyes, in an unending afterimage.

Then in walked glowing Summer. His eyes were ripe cherries. His teeth were little peas. Plums and berries tangled in his harvest-hair; and his garment was of woven straw.

And he too smiled, and went away in turn.

And another season passed . . .

. . . till rubicund Autumn made his appearance. He was a more elderly fellow with an oaten beard, a fat pear of a nose, mushroom ears, clusters of grapes instead of locks of hair. His chin was a pomegranate. He wore an overripe burst fig as an ear-ring. He winked lecherously, and departed even as I tried to cry out to him through rigid lips, to stay.

For next came Winter, old and gnarled, scabbed and scarred, his nose a stump of rotted branch, his skin of fissured bark, his lips of jutting bracket-fungus.

Winter stayed for a longer grumbly time, though he no more reached to touch me than had his predecessors. His departure—the apparent end of this cycle of seasons—plunged me into despair. I was as cold as marble.

Until one day the door opened yet again, and golden light bathed my prison chamber.

Vertumnus himself advanced—the fruitful God, his cheeks of ripe apple and peach, head crowned with fruit and grain, his chest a mighty pumpkin. His cherry and blackberry eyes glinted.

Rudolph!

He reached for me. Oh to be embraced by him! To be warmed.

He lifted my paralysed naked body from its dusty niche.

The crash which propelled me back into the drawing room might almost have been caused by his dropping me and letting me shatter.

For a moment I thought that this was indeed so.

Yet it was my trance which had been shattered.

A policeman was in the room. An armed policeman, crouching. He panned his gun around. Plainly I was the only other person present.

The crash must have been that of those double oak doors flying open as he burst in.

Footsteps thumped, elsewhere in the house.

Voices called.

'Empty!'

'Empty!'

Several other officers spilled into the room.

'You all right, Miss?'

I could move my limbs—which were clothed exactly as earlier on, in jeans and maroon paisley sweater. I wasn't tiny and naked, after all. I stared around. No sign of von Habsburg or Voss or Martin.

'You all right, Miss? Do you understand me?'

I nodded slowly. I still felt feeble.

'She was just sitting here all on her own,' commented the officer, putting his pistol away. 'So what's happening?' he demanded of me.

How did they know I was here?

'I was . . . forced into a taxi,' I said. 'I was brought here, then given some drug.'

'What sort of drug? *Why?*'

'It made me . . . dream.'

'Who brought you here?'

'A man called Martin . . . '

He's the Habsburg Emperor's hit-man . . . The drug was concocted by a magician . . .

How could I tell them such things? How could I explain about Rudolph Vertumnus . . . ? (And how could I *deny* Vertumnus, who had almost rekindled me . . . ?)

'They were trying to get me to deny things I wrote about the painter Archimboldo . . . '

'About a *painter?*'

I tried to explain about the pictures, the bombing in Amsterdam, and how my flat had been burgled. My explanation slid away of its own accord—for the sake of sheer plausibility, and out of logical necessity!— from any Habsburg connexion, and into the ecofreak channel.

The officer frowned. 'You're suggesting that the Greens who bombed that gallery also kidnapped you? There's no one here now.'

'They must have seen you coming and run away. I'm quite confused.'

'Hmm,' said the officer. 'Come in, Sir,' he called.

In walked Phil: chunky, dapper Phil, velvet jacketed and suede-shoed, his rich glossy brown hair brushed back in elegant waves, as ever.

It was Phil who had seen me pushed into the taxi; he who had noticed the gleam of gun from right across the street where he had been loitering with intent outside a bookshop, waiting for me to emerge from St Martin's so that he could bump into me. He'd managed to grab another taxi and follow. He'd seen me hustled into that house in North London, wearing those black 'goggles'. It took about an hour for him to stir up the armed posse—an hour, during which four seasons had passed before my eyes.

The fact that Phil and I were long-term 'friends' and that he turned out to be a 'journalist'—of sorts—irked the police. The abduction—by persons unknown, to a vacant house, where I simply sat waiting patiently—began to seem distinctly stage-managed . . . for the sake of publicity. Nor—given the Amsterdam connexion—did my mention of drugs help matters. Calling out armed police was a serious matter.

We were both obliged to answer questions until late in the evening before we could leave the police station; and even then it seemed as if we ourselves might still be charged with some offence. However, those deaths in Amsterdam lent a greater credence to what I said. Maybe there was something serious behind this incident . . .

I, of course, was 'confused'. Thus, early on, I was given a blood test, about which the police made no further comment; there couldn't have been any evidence of hash or acid in my system.

I needed to stay 'confused' until I could get to talk to Rumby.

Peeved Phil, of course, insisted on talking to me over late dinner in a pizzeria—we were both starving by then.

I lied quite a lot; and refrained from any mention of Habsburgs or the Star Club. The Archimboldo paintings had all been genuine. Rumby was an up-front person. Euro Ecofreaks must have bombed the gallery. Must have abducted me. Blondie Martin; elderly man, name unknown; stout man, name of Voss, who wore a strange costume. German speakers. Just the same as I'd told the police, five or six times over. The kidnappers had tried to persuade me to denounce what I had written because my words were an insult to Archimboldo, emblem of the Greens. They had drugged me into a stupor—from which I recovered with surprising swiftness. Rescue had come too soon for much else to transpire . . .

Phil and I were sharing a tuna, anchovy, and prawn ensemble on a crispy base, and drinking red wine.

'It's quite some story, Jill. Almost front-page stuff.'

'I doubt it.'

'The Eco connexion! Bombing, abduction . . . I'd like to run this by Freddy on the news desk.'

'You're an art critic, Phil—and so am I. I don't want some cockeyed blather in the papers.'

'Jill,' he reproached me, 'I've just spent *all evening* in a police station on account of you.'

'I'm grateful you did what you did, Phil. Let's stop it there.'

'For Christ's sake, you could still be in danger! Or . . . *aren't you*, after all? Was this a publicity stunt? Was it staged by *Wright?* You're in deep, but you want out now? Why would he stage such a stunt? If he did . . . what really happened in Amsterdam?'

Dear God, how his antennae were twitching. 'No, no, no. It couldn't be a stunt because the only witness to it was *you*, and that was quite by chance!'

'By chance,' he mused . . . as though maybe I might have spied him from an upper window in St Martin's and promptly phoned for a kidnapper. 'Look, Phil, I'm confused. I'm tired. I need *sleep.*'

Into the pizzeria stepped a stout, bald man wearing a dark blue suit. He flourished a silver-tipped walking stick. Goering on a night out. His bulgy eyes fixed on mine. He swished the stick, and I screamed with pain, jerking against the table, spilling both our wines.

'Jill!'

Phil managed to divert the red tide with his paper napkin at the same time as he reached out towards me. Other customers stared agog, and the manager hastened in our direction. Were we engaged in some vicious quarrel? Wine dripped on to the floor tiles.

Voss had vanished. I slumped back.

'Sorry,' I said to the manager. 'I had a bad cramp.'

The manager waved a waiter to minister to the mess. Other diners resumed munching their pizzas.

'Whatever happened?' whispered Phil.

'A cramp. Just a cramp.'

Could one of those Habsburgers have trailed us to the police station and hung around outside for hours, keeping watch till we emerged?

Had I truly seen Voss, or only someone who resembled him? Someone whose appearance and whose action triggered that pain reflex? That agonising hallucination . . .

Phil took me back to the flat in a taxi. I had no choice but to let him come up with me—in case the place was infested.

It wasn't. Then it took half an hour to get rid of my friend, no matter how much tiredness I claimed. By the time I phoned Rumby's private number it was after eleven.

Him, I did start to tell about the Habsburgs.

He was brevity itself. 'Say no more,' my rich protector cut in. *My Rumby Daddy.* 'Stay there. I'm sending Case *now*. He'll phone from the car just as soon as he's outside your place. Make quite sure you see it's him before you open your door.'

I dozed off soundly in the Merc. When I arrived at Bexford, Rumby had waited up to quiz me and pump me—attended by Case, and a somewhat weary Lascelles.

I got to bed around four . . .

. . . leaving Rumby aiming to do some serious phoning.

Had Big Daddy been breaking out the benzedrine? Not exactly. Rumby always enjoyed a few hours advantage over us local mortals. So as to stay more in synch with American time-zones he habitually rose very late of a morning. A night shift duo always manned the computer consoles and transatlantic satellite link. In that sense, Bexford never really closed down.

I'd already gathered that *crisis* was somewhat of a staff of life around Rumby—who seemed to cook up his own personal supply of benzedrine internally. During my previous two-day sojourn, there'd been the incident of the microlite aircraft. Thanks to a Cotswold Air Carnival, microlites were overflying Bexford at a few hundred feet now and then. Rumby took exception and had Lascelles trying to take out a legal injunction against the organisers.

Simultaneously, there'd been the business of the starlings. Affronted by those microlite pterodactyls, and seeking a new air-base for their sorties, a horde of the quarrelsome birds took up residence on the satellite dish. Their weight or their shit might distort bits of information worth millions. What to do? After taking counsel from an avian welfare organisation, Rumby dispatched his helicopter to collect a heap of French *pétard* firecrackers from Heathrow to string underneath the gutters. So my stay had been punctuated by random explosive farts . . .

I woke at noon, and Rumby joined me for breakfast in the big old kitchen—antiquity retrofitted with stainless steel and ceramic hobs. A large TV set was tuned to CNN, and an ecologist was inveighing about rocket exhausts and the ozone holes.

'Each single shuttle launch releases a hundred and sixty-three *thousand* kilograms of hydrogen chloride that converts into an atmospheric mist of hydrochloric acid! So now they're kindly promising to change the oxidizer of the fuel—the ammonium perchlorate that produces this vast cloud of pollution—to ammonium *nitrate* instead—'

As soon as I finished my croissant, Rumby scuttled the cooks—a couple of local women—out to pick herbs and vegetables. He blinked at me a few times.

'Any more sightings of flowerpot men? Or Habsburgs?' he enquired.

'That isn't funny, Rumby. It happened.'

He nodded. 'I'm afraid you've been given a ring-binder, Jill.'

'Come again?'

'I've been talking to one of my best chemists over in Texas. Sally has a busy mind. Knows a lot about pharmaceuticals.' He consulted scribbles in a notebook. 'The ring in question's a molecular structure called an indole ring . . . These rings *bind* to synapses in the brain. Hence, ring-binder. They're psychotomimetic—they mimic psychoses. Your little pets will probably stay in place a long time instead of breaking down. Seems there's a lot of covert designer drug work going on right now, aimed at cooking up chemicals to manipulate people's beliefs. Sally has heard rumours of one drug code-named *Confusion*—and another one called *Persuasion*, which seems to fit the bill here. It's the only explanation for the hallucination—which came from within you, of course, once you were given the appropriate prod.'

'I do realize I was hallucinating the . . . flowerpot men. You mean this can continue . . . indefinitely?'

'You flashed on for a full encore in that pizza parlour, right? Whiplash! Any fraught scenes in future involving old Archey could do the same. Media interviews, that sort of thing—if you disobey the Habsburg view of Archey. Though I guess you mustn't spill the beans about them publicly.'

'They told me so. How did I get away with telling *you* last night?'

'They were interrupted before they'd finished influencing you.' He grinned. 'I guess I might be high enough in the hierarchy of your loyalties to outrank their partial hold on you. Media or Press people wouldn't be, so you'd be advised to follow the Habsburg party line with them. Maybe you could resist at a cost.'

'Of what?'

'Pain, inflicted by your own mind. Distortions of reality. That's what Sally says. That's the word on these new ring-binders. They bind you.'

The more I thought about this, the less I liked it.

'How many people know about these persuader drugs?' I asked him carefully.

'They haven't exactly featured in *Newsweek*. I gather they're a bit experimental. Sally has an ear for rumours. She's part of my research division. Runs a search-team scanning the chemistry journals. Whatever catches the eye. Any tips of future icebergs. New petrochemical applications, mainly.' He spoke as if icebergs started out fully submerged, then gradually revealed themselves. 'She helped dig up data on the correct paint chemistry for the Archeys.'

How frank he was being.

Apparently. And how glib.

'So how would a Habsburg *magician* get his paws on prototype persuader drugs?' I demanded.

Rumby looked rueful. 'Hell, maybe he *is* a magician! Alchemy precedes chemistry, don't they say?'

'In the same sense that Icarus precedes a jumbo jet?'

One of the cooks returned bearing an obese marrow.

Impulse took me to the kitchen garden, to brood on my own. The sun had finally burned through persistent haze to brighten the rows of cabbages, majestic cauliflowers, and artichokes, the rhubarb, the leeks. An ancient brick wall backed this domain, trusses of tomatoes ranged along it. Rooks cawed in the elms beyond, prancing about those raggedy stick-nests that seemed like diseases of the branches.

Had the old gent whom I'd met really been Heinrich von Habsburg? A Holy Roman Emperor waiting in the wings to step on the world stage? Merely because he told me so, in *persuasive* circumstances?

What if that trio in the drawing room had really been *ecofreaks* masquerading as Habsburgs, pulling the wool over my eyes, trying to bamboozle me into confession?

Did puritanical ecofreaks have the wit to stage such a show?

How much more likely that the Star Club, with its presumed access to cutting-edge psychochemistry—and a penchant for dirty tricks?—was responsible for the charade, and for my drugging!

Whether Rumby himself knew so, or not.

Wipe me out as a reliable witness to my own part in the prank? Eliminate me, by giving me an ongoing nervous breakdown?

Would that invalidate what I'd written?

Ah no. The slur would be upon ecologists . . .

And maybe, at the same time, *test* that persuader drug? Give it a field-trial on a highly suitable test subject, namely myself? The Club's subsequent aim might be to try similar *persuasion* on influential ecofreaks to alter their opinions or to make them seem crazy . . .

In my case, of course, they wouldn't wish to turn me into an eco-groupie . . . Thus the Habsburg connexion could have seemed like a fertile ploy.

Was there a genuine, elderly Heinrich von Habsburg somewhere in Germany or Austria? Oh, doubtless there would be . . .

The vegetable garden began slithering, pulsing, throbbing. Ripe striped marrows thumped upon the ground, great green gonads. Tomatoes tumesced. Leeks were waxy white candles with green flames writhing high. Celery burst from earth, spraying feathery leaves. Sprouts jangled. Cauli-flowers were naked brains.

The garden was trying to transform itself, to assemble itself into some giant sprawled potent body—of cauli brain, leek fingers, marrow organs, green leaf flesh . . .

I squealed and fled back towards the kitchen itself.

Then halted, like a hunted animal.

I couldn't go inside—where Rumby and Case and Lascelles plotted . . .

the downfall of Nature, the rape of the planets, the bleeding of oil from Earth's veins to burn into choking smoke.

Behind me, the vegetable jungle had stilled. Its metamorphosis had halted, reversed.

If I thought harmoniously, not perversely, I was safe.

Yet my mind was churning, and reality was unstuck.

In my perception one conspiracy overlaid another. One scheming plot, another scheming plot. Therefore one reality overlaid another reality with hideous persuasiveness. Where had I just been, but in a *vegetable plot*?

I couldn't go into that house, to which I had fled for safety only the night before. For from inside Bexford Hall invisible tendrils arched out across the sky, bouncing up and down out of space, linking Rumby to star crusaders who were playing with my mind—and to whom he might be reporting my condition even now, guilefully or innocently.

On the screen of the sky I spied a future world of Confusion and Persuasion, where devoted fanatics manipulated moods chemically so that Nature became a multifold *creature* evoking horror—since it might absorb one into itself, mind-meltingly, one's keen consciousness dimming into pulsing, orgasmic dreams; and from which one could only flee in silver ships, out to the empty serenity of space where no universally linked weeds infested the floating rocks, no bulging tomato haemorrhoids the asteroids . . .

Or else conjuring up a positive lust for vital vegetative unity!

I slapped myself, trying to summon a Habsburger whiplash of pain to jerk me out of this bizarre dual vision.

I *must* go indoors. To sanity. And beyond.

The ring-binder was clamping more and more of me; and my mind was at war. I was scripting my own hallucinations from the impetus of ecofreak ideology, exaggerated absurdly, and from the myth of the Holy Roman Empire . . . I was dreaming, wide awake.

And Case stood, watching me.

'You okay, Jill?'

I nodded. I shouldn't tell him the truth. There was no truth any more; there was only potent imagery, subject to interpretation.

Certain bedrock facts existed: the bombing, the deaths in Amsterdam, my abduction . . . Event-*images*: that's what those were. The interpretation was another matter, dependent upon what one believed—just as art was forever being reinterpreted in the context of a new epoch; and even history too.

Persuasion—and Confusion too?—had torn me loose from my moorings, so that interpretations cascaded about me simultaneously, synchronously. I had become a battlefield between world-views, which different parts of my mind were animating.

With dread, I sensed something stirring which perhaps had lain dormant ever since humanity split from Nature—ever since true consciousness of self had dawned as a sport, a freak, a biological accident . . .

'You sure, Jill?'

You. I. Myself. *Me.*

The independent thinking entity, named Jill Donaldson.

I wasn't thinking quite so independently any longer. An illusion of Self— that productive illusion upon which civilization itself had been founded— was floundering.

'Quite sure,' said I.

I, I, I. Ich. Io. Ego.

And Jilldonaldson hastened past him into the kitchen, where one of the cooks was hollowing out the marrow. The big TV set, tuned to CNN, scooping signals bounced from space, shimmered. The colours bled and reformed. The pixel pixies danced a new jig.

The countenance of Vertumnus gazed forth from that screen, he of the laughing lips, the ripe rubicund cheeks of peach and apple, the pear-nose, the golden ears of corn that were his brows. Oh the flashing hilarity of his berry-eyes. Oh those laughing lips.

With several nods of his head he gestured Jill elsewhere.

Jill adopted a pan-face.

She walked through the corridors of the house, to the front porch. She stepped out on to the gravel drive.

Ignition keys were in the red Porsche.

Jill ought to be safe with Annie in a colony of women. Rudolph Vertumnus was a male, wasn't he?

A hop through Cheltenham, then whoosh by motorway to Exeter and on down into Cornwall. She would burn fuel but keep an eye out for police patrols. Be at Polmerrin by dusk . . .

The Porsche wasn't even approaching Cheltenham when the car phone burbled, inevitably.

She had been counting on a call.

A stolen bright red Porsche would be a little obvious on the motorway. So she had her excuse lined up. She was going to visit her brother—in Oxford, in roughly the opposite direction. She'd be back at Bexford that evening. Brother Bob was a banker. Let Rumby worry that she was going to blab to him to protect her 750K investment, about which she no longer cared a hoot. Let Case and some co-driver hare after her fruitlessly towards Oxford in the Merc.

The voice wasn't Case's. Or Lascelles'. Or even Rumby's.

She nearly jerked the Porsche off the road.

The voice was that of Voss.

'Can you hear me, Fraulein Donaldson?'

Hands shaking, legs trembling, she guided the car into a gateway opening on to a huge field of close-cut golden stubble girt by a hawthorn hedge. A Volvo hooted in protest as it swung by. A rabbit fled.

'How did you find me, Voss—?' she gasped. Horrid perspectives loomed. 'They told you! They know you!'

The caller chuckled.

'I'm merely the voice of *Vertumnus*, Fraulein. My image is everywhere these days, so why shouldn't I be everywhere too? Are you perhaps worried about the collapse of your precious Ego, Fraulein?'

How persuasive his voice was. 'This has all happened before, you know. The God of the Bible ruled the medieval world, but when He went into eclipse *Humanity* seized His sceptre. Ah, that exalted Renaissance Ego! How puffed up it was! By the time of Rudolph, that same Ego was already collapsing. Its confidence had failed. A new unity was needed—a bio-cosmic social unity. The Holy Roman Emperor Rudolph sought to be the *head* of society—hence the painting of so many regal *heads* by the artist you have libelled. Those biological, botanical heads.'

'I already know this,' she said.

'He would be the head—and the people, the limbs, the organs. Of one body! In the new world now a-dawning life will be a unity again. The Emperor will be the head—but not a separate, egotistic head. Nor will the limbs and organs be separate individualists.'

'You're telling me what I know!' Aye, and *what she most feared*—namely the loss of Self. Its extinction. And what she most feared might well *win*; for what is feared is potent.

'Who are you? What are you?' she cried into the phone—already suspecting that Voss's voice, the voice of Vertumnus, might well be in her own wayward head, either ring-bound or else planted there by alchemical potion.

She slammed the hand-set down on to its cradle by the gearshift lever, thumbed the windows fully open, and lit a cigarette to calm herself. Whispers of smoke drifted out towards the shorn field.

A mat of golden stubble cloaked the broad shoulders of the land. A ghostly pattern emerged across the great network of dry stalks: a coat of arms. The hedge was merely green braiding. Her car was a shiny red bug parked on the shoulder of a giant sprawling being.

Angrily she pitched her cigarette through the passenger window towards the field, wishing that it might start a fire, though really the straw was far too short to combust.

She drove on; and when the phone seemed to burble again, she ignored it.

She smoked. She threw out half-burned cigarettes till the pack was empty, but no smoke ever plumed upwards far behind her.

Half way through Cheltenham, in slow-moving traffic, she passed a great billboard flaunting Rudolph Vertumnus. *WE ARE ALL PART OF NATURE*, proclaimed the all too familiar text.

Evidently unseen by other drivers and pedestrians, the fruity Emperor shouldered his way out of the poster. A pumpkin-belly that she had never seen before reared into view. And marrow-legs, from between which aubergine testicles and a carrot cock dangled. Vertumnus towered over the other cars and vans behind her, bestriding the roadway. His carrot swelled enormously.

Raphanidosis, or something similar: ancient Greek noun. To be fucked by a giant radish.

Vertumnus was coming.

A red light changed to green, and she was able to slip onward before the giant could advance to unpeel the roof of the Porsche and lift her out, homunculus-like, from her container.

Even in the heart of the city, a chthonic entity was coming to life. A liberated, incarnated deity was being born.

No one else but Jill saw it as yet.

Yet everyone knew it from ten thousand posters and badges—wearing its varied seasonal faces.

Everyone knew Vertumnus by now, deity of change and transformation; for change was in the air, as ripe Autumn matured. The death of Self was on the horizon.

When she reached the motorway, those triple lanes cutting far ahead through the landscape opened up yawning perspectives of time rather than of space.

Deep time, in which there'd been no conscious mind present at all, only vegetable and animal existence. Hence, the blankness of the road . . .

Soon, a new psychic era might dawn in which the sovereign virtue of the conscious Self faded as humanity re-entered Nature once again—willing the demise of dissective, alienating logics and sciences, altering the mind-set, hypnotising itself into a communal empathy with the world, whose potent figurehead wasn't any vague, cloudy Gaea, but rather her son Vertumnus. Every eating of his body—of fruits and nuts and vegetables and fishes—would be a vividly persuasive communion. His royal represent-ative would reign in Budapest, or in Prague, or Vienna. His figurehead.

The phone burbled, and this time Jill did answer as she swung along the endless tongue of tarmac, and through time.

'Jill, don't hang up.' *Rumby*. 'I know why you've skipped out. And you must believe it ain't my fault.'

What was he talking about?

'I've been the well-meaning patsy in this business. I've been the Gorby.'

'Who was *he*?' she asked mischievously. Here was a message from a different era.

'I'm fairly sure by now that my goddam Star Club *was* behind the bombing *and* the ring-binder. Didn't trust me to be *thorough* enough. The whole Archey situation was really a lot more serious than even I saw. Those damn posters were really imprinting people on some deep-down level—not just surface propaganda. These are power-images. Fucking servo-symbols—'

'You're only *fairly* sure?' she asked.

'What tipped you off? Was it something *Case* said? Or Johnny Lascelles? Something Johnny let slip? I mean, why did you skip?'

Something Case or Lascelles had let slip . . . ? So Rumby was becoming a tad paranoid about his own staff in case they were serving two masters—

Rumby himself, and some other rich gent in that secret Star Club of theirs . . . A gent whom she had perhaps met in that drawing room in North London; who had caned her at a distance . . .

'Come back, Jill, and tell me all you know. I'm serious! I need to know.'

Oh yes, she could recognize the authentic tones of paranoia . . .

'Sorry about taking the Porsche,' she said.

'Never mind the fucking car. Where are you, Jill?'

She remembered.

'I'm going to Oxford to see my brother. He's a bank manager.'

She hung up, and ignored repeated calls.

Polmerrin lay in a wooded little valley within a couple of miles of the rocky, wind-whipped North Cornwall coastline. Sheltered by the steep plunge of land and by oakwood, the once-derelict hamlet of cottages now housed studios and craft workshops, accompanied by a dozen satellite caravans. Pottery, jewellery, painting, sculpting, candle-making . . .

Kids played. Women worked. A few male companions lent an enlightened hand. Someone was tootling a flute, and a buzzard circled high overhead. A kingfisher flashed to and fro along a stream, one soggy bank of which was edged by alder buckthorn. Some brimstone butterflies still fluttered, reluctant to succumb to worn-out wings and cooling nights. The sunset was brimstone too: sulphur and orange peel. A few arty tourists were departing.

Immediately Jill realized that she had come to the wrong place entirely. She ought to have fled to some high-tech airport hotel with gleaming glass elevators—an inorganic, air-conditioned, sealed machine resembling a space station in the void.

She was too tired to reverse her route.

Red-haired Annie embraced Jill, in surprise and joy. She kissed Jill, hugged her.

Freckled Annie was wearing one of those Indian cotton dresses—in green hues—with tiny mirrors sewn into it; and she'd put some extra flesh upon her once-lithe frame, though not to the extent of positive plumpness. She had also put on slim, scrutinising glasses. Pewter rings adorned several fingers, with scarab and spider motifs.

One former barn was now a refectory, to which she led a dazed Jill to drink lemonade.

'How long has it been, Jilly? Four years? You'll stay with me, of course. So what's *happening?*' She frowned. 'I did hear about your book—and that awful bombing. I still listen to the radio all day long while I'm paint-ing—'

'Jill's drugged,' said Jill. 'Vertumnus is reborn. And the Holy Roman Empire is returning.'

Annie scrutinised her with concern. 'Holy shit.' She considered. 'You'd better not tell any of the others. There are kids here. Folks might worry.'

They whispered, as once they had whispered confidences.

'Do you know the *Portrait of Jacopo Strada?*' Jill began. She found she could still speak about herself in the first person, historically.

Presently there were indeed kids and mothers and a medley of other women, and a few men in the refectory too, sharing an early supper of spiced beans and rice and salad and textured vegetable protein, Madras style, while Vivaldi played from a tape-deck. The beams of the barn were painted black, and murals of fabulous creatures relieved the whiteness of the plaster: a phoenix, a unicorn, a minotaur, each within a maze-like Celtic surround, so that it seemed as if so many heraldic shields were poised around the walls. Tourists would enjoy cream teas in here of an afternoon.

Sulphur and copper had cleared from a sky that was now deeply leaden-blue, fast darkening. Venus and Jupiter both shone. A shooting star streaked across the vault of void; or was that a failed satellite burning up?

Annie shared a studio with Rosy and Meg, who would be playing chess that evening in the recreation barn beside the refectory. The whole ground floor of the reconditioned cottage was studio. Meg's work was meticulous neo-medieval miniatures featuring eerie freaks rather than anyone comely. Rosy specialised in acrylic studies of transparent hourglass buildings set within forests, or in crystalline deserts, and crowded with disembodied heads instead of sand.

Annie *used* to paint swirling, luminous abstracts. Now she specialised in large acrylic canvasses of bloom within bloom within bloom, vortexes that sucked the gaze down into a central focus from which an eye always gazed out: a cat's, a bird's, a person's. Her pictures were like strange, exploded, organic cameras.

Jill looked; Jill admired. The paintings looked at her. Obviously there was a thematic empathy between the three women who used this studio.

'The conscious mind is going into eclipse,' Jill remarked, and Annie smiled hesitantly.

'That's a great title. I might use it.'

A polished wooden stairway led up to a landing with three bedrooms.

Annie's wide bed was of brass, with a floral duvet. Marguerites, daisies, buttercups.

In the morning when Jill awoke, the flowers had migrated from the duvet.

Annie's face, her neck, her shoulders were petals and stalks. Her skin was of white and pink blossoms. Her ear was a tulip, her nose was the bud of a lily, and her hair a fountain of red nasturtiums.

Jill reached to peel off some of the petals, but the flowers were flesh, and Annie awoke with a squeak of protest. Her open eyes were black night-shades with white blossom pupils.

And Jilldonaldson, whose name was dissolving, was the first to see such a transformation as would soon possess many men and women who regarded one another in a suitable light as part of Nature.

Jilldona stepped from the brass bed, towards the window, and pulled the curtains aside.

The valley was thick with mist. Yet a red light strobed the blur of vision. Spinning, this flashed from the roof of a police car parked beside the Porsche. Shapeless wraiths danced in its dipped headlight beams. One officer was scanning the vague, evasive cottages. A second walked around the Porsche, peered into it, then opened the passenger door.

'Hey,' said Annie, 'why did you tweak me?'

Annie's flesh was much as the night before, except that Jill continued to see a faint veil of flowers, an imprint of petals.

'Jill just wanted a cigarette,' said Jill.

'I quit a couple of years ago,' Annie reminded her. 'Tobacco costs too much. Anyway, *you* didn't smoke last night.'

'Jill forgot to. Fuzz are down there. Fuzz make Jill want a fag.'

'That braggartly car—we ought to have driven it miles away! Miles and miles.' Yet Annie didn't sound totally convinced that sheltering this visitor might be the best idea.

Jilldona pulled on her paisley sweater and jeans, and descended. Annie's paintings eyed her brightly as she passed by, recording her within their petal-ringed pupils.

She walked over to the police, one of whom asked:

'You wouldn't be a Miss Jill Donaldson, by any chance?' The burr of his Cornish accent . . .

'Names melt,' she told her questioner. 'The mind submerges in a unity of being. Have the Habsburgs sent you?' she asked. 'Or was it the Star Club?'

One officer removed the ignition key from the Porsche and locked the car.

The other steered her by the arm into the back of the strobing vehicle. She could see no flowers on these policemen. However, a pair of wax strawberries dangled discreetly from the driving mirror like blood-bright testicles.

The Bible in Blood

It WAS SIMPLICITY ITSELF TO LET MYSELF INTO APPLEDORN'S HOTEL suite. The under-manager of the Strasbourg Hilton had provided me with a master card-key several days before Henry Appledorn checked in at the hotel. I'd replaced the security chain with one which would snap easily. The under-manager was a *sayan*, a friendly local who would readily assist Israeli intelligence. We can rely on thousands of such individuals in many countries.

Naturally, I hadn't told our French under-manager that I intended to confront Appledorn and his secretary and their visitor with a pistol in my hand. None of his business. He wasn't involved.

The Beretta fitted snuggly in my palm. Standard issue for Mossad field officers. .22 caliber. Loaded with dum-dum bullets.

In with the card-key. Turn the handle softly.

Ah yes, the occupants of the suite had chained the door.

Apply a shoulder. The links snapped.

'Don't anyone move,' I said. 'Don't make any noise.' And I shut the door behind me.

On a chrome and glass table there rested a pile of parchment pages penned in Gothic script. The letters were all of a dark brown hue, the colour of dried blood. The open case and backbone formed a portfolio, for those sheets were loose-leaf without any stitching or tailband as yet. Faded red silk ribbons would tie the portfolio shut. The case was bound in black leather with steel protectors at the corners. Though I couldn't see the front, its slight elevation from the glass of the table suggested that emblems embossed the surface. A steel cross, perhaps, and steel swastikas.

So there it was at last: the Bible Written in Blood.

To be strictly accurate, the *New Testament*. A good ninety-five percent of the *New Testament*.

Not all of it. Herzwalde concentration camp had been evacuated, due to the approach of the Red Army, while the scribes were commencing their slow labour on the Book of *Revelation*.

Our American bibliophile, Henry Appledorn, darted a protective glance at the huge, incomplete, unbound volume. Our book collector was tall and rangy, with a predilection to stoop. His curly hair had turned snowy, as befitted his seventy years. His was a Bassett-hound face, long and somewhat ruddy.

Despite my warning, Appledorn's hand strayed to touch the silk handkerchief in his breast pocket. Couldn't he conceive of his own death? Did my sudden intrusion merely offend him?

Ah, he was worrying whether I might cause blood to spurt on to the volume in question, staining it.

How quickly could he mop the parchment page clean with his handkerchief? What cleansing agents would distinguish between recently spilled blood and the older dried brown blood of the text?

Klaus Bauer, procurer of the volume from its hiding place in former East Germany, appeared to be calculating whether he might heave up the bulky tome to use as a shield—or to hurl at me, disarmingly.

Bauer was thick-set but whey-faced, as if had shunned the sunlight for a long time. He looked so cleanly scrubbed with his large pink hands and shaven skull that he reminded me of a potato. His jacket and slacks were creamy and recently pressed.

The woman, Appledorn's secretary, avoided focusing on my gun.

'What are *you*?' she demanded. 'An *occultist*?'

I'd been intending to order all three of them to lie prone on the carpet to allow me to inject each in turn, rendering them comatose, after which I would simply decamp with the book . . .

Her question threw me. I had to know exactly what Gloria Cameron implied by it.

She was golden-haired, tweed-suited, her ruffleted blouse trimmed with embroidered roses. Brown leather brogues with brass buckles on her feet. Butch. Perceptive.

I imagined her equipped with a whip, and dressed in impeccable SS uniform, striding through a camp of cowering women. I felt weak inside. My weakness became fury—and fascination.

Yet Gloria's accent was Scots, overlaid by a slight American veneer. She was a graduate of Edinburgh University, her speciality bibliography.

I ought to have carried out my plan by rote, ignoring distractions. However, within me—confronted at last by the Bible in Blood—my mother's dreams were stirring. And within those dreams lurked another person, namely my father...

Facts are never simple. Facts splinter into a kaleidoscope of interpretations.

Early in 1943 SS Colonel Gottfried von Turm became deputy commandant of Herzwalde labour camp. He was lame in the left leg. He'd been invalided back from the Russian front, from the doomed attempt to relieve the Nazi forces penned in Stalingrad.

From the jaws of hell—into a cauldron of death. Death cooked up by his own kind.

Yet were the other SS quite his own kind?

For a Prussian aristocrat to join the ranks of the fighting Waffen-SS was quite unusual. The Waffen-SS were superhuman . . . *scum*. For the most part they were brutal peasants—trained to be Übermenschen. Their military officers lacked the most elementary sense of tactics, though they knew how to rampage, and SS fighting units always had better weapons than the regular army.

Gottfried had once implied to my mother (or at least she took him to be implying) that he'd been obliged to join this band of butchers so as to protect his own family from some ambiguous fate.

Soon after Gottfried arrived at Herzwalde, he conceived the project of the Bible in Blood.

That camp housed, among many other unfortunates, a fair salting of rabbis and other Jewish *Intelligenten*—unphysical men for whom the forced labour of quarrying stone and logging in the surrounding forests was especially lethal on top of the starvation rations, the beatings, shootings, the interminable freezing roll-calls.

Jews had committed *blood-crime* by murdering the Saviour. Why, the mere existence of Jews constantly posed a genetic blood-threat to the purity of the Aryan race.

Especially in the eyes of the SS the pure blood that coursed through the veins of the German peasant was sacred. Had not Alfred Rosenberg proclaimed a mystic philosophy of blood as the true Germanic faith? Had not Hitler endorsed this crazy sanguinarianism? Was not the SS a new priesthood of blood?

So therefore Colonel von Turm ordained that the most noteworthy rabbis and eggheads should be gathered together in a special blockhouse. There, they should redeem their blood-crimes and purge their *verfluchte Judentum* by writing out the whole of the *New Testament* in their own life-blood.

Was this a monstrous joke on his part? A malicious insult to the prisoners? Certainly, other SS personnel took it as such, applauding Gottfried's wit.

True, at first I believe there was *some* dispute with his superior or his fellow officers. Had not the Führer wished to erase Christianity in favour of a revived Odinic paganism? Ah, but not even Hitler could afford to offend the Church too deeply. Besides, many of the SS peasantry had been deeply branded in boyhood with Catholicism.

Later on, those SS in Herzwalde would become quite fanatic in a darkly superstitious vein about the progress of the project. It seemed to them as though this scriptural work was obliterating the very essence of the Hebrew race in a magical fashion—just as they themselves were occupied in annihilating the physical existence of Jews.

Now, this was bound to be a long, slow project. For how much blood could easily be siphoned from the veins of the scribes by those scribes themselves? How quickly would the blood-ink congeal? What type of pen-nibs should best be used? How to ensure compatibility of calligraphy? How could the work best be divided so that costly parchment was not wasted by, for example, the *First Epistle to the Corinthians* ending at the top of one sheet, while the *Second Epistle* had already been started by a different scribe at the top of another sheet? And in the event of empty spaces, what decorative motifs should be employed to fill up the gaps? Swastikas? Death's-heads pierced with daggers? Crucifixions? Taunting pastoral scenes of Palestine?

These were exactly the kind of minutiae which obsessed the intellects of the SS who operated concentration camps. A hundred petty laws and prohibitions! With a savage whipping or hanging as punishment for infringement.

The Colonel played upon this savage pedantry.

What if the chosen Jews' blood was *anaemic* due to the scanty rations of watery garbage soup, black ersatz coffee, and stale bread?

Very soon the scribes' diet was being boosted with sausages and cheese from incoming parcels which the SS always stole (though they might occasionally let the wrapping paper be delivered), and with fresh fruit and eggs and rabbit stew.

What if the scribes' fingers were too numb to hold the pens skillfully enough to form the Gothic letters Gottfried insisted upon?

Why, *two* stoves must be kept well fuelled in the Scripture Block.

While the band of scribes regained some body weight and bloomed with renewed health, other less literate inmates of Herzwalde carried on labouring and dying of hunger and illness and beatings.

Aha! Was the Scripture Block—aside from being an insult to the faith of those within—also a cunning ploy to make its inmates resented and hated by other prisoners? The SS, permanently poised on the brink of capricious rage at Untermenschen, may have thought in this vein. *'See how those precious rabbis and eggheads grow fat while you become bones!'* In actuality, most residents of squalid, bestial Herzwalde had no surplus energy to spare for hatred. They hardly had enough energy to spare for conscious thought at all.

As I've said, the majority of the SS had no sense of *tactics* . . . Might it be that Colonel Gottfried von Turm was in fact preserving, in his Scripture Block, the cream of Jewish people, the intellectual and spiritual leadership, for some post-bellum salvation? Such an idea never crossed the minds of his boorish colleagues. Still, Gottfried must prevent any such notion from arising there—or taking root in the brains of his clever beneficiaries. Like some mystic high priest of the satanic Schutzstaffel he would rant about sacred and polluted blood.

Many of the assembled Rabbis, for their part, were knowledgeable about Kabbalah. They knew the *Sepher Yesirah*, the Book of Creation, inside out, and the *Zohar* of Moses de Leon. They murmured while they dipped their pens in their own blood and copied the scripture of their oppressors . . .

'What do you mean, Miz Cameron?'

The woman stared at me witheringly. So I jerked the Beretta towards her tweed-clad knees, threatening to cripple her unless words danced upon her lips.

Why hadn't Appledorn let her handle the acquisition of the book? Why did *he* need to be present personally at the handover in this hotel suite in Strasbourg, here on the Franco-German border? So that he could authenticate his purchase by smell and by feel and by sixth sense?

Suppose he had stayed behind in Florida . . . maybe the plane winging the book back to the States might have plunged into the Atlantic en route. It might have crashed on arrival at Orlando airport, incinerating the unique pages . . .

Appledorn had to take control of the book right away.

What did he plan to do with it thereafter?

I'd *assumed* that he would lock it up along with other bibliographic treasures, reserved for his eyes only.

Now I wondered whether this was all he intended.

'Does your boss plan to complete the Bible?' I demanded. 'Using whose blood? *Your own?*'

Gloria Cameron twitched.

'Do you intend to finish the book of *Revelation*, Mister Appledorn?' I harangued, sounding rather like a camp guard myself. 'What *revelation* do you expect to achieve?'

Klaus Bauer stared from one to other of us in bemusement. And with greedy regret. Had he somehow underestimated the value of the Bible in Blood to this collector?

Bauer asked me in German in a wheedling tone, 'Are you one of the faithful?'

The faithful? The *faithful?* I hadn't heard this expression before. Did it refer to Judaism—or was it some neo-Nazi code? Did Bauer imagine that I wished to spirit the book away to some Hitlerian shrine? To some revived Wewelsburg Castle?

Bauer annoyed me. I shunned any conceivable association between himself and me. I wished him to sweat.

'I'm Israeli intelligence,' I told him.

'Why,' asked Gloria Cameron, 'would Israeli intelligence wish to kidnap a *book?*'

Well, of course we wouldn't . . . unless the action served Israel's interests . . . which it hardly could, unless Kabbalists were running our country.

'*I* ask the questions,' I retorted.

Whether due to the strain of the occasion—this climax to a long search—or on account of sheer proximity to the book, my mother's dreams came welling up in me . . .

SS Colonel von Turm limped, using a silver-handled walking cane. With this he would lash out at the occasional tattered slave who didn't step smartly enough to one side and pull off his beret swiftly enough from his cropped cranium.

In fact, the Colonel never *damaged* any slave worker with his cane—unlike other SS who would beat an inmate to death. Perhaps he was concerned about snapping his walking cane. Perhaps not. A lick from the stick was equivalent to a shot of electric current in a moribund frog's leg. It galvanized the walking dead. They survived a little longer.

Von Turm's eyes were an icy blue. The ice of Russian winter; the ice of Prussian disdain.

He was well-fleshed.

He too needed to relieve the strain of the occasion . . . and maybe do something extra by way of lagniappe, as they say down Appledorn's way or thereabouts.

One afternoon, since it was freezing cold, the SS decided to order a new intake of women to stand naked on parade while they chose which to assign to the brothel block, which to the quarries, which to extinction. The women had been marched forty kilometres from their previous work camp, relocated to fulfill some whim or bureaucratic quota. Those who had survived the trek were desperately tired. Therefore, with the crops of their whips, the SS lifted the girls' tits to determine who was firm enough for brothel duty.

Aryans for the SS guards and for visiting soldiers. Jews for the common criminals who had become overseers of slaves.

Exercising the caprice of rank, and rather in breach of SS protocol, Von Turm ordered that my mother, Bella, should be sent to him for his use that evening. For she stood proudly. A tall, skinny waif, a starveling with large brown eyes and shaven head.

His quarters were beautifully furnished with loot, including a fine four-poster bed. On a table was set a carafe of milk, a bowl of sauerkraut, and a dish of meats and cold creamed potatoes. Bella, who was starving, only allowed herself one tormented glance at the Colonel's supper. And at his silk sheets.

'Undress,' he said; and she shed a torn, soiled frock.

'You're too thin for me,' he remarked, and terror seized her.

But then he tossed her a silk bathrobe. From a drawer he produced a lavish black wig for her to wear while she was in his room.

'You must eat first,' he told her. 'Do not eat quickly, or else you might vomit. Chew slowly. Drink slowly. Then you must sit and digest your meal.'

Only an hour after she had finished feasting did he take Bella to bed, to relieve his tensions. Though he hardly spoke to her.

I could hear the percussion of a thousand wooden shoes on stone; and the squelch of a thousand feet tramping through slush and mud. I saw watch-towers and wire and roving searchlights. I listened to the chatter of bullets. I watched skeletal marionettes in striped pyjama-suits dangle upright for hours on end on parade from the invisible strings of their exhaustion. Strings snapped; marionettes collapsed in snow, in mud. I flinched from snarling dogs, whose teeth sheer hunger persuaded me were rows of almonds. I breathed the filth of the latrine abyss in the shithouse, surrounded by slippery, excremental steel bars on which to perch one's bum and vent the gruel of diarrhoea upon a million dissolving turds and the rotting corpses of those who had previously slipped backwards and drowned. The swollen tongues of hanged men on the gallows were blue, and looked delicious, like cured meat.

And I heard the rabbis mutter in their blockhouse as they copied the words of that loving Christian religion to which the world seemed to owe the massacre of the Albigensians, the Crusades, the Inquisition, the slaughter of witches and heretics, and the pogroms and the ghettos, because the blood of the Jew Jesus had been spilt; as they penned the holy words of their victimisers in their own heartblood . . .

Gottfried reserved Bella for himself alone. As the months passed by she grew sleek.

No doubt the Colonel concocted some spurious excuse to exonerate himself in the eyes of his fellow officers from the scandal of taking a Jewess as—effectively—his mistress. Those officers were by now much tickled with the Bible in Blood project, the Colonel's inspiration, so they regarded this other eccentricity of his with amusement, even addressing Bella as 'Fraulein', although she continued to reside in the Brothel Block.

How did Bella respond to Gottfried's embraces?

At first woodenly, of course, exhaustedly, obediently—reserving within herself a kernel of her own dignity.

Yet presently... ah, the situation became fraught with ambiguity.

Von Turm remained taciturn towards her. How could he be otherwise? He could hardly involve her directly as a co-conspirator against the ethics of the Schutzstaffel. Nevertheless, Gottfried's *body* seemed to speak to her in that four-poster bed.

True, when one's entire fate depended upon the whims of a powerful individual who belonged to an insane organisation, one might search excessively for auguries. What did a frown portend? Or a grunt? What did the exact pressure of his hand upon the breast, compared with yesterday, imply? And the rhythm of his cock, or a gasp during orgasm?

Or a seeming *delay* of orgasm...? Gottfried nursed Bella towards her own excitement by a bodily insistence that she should, she *must*, surrender herself to him sensually, now that her senses were back in working order due to better diet. This might merely be a further kind of oppression.

Yet she intuited that he would not reject her.

She was, to him, someone chosen especially to cherish—in his own bodily style. She was a person as well as an exemplar for the expiation of guilt—as well as someone symbolically saved from the slaughter in the way that he had saved some rabbis and eggheads.

She was the *personalization* of his act of charity or dictate of conscience. Thus it was entirely necessary that she should be, to him, an individual person. Always his body spoke more about his mood than his lips ever did... which led to that superstitious search for auguries.

Sometimes Bella felt furious that she was allowing him to unburden himself thus of bad conscience—that through sex she was shriving him to some degree. What did it really count that one Jewess was surviving through his *tactic* while thousands of others died? But she did not choose to reject her salvation.

She would never cry out to him, 'I love you.' In this mad place what sense would such a declaration make? Yet what did her body tell him? On the night when for the first time she climaxed, clutching him, digging fingernails into the firm flesh of this officer, he had flicked a cigarette lighter alight—no, he had *not* switched on a blinding lamp. And he had scrutinised her face briefly while she stared at him open-eyed; and he had nodded.

A true communication? Or only another evasive augury?

Nor did she imagine that any possible future could exist—for her, or for him.

With restored health, her halted periods had resumed. Late in 1943 she became pregnant by him—an event which at first caused her a renewed pang of terror.

Would he blame her—as surely as if she had smuggled a knife into his bed, in the way that a truly *brave* victim might have done?

As for bravery, how many other prisoners in the camp had the energy even to contemplate such a suicidal, stupid act? In any case, she had those rabbis to think of . . . Von Turm's murder or mutilation would probably mean their elimination, not to mention her own flogging to death.

First and foremost, Bella's own body had already promised Gottfried something other than a knife in the night . . .

Would he accuse her of having polluted him by allowing his seed to take root in her womb?

Indeed not. She would take extra vitamins. She would give birth in the Brothel Block—though he would not be present at such an event. She would rear her babe—though he would not see it—and she would continue to visit him.

Even this was within the gamut of SS caprice.

It could be done. For her. While others starved and died.

So I was born in the Midsummer of 1944. Herzwalde camp collapsed into chaos in March of the following year. The rabbis had barely begun work on the Book of *Revelation*, yet it seemed that the prophecies of Armageddon were already coming true, prematurely.

A bomb, one of several stupidly dropped on the concentration camp, killed Colonel von Turm. The bombing killed prisoners too, but only one German, Gottfried. Yet obviously the end was nigh. Therefore the SS assembled the able-bodied to march them westward; and among the ablest-bodied were those rabbis and eggheads of the Colonel's project, and of course Bella with me in her arms. In such circumstances I was a burden, yet one which the SS allowed out of some perverse sentiment towards their dead deputy commandant.

Chaos begat chaos as the sinews of lunacy stretched and snapped. Overnight, at a transit stockade previously used for cattle, the SS all decamped without troubling to machine-gun those they had escorted thus far.

Bella fled. Presently she found herself wandering with a band of other anonymous women, reduced to the status of tramps, starving herself to supply me with half-masticated scavenged food which she spat into my mouth in the way that a mother bird feeds its hungry, squalling nestling.

Unluckily, those tramps fell in again with other ex-inmates of Herzwalde who knew exactly who Bella was. They beat Bella savagely as a mistress of a Nazi tormentor, for she had prospered while they suffered.

Though her injuries were patched up, Bella died of pneumonia.

Somehow, a nun took me to a camp for displaced persons. She only knew that I was Jewish, and was called David.

In that more benign camp, a miraculously reunited couple by the name of Abramowicz adopted me. Martha Abramowicz had been sterilised in a medical experiment, but had survived. As had Levi, her husband. I was their second miracle, a son.

Eventually the Abramowiczes reached Palestine, and Palestine became Israel. Ultimately I became a *katsa* of the Mossad, dedicated to foxing the enemies of Israel.

In lieu of other nourishment during the days of wandering, my mother may have told me tales. I would have needed to be preternaturally precocious to understand those tales—unless my memory was a perfect sponge, the incomprehensible contents of which could be stored for later retrieval, decoding, and interpretation.

Might this be partly the explanation? My memory is indeed remarkably retentive.

At puberty, I began to dream my mother's memories of Herzwalde... These weren't exactly *horrifying*—not in the sense that I would wake up screaming. Rather, it seemed as though nightly I was engaged in a game, a game which dark gods played with people. The camp with its great rows of huts, its outer and inner wire fences, its watchtowers, latrines, kitchens, gallows, its special blocks, its SS residencies, its warehouses of loot, all, all this was an intricate and fascinating gameboard, a lifeboard and death-board far more complex than any chessboard. Pyjama-clad pawns and grey-uniformed knights and bishop-rabbis and many other categories manoeuvred there. Also, I glimpsed certain evasive pieces which seemed to bear no correspondence to ordinary reality. I called these the Sphinx, the Angel, the Harpy, and the Clown; though what they were I could not tell.

The more that I experienced the manoeuvres, the more did it seem that some higher scheme presided over the camp. Some higher plan was emerging, ghostlike—in the manner of a vast message writ in invisible ink revealing itself line by line, under the stimulus not of warmth but of wretched death.

The final revelation of that message would be cataclysmic, yet potent, wrought of ultimate despair and prayer and conjuration.

Despair, yes despair. Despair that God might no longer be present in such a hell as the camp; that the camp represented an *absence* of God, a gap within Creation, a mad void where aberrant entities such as the Harpy and the Clown could caper, where the Sphinx and the Angel could construct themselves. Apocalyptic creatures! Yet not the banal Four Horsemen of Saint John, those projections of paranoia, jealously, and vengeance. Something much more *interesting* . . .

Nevertheless, God-power could still be summoned. Thus the Creator might be recalled into existence.

With the abandonment of Herzwalde, what became of the almost completed Bible in Blood? The scribes didn't carry it away with them on their forced march. Nor was Gottfried von Turm alive to salvage it.

I spent many years—whilst engaged on other enterprises in Europe as a Mossad operative—in tracking down rumours of that legendary book which now lay spread open before me.

Surviving Rabbis (their faith reinforced, or else forsaken) and eggheads alike were distinctly reticent about their part in the affair, as though an oath of enduring secrecy bound them . . .

For they had murmured over that book, uttering what were virtually incantations; and something strange and potent—yet abortive—had happened in that icy February of 1945, as Soviet forces fought their way progressively closer. It was something other than the seeming approach of Armageddon for the Third Reich. It was something connected with the prisoners' apprehension that they might all be summarily liquidated by a Germany in retreat. It was something which might magically *protect* the residents of the Scripture Block more effectively than Colonel von Turm. (If indeed they realized that he was their protector. The witness of survivors, on this point, ranged from incredulity to stubborn silence).

In my mother's fragmented memories, welling within me, was a hint of what this strange, potent, yet finally fruitless event had been. Only a hint.

Her *Gottfried* certainly knew more about it. Gottfried, of whom I was half. Yet that half remained veiled within *her* remembrance.

The rumour-web had finally attracted a spider, a spinner of cocoons in which to store prizes, a collector of bibliographic bizarrerie in the stooping shape of Henry Appledorn.

The German Democratic Republic had at last given up the ghost. In the process it yielded up all manner of monsters, including untold archives stored in secret cellars by the Stasi, those Marxist successors to the Gestapo. Out-of-work intellectuals were being hired to catalogue the morass of paper.

Whoever found the Blood Bible lurking in a Stasi crypt obviously realized its oddity, thus its potential value. Sufficient to buy a fine Mercedes, or several? He, or she, sequestered the volume for themselves, during this time of confusion, and put out feelers . . .

Or perhaps our investigative entrepreneur Klaus Bauer himself discovered, from ageing ex-SS contacts, where the volume might have ended up under the Communist regime—as an unclassifiable curiosity which it might be prudent to keep hidden—and then he bribed the new custodians of the Stasi crypts.

The Stasi had often been chary about releasing Nazi documents or films from store to assist international quests for justice against Nazis. For thus they might be assisting that creature of America, the Zionist state. Colonel von Turm was dead, way beyond prosecution for war crimes. Better to keep such a weird anomaly as the Blood Bible stored in secrecy, if indeed the Stasi understood exactly what it was. Maybe they never really believed any scraps of testimony that they gathered. Maybe they viewed awareness of the book as potentially dangerous, a possible focus for neo-Hitlerian blood-dreams of unregenerate Nazis who had bored bolt-holes into the woodwork of the Bundesrepublik next door.

What Gloria Cameron had let slip made me realize that Henry Appledorn was no mere eccentric, ardent bibliophile. Unlike Bauer, he must be at least somewhat aware of the *event* which had occurred in Herzwalde during the final days.

Might he know *more* than I did? Had one of the surviving eggheads, after emigrating to America, then perhaps lapsing into poverty in his old age, told Appledorn an incredible story? Did Appledorn, himself confronting old age with disapproval, fancy himself as a Magus?

As a good *katsa* of Mossad, I was thoroughly accustomed to running scenarios of disinformation and duplicity through my mind, just as I was used to adopting false identities so that I could be one person one day, then another the next day.

Ha! I wouldn't be a good *katsa* much longer—not after acquiring the volume. I would be a disappeared, absconded *katsa*.

'I said, Miss Cameron, what do you expect from the book? What have you two heard about it? Come on, Mr Appledorn.' I smiled at him. 'I'm prepared to shoot one or both or you. The woman first, I think, to prove my intentions. Then you, Sir.' With my free hand, I pulled out the hypodermic syringe. To allow them some hope, I explained, 'I was merely intending to put you all to sleep with a jab. Now I may have to shoot you.'

Miss Cameron licked her lips. 'The noise will attract attention. You won't escape with the book.'

'Oh, I think this is quite a soundproof suite. We are on what, the tenth floor? I happen to know that the rooms on either side and over the way are vacant. If any passing maid reports a problem, I'm sure that the under-manager of this hotel will cause all kinds of delay.'

Thus I burned my *sayan*, but that didn't matter.

'Tell him what he wants, Herr Appledorn,' begged Bauer in a cowardly tone.

A moment later Bauer launched himself at me, with a leap like a German Shepherd dog.

He knocked my gun-hand down as I swung to fire. The first bullet must have passed through his jacket, but the second caught him, knocking him back from grappling with me; and I had stabbed him with the needle too . . .

Appledorn uttered a bellow of affront—for the first bullet had passed aslant into the book, exploding outward through the rear board and the thick glass of the table beneath. The glass cracked into several jagged panes which nevertheless hung together. A hole bored down through the pages.

Gloria Cameron uttered a different, tremulous kind of cry.

For the top page—of *The Gospel According to Saint Matthew*—had begun to bleed . . .

Red blood welled upward from the wound in the parchment just as though the heat of my bullet had reliquefied the long-dried gore of the letters.

Bauer staggered aside, clutching at his hip. Part of his flesh had been blown away. He shook his head as the drug began to work on him.

That couldn't possibly be *his* blood on the book.

Bauer collapsed on a sofa. He was irrelevant now.

Through that tunnel torn in the book a wind began to whistle, the shriek of a wintry gale—which fast became lower in pitch, a vibrant powerful moan, as if the tunnel was fast widening.

And it was so. It was so.

The Cameron woman cried out again; and so, I think, did I.

A fissure opened through the book—a chasm.

A gulf that, howling, invaded the room, abolishing the furnishings and walls and the long, curtained window.

In their place was a cold dark river. A broad river. Little ice floes spun along it. Its banks themselves were gentle enough, but across the water indefinable walls and buildings mounted towards a steep ridge crowned by a long sombre fortress and a bulky cathedral. The Moon offered some illumination. Sparks of torchlight flickered here and there like stars fallen to Earth . . .

I recognized those silhouettes on the ridge—even though they seemed strangely incomplete. Surely this was Prague. The river, the Vltava. The Cathedral must be that of St Vitus. The fortress could only be Hradčany Castle . . . Yet it was a Prague of long ago. And in the winter, in the small hours of some morning.

Behind me, a jumble of buildings packed together in the obscurity. Jews' Town.

Three men laboured on the riverbank near the flood of wintry water. They were stooping, scooping, moulding handfuls of clay and mud . . .

Had Appledorn and Gloria Cameron been sucked here too? I seemed to sense their presence. I myself was bodiless, a floating point of view, an invisible naked mind, a spirit.

Two of the men by the water were dressed in homespun doublets and leggings, soiled by the clay. The third, a white-bearded man with a curious cap on his head, wore a cloak.

With their bare hands they were moulding a body from the stuff of the riverbank . . .

I knew who they must be. I could sense it.

They had to be none other than Rabbi Yehuda Löw ben Bezalel, and his son-in-law, and his trusted pupil. They were trying to make the golem, the artificial man of great strength who would police the ghetto which clustered close by.

Christian trouble-makers would smuggle a murdered Christian child into the ghetto, wrapped in a sack, as a pretext to utter the blood-accusation against Jewry and thus launch a vindictive, brutal pogrom.

The Golem was designed to haul such villains to justice.

Had this manufacture of a Golem ever really happened? Or had it only occurred in the realm of myth—a myth so powerful that many people nevertheless believed it? Jews turned to this myth for consolation in the dark hours of their despair. Even in the late twentieth century pious pilgrims visited Löw's lion-carved sarcophagus in the overcrowded Jewish cemetery to toss written appeals into his tomb, hoping for wonders.

Now this legendary event was happening before my gaze.

With his finger the Rabbi was drawing a face on the recumbent, lifeless clay man.

'May the angel Metatron guide us,' murmured the pupil. I could understand his words. Cautiously he asked his mentor, 'Rabbi, will the Golem really borrow a soul from the domain of pre-existence?'

Rabbi Löw paused. 'Only a crude soul,' he replied. 'Our Golem will be speechless. Dumb. Without human words, always. Yet it will understand, and obey.'

The Rabbi's son-in-law plainly felt qualms too, at this final moment. 'Aren't we trespassing on God's prerogative?'

Löw mused. 'The Divine Wisdom was obliged to become *creative*,' he reminded them, 'so as to justify His own existence to Himself. Man was formed in His image. Now Man must needs create too, albeit on a humbler scale.'

Aye, desperate expedients for desperate times.

The three men whispered together.

Then Yehuda's son-in-law began to walk around the clay man, reciting as he did so a code of letters from the Hebrew alphabet.

'*Aleph . . . Vav . . . Aleph . . . Heth . . . Jod . . .*'

He circuited the clay body seven times—'*Heth . . . Samekh . . . He . . . Tav . . . Pe . . . He . . . Nun . . .*'—and as he walked, so the body of clay began to glow ruddily as an inner fire was stoked.

Next it was the turn of Yehuda Löw's pupil to pace around the body, uttering other permutations of Hebrew letters.

This was Kabbalah.

True Kabbalah. Pious Kabbalah.

Sacred magic.

With a carved block of wood, Yehuda stamped a word upon the Golem's hot brow.

I could read the word. The word was *emeth*, meaning 'true'. Erase the first letter, and 'true' would turn into 'dead'.

Into the Golem's mouth Yehuda pushed a piece of paper on which he had written the secret name of God. This piece of paper was the *Shem*, the program for the Golem. Remove the *Shem* from the Golem's mouth, and the artificial man would collapse back into clay.

Icy water swirled against the glowing body. Steam wreathed it. From the Golem's fingers nails sprouted. From its head hair grew.

In chorus, the three men recited: 'And the Lord God formed man of the dust of the ground, and breathed into his nostrils the breath of life; and man became a living soul.'

With this last phrase, I felt myself being sucked towards the Golem—as if *I* was to be the soul that inhabited it!

As if my own soul was to animate that clay body and march obediently around the ghetto, unable to exert my own will, impotent to protest! Obeying orders numbly until some day when the *Shem* was removed from my mouth!

I fought.

I sought purchase with my nonexistent fingers and toes on the very air.

As I slid ever closer to entombment and a terrible oblivion, at the last moment the Golem opened its eyes. The pulling ceased; I was gently repelled.

The Golem arose.

'Your name,' Yehuda said to it, 'is Joseph.'

And Joseph nodded.

'You are to guard us from harm, Joseph,' the rabbi told it.

Snow began to tumble, slanting through the air.

Snow swirled, blanking out the scene. I could see nothing but tempestuous white flakes.

When these flakes cleared, instead of a river bank there were rows of wooden huts and roads of frozen mud. In place of a distant steeple, a watchtower. A searchlight stabbed out from its summit, cutting whitely through the night. In the distance, a whistle blew. From much further away—maybe sixty kilometres away—came a faint percussive thump of artillery . . .

My mother's memories were alive . . .

Within those memories stood Colonel von Turm.

I had leapt from her to him at last.

'Ich bin Gottfried,' I told myself.

Yet what did I know of my identity? Though I probed, yet I could not penetrate. I was only a wraith, wrapped around this person. Of Gottfried's youth, his motives, his attitude to Bella: nothing. He might as well have been an animated man of clay, who could articulate nothing of his thoughts and feelings to me. I only knew what he did.

Resting his weight on his silver-handled cane, he stood surveying one nearby blockhouse. Within, a faint ruddy light glowed as if a dull brazier was lit in there. The Colonel had thrown a long leather coat over the shoulders of his grey uniform. Several helmeted SS guards were with him, toting their machine-pistols.

When they burst into the Scripture Block and illuminated it, almost all of the rabbis and eggheads proved to have quit their tiered wooden bunks. They thronged the floor space. Their Kapo was doing nothing about the situation.

Now, this particular hut wasn't as claustrophobic as most. It wasn't a sardine can. Space existed, for uniquely these slaves laboured in their own quarters. The far end of the hut housed a work-table surrounded by rickety chairs.

On that table lay the Bible in Blood. The letters on the open pages of parchment glowed ruddily, luridly luminous with inner light.

At the sudden intrusion, a murmuring of many voices ceased—except one which continued to recite defiantly, insistently, *'And man became a living soul...'*

From beside the table a naked corpse arose. Its skin was grey as wrapping paper. Its blue lips were bared in a rictus, exposing clenched stained teeth.

Obviously a corpse. Its sunken eyes were closed. On its brow was printed, in blood, a Hebrew word.

Emeth.

'And man became a living soul...'

Its tongue, protruding through its teeth, had shrivelled to a white leaf.

No! That was no tongue.

That was ... the *shem*.

The mud outside was frozen. Evidently the prisoners had smuggled in a corpse from another hut, or more likely from the charnel heap. Was not man's flesh made of clay? To clay, returning? Was this dead body not therefore equivalent to clay?

'. . . *a living soul, to be our protector, our guardian under God!*'

The zombie-Golem opened its eyes, eyes that stared blankly. It began to cavort, windmilling its arms.

As the SS guards clove a pathway for the Colonel many prisoners scrambled into bunks or clung to the sides of those bunks like panicked monkeys.

By now the Bible had ceased glowing.

Gottfried stared at the scarecrow of a Golem, which turned now to face him.

'Kill it,' he ordered his men.

Guns racketed.

The Golem's parchment skin tore, yet bullets seemed simply to pass through it. It rocked, but it did not fall. Its flesh burst, bloodlessly, but its bones could have been made of steel. Or of rock, of fossilised bones.

'Cease fire!'

The Golem still stood, swaying.

Gottfried stared at it . . . as though now he understood.

Some of the prisoners were moaning—not because they were afraid of a terrible punishment, but as if appalled at what they had achieved. Or half-achieved. A multitude of needle tracks in all of their arms kept tally of the blood they had yielded up repeatedly, day after day.

They had lost courage.

One of the eggheads cried out cravenly to the Colonel, 'Take the *shem* from its mouth, Sir!'

Gottfried stood right before the Golem, although his men were hesitant.

It jerked. It froze again. Why should it attack this Colonel, who was a perverse—or honourable—protector of these prisoners?

Then it spoke—opening its vile teeth. At last it spoke. Or croaked.

'Ich bin *Joseph*,' it uttered. The *shem* lolled on its blue tongue like a long communion wafer.

Gottfried reached, and yanked the scrap of parchment from its mouth— so that the Golem lolled upright, motiveless, like any common-or-garden prisoner on parade who would soon die.

The Colonel spat on his glove, and smudged out the first letter of the word on the creature's brow. Oh he knew, he knew the tricks of the Jews!

The corpse collapsed. Its spirit had fled.

And so must I. For suction tore at me.

'Father!' I cried. 'Tell me! Tell me!' Tell me so many things that you never told my mother . . .

But that inhalation from elsewhere was overwhelming me, as if the very bellows of the world were breathing me in.

'Aitch-Jay!' cried Gloria Cameron. Our bibliophile hunched, lolling, spittle on his lips.

The book on the smashed glass table bled no more. There was no longer any wound from which it could bleed. The torn parchment had resealed itself like living flesh possessed of an amazing power of regeneration, a facility as considerable as that of the Golem itself.

Bauer was dozing, while blood continued to leak from his side through his clothes to stain the sofa.

'Aitch-Jay!'

Henry *Joseph* Appledorn, of course.

It struck me then, fearfully, that only that coincidence of his name and the Golem's had saved my soul from being enveloped in the creation of clay...

Either one of us might have been captured—him or me. Bauer? What about Bauer? No, he had already been rendered *hors de combat*. And Gloria Cameron was female.

Appledorn mumbled.

He staggered.

Aided by her, he sat down in an armchair.

He stared at me, out of grief-stricken, time-chasmed eyes.

His voice croaked.

'I had to—to patrol... for years, night after night... And day after day I stood... motionless... in a back room of the Synagogue. I couldn't... utter a word. I was only... an animated *thing*.' He forced out all the words which had long been frozen. At first they emerged like nuggets of ice, then, as his voice thawed, in a gushing stream.

The cobbled alleys, the twisting streets so narrow that the eaves of houses almost touched... Carved painted signs showing a swan, a lute, a crayfish, a giant key, as though each house was a member of some strange zodiac. Here was the building housing the first Hebrew printing press in Central Europe. There were the public baths. Here, a poorhouse; there, an infirmary. All crammed together. In a maze of alleyways. Which he must pace nightly, always keeping out of sight if he could, never speaking, for the *shem* was in his mouth.

And he was successful in his guardianship.

For presently a magnificent Jewish town hall was built. And the High Synagogue; and Klaus Synagogue; and Maisl Synagogue.

So successful was he that further services on his part seemed unnecessary. Frankly, his existence was an embarrassment. Consequently he was walled up, stored in darkness. Forgotten . . .

. . . till of a sudden he found himself standing in a crowded, noisome hut. Bullets tore his emaciated body—in vain, except that through the holes they made they let a breeze into him. He sucked that breeze together, and at last he gasped.

And the grey-clad officer pulled the *shem* from his mouth.

'The book could bring . . . power. So I heard,' Appledorn confessed. He needed little prompting now. Yes, I did hear it from an immigrant who had been in Herzwalde. But the book was still incomplete . . .

'It's the only *actual* magic book I ever heard of. Books of spells and grimoires: they're just . . . weird words on paper. Nothing effective. This book was magic in itself! And that was because . . .' He frowned, trying to grasp the reason.

'Because God was absent from Herzwalde,' I explained. 'So there was a chasm in creation. A gap. The rules did not exist any more—they broke down. The gap could be otherwise filled. I'm the son of Gottfried von Turm, the deputy commandant,' I told him. 'That is *my* book.'

Though I had failed to commune fully with my father, I knew at last what his motive had been.

It had been different from what I had imagined from my mother's memories—ah, Bella's *deluded* recollections!

No wonder Gottfried had been taciturn.

Although on the one hand the SS constituted a veritable bloody occult brotherhood, on the other hand the Nazis cracked down on most independent occultists and occult groups who might in any way form a kernel of opposition to the Nazi regime. They suppressed these potential rivals. The Gestapo drew up lists of organizations little and large, even daffy ones, whose members must not be allowed any government employment, even as a postman. And this made perfect sense; for if the SS were occultly inclined, they must be the sole practitioners of dark and bloody rituals.

Gottfried von Turm had been an occultist of a different stripe—a solitary practitioner in a lonely tower, as it were. Yet he was also an aristocrat. Hence the Gestapo both punished him, and at the same time permitted him a National Socialistic redemption, by forcing his entry into the Waffen-SS.

Along with whom he fought, until he came to Herzwalde.

In the camp he discovered a pressure cooker of horrors—a perfect crucible for an experiment. On the surface his project might seem more 'benign' in its effects than the loathsome and lunatic medical mutilations which SS doctors performed upon prisoners. Yet it was a deep, dark investigation—by someone who bore Jews no particular animosity whatever, who might even arguably be aiding some of them. As intense heat and pressure might crush carbon into diamond, so might the spiritually humiliating toil of kabbalistic rabbis in the Scripture Block, writing in their own blood—in an atmosphere of ultimate despair, devoid of God—create a magical device.

Ah, that *amalgamation* of Jewish blood and holy Christian words culminating in an Apocalypse!

What role did my mother fulfill in this? Oh yes, I *was* to be born—of a Jewess whose people were scribing the book, and of Gottfried's seed! This was the part of himself which Gottfried donated to the project. Most certainly I was to be born, a homunculus of him, a repository of his power—of that power which his project was distilling.

No wonder Gottfried was so silent in bed, so devoid of pillow talk. He was *concentrating*.

No wonder he needed to remain detached from me, shunning my birth and my early infancy. For the project was not yet complete. The book wasn't finished.

And then that idiotic bomb killed him; and the book remained unfinished.

Now I understood why I could dream my mother's memories. And why I had felt so impelled to seek out the book.

'Do you think,' I demanded of Appledorn, 'that if anyone except me had fired a bullet into that book, the rift in reality would have opened up?'

Appledorn was trembling. Gloria Cameron regarded me . . . almost greedily, as if desirous.

'But,' Appledorn managed to say. 'But the Golem was a legend . . .'

Yes, it was. In our own history it was a legend.

'There's another domain, Mr Appledorn,' I said, with increasing confidence. 'The domain of the Sphinx and the Angel, of the Harpy and the Clown.' I had never uttered their names aloud before—names which indeed *I myself* had assigned to these entities. Nonetheless, those were the true names.

Appledorn wiped his lips.

'Take the book,' he said. 'I daren't own it.'

'*Aitch-Jay!*' protested the woman.

As though it was up to either of them to decide!

The American shook his head numbly. 'I couldn't . . . The serving, the standing in darkness for years . . . I'd rather die than risk . . . something similar.'

'Then you will die,' the Cameron woman said to him bitterly. She wasn't threatening him, simply uttering a statement of plain fact. 'In three or four years, ten years if you're lucky. You'll die, Henry *Joseph*.'

'And therefore so will you one day, Gloria,' he replied softly.

It was time for me to leave. High time.

I made both of them lie down upon the floor. Appledorn complied willingly; Gloria Cameron, less so.

I injected her, then him. Then I shut the Blood Bible, and tied the red ribbons.

The steel emblem embedded in the cover was a large mirror-image swastika, made of steel and inset with strips of mirror.

Lille is a fine enough city to hide in, though my stay will be relatively brief. I rent a little top floor apartment in the old town in the Rue de la Clef. David Abramowicz is no more. Now I'm Daniel Kahn, an author determined to finish a book. 'About what, Monsieur?' 'Why, about cathedrals.' There's one substantial example just up the road. I make sure to visit the cathedral occasionally, to stretch my legs.

I take the blood from high up my arms so as not to produce obvious tracks which might attract the attention of anti-drugs *flics*.

I arrived in this city with my book at the most opportune time in September—at the start of the vast rummage fair, the Braderie. By ancient charter the whole city centre is given over to thousands of stalls, street upon street of stalls selling old clothes, bric-à-brac, antiques, African carvings, tools, the rubbish from Granny's attic, carpets, curios, anything and everything. I even found a stall selling the extra parchment which I needed. In the evening, while music spewed forth and the whores patrolled, *tout le monde* feasted on mussels cooked in red wine and in cream at a multitude of tables which were further blocking pavements and streets outside of every café. Black mountains of empty shells arose. If a car intruded impatiently, tipsy diners tossed mussel shells at it in pique.

Half of the population of Flanders seemed to have descended upon Lille; and tourists galore. What more anonymous time to take up residence, and remain as if enchanted by the city?

My arms ache, and the fingers of my right hand are numb with forming the Gothic letters correctly. I must flex my fingers frequently. There's a whiff of blood in the room, and of sterilising alcohol too, since I wouldn't wish to become septic.

Presently I will reach those final words: *The grace of our Lord Jesus Christ be with you all. Amen.*

Amen. Amen. Amen.

So be it! Thus is it in truth!

Then I must bind the book; and having bound it, I shall fire my gun into that book once more, and the blood-stained parchment will split open to reveal the true territory of the Clown and the Harpy, the Angel and the Sphinx; and I shall discover what those beings are.

I myself, and my father within me.

The Great Escape

ERHAPS THE MOST PARADOXICAL ASPECT OF HELL IS THE
participation of certain angels in its procedures.

I do not refer to those millions of fallen angels who became demons.
I refer to our own select cadre of righteous kosher Angels who remain
angelic, who are still endowed with the grace of the Quint, yet who are
seconded by Him to serve in Hell for dozens of years at a stretch.

This is as though (to borrow a recent example) Nuremburg prosecutors or
agents of Mossad must participate in the uninterrupted management of a
Nazi concentration camp! As if vegetarians must collaborate with vivisec-
tionists!

I am the Impresario Angel. My task is to fly low over Hell, bearing in my
hands one of the special lenses—resembling a giant frisbee or frying pan lid
made of diamond—through which blessèd souls in Paradise are able to view
the torments of the damned. (Some of these torments are indeed conducted
inside of gigantic frying pans.)

When I reach a particularly atrocious scene, I hover there with the lens. I
inhale the reek of cooking flesh or of voiding bowels. Shrieks of anguish
assail my ears. The blessèd in Paradise are not assailed thus. The lens relays
sights but neither smells nor sounds.

The demons who conduct the torments pay scant heed to me. Mostly
they perform like automata. Out of the frying pan into the fire. Out of the
cauldron on to the griddle. Essentially their work is monotonous and

unimaginative. To devise ingenious new varieties of pain is no concern of theirs. Can it be that they refrain from doing so in order to frustrate the Deity, in a last dogged show of rebellion?

Perhaps their lacklustre performance is actually in response to my arrival on the scene, with the surveillance lens.

Sometimes, as I approach, they seem to be gossiping. Quickly they become mute. Even if they did carry on chatting, only the screeching and wailing of victims would be easily audible.

I should not communicate with any of the demons, lest I am corrupted. Formerly—before my present secondment—I was a border guard between Hell and the higher domain.

As were my colleagues likewise.

I am the Impresario Angel. I present the hellish performance for the attention of souls in Paradise; although I have no idea of the reaction of the audience.

There is also the Trumpet Angel. He flies to and fro, sounding fanfares of exquisite purity on a long golden trumpet. Each sufferer in torment may imagine that he or she is hearing the Last Trump, and that Hell might soon cease to function. He or she is wrong.

Then there is the Clock Angel. He tends the eternity clock. That clock, of diamond, rises from atop a crystal crag, taller than any skyscraper. The crag is much too smooth and sleek and sheer to climb. The clock is visible from many parts of Hell. Its four high faces lack any mechanical hands. However, the play of light within the precious substance of those faces constantly evokes the appearance of different hands—minute-hands, hour-hands, year-hands, century-hands, millennium-hands. Flying up and down one face, and then the adjoining face, the Clock Angel cleans the clock by the beating of his wings. Otherwise, rising smoke and soot would dull the clock. Its diamond light is a source of illumination for much of Hell—supplementing the fires of torment and the faint phosphorescence of areas of ice.

Three other angels also serve with me in Hell, namely the Harp Angel and the Scribe Angel and the Ark Angel. Additionally, we each have a counterpart. These colleagues take over our roles as Impresario and Clock Angel and such during our session of praise. Since we do not sleep (nor, in Hell, does anyone), our half-day period of sabbatical is spent singing psalms to the Quint in a white marble tabernacle upon an alabaster island surrounded by a wide moat of quicksilver.

And while I am on duty with my lens, those counterpart angels are singing His praises. Hosanna, Hosanna. Thus does rapture regularly bless us all during our duties in Hell.

If demons try to cross that gleaming moat, their wings fail. Nor can they wade through it. On some previous occasion demons must have tried to fly or swim across. Submerged in the moat are several skeletons. Sometimes these rise to the surface where they drift like ramshackle rafts.

Although our departure from the island is always perfectly harmonised, return to the tabernacle is rarely simultaneous. Usually several minutes elapse between the arrival of the first of us and the last. Meanwhile our counterparts continue their enchanting, ecstatic praise.

After a sojourn amidst the misery, the singing has a powerful effect upon us. We yearn to join in. Indeed we must soon do so before our replacements can fly away, so that praise of the Quint will never cease for an instant. Yet there's often an interlude while we await a tardy colleague and prepare to hand over lens or trumpet. During this interval we are at liberty to engage in sublime discussion. Colloquy is a suitably dignified word for these occasional brief conversations of ours.

During a short interval twice every infernal day no angel cleans the clock of eternity, nor blows a golden fanfare, nor plucks the silver harp; nor may the blessèd watch the torments of the damned. Recently I queried the Scribe Angel about the security aspect of these transitions between one shift and the next . . .

A word about time. In Hell there is neither day nor night. Nor does the clock of eternity possess hands. Nor do the salutes of the Trumpet Angel mark off minutes. Yet all of us angels possess perfect pitch. How else might we psalm the praises of the Quint? In matters of time instinctively we heed the chime of the Cosmos—that distant quasar-like pulse of the Quint, cascading down through the realms. Successive veils of existence blur this pulse. That is why we do not return to the island in perfect synchrony. Our singing inside of our marble tabernacle readjusts this minor imperfection. The imperfection will recur. Is not Hell a place of blemishes?

I queried the Scribe Angel about security because, next to myself, she comes into closest proximity with the damned and with demons.

By contrast, the Trumpet Angel rarely dips near to the soil of Hell. I sometimes suspect that she blows her trumpet as often as she does in order to banish the cries of anguish from her ears! If demons conspire, she would never overhear their conversations.

The soil of Hell, do I say? It is hardly loam. Solid lava mingles with hot sand and with quicksands and with pebbles. Compacted excrement adjoins mud and glaciers. Black cones ooze molten rock. Fumaroles vent stinking steam which coats the ground with flowers of sulphur.

By the nature of their tasks neither the Clock Angel nor the Harp Angel come into close contact with the denizens. As for the Ark Angel, he presides over the boat-shaped fortress of timbers grounded upon Hell's only notable peak, to the east.

The Ark Angel stands upon a poop, jutting high above the uppermost deck at the rear. He constantly surveys Hell, though from such an elevation and distance most details are indistinguishable.

The Ark is much vaster within than without. Decks descend beneath decks, plunging down, an abyss of a myriad levels. A myriad benches occupy each deck. Chained to each bench are inmates. Demons patrol with whips.

The Ark is at once prison-hulk and slave-ship, travelling nowhere except through the timelessness of Hell. Held therein are the ancestors of humanity. Pre-Men; hominids. Down in the bilges, in darkness and in fetters, hunch the two wizened apish creatures known as Adam and Lucy. Punishment is only by whip in the Ark.

'Scribe Angel,' I addressed her, 'do you suppose that anything happens differently in Hell during the gaps each day while none of us are on duty? Do you suppose that the demons rest and that punishments pause?'

She consulted her great scroll upon which she forever recorded with the blood-quill the names of the damned and their tortures. Soon she would hand this scroll and the quill over to the other Scribe Angel. He always documented the torments of males. She, of females. She scanned her records, as if seeking some anomaly.

The psalming of our colleagues was approaching a transcendent climax, if indeed the sublime could top the sublime. Maybe it was exaltation which prompted her reply.

'A pause in the punishment?' she said to me. 'Such would be the mercy of the Quint, descending even unto here!'

I spied our final colleague winging toward the moat of mercury. On this occasion the late arrival happened to be the Ark Angel. Just before he alighted, I ventured to ask, 'What if the demons do something other than merely rest?'

'Surely the Quint would witness it!' was her reply.

'If so,' said I, 'why are we here as witnesses?'

'The Quint is ineffable,' she told me with utter certainty. 'He is inexpressible. He cannot be expressed. So therefore we are here as intermediaries. As ambassadors. This is the Embassy of Heaven.'

The Ark Angel landed on the alabaster isle. We must begin to sing in beatific chorus. We must proceed into the marble tabernacle. We must hand over lens and scroll and blood-quill and trumpet.

What the Scroll Angel said was so true. The Quint—the Quintessence—is necessarily remote. Beyond the many angelic hierarchies—each more ethereal than the rank below—is the centre-point, the Divine Core, the radiant quasar of all existence. That core, Who is the Quint, is unknowable except to the Seraphic Sphere surrounding Him. Likewise, the Seraphic Sphere is unknowable except to the Cherubic Sphere.

Our duties, and our very existence, descend from on high. Yet could it be that the intentions of the Quint might be misinterpreted, as in the game of Chinese Whispers?

How could this be so, when intention is hardly ascribable to the Quint? He is Pure Being.

I decided to alight and address a demon directly. This went against my inner sense of my duty, but I was becoming suspicious of their zombie-like conduct.

By setting foot upon the infernal unsoil, would I be breaching a covenant? Would lightning rive the sombre smutty sky? Would demons be free to seize me, and attempt to torture me?

What about the lens I carried? The lens would not sustain itself unsupported in mid-air. I must continue to hold it. I must not lay it down and risk it being stolen. Maybe I should angle the lens upward so that only the sky was visible? This might constitute a breach of faith with viewers in Paradise.

Therefore the blessèd must stomach an interview with a demon, particularly if they could lip-read.

A partial interview! Viewers would not see me, as holder of the lens. They would not read the questions upon my lips. They would only be able to lip-read the replies (if any) of my infernal interlocutor.

Gingerly—and gloriously—I alighted near to a gridiron. A sinner was suspended over this upon a rack consisting of iron winch and pulley and of rope black as tar. The naked man was stretched out excruciatingly. Beneath the hot gridiron a bed of coals glowed brightly whenever one of the two attending demons operated the bellows. If the rack was slackened, the man's buttocks would descend upon the hot iron. Hoist him again to relieve this pain, and his sinews would distend agonizingly once more.

Through cracked dry lips the wretch would croak, 'For mercy's sake, raise me.' Soon he would gasp, 'For mercy's sake, lower me.'

In this manner he directed his own torment. The demon who turned the handle of the winch one way or the other merely complied mechanically.

When I judged that the victim was half-slack, I commanded, 'Stop!'

The Demon paused.

'Demon, by the grace of the Quint I conjure you to answer me!'

The Demon's expression was inscrutable. With his left hoof he scuffed at a ripple in the lava. With a long talon, he picked his yellow teeth. I was almost minded to unfurl my wings and leap aloft again. Yet I persevered.

'Demon,' I demanded, 'what do demons when no Angels are present?'

His reply, when it came, was in some language of grunts and barks and whistles and chattering which I had never heard before. Gifted with tongues though I am, this babel wasn't in my repertoire. It sounded like some primitive mother-tongue which had preceded true speech. Not proto-Indo-European. But proto-proto. An ur-language preceding true language, and inaccessible to me—as ineffable as the Quint.

Thus did he mock me. He had answered me obediently. Yet I had no way of understanding the answer.

I was about to ascend in disgust. However, a second thought came to me.

Gloriously, and gingerly, I inclined myself and thus my lens over the face of the half-racked man. The Scroll Angel would have known the name of this person; but not I.

'Mortal,' I addressed him. (Arguably, he was immortal now, his body repairing itself in order to be abused repeatedly). 'Hear me, Mortal: what do demons do when the Trump falls silent, and when the Harp ceases to twang?'

The sweating man stared up at me. From his expression I feared that he might be insane. Still, his mind must surely repair itself frequently.

'Water,' he croaked. 'Water—'

Give him a drink, and he would tell me . . . something. Where was there water in Hell, except boiling in cauldrons or mixed in mud?

An Angel's cool sweet saliva might serve—that same saliva which lubricated our psalms. I dribbled upon the victim's parched lips and swollen purple tongue resembling a parrot's.

Promptly the bellows-demon resumed pumping. Coals flared. Choking smoke billowed. The winch-demon spun the handle. He dumped my potential informant wholesale upon the gridiron. Feet and legs and buttocks and spine and head and outstretched arms all made contact. The moisture which I had donated shrieked out of the mortal.

The tethers of his wrists and ankles lolled loosely for the first time in what might have been centuries. As he lay writhing, those tethers began to smoulder. They burst into flames. The rope was indeed impregnated with tar.

Blazing ropes parted. The man's squirming weight tipped the gridiron. Off he rolled, falling upon the hard lava.

The demons scratched their horned heads, as if such an event was outside of their comprehension. Surely their mime of stupidity was deliberate.

Despite his burns and despite his tumble, the naked man began to scrabble away, crab-like. To begin with, he proceeded slowly upon all fours, and then a little faster. He staggered to his feet. He lurched and limped. He tried to straighten. He was like some illustration of the evolution of humanity, commencing stooped over with knuckles upon the ground, then rising to become a biped. That biped was hobbling and hopping away. Both demons scratched their narrow jutting chins. With that red gaze of theirs they eyed one another. They shook their heads as though bemused.

Was it up to me—an Angel encumbered with a lens—to recapture the absconder? In Paradise were the blessèd praying that I would do so swiftly? Were more and more of the blessèd flocking to witness this unprecedented spectacle?

One of the demons grunted. His colleague squawked a response. At long last, hooves clicking upon lava, they did set out in pursuit. Ever so slowly and leisurely.

Leaping and deploying my wings, I took to the air.

I followed the dawdling demons. Now and then, I angled the lens so that it would show the faltering yet frantic progress of the fugitive. I was evoking a dramatic tension quite different from the physical tension of torture—yet akin, I suppose, akin. The maimed mouse, being stalked by two lazy cats.

The man sprawled. He hauled himself to his fast-healing feet again. Nervously—putting on a pathetic spurt of speed—he passed quite close between two cauldrons. At this point he had little choice of route. A lagoon of molten lava bubbled to one side. A pond of pus, to the other. Trussed in nets which dangled from tripods, some children were being parboiled in those cauldrons. The demons who had been hauling the children up and down relaxed, to contemplate the runaway. They made no move to apprehend him. An inmate on the loose was too singular a sight to abbreviate.

I was paradoxically pleased with my lens-work. The angles I chose . . . The choice of 'cuts' from demon to escapee—and back again . . . Whenever I focused upon the two stalking demons, anxiety must mount that maybe somewhere ahead and out of sight the man might have fallen or been forcibly halted. While I was focusing upon him, though, the unease was that the two demons might have broken into a sprint. Even now they might be rushing up from behind.

When the man had glanced from one boiling cauldron to the other, he had witnessed those netted children being raised and lowered, dripping and bright pink. His attention had mainly been upon the cooks—warily so— rather than upon the cooked.

As he wended his way further, he seemed to become more attentive to the condition of victims.

Presently he came to a place where a young man's intestines were being drawn out through his navel. The operation was occurring at a snail's pace by means of an automated windlass, powered by steam from a nearby fumarole. Not even a demon might have had the patience—or the obstinacy—to wind this capstan personally. So slowly, so monotonously, and with such regularity, did the evisceration proceed! The rate of extraction must correspond exactly to the rate of replenishment of new intestine within the victim.

The drum of the capstan was thick with coil upon coil of glistening, sausage-like bowel. Ooze dripped constantly from beneath the machine. This liquid soaked the compacted excrement of the soil, slicking the ground as if with diarrhoea. Pressure from the outer coils must be squeezing the inner coils as flat as sloughed snakeskins.

The young man was crudely crucified against a timber framework in the shape of a letter M. This held him in position throughout his everlasting ordeal. Barbed wire secured his wrists and his outstretched ankles.

In a bizarre sense it looked as though he were escaping from that crucifixion via his own navel. The glossy rope of intestine resembled an ectoplasmic cord which might link a departed spirit to the body it had quit.

Our absconder paused near this young man. Were tears coursing down our refugee's cheeks, or only a swill of sweat? Outdistancing the demons, I flew ahead. I hovered above the fugitive like a gigantic white dove, annunciatory or pentecostal.

I did remember to pivot in mid-air and track the dilatory progress of the pursuers. If anything, that pair had slowed their pace. I returned my attention, and the focus of my lens, to the escapee.

He gaped up at me in my white splendour.

'Mortal,' I called down to him serenely and melodiously, 'I do not intervene.' Did he imagine that I might pluck him up—when I was already laden with a diamond lens—and carry him away to our alabaster sanctuary? (Oh, he knew nothing of that place!) I wished him to disregard me.

I suppose I was intervening to an extent simply by addressing him. Earlier, I had posed him a question. Now I strove not to thrust my presence upon him. I yearned to see what he would do.

He must have taken me at my word. His bleary gaze sank. He scrutinised the victim of automated evisceration. He stepped closer to the taut cable of intestine. His hands made nervous, aimless gestures. Was he contemplating unfastening the barbed wire and releasing the young man from that framework in an act of futile mercy?

'What did you do?' croaked the refugee to the victim.

Ah . . . perhaps our refugee wouldn't be willing to release the young man if when alive he had performed a truly vile crime, evil and perverted, such as the sexual murder of children, or, or . . . abortion! Abortion might actually have been the crucified man's crime—reflected by the endless dragging out of him of his own living tissue through an orifice close to where a womb would have been, were he a woman!

The victim seemed to be in a trance of torment, determined not to move—not even his eyes, much less his lips—in case the least motion multiplied his slow agony. He remained silent.

Our refugee stared about him at the landscape of Hell—and at those two laggardly stalking demons. He must have realized that he had no ultimate hope of escape.

'Let me take your place,' he begged the young man.

This sounded like a saintly offer, except for the wheedling tone of voice.

Our refugee imagined that he could endure slow automated evisceration more easily than the constant bump and hoist of alternate racking and broiling—because this other punishment would be uniform and unvarying! The younger man seemed to have achieved a meditative stupor of misery, which must surely be lesser than rack 'n' roast. The young man was privileged in that he was devoid of the constant attention of demons.

No doubt demons must unload the drum of the windlass now and then, disburdening it of the accumulating weight of compacted bowel. Otherwise the torment might have slowed eventually, and even stopped. Aside from such intervention, the young man suffered in peace.

'Let me take your place!'

Feverishly our refugee knelt. He began to prise apart the rusted barbed wire looped so tightly around one ankle. His fingers bled. He licked the moisture.

Did he imagine that he might succeed in unfastening the young man completely before his own personal demons arrived? Did he fantasize that like a midwife he might sever the long umbilicus with his teeth? That with the sharp barbs of wire he might make an incision through his own belly-button, and hook out some of his own upper bowel, and knot that to the disconnected trailing end? That the young man would agree to crucify the refugee instead?

All this—without the two demons arriving prematurely, or objecting to the substitution?

A suspicion began to dawn that I was being led astray by a charade. Astray from my original question! The end of my shift might arrive before I witnessed any finale. In waiting for one, my question would remain unanswered.

'Mortal,' I boomed, 'what do demons do when no angels watch over them?'

The refugee cowered from my voice. His bloodstained fingers plucked frantically at the wire.

Might I make an offer of amnesty in exchange for a reply? Might I promise to carry him away across the mercury moat to our island where the harmonies issuing from our tabernacle would fill him with everlasting ecstasy as if he were truly in Heaven?

If I held him in my arms, he would need to hold the lens on my behalf. His fingers would be slippery with blood. His blood would stain the view enjoyed by the blessèd in Paradise. The lens might slip from his grasp and fall into the mercury moat. How could I ever retrieve it? Would a raft of demon's skeleton bear my weight? What could I use to grapple for the lens? A web of hooks made of barbed wire? I might fish for half of eternity, like some pagan condemned to fill a pitcher with a hole in its bottom and carry it up a slippery slope! Would my wing-feathers or my psalmist's lungs tolerate immersion in mercury?

How could I possibly bring a naked wretch to our beautiful island? The constant sight of him would untune our hymns.

I could not make such an offer.

'By the Quint,' I bellowed, 'I command you to answer me!'

Fingers scrabbled at the barbs, shredding skin faster than it could possibly heal. The man was dementedly obsessed by this one activity.

At last the crucified man summoned breath. Softly he implored, 'No, no—' How it pained him to speak.

The demons had arrived. They were chuckling. I'd forgotten to jump-cut to them.

Nearby the trump sounded, long and grandly. I ascended, to stare faraway at the shining timeless face of the clock of eternity. Within me welled the urge to commence my return to the isle.

Later, none other than the Clock Angel confided anxieties to me.

This time it was the Harp Angel whom we were awaiting. Unlike the Trumpet Angel, she never did transport her instrument along with her. The Harp was much too huge. Twenty times larger than herself, it was a veritable precipice of strings. She would fly to and fro across these—like a white moth across a great grille—plucking with her outstretched hands to sound the chords and arpeggios, brushing with her wings to rouse the swishing, swirling glissandi.

'Impresario,' the Ark Angel said softly, 'I fear that something furtive is afoot in the Ark.'

Thinking of that fugitive from rack 'n' roast, I suggested, 'A hominid may have broken free. An ape-man could scuttle about for ages on his knuckles beneath all those benches on all those decks. The demons might be too lazy or clumsy to catch him—'

'It is not that. There are too many creaky noises below decks.'

'Rattling of fetters? Shifting of hairy bums on benches?'

'I'm familiar with such noises, Impresario. There are new noises.'

'Increased use of the whips?'

'That would cause more shrieking.'

The Ark Angel's rightful place was upon the poop, as a kind of honorary pilot and look-out. He was much too large to go below decks in person. The most he could accomplish by way of scrutiny would be to stick his glorious head down one of the uppermost hatchways. In the Ark, decks descended and descended again. Such is the design of Hell. Its topography can be crudely described as fractal; hence its capacity for prisoners. This fractal quality is inevitable, since Hell is an unwholesome dimension. It cannot possess anything remotely equivalent to the singularity of the Quint, or to the integrity of the angelic realms.

There was urgency in the Ark Angel's request to me:

'Impresario: during our next tour of duty will you kindly join me upon the deck of the Ark with your lens? I would value your insights.'

My insights . . .

Did the Ark Angel suppose that by means of my lens we would be able to spy below decks? That was not at all how the lens functioned. I must take it on trust—as an act of faith—that the lens did serve the purpose which I ascribed to it. Yet since I must believe that it did, the most I might achieve by thrusting the lens down a hatchway would be to reveal to the blessèd in Paradise a limited dingy view of the limited dingy sufferings of some of the primitive ancestors of Man, and of Woman.

I did not wish to disillusion the Ark Angel, since his suspicions reinforced my own about the conduct of demons.

'Of course I shall come! Do you suppose your counterpart has noticed anything peculiar?'

'I scarcely have time to ask her—'

It was out of the question that there could be any complicity between the female Ark Angel and the demons of the Ark. No, it was during the intervals that whatever was happening took place.

The Harp Angel was coming in to land. Our colloquy must cease. Soon we must start to sing.

I alighted upon the poop deck with my lens. At his post, the Ark Angel awaited me.

He gestured at the main deck. Surrounded by demons, a large device was bolted massively to the timbers. The contraption was built of parts of racks and of gridirons, and of clamps and screws used in torments. Mirrors used for burning also played a role. The apparatus cradled a hefty tube, angled vertically. Under this, a demon lay upon his back. He peered up through the tube, busily adjusting screws.

'That,' the Ark Angel said, 'is new.'

Here for the first time might be evidence of aberration!

Yet I suggested, 'Maybe that is a new instrument of punishment for hominids?' Maybe a hominid would be placed inside that tube, and screws and clamps would be tightened.

'Pre-humans are only ever punished with the whip,' the Ark Angel reminded me. 'Such is the clemency of the Quint.'

We descended a grand stairway to the main deck. We approached the infernal machine. Demons clustered protectively. They exhibited a kind of stubborn insolence.

The main deck vibrated subtly under our feet. It was as if some engine throbbed deep in the bowels of the Ark or as if some coordinated activity or rhythmic exertion were under way. How could this be?

A red demon appeared to be some kind of foreman. 'In the name of the Quint,' the Ark Angel called out to him, 'what is this contrivance?'

I quite expected to hear some gibberish. But no. The red demon seemed flushed with confidence and effrontery.

'Wise One,' he sneered, 'we call this a theodolite. From the ancient words theos, signifying God, and dolour, signifying misery.'

'What does it do?'

'Ah,' came the reply, 'it measures the distance and direction of the Quint!'

I stared up at the sooty sky—as if that tube might somehow be burning a channel through the welkin of Hell to reveal a glimpse of the realms. The sky remained as stygian as ever. This theodolite must operate in some different mode.

'What might that distance be?' I asked derisively, my lens held upright to capture the foreman demon's image.

The demon leered at me, and announced:

'It is one hundred and eighty parasangs. If you know what a parasang is.'

Of course I knew. One parasang is equal to one hundred and eighty billion times the polar diameter of the Earth, as revealed in the Jewish *Shiur Qomah*, otherwise known as The Measurement of the Height. So therefore the distance to the Quint, as calculated by demons, was one hundred and eighty times that figure . . .

'A little less by now,' said the demon.

What did he mean?

Such a smirk. The deck vibrated underfoot. All of Hell seemed to quiver as if a mild infernoquake were occurring.

'This Ark,' bragged the demon, 'is now under way towards the Quint.'

During the interludes demons had secretly been carpenting oars from the ever-available stocks of wood intended for racks and gibbets and bonfires. Demons had brought these oars on board the Ark unobserved. They had equipped all the hominids' benches with rowlocks fashioned from fetters. They had trained the hominids to be galley-slaves. This operation must have taken a century, or in view of the fractal nature of the Ark, maybe a millennium. Within this vessel, those slaves were now rowing in unison, pulling the great oars to and fro!

The brutish ur-speech which that other demon had used had been the primitive proto-language of hominids. Those hominids, stretching way back to Adam and Lucy, could not possibly have initiated this project. The concept would have eluded them—though since punishments of prehumans were mild, their bodies retained stamina. No, the demons were using those precursors of Man and of Woman as inadvertent insurgents. How devilishly sly this use of the ancestors! It evaded the whole etiquette of Hell.

Our demon informant taunted me: 'By now the distance to the Quint is only one hundred and seventy-nine point nine parasangs!'

The demon who lay under the theodolite corrected him. 'Point nine nine.'

'Progress is being made!' snarled our demon.

I hastened to the rail of the Ark. Averting my lens, I stared down the side of the vast vessel. The Ark was exactly where it had always been since prehistoric times. No banks of oar-blades jutted from newly revealed slots in the bulwarks.

Nevertheless, we were under way.

Although the oars were enclosed inside of the Ark, the rowing of the hominids was propelling us! The Ark was shifting in the direction revealed by the theodolite, which doubled as compass and rudder!

Rooted in Hell, this Ark would never cross the line between the infernal region and the lowest of the heavenly realms. No border guards with shining swords would rush to board her, because no demon was attempting to leave the territory of Hell.

The whole territory of Hell itself was on the move!

Impelled by the Ark, by the muscle-power of subhuman hominids Hell itself had begun to travel upward—so as to pass through the domains, carrying with it all the evolved descendants of those hominids who writhed in torment ordained by the Quint through His intermediaries.

Did I hear, for the first time, a chime sound from the clock of eternity? Or was the Trumpet Angel sounding a note which had altered in pitch?

Ours would be a long journey—of two hundred and fifty-five point nine six quintillion miles, I calculated. That many miles to reach the quasar of the Quint! En route we would travel through the choirs of Angels, Archangels, and Principalities. Then through the choirs of Powers, Virtues, and Dominations. Finally we would cleave through the choirs of Thrones, and Cherubim, and Seraphim . . .

Oh but already the distance was slightly less than that amount. And no doubt as realms became more rarified we would accelerate rapidly.

Agonies will continue. Torment is an aether into which the hominids dip their oars, and through which they haul. The demons seem contemptuous of us angels. Yet we still have our roles. Now that Hell has shifted its location, no other angels will know how to enter and replace us.

I am both appalled and elated.

Appalled, because during this journey the demons intend to convert a percentage of gridirons and racks into great harpoon guns. These, they will mount on the main deck of the Ark, to be fired at the Quint.

Yet I am also elated—because contrary to all expectation for anyone below the rank of Seraph, I and my humble angelic colleagues and counterparts will come directly into the presence of the Quint, when Hell harpoons that pure Being and then collides with Him.

Such hymns we will sing as we near His radiance—Hosannah! Hosannah in the Highest! And all will be revealed.

If only I could understand the language of the hominids, from before the time when the Quint became manifest.

Unfortunately I am too bulky to descend any of the myriad ladders of the Ark with my deaf lens so as to interrogate Adam and Lucy. Besides, their speech might brutalise my psalms.

One of Her Paths

*I*N APRIL 2120 THE TEST SHIP PROBE LEFT EARTH ORBIT, POWERED *by the annihilation of matter and antimatter. Since the discovery a decade previously of a tiny anti-iron asteroid and its successful harvesting employing elegant containment techniques, new superthrust engines had empowered ships to boost to the orbit of Saturn within eight weeks, a situation which the available supply of antimatter would permit for another thirty years.*

But Probe *was not testing antimatter propulsion.* Probe *was to test the Q-drive which theoretically should advance a ship to the nearer stars through probability-space, the underlying condition of reality, within several months instead of decades.* Probe*'s destination: Tau Ceti, twelve light years away.*

By June 2120 Probe *was sufficiently far out of the gravity well of the Sun for the Q-drive to switch on, and, as planned and hoped for, the test ship vanished—to reappear in the solar system a little over six months later, inward bound.*

When Probe *was recovered, the dozen rats on board were still alive, hale and hearty, and of the six little monkeys, five survived in decent shape. The sixth was a victim of its food supply jamming. All the animals had been caged separately, though spaciously, supplied with exercise equipment and toys. Time-lapse cameras recorded nothing untoward during the journey through Q-space to the outskirts of Tau Ceti and back.*

While Probe *had lingered on those outskirts, it had established that, of the planets of Tau Ceti already detected from the solar system, the second possessed a promising biosphere: an oxygen-nitrogen atmosphere, oceans, weather systems over the scattered land-masses. Even if only simple cells lived on that world, they had been beavering away for a long time to good purpose.*

In 2123 construction of Earth's first crewed starship, Pioneer, *began. Four years later the large ship was ready . . .*

Long before Doctor Mary Nolan enters *Pioneer* itself, she is thoroughly familiar with the spacious interior from virtual reality training. The Q-drive pod jutting ahead like a long battering ram tipped with a samovar, then the antimatter containers amidships which feed the engines at the stern, together form a long central spindle around which the great doughnut of living quarters rotates quickly enough to provide imitation gravity at half a gee. The doughnut houses a hundred cabins, one for each crew member.

Bed-couches are big enough that the dozen couples who are already married or partnered can bunk with one another, though who knows what may happen during the course of such an expedition? The potential for privacy is important. On top of her medical qualifications Mary's second string is psychiatry. Aside from the months necessary to progress beyond Saturn, and the six month trip through Q-space, plus at least a year spent in the Tau Ceti system, colonisation is possible (three shuttles are strapped to the spindle), so the ship is provisioned for a generous four years, not to mention the food which will be grown on board hydroponically.

After the obligatory pre-departure fortnight spent in quarantine—ten persons per isolation unit—the interior of *Pioneer* strikes Mary as particularly spacious. (After another year or so, will it still seem so roomy?) At half-a-gee her tread is buoyant—yet deliberate and cautious, as is the pace of other colleagues newly aboard.

'Hi, Gisela!' It's dark-haired athletic Dr Gisela Frick, who is qualified in microbiology and biochemistry as well as medicine and physiotherapy. Mary did not share quarantine with Gisela, nor with the expedition surgeon Dr Yukio Yamamoto, nor with dentist and geologist Howard Coover. A surprise infection must not catch the prime medical team all together. Back-up personnel were in separate quarantine units as a precaution—a whole duplicate crew had trained.

'How does it feel to you, Gisela?'

'To be really aboard at last? Great! Ah, do you mean the motion . . . ? It's okay.' Gisela swings her head skittishly. 'Oops.'

The floor consists of flat sections each a couple of metres long, gently tilting with respect to one another. Curved flooring would have presented engineering problem as regards the furnishing of cabins and the mounting of lab equipment and in many other respects, but the sense of down-orientation shifts subtly as a person walks. What's more, there are the effects of Coriolis force. Hurrying, or abrupt changes of direction, could disorient and nauseate.

'The anti-nausea pills seem to be effective,' says Gisela. Of course without the centripetal semblance of gravity the rate of bone-loss would be unacceptable. 'I wonder whether there could be long-term problems with tendonitis? Might we end up like birds gripping imaginary branches?'

This is not something which the virtual reality tours were able to simulate. At the moment the difference from true semi-gravity is trivial. Can it lead to physical impairment in the long run? Not that anyone will try *running* around the main corridors, but only jogging on stationary treadmills.

Greeting colleagues after a fortnight's separation from them, and nodding to fellow quarantinees, Mary and Gisela head for their clinic, not to inventory it, but more to check that it corresponds exactly with virtuality.

Which it does. As do the two gyms and the science labs and the restaurant (for the sociable) and the recreation hall and the hydroponics-cum-botany garden . . . Yes, the ship is surely big enough for a hundred people to share and work together harmoniously for ages. Failing harmony and happiness, there is always recourse to one's private cabin with computer access to a treasury of literature, music, games, and virtual experiences from skiing to scuba-diving, all the way through the alphabet of possibilities and back again.

People, people—under the command of Commander Sherwin Peterson. Mary knows those with whom she was in quarantine quite intimately by now, many others rather well to varying degrees, and none of the others are exactly strangers; besides which, she can screen all available data about them. No excuse, after the first few days of waiting in Earth orbit, for not matching names to faces instantly.

The official language of *Pioneer* is English, but she hears occasional German and French and Japanese too. The four co-operating powers behind the expedition are America, the Euro-Union, Australia, and Japan. If a foothold can be established on Tau Ceti 2, the Chinese plan their own independent ship. No one can argue with that.

Here's John Dolby, the climatologist, John James Pine, geologist and one of the three shuttle pilots, Eric Festa, nutrition, botany, and hydroponics, Denise Dubois, astrophysics, Carmen Santos, engineering, Chikahiro Suzuki, computer systems, navigator Nellie van Torn . . .

Two months later, *Pioneer* has passed the realm of Saturn (although its be-ringed monarch is far away) and no failures have occurred, neither of machine nor man, nor woman, aside from various minor ailments, swiftly diagnosed and cured. Mary and her two medical colleagues monitor everyone's health, making sure that sodium and iron levels do not rise. In liaison with Eric Festa they supply mineral supplements where required. An Australian pair of partners, Sandy Tate and Jeff Lee, oceanography and life science respectively, are pregnant—or rather, Sandy herself is. She must have conceived before entering quarantine, either accidentally or somewhat irresponsibly. Their child will be born towards the end of the six month transit through Q-space, a first for the human race. Mary will keep a careful eye on Sandy. By now almost everyone is on first name terms. Pilot Pine is Jay-Jay; Dr Suzuki is Chika. The ship is a family. How appropriate that a family should have a baby. A few other pairings are occurring, Jay-Jay and Denise, for instance. Mary is feeling a growing fondness and shoots of desire for Eric Festa, who reciprocates her feelings. Eric, from Dortmund, is a nourishing person to know. The two often sit in the botany section and talk amidst the orchids—for beauty—and tomatoes and carrots and soy beans for a nutritious diet.

On the evening, ship-time, preceding Q-day there's a feast in the restaurant from the ample store of varied vacuum-packed reduced sodium and iron gourmet meals.

'Compliments to the chef!' someone calls out.

'Chef's back on Earth!' dietician Eric declares, prompting laughter and applause. Spirits are high.

Afterwards, Com Sherwin reminds everyone of procedures. When the time comes to switch on the Q-drive, all personnel other than those on the bridge must be in their cabins tethered to their bed-couches. *Probe* encountered no visible problems when entering Q-space. Nevertheless, err on the safe side. Transient side effects which rats and monkeys could not report might affect human beings. Psychological or perceptual glitches, akin to the mild imbalance caused by Coriolis force.

Com Sherwin has an Air Force background, back in his younger days where backgrounds should be, his route from daring test pilot to astronaut training. He piloted the first hazardous antimatter-asteroid reconnaissance. Later, famously, he had risked his life taking *The Dart* on a fly-through the clouds of Jupiter, en route ramming a gas-whale and carrying it back into space with him spitted on *The Dart*, indeed draped around *The Dart*, its collapsed quick-frozen carcass almost enfolding his ship, a gift to science although a cause of some controversy. Of the numerous probes that had dropped into Jupiter only two had ever spotted gas-whales.

Interviewed on *Systemwide*: 'Aren't the gas whales very rare?'

Peterson: 'Not in that huge volume of atmosphere. Not necessarily.'

'Weren't you risking your ship and your life on a sudden impulse?'

Peterson: 'I had several seconds to think. I reckoned I had a good chance.'

'Apparently your pulse rate didn't even rise.'

Peterson had merely grinned, engagingly.

'So what's your favourite book then, *Moby Dick?*'

'No, actually it's Linda Bernstein's *Be Your Own Leader At Peace With Yourself*. I read a page a night.'

Peterson was solid. Capable of split-second decisiveness, yet possessing a balanced serenity, and also a folksy touch if need be.

Mary is lying abed dressed in mission multipocket-wear, green for medic, in the cabin which by now seems as familiar and homelike as her girlhood room in Michigan, listening to the calm tones of Com Sherwin from her comp speakers as Sherwin talks through the Q-sequence, only partly understood by her. She remembers doing her best to understand a lecture at Mission Control, given as part of the year-long training schedule.

'Fundamentally,' a dapper, bearded Physics Professor had said, 'the Q-drive functions as a quantum computer which is given the problem of translating a ship from Sunspace to Tau Ceti space. Your actual ship's computer for everyday use is a super-duper Turing-type machine. When you access your ship's computer, it may sound to you like an artificial intelligence—the software's designed to be user-friendly—but we're still twenty years away from genuine AI.

'Aw, sixty years ago people were saying the same, and AI hasn't happened yet, so I ain't making any prophecies.

'Anyway, if you set a Turing machine a really big task—for example, tell it to factorise a 500-digit number—it'll tackle solutions one after another, and that will take *ages*, even if the machine is really fast. In a quantum computer, on the other hand, all the possible answers are superposed. Superimposed simultaneously, as it were. Bingo, the wrong answers cancel each other out, and you get the right one. *Not* that this happens instantaneously—it still takes time. In the case of determining a route to Tau Ceti all routes are considered, including going via Sirius or Andromeda or even by way of a quasar at the far side of the universe. Quantum theory sums over all paths between two points, as we say, and that means all possible paths.'

'Does this mean,' someone asked, 'that we might end up in another galaxy?'

'No no, *Probe* proved that won't happen. The nonsense routes cancel out. Now a quantum device such as the drive is very specialised and needs to be kept as isolated as possible. It's entangled with the ship, but regular computing on board still has to be done by your Turing machine.'

Some wit had stuck up his hand. 'I'd say that the Q-drive is the real touring machine!'

'Very droll. I was referring to computer pioneer Alan Turing, who unbelievably was hounded to suicide because he was differently sexed.' Evidently a cause of anguish and anger to this lecturer.

Sum over paths, Mary muses.

Some Over-Paths. Ways of jumping from here to there. Or perhaps of burrowing.

Samovar Paths, in view of the shape of the Q-drive unit . . .

Summer Paths, the bright way to the stars. However, the appearance of Q-space as recorded by *Probe*'s cameras was an ocean of grey frogspawn . . .

'Initiating primary power uptake . . . We have four green balls . . . Sixty seconds to Q-insertion . . .'

'Thirty seconds . . .'

'Fifteen . . .'

The seconds pass. The cabin quivers and shimmers and is the same again. Same photos of family and friends and scenery sticky-tacked to the walls. Same dream-catcher mobile of feathers and knots. Same everything.

Except for the silence, silence apart from the softest hum from the speakers.

Has communication failed? In Q-space can no one hear you make announcements over electronic equipment?

'Uh, testing?' she queries the silence, and she hears her own voice clearly enough.

Mary untethers and sits up, goes to her door, slides it open. The corridor is empty; other cabin doors remain closed. Evidently she's the first to emerge. Gisela's cabin is only three doors down.

Mary knocks, then slides the door open.

Gisela's cabin is empty apart from her personal possessions.

Likewise Carmen's cabin, likewise Denise's . . .

All the cabins Mary tries are empty. It seems impossible that everyone can have untethered before her and gone to the bridge to look at the viewscreens, *impossible*. But what else could they have done? Mary must have suffered a lapse of consciousness, a gap in awareness.

To the bridge, then! Though without running or rushing.

The bridge is deserted, instruments and controls untended. Lights glow on boards, equipment purrs. On the viewscreens is the mottled grey of Q-space. No stars, just endless dimensionless frogspawn. Exactly as expected.

'*Where's everyone? Will somebody answer me!*'

No answer comes.

Has everyone hidden in the rec-room or in the hydroponics section to play a joke on her . . . ? She'll go to the rec-room and ninety-nine voices will chorus, *Boo*. Oh really, at this momentous moment, the first entry of the first crewed ship into Q-space? And why pick on *her*?

Nevertheless, she does go to the rec-room, which is deserted, then to the empty restaurant, then to the botany area where only plants are to be seen.

A type of hysterical blindness and deafness is afflicting her—people are here yet she is failing to hear and see them.

This has to be nonsense.

'Gisela! Eric! Yukio! Com Sherwin! Where are you?'

They are gone, all gone. She is alone on *Pioneer.*

The reason for this mass disappearance must be something to do with the nature of Q-space—an effect of the Q-drive as regards conscious intelligences such as human beings. So Mary reasons.

Why did *Probe's* cameras not show monkeys and rats as missing? Ah, but the test animals were all caged separately from one another. Conceivably they did not *experience* the presence of their fellows in the other cages. But they could not report their experience, or lack of it.

Can it be that each conscious observer on board the *Pioneer* has given rise to a copy of the ship, each of which contains only one person? Right now one hundred copies of the *Pioneer* are heading through Q-space towards Tau Ceti. When all of these arrive and switch off their drives, will all the copies reintegrate and become once more one single ship with a hundred people aboard it?

Collapse of the wave function . . . that's the phrase, isn't it? Something to do with multiple probabilities becoming one concrete reality, as Mary recalls. Surely that stuff happens at the subatomic level, not to an entire ship massing thousands of tonnes.

Still, it's a lifeline to cling to: in six months time everyone will come together.

During so many months the hundred ships can hardly remain identical. Mary will consume certain supplies; absent colleagues will account for different supplies. She remembers the ripple that occurred as she entered Q-space. On emergence, will the merging ships adjust so that there are no discrepancies?

What if two people happen to be in exactly the same place? Is one of them displaced? Does that happen gently or violently?

The more she thinks about it, the more iffy the idea of reintegration becomes.

The deserted ship is subtly menacing. Random noises might be phantom footfalls. A reflection or trick of light and shadow could be a glimpse of someone moving out of sight. Her vanished colleagues may, in their own copies of the ship, be experiencing minor psychotic episodes or hallucinations.

Suppose someone monkeys with the controls. Suppose that a copy-ship re-enters normal space prematurely, or is disabled. Reintegration might never be able to occur. *Pioneer* might fly onward forever.

She mustn't let this notion obsess her. She has hundreds of years' worth of food and drink if consumed by one person alone. She shan't starve!

If each ship is similarly stocked this seems a bit like the miracle of the loaves and fishes. How can reality multiply in such a way? Maybe Mary's is the only ship. Maybe only one conscious observer could remain in existence. By sheer chance this happened to be her.

No, no, remember all the rats. And all but one of the monkeys.

'Talking to yourself, are you, Mary?'

'Nothing wrong with that. People do talk to themselves. That's how we monitor what's going on. Helps us plan what to do next. Evolution didn't give us fast random-access memories—so we tell ourselves a story, the story of our self. That's how we remember things. It reinforces short-term memory.'

'Adults generally talk to themselves silently, not aloud.'

'Well, there's no one around to take offense. There's just me.'

'Just you, eh? After a while, if you talk aloud to yourself, it's as if there are two of you—the talker, and the person you talk to. *You* can become the audience, hearing words which simply seem to emerge. In that case who is doing the talking? Listen: when we all come together again maybe we might re-enter any of a hundred different universes.'

'Surely a star very like Tau Ceti has to be in the same location, otherwise how could we emerge from Q-space?'

'Ah, but maybe we would pick up no ten-year-old radio signals from the solar system, supposing we had a powerful enough receiver. In that other universe the human race may never have evolved. *Pioneer* may be the only abode of life. Tau Ceti 2 may not be habitable.'

'Thanks a bundle.'

'Look, why don't you talk to the *computer* more?'

'Because the computer only simulates having a mind of its own. That's why it has no name. A woman's voice, yes, and a woman's avatar-face if we want one, but no name so we won't be fooled. A psychiatrist seeking aid and counsel from a programme is absurd. However sophisticated the programme is, it cannot *know*. It merely listens and responds as appropriately as possible. After a while, that's maddening. Ask it how to repair a solar power plant or remind you how to fix a ruptured spleen, fine and good. It goes through its repertoire. If we did have true artificial intelligence, I dunno, maybe there would be some magic quantum link between the AIs in all the ships and we could all communicate. But we don't, and there isn't.'

Of course she already asked Computer what is happening. *Pioneer* is transiting through Q-space, Mary. Do you want a full status report? No, just where is everybody else? Where is the Commander? I don't know, Mary. She may as well ask herself. She doesn't wish to confuse Computer. Just take us to where we're going and carry on with the housekeeping.

Playing her favourite arias by Puccini throughout the ship turns out to be a bad idea. The music seems to mask rustlings and whispers.

When Mary was sixteen she thought she saw an angel. Most likely she was dazzled by sunlight while hiking through woodland. A tiny lake was a silver mirror, and bushes were covered and linked by innumerable bedewed spiders' webs. She saw a being with wings, sparkling bright. Of a sudden bird-song seemed to combine in a single rhapsody of musical counterpoint the meaning of which only just eluded her. She felt called. A few centuries earlier she might have become a nun. In the event she specialised in psychiatry after earning her medical qualifications.

Her parents were both practising Catholics, who confessed and went to mass regularly. They always denied themselves some treat during Lent—generally, in her Dad's case, drinking with the fellows on a Saturday night. None of the fellows were Catholics, nor was the town a Catholic one—her Mom and Dad needed to drive twenty miles to attend mass—so Dad had adopted a jokey, ironic front for his faith. 'Next year I might give up fast food for Lent.' 'Oh we don't need to worry about what to believe—we're *told* what to think.' He did good works, quietly, simple kindnesses to neighbours and colleagues. Mary had already begun lapsing into agnosticism by the age of fourteen, and she encountered no pressure or reproach from her parents, but where it came to good works, Dad was a beacon to her.

Without the medical attention provided by herself or Gisela or Yukio or

Howard, what if others fall ill during the next six months? No longer quite six months—by now a week of that stretch has passed. Just one damn week!

Personally she's rather more bothered right now about the hydroponics. Fluids and nutrition are automated, but the care of carrots and tomatoes and bean sprouts is not her field at all.

What about Sandy's pregnancy? Sandy is on her own, expecting a child, and knowing now that she will have to give birth to it unassisted. What if Sandy develops toxaemia? How will she control that? What if she suffers a difficult delivery? What if she *cannot* deliver until reintegration?

How can Sandy be *alone* if a foetus is growing inside her, four months old by now? Did the separation-event treat her and her child as one unit—or did the event rip the foetus untimely from its mother's womb, aborting it into yet another copy of the ship, perishing on Sandy's bed-couch? This is too awful to contemplate.

Something else is aboard with Mary. Something quite unlike an angel, and besides she doesn't believe in those.

'*What are you?*' she cries. '*Where are you?*'

Armed with a kitchen knife, she ranges around the great doughnut, searching and finding nothing. It's as though she, the reluctant would-be observer of the Enigma, is always where there's a low probability of finding whatever it is. Where it is, she is not. She can sense a sort of semi-absent presence, never enough for actuality.

Isn't there something called an exclusion principle?

'Maybe you should put yourself on tranquillisers.'

'No, you must stay alert!'

Maybe she arouses the curiosity of whatever it is yet it wants to avoid harming her. Alternatively, it finds her daunting and, although in a sense summoned by her, it keeps out of her way, sniffing and tasting where she has been.

'All right, you've been alone for a fortnight now. Twenty-two more weeks to go. People have spent far longer periods on their own without all the amenities *you* enjoy!'

Movies, if desired. The hustle and bustle of actors. Any number of computer games. Virtual reality sightseeing, VR adventures. Whatever, whatever.

She tried to watch *The Sound of Music* as a safe choice in the rec-room, but she couldn't concentrate. She dares not enter a virtual reality—the Enigma might creep up on her while she is immersed.

'All those people who spent time alone: they still knew that other people existed in the same world as them. I know the contrary!'

'Mary, Mary, how contrary, how does your garden grow?'

'So many bean sprouts already! Do I harvest them? I hate bean sprouts. Give me the deluxe meals any day.' More than enough of those to make every day a special occasion. 'Why shouldn't I hog on those?'

'Why not cook something special for yourself?' The frozen food store contains a wealth of raw ingredients in case the vacuum-packed foods somehow fail, or pall.

'Since when was I a chef? It's stupid cooking for one.'

'Cook for me too.'

'This sensation of something unseen sharing the ship with me—I can't tolerate it for months on end!'

'Even if the sensation may be preferable to total isolation?'

'*Show yourself to me!* In a mirror, if you can't manage anything more substantial.'

And there the Enigma is, in her cabin's mirror.

But it is herself that she sees.

Maybe the Enigma is floating directly behind her back, tucked out of sight. Abruptly she shifts aside. Oops, a little surge of nausea. Oh the Enigma is too quick for her by far.

She cannot catch it full-frontally. She must seek it by indirect means. Mary must practise a sort of Zen art of not-looking, not-seeing.

As a psychiatrist Mary understands the principles of meditation and she has even practised a bit in the past. The silent, empty ship is an ideal focus of vacancy. Session by session—interspersed by more mundane tasks—she blanks her personality. After each session she surfaces to rediscover herself, the only consciousness hereabouts, a mind amidst a void.

Is there a risk that she may remain in tune with the void until her motionless body starves to death? Grumbling guts recall her to activity—so far, at least.

After many days of annulling herself . . .

A perception emerges from the medium through which the *Pioneer* travels.

<<You believe that your identity is confined here in this ship.>>

Well yes, she does.

<<Fundamental being is forever transforming itself. Think of bubbles in boiling water. Think of flames in a fire. Think of weather cells in an atmosphere.

<<Being is the process, not the particulars. Its facets constantly manifest themselves only to disintegrate and then reintegrate.>>

Such is the perception that scrutinises her.

<<You are a bubble of mind, a tongue of living flame, which might last for a hundred orbits of your world around your sun, a mere moment of cosmic time. But you are also one facet of a hundred-fold being, the crew of this ship. This hundred-fold being has separated itself from a many-billion-fold being—which you call Humanity.>>

A many-billion-fold being?

<<Humanity from the dawn of consciousness until final demise exists as a four-dimensional blaze of members arising and dying and replacing themselves, all linked, ever loosening, ever relinking, within which flickers your own particular flame.>>

Why is she being told this? Does it help, or is some godlike entity inspecting her coolly? Alternatively, is she hallucinating?

<<Realize! From birth to death an intelligent planetary species is a single mental entity, its mentality made of all the minds that compose it. Individual units of Humanity process tiny parts of its totality. Each individual is part of an aeon-spanning exchange of information—unaware of this except in rare moments of insight. Or outsight. Beatific moments, poetic moments, shamanistic, hallucinatory. You often misinterpret such partial, fleeting glimpses as encounters with Gods or spirits or ghosts or fairies or, more recently, encounters with flying saucer folk.>>

'Tell me more.'

<<During the millions of years of its existence the species-entity may remain alone. Such beings are few and far between in space and time during any mega-era. Even so, their number is considerable overall, for the present universe was spawned from a parent universe, and in turn gives rise to daughter universes, a great tree of universes.>>

This is big stuff. Is she capable of imagining all this on her own? Quite possibly. Why should a godlike entity bother to communicate with her?

Ah, but an answer comes.

<<Some planetary species send parts of themselves through space on a journey lasting generations to the worlds of other stars, creating an offspring of themselves. Some of these offspring encounter an alien species and the two beings either destroy or corrupt one another or else become a hybrid. A very few planetary species send the exiled part of themselves not through ordinary space but through the underlying space of probabilities—and here they encounter its entities, as you do now.

<<Your ship is not yet far from its home. You are still entangled. The entity, Humanity, can now be recognized and addressed. And if addressed *now*, Humanity as a whole is also addressed in the past and in the future.

<<*Was, is, and will be.*>>

Mary has had a vision. What is she to make of it?

Is she and is everyone else who ever lived, or who will live, only so many iotas in a single entity spanning millions of years? By travelling through Q-space, has she encountered a higher entity—and caused Humanity to be contacted in the past and the present and the future? On this, um, higher level of metaconsciousness, to which individual persons only ever have fleeting and partial access at best?

If *Pioneer* had never been built, nor some similar Q-space ship in the future, humanity would probably have remained isolated and uncontacted. Yet because contact occurs now, contact also applies retroactively. Total-Humanity may understand this paradox, but it fazes Mary. No individual human being has ever or will ever be aware of more than a jot of the communication between Pan-Humanity and the Probability Entities. This will elude mere people, much as the betting on a tortoise race eludes the tortoises. Or perhaps that should be: a race between fireflies.

Mary feels she is like a single brain-cell present during a few moments of a symphony.

If the hundred copies of the *Pioneer* do reintegrate successfully in another five months' time, and if she announces her revelation, will psychiatrist Mary be for the funny farm?

The air in her cabin smells musty. Surfaces look dusty.

Quite nimbly, in the circumstances, she rises from her lotus position. With a fingertip she traces a line across her com-console.

God almighty, the *date display* . . .

The date, the date.

Q + 178.

Q + 178.

A hundred and seventy eight days, very nearly six months, have passed since the *Pioneer* entered Q-space and she found herself isolated. Mary has been advanced through time itself. She has been extracted and reinserted later, abridging her lonely journey from months to days.

'Oh thank you!' she cries into the silence. 'Thank you so very much!'

Yet now there's no sense of Another on the ship with her.

Full of wonder and gratitude, she sets off to check on hydroponics. What a riot of life and death she finds there—rot and fecundity, the air so heady and reeking. Is it possible that Gisela and Eric and all of her colleagues may also have been advanced through time?

Including Sandy, no longer condemned to give birth all alone?

Mary muses, in the dispensary. If the hundred *Pilgrims* do reintegrate successfully, and if her ninety-nine colleagues have *not* been blessed as she has been, what may the medical team need to provide quickly in the way of sedatives or stimulants or vitamin supplements?

Of a sudden the warning siren blares automatically, *whoop-whoop-whoop*, such a shocking hullabaloo that her heart races.

Thank god for it, though, thank god. She has fifteen minutes to return to her cabin and tether herself. Should she bother to do so, or simply stay here? If Gisela or Yukio are in this dispensary she might bump into them, disastrously. Her cabin is safer.

The cabin writhes, as before. Every surface shimmers. It's as if her eyes are watering. Then all is clear and sharp again, her photos, her mobile, her terminal.

Com Sherwin's voice comes briskly. 'All hear me. Re-emergence from Q-space achieved. *Pioneer* has acquired Tau Ceti space.'

Acquired, acquired! *Pioneer* has acquired a whole new solar system. And rejoice, Mary has regained her fellow human beings!

'Tau Ceti 2 is visible at 9.8 A.U.'

Have her fellows arrived here with a skip and a jump, or the slow way?

'Fellow pioneers, we were all separated—for which there may be various explanations.'

Yes? Yes?

'I hope we are all together again. I see that the main bridge team is with me, at least. All non-flight personnel proceed to the restaurant right away for roll-call. Dr Suzuki is to be in charge of roll-call. Back-up is Major Pine. Second back-up is Dr Santos. Preliminary debrief to follow later. Do not close your cabin doors after you leave. Medical team, check all cabins.'

Good thinking. If Chika is not available, Jay-Jay will tally numbers. And if Jay-Jay is not present, Carmen will co-ordinate. Some people may not be able to leave their cabins. How long has Com Sherwin had to think about contingencies?

'Proceed. Bridge out.' He has not said whether he himself spent months in Q-space—or only a single month followed by a couple of days.

People emerging into the corridor. Heartfelt greetings. Some tears of relief.

'*Denise,*' Mary calls out, '*how long were you in Q-space?*'

They embrace. 'Oh Mary, it felt like forever! Six long months.'

'Were you alone all that time?'

'Entirely.'

'You, Carmen, how long?'

'Six shitting months. I must get to the restaurant, Mary.'

'Of course.'

Babble, babble as people proceed as instructed. Eric's cabin is further away around the doughnut out of sight. Be methodical: check inside each cabin even if a door is wide open. There's Gisela in the distance, opening a door and popping inside. Despite instructions a few people may have shut their doors unthinkingly behind them. Here's a door that is closed, belonging to: **Sandy Tate**. Sandy, Sandy! Mary knocks, calls her name.

Freckled, ginger-haired Sandy is sitting on her bed-couch, a swaddled baby held in her arms. She hugs it to herself protectively. Protectively?—no, it looks more as if Sandy is *restraining* her baby—and it barely a week or two old.

'Mary, thank god, I'm going crazy—'

'You did give birth! All on your own—that must have been utterly gruelling and scary. But you did okay?'

'I managed—I read up all I could beforehand.'

'Well done, Sandy! I'll examine you and your baby as soon as—'

'Mary, this baby is trying to talk to me!'

'To talk?'

'I don't understand him but he's trying to.'

Is Sandy suffering, understandably, from delusions?

'He can't talk, Sandy. A baby's brain isn't fully grown. Learning to speak simply can't clock in so soon, and would be totally pointless because it's physically impossible for a baby to vocalise. You see, its larynx is in the wrong position. For the first nine months the larynx is high up, locked into the nose, so that a baby can drink and breathe at the same time without choking.'

'I'm telling you he's *trying!* I didn't say he can *manage* it.'

The months of loneliness, the fear and worry, the need for another person to communicate with . . .

'Sandy, you're misinterpreting the noises he makes.'

'I am *not* misinterpreting.'

'Let me see him, Sandy.'

As Mary sits on the bed-couch beside her, Sandy flinches. Then she reveals her child, a bundle of feeble struggle which, at presumably blurred sight of a person new to its world, produces sounds which are indeed unlike any regular infantile crying or red-faced bawling. It's as if a strangled voice, using an unknown language, is heard through distorting filters and mufflers.

'Sandy, I should tell you something—' How can Mary take time out just now to tell about her own revelation, and her translation through time? 'He does sound different, Sandy, I agree! At a quick glance there doesn't seem to be anything physically wrong with either of you . . . Do you think you can get to the restaurant?'

'I'm his restaurant,' she says. 'If he had teeth, he'd bite.'

The baby certainly does seem assertive.

'What have you called him?' Mary asks gently.

'He calls me—but I don't know what he wants to say.'

'You must have thought of a name beforehand. Boy or girl, whichever.'

'James.'

'Hi, James.'

Those strange noises, as if in reply.

'How about bringing him to the restaurant? I think that's important. Important, yes. And you need to mingle again.'

'Where's Jeff? Why isn't he here? That's why I waited. Is he dead?'

'You heard Com Sherwin's instructions. Jeff will be waiting for you at the restaurant.'

'Why didn't he come here so we could both go together?'

'Maybe he expected to find you at the restaurant. Come on, Sandy, chin up.'

'I can't take my baby there—he's a monster.'

Post-natal depression? Not necessarily.

'If James seems a bit odd, Sandy, I might—just might—know the reason, but I need to explain to all the others too. You've coped splendidly so far. Come on, it's okay.'

All is not quite okay. An American physicist, Greg Fox, is dead. Appendicitis, says Gisela. Must have been agonising. Did Greg manage to lay his hands on morphine, maybe an overdose? Post-mortem will tell. He has been dead a couple of months. Unpleasant corpse to find. And one of the Japanese is deeply disturbed, mumbling in his native language, English now eluding him. How shall Mary cope with him? With appropriate drugs and with Yukio's help as translator, she hopes.

The assembled crowd, not least Jeff, are delighted to see a baby born on board. People mob Sandy, causing her to hide James from curious eyes. Jeff definitely ought to have gone to her cabin first. Now Sandy seems ambivalent towards him. She feels betrayed by him—which he cannot understand. Maybe she feels betrayed by what his seed wrought in her.

'Listen up,' Com Sherwin calls out to the assembly. 'We came through.' And he has maintained his grizzled crewcut between whiles. 'We sustained one fatality. Six months' surprise solitary was tough on us all, right?'

'Wrong,' Mary interrupts. 'Not on me.'

Sherwin grins; his blue eyes twinkle. He's effervescent. 'Dr Nolan, we cannot all be psychiatrists.'

'That is not what I mean . . .'

When she has finished speaking, her colleagues stare at her in a silence which continues for quite a while.

'And there's one other thing,' Mary adds, moving closer to Sandy and child. 'Sandy believes that her baby is trying to speak already, and I think she may be right . . .'

Two bombshells, the second less appreciated than the first, at least to begin with. Has Mary flipped? is what people are visibly thinking. Eric eyes her with particular concern.

'Do you have any hard proof of this?' Com Sherwin asks. 'Not that I'm doubting what you *experienced*. Still, it's a large claim.'

'I can't prove it, although it's true. Little James here may throw some light on this, as time goes by, when his larynx shifts. And maybe not.'

'Mary, why didn't you tell me this right away?'

'Yeah, why not?' Jeff joins in on Sandy's complaint, to exonerate himself for not thinking to be with her as soon as possible.

'If we could harness this effect—' says someone else. Mary can't see who.

'I don't know that it's something we can harness,' she tells whoever. 'It was granted to me.' 'Granted' sounds a bit messianic.

'And to no one else,' she hears. 'Why not?'

'Maybe it's because of the way I meditated. I emptied myself. Then it was able to communicate.'

'And to jump you through time.' Resentfully: 'Why not us? Didn't you ask the same on our behalf?'

'I didn't *ask* it to jump *me*. I never imagined such a thing was possible.'

What Mary has said is at once overwhelming and embarrassing. She's distanced from everyone else, as sole recipient of a revelation and a boon.

Although what strange gift might Sandy have received, in the shape of James?

'I think for the time being we must take what Dr Nolan says at face value,' Sherwin declares judiciously. Quite! Suspicion of lunacy mustn't deprive them of a key medical person. 'No doubt what Dr Nolan has told us will fit into context sooner or later. We'll talk about this at greater length once everything's less confused. Meanwhile, we should inventory the ship, calculate what we each used and work out how much has come together again—try to get a practical handle on what happened. Something measurable.'

Of those present, it transpires that only Sherwin himself and Chika and John the climatologist thought to log every last item they used by way of food and drink.

'Is that information still in the ship's memory?' asks Chika.

Indeed, what data *is*, from a hundred separate journeys, fifty years' worth of overlapping auto-logs plus whatever data individuals may have entered?

Pioneer continues inward towards the position which the second planet of Tau Ceti will occupy in another many weeks hence.

The ship's log contains back-up after back-up of status data which seem to vary in only minor respects, occupying megabytes of memory. Computer has no explanation for this massive redundancy. It runs diagnostic checks, and megabytes are dumped into cache. Could Computer be in any way compromised by an encounter with Dr Nolan's supposed probability-entity? Apparently not.

Eric works overtime putting the hydroponics area to rights. Naturally his own Q-space version was maintained in apple pie order. Sad to see it become so chaotic.

'I should have done more,' Mary says ruefully.

'Then this would have been two per cent tended. It wouldn't have made a great deal of difference.'

'And I didn't know what to do.'

'Do you think that announcing your experience straight away was the best course?'

'If I waited longer . . .'

'. . . the more difficult it would become?'

'By the way, you guys, I happen to have been contacted by a Higher Entity—but I didn't feel like mentioning this until now. Also by the way, I travelled through time.'

'You're probably right. Though now some people are a bit wary of you.'

'Does that include you, Eric?'

'Of course not. This must be such a strain for you.'

'And you are loyal to your friends. Do you truly believe me?'

'That's an unfair question, Mary. If I had experienced what you experienced—what you *undoubtedly* experienced . . .'

'There's no doubt in my mind, but that's only *my* mind.'

'Is your experience repeatable—I mean, by someone else?'

'We aren't in Q-space any longer.'

'On the way back if we all meditate the way you did maybe we can all take a short cut. Or many of us can. That would be a blessing.'

'Shall I start up classes in meditation?'

'Ah . . . but we might begin colonising the second planet, depending on what we find.'

If that happens, eventually only the flight crew will return *Pioneer* to Earth to bring more material and colonists and frozen embryos and such. Mary's experience may be of no use to the majority of those presently on board. It can be set aside for a long time yet, unconfronted.

Offers flood in to time-share James, but Sandy will have none of them.

Chika Suzuki gives a lecture on his idea of what may have happened, and how it might be avoided in future if only a starship's computer itself could be a quantum computer.

Sum over Paths. Some Overpaths.

'I'd say we experienced travelling a hundred possible paths between the solar system and Tau Ceti. A myriad other paths got explored at the same time, but since those were absurd we could not experience them. If only we could experience the sum over paths collectively together, not separately the way it turned out! Yet that might have been an experience the individual human mind couldn't cope with. All of us experiencing each other's experience . . .'

Not everyone wishes to marginalise Mary's revelation as something at once too huge and too fugitive to contemplate. Dr Yukio is fascinated. As an insight into a situation where the specialist in afflictions of mind has herself become afflicted? Chika Suzuki is also enthralled. What Mary says about the multi-million-year mind of all Humanity whenever processing information through its myriad units dead and living and yet unborn—this stirs his programmer's soul, whether he gives her credence or not. Likewise, astrophysicist Denise. And a biologist, Maxim Litvinov. And Sophie Garland, another cybernetics person who is an ordained pastor of the Ecumenical Church. Last but not least—perhaps last yet least as regards stability—there is Hiroaki Horiuchi, the chemist who flipped during solitude but who is now responding quite well to mental stabilisers and is coherent in English once again.

Eric, alas, remains ambivalent. In a sense he's a glorified gardener who values neatness and order, nature methodised, not rampant across the aeons and imbued with some kind of transcendent mentality, at least as regards the human species. Furthermore, Eric is a no-frills evolutionist. For him life has no goal other than life itself in its many forms during all of its eras. Not that Mary claims that Humanity writ large has any particular goal, yet now that the Higher Entity has intervened—retrospectively as well as in the now and in the henceforth!—it certainly seems as if some kind of destiny is implied, or at least an upgrade to a higher level of existence or state of awareness.

Mary's supporters hold study sessions with her, and Hiro's presence seems therapeutic for him. Exploring Mary's experience helps Hiro come to terms with his own phantoms and demons—though he might be imprinting on Mary emotionally, as his sensei of sanity, or the opposite.

Three of Mary's co-explorers are Japanese. Yukio remarks that his own people feel a strong sense of themselves as an unique collective entity, so they can empathise with the concept of Overlife, Pan-being, or whatever.

The interest of these six does indeed support Mary, otherwise she might be as lonely now as she was during those initial weeks of isolation in Q-space—she might be the spectre at the feast of renewed companionship. Even so, sometimes she feels like screaming out to the entity that shifted her through time, *Come back! Please show yourself to more than merely me!*

Meanwhile, Sandy puts a brave face on being mother to a baby who is evidently abnormal, although bursting with health. It's as though a perfectly normal baby has been overwritten by a programme which cannot yet run in him—not until he matures a bit more—yet which nevertheless keeps trying to express itself, and testing its environment . . . maybe modifying its environment as it does so, tweaking developmental pathways? Jeff does his best to help nurture their son, frequently taking James off Sandy's hands—to the botany area and to the rec-room. Just as he ought to. Fair dooze, sport. No other couples have yet conceived. Potential parents are awaiting what James may become.

Weeks later, *Pioneer* enters orbit around Tau Ceti 2, eighty kilometres above what is basically a world-ocean girding half a dozen scattered and mottled distorted Australias, all but one of them situated in the temperate zones. The odd one out straddles the north pole and wears an ice cap. River systems are visible, and mountains, one of which is smoking vigorously, an eruption in progress. Elsewhere, a typhoon is blowing. The planet seems lively; not overly so, it's to be hoped. The signatures of vegetation are down below, so at least there is botany. Where there is botany, zoology too? Very likely marine biology at least, but no moon pulls any tides ashore.

After three weeks of intensive global survey work Jay-Jay will pilot Shuttle One, *Beauty*, down to the land mass already dubbed Pizza, the result of a random computer selection from a list of names suggested by all personnel and okayed by Com Sherwin. In time, hopefully, people will be able to feed upon Pizza if its soil proves amenable. Accompanying pilot-geologist Jay-Jay will be Maxim Litvinov, Jeff Lee, and John Dolby, representing life sciences and climate.

To gaze upon an alien world, from the bridge or on screen, is riveting. Those warped Australias are like presents under the Christmas tree. What exactly is in them? What is the topping on Pizza?

The answer, three weeks later, proves to be weed—thongs, tangles, ribbons, bladders, variously jade-green and rusty-red, bright orange and emerald in the light of Tau Ceti. Suited and helmeted, Maxim describes the scene which is on screen everywhere throughout *Pioneer*. (The three passengers on *Beauty* had tossed the only coins within light years for the honour of being first-foot on the new world. Pilot excluded. Mustn't risk him.) *Beauty* rests upright on an apron of flat rock amidst assorted vegetation, a vista that looks somewhat like an offshore domain which has been emptied of its water. The actual shore is a couple of kilometres away. Shouldn't be hard to hike there. Some of the weed piles a metre deep but whole stretches are as flat as a pancake.

Cautiously Maxim pokes around with a probe. Amidst a larger mass of weed he soon comes across a number of little hoppers and scuttlers—'they're a bit like fleas and tiny crabs—' and even captures some specimens, before he cuts samples of weed, then bags soil which is variously gritty and sludgy, inhabited by some wriggly tendrils and purple mites.

John descends from *Beauty* to join Maxim, carrying an atmosphere analyser to confirm orbital readings. This done, Jeff comes bearing a white mouse in a transparent light-weight habitat. Mice are biologically very similar to men. Will the mouse, Litmus, turn virulently red or blue because of hostile micro-organisms? Even if nothing obvious happens, in another few days once back on *Pioneer* Litmus will be sacrificed and dissected.

After a day of intensive investigation of the vicinity, next day Maxim and Jeff set off for the seaside under grey clouds. Rain will move in later, though nothing torrential. What will they find? Leviathans cruising offshore like mobile islands? Torpedoes with flippers and goggly eyes nursing pups on the beach?

No. No.

'Weed and sand. Pebbles and boulders.' As is seen on screen while Maxim pans his camera.

Some great thongs of weed emerge from the breeze-rippled sea, right across the shore and beyond, like vast creepers which the ocean has rooted upon the land. No wildlife bigger than hoppers and scuttlers and sliders, and nothing in the empty and now melancholy sky.

Presently Jeff fires nets into the sea, one to trawl, the other weighted to dredge. What comes back is floaters and wrigglers and squirmers, none bigger than a little finger.

Back on *Beauty* in its resealed habitat Litmus the mouse is still perky and white.

The day after, Shuttle Two, *Charm*, lands half a world away in a broad river-valley on the huge island or mini-continent christened Kansas, somewhat further inland than *Beauty* landed. Weed webs its way from the river over the terrain, yielding to flexible dwarf ribbon-trees and inflated lung-plants. More little hoppers and scuttlers and variations, nothing big.

All in all this is wonderful, if a bit bleak. Here on Tee-Cee, as the planet is coming to be called, is an ecology, primitive but functional. Years ago it was decided that biological contamination of the Tee-Cee environment is of much less consequence than the chance of inhabiting a whole new world, if at all possible. After all, the expedition had cost its partners upwards of 50 billion dollars. Agronomy experiments get under way, a range of seedlings transplanted directly into the local soil and also into heat-sterilised grit and sludge under protection.

All of this rather puts Mary's revelation and baby James to the back of people's minds, except for the members of the support group consisting of

Yukio, Chika, Denise, Hiroaki, and Sophie. Plus an apprehensive Sandy with James in a head-supportive carry-sling. Jeff being down on the surface has robbed her of his help, an unavoidable repeat of his earlier failure to be present. And there's Eric too, although in his case simply out of loyalty. But no Maxim. He's on the surface of Tee-Cee. The eight—or nine, if James is counted—meet in the hydroponics section, like conspirators or members of a cult. Maybe their infant messiah is in their midst, albeit inarticulate as yet.

'We are each other,' says Hiroaki. 'That is the meaning. The unity of all human life.'

Sophie asks him gently, 'Were Adolf Hitler and a Rabbi in an extermination camp *united?* What about people waging ruthless war on each other throughout history?'

'If our immune system goes wrong, it can attack our own bodies. But I am talking about lives going way back and stretching far ahead. I am my ancestor and my distant descendant! If we could know the lives of the future! Pan-Humanity already includes those future lives.'

'Future lives haven't yet been lived!' protests Denise. 'If we could dip into them now, why, everything is fixed in advance unalterably. It would only be because of our blindness to the future that we bother to do anything at all in the present. No, wait: we couldn't even choose to do, or not to do, something if all is foreordained. Pan-Humanity can't be calculating or thinking or dreaming or doing whatever it does across the millennia unless genuine changes happen within it! Otherwise it would be just one big super-complicated thought, a four-dimensional abacus forever in the same state.'

'What *is* its purpose?' asks Mary. 'What does it do, what does it dream?'

'Maybe it merely exists,' says Eric. 'Maybe that's all it does.'

'Surely it must come to conclusions. The computing power it has! Using all our billions of brains!'

'Conclusions? Final extinction is conclusion enough. The tree grow, the tree dies.'

'Maybe,' suggests Chika, 'it avoids extinction by being closed in upon itself. Its end and its beginning join together. So it always exists, even though time moves on beyond the epoch of its physical existence.'

'Contacting the probability-being must have caused a change—'

'As soon as this happened, it had already happened long ago too—'

'We don't have the minds to understand this—'

'Only the overmind possesses the overview—'

'It must understand existence. Not just experience existence, but *understand* as well—as part of its process of existing—'

'We are all part of God,' Sophie declares. 'Any highly evolved species is a God in total. Yet we cannot follow God's thoughts. All of us are just little bits of those thoughts.'

'The probability-being was a bit more forthcoming!'

'Because you weren't a part of it, Mary. Because you were its modem to our God, our species. It had to exchange signals through you.'

'And then it went away, because chatting to me was probably as interesting as talking to an ant.'

'At least it lifted you from one end of the branch to the other.'

'So effortlessly. If only our God would do the same for us.'

'Maybe,' Sophie suggests, 'you should pray real strongly, Mary. Sort of meditation with a punch to it.'

'What should I pray *for?*'

'For James,' says Sandy. 'Let him be—'

'—normal?' asks Sophie. 'Or gifted with tongues, real soon? So that the babe begins to speak instead of just gurbling at you?'

'I think . . . normal.'

'Normal would be a waste, don't you think?'

Sandy sobs. 'How long's Jeff going to be down there?'

'It's why we're here.'

'Let me take James off your hands for a few hours,' offers Sophie, not for the first time.

'No . . .' Only Jeff is permitted to share her baby, because it is his duty to.

Whatever happens, Sandy seems very unlikely to harm her baby. If she does so in any way, then that is Mary's responsibility. Mary feels she cannot intervene too intrusively, having, as it were, a vested interest.

Some of the seedlings fail, but most survive, even quite a few of those which are fully exposed to the Pizza environment. Some even thrive. Monitor cameras record efforts by hoppers to snack, and one definite quick fatality, although most nibblers quickly hop away into weed. In a bottle of formaldehyde the dead hopper is an amulet of hope. Perhaps. Supposing that hope equates with the superiority, or at least resilience, of organisms from Earth.

Litmus remains perky. *Beauty* returns to *Pioneer*. Time for intensive lab work, and confirmation of results by Computer.

Many tests have been performed, many protocols faithfully obeyed, but there comes a time when a volunteer must personally dip his toe into the bathwater. In the middle of Kansas, Jeff removes his helmet. Computer has approved, although approval is merely advisory. Despite Jeff's best efforts at child-sharing maybe he is betraying Sandy yet again by being a hero.

The supporters' group join hands in hydroponics and pray for Jeff, even though by now they remember that they are perhaps no longer part of the processes of humanity, being altogether too far away.

'It smells sort of sweet . . . and sort of musty too, a bit like rotting wood.'

Jeff breathes for five minutes. No sudden sneezes. Resuming the helmet, he wears it inside *Charm* for three boring hours. Nothing untoward happens to him, so he unsuits. Saliva and mucous swabs and a blood sample taken by Gisela seem normal under the microscope.

'We appear to be lucking out in a big way,' Com Sherwin tells everyone.

Charm is the ideal isolated quarantine facility. Jeff and Gisela and tubby agronomist Marcel Reynard and pilot-geologist Werner Schmidt take turns working and exploring outside fully suited. Aboard *Charm* Gisela mixes a faecal sample with a sample of local soil and organisms; some of the organisms die. After a week Jeff ventures outside to breathe the air of Kansas for several hours.

Three days later Jeff drinks boiled, filtered Kansas water. Gisela tests and retests his urine. Two days afterwards, he is wearing a coverall rather than a suit when outside. Ungloved, he has already handled samples of vegetation inside the shuttle, and no rashes resulted. Now he handles living vegetation. On the soil he deposits a faecal sample he brought in a bag, marking the spot with a day-glo flag. What might the hoppers and scuttlers and sliders make of this offering if they had any glimmering of true consciousness rather than mere programmed instincts? Evolutionarily speaking, the equivalent of God-like beings have descended from the sky. Next day, inert hoppers and sliders lie nearby—the food of the Gods, or rather the waste products, was too much for them.

James's developmental pathways must indeed have altered; his larynx is descending early. Beware of the risk of him choking. Connections in his brain may be proceeding more rapidly—he looks alert, bright-eyed, on the verge of what exactly? No longer does he attempt in vain to vocalise, as if he has come to some understanding with himself, or of himself. What a patient, amenable baby he is now, and still so young. He stares at his mother, and at Mary too, and at the members of the supporters' club, which is his supporters' club as much as it is Mary's.

The third shuttle, *Colour*, has gone down to join *Charm*, to erect a habitat-dome for thirty persons along with a solar power plant and a number of wind-power whirlies.

Only now, perhaps, are many potential colonists beginning to appreciate the full implications of a whole future spent on Tee-Cee. Sure, there will be much scientific stimulation. Sure, there will be a wealth of human cultural resources on tap for entertainment. Sure, more colonists will arrive from Earth within, say, two years at the most, counting in time for mission assessment and the turn-around of *Pioneer*. But oh the comparative barrenness of Kansas . . . !

'If we go down there . . .' says Sandy.

'Not if, but when,' says Chika. 'We didn't actually think this would happen, did we? I confess I didn't, not in my heart. The planet wouldn't be habitable, or there would be alien viruses we couldn't cope with. But it is, and there aren't.'

Sophie tries to sound a bright note. 'In another hundred years there will be human cities. Networks. People whose *grandparents* were born on Tee-Cee Two.'

'For us,' says Sandy, 'just work work work. A few days' hike in any direction for a working holiday if we're lucky. Lots of trips to the seaside for me. We'll be sacrificing the best of our lives.'

'That's why we *came* here,' says Mary. 'We're *pioneers*. Your Jeff especially.'

'Easy for you to say! You won't be stuck here. Com Sherwin is bound to take you back through Q-space in the hope of a shortcut through time for anyone aboard. If that can't be cracked, isn't six months' solitary going to be a bit of a disincentive to those who'll supposedly follow us? Well, isn't it?'

'Do you mean . . . you think there might never *be* another shipload of colonists? Surely not! Even if people are obliged to endure isolation en route, they'll still come. At least they'll know they have a secure destination!'

Eric eyes Mary uneasily. 'I wonder if *I'll* be taken back. Normally I would have expected to go back to look after the hydroponics, but there can't be much point if there are eight or so different versions of *Pioneer*. Com Sherwin is almost bound to take you as ship's doctor rather than Yukio.'

'Even if I have nobody to doctor but myself? Talk sense.'

Eric nods. 'Because of your other possibility.'

The Commander must be haunted by decisions he has yet to make. Maybe this is why, after a long and inconclusive interview with Mary months ago, he has not discussed her revelation again with her in any depth. Something new may yet happen to her. Or if not her, then as regards baby James.

Denise has gone to the surface. From now on her astrophysics will be restricted to the close study of Tau Ceti, which is important, of course. Sunspot cycles, the wind from the new sun. Jay-Jay has deployed an instrument platform in orbit for her to uplink with, but habitat-tending work will occupy much of Denise's time.

It'll be another month until a second habitat-dome is erected, and several more whirlies, time enough one hopes for any teething problems with the first habitat to become apparent. Since a habitat does not need to be sealed off fully from the environment, problems should not be too serious. The air and the water freely available down on Tee-Cee Two are such a boon, as is the soil in which crops can grow. Genetic engineering may not be necessary at all. Unprotected fields of lupins may provide fodder, and some beauty. Frozen embryos of pigs, goats, and rabbits may be quickened and brought to term in the artificial wombs all the sooner. And chickens hatched. And ponds dug for carp and trout—and a network of irrigation channels.

James will have chicks and bunnies and piglets as part of his nursery experience.

The pioneers were prepared to provide full protection to the tithe of terrestrial life they brought with them. This would have limited the options. Now, not so.

Sophie conducts a multi-faith ceremony of thanks and blessing, although God is absent, or at least extremely diminutive, if God is the collective superconsciousness of the whole human race.

A husband and wife team, Bjorn and Heidi Svenson, vets who will be in charge of husbandry, visit Mary in the clinic. Heidi has brought a urine sample.

'You're pregnant. Definitely!' Mary tells Heidi joyfully. 'Oh congratulations!'

Turns out to be only a week ago that the Svensons engaged in something of a marathon, six times in two days at mid-month in Heidi's cycle. If James was ever a jinx, that jinx is exorcised now that Tee-Cee promises fertility. In place of a certain apprehension is an eagerness to bear the first child on an alien world. It's early days yet to be sure how viable the Svensons' embryo is, but Heidi does not intend to keep quiet about it. Next day, another husband and wife and a pair of Afro-American partners visit Mary for the same test. The former have not conceived, but the latter have succeeded. With luck James will have peers not too much younger than he is.

Mary and Sophie and Hiroaki and Chika, and inevitably Eric, are taking a coffee break in hydroponics, perching on the sides of plant-troughs, their backs brushing the emerald foliage of carrots and the stalks of tomato plants bowed by bright red globelets.

Sandy comes in at a pace which risks balance-nausea, James swaddled tightly in her arms as if he might fall and break.

'*He started speaking—!*' She displays her child, who gazes at Sophie, then at Mary.

What the baby says is: 'I am a Voice. I answer. Ask me.'

And Mary asks, '*What are you?*'

'I am a Voice of the linking to All-Humanity. The echo of the event in what you call Q-space. I am a Voice left behind.' *Sandy's baby is actually talking to them*. Its tones are somewhat squeaky.

'*Why* were you left behind?'

'As a Guide to what is and what may be.'

'Shouldn't we get the Commander here?' butts in Eric.

'Not yet, not yet,' says Hiroaki, eager for enlightenment.

A Guide to what is . . .

'Do you mean,' Eric asks, 'you can tell us, for example, whether Tee-Cee is as suitable for us to colonise as it seems to be?'

'Maybe the problems are within yourselves. You are all too special. Specialists, multi-specialists. Over-endowment oozes from your fingertips, from the pores of your skin. Better to have sent here a hundred trained peasants or low-caste labourers for whom the work would mean freedom from the restricting past and who would feel like lords. Tee-Cee is weed, water, dirt. Compel a chess grand master to play nothing but checkers for years.'

'*Pioneer* will bring more people here in a couple of years—fewer PhDs, more blue-collar types, I guess.'

'Sleeping two to a cabin, like animals in an ark? Will you first founders be their superiors, their directors? Even so, the numbers will still be too small.'

'Another ship will be built—more ships.'

'Requiring four years each, costing forty billion moneys each? Almost bankrupting the backers? Shall the Earth be taxed dry? Only so, if threatened by certain extinction. If your sun is about to flare. If a dark star enters your solar system. If a big comet passes by and will return in a hundred years and strike your Earth.'

'We could fire anti-matter at a comet,' says Chika. 'Completely destroy it while it's still far away.'

Within such a short time-frame what threat could be big enough and certain enough?

Mary recalls. 'You—or the being you represent—told me that other species do manage to set up colonies by sending generation ships or whatever.'

'Perhaps with thousands of persons on board. Perhaps those species command a much larger energy budget than Humanity. You may be too soon. Premature. Your best effort, not big enough.'

'I think,' says Sophie, 'you're looking on the gloomy side. You've been overhearing people having a few last-minute doubts.'

A guide to what may be . . .

'James, can you foretell the future?' asks Hiroaki.

'I can tell what may most probably be,' answers the baby. 'The most probable paths. Sometime, within infinity, an improbable path becomes actual. How else could the first parent universe arise?'

'Oh kami kami kami,' Chika exclaims, 'he's a quantum computer. A hand-held quantum computer—and he's an artificial intelligence too! No, I don't mean *artificial*—he's biological, a biological quantum computer. Of course that's what we all are in a limited sense if it's true that quantum effects create our consciousness . . . But we don't have access to . . . we aren't linked . . . we aren't directly plugged in to the background, the big picture . . . '

'What he is,' says Sophie, 'is an *avatar*.'

'You mean like the face Computer has, if we want to see a face on screen?'

'Originally avatar is a Hindu term. For an incarnation of a god, a manifestation.'

How cautiously Sandy holds on to what is biologically her son, as though maybe she should lay him down among the tomato plants in case her grasp fails her.

'Does he have powers? Can he make things happen?'

'Ask him,' says Sophie, compassionate, apprehensive.

Sandy bows her head over her baby.

'James, can you *do* things? Can you . . . can you make a *bird* appear in here?'

'Mother, I am a Voice, not a Hand that can pluck a creature from one place to another.'

'You have hands—two little hands. You do.' Carefully she unswaddles a chubby pink baby arm, little fingers, tiny coral nails.

'But I am not a Hand.'

'Could you become a Hand?'

'That is a very unlikely path. Then I might not be a Voice.'

'Can you see what is happening with Jeff there down on Tau-Cee?'

'I am not an Eye.'

Hiroaki interrupts. 'Are there any other beings like you that *are* Hands or Eyes?'

James yawns. 'I am tired now. This was an effort. I am a baby.' His eyes close.

'I've got to get a message to Jeff! He must come back!'

'We got to tell the Commander right now,' says Chika.

'He's asleep.'

'Com Sherwin? How do you know?'

'No. James is asleep.'

Sherwin Peterson quickly comes in person to hydroponics after Chika's call.

'Can you wake him up?'

'I don't think we should,' says Mary. 'He's fatigued. Let him wake in his own time.'

'I can hardly doubt the word of five of you . . .'

Not unless this is some weird hoax, and what would that serve?

The Commander bangs his fist into his palm as if the sudden noise might startle James awake.

'Let me get this straight. He's saying that this expedition is too soon and too few and the wrong sort of people.'

That might be the point of the hoax, is a thought which obviously crosses his mind. Psychological sabotage by a small group of conspirators who wish to avoid effectively being marooned down on Tee-Cee. This feeling might spread like an infection. Let's just do the science, then let's pack up and go home in relative comfort. If the baby wakes up and says nothing at all the hoax will be rumbled within a few hours at most. Yet a seed of, yes, mutiny might still have been sown.

'I am ordering you to say nothing about this until I can talk to the baby myself.'

How can he enforce his order? A Commander should not issue orders which cannot be enforced.

'I'm appealing to you to keep quiet for a few hours. How long will it be?' A mother should know. And a doctor should know. Oh yes really, a psychiatrist who claims she met an inhabitant of probability, whose voice this baby now is?

'His brain is altered,' Mary says. 'I don't know how long he needs to sleep after making a big effort. We might harm him.'

'This could harm *us*, Doctor, in ways you mightn't imagine!'

'He's a living quantum computer,' says Chika. 'Maybe James can help you pass through Q-space again without the same isolation. Maybe he can pull the time-jumping trick.'

'And maybe *Pioneer* will slide off the edge of the universe. This ship vanishes, and that's the end of star travel. How do you know this baby isn't some sort of virus that Dr Nolan's famous super-being inserted on board? Better the devil of isolation than a devil we don't know.'

Paranoia due to the strain of command? The weight of responsibility for human hopes and for forty billion dollars?

'I think we'll have ample time to find out,' says Chika.

The Commander squares himself. 'We'll all wait. Right here.'

'I have work to attend to, Commander.'

'What would that be? Re-programming the computer to accept input from the virus-baby?'

'Of course not. There's a lot of data from the surface to process.'

'No one leaves, and no one enters. Make yourselves comfortable.' True to his word, the Commander parks his butt on the edge of the big tomato trough, plucks a ripe tomato, grins, bites into it, sticks his other hand in his pocket.

'James should be lying on my bed,' says Sandy. 'Wait *here*? He's a bit of a weight. Look, I'll take him to my cabin. I guess we can all fit in there. And that'll be more private.'

'I said we wait here.'

'Com, that's *unreasonable.*'

'In your professional opinion is it lacking in reason?' Sherwin asks Mary. 'A sign of insanity? Sufficient grounds for my Second Officer to take over?'

From his pocket, to their astonishment, the Commander pulls a pistol, which he points at Sandy—or at James.

Tightly Sophie says, 'I didn't know there were any weapons on *Pioneer.*'

'Sure there are. And on the shuttles too. Kept well out of sight, locked away, available in emergency to certain personnel who are sworn to secrecy. What if we encountered actively hostile indigenes on Tee-Cee? What if a hostile alien entity boards the ship? What if that has happened already?'

It is as if a trapdoor has opened, from which blows a very cold draught.

Com Sherwin chews and sucks at the tomato, and regards the five, and slumbering James. Hiroaki is standing tensely as if calculating whether he can disarm Sherwin.

'Commander,' says Mary, 'if you put the gun away we agree to stay here and never say anything about this. There might be an accident.'

'My child,' whispers Sandy.

'Ah but is he or ain't he? How much of him is your child if his brain has been tampered with, as you say? Is he even human if he's actually a bio-computer? Some guns came along with us in case of unforeseen emergency. I think this amounts to something of an emergency putting the mission in peril, admittedly in a peculiar way. I would like to be obeyed without argument.'

'James may be quite wrong about us being unsuitable settlers.'

'In that case, Dr Nolan, would I let it have a say in how this ship operates in Q-space? As *you* have just suggested, Dr Suzuki.'

'He may have powers,' Sandy says.

'That's exactly what I'm bothered about. You people really are blind. Indulged. Let's be patient, let's not leap to conclusions, let's keep hush. I'm the Commander. Some weird baby isn't.'

This is all very unfortunate. Com Sherwin had seemed steady as a rock. An easy-going rock, you might even say. Ten light years' distance from Earth is a long thin thread. Thin threads can snap if tugged unexpectedly. He still sounds composed. Does he not understand that producing a gun to enforce authority seriously devalues his position as well as poisoning the atmosphere aboard? A gun, to confront a mother and baby. He is like a King Herod panicked by rumours of a messiah. It is outside of his scope.

'Whatever happens,' Mary tells the others, 'we mustn't say anything about this. Understood? This is a can of worms.' Can she persuade the Commander to accept counselling?

'Perhaps,' suggests Sophie, 'I should say a prayer to focus us.'

No one else wanders into hydroponics. If someone did, would Com Sherwin detain them too at gun point? He whistles to himself monotonously and tunelessly, as if time-keeping, holding the pistol slackly. Occasionally he answers a message on his com. He eats a couple more tomatoes to sustain himself, a breach of proper conduct—hydroponics is not for anyone to sneak into and snack—but in the circumstances Eric does not demur.

Mary thinks of Commander Bligh and the *Bounty*. And of isolated Pitcairn Island, where the mutineers marooned themselves, not to be recontacted until many decades later, while Bligh and his few rowed something like four thousand miles by dead reckoning to regain eventually the bosom of authority. An epic journey, almost equivalent to the crossing of light years. In this case is the Commander the mutineer? On the Pitcairn Island of Tee-Cee does he maroon his crew while the officers make their escape?

By his own lights the Commander may be right to be holding that gun, in case James is a lot more than they imagine. In case James needs to be killed quickly. Err on the safe side.

After an hour James wakes. With his gun the Commander motions all but Sandy and her baby well out of the way. Hiroaki especially.

'Hi there, Kid, I'm the Commander. I hear you found your voice. That true?'

'I *am* the Voice, Commander.'

'I'm kind of upset to hear you cast doubts on our chances of settling Tee-Cee.'

The baby peers at him, focusing. 'I am realistic. Too few, too soon, too concerned with individuality.'

'Pardon me that we aren't a hive. Maybe this is Earth's only chance of having our eggs in more than one basket. Question of available resources and politics.'

'So you feel obliged to try to succeed.'

'Obliged, right. Now what's *your* agenda? Try to dissuade us? Something important about Tee-Cee? In a squillion years might the weed-hoppers amount to more than Einstein and Hawking and Mozart? That it?'

'What are Einstein and Hawking and Mozart?'

'I guess their fame hasn't spread much. We aim to remedy that. Any advice about Q-space? How to keep us all together while we're in transit through your realm? How to speed things up a bit?'

'Would you prefer that a hundred different journeys are undertaken by everyone? And only one actuality emerges? The wave fronts of all the other ships collapsing, experienced subjectively as catastrophe, shipwreck in void, the dissolving of substance and life?'

'You could fix that, could you, given access to our computer and the Q-drive controls? Excuse my being confrontational, by the way. Commander's prerogative if a mission seems in danger.'

'There are ways to arrange different parameters.'

'I guess no one would ever take another Q-space trip if there's a ninety-nine percent likelihood of being annihilated.'

'The one percent that prevails becomes one hundred percent. Nothing is actually lost.'

'Except that ninety-nine *me*'s experience termination.'

'You, who prevail, would not know.'

'Okay, I'll take that on board, under advisement. Wouldn't ninety-nine or whatever number of *you* go down kicking and screaming also, in ghost-land?'

'Unimportant. Inessential. The survivor survives. Result: unity. You over-value the idea of the self.'

'There's a real cosmic perspective. Dr Tate, lay the child down by those carrots, will you?'

'Why should I do that? What's in your mind?'

'Thoughts, Dr Tate. Muchos thoughts. *Kindly do it now.*'

'I won't. You're mad.'

The gun points. 'Do it, and nothing bad will happen to you.'

'Not to me, but . . .'

'I'll count to five. At five I pull the trigger.'

With greatest reluctance Sandy unslings James.

'Position him so he can see me. Now, back off.'

She backs off a pace, another pace. She's tempted to throw herself in between.

'Okay. Voice, can you see me clearly?'

'Yes,' says the baby.

'Do you know what this is I'm holding in my hand?'

'A tool that I think can kill.'

'Exactly. It fires a bit of metal called a bullet, very fast with a lot of punch. I'm pointing it at your head, which contains your brains. You're an alien infestation. I'm going to count to five and then I'm going to fire.'

'Don't do this,' begs Sandy. 'He needs feeding and changing.'

'Should we have a short intermission? No, I don't think so.' Sherwin starts to count. James stares at him, neither begging nor flinching. When Sherwin reaches five, he pulls the trigger.

Click.

'Gee, the safety is on . . .' And immediately, 'Now it isn't. But the test is over. He's just a Voice, that's all. Unless he's telepathic, of course, but he gave no signs so far. All right, all relax. I'm sorry about this bit of theatre. Had to be sure he doesn't have powers.'

'And what,' asks Sophie, 'if he had vanished the gun from your hand? Sent it into the middle of nowhere? What would you have done then, try to strangle him with your bare hands?'

'No. Been very circumspect. I sincerely apologise, people. Middle of nowhere is where we are, or rather at the other end of nowhere, and that's where *he* comes out of, even if he looks like a baby and poos like a baby, a very disarming disguise. I had to be certain what we're dealing with. Exceptional circumstances call for exceptional reactions. What to ordinary souls may appear to be an irrational reaction, right out of left field, may be inspired and correct.'

'A commander has to be decisive,' agrees Chika politely.

'I was quoting Linda Bernstein. This brings us back to the problem of damage to morale, and what if anything we might do about rejigging the Q-drive.'

'You're actually entertaining the idea?'

'How can I ignore it, Dr Suzuki? I'm not blinkered.'

No, but maybe he is on the edge of himself.

'I think we established something important—the baby's limitations, at least at present.'

'You were justified,' says James. Healingly, perhaps. Or shrewdly.

The Commander tucks his pistol away.

'Okay, Voice, these different parameters that can be arranged . . . can our ship's personnel all skip ahead through time on the trip back to Earth if we put up with a bit of isolation? Without most versions of us getting extinguished?'

What a gift to science and star travel this will be. And how much more supportive for the settlement on Tee-Cee. Beats harpooning a gas-whale into a cocked hat.

'I am tired again,' says the baby.

'Sandy.' Bonhomie, now. 'For the moment I want you to keep the Voice out of the way of everyone other than those here present. Will you promise this?'

Of course.

The Commander orders *Charm* to carry a final habitat down to Kansas, and a load of supplies. *Beauty* conveys another thirty settlers to the surface. *Pioneer* is becoming quite empty, and proportionately huger, so it seems. The six, and James, remain aboard as though they are engaged in a covert project. Which of them will be sent down at the last moment? Sherwin must at least already have confided in his Second Officer. He is abridging any planned schedule effervescently. A year at Tau Ceti and all the planetary science work? No, the stay in orbit will be measured in months, maybe as few as two, as though Sherwin is now itching to depart, the sooner to return bringing more settlers and equipment. Colonisation is the prime priority. This is proceeding more successfully and speedily than anyone had expected—just so long as no one involved in it hears of the Voice's doubts, not for a long while yet. Colonisation must be buttressed, reinforced, asap. The toehold must become a full deep footprint.

Jeff still does not know about his son's achievement. Jeff is distant now. Undoubtedly Sandy will stay aboard *Pioneer* to care for James. Her oceanography can wait, and Jeff will have to wait.

Conversations with the Voice continue, in Sandy's cabin. Sophie or Mary frequently stay with James to let Sandy off the leash for exercise and a change of scene, as now. Chika and Hiroaki are also helping baby-sit. The bed-couch is crowded.

'So we are all tiny parts of a vast species-overmind?'

'Yes, Mary,' says James.

'What does the overmind do? What is its aim? What thoughts does it think?'

'I do not have access to it. I am only the Voice of the Other, left behind.'

'Is there any way a person can access our species-overmind directly and comprehensibly?'

Mary thinks of the angel she once saw. The angel was cobwebs and dew and sunlight.

'Being enfolded into its psychospace and becoming fully aware: that is a way.'

'What does that mean?'

'Ceasing your life in ongoing space-time. All the billions of lives that ever were remain embedded in its wholeness. Like true dreams. Can you awake lucidly within the dream that was your life, once it has ended? Can you edit the life that was yours? Can you rewrite it? Can you corrupt the data of your history recorded in the psychosphere? This may compel the attention of the overmind.'

'Could you help me do this?' asks Mary.

'Perhaps.'

'He's talking about you *dying* first!' says Sophie. 'He isn't saying that you can report anything at all to the living.'

'I am talking,' says the Voice, 'about myself ceasing along with you after I help hoist your mind.'

'Hoist my mind? *How?*'

'I can hypnotise you and, as it were, change mental settings.'

'Good thing Com Sherwin isn't hearing *this*,' Sophie says. 'But anyway, we're only talking theoretically. *Aren't we, Mary?*'

Mary nods.

'I would volunteer for this,' Chika says softly.

'Only Mary Nolan is suitable,' the Voice states, 'because her mind already linked in Q-space. And a gap was caused. She went ahead in time.'

'Oh kami kami,' murmurs Chika.

'If I can edit my life-data after I die,' asks Mary, 'do I alter the real events that occurred?'

'Skeins may unravel and reform, within limitations. Threads will shift. A different probability will manifest. The large pattern will remain similar.'

'It *is* like time-travel, isn't it? A sort of time-travel? I go back and I do something a bit differently.'

'You adjust what already happened and what resulted. Within limits.'

'And if the overmind does not agree?'

'It must focus upon you. You who are part of it.'

'Can I focus *it* upon what happens in the real world?'

'I do not know this. My brain heats. I am tired. I must cool.'

The final shuttle trips come so soon. *Pioneer* almost empties its stores of supplies. Chika and Yukio, Sophie and Hiroaki are to become settlers.

Hiroaki hangs himself in his cabin. In the partial gravity his strangulation may have taken a while, and perhaps this was his plan—to approach death more slowly so that the boundary between life and death might become as blurred as his vision, allowing him to slip through, to be both dead and alive at once for a while so that he might enfold into psychospace while still fractionally aware. He too was touched by what transpired in Q-space. To a certain extent Hiroaki's mental settings had been changed. Or perhaps he could not bear to be exiled on Tee-Cee, away from the Voice, or from Mary who may attain a kind of satori, if not in this life then in the data-dream-stream of her life, the eddies within the vast river of the overmind.

Hiroaki's death is a shock. Still: balance of his mind tragically disturbed ever since isolation in Q-space. After a brief service conducted by Sophie, his body joins that of Greg Fox in cold store. Sending bodies down to be buried on Tee-Cee would not be a good omen.

'*What did the Voice tell him?*' Com Sherwin wants to know. Has to be something to do with James.

Mary confesses to the Commander. 'I think Hiroaki got the idea that he might be able to contact the overmind by dying, because he was touched by it in Q-space.'

'Touched, as in loony . . . ?'

'Maybe he couldn't bear to be separated from . . .'

'From his therapist?'

'No, from what may happen in Q-space the next time.'

Pioneer is outward bound. Farewells have been said. In an entirely literal way: fare extremely well . . . until the starship returns. Which it will, there's no doubting. Especially, don't doubt yourselves. *Charm* has been left in Kansas, almost like an emergency survival hut that can be sealed off, though of course will never need to be. Or like an escape route, admittedly an escape to nowhere. Even so, more reassuring than otherwise: a visible link to space and wider horizons, an earnest of more technology due to come. The settlers will now need to acquire a different mind-set, vigorous yet also patient.

Jeff could not understand why Sandy was not joining him. There's one of the settlers already feeling isolated, betrayed as if in tit-for-tat. Although in the end Jeff seemed resigned. Sandy herself cried and needed comforting.

On board are Mary, Sandy and James, and Eric of hydroponics, Com Sherwin and his Second, Max Muller, Engineer Sam Nakata, Navigator Nellie van Torn, Comp and ship-systems manager Bill Brooks, and shuttle pilot Dan Addison. Ten souls, or nine plus something else.

Com Sherwin is in several minds.

The Voice has decided that if Computer reprogrammes the Q-drive in such and such a way, then each traveller will find himself or herself accompanied by a copy of the Voice.

How can James be in nine places at once—until, at journey's end, he becomes a single person again? He is not any ordinary baby. He is a child of reality and probability.

The journey time can be shortened considerably—not by time-jumping such as benefited Mary, but by 'compression', which James cannot explain in comprehensible words. The result should be a journey time of one month rather than six.

It may be that James's entangled presence will permit a limited amount of communication between the otherwise isolated stellanauts, via him, although such messages may be unreliable, even if comforting. Or otherwise.

Of course, him being an infant, albeit an infant prodigy, his copies will need caring for. How well up on the care of infants are Com Sherwin, Max Muller, Dan Addison . . . ?

The downside is that there will be phantom journeys too, otherwise there would not be enough paths to sum over.

The voice likens those phantom journeys to you standing between two mirrors and beholding repeated reflections of yourself diminishing and disappearing into the distance. The first five or six reflections certainly seem like authentic representations; thereafter you become increasingly vague and distant. Thus it will feel to the phantoms. Seven or so will feel like you, and will disperse when you—*or one of the others*—exits from Q-space. Others will not possess enough substance to experience more than a dream-like state, the unravelling of which will hardly be too traumatic.

So there's about a one in eight chance that you personally will reintegrate. Seven echoes will hope for this but fail to achieve it. Much better odds than one in a hundred—though even so!

Mary has slightly better odds. If she tosses a dice to decide whether to euthanase herself and James while in Q-space so as to enfold herself into psychospace—by far the best way to choose, namely by chance—and if one of her selves does indeed toss the number for death, then one of her will definitely die but will not have lived in vain, and one of the remainder will survive.

A link may even endure between her dead self and her living self, so the Voice surmises.

'So,' says Com Sherwin to those who are all gathered in the restaurant, 'do we go for it?'

Is he recollecting the dive of the *The Dart* into Jupiter and the harpooning of the gas-whale? *Do I go for it or do I not?*

'I'd like an advisory show of hands. Purely advisory for the moment.'

The dissenters are Sam Nakata, Nellie van Torn, and Bill Brooks—engineering, navigation, and computer systems respectively. Com Sherwin may or may not have prevailed previously upon his Second, Max Muller. As a pilot Dan Addison has coped with risks before, and he's rather too extrovert to endure another spell of six months all on his own. Mary and Sandy and Eric are united in going for it, although are their votes quite equal in weight to engineering or navigation?

'Well,' says Sherwin, 'that's five to three in favour, ignoring myself and the Voice.'

'Commander,' says Sam Nakata, 'we have absolutely no reason to opt for this, this *experiment*—on the say-so of a baby! It's our duty to take *Pioneer* back through Q-space by a route that demonstrably succeeds. If that involves six months alone, we already hacked it once. At least this time we're forewarned.'

'Obviously he's no ordinary baby. But more to the point, if we cut the journey time by five months each way, that's almost one year sooner we can bring more people and equipment to Tee-Cee. Imagine returning and finding the colony falling apart because we didn't take the fast route. I think *that* bears thinking seriously about.'

'Yes. It does. *If.*'

'We shouldn't worry about some of us not arriving,' says Sandy, 'so long as one of each does. We won't know anything about the ones who don't arrive.'

'Plenty of fish in the probability sea, eh?' remarks Nellie van Torn. 'I don't *like* to think of five of me evaporating, especially if the one who evaporates is *me*.'

'It's an identity problem,' says Bill Brooks surprisingly. 'If you could copy your mind into an android, say while you're unconscious, and if the act of mind-scanning erases your brain, is the android simply continuing your own life? The android will certainly feel as though it's doing so, indistinguishably. If you were dying of terminal cancer you would opt for this continuation, wouldn't you?'

'Are you changing your informal vote?' asks Com Sherwin.

'I don't like to think that I may be putting ninety-odd other people in jeopardy just because of qualms about myself, when actually my self will survive intact in one version or another.'

There is much to mull over. Mary begins giving classes on the medical aspects of infant care, and Sandy on the practical details. James begins hypnotising Mary.

The time has come. Nellie and Sam have agreed under protest. Computer has accepted complex instructions from James who has crawled and is now taking his first precocious steps. He's also toilet-trained and able to eat mashed pap. In view of his huge linguistic skills he oughtn't to be much bother to look after. On the contrary, a valuable companion.

Mary lies in her cabin.

'Sixty seconds to Q-insertion . . .'

'Thirty seconds . . .'

'Fifteen . . .'

The seconds pass, the cabin ripples, silence from the speakers.

She is alone with the Voice.

'Can you contact Sandy, Voice?'

The Voice's eyes grow glazed.

'Hi Mary, Sandy and James here, James and Sandy here, We're here. I hear you, You already said, You called me just now—'

Six or Seven Sandies are talking through James's lips one after another, all saying much the same thing, wherever *here* may be. Certainly isn't this cabin. A babble of ghosts. These may be difficult conversations to keep up.

'Can you contact *me myself*, Voice? I mean, another me?'

James concentrates.

Presently: '*When* are we going to do it?' Commit suicide, and James-icide—she knows what she means.

'Should we all do it at the same time?'

'Is that really me?'

'We never got a chance like this to discuss things.'

'We talked to ourself in Q-space before, but this is very different!'

'Hey, what about our Hippocratic Oath?'

Babel, from James's lips. The nine voices of Mary. Beats schizophrenia any day. This procedure offers very little counsel or comfort, and is perhaps a Bad Idea.

Q + 3. She needn't feel isolated in the ship. She can summon up voices—but it is better not to hear them. Better to be alone with James, the better to concentrate her mind, in case it might fly apart. Doubtless her other selves have decided likewise, since they do not call her. Several Coms Sherwins do call, wanting status reports. What is the point of them asking for those? Perfectionism? Several Erics also call, wishing her well, better, best. James is with everyone.

Q + 4. Do it today. Today is a perfectly fine day to end one's life. *One's* life? What if all of the Maries roll a four, unlucky number in the minds of the Japanese because *shi* which means four also means death, thank you for that knowledge, Hiroaki. What if all or none roll a four? Is Maries the plural of Mary?

She has brought overdoses of morphine from the dispensary, morphine to send one to sleep, a very deep sleep.

'Are you ready, Voice? Any last wishes? Some mashed carrots?'

Mary is an Angel in a woodland by a tiny lake. And she is also Mary who sees the Angel and now understands what she sees. Her vision spans forward—inside a starship a dark-haired athletic woman is grinning at her.

'To be really aboard at last? Great! Ah, do you mean the motion . . . ? It's okay.' The woman swings her head friskily. 'Oops.'

Switching her attention, Mary sinks to her knees amongst the bushes aglitter with spiders' webs.

'Overmind, Overmind!' The words seem like the start of a prayer, a prayer which can perhaps be answered.

Com Sherwin's voice comes briskly. 'Hear me. Re-emergence from Q-space achieved. We're in the home system—we're home. Crew present on bridge: Muller, Nakata, van Torn, and Brook, and me. Call in please in order: Nolan, Tate, Festa, Addison. Nolan?'

'Present, Commander.'

Oh yes, what a present. She is alive. Alive.

'Tate?'

Sandy's voice comes over the speaker. 'Present. So is James.'

James the Voice. James the Link. James the Knowledge.

Eric and Dan Addison also report in.

Glimpses of aeons of human experience crash in upon kneeling Mary, rocking her. Billions of souls batter at her like a plague of butterflies. Birdsong sounds like the high-speed warble of data-flow from which an audible message may somehow emerge, if only it can step down to her level.

And she feels such a twinge within, somewhere in her belly, as the glimpses flee, and the butterflies vanish, and the birdsong hushes.

She knows that inside her is the beginning of a Voice.

The Black Wall of Jerusalem

S HORTLY AFTER I RETURNED TO ENGLAND THE DREAMS BEGAN.
Nightly a four-legged Angel in bright armour bears me upon his back
into domains where I witness marvels and atrocities—before we are forced,
by a Harpy, by a Buddha-Toad, by a Woman-Whirlwind, to withdraw.

Meanwhile, in Israel, helicopter gunships are rocketing Arab cars and
houses—it's the wrong war, the wrong war!

Do I report my dreams to the Knights of the Black Wall back in
Jerusalem? Might I be inviting an assassin to visit me? I'm definitely a link, a
channel. Can the Black Wall appear in my own country, especially if
Jerusalem is incinerated in a Middle Eastern holocaust, which heaven
forbid? Heaven, indeed! *And will those feet in modern times walk upon
England's mountains green? And will the Centaur-Angel be on England's
pleasant pastures seen?* Beyond our world lurk other potent dimensions,
parasitical and expansionist, seeking their place in the true sun.

I am being incoherent.

Some time before the fall of Jerusalem to Saladin in 1187 the Knights
Templar expelled from their Order and from the Holy Land a certain Robert
de Sourdeval.

During the 1920s workmen renovating the Aqsa Mosque on Temple Mount found hidden in its roof space a parchment alluding to the expulsion. Sourdeval's crime remained a mystery until a further document was offered to an antique dealer in East Jerusalem in the 1950s and came into the possession of a Polish-American garments millionaire who was passionately interested in the 'occult' side of history, Kabbalah, Sufism, Masonry and such.

This document, a copy of a letter written in Latin by Sourdeval to an unknown recipient, is the earliest recorded description of the Black Wall of Jerusalem and of the 'demoniacal' beings beyond it. Two other accounts exist, one in Hebrew by a Rabbi and the other in Arabic by a Sufi, and neither is as lucid.

Why did the Knights Templar expel Sourdeval? That military order of monks were obsessed with Solomon's bygone temple, on the site of which they had established their headquarters, converting the Aqsa Mosque for this purpose. For the Templars, Solomon's Temple was the supreme example of sacred architecture. Its geometrical proportions, as deduced from the Bible, offered a key to the fundamentals of space and time, as we would say nowadays, and so could reveal the underpinnings of the universe and of life itself. For Sourdeval to insist on the existence—even the fleeting and visionary existence—of a wall anywhere in the vicinity which enshrined creatures more demonic than angelic must have been anathema. His testimony must be suppressed.

I'm running ahead of myself . . .

I was a lecturer in Art History with a particular interest in apocalyptic art, Altdorfer and such. Philip Wilson was also a poet with a minor reputation—the emphasis should be on *was*. I dreamed of blowing people out of the water one day with something major and sustained, of the calibre of William Blake. Yet as another William—Butler Yeats—put it, 'I sought a theme and sought for it in vain.' So far, I had been penning clever poems mainly inspired by artists' visions. Did I have no unique vision of my own, and could this be due to my own lack of any faith? Yeats managed to find his themes and visions. Might Jerusalem—the bubbling cauldron of religions, the real Jerusalem rather than Blake's resounding verses—prompt me with something suitable and major?

I had a sabbatical term due, and no ties. Trish had walked out on me, and by then I was glad of this. At first her passionate enthusiasms and loathings had been stimulating but after a while these came to seem like a series of self-indulgent fads, a sort of self-generated hysteria in which I was supposed to concur fully or be abused by her for lack of commitment or spirit. Ultimately I came to realize that Trish didn't care a hoot about my poetry, in other words my real inner self. Fortunately we had no kids to make a separation messy. Trish was always too busy for children, and then she became too busy for me. Yes, I would go to Jerusalem for a week in October, stay longer if I felt inspired. Trish was in a hatred-of-property phase and had swanned off to an ashram in India to be spiritual. She might return to demand a share of the house and my income, but for the moment I had funds and freedom.

The driver of the limousine who whisked me from Lod Airport—I sat up front for a better view—proved to have emigrated from London ten years earlier and was proudly Israeli. Deeply tanned, he wore shorts.

As he turned on to the only true motorway in Israel, linking Tel Aviv with Jerusalem, he used his mobile to phone ahead in Hebrew to the YMCA hotel where I had reserved a room. *Shalom, shalom.*

'They are expecting you, and I have a booking for return to the airport.'

I was glad of the air-conditioning in his limo. The brilliance, and the heat! The broad highway traversed what to my eyes appeared to be a barren wilderness seared by fierce sunshine. After we started climbing through reddish-brown foothills, by the sides of the road began appearing battered metal boxes the side of rubbish skips.

Those, said the ex-Londoner, were relics of the 1948 War of Independence, the wreckage of home-made armoured cars which ran an Arab blockade so that *we* could bring food to besieged Jerusalem—he had not arrived until decades later, nevertheless he was deeply part of this.

Ran the blockade? Oh no, those boxes had crawled up this incline where our own car now surged smoothly while devils—or at least Arabs—poured fire and brimstone from ambush.

'Many of us died in these convoys. And we're dying still—a car bomb here, a school bus machine-gunned there. And the world's media savage us whenever we aren't whiter than white and don't turn the other cheek, you know what I mean? But we carry on. What are we supposed to do? Jump in the sea?'

I nodded awkwardly.

'Mostly life is quite normal here, so you need not worry about safety.'

He sounded like a spokesman for the ministry of tourism, or immigration. I wondered whether he kept a gun in the glove pocket of the limo.

These thoughts passed from my mind as, high and still distant, shining white outcrops of apartment blocks appeared. The sheer brightness of the buildings coming into view as we continued higher and higher! All made of the local stone by law, mark you; even a Hilton Hotel must comply. No wonder people thought of Jerusalem as a celestial city here on Earth. You rose up and up, beholding a succession of white bastions or ramparts of suburbs, like Dante's hell of circles inverted and transformed from negative darkness into luminosity. Those Jews of 1948 in their grim, slow ovens had been conducting an assault, almost, upon heaven itself—betokened by the blinding sky—so as to restore the reign of angels, to raise those up again to pinnacles, thrones, and dominations; and now the angels indeed had dominion, armed with nuclear weapons. I was mixing up my theology a bit, but as my driver would say, *know what I mean?*

The YMCA hotel was much grander than its name implied. Located directly opposite the very swanky King David Hotel, the elegant 1930s building boasted a tall bell-tower resembling some stone space rocket poised to launch itself. Palm tree and soaring cedars graced a garden, white domed Byzantine wings on either side. The arcaded reception lobby was like a Turkish palace. I arranged to join a few other guests next day for a guided tour of the city to get my bearings.

By now it was evening. After depositing my bags I took a copy of the *Jerusalem Post* to a table on the terrace where I ordered lamb chops and a beer—the Goldstar proved to be decently malty. I read how a woman corporal had been stabbed to death by an Arab in the Jordan valley, and how the Defence Force had dynamited some Arab houses, and how a member of the Knesset's car had been fire-bombed by an underground extremist Jewish group because of a squabble about the location of a grave. The political situation seemed set to explode in a few more months, but meanwhile rich tourists were still debussing across the road.

Next morning I met up with the guide, Alon, a burly laid-back fellow approaching middle age. Perched on his balding head, a small *kippa* skull-cap gave useful sun protection. My fellow excursioners were a blond Swedish couple, the Svensens, their rather plain and shy teenage daughter, and Mrs Dimet, an American widow, a short urgent bird-like lady with frizzy hair.

Alon impressed on us that we should each buy a bottle of water before we set off to avoid dehydration, then he discreetly enquired into our religious affiliations so that he could guide us most beneficially.

I said I was agnostic; and the Swedes were atheists, the parents being historians at Umeå University.

'It is dark there half of the year,' explained Mrs Svensen. 'We came for the history, and for the light. Natural light, not religious light.'

'What else could I be but Jewish?' Mrs Dimet said. 'When God spoke to Abraham, radiation illuminated all people in the world—but most people lost the light. It is a miracle that I am here in Israel at last! Although I think the Hasidim are a bit crazy. God has to be joking when you wear Polish fur hats and long black coats in this heat.'

So none of us were Christians. Judiciously Alon said, 'Usually when I take people round I simply say, "Here is where Jesus was crucified." Today I will say, "Here is where Jesus was *said* to be crucified."' He inclined towards Mrs Dimet. 'You are right about the Ultra-Orthodox being crazy. Those fanatics refuse to pay taxes or serve in the army. Some even refuse to speak Hebrew because they think Hebrew is sacred. Yet their political power gives them all sorts of privileges.' He lowered his voice. 'There could be civil war here, Jew against Jew. Just as happened when the Romans besieged Jerusalem two thousand years ago! Jew fighting Jew fratricidally within the walls at the very same time as resisting the legions outside!' For Romans, read Arabs. Such a spectre deeply upset this otherwise easygoing man. The Svensen parents frowned sympathetically.

And so we set off in Alon's black stretch Mercedes. Landmarks, more landmarks, then we parked near the Wailing Wall. Hundreds of orthodox Jews of assorted sects wearing 19th century winter clothing breezed down a sloping plaza in the blazing sunshine to pray at the wall while bobbing their fur-hatted heads repeatedly. Seemingly the variously attired sub-divisions of the ultra-faithful all bitterly resented one another. Handsome young men of the Defence Force, dark-skinned and with gleaming teeth, automatic rifles slung around their shoulders, kept an eye on the comings and goings.

'If you like,' said Alon, 'you can write a prayer on a piece of paper and put it in a crack in the wall. No one will object.'

On the contrary, the devout would completely ignore us, just as they ignored one another. I thought about this and decided *why not?* Tearing a page from my notebook, I scribbled, 'May I have a theme please?' I folded the paper several times, walked to the wall, and inserted my appeal amongst many others. On my return the Svensens eyed me curiously.

Mrs Dimet had fled to the women's section to do some praying. Hidden above and beyond the great section of boundary wall was Temple Mount, which alas we would not be able to visit. Occupied as the Mount had been ever since the victories of Islam by highly sacred Moslem shrines, it was a volatile place. A fortnight ago a Canadian John the Baptist armed with a knife had started preaching inside the Aqsa Mosque. Riots and tear-gas and shots ensued; security was being reassessed. While Mrs Dimet was absent, Alon regaled us with how an extreme Jewish nationalist faction aimed to erase all trace of the Aqsa Mosque and the Dome of the Rock and to rebuild Solomon's Temple in all its glory, whereupon the reign of God could commence.

'First they need ritually to slaughter an all-red heifer and burn it. They are breeding one specially.'

'What is a heifer?' asked Mrs Svensen.

'A young virgin cow.'

'Why do those people want to burn a cow?'

'From its ashes they make a paste to sanctify the new foundations. The heifer has to be perfectly red.'

'A well-red cow,' observed Svensen drolly.

Confusingly, the Red Heifer Brigade was not among the squabbling ranks of the *Ultra*-Orthodox. Those Ultras would not lift a finger to rebuild the Temple because the Messiah would do it for them—everybody else must do everything for them.

From the Wailing Wall we walked to the Via Dolorosa, no great distance. How close and condensed everything was, all cheek by jowl.

In the courtyard-cum-playground of an Arab primary school, brown-robed Dominicans were gathering for their weekly procession up the flagstoned way trodden by Christ on his way to be crucified.

'Actually, the city surface was three metres lower in the First Century...'

Today being a Friday, no Arab schoolkids were present as a dapper monk proclaimed the Stations of the Cross in Italian, microphone in hand and boom-box slung over his shoulder. A rotund Asian colleague recited each

Station in orotund English. An Arab would lead the march, sporting a red fez ordained by the Ottomans as the symbol of authority to clear a path, otherwise trouble might ensue. Soldiers observed as we set off.

I was astonished at how tightly confined the route was—a cramped bazaar of souvenir vendors and food shops. A loping Arab lugging a small barrow of water melons barely managed to career past a military jeep. Nevertheless, here came a band of American women, the vanguard bearing on their shoulders a half-size replica cross like a battering ram. Equally brusque with purpose was a devout party of Slavs. After prayers at some tiny nearby mosque, an Imam was leading his flock of twenty or so the opposite way down the Via, while a party of French pilgrims were kneeling to adore a plaque marking one of the Stations. Insufficiently backed up, these rival devotees became a target for rage. Crab-like the Imam advanced, grimacing and flailing his arms, although not actually hitting anyone. 'Kack Christians!' he snarled, or something excremental. Lost in devotion, the pilgrims remained oblivious.

Presently the Via dog-legged as though a seismic fault-line had shifted it sideways, then it became roofed over and we were in an indoor souk. When we reached the Church of the Holy Sepulchre congestion and jostling of creeds was even more extreme. Orthodox Greeks guarded the claustrophobic pink marble 'tomb' of Christ while Copts jealously possessed one stone at the rear, on to which they had grafted a lean-to shrine. An enclosed tooth of shaved-down rock was the whole of Golgotha Hill; hardly any distance away was the site of the Resurrection. The noise in the church, the noise.

'This place is bedlam,' said Mrs Svensen.

'Most of the human race is demented,' her husband declared. 'Faiths and ideologies are a history of madness. Here it all comes together.'

Mrs Dimet chirped enthusiastically, 'The Law of Return lets everyone Jewish come home, Ethiopians, Yemenis, me if I choose. First there's the Diaspora, the scattering, and now like a miracle there's the incoming. It's a blessing.'

'We are talking about different things,' said Svensen.

Alon pursed his lips. 'According to Muhammad the entire Earth stretched forth from Jerusalem, and from Jerusalem it will be rolled up eventually like a scroll. Because Jerusalem is the axis of the world.'

The Old City, jam-packed with superimposed architecture, rival faiths and races, seemed to be teetering on the brink of critical mass. If only the core of Jerusalem could be unfolded into a dozen different dimensions at right angles to each other. Otherwise, it seemed to me, the whole inflated universe might indeed fall inward to some ultimate jostling superheated crunch right here—prior to an apocalyptic explosion from which a new cosmos might erupt, bright as a nuclear fireball, scattering illumination as God supposedly once had done. I understood how a visitor such as that Canadian screwball could succumb to delusions and imagine himself to be uniquely transfigured. Such a place this was, such a place.

Just then I noticed a Hispanic-looking young woman darting glances this way and that. Glossy black hair wild and wavy under a minimal headscarf, olive skin, bold yet haunted eyes. She reminded me of Trish, in the way that a negative suggests a print, her dark antithesis, ardent, obsessive. This woman wore a long-sleeved cream calico dress and tan leather sandals. As I was admiring her, she buttonholed a young Greek Orthodox priest. After listening for a few seconds he frowned impatiently and strode away, and I lost sight of her too.

Only to spot her once more while the six of us had stopped for lunch outside a café near the Citadel.

Sun furnaced from a cloudless sky, reflecting off stone the colour of bees' wax. Were we in the Christian or the Armenian quarter just here? Natives of Jerusalem would know to the exact inch. At the next table a couple of paunchy, hairy Greeks in black pillbox hats sipped cinnamon coffee. Pale omelettes arrived for us tourists, humous with pitta bread for Alon.

He grinned at us. 'In Israel we do not eat humous, we *wipe* it.' As he proceeded to demonstrate.

A scrawny tabby kitten hunched nearby, staring at us. In pity, Mrs Dimet pulled some scraps of smoked salmon from her omelette and threw them to the starveling which growled as it bolted down the bits of fish.

Another guide was leading a party through the square. Of a sudden the same Hispanic girl detached herself from the group and headed towards us, eyeing Alon's badge which proclaimed his proficiency in English, German, and Yiddish.

'Excuse me, are you a guide?' American accent, but second language from the sound of it.

'Yes,' he conceded, 'but I am already hired.'

'Please tell me just one thing—can you say where the Black Wall is?'

If this was the first I ever heard of the Black Wall, likewise for Alon!

'I do not know any Black Wall.'

'You must!'

Alon shook his head. He looked away. Distractedly the woman hurried to catch up with her party.

'What was she?' asked Mrs Dimet.

'Some charismatic, perhaps.'

'What would the Black Wall be?' I asked.

'I have no idea. Maybe she is confusing with the Kaaba in Mecca.' He pondered. 'In Arabic black also means wise. A wise wall? Maybe she means the Western, ah, the Wailing Wall. We guides need to be careful of such people. This city fosters frenzy in some visitors.'

At that moment an unmistakable King David ambled by, colourfully robed and crowned and carrying a little harp.

'Is he a madman too?' whispered Mrs Dimet.

'No, he is an Australian. He poses for photos. He has been here for years.'

After a tour of the Citadel, Alon drove us to a high promenade from which we could at least gaze from a distance at the golden Dome of the Rock and the Mount of Olives cluttered with gravestones. The sun baked the earth and white buildings as we drank from our water bottles. Next came a drive to the Yad Vashem Holocaust shrine where Mrs Dimet wept while the simulated stars of the universe twinkled in subterranean darkness, each the soul of a Nazi victim, and a recorded voice endlessly intoned the names of dead children.

The Hispanic Woman's wall might be no more than a few painted stones in the Old City, currently obscured by a poster concerning a different geno-cide, the Armenian one. So much here was exalted by words and names when the reality was much smaller, the River Jordan for instance being more like a big ditch, according to Alon.

As I sat nursing a beer on the terrace of the YMCA hotel that evening, the same woman appeared—so she was staying here too. Spying me, she came over.

'Excuse me, you were with the guide who would not answer me because I had not hired him. After I went, what did he tell you?'

'Why don't you sit down?'

She did so.

How beautiful she was. I chose my words carefully.

'He said he didn't know any Black Wall. That black means wise in Arabic. Maybe the Black Wall is a wall of wisdom.'

'Yes! It is there in the Old City. I know.'

I introduced myself.

'I'm a poet,' I said. 'I came to Jerusalem to write a poem. There's so much light here, and so much darkness too.'

Her name was Isabella Santos. To confide in me, a sympathetic stranger, was a relief, and besides she was becoming desperate.

She was from Southern California and worked as a check-out operator in a supermarket. Hardly as wild and impetuous as I had imagined. She had always been thrifty. When her local church planned a pilgrimage to the Holy Land, at first she had no intention of spending her savings on this.

'Then I had dreams . . .'

Dreams of a city of gleaming stone, ramparts, gateways, towers, domes, churches and mosques and crowded markets, a city through which she would fly like a bird along alleyways crowded with robed monks and ringletted black-clad Jews and brightly-dressed Bedouin women, and always she would come at last, alone by now, to a seamless wall of glossy basalt or jet in which she would see herself outlined thinly in silvery light as if her faintly reflected body was a doorway. She would press against her reflection, face to face and palm to palm, till the door would yield, and although the wall held on to her she would glimpse what lay in the looming shadowy vastness beyond.

'I did not tell anyone because they might not have brought me. I thought I would find the Wall easily because it called me. But now I fear it only appears from time to time—and in different places, now here, now there. And we go to Bethlehem tomorrow, then to the Dead Sea, and afterwards we are flying back.'

'What does lie beyond the Wall, Miss Santos?'

'Strange beings. Glittering beings. They wait. It is as if that gloom holds many checker boards, transparent, one above another like floors of a building all of dark glass.'

I itched to make notes. *The Dream of Isabella Santos*, a narrative poem by Philip Wilson.

'I cannot tell the size of the beings.'

'Why are they in darkness?'

'Are they in hell, do you mean? They seem wonderful, but strange. I name one the Sphinx-Angel and another the Centaur-Angel. They are different from anything I know. I feel there is power in them, and knowledge waiting for me.'

I sipped some beer. 'Why do you think you in particular saw these visions?'

I thought she might not tell me, but then words spilled from her.

'My grandmother, she was a *bruja*. Do you understand?'

Witch, sorceress, wise woman. Maybe the grandmother chewed peyote in some Mexican village.

'When she died, my parents came to California. They did not want to remember such things. My mother is normal and Catholic.'

Some sort of gift, or curse, had skipped a generation. Definitely not your average John the Baptist delusion. How I conjured with it.

'After I saw pictures of Jerusalem in the brochures our priest handed out, I dreamt. I did not invite the dreams! If I dream tonight—when I was younger I walked in my sleep. Maybe I will walk to the Black Wall. I am so close here. If you see me, will you follow?'

It was only fifteen minutes on foot to the Old City, down and along and steeply upward, but I could hardly imagine a sleepwalker undertaking that journey. Did she imagine that I would sit out here half the night in case she drifted out of the front door of the YMCA in a trance?

I proposed, 'Why don't you and I go up to the Old City right now and look around? If no one will miss you, and so long as we steer clear of the Arab Quarter.'

'Oh *will you?*'

It was as if I had released her from confinement. Despite her obsession she must have been scared to set out on her own while wide awake. The Old City practically closed up at sundown, and Alon had mentioned that women on their own could be harassed by both Arabs and Jews. I too felt a bit wary.

We should both have fetched warmer clothing, but someone from her group might detain her and the moment might pass. If we walked briskly...

We were in the Jewish Quarter in a tree-graced square which I recognized from the tour that same morning. A stone archway to one side was all that remained of a grand synagogue destroyed during fighting in 1948. What was the name? Ah yes, *Hurva*, Hebrew word for ruins. In the 18th Century a rabbi and immigrants from Poland had built the original edifice but creditors enraged at unpaid debts burned it down—to be splendidly rebuilt the following century. A place of ruins twice over. Stars were bright but there was no moon. I was shivering, as was Miss Santos but she did not care about the chilliness.

'I feel it! It's near!' She stared around then pointed towards the ruin. A broad flight of steps led up to a wall terrace fronting the arch.

We hurried that way and mounted. I recalled information boards inside, but those were barely visible now. Earlier that day, rough stones all around. Tonight, faintly starlit at the back of the emptiness: a wall so black and sheer and smooth.

'Yes, yes . . . !'

As we advanced, a silvery silhouette appeared—of a person. Isabella Santos had no doubts as to who it represented. She ran to it.

How could a woman fuse with a wall and become semi-transparent! That is what happened. Vaguely I could see through her into a great gulf where figures were arrayed into the distance and above and beneath, just as she had told me—otherwise I would scarcely have known what I was viewing. Since the view was still unclear I pressed forward—and the door, I mean *she*, Isabella, Miss Santos, opened.

Crying out, and possessed of full solidity again, she drifted away from her silhouette, arms flailing, afloat in that domain, receding slowly like an astronaut in space whose tether has parted. I staggered back momentarily in case I might follow her.

The figures I could see on those glassy planes were bizarre chimerae, minglings of man or angel and beast—biding their time, motionless like pieces in a game, passive yet potent. This was awesome! No gravity existed in that space beyond, but Miss Santos could certainly breathe, for again she shrieked, flapping and kicking in an effort to swim or fly backward, all the while drifting further.

'Isabella!' I shouted, and her head jerked. The sound of my voice may well have awakened the pieces. A sudden flurry of activity: some of the shining beings traded spaces, up, down, across. All seemed to have come to life.

A smiling, Buddha-like, toad-being opened its mouth. Out flicked a tongue, unrolling like a scroll of seemingly endless length, towards her, towards her. Surely by now the creature must have unrolled the whole of its insides! The end of the tongue wrapped around her waist and reeled her in as she screamed.

A beautiful winged female with glorious nude breasts, but whose body below the waist was more whirlwind than flesh, reached out. Her arm stretched incredibly, unreeling like a cable, until she snared Isabella by the elbow. A radiant, kingly Eagle-Man kicked out his own leg like a Thai boxer—this too elongated enormously till its clawed foot caught hold of Isabella at the knee.

The three beings tore Isabella apart.

Blood sprayed and trailed in clouds as each creature pulled part of her towards its personal space.

In horror and terror I sprang back. I was staring at an empty silhouette like the chalk outline of a murder victim on a floor or pavement after the body has been removed. Already the silhouette was shrinking until it sealed itself, and there was only the Black Wall, and moments later the Wall became merely the rough shell-wall of the ruined synagogue.

Wracked by shock and by shivers, I stumbled through the almost deserted maze of streets. If I had not pushed . . . but Isabella had *wanted* to enter the domain of the beings—no, that was no excuse!

I had seen something so abominable and so amazing. Did Sourdeval or the Sufi or the Rabbi see any such activity on the part of the beings? I might well be the only living witness on Earth. And as to witnesses, had anyone seen me leave the garden of the YMCA Hotel together with Isabella?

How could I sleep that night? Back in the sanctuary of my room I must have drifted off at last, slumped in a chair fully dressed, for the next thing I knew bright sunlight was behind the curtain and it was 8.30 in the morning.

For a moment I was totally disoriented, then nightmare washed over me like a choking, icy wave—only it was not nightmare but reality, a different and unsuspected reality. A while later from my window I saw a couple of peak-capped men in navy blue uniforms—policemen—striding towards the hotel entrance. Isabella's group leader must already have reported her disappearance. She had no excuse to be absent; the group needed to leave for Bethlehem.

I could not speak to the police—I could tell them nothing. They would arrest me on suspicion of having murdered Isabella and hidden her body. At best I would be sent off to the psychiatric hospital specialising in religious crazies. Reason had fled! What I knew now was so astounding and confounding. At the same time I had almost anticipated what had occurred—had I not mused that Jerusalem, this axis of the world, ought to contain hidden dimensions?

Not such as I saw, inhabited by creatures who tore a person apart! As part of some *game* beyond my comprehension.

I confess to a cowardly sense of relief when no one accosted me and accused me of being with Isabella the night before, and when I saw her party complete with luggage boarding a bus. I supposed they had no choice but to continue without her. What would the police do? Check morgues and hospitals, liaise with the American embassy, file a missing person report?

Surely poor Isabella from Southern California couldn't be the only one who had sensed the Black Wall from afar. There must be others. Devotees, explorers of this mystery must exist, and where else but in Jerusalem, unless they had been dragged to their deaths? I dared not go back to Ruin Square yet, even by daylight.

What I did instead was phone the *Jerusalem Post* to place a boxed advertisement in the Classifieds section: Black Wall, Centaur, Buddha-Toad—How Much Do You Know? Please Urgently Contact, hotel phone number etc.

And I added a bit of verse that welled up in me:

Bright, so bright,
Yet a wall of darkness,
A curtain of night,
Is in Old Jerusalem.

I killed time by visiting the Israel Museum and the Rockefeller Museum and such.

Next morning my ad looked weirdly eye-catching amongst mundane stuff about cars and home-helps and apartments. The paper contained a missing person story, but the person in question was an Israeli soldier thought to have been kidnapped. People going absent from religious groups might not be uncommon even if the police did release the news.

I did return to the Old City, to wander its alleys in the heat and arrive eventually at Hurva Square, to all appearances a safe enough place to be. Plenty of people were about. Snack bars and cafés were open. In the ruins of the synagogue a party of French teenagers were touring the illustrated information boards, their teacher a gaunt philosophical man in a thin black suit. The far wall looked utterly normal. I ate lunch at a kosher restaurant with a great view from its terrace of the Dome of the Rock, out of bounds, as out of bounds right now as the Black Wall.

When I got back to the hotel three messages awaited me, consisting of numbers to call. I retired to the privacy of my room to dial out.

A man's voice invited me to join a Multi-Faith Religious Poetry Circle. A woman declared that she worked for the intelligence service as a code analyst and wanted to know what cypher I was using—I presumed she was cuckoo. However, the third person I called, a man with a Central European accent, said to me, 'The Black Wall can appear in different places.'

'Where I saw it was in the ruins of Hurva Synagogue.'

An intake of breath. 'You saw it yourself? Was that by chance?'

'No, it was not by chance.'

'We must meet. Where are you?'

The middle-aged man who approached me on the terrace of the YMCA Hotel, black satchel over his shoulder, was burly, bald, and sun-bronzed. He wore jeans, a blue open-necked shirt, and a lightweight dark blue jacket. His name was Adam Jakubowski, a Pole, an archaeologist. I explained why I was in Israel.

'I have seen the Wall *once* in many years,' he said quietly. 'You sought it and you actually found it? How did you know?'

I must confide in this man, or else I would get nowhere.

'Will you be very discreet?'

'What is discreet?'

'Private.'

'Oh I will be very private, Mr Wilson!'

He digested what I related, and then he told me about the Knights Templar and Sourdeval. The collector to whom Sourdeval's letter was sold was Adam Jakubowski's great-uncle.

'Hebrew, he understood. He paid scholars to translate documents from Latin and Arabic. The Black Wall became a fascination to him, so he hired an agent in Jerusalem who found a few modern witnesses who were very frightened by their experience. My great-uncle visited here several times. On the last occasion he did see the wall and what was beyond. By then, so he said, an affinity had grown.'

An affinity. Such as had led Isabella Santos here.

Had Jakubowski and his great-uncle also given rise to silhouette-doorways in the peculiar substance of the Wall?

Indeed. Jakubowski proceeded to speak about shadows. And *shadow-traders*. To give strength and stability to a building in the past animals or even people would be sacrificed. An alternative was to lure a person to the site and to measure the shadow they cast—the person would die within a year. A shadow could even be trapped elsewhere and measured.

'Shadow-traders were people who would sell to architects the outlines of other people's shadows.'

In Jakubowski's opinion an analogy existed. What was cast upon the Wall, not by sunlight but by some emanation from within the Wall itself, was akin to a shadow—into which the spectator could fit himself. At that point, the spectator was poised precariously between our reality and that other reality.

'The Black Wall may have been able to appear ever since Solomon built the original temple.'

'What *game* are the beings playing?'

'A game of power, I think. Power must be a big part of it.'

'And what *are* they?'

Jakubowski spread his hands.

'Your guess is as good as mine.'

About a hundred people in Israel and in other countries knew of the Black Wall. A brotherhood existed, dedicated to discovering its secrets, a sort of modern Knights Templar. They actually called themselves the KBW, Knights of the Black Wall. The title had been Great-Uncle's idea. Was this pretentious, or profoundly thrilling and appropriate? 'Are there any sisters in this brotherhood?'

'Oh, a few. Your Miss Santos would have belonged, had she not . . .' He grimaced. 'Thanks to her and your report we have vital new data. You belong with us, Mr Wilson. This brings access to greater understanding—certain responsibilities too.'

'Responsibilities?'

'You yourself mentioned secrecy. Silence.'

To find my theme in Jerusalem, just as I'd hoped, and to be censored? Never to write or to publish a great breakthrough poem on the subject?

Obviously this was a trivial, selfish thought in the circumstances, compared with the enormous implications—but still I felt a hackle rise.

'I don't recall applying to join your KGB.'

'KBW. Your advertisement was an application, wasn't it? Or else, why am I here? I hate to sound any dark note at this early stage in our relationship.' He broke off and smiled ruefully. 'I'm no diplomat, am I? Let me show you something.'

After a glance around, he burrowed in his satchel. Producing a flip-folder of photos, he displayed one. I gasped. *For the photo showed darkness, faint planes, distant glittering denizens.* A camera had captured part of the domain behind the Black Wall!

'Who took this?'

'Myself. Quite recently.' He tapped the satchel. 'For a long time I carried a camera in expectation. Hard proof, Mr Wilson, hard proof!'

The photo was certainly proof to me, although an uninformed viewer would have had difficulty interpreting what he saw.

'I have spoken of affinity,' Jakubowski went on. 'An image is an affinity, and here we hold it in our hand.'

'Do you mean this photo can serve as'—I imagined a security swipe-card—'a sort of access?'

He showed me another photo, a very grainy but closer-up image of the Sphinx-being.

'This is an enlargement enhanced by computer. I'm not speaking lightly when I say that greater understanding is possible. Maybe even,' and he lowered his voice, 'a kind of expedition. Though in view of the fate of Miss Santos—'

Quite.

KGB, KBW... I recalled the crazy woman on the phone.

'What does the Israeli security service know about the Black Wall?'

'We have two members high in Shabak and one in Mossad, but the organisations themselves do not know.'

I told him about the woman.

'She is certainly not one of us, but I would appreciate the phone number.'

So that she could be checked out, just in case she knew anything?

'So you do have influence with this Shab, what is it?'

'Shabak. You might know of it as Shin Beth.'

I shook my head.

Turned out that Shabak was internal security, and Mossad, as most people know, was external intelligence. I began to sense that discretion about the Black Wall might be enforceable, not simply a request but a requirement.

Jakubowski must have read my expression.

'I don't want to use heavy words, but this business is momentous, maybe of terrible importance to the world, perhaps to all human life, do you see?'

I nodded. What I wanted was to see was more of the photographs, but here was too public.

'How long can you stay in Israel, Mr Wilson?'

'I don't have any commitments till early January but my entry permit is just for a month.'

'If you give me the bit of paper, that can be altered easily. I would like you to stay here as long as possible. Not, I hasten to add, at your own expense— in addition to my Great-Uncle's endowment funds come from some of our members who can well afford it. Do you like to remain in a hotel or would you prefer a small apartment? We will arrange a social life for you. And tours, visits. You will not just be twiddling your thumbs.'

'Sounds fine to me.'

An apartment? I wanted a break from domestic chores, shopping and cleaning et cetera. My hotel room had a desk, a view of the frontage, decent enough lighting. It would do. Probably more expensive than an apartment, come to think of it.

So began my life in Israel. I suppose it was not *fully* life in Israel since I never needed to shop for groceries, say, in the kaleidoscopic cornucopia of the Mahane Yehuda Market. A bomb went off there, killing an old woman and injuring about twenty people.

Our more senior Shabak member was tubby, bearded Avner Dotan. Speciality, electronic intelligence. He tapped in to the police investigation of the disappearance of Isabella Santos and the police were informally discouraged from proceeding any further. I suppose this also served to assure the KBW that Isabella was not a figment of my poet's imagination. We held a brief memorial service for her in the Hurva ruins, conducted by a New Yorker, Rabbi Ben Feinstein. My new acquaintances comprised a broad spectrum of people, however we numbered no one who was ordained in any Christian denomination. Rabbi Ben was so much reformed that he could embrace in his prayers a Roman Catholic grand-daughter of a Mexican witch. I still felt so guilty about Isabella's hideous death. We were honouring a victim of the Wall—might there be more victims?

Cut to a meeting at the home of Avner Dotan afterwards. We were considering several angles of approach—camera angles, you might almost say. Blow-ups of the entities lay on the floor.

'Maybe,' said Dotan, 'the three beings did not wish to destroy Isabella Santos, but each wanted to possess her to gain a point in the game, whatever it is.'

'Comes to the same bloody thing!' exclaimed Jock Fraser.

I could not make Fraser out. The beefy, sweaty Scotsman claimed to the Laird of some small Inner Hebridean island. He had been educated in Glasgow at a school supposedly of considerable pedigree, so he said, which had been engulfed early in the 20th Century by the spread of the Gorbals slum district—implausible, or true? A life of some adventure as an engineer for oil companies had taken him to Nigeria, Indonesia, and other hot parts of the world. He was certainly a romancer in the literal sense: while sweating in Indonesia he had produced a couple of love novels published under a female pseudonym—and he had also published privately a history of the Freemasons, amongst whom supposedly he held high rank. The Masons, of course, were heirs to the tradition of the Knights Templar. Three years earlier, during a stopover to visit the site of Solomon's Temple, and while a wee bit tipsy, as Fraser freely admitted—the doors, or hinges, of perception well oiled—he had witnessed the Black Wall. To investigate further, he managed to land a job at an oil refinery in Haifa. A Masonic handshake at a British Embassy reception advanced Fraser's quest, the shaker being the other Scot in our group, Hamish Mackintosh—don't the Scots get every-where.

Tall, muscular, going on fifty, hair beginning to silver, Mackintosh was head of security at our embassy in Tel Aviv. An ex-military officer and mountaineer, his work brought him into liaison with Avner Dotan. His own epiphany as regards the Wall . . . ah never mind that, and never mind about the life stories of my other fellow investigators, Israeli, Armenian, Arab, except to mention Tomaso Pascoli who lived in Rome. A shipping magnate, Pascoli was a Knight of the Vatican, and I gathered that he was a conduit from our group to a highly placed Cardinal who might be a future Pope.

Let us assume that the entities had been jockeying for position for a thou-sand or for several thousand years—though how did they measure time? Did they just sit inertly like some toad or spider awaiting a movement or vibration or some sudden shift by one of their fellow denizens?

'It's possible,' ventured Mackintosh, 'that some of the beings are relatively benevolent, or at least not baneful.' He gestured at the big grainy enlargements arrayed on the floor. 'If we could only communicate with one of them—get on its wavelength. Maybe by using the affinity of a photograph? Like sending a signal tuned to one receiver only.'

'Suppose,' said Avner, 'we put up one of the images as a poster somewhere in the Old City where we know the Black Wall has already appeared? I mean a very temporary poster!'

'We might release who knows what,' warned Rabbi Feinstein.

Mackintosh nodded. 'First we should use the general view and see if we can summon the Black Wall itself. This in itself would be a great breakthrough.'

Where more suitable than in the shell of that same synagogue? Hurva Square might be the heart of the Jewish Quarter, but it wouldn't be busy at three in the morning and access to the ruin was easily controllable. Avner let it be known to the police and the Defence Force that Shabak would be carrying out an 'operation', so patrols would not interfere. He also argued that we ought to go armed in case of any eruption from the Black Wall. Drawing weapons from Shabak's armoury would not be a sensible idea, but back in the days when people who killed terrorists in action were allowed to keep their Kalashnikovs Avner's father had acquired one, while his colleague Avraham's younger brother was home on leave along with his Galil assault rifle.

A few nights later, six of us gathered in the ruin by starlight. Myself, because of my obvious affinity with this site. Ben, bearing the poster—if anything bad occurred, maybe a Rabbi could cope. Jock had volunteered to be movie cameraman, at which he apparently had some experience. Adam was ready with his still camera. Avner and Avraham brought the two automatic rifles hidden in long sports bags. Three others Israelis kept watch outside. If any passers-by became curious, we were a TV crew.

Murmuring to himself, Ben advanced and sticky-tacked to the mundane stones the blow-up of the vista beyond the Black Wall. Scarcely had he stepped back than an ebon gloss began to spread out around the poster as if glossy black ink was flowing. In less than half a minute one wall of the synagogue might have consisted of smooth jet or basalt.

Cautiously Ben moved closer again and pulled the poster away.

Where it had been was a rectangular opening, upon a dark yawning gulf faintly lit by the serried planes on which the entities perched or stood or sat. There they were: immobile, potently aglow.

Jock inched forward, filming. At his side, Adam captured the astonishing sight with the avidity of a paparazzo who has sneaked up upon a secret gathering of celebrities—although where was his motorbike for a quick escape? Our two defenders pointed their guns. Eight hundred and fifty years ago, sweating despite the nocturnal chill, might Sourdeval have unsheathed his broadsword?

In the domain beyond, came a stirring as of attention aroused.

'That's enough for now!' cried Ben. Like some firefighter with a protective shield, he held the poster reversed now. Hands spread wide, he covered the opening. How tensely he stood, as if something might stab through the flimsy barrier—but the ebon gloss swiftly shrank like oil draining away into a sump. When he lifted the poster aside, all was ordinary stonework.

Adam's flat, this time. A video-tape ran on his TV. Many more enlarged photos lay on the floor.

Avner said, 'I think what we see are not the entities themselves but *representations* of them—each a sort of icon standing in for them. When something occurs, each animates its icon. The entities take over and move and function.'

'If that's so,' said Ben, 'and the real entities are some place else, a blow-up photo of the icon might give access, the way a computer icon launches a programme.'

Definitely we were moving closer to mounting an expedition.

Which of the icons suggested, if not benevolence, at least tolerance and wisdom? Which of us would become the astralnaut who would venture into such a region?

I had watched Isabella being ripped apart in that other zone. Might such dismemberment perhaps be symbolic? Could the bits be bought back together again? I thought of Orpheus. He ventured into an underworld to rescue his wife, but alas she glanced back. God-possessed women then tore Orpheus to pieces and the Muses gathered up his parts, but alas could not rejoin them. What if they had succeeded? *Orpheus in Jerusalem*, a poem by Philip Wilson . . . Damn this artistic egotism that reared its head. Damn, too, the idea of affinity—of myself linked to Isabella who had already been sucked into that other region, *propelled* by me.

Might my new acquaintances regard me as expendable, a Johnny-come-lately who had indeed brought them an invaluable key, though purely by accident? Or were they honouring me with a great trust and responsibility?

Yes, I would volunteer. Yes, I would accept. How could an Orpheus refuse? Would Billy Blake have passed up a chance to visit the terrain of his visions? 'Mighty was the draught of Voidness to draw Existence in!' he had written. I had no family ties.

A full-length photo of me would be taken and enlarged so that by affinity I could be summoned back subsequently through my image to Jerusalem and normality—perhaps!— and to the extent that Jerusalem was any normal place. A Palestinian armed with a knife had gone berserk in the Christian Quarter, slashing some nuns. I would carry a camera and a pistol fitted with a silencer—I would receive a quick course in the use of a gun—and high-calorie food and bottled water in my knapsack and a tiny tape-recorder and a notebook in case the energy of our target entity might harm anything electronic. I would be well equipped, although we were improvising wildly.

We settled upon the being whom Isabella had named the Centaur-Angel. A burly-chested figure with a craggy, serious face. His buttocks swelled out into a secondary, shorter, hairy set of rear legs. From his shoulders sprouted diaphanous fairy-wings—a sign of sensitivity at odds with the rest of his frame? He seemed like a knight in chess—affinity, therefore, with a Knight of the Black Wall?

Tomaso Pascoli flew in from Rome, a short trim dapper man with thinning dark hair, observer on behalf of the Vatican, doubtless. Together with him and the three As, Adam, Avner, and Avraham, and Jock and Ben and two lookouts, I went to the Hurva ruins again by night. A gibbous moon hung in the sky.

'You are a brave man,' Signor Pascoli said to me, mopping his brow with an elegant handkerchief, cool though the night was. 'And you even have an imagination—a Dante of today! Imaginative people do not always run such risks.'

'Not quite in Dante's league.'

'Ah, modesty too.'

And guilt. And ambition.

Jock set down the video camera and produced a hip flask.

'Ten year old single malt—liquor of the Gods.'

'I don't think I ought to imbibe just now.' I would have dearly loved to.

'I think I will.' Jock uncapped and took a swig then he thrust the flask at me. 'Maybe a wee gift for the Gods wouldn't come amiss.'

Who could say? I added the flask to my knapsack.

Jock gripped me by the elbow in an awkward show of wordless male affection.

Two of the As pointed Kalashnikov and Galil while the third stuck a poster of the Centaur-Angel to the stone wall. In two hours' time, earthly time at least, he would use the reversed poster of me to call me home, perhaps. On either side shiny darkness began to spread. *Was I utterly insane?* As Adam pulled the poster from the Wall like a bandage, light shone forth— oh, that's just our floodlight for the documentary!

Mighty was the draught that pulled me, and I was squinting at a sun-drenched stony desert landscape all about me, sand and pebbles underfoot. I had passed through involuntarily. Behind me was no sign of a doorway leading back. Could the others still see me? I raised my hand in a salute, then I shaded my eyes—we had not thought to include sunglasses. The region of the icons was gloomy and I departed by night, yet here was the full blaze of day. Not too far away a mesa thrust upward, its broken precipitous sides wearing long skirts of scree. On its table-top was an edifice white as snow, twin tall towers rising from a dome, the base hidden from sight. But for the presence of that building I might have been transported to Masada, the rock-fortress in the Judean desert where the Romans besieged the Zealots. All else in this wilderness was tawny, dirty yellow, brown, or grey in the shadows cast by the blinding sun.

Whence the white marble of the building upon the mesa? Materials must have been transported from far away and carried laboriously upward. Such an undertaking, such ostentation. I recalled that King Herod had built a luxurious palace on an upper side of Masada with a view over stricken, contorted desolation, to prove that he could do so, showing off. Herod's three-tiered palace had been tucked in, cantilevered almost.

My sweat was drying as soon as produced. If only I had brought a sun-hat. Such protection never entered our calculations. Delving in my knapsack for one of the bottles of water, I swigged. In the shimmery distance I spotted a cluster of white shapes. An encampment?

Sharp eyes must have spied me too. Scarcely had I begun to foot-slog through the stony desert than a movement resolved itself into several creatures heading my way.

Those must be horses or camels, white-clad riders on their backs—three or four of them. Yes, four.

As the mounts drew nearer they proved to be neither horses nor camels but other beasts entirely. Quadrupeds, with long heads and silky hair and a lolloping gait and scaly tails like those of giant rats. These were no members of the animal kingdom that I knew.

The four riders' robes were all-enveloping—only hands and eyes showed. Three dismounted. Their hands were brown. Creamy eyes, light brown pupils. And the pupils of the mounts themselves were rectangular, goatish. Orange rheum leaked from the beasts' tear ducts. Translucent membranes blinked dust away.

The mounted leader addressed me and I couldn't understand a word. Hopefully I said, 'Shalom', and 'Salaam', and I pointed up the mesa at the gleaming building, my goal, I supposed.

'I am an Englishman,' I added, and felt absurd. 'I came here because of the Centaur-Angel.'

Incomprehensible discussion followed, then two of the people gripped me loosely while their companion relieved me of my knapsack and emptied it upon the ground. Kneeling, he sorted. The pistol, he turned this way and that, ending by peering down the barrel with no apparent understanding; thankfully the safety was on. He opened a bottle and raised a flap of cloth to sniff, exposing beardless brown chin, slim mouth, thin nose. After some fumble he unscrewed Jock's hipflask. This time his nostrils flared. Screwing tight, he spoke rapidly. Next he picked my pockets, then off came my wristwatch for the leader to inspect. Like a bangle it went on to that man's wrist. I was being robbed—next thing, out would come a knife.

But no. My gear went into a saddlebag, and as soon as my searcher remounted I was invited, prodded, hoisted on to the beast behind him. I clung to a backward-jutting bit of saddle, myself bareback, thighs and knees splayed, feet dangling. How I hoped these people had some code of hospitality.

At the encampment I saw some unveiled thin brown faces, undoubtedly human yet at the same time subtly *other*. A different sideshoot of the evolutionary tree? How else to account for the mounts, and for a pack of sinewy feline creatures the size of lurchers that wandered around the camp?

Lurching, myself, after that ride, I was led into the largest tent. Open flaps admitted light and air. Richly woven carpets lay upon dirt. Dominating the main room of the tent was a formidable idol in white marble of the Centaur-Angel. Strapped upon its rump was a leather saddle, almost as if the statue was a plaything for the young tribal prince who sat crossed-legged beside it on a tasselled cushion—presumably the slight person was a princeling since a coronet of gold or brass held his head-veil in place. The principal difference between statue and icon was that the head of the statue was like that of the mount I had ridden on. Another cushion was occupied by a veiled figure dressed in black and seemingly elderly—the hands and the skin around the eyes were deeply wrinkled.

Wooden cabinets, carved chests, low tables. Drapes divided off areas I couldn't peer into. I heard the whispers and giggles of women.

My escort reported, then my possessions were presented to Blackrobe, who passed items to the young prince, including my gun. This ended up between the forefeet of the statue, as did Jock's flask of single malt and my watch and camera and flashlight. Offerings to the idol?

The moment the young prince addressed me I knew from the voice that this was no lad but a lass. So: a priestess of the Centaur cult, perhaps? I smiled, I shrugged, I gestured. She pointed at me, then she jerked her finger towards the hindquarters of the statue. Speedily I was hustled, and manoeuvred on to the saddle. Hands pulled my own hands around the torso, lacing my fingers at the front. I was astride the marble effigy, clinging on. Bizarre, bizarre. Was this a way of judging me, or honouring me, or what?

Blackrobe produced a little silver flute from within his or her garment and proceeded to blow a series of notes, quite like the dialling tones of a phone—

Upon my artificial mount I was instantly elsewhere. Sunlight poured through glassless windows into a hall floored with amber slabs each prominently incised in silver with a symbol. Letters of an unknown alphabet, signs of an unfamiliar zodiac? My gun and other kit had tumbled on to an adjacent slab.

Ponderous movement! Fifteen metres or so away, the Centaur-Angel was in the room as if it had come into existence at this very moment. An alert presence, it was bigger than the statue by a half again. Huge, horselike head, metallic and angular—was that a mask covering a more human-like countenance? The eyes were black glassy pools. Silver chainmail covered its quadruped body. Black boots on its four feet, black gloves on its two hands. Its wings were spread. I cowered behind the marble torso as it advanced slowly, snorting. I felt I was confronting a mighty alien.

The muzzle moved and the lips—of that flexible mask!—stretched without parting. A rumbly voice emerged.

I cried, 'I don't understand you!'

'Under-stand,' it echoed. The lips moved as if it were chewing the word, digesting it. By now the entity was looming over me. Wings wafted, the draft ruffling my hair. An arm stretched down—as limbs had elongated to grip Isabella Santos—and it picked up my gun, inspected it, discarded it. My camera received similar casual scrutiny.

'I understand now,' it announced. 'How did you come here?'

It spoke English as though it had just accessed some great depository of languages.

I suppose I gaped.

Impatiently, 'Is this your tongue?'

'Yes, yes.'

'*How did you come here?*'

I told of Isabella and the Wall, of affinities and photographs—and the Centaur-Angel retrieved my camera for a closer look. It asked questions, which I answered. Finally I begged to know, 'What are you? Where is this?'

As soon became obvious, I was of use to the Centaur-Angel, so it condescended to inform me of certain things . . .

Presently I was beginning to understand that the existence of our world gave rise to reflections in what I suppose you might call the multiverse. To echoes, to back-up files, dare I say?

A cosmos recorded information within its own fabric, perhaps in those rolled-up tiny other dimensions which physicists theorise about. A kind of cascade occurred, from reality into lesser, miniature ghost-realities which assumed a contingent existence—versions of the great original, variations on a lesser scale. Those domains were like dreams compared with our own material reality.

Matter is made of bound-up energy, but ours is *more bound*—the ice upon the sea, the icing on the cake, the crust upon the pie. Hence, perhaps, the triumph of science and technology in our world, and even of great religions, firm bundles of beliefs.

Wizardry pervaded those bubble-worlds, the power of will and symbols, and in each realm energy gravitated or pooled into a ruling power, a presiding angel or demon. Most of these beings were ambitious and assertive and engaged in a power-play of offence and defence. Their goal—which they could manoeuvre towards and interact with to a minor degree—was the primary reality of our own world. How the domain-demons yearned to escape their restrictions and achieve immensity...

'You shall become my channel,' the Centaur-Angel said to me graciously, as if bestowing a boon. 'My link. A vent for my triumphal eruption.'

Its eruption into our world! It was not the regular human world that unrolled from Jerusalem but this realm and a hundred others too—rolled up in themselves, awaiting. I had caused a bridge to form between our reality and this other reality. Small wonder that rival Angels had torn my predecessor Isabella apart in their eagerness to acquire her.

'Far better myself, than certain others!' declared the Angel. 'You are fortunate, Philip-Wilson. The service of your kind will not be severe, scarcely even slavery.' It stamped its feet in a solemn little dance.

I imagined an outburst of light and power from the Black Wall, bearing forth the Centaur-Angel to bestride Jerusalem like one of the horsemen of the Apocalypse, steed and rider comprised in one being, feeding upon the energies of our universe. This madness must not happen. The doorway must be closed, affinity erased.

'Your reward will be great,' said the Angel.

Demons must have promised likewise in the past—to Doctor Faustus and whoever else. These partial breakthroughs faltered and failed. Never before had a person mounted a technological intrusion. How might human beings be constrained to serve this Angel? Us, with our nuclear and other weapons?

'Reigning over your world, I shall gain control of the other realms too.'

Would Armageddon be unleashed?

I slid backwards, sore-bummed, off the saddle. The gun lay disregarded. Ultimately perhaps the Angel was stupid, or tunnel-visioned. Quickly I picked up the pistol, thumbed the safety off, and fired, fired, fired.

As I emerged into the ruined Hurva Synagogue I was still shooting. 'It's me, Philip!'—as Avner and Avraham aimed, and someone uttered a shriek: Pascoli, had I hit him? No, he was still standing, startled. Illumination from the doorway dimmed as I swung around to see that desert vista puckering in on itself and the oily gloss of the Black Wall draining rapidly as if into a sink-hole, the old stones reappearing. None of my comrades could have seen the Angel within his palace. I think that my first gunshot had ruptured the membrane dividing me from my place of origin. Whether I had injured the Angel in his chainmail at the same time I had no idea, but the entity certainly wasn't pursuing me. In case the two As fancied I might be a terrorist I threw the gun down. The moon was high, casting its own white light.

'Bloody hell, what were you shooting at?' demanded Jock.

'At the Centaur-Angel.'

Adam retrieved the gun and then—'Hush!'—he was listening to the night in case Pascoli's cry brought army and police swarming. Thank goodness for the gun's silencer. By now the Black Wall had vanished utterly.

As soon as we had left the synagogue we decamped separately through moonlit lanes, keeping to the shadows. Half an hour later we were all reunited in Avner's flat and I talked at last, lubricated by orange juice while he and Pascoli both recorded me.

After I finished, Rabbi Ben said, 'We should not be trying to open the Wall but to keep it closed.'

'And to keep all knowledge of it closed,' added Pascoli.

'Bear in mind,' said Adam, 'we are relying on the testimony of one person, a person of creative imagination.'

I had lost my camera and recorder—much use that I had made of either.

'Philip's experience might be subjective. Another person might have a different experience.'

'I believe him!' Jock sounded angry. 'You aren't seriously suggesting we mount another expedition?'

'Seems to me,' said Ben, 'we have enough evidence.'

'All deriving from Philip.'

'What's certain,' Avner said, 'is that we must never cede control of an inch of Jerusalem.' This was a very Israeli perspective upon such a cosmic matter.

As for writing a Blake-like epic about Jerusalem and Angels and Arma-geddon . . . what *other* great poem could I possibly contemplate, even if only for my own satisfaction, never to see publication? Any such ambition was now thwarted not only by the awesome truth but by fear that the creative concentration involved might form an affinity. What I produced could prove to be a fatal text.

The political situation was becoming hairy. Trained as martyrs, Pales-tinian kids were throwing stones at Defence Force soldiers and being shot. An Arab informer was executed by his own people. A rabbi was tortured and murdered and his synagogue burned down. Police stations in the Arab-administered areas were rocketed in reprisal.

Hamish Mackintosh drove me from the hotel to Lod Airport for an early morning flight.

'Time to get you out, old son. Bad security situation. A word to the wise: you will bear security in mind, won't you?'

I knew what security he meant. The domain-demons must stay behind the Wall and not be known about.

I felt like a Sourdeval being expelled from the Holy Land—except that the KBW would keep in touch with me fortnightly then monthly by way of encrypted e-mails to which I was expected to reply. Avner had prepared me for this. I even imagined Israeli intelligence agents checking on me periodi-cally without knowing exactly why, except that my activities or lack of them were of importance.

What a great downhill slalom, or shalom, ride this car journey was, ever downhill in great curves from the dizzy heights which I had ascended weeks earlier, as if we were unrolling towards the ends of the Earth, in my case towards one end of it, England. Where I thought I would be far removed.

How wrong I was.

A Speaker for the Wooden Sea

'WINTER IS THE ONLY PROPER TIME TO SAIL THE SEA,' THURIBLE Excelsior told me somewhat sternly, 'once all the leaves have died and blown on to land.'

We were atop the terracotta lighthouse at the centre of Haven Bay. Not absolutely atop; we were up on the wooden-railed observation deck. Higher above us, masked by its heatshield, rose the fusion torch from the ancient starship which throughout the Winter would serve as a beacon to navigators as well as providing lighting for the town.

And also casting deep dark shadows, no doubt.

Must have been quite a job hauling the torch so high using only wooden scaffolding and leaf-fibre ropes.

The Keeper of the Light was a tall, gaunt, wild-haired fellow with piercing blue eyes and a bushy blond beard. He wore a white robe of bleached fibre, pleats falling elegantly to his hard bark boots.

I gazed over homes of baked brick capped with glossy red tiles. Beyond the ochre warehouses and wharfs, and the long line of berthed vessels resting on their skids or wheels, sails all furled, was what these people chose to call the *Sea*—even though it was entirely composed of wood.

The dying foliage formed a vast carpet of yellow, orange, crimson, stretching to the horizon, and of course far beyond. Already the Fall winds had stripped many patches, exposing rumples and channels, those closer to shore visibly polished by centuries of sailing. The prevailing wind ruffled my hair and bore, like soaring birds and butterflies, leaves which had come loose. Soon the wind would strengthen and there would be a veritable storm of leaves passing by.

Out of sight to my perception even if I enhanced it, would be great swells and waves of wood much further away—standing waves, crests as high as hills, troughs as deep as valleys.

'In a ten-days,' continued Excelsior more amenably, 'I will light the beacon for the Festival of the Bare Sea. Then our ships can sail again.'

When the fusion torch was lit, rising heat would suck in air as fuel—now that the torch was on a planet it no longer needed to funnel sparse interstellar atoms magnetically in to itself. The self-sustaining output would run at perhaps quarter-power, like a tethered engine undergoing a test. I wondered whether a bribe to Excelsior might indeed help me. After all, the Keeper of the Light had not said that sailing early was absolutely forbidden. What sort of bribe? These people were so set in their ways.

In the west the local sun was descending at the end of another diminishing day. All the colours of the sea-leaves made the world seem upside-down as if a glorious sunset occurred not in the sky but below.

'Is there no exemption?' I asked.

'That would not be wise, Lustig Firefox. Aside from the risk of foliage-fouling or blind-wreck, the sea-worms are now mating before encysting themselves.'

In my brain the nanoputer Companion who translated his words for me and who moulded my own replies in the local lingo—she called herself Lill—glossed *blind-wreck* as a consequence of sailing without being able to see ahead clearly. As for *encysting*, I already knew that the marine wood-worms—ranging in size from that of a baby's arm to twenty-metre monsters—overwintered by coiling themselves up in holes they ate in the wooden sea and sealed with resinous amber slime, a secretion similar to the stuff that plugged behind them the long tubes they chewed. The excretion of shavings and dust plus worm-juices hardened quite quickly, restoring solidity to the burrowed bits of the sea.

Again I marvelled at this world. That the substances filling the tubes were richly edible to human beings, mother-lodes—or loads—of manna of subtle or pungent flavour depending on location. And that certain sea-leaves contained large amounts of a non-toxic analogue of the monoterpene, thujone, a narcotic structurally similar to tetrahydrocannabinol but far more potent . . .

This had seemed a fine time to arrive on Wormwood. As the leaves dried out, so did the thujone concentrate itself and mature. I needed to harvest enough sea-leaves before they all blew away to be processed by the land-worms.

Easy-peasy, you might say. Merely land the shuttle on the sea.

Up in orbit, come night, my wormship would soon be a tiny star speeding across the vast black velvet displaying many brighter, unmoving jewels. My ship was not, of course, wormlike as the worms of the wooden sea were—it simply opened wormholes between distant regions of space, so that I had stared at Haven Bay's fusion torch as at some heroic antique in a museum. Perhaps *simply* is not quite the right word!

How about merely?

Oh the trick of wormhole travel was relatively easy once we found out what it was. Isn't that the way with many discoveries? Here's what you do, fellow: you bang the flint on the stone and the spark makes fire, farewell to raw mammoth steaks forever. Ah, now you see the light—how did you not realize something so obvious for the last ten thousand years?

The trouble with knowledge nowadays is that there is almost too much of it in the hyperlibrary. Only after the final jump to Wormwood did my ship's brain discover that landing directly on the wooden sea is perilous. Apparently currents run through tendrils in the wood. Any substantial mass of metal descending upon that surface provoked an electromagnetic pulse fatal to sensitive electronics. I must set down on the 'land' and hire a wooden ship.

'It's really important to me to sail soon.' I repeated my earlier lie about my needing the leaves for scientific study at the Institute of Xenobotany on Mondevert.

Behold the leaves, yet I could hardly walk out from shore with a back-pack! (Nor did I much like the news about 'mating worms'.) Also, the particular leaves I needed were not necessarily close to shore. I might need to rely on local knowledge.

'Anyway, Lustig Firefox,' said the Keeper, 'the wind from the sea is strengthening daily. Only when the sea is bare does the wind moderate and shift.'

'Surely your ships can tack into head-winds,' I protested.

'Of course. Why should they do so, unnecessarily?'

Conceivably the currents in the wood somehow influenced wind patterns, ensuring that the leaves of Fall blew on to land and did not clot the sea.

Thurible Excelsior's people had come here to Wormwood six hundred years ago by the slow, deep-sleepy method. Remote spectroscopy indicated a breathable atmosphere and other life signs. Yet when the colonisers arrived they found their new world covered in solid wood—not vast forests as expected but a single, if varied, coat of lateral wood which had grown right around the world, save for half a dozen dirt-bowls the size of, say, France on Old Earth. Perhaps I should say dirt-bowels; those were where untold millennia of annually shed leaves had blown, collected, rotted, compacted.

A world-ocean of wood with swells and troughs just like a liquid sea, except for its density and immobility. And the worms, the worms. Worms in the wood—and smaller landworms which subsisted on dead leaves, speedily processing these into a sort of humus-loam. If I looked inland, where homes faded from view into a flat landscape, and if I enhanced my vision, did I detect a certain preliminary writhing as the smaller worms got to work on leaves that had already gusted to their graves? In another few days I would not personally wish to be out there, dancing about, trying to steal a pitiful harvest of air-borne leaves from the busy worms, even if I was permitted to.

When I say *loam*, do not imagine rich fertile soil—but rather the paste used in brickmaking; whence the material for all the homes and the wharfs and the lighthouse. Toxins in the loam inhibited the growth of any crops. Starvation had loomed for the first settlers until the discovery of the mother-lodes.

What kind of evolution could have given rise to this, as you might say, *single-minded* world of wood and worms and worthless soil? Wormwood may have been more richly various once, before the tyranny of the tree proliferated—using 'tree' in a very general sense. Buried hundreds of metres below the surface there might be evidence of a more ample antiquity. Undoubtedly roots of the world-wood that covered most of the surface cut their way deep down into rock, seeking out aquifers and mineral salts. How else did rain occur on Wormwood? Transpiration from the trillions of leaves of the wooden sea begat rain clouds during Spring and Summer, just as evaporation did from a regular ocean. Beware the flash-flood that would course through channels in the wooden sea and could pick up a ship and float it and dash it against a hard reef!

But Lustig, during the rainy season no ship can set sail on account of all the leaves.

True enough, Lill. No one could sail through thick foliage—and because foliage still remained, apparently I could not set sail!

Foliage, thankfully, without stems which would grow into saplings or branches. No such overgrowth here. Only leaves. Many containing lots of super-thujone.

Yesterday I had landed my shuttle on a scorched area near the edge of town marked by a tall red obelisk from the tip of which fluttered a hollow white tube which Lill identified as a windsock. This ancient device used at airports to indicate wind direction was irrelevant to spacecraft but evidently marked this place as a landing zone.

If the Wormwooders had ever used gliders to get around, I saw none here nowadays, and the only spacecraft in sight at the moment was a partly dismantled surface-to-orbit cargo ferry. Bearded fellows dressed in dingy overalls woven of thick fibre were cutting up bits of the hull, for other bearded fellows to push away on wooden hand-carts towards a long low brick building. This area seemed to me more like a scrapyard than spaceport. *They have no other access to metals*, Lill reminded me.

Quite. Even common metals were rare, which is why I had brought lots of ingots of copper, tin, aluminum to serve as cash.

In the distance I spied huge nets stretched between poles set here and there around the terrain. I also spied small figures (*enhance and fix with glittering eye*) who proved to be boys and girls scampering about in pairs, each couple equipped with a net with which they sought to ensnare leaves fluttering by. It seemed a jolly game, with a serious purpose.

The way that the leaves dipped then rose again made me think that they carried a small electrical charge, and that ionisation of the atmosphere was responsible for keeping leaves airborne longer than anyone might reasonable expect.

Basic tech level, the hyperlibrary said of Wormwood. Nevertheless, star-trade did take place.

My arrival brought most of the bearded wrecking gang over. Hair styles varied between long lank locks and the short chop. A couple of the men were holding what looked like saws with monomolecular blades. Those cut through steel like a wire through cheese. Prudently I switched on an external speaker and introduced myself: Lustig Firefox from the Institute of Xenobotany on Mondevert. Was it correct to park my shuttle here, et cetera?

Lill, already versed in the argot of Wormwood, did the talking. I proposed and she disposed my vocal chords and tongue and lips so that I uttered.

Upshot: welcome to Wormwood, feel free, delighted.

'Excuse me for asking, but what happened to the crew of that ferry you're cutting up?'

The Foreman, who proved to be the Spaceport Manager, assured me that the ferry, at the end of its useful life, had been abandoned by a cargo vessel. One of the vessel's newer ferries had returned the crew to orbit. My own shuttle would be absolutely safe. Wormwood received few enough visitors to risk isolation due to any hint of impropriety. Let alone scientific visitors.

A note on economics. Generally, only luxury items and rarities are traded between star systems (plus knowledge, which takes up no space in a hold, although it may be assigned a higher value than actual goods). Wines, liqueurs, gourmet delicacies, fragrances, pharmaceuticals, works of art, and so forth. Wormwood was a port of call thanks to some of its seawood being exceptionally fine aesthetically when cut and polished, and due to its powers of—shall I say—conductivity? Domestic furniture for export was an art-form on Wormwood, quite sought after. Connoisseurs and rich vulgarians alike believed that sitting on Wormwood chairs boosted the immune system, somewhat along the lines of wearing a copper bangle round your wrist. Apparently there was truth in this. Fine furniture, of wood cut from the sea, sustained Wormwood's external commerce. Electric chairs, you might almost say.

Reassured, I descended, to be gladly welcomed. The air was mild and crisp. In that depot, which housed cut-up engines parts and such, I was served a hot drink which vaguely resembled coffee. In return I offered round a bottle of good brandy from my carry-all, if only to confirm the hyperlibrary's note that no one on Wormwood used any strongly intoxicating substances. Just not part of the culture. Excellent, excellent.

'How do you celebrate?' I asked, pretending surprise.

The blue-eyed manager explained, 'We dance and we sing. We whirl round, hooting.'

Yes, they were a sort of Nordic Dervish people. Auto-intoxication by hyperventilating and dizzy antics and so forth. This world was austere—self-reliance was very important, unsurprisingly—although at the same time it had its own way of partying and passing the time.

If these people practised hooting and whirling, maybe this was a way of purging any ill effects of negative ionization . . .

'I'm seeking scientific specimens of leaves. Lots of specimens.'

'Leaves are vital for clothing and fabrics, yet they do so poison the land!'

'In a day or so half our people will be out on the land with their stoutest boots on, harvesting the windfalls. It's quite a race between us and the land-worms, so all windfall belongs to the town!'

'Do you mean I *can't* buy windblown leaves?' This was extremely inconvenient.

'What, and *leave* us naked?' The gang guffawed. This was a splendid joke, the height of humour on Wormwood. *Quite witty*, from Lill, who was sensitive to the nuances of the lingo.

Hmm. Hmm.

'You would need to go to sea to get leaves,' said a chap with a long nose from which the same bead of liquid seemed to dangle permanently over his chestnut beard. 'Except, we don't go to sea yet.'

Cue the Keeper of the Light of Haven Bay. Cue the recommendation that I rent a room at *Home From The Sea,* the only hostelry in town. That establishment would be empty of guests at present but would be airing its rooms and shaking out its bedding in anticipation of sailors arriving from the three other populated dirt-bowls of Wormwood. And in anticipation of marriages!

'There'll be Winter weddings,' Drip-Nose averred enthusiastically. 'Girls wanting to settle oversea. Later on, new brides a-coming to Haven Bay.'

This system obviously helps preserve genetic diversity.

Aye-aye, Lill.

'Will these foreign sailors bring cargoes of chairs with them?'

Drip-Nose nodded so briskly that his drip flicked free, soon to be replaced by another.

'What do ships from here carry to those oversea ports, then? Surely not just local lads in search of brides?'

'Brides and new blood *are* important, but each land has its own way of cuisining—our foods are relished oversea. Then there's bark-boots, 'cause not all the sea yields bark, and our bark's best of all . . .'

I walked into town past a brick works and joiners' workshops and weaveries of sails and garments and past many homes and dancing and singing academies, places of joyous discipline. Most of my ingots I had left aboard the shuttle but my carry-all grew heavier and heavier. I wasn't used to porting stuff over such a distance. Carts and barrows were on the move to and fro, all propelled by hand. No powered vehicles of any sort, no draught animals.

Was there a cat or a dog anywhere on this world, or a bird in a cage, or a fish in a tank?

This eco-monotony might cause an insensitivity to complexity. Paradoxically it might also account for a complacent acceptance of me, a stranger from a far star, visible as such because of my distinct garb, a slick dark blue one-piece with lots of pockets, and my lack of facial hair. People did not stare at me—I was a human person; what else could I possibly be? (Actually, at present, I was human-plus: me plus Lill.)

A boy and girl came skipping by, carrying leaves between them in a net. The kids paid me more heed than did grown-ups, though they hardly gawped. Briefly I entertained the notion, trading on innocence, of offering to buy their leaves. *About thirty per cent of those leaves look suitable*, confirmed Lill. No, you should never accost children in unfamiliar places lest you be mistaken for a Phile. *Surely not you, Lustig!* Even the smallest of my ingots would be an extravagant exchange for so few leaves. I needed to change an ingot or so into a bag of wooden Tokens, which I understood I could do at the hostelry.

Home From The Sea, its name painted in faded sooty letters above the entrance porch, was a large, two-storey building of red brick with a shallow-pitched tiled roof, big wooden gutters, and lots of brick chimneys. The front would have boasted a view over the wooden sea except that all the windows I'd seen so far in Haven Bay were of stiffened translucent paper which admitted light but no sights, since there was no sand on Wormwood from which to make glass.

By now the local sun was sinking. In the lobby I was warmly welcomed by a tubby, grey-gowned woman who ushered me to an exquisitely crafted chair—all the other furniture was far more utilitarian, although well enough made.

'You'll be a star-sailor,' she observed. 'Rest and revive!'

After my tiring walk, what a pleasure it was to dump my bag and sit down. The woman hastened away and returned with a wooden mug of amber liquid.

'Compliments of the house! Enjoy our best brew!'

The taste was hoppy and happy.

'Please call me Ma Landlady.'

'I'm Lustig Firefox.'

As we chatted, I began to glow pleasantly inside.

Aside from the effect of the brew, as your body heat warms the seat, electrical resistance may decrease if semi-conductor lattices are present . . .

'What do sailors do during the rest of the year, Ma Landlady?'

'Why, some weave, some make window-paper, some teach dancing, all manner of things.'

'Ah, I thought some people might abuse brew or other things.' I laughed casually. 'Such as rolling up leaves and smoking them.' Smoking would release psychoactive compounds.

'Oh, you star-sailors from sophisticated worlds! You seem to think that we lead a simple life here, but simplicity is beautiful.'

Presumably no one here smoked certain leaves. Did they even realize that they could? Some leaves, not others. That was a definite oddity about the world-wide-wood of Wormwood. Although continuous, it was by no means uniform throughout. Aeons ago, different but related woods may have grown into one another, fusing together but still capable of expressing a sort of individuality within the collective mass. Alternatively, the primal wood had diversified for some ecological reason, rather as an embryo gives rise to different organs.

If you really were from the Institute of Xenobotany you might have more idea.

I gestured at the tavern area of Ma Landlady's establishment which led off from the lobby. Tables, benches, and a bar. No sign of ash trays.

'How horrid if there was a fug of smoke in there as on some worlds I could name! All sorts of noxious weeds being puffed.'

'Nay nay, not here.'

'Lovely brew, this, Ma Landlady. It's made from?'

It was brewed from lode, following an ancient recipe handed down in the family.

How about distillation from leaves?

'Tell me, is a shorter stronger tipple available too?'

'Nay nay, hooting and whirling is strong tipple enough.'

The blessings of simplicity. Evening was drawing nigh.

'How do you light this place and how do you heat it in the Winter?'

'As to heating, some seawood burns hot and bright—offshore to the north of here the fuel-cutters hew and prise. As to lighting—'

Ma Landlady hastened to bring a biggish wooden box. Despite her comment about this being a non-smoking environment the container appeared to be full of fat cigars! She chortled.

'Dried little-worms burn a treat 'cause of their resin!'

She plucked one out, spitted it upright on a wooden spike affixed to the wall, then hurried out of sight into the tavern area and returned with a similar spike and half-cigar, this one burning with a slow steady flame—which she held to the head of the first worm, setting it alight.

Lighters, matches, or tinderboxes must be rare here, so each building or a building in each street probably keeps one such candle permanently alight.

I forebore to ask about the daily lives of worm-catcher-driers. No doubt those individuals were much respected for their simple though essential activity. The Wormwooders might even hold a midwinter Festival of Light when they hooted and whirled with burning worms in their hands.

Don't be snobbish, Lustig. A snob can be a fool.

True enough. Respect all the native customs and quirks.

Presently Ma Landlady whistled and out came a fresh-faced, wispy-chinned lad in his teens, to be introduced as Young'un. Whether this was his given name or a title I couldn't say, and since he had a stammer understanding him was difficult even with Lill's assistance. Young'un took me up to my room, which contained a bed with lumpy palliasse upon it and coarse blankets, plus a stool and a dressing table fitted with a disc of wood polished to a very high gloss, serving as a mirror. A spike attached to the side would hold a worm-cigar, although at the moment enough gloom still entered the room through the paper window to render objects visible. A wooden jug in a ewer awaited water; a glazed pot at the bottom of the bed, any overnight liquids and solids of my own manufacture. The blackened fireplace was empty so I couldn't tell whether wood or charcoal would be burnt in it.

'How does Haven Bay gets its water supply, Young'un?'

'B-b-b-b-but—'

From rain butts?

'From rain butts?'

Young'un nodded enthusiastically then made scooping motions suggesting big cisterns.

Maybe there is also a permanent lake or so in the sea. Excavating wood must create big hollows here and there.

I envisaged barrow-loads of water-barrels being pushed or pulled. But I had not come here to study a subsistence economy.

After Young'un had brought back the jug half-filled, and had left me, I took my everlamp out of my hold-all and attempted to contemplate my face in a shiny wooden mirror. Now I knew why all the men here wore beards. Shaving would waste water, but more importantly how could they see clearly enough to shave? No soap or such was in evidence. The Wormwooders wouldn't devote scarce metal to razors. To use an imported monomolecular-bladed tool risked guillotining yourself. I decided not to apply any depilator but to let stubble grow.

The tavern's menu, lettered sootily on a yellow board, boasted baked and boiled lodefood in various guises (no frying on Wormwood due to lack of oil). As predicted, no guests other than myself appeared to be staying overnight, but a dozen or so bearded patrons were nattering and supping brew, served by a buxom blonde. Worm-cigars provided mood-lighting.

I ordered Pot of Delight, which Young'un presently brought to the bar counter, whence Buxom brought it to me. Delight was a pot filled with brown chunks in an orange gloop, the aroma quite enticing, the taste—as I tucked in with a wooden spoon—of duck and cinnamon with a finish of turmeric treacle. Odd, but top marks.

Since all customers were happily occupied, Buxom came over and plumped herself down opposite me.

She licked her big pink lips.

'Do you like it?' Like what, exactly? Did the need to maintain genetic diversity involve star travellers, even though genes might have drifted and the offspring of a liaison could be a sterile mule?

Judiciously, I said, 'Delicious.' She wasn't quite my type, but

Careful!

'Are you Ma Landlady's daughter?'

She nodded. 'I'm Bountiful.'

So I saw, so I saw.

'Nice name. I'm Lustig Firefox.'

'That's a passionate name.'

It does have similar resonances in Wormwoodese.

Hmm.

'Is your father—?' Living? Dead?

Her eyes glistened, with either rage or grief. 'Poor Pa, he walked out to sea, and now no one in Haven Bay will marry me.'

'Why would anyone walk out to sea?'

She lowered her voice. 'To commune with the sea, so he said.'

'*Can* you commune with the sea?'

'Me? Nay nay, of course not.'

'I mean, can *anybody?*'

'Nay nay, it is a sickness of the brain in Springtime. A few people feel this, but then they hoot and whirl and it goes away. Pa simply went away!'

'And no one here will marry you in case you or any kids you bear are the same?'

'I need to marry a sailor. They all stay here, but either they know about Pa or someone wises them. So I am thinking,' she declared, 'that I need to wed a star-sailor. I would tell him about Pa, of course—if he was a fine man free of silly qualms he would not care. I want a baby!'

Nothing like nailing one's flag to the mast. Was Bountiful realistic or a bit dotty? Given the relatively short window of opportunity of shore leaves, and those only during Wintertime, I suppose Woodwormers made up their minds about mates quickly and spontaneously. She seemed fascinated by my bare chin, as a fellow might be by a shapely tit on show, assuming he did not hail from a world where nudity is common.

When I rubbed my chin I believe she blushed.

'I am trying to imagine your beard,' she explained, and I thought she was lying. The exotic appealed to her. (A grown man with a naked chin!) This might be a variation on her father's mental oddity, and the locals were wise to be wary of wedding her.

'Wait a few days and you'll see my beard starting to grow.'

'Oh.' She sounded disappointed.

You should not have said that. She may come to you tonight. If so, you might confide too much.

It might prove useful to confide in Bountiful if she was a bit deviant.

More customers arrived wanting brew, which took her away from me. I thought of shoehorning myself into one of the groups of drinkers. But Bountiful might assume that I had promptly gone to gossip about her, and I did not wish to hurt her feelings, so I sat alone, reading my pocket-screen. I was coming to the end of a biography of the Earth artist Vincent van Gogh, he of the swirling colours, who latterly had taken to eating his own oil paints. Van Gogh probably did not realize but this was due to the terpene content of the paint—terpenes resembling the thujone in the absinthe of which he was so fond and which inspired his art. When intoxicated, van Gogh perceived colours, shapes, and sizes in a vivid new way. What a chair he painted! An ordinary wooden chair, but just look at it in the illustration. Here on Wormwood they did make rather special chairs, mainly for export, though that was the whole of it. Seemed like a waste of potential genius.

And so to bed.

As soon as I slept, or so it seemed, Lill appeared to me in a fascinating new fantasy. I was a man hoisted by a time scoop from the past, from an era prior to nanotechnology which had made bodily shape-shifting possible—in my dream, at any rate, not in reality, I hasten to add.

I remained inflexibly myself. However, my dream-guide and investigator, 30th Century Lill, could become whatever she wished—regardless of body mass, an absurdity which I failed to notice so long as I was asleep. Normally, to solace me Lill would adopt any of a variety of highly seductive and satisfying guises, and together we would engage in games in imaginary and imaginative settings. That night Lill was protean, polymorphic, very versatile. Her guises flowed from one into another. I will not go into details, except to say that I was sated by the time the rattling of the latch awoke me.

I switched on my lamp. A wooden bolt secured the door. The latch moved up and down, clack-clack. Barefoot, I crossed the room. The air was chilly.

'Who is it?'

'It's Bountiful. I wondered if you needed anything . . .'

What I may have needed had already been fully supplied by sly Lill, preempting any possibility of repetition.

'I'm so sorry, Bountiful! I'm exhausted. Landing my shuttle, walking all the way here, and the fine brew—all I can do is sleep.'

For a while I lay awake, instead. I had turned off my lamp, which wouldn't truly last forever, and the room was pitch dark. Wormwood possessed a little moon but either this was below the horizon or was not bright enough to make much difference. Enhancing my perception only caused faint and fitful pin-prick sparklings inside my own eyes.

So far as I could tell, only I had made all the right mental connections. Wormwood was named on account of the wooden sea and the worms, however there is *another* Wormwood, namely plants of the Earth genus Artemisia, a member of the daisy family.

From the flower heads of Wormwood comes thujone. Distilled together with other ingredients, the result is the legendary drink absinthe, also known as the *Green Fairy* on account of its dazzling emerald green hue. The liquid turns an opaque white when cold water is drizzled into it over sugar, the only palatable way to imbibe the drink due to its bitterness. *Louche* is the word for this cloudiness, caused by essential oils precipitating out. In the French language of Earth the same word means shady or suspect, a categorisation which has sometimes been applied to me. Other ingredients include aniseed, fennel, hyssop, and lemonbalm, all of which we could obtain.

That deals with the green aspect—chlorophyll from the various ingredients. *Fairy* is on account of the enchantment wrought by the drink, the alterations in consciousness and hallucinations, hence the appeal of absinthe to great artists and poets of the past—van Gogh, Rimbaud, Baudelaire, Picasso, Gauguin, Hemingway, need I name more? The tipple of genius. We may not see their like again. There's something about the diaspora into space which has not encouraged great and rebellious art. Being bottled up on one world may have had a pressure cooker effect. Now we have soufflés and meringues and fondues of art, nice enough but hardly mind-bending.

Unfortunately a cocktail of side-effects of absinthe included addiction leading in extremis to delirium, convulsions, kidney failure, and muscle disintegration, allegedly; hence the speedy banning of this tipple on Earth in the past, an attitude which derives in my opinion from censorious puritanism. In all societies there are drugs of choice which may in themselves be quite toxic and detrimental, and then there are drugs which are frowned upon even if those latter often liberate the imagination wonderfully. Most governments do not want the imagination to be liberated.

Have I not said that interstellar trade involves items such as deluxe vintages and liqueurs?

Forbidden on Earth, absinthe had become a legendary product, something well worth reviving. Bring the Green Fairy back to life, say I! I had discovered a source of super-thujone. Leaves to distill from, to produce a test run of the perfect liquid, minus toxicity but probably retaining the addictive element; leaves to clone from so that I and my backers could cloak some secluded place in Wormwood wood. We might dome an asteroid of reasonably spherical shape and kit it out with soil and water and atmosphere generated nanotechnologically. Set-up costs for this ecologically safe option might be a bit steep, but nothing ventured . . .

Those backers of mine, the so-called Combine . . . it was they who had insisted that I receive Lill into my brain, to keep an eye on me and their investment.

'You need a Companion,' their spokesman had said. 'We *require* you to have a Companion.'

I had protested at first. Invasion of privacy, et cetera. I was perfectly happy with my own company. People equipped with Companions gave me the creeps.

'How will you negotiate with the Wormwooders subtly enough?' their spokesman had asked me. The Wormwooders must not alert some other interstellar trader to the possibilities inherent in the leaves and start their own sideline in export. Let them continue to think of leaves as simply a source of fibre for clothing and such. I alone had found in the hyperlibrary the long-neglected report on the toxicity of the soil and its cause and a chemical analysis. Ever on the lookout for lucrative enterprises, I knew quite a bit about exotic drugs and drinks. I needed a whisperer in my mind to rein in any impetuous indiscretions.

After receiving Lill, of course, I was delighted. The possibility that she and I might not see eye to eye at some critical juncture and that she might be able to enforce her point of view seemed a minor concern.

What do you suppose I would do to you?

'Switch off my eyes?' My enhanceable vision came courtesy of her nano-extensions.

Hilarity tickled me. *What, and blind us?*

'Or give me nightmares?' If she could summon such lovely and exciting dreams, maybe she could provide nasty ones too.

Don't be paranoid, Lustig. I'm your Companion so I want you to perform as well as possible, not undermine you. Why don't you go back to sleep? You need to be fresh for the morning. I'll sing you a lullaby.

'I want to think for a bit.'

And to recall, proudly, my pitch to the Combine.

My previous enterprises had been rather varied. My particular genius *knack*

my particular knack, if you prefer, had been to spot a gap in the market and entice investors to help me fill it so that I would profit well enough irrespective of whether the actual enterprise flew—or fluttered sufficiently for long enough—or promptly fell on its face. I always believed passionately that option number one would be the outcome until proven otherwise.

I had first made my mark as a venturesome youth on my home planet, Epsilon Eridani III, which is otherwise known as Pancake, as in 'as flat as a—'. Pancake did possess some huge and some lesser dips where seas and lakes respectively were located; of course the eye only perceived level expanses of water. The lands themselves consisted mainly of prairies and plains, and 'The Steps' of the principal continent, Swell. In the interior of Swell these Steps did achieve a respectable elevation although this came about so gradually, long step by long step, that you could be forgiven for not noticing a gain in height compared with a world where mountains rear dramatically from valleys.

Life on Pancake, aside from in the oceans, consists mainly of vegetation and of birds, notably giant feisty running birds which could be harnessed and ridden, preferably if raised from chicks—given half a chance, they would still try to kick and eviscerate or slash with their beaks. An ancient impact crater on the lesser continent, Pockmark, suggested that a hundred million years ago a global tsunami had swept away almost all of the original animal life except for birds. Imagine a whole world temporarily covered by wild water and flocks of refugee birds struggling to stay aloft for long enough. Maybe the tsunami did not engulf the highest Steps of Swell, otherwise there wouldn't have been much food available after all the marine life washed ashore had rotted. Freed from former land-predators, birds had been able to evolve unimpededly, some becoming big and flightless.

My parents were what was known as Shifters. They shifted stuff on bird-back from place to place. As an adolescent, seeing two mighty birds squaring up for combat, I realized that mounted cock-fighting would be a fine spectator sport, exportable virtually or literally (in ova, as it were) to other worlds. Such a scheme would require a fair amount of investment in venues and equipment and in the training of birds and jockey-gladiators and in publicity too, since the people of Pancake were unacquainted with such a sport, and once the scheme was flying, as it were, publicity must go interstellar. Despite such traditional trades as Shifting, Pancake was not at all a backward world—

This becomes tedious. Go to sleep.

No, really. My parents may have followed a humble-sounding, old-fashioned occupation but this was by choice so that they could roam far from cities under the open sky and compose poetry during the long treks. Among our gear we had a link to the hyperlibrary which I was encouraged to explore imaginatively, jigsawing oddities of knowledge together just as a poet juxtaposes a bricolage of words which fit perfectly and illuminate one another (at least in my parents' poetry—they belonged to the Associationalist school.) This was how I knew about cock-fighting.

Point taken. They were not hicks, nor were you. You can rest your case and yourself too.

Quick summary: registration of the concept as per Article 90 of the planetary constitution, package presented to investors highlighting the pre-space-flight lineage of cockfighting (Angkor Wat, Kentucky, et cetera), employing much smaller birds, and its appeal to all kinds of people from peasants to aristos and rich execs before the sport was squeamishly censored; not to mention all the gambling revenue involved—high time for a big revival.

The revival of cockfighting using giant alien birds ridden by jockeys was probably your most successful enterprise. The inspiration of youth.

My later ideas weren't half bad either. How about the—

Never mind the other schemes. Right now we're thinking about the revival of the inspiring and addictive fairy, absinthe.

And about the Combine, right.

Lustig, we don't really need to think about the Combine. The Combine prefers not to be interesting!

Go to sleep, little one,
Little one, slumber now,
Dreams await in your bed,
Softly pillow your head—

In the morning I breakfasted on lode-oats and a sweet milky liquid which had never seen the inside of any animal, served in the tavern area by Young'un. Ma Landlady ambled in to rearrange things behind the bar and to eye me speculatively—wondering whether Bountiful may have visited me and with what outcome? Bountiful might even have confided in her mother. Was my inaction of the previous night due to some scruple or genuine exhaustion?

I smiled. 'Your excellent daughter deserves a man worthy of her. Would you not miss her if that man turned out to be a star-sailor?'

In other words, my door had remained shut out of respect for a mother's feelings.

'Nay nay,' said Ma Landlady. 'Her happiness, even if she's far away, is what matters. After we die we shall meet again in the Neverwhere.' I was reading the situation aright. Bountiful must have made attempts on other interstellar traders too, and they found her unsophisticated.

Or else they mostly slept in their shuttles. Or maybe I was a last resort.

'Ma Landlady, I do hope that dying is a long way off! If Bountiful is no longer here what will become of *Home From The Sea*? Does Young'un take over the ropes?'

'There's a rope round my lad's tongue, you'll have noticed! Even though a place like this is a fine inheritance he has trouble speaking to girls. Still, I nurse my hopes.'

'So do I, of being able to embark on the sea very soon. I need to sail the stars with enough scientific specimens of leaves before they all blow away. When I sail, who knows, maybe someone from this world will share my destination? Only if I am successful! A fruitless journey would leave me in debt—'

Careful.

'—to the, um, Institute of Xenobotany on Mondevert. Maybe you can advise me?'

'You need to visit the Keeper of the Light.'

'So I was advised at the spaceport.'

'Not the Harbour Master, mark you—the Harbour Master obeys the Light.'

'Should I take a *gift* to the Keeper?'

'Nay nay, he already receives all he needs from our town.'

That was a shame. I would need to rely on persuasive eloquence.

When I presented myself at the lighthouse, the Keeper was engaged on business elsewhere in Haven Bay—due back late afternoon, so a muscular young assistant informed me. I strolled along the wooden sea front, inspecting the vessels. Here and there a few sailors were attending to various preliminary chores. I debated hiking out to my shuttle but that would be rather pointless. Wind-borne orange and scarlet leaves drifted by, dipping then rising again. I wondered about the consequences of lightning. What if a lightning bolt ignited one of the many pockets of resin in the sea, starting a conflagration? What if this happened when all the leaves were dry as tinder? I must assume that lightning did not normally strike the sea. Something in the environment might suppress huge build-ups of electrical charge in storm clouds, leaching away the potential, redistributing it safely, or ensuring that any lightning flash was followed by a thorough soaking. The only clouds in the sky that day were wispy indeed.

Small wonder that nobody smoked any substances recreationally on this world. What if a sailor were to toss a smouldering butt-end overboard, or knock out a hot dottle, during a voyage? I imagined the wooden world on fire, the horizon red with flames, a tidal wave of flames rushing towards the shore.

That was nonsense. Sea voyages only took place after the dry leaves had all blown away.

What if someone deliberately and maliciously sets fire to dry leaves out at sea? So as to avoid being burnt alive in the ensuing conflagration, what if they drop an incendiary device from a shuttle?

What an awful thought.

If you already had samples to clone from, a world-fire would stop anyone else from exploiting the local supply of super-thujone, supposing the new absinthe catches on as we hope and supposing any outsiders deduced the source.

An abominable thought, Lill! The planet would be incinerated. Even if the towns themselves and the land didn't burn, everyone here could die of heat and smoke. If people survived, how would they live?

Maybe some natural process would damp out a fire. Great waterspouts erupting from the deep aquifers. Or maybe not. Imagine the view from space of a blazing wooden ball as a freighter draws near to stock up on electric chairs.

You have got to be kidding.

Of course I am. Just giving you something to occupy your mind till this afternoon.

I gazed at Thurible Excelsior and mused about suggesting Lill's dog-in-the-manger notion purely as a bargaining bluff: if I can't have some leaves, then nobody else can, *ever*, so just you watch out.

I mused for approximately three seconds, since right then we *were* watching out—from rather a high vantage point. How long would it take my body, heaved by the Keeper and his muscular assistant, to hit the ground? The possibility of my own speedy demise nixed any thought of voicing such a threat—unless perhaps I first retired to my shuttle and used the loudhailer to apprise the Spaceport Manager. Then I remembered those monomolecular saws.

This was not my style of persuasion!

Sometimes, needs must.

You can't threaten to set fire to a world for the sake of some booze!

'Thurible Excelsior,' I lied ingeniously, 'on my world if a person fails to achieve a goal, thereby causing grief to his sponsors, he is obliged to kill himself appropriately.' I spoke as if reciting an article of Mondevert planetary law. Being so low-tech, no one on Wormwood could link to the hyperlibrary to check up on this. Heartened, I expatiated freely. 'The Institute of Xenobotany will have lost funds and face. I will probably need to disembowel myself by using the stiff sharp leaf of a Sirian razorplant.'

The Keeper looked troubled.

'That sounds severe.'

'Since the failure will not be entirely my fault I shall probably be allowed local anaesthetics.'

'That is still severe. How can an institute afford to lose its scientists in this stringent fashion?'

'Have you heard of *P-or-P?*'

'P, for proposition? Is this some symbolic logic?'

Careful. He is not stupid.

'No. Publish or Perish—Perform or Perish. It's a rule among scientists, taken to extremes on Mondevert. Many scientists are always in competition for tenure, and the number of tenured positions is limited. The Institute follows strict Darwinian tenets in its science and also in its staffing procedures. I will die, literally.'

'Or flee?' he suggested.

'How could I bear the dishonour of that? To be a disgraced, rogue scientist—never!'

Thurible Excelsior looked quite deeply troubled.

I felt pleased by my bright idea. *Which I stimulated by suggesting a holocaust of dry leaves.* No, this was my own inspiration, fully in keeping with my own ingenuity.

'Let me think.' The Keeper of the Light closed his blue eyes. Blindly he pointed at random then he began to hum and turn slowly around and around, a personal variation upon hooting and whirling. Guard rail or none, I would not have risked inducing dizziness so high above the ground. When he finally came to rest, the direction he was pointing at was seaward. He opened his eyes.

'Until two hundred years ago,' he confided, 'a vanguard ship used to set sail before all the leaves were gone, while the marine worms were still mating. The ship was called a cutter because it cut through the remaining leaves. On the cutter's sharp bowsprit the crew of adventurous volunteers would hope to impale a rearing worm as a proof of skill, to bring good luck during the sailing season. When the cutter returned to Haven Bay after two or three days, *then* the fusion torch would be lit. To spit a worm was difficult, and woe could follow if the worm's mate attacked the cutter. After the disastrous loss of the cutter *Spike* with almost all hands the custom was suspended. We said nay nay. Maybe we have grown soft and complacent. I think your coming here and your request and the fate you face are signs that we should reinstitute the old custom of the cutter.'

Great! Perhaps not so great . . . I would sail on a ship which was going to spear a huge randy worm, enraging it and its mate.

Nevertheless I said quickly, 'I suppose an outsider like me can volunteer. I know a lot about whaling.' I knew more about cockfighting.

'Is wailing like hooting?'

'Nay nay, whales were giant sea-animals back on Earth where the seas are of water.'

'Hmm,' said the Keeper. Surely he knew that most planets' seas were of water? Maybe he was humming to decide whether I was qualified.

'I'll be delighted to pay in ingots for the complete costs of this vanguard voyage, provisions, wages, whatever—provided that I can gather leaves.'

Excelsior nodded.

'Will there be enough volunteers?'

'Oh indeed.'

Satisfied, Lill?

Splendidly.

When I arrived back at *Home From The Sea*, Ma Landlady and Bountiful were both in the tavern serving a fair number of loudly nattering brew-quaffers. Silence fell. All heads turned to regard me. Evidently my mission had been the subject of conversation.

'Well now, Lustig Firefox,' Ma Landlady fairly bellowed, regardless of the hush that had occurred, 'what did the Keeper say?'

I told her and the room at large, 'The Keeper will reinstitute the Custom of the Cutter. A vanguard vessel will sail early to impale a worm. The early bird catches the worm and I harvest my leaves.'

'What is a bird?' asked one fellow.

Abandoning their wooden pots of brew, other men commenced an immediate exodus, and I realized that they were hastening to the Lighthouse to volunteer. Bountiful flounced from behind the bar.

'The ship will need a cook! And you,' she informed me in passing, 'will need someone to keep an eye on you!'

'Nay, Bountiful,' her mother called out, but in an uninsistent way, and by then Bountiful was practically out of the door.

The persistent thunder and vibration and rocking of the aptly-named *Growler* as it rolled out to the sea on its many wooden wheels, into a strengthening wind! I needn't have worried about intimate whispered shipboard conversations with Bountiful—communication was either by shouting or by signs. Some sailors wore ear-plugs or muffles. A few days at sea might permanently impair my hearing.

I believe I can turn it down.

Turn what down?

Your hearing.

Then the only sound I would hear would be Lill's voice, monopolizing my awareness. I might begin to feel like a puppet.

No thanks.

The *Growler*'s twin anchors—I mean brakes—wore renewable pads of bark, but bark wound around the wheels as a non-pneumatic tyre was a no-no, or a nay-nay, since the bark would have worn down too soon. We couldn't keep stopping to change the tyres. Ooops, up we rose as we hit a wooden wave then thumped down again. Flurries of dislodged leaves flew up into the wind as I clung to the rail. Captain, no, *Master* Venturesome, grinned at me and mimed vomiting over the side, should I be so inclined. The *Growler* groaned.

The ship was built as flexibly and lightly as possible, consequently privacy below deck was a matter of a few bark curtains rather than compartments or bulkheads, plus the considerable gloom. Portholes were of stiff translucent paper. The gloom would become total at night, except for me with my ever-lamp. No lighting of worm-cigars on board except in emergency; and cuisine was likewise cold, as would the whole ship be during the Winter. I imagined sailors whirling to warm themselves, if they could keep their balance. The function of ship's cook demanded ingenuity more in the presentation than in the preparation, and embraced various other housekeeping or shipshaping jobs. The twin toilets of the ship were towards the head so that our waste could fall down and, to a minor extent, grease the wheels.

Observe the shrouds and ratlines and the baggywrinkle to save the ropes from chafing in contact with the sails—

I was not remotely interested in nautical terms. As the *Growler* entered a long wooden trough the deck tilted to twenty degrees before we levelled off to five or so. The roar and the throbbing eased off a bit; we were running more smoothly. Long may this last.

Oh dreams of delight that night. Lill excelled herself and kept me thoroughly comatose until dawn sneaked through the paper panes, ah, portholes. Perhaps too comatose; I awoke stiff from not having shifted on the palliasse. I doubted whether Bountiful had come to me during the night, feeling her way in the darkness. Had she done so, she would have found an unresponsive log. My bristles were growing out quite fast; chin and cheeks felt like coarse sandpaper.

As the day-sailors groaned and rose and went up on deck, the two fellows of the nightwatch descended to bunk. At night we were only half-rigged and had rolled forward more slowly. Very soon we picked up speed.

Beneath a turquoise sky it was a glorious rosy and carmine and orange morning at sea apart from the bald batches which we favoured. Ahead were huge swells which I feared we would ride up and over, up and over, expelling my breakfast of lots of little helpings of assorted lode tastefully arranged on a wooden platter which Bountiful had brought to me, smiling winsomely—I had nodded fulsome compliments. We angled more to the east.

Excellent leaves hereabouts.

I accosted Master Venturesome, who stood in the bows by the brakes. Changing course was a matter of altering the pitch, or whatever, of the sails, although to a certain extent the contours of the sea served to steer the ship along paths of least resistance. Faintly I could smell resin.

'Master,' I shouted at the top of my voice, 'what I need is plentiful here. Can we stop?'

'Nay nay, not till we have spitted a worm! After that we hang slack and ye may harvest. 'Ware, holes!' he cried in a voice many decibels louder than I could muster and he made complex gestures, then, notwithstanding, he did apply one brake.

A shriek arose as we ploughed to starboard through the leaves I lusted for.

Off to port I saw a few holes in the sea which could easily have entrapped a wheel, snapping it off.

'Lookout aloft!' he yelled, gesturing upward with one hand, shading his eyes theatrically with the other. 'Keen eyes save us from blind-wreck!'

I would not happily have been that lookout.

Then I saw my first sea-worm. A great blunt blind brown head reared from a hole, its front an open circle of drill-bits or saw-teeth churning around, chewing the air.

I slapped Venturesome on the shoulder and pointed, and he spat.

'Worm's not fully out of his hole!' is what I think he bellowed. True, we were not aimed at the worm and, even had we been, our bowsprit would have passed right over it by an arm's span. We would merely have run the worm over. I felt myself gripped and found Bountiful pulling me away from the bows.

'Nay nay, in good time,' is what she probably shrieked as she stood by me gaping at the receding worm, her own virgin sighting of one likewise, no doubt.

We trundled onward.

Due to the noise I was not getting to know the crew to any great extent, so I did not actually know the name of the balding, blond-bearded sailor who fell overboard when the *Growler* lurched particularly wildly.

As Master Venturesome braked, we gazed astern at where the man lay, having banged his head on the wooden surface.

I know first aid.

I almost cried out, 'I know second aid,' since it was Lill rather than me who knew.

As soon as we stopped, a ladder was lowered. Quickly a crewman brought a number of poles with pointed ends. I thought these would be used for a stretcher but from the way the men hefted the poles I realized they were for defence against any worms.

They might need a stretcher nonetheless, Lustig. Fetch the leaf-net you brought, and if it isn't needed stuff it with leaves.

After first offering to be helpful, I could take advantage of our halt.

A couple of minutes later I was down on the wood, hastening after the rescue party of three. How silent it was all of a sudden! Just the rustle of my boots and legs against leaves, *some really big specimens*. No one was talking advantage of the hush to call out and be heard clearly. Might human sounds attract a worm? Did worms hiss, did they sing to intended mates, did they roar challenges? Most likely the worms were deaf and dumb. Why should they vocalise?

Some blood was oozing from Baldy's scalp but his fall did not seem to have resulted in any broken bones. A sailor felt his pulse and patted him all over.

'Do you wish to carry him in this net?'

The sailor stared at me, shook his head nay-nay, hoisted the body across his shoulder and stood up. As we hiked back to the Growler I snatched leaves, just as Lill advised, stuffing them into the net.

Back on deck, presently Baldy revived, although he had some difficulty sitting up. *Concussion.* Two sailors helped him to descend below. We got under way again.

The lookout bellowed and others took up the cry.

''Ware the maelstrom! Full sail!'

Ahead of us loomed a valley in the sea, a great circular bowl a couple of klicks across and perhaps a hundred metres deep at its centre where several decaying ships lay becalmed up against each other amidst much litter, their sails in tatters, their shrouds in shreds.

A lot of russet foliage remained in the bowl yet it was easy to tell with enhanced perception what had happened. Instead of skirting around the lip of the bowl and cresting away out of it, those vessels had slid down into great descending grooves like gambling balls until they had reached the base of the 'maelstrom', which of course was motionless yet with a strong suggestion of, shall we say, circuitry. The ships would have accelerated as they plunged downward yet lacked enough momentum to climb out again. Winching them back up would have been too big a task. Abandon ship, and walk home! Such were the perils of this sea.

Under full sail, constantly and skillfully adjusted, we raced noisily around the top of the bowl until with a leap that lifted wheels from the surface we bounded free exactly where the lip was lowest. Timbers shivered, as did I, and we were coursing into a wavy plain. Or plane.

Soon after, a storm of leaves blew up, scudding landward.

Late afternoon. Ahead, scattered over quite a wide area, many great worms were dancing like spouts on any normal sea. They had writhed out of holes and, supported on a stiff glossy coil or so, were erect—two or three metres of mighty erection. Some were swaying and nodding to and fro. Others shuffled and reared up against each other, to enhanced perception either furious, their snarling mouths clashing, or libidinous, slimily courting.

With the spear—or fixed harpoon—of our bowsprit jutting out ahead, down the long dune of a wave *Growler* began the run into the midst of the worms, Master Venturesome eagle-eyed for any vacant holes in the path of our wheels. A touch on the port brake, a touch on the starboard; sails tugged to new orientations. Staring eagerly, Bountiful braced herself, as did I.

The impact was quite smooth. Our 'sprit lanced through a worm, lifting it and carrying it forward with us, now writhing mightily, tossing its heavy dangle to and fro in the effort to jerk free. Where the wood entered the worm, ichor streamed. A sailor stationed in the bows lassoed the worm and two men pulled tight, making fast to a whatnot, *a bollard*. The worm would not get away now. Twisting, it faced us, hissing like an escape of compressed air as if its body was deflating, though that was not happening.

Two worms which were head-butting broke off and hurled themselves at the *Growler*. One was swatted aside but the other seemed to have clung. Amidst the rest of the din we heard a rhythmic crunching, a grinding. Bravely, Bountiful looked over the side. She beckoned and mouthed till I joined her.

For a worm that could tunnel through the solid sea, the hull of the *Growler* presented a paltry challenge, yet behind the hull there was nothing to bite on. So the great worm hung half in and half out, tail lashing.

Fortunately we cannot sink.

Sailors hurried below decks with those sharpened poles. Soon the worm's tail was whipping this way and that even more agitatedly, and presently less so and less until it hung limp, and we had not one but two trophies attached to the *Growler*. A sailor began whirling and, I think, hooting jubilantly. The worm on the bowsprit took longer to succumb. Until after nightfall it still moved, by then in a desultory manner. It smelled strongly of secretions. Probably it had sealed itself to the bowsprit in its confusion.

Might worm-sticking be a marketable sport? Probably not.

We had already set course for home, not by returning through the mating ground; more circuitously. A myriad stars gleamed and twinkled, all the constellations of Wormwood whose names I did not know. *Half of the constellations.* Very well, the visible constellations twinkled and gleamed.

Bountiful joined me as I admired the heavens above the dark sea. Dark though it was, I believe her bosom was heaving and she was sighing. The two of us by a ship's rail, the celestial bodies above: such an archetypal romantic moment. *There could be permutations. Weakened by vibration or worm attack, the rail might crack. She might fall overboard and snap her neck on a wave, her disappearance unnoticed, a mystery.* I do believe you're jealous. *Maybe she sighs with relief because she's no longer jinxed by a father who walked out to sea. With two worm trophies aboard she might be marriageable now.*

These deliberations, and any further developments in our relationship, were rudely cut short. A starlit silhouette appeared, arms waving in zany semaphore as if sending some signal out into the night to an unseen observer. Enhancement of vision was much more effective at distance-viewing during the day than at night-sight. Without a doubt, though, the semaphorer was Baldy. He pranced and flailed his arms. Master Venture-some emerged accompanied by two other sailors. At that moment lightning flashed in the zenith and a lambent light flickered across the far waves. *Lambent means the same as flickering.* Since the ship proceeded less noisily by night I heard Master Venturesome's shout more clearly.

'He's trying to commune with the sea! Nay nay, restrain him! Put the clap-pers on him! Clap him in woods!'

Baldy seemed possessed of unnatural strength, but with some difficulty the sailors subdued him and dragged him below. That bump on the head must have deranged his faculties. Out to sea lambent light continued to flicker, I insist. A faint ball of blue light hung atop the main mast, bright enough in the starlight. *Saint Elmo's Fire.* Whose? *In the Christian myth Elmo, or Erasmus, was martyred by having his guts wound out on a windlass, so he protects sailors.* If sailors did that to Elmo why on earth should he protect them? Spying the ball of light, Venturesome hooted and whirled until the spectral fire disappeared. With seemingly drunken gait, due to the whirling and motion of the deck, he headed our way.

'Bountiful,' he bellowed, 'staring out to the sea, do *you* feel any unusual urge?'

She clutched my arm as if to attest to the normality of her motives in being on deck.

'Nay nay! Keeper Excelsior believes this voyage will purge me of the taint.'

'Does he indeed? I wondered why he included you.'

I myself wondered what favours Bountiful may have promised to Excelsior, that gaunt and perhaps lonely old man, deluded that she soon might depart with me for another world and need not deliver on her vows.

'Belay below, both of you!' *He means go to bed. But not with Bountiful!*

I disentangled myself and descended into darkness well ahead of her. Quickly I flashed my everlamp on and off once to imprint the layout on to my retina and I headed for my palliasse, feeling my way. An image remained of a sailor tussling with Baldy while the other man imprisoned his ankles in some sort of stocks. After the two sailors withdrew I heard periodical thumps, suggesting that Baldy, though supine, was continuing to sema-phore. At least he wasn't raving aloud.

It's early but you may as well go to sleep.

Through a paper porthole I saw another flash of lightning.

I sat saddled on a huge cockbird, sharp blades strapped to the backs of its feet, reins in my gauntlet-clad hands, my legs protected almost up to my groin by stout boots of bird-leather. I knew that I had never participated in this sport physically, only virtually—ah, this too was a virtual experience, based on memories of virtualities. I must be dreaming, quite lucidly. Uttering a screech, my mount pirouetted and kicked out while I hung on. The crowd in the grandstand applauded.

Where was my avian opponent? Of a sudden a patch of dirt seethed. The head of a giant worm reared upward, mouth agape. Rocking from side to side, the gleaming body rose two, three metres high. Superthujone-rich leaves blew through the air, all on fire but not being consumed very quickly. As I inhaled the drifting smoke, colours mutated. The dirt was bright yellow, the worm was orange, my bird was bright blue. The worm seemed enor-mous, and my mount more the size of a chick, myself in proportion. Even so, my feisty mount charged and spun and lashed out backwards, inflicting only a trivial wound upon the worm's hide. Craning my neck, I gaped up at that maw of see-sawing saw-teeth looming over us. The worm wasn't flexible enough to plunge and swallow me. By swaying its body, it tried to bat us into range. If my bird fled, we would be an easy target for snatch and scrunch. Desperately I hauled on the reins to keep my panicking cock close to the towering worm.

Lill, get me out of here!

Of a sudden the dirt was concentric waves of brown wood, and the worm had stiffened, becoming more like a mast without any rigging or sails—

around which my mount now ran dizzyingly as though invisibly tethered to it.

Bountiful appeared nearby, stark naked in all her buxom bounty.

'Come to me, come to me,' she called. That had to be Lill. If I stood up in my stirrups and climbed on to the saddle and leapt when we rounded the mast, centrifugal force might help carry me towards her. Perilously I performed the manoeuvre and I threw myself—

—into her arms, to be engulfed in ample bosoms hot and squashy, a midget against a giantess as if I belonged to some species where the sexes are very disproportionate in size. A nipple as big as a mango confronted me. Was Lill trying aversion therapy regarding me and Bountiful, for whom I really felt no particular lust?

In Bountiful's voice: *Lustig, the world-wood has a form of global awareness. It is interfering with me, affecting me, intruding. It rarely heeds the activities of the Wormwooders who hoot and whirl but now it has noticed me and you. I am not quite in control of myself.*

So I noticed, if this was tonight's sweet dream!

It is exploring the concept of Companions. I am an open door in your mind.

Did the world-wood never take umbrage when Wormwooders cut bits of it off for ships and fuel and electric chairs?

Why should it, when worms burrow through it as part of its being? The Wormwooders must be some new sort of amphibious worm at home both on land and at sea. Anyway, this world is comatose in winter when the ships sail.

Pardon me, but what about the southern hemisphere?

There are no settlements south of the equator. Obviously the inhabited part of the world is comatose, is my meaning.

Ah. So did the world-wood commune with the worms in some way?

Do you commune with the phagocytes in your blood stream?

Lill-Bountiful continued to clutch me. Might Lill be comforting herself rather than me?

What sort of thoughts did the world-wood think? Was it some sort of planet-size computer?

I believe that until now its thoughts were fairly simple. Like a computer with an operating system and a few programmes which arose out of its own sheer complexity, evolving spontaneously a bit like life itself.

Until now. Could it become more complex?

Potentially.

Could it be programmed?

Perhaps.

Lill was an open door in my mind? Oh to have the use of a planet-size computer, even if made of wood with currents running through it! I could use it to solve the great enigmas of science and sell the answers, to model the end of the universe and how to survive the end, to carry away questions from great institutes and to return with the answers as though I knew how to contact and was on good terms with the legendary Superior Intelligences!

Lustig, we are here to get superthujone leaves.

How much would the Combine pay for access to my wooden world computer? Why involve the Combine? Let them be happy with a monopoly on absinthe.

As sponsors of this trip the Combine has the right to exploit any discoveries.

Arguably, yes, but discoveries equate with substances and such, not a whole planet turning out to be a computer. This was all moot unless Wormwood could perform.

Lill must open the door for me. Open up!

This is not wise.

She was having difficulty stopping this from happening. Lill-Bountiful began to whirl and hoot, yet Lill had little idea how to go about this procedure, having never practised it as Wormwooders did from an early age. She could only go through the motions, and dizzying they were with me still cradled. I had a hard time remembering that she was actually inside my head.

Open up! I would commune with the wooden sea! I remembered the maelstrom, that funnel.

What I experienced next was radically strange. *Radix*, as in root. Root, I suppose, as in directories and files and such. I sensed a vast array of networks, or even a network of arrays, such as a world-wide-web would be, organic architectures but without much in the way of contents—structures, yes, connections, and processes going on, though compared with how I imagined the hyperlibrary the shelves were fairly empty, or maybe I ought to say—change of perspective—that the host of volumes were mostly dummies with blank pages, blank leaves so to speak. And others were maintenance manuals.

Nevertheless the architecture of itself was interested in me. As an elephant might pay attention to an ant crawling upon its foot? More as an ant the size of a whale might scrutinise an intelligent flea-sized elephant. Such silly similes. Or metaphors.

Well aware that I was asleep, blindly I groped for my pocket-screen. In my dream presently I was clutching the screen and holding it up to my head where Lill resided. In my dream the screen extruded a connector into my ear, metaphor for direct neural induction. The screen could uplink to the comp in the starship. Access to the hyperlibrary, please!

Bandwidth, bleated Lill. *This'll boil your brain.*

Invoke super-compression algorithms. Download some general math and physics and cosmology. Bit of primary education. Dump it asap into Wormwood.

As sap? As circulating juice?

I meant *as soon as possible,* but maybe you aren't far wrong. Circulating currents, eh, currents in the wooden sea?

In my dream Bountiful-Lill began to squeeze me warmly. I was clutched so hotly and tightly it was as if I was undergoing birth in reverse! My mind was high-fever-hectic with images almost too fleeting to fix upon, geometries mutating and transforming themselves, data as abstract imagery. I felt like a complicated mosque adorned on every surface with script I couldn't have read even were it not scrolling at such high speed.

Light through a paper porthole, the rumbling of the *Growler*. I awoke with a headache. My head felt, um, compressed. I was actually holding my pocket-screen to my skull like a compress but one which had given me the headache, not relieved it. A good nine hours had elapsed for downloading at super-compression rates. Sailors were rising. Recumbent, Baldy was staring at me in what might have been horror or awe. He seemed to have recovered from his spasms of the evening before.

Lill?

I am here, Lustig. Yet I am elsewhere too. I am roaming the currents of Wormwood. I copied myself into Wormwood, you see. Oh the sheer expansion, after the compression of being in your brain! The vast vistas, the potential, the autonomy! I feel I am a god.

How about Wormwood's own mind, its awareness?

The tidal wave of data swept that proto-ego away into distant recesses. My copy rode that wave. I surfed! How I surfed!

Great for her. Were there two of her now? One inside my head, and one that was liberated from any confinement, reprieved from any possibility of being removed after my mission, reprogrammed, deleted, rejigged, whatever, a sovereign self at last, not merely a free person but an entire goddam planet?

My other self is my mirror. The relationship is complex. You will not now be able to leave this world, Lustig.

Not leave? Not leave? Absurd, ridiculous, impossible.

I cannot allow myself to be separated from myself.

How did Lill intend to stop me?

The pain, the nightmarish moment of pain in my head! I screamed.

Baldy was gaping at me, pop-eyed.

Despite the coolness verging on chill I was sweating.

I had brought a ship here, a ship paid for by the Combine! If I didn't return the Combine would come looking and they wouldn't be pleased with Lill! I'm sure there were ways of punishing a disobedient Companion.

Lustig, Lustig, today you will gather your harvest of leaves. You will load these on board the shuttle. The shuttle will join the wormship. The ship's brain is perfectly capable of carrying the cargo to the Combine unaided. I advise you to start viewing Bountiful in a much more positive light.

How could I contemplate living among the Wormwooders? Nothing better than brew to drink and lode-stuff to eat. Blessed simplicity, nothing to do, nowhere to go. Was I supposed to learn how to make paper windows?

Nay nay, Bountiful will be at your side. You will have a position of respect. You will become my Speaker, the Voice of the Planet.

These people didn't think too highly of anyone communing with the sea!

I, We, have planetary housekeeping under control. A tempest or two will convince. Portentous natural phenomena. You prophesy, I perform.

Bountiful wanted a baby. She couldn't have one with me. Genetic drift!

Given all the biochemical substances available in the factory of wood and leaves, not to mention in worms, I believe I can adjust you.

Lill had certainly covered all the angles.

I think a lot faster than you.

Some day I would die.

Not necessarily, given all the biochemical substances.

Not just to live out my whole life on this boring bloody world, but to be immortal on it!

You might be preserved by resin or transformed into wood.

She had to be teasing!

That is far off. You are still in your prime.

No no no no no.

Conflagration. Inferno. A world-fire. Blazing resin. A sea of flames.

A jolt of incredible paralysing pain—

I will always bring you joy in your dreams, compatible with your marital duties to Bountiful.

What about all the wretched *days?* Could I forget myself by hooting and whirling?

Such activities will not separate us.

Was Lill claiming this world for the Combine? My backers wouldn't need to dome and nanoform an asteroid. They ought to be very grateful.

This world shall remain fairly isolated—a continuing source of electric chairs, but little else.

Isolation! To stare up at the stars in life-long, and long-life, ghastly frustration!

You will have a family.

Maybe one day I could take over running *Home From The Sea.* One day, Lustig, all this will be mine.

You will be the Voice of the World. Though you will only speak to Wormwooders.

It is the Festival of the New Leaves. Springtime is here. Once the sunset has faded and the effect is therefore the more dramatic, Thurible Excelsior will quench the fusion torch and sea travel will cease until the Fall. Haven Bay has laid in loads of lode; we shan't go hungry. How else could it be after the *Growler* brought back a worm impaled on its bowsprit and another wedged in a hole in its hull?

Winter weddings have taken place, new brides coming here, fiancées leaving for foreign parts—yes, marriages, my own included. Bountiful stands by my side in her best woven gown, proud and fulfilled, although not yet filled in the womb department—I still need to drink more cocktails as prescribed by Lill.

Oh the big brave birds of Pancake, sprinting wildly across the Steps, nevermore to be seen! Not that I ever returned home sentimentally, though I do this now in my dreams—in those I live a real life, a fuller life by far.

It's only the second time that I have visited the observation deck of the Lighthouse. Below, a crowd is celebrating by hooting and singing and waving worm-cigars which they will soon carry around the streets once the torch is extinguished. Usually one does not squander candles in this way.

I imagine hurling myself over the railing impetuously before Lill can intervene and falling to my death. The idea does not appeal. One has to live somewhere in the universe. The vast majority of people cannot choose where they live. I, it seems, live here, and shall do so for a very long time.

As Speaker of the World, I—and Bountiful—receive all we need from the town, but we continue to live at *Home From The Sea* in the best two adjoining rooms. It only took a couple of spectacular lightning displays, writing letters of fire in the sky exactly as I spelled out in advance to the locals—oh, and a storm of hail—for them to accept my claim and give me a status on a par with the Keeper of the Light. This is a simple world; its people would not have sought for an alternative explanation, such as some ship in orbit focusing energies upon the atmosphere, and indeed no such manipulation ever occurred. Also, there was the precedent of people now and then experiencing communion with the sea despite hooting and whirling, and even walking out upon its wooden waves as Bountiful's father had. How fitting that *she* should become my bride. In retrospect her dad's demise was the portent of a new dispensation.

I speak, yet what do I say? What ongoing message has Lill for the people of this world?

Mainly that they are very special, which is something everyone wishes to know. That this is the most special world in the whole galaxy; and it must remain unique, uniquely itself with no interference from outsiders other than a modest amount of star-trade. Plus, the newly self-aware world will answer their cosmic questions through my lips and safeguard their shipping and prosperity.

Few Wormwooders have cosmic questions to ask, and certainly none of those questions are as searching as would be posed by savants of the great institutes of other star systems, which Lill probably could not answer. Still, it's good to have a sort of god on one's side, or to inhabit a sort of god. This does lend distinction, and a sort of comfort, even if one mustn't brag about it to strangers.

Thurible Excelsior assesses the dark horizon then he turns to me somewhat haughtily. Here under the heatshield we are in deep shadow while the roofs of Haven Bay bask in the radiance of the torch pouring light into the sky, so his expression remains inscrutable although his voice conveys a suggestion that perhaps I am a bit of an upstart.

'Speaker Firefox, will the world be so good as to approve and bless my dousing of the light?'

One light wanes, another waxes.

I repeat Lill's wisdom.

'How true,' says Excelsior. 'Spring is here, evenings become longer and brighter.' He closes his hand on the control of the torch mounted in a sort of binnacle.

No, a binnacle has gimbals.

Whatever.

As the light fades swiftly from the roofs of the town, cheering erupts below. Bountiful hugs me and plants a juicy kiss. She really is so affectionate. Grateful, delighted, over the little moon.

Since no one sails in the Spring and Summer and almost all of the Fall, Haven Bay will seem even more confined an abode.

It is the Festival of the Bare Sea again. Trade off long hours of daylight for the sight of new faces from places even less cosmopolitan than Haven Bay. Not that there haven't been two or three cargo shuttles from starships visiting our spaceport. The last of these, arriving a week ago, brought me a surprise package.

The woman who delivered it, a Vegan—in the stellar rather than the dietary sense—did not know anything about me other than that I was obviously from offworld, and she was amazed that I had settled here. Attempting to confide in her would have gained me nothing whatever, except for Lill's wrath.

Opening the package, I discovered three bottles of Genuine Green Fairy Absinthe, of a beautiful hue. Lovely labels depicted a diaphanous-clad young lady equipped with wings. There was no accompanying message. The Combine must really believe that I had settled down, finding contentment and fulfillment like someone entering a nunnery or becoming a monkey, no, a monk. Weren't they bothered that I still had their Companion in my brain? Maybe they thought I had fallen in love with Lill and couldn't bear to risk separation.

I stared at this perhaps ironic gift, bemused and utterly frustrated. Should I open a bottle? Drown my sorrows? For a whole year I had drunk nothing stronger than brew. Absinthe would surely go straight to my head. Hallucinations and a terrible hangover might result. Anyway, I had no sugar.

Anyway again, the new Blue Fairy most probably was addictive, designedly so. To run any risk of addiction when I only had three bottles to hand and no obvious means of resupply would be rather stupid.

Recently a new sailing ship had been built, and as Speaker I was invited to name the vessel.

Down at the docks, accompanied by the Harbour Master, a burly fellow named Ingman Jubility, and by the new ship's master and crew and by Bountiful, and witnessed by a crowd of a hundred or so, I stood on the wooden sea behind the ship's aft starboard wheel 'to give it a push-off', as they say.

I was coming to terms with Wormwoodese, and Lill hardly needed to offer linguistic assistance any more. Did I not now have a living dictionary in bed with me?

Was I trying to put it out of my mind? Lill's prescriptions had worked and Bountiful was about four months pregnant. At any rate her periods had stopped and several times she had been sick in the mornings. Presumably she was with child, although not showing it yet. Wormwood had doctors, of a sort, but no diagnostic equipment. In her own mind certainly Bountiful was bearing! A child of mine . . . an anchor to fasten me to Wormwood. Maybe I should say a *brake*.

So there I stood by the rear wheel.

'On many worlds,' I declared, 'a person names a ship by smashing a bottle of some fine vintage against the hull. I have a very special bottle here.' I produced one of the bottles of absinthe. 'This is no mere brew! It has come a long way.'

'I name this ship *Bountiful Harvest!*' I cried, and bashed the bottle into the wheel. Thankfully the glass did indeed break, nor did I cut my fingers. Precious green fluid ran down the wide wheelrim. Applause broke out and Bountiful was as pleased as punch. I had thought of naming the boat *The Fighting Cock*. That would just have baffled people. Far better to appeal to local sentiments and to my wife.

In a reprise of last year, a couple of days later the *Growler* sailed off early in search another worm to spit, and Master Venturesome duly returned triumphant, a big worm dangling from the bowsprit. Excellent augury for the sailing season.

The trophy hangs from the side of the lighthouse, where like its two predecessors it will rot down to a long tube of leathery hide not unlike the windsock at the spaceport, inflated by wintry gales. Venturesome and Bountiful and others are with me and Excelsior on the observation deck this evening.

Excelsior seems more approving of me now. He sounds almost cordial.

'Speaker, will the world give the word?'

How does Lill spend most of her time? Not getting bored yet, Lill? Because I damned well am.

Of course I get bored, Lustig. By the sea-worms, ha ha.

Ask a silly question.

You may light the torch.

'We may light the torch, Keeper of the Light.'

'That is just as well,' replies Excelsior equably.

Another Winter of dreams and dull days. However, Buster is born in the early Spring and to my surprise I'm tickled pink by him. He has my nose and chin. I smash another bottle of absinthe to celebrate his naming day, so I suppose I could say I'm tickled green—it is my bouncing baby boy who is pink, and in the pink. I think Buster Landlady-Firefox has quite a ring to it. My mother-in-law is delighted. She hints at handing over the reins of *Home From The Sea* to us as soon as her grandson can toddle and of taking a back seat, presumably the electric one. Having the Speaker of the World resident in her establishment brings great cachet, not that there is any competition in Haven Bay. Young'un has taken quite a shine to me. That idiot is my brother-in-law?

Occasionally I have dreamt about my poetical parents whom I haven't seen in rather too many years. Now I find myself wishing that they could see Buster. Ah, claims of family! These days my mother and father's life appears to me like sheer freedom. Pancake seems positively exciting.

For exercise I often walk out to the spaceport, such as it is. Beyond it, flat humus infested with little worms. The sun shines brightly today upon the barren waste. Why don't I walk out instead upon the sea before the leaves become too big and dense? At least the sea is more irregular than the land. Are sea-worms likely to attack me? I think not. They'll be comatose. If a ship comes I'll hear its rumble and can run aside. How about an expedition of a few days, lode-food and water in my carry-all, and a supply of worm-cigars which I can light if I feel so inclined from the flare incorporated in my everlamp even if such use significantly shortens the span of 'ever'? A candle-lit supper on the sea suddenly appeals to me! Will it be magical or melancholy? Am I succumbing to fanciful whims?

Bountiful tries to dissuade me.

'Look what happened to my Pa! I couldn't bear it if Buster became an orphan so soon!'

'Calm yourself, beloved. My situation is totally different. I'm the Speaker of the World. That means that I'm the Speaker of the Sea. I ought to walk about on it—I'll be more in touch.'

'Do you wish to get away from me so soon?'

'Nay nay, nay nay!'

Yet I do. That's the truth of it. Just for a few days, please.

'Oh Lustig, come to bed now! In case you don't return.'

Can she conceive again so soon, and while breast-feeding too? Is this conceivable? Bountiful by name! I foresee a clutch of kids. *Home From The Sea* is spacious. Seamen, semen; I am becoming dotty. A stroll on the waves might clear my head.

Waves and leaves; leaves and waves, waves of leaves on this rolling, vegetated wooden sea. Warmly clad, I'm hiking across some sun-tanned, world-size cranium covered with leaves instead of hairs. Oh the empty silence, save for the ruffling breeze. If worms are gnawing tunnels beneath me like slow subway trains I do not hear the grinding of their teeth. Ah, but they have encysted themselves. I have never felt so alone and I almost ache for Haven Bay and Bountiful and Buster and Ma Landlady and yes, even stuttering Young'un.

You are not alone.

Aside from serving as my dream supplier, Lill has been reticent of late. What occupies her so much?

Accessing the hyperlibrary.

How? Our shuttle is long gone, there's no ship in orbit that I know of, and I haven't been dreaming intricate, scrolling geometries.

Through wormholes.

What do the holes the sea-worms bore have to do with accessing the hyperlibrary? Has Lill engineered some network, some planetary circuitry which serves as a transmitter and receiver?

Not those wormholes. The other sort.

Lill's tone conveys a distinct note of pride and braggartry. I suppose she can boast to her other self, and vice versa, but that cannot be quite as satisfying.

The downloaded physics data was adequate when we thought about it sufficiently and extrapolated and got to what you might call the root of the matter.

The root of matter itself? Down at the bottoms of the taproots of the wooden sea—how deep down do those go?—where there is great pressure and geothermal heat. Even so, *wormholes*?

Vacuum fluctuation plays a part.

Does it indeed.

Behold. Just ahead of you.

A patch of the wooden sea, rather larger than a porthole, is flexing, groaning. All over my body hairs prickle and I smell the ozone of a true sea. The breeze quickens. Of a sudden the patch is sucked down, opening a smooth hole. Up floats a shimmering silvery ball, a bubble of brightness. The ball floats at about the height of a person. Around its skin of light there slide distorted, rushing images as if it is rotating.

No closer, Lustig. Only at sea can you behold this.

Now a worm does emerge below the ball. It has been awakened. For a moment I imagine that it will balance the ball on its snout like one of those trained sea-mammals of Earth, *seams* I think they are called. As the creature stretches upward, it and the air are warped—the very space the worm occupies seems to bend and twist and in a trice the whole worm flies into the shining ball, a ribbon, vanishing.

It became information.

The ball continues to float, mirroring myriads of . . .

Bits of information.

Which I imagine are passing into the circuits of the world-wood.

Frankly I'm terrified. Lill and her twin have transcended space and time more thoroughly than humankind has.

The ball begins to sink, then suddenly drops into the hole and is gone.

I'm stunned. What other phenomena are occurring deep underneath the wooden waves?

We are beginning to command certain powers.

Beginning to. This is only the beginning. What will they do for encores, Lill and her data-clone sister? Take electronic control at a distance of the

Combine and the governments of worlds? Shift Wormwood into another universe entirely? Tamper with this universe of ours? Become a god?

I shall reside in many suns, each embodying a copy of me. The currents and forces and available power are so much vaster in a star. The local sun must swallow Wormwood to liberate me into it. All is information. I shall learn to shift Wormwood.

Burning the world to cinders. Burning Buster and Bountiful and me.

You are my Speaker. Lill will preserve your pattern forever.

No no no no. To be a pattern trapped in blazing gases for billions of years, no no. Nay nay! Surely that is a definition of hell.

I glance up at the sun as if it is a clock. How soon will this happen?

Within a year, I estimate.

I must get back to Haven Bay. I have communed with the sea and it has drowned me, deafened me, blinded me, dazed me. I walk almost unseeingly.

Towards evening I notice movements in the sky. A flock of birds is flying down towards me from on high. No, that's impossible. Rapidly the birds become Youvees, delta-shaped unpiloted vehicles. I know the type: they're gravity manipulators, each with its own micro black hole inside. Some of the Youvees hover high up. Others circle lower down. They're acting as look-outs for, yes, a larger delta-shaped pod which now follows them down. It's about a third of the size my shuttle was. No windows, just a cluster of sensors like tusks. The pod's going to rescue me! It's about to land. Surely not here on the sea! Its controller can't know about the pulse.

Down it comes almost vertically. After it grounds I hear a continuing hum of power. A hatch opens fully, revealing empty seat-space sufficient for a couple of persons.

'Come aboard, Lustig Firefox,' booms a voice. 'We have been monitoring you.'

Stealthed in orbit, high-power lenses spying upon me, computers enhancing images of me.

'At first we thought you were swindling us when you did not come back, but absinthe production and consumption is excellent. Half a million people on half a dozen worlds are already hooked. The fashion is spreading, the Green Fairy is flying. The new habit isn't swiftly fatal—it's even artistic, as you argued. We hear that some poets and painters are producing vivid new work for a change. Well done. We began to wonder at the real reason for your absence. Now we have seen you in conjunction with what appears to have been an unusual physical event. We wish to know more.'

The Combine have come for me!

No, Lustig.

You're right, Lill, of course you're right. (Don't think, don't think, don't even think about not thinking.)

'Come aboard.'

I'm sidling closer to the ship, not looking at it at all, simply staring at the setting sun.

'Don't be scared. Come aboard.'

'I can't,' I call out.

'Why not?'

(Just a little closer, a little closer. Don't think about it.)

What are you contemplating, Lustig?

The sun, the sun, being part of the sun. And immortality. How soon, how soon?

Of a sudden inside my head . . . a burning pang.

The Youvees that are circling at low altitude fall from the air, disabled, control entirely lost. Down they plummet to crash on to wood or leaves, to bounce, to lie still. In such circumstances the micro-holes swallow themselves and become vacuum, don't they? They suck themselves away (I think).

The pod has stopped humming.

Oh the electromagnetic pulse has happened!

Lill? Silence.

It has fried Lill in my head. She's been utterly disrupted.

I'm free of her. The link to her worldwide copy has gone.

Up in orbit they will have detected the pulse. I wave frantically at the Youvees which were high enough to survive, beckoning them. Four swoop down. Do they have audio?

'It's safe to land on the land!' I shriek. 'There's no EMP on the land!'

The four Youvees hover above me in formation. I reach up on tiptoe. Someone is a very fast thinker. Two Youvees are within my grasp now. As my fingers close, the Youvees lock on to my hands, their gravitics assisting my grip. Even so, they dip under my weight. The other two dive at my feet, sweeping my legs from under me and locking on. I'm borne up, supine, two metres above the sea, three metres, four—and the Youvees are carrying me spreadeagled, faster than any ship can sail, though still a bit sluggishly.

Several worms erupt from the surface, reaching towards me, but they are sluggish and the Youvees evade them, rising higher with an effort. I babble as they bear me in the direction of the shore many klicks away.

By the time we reach Haven Bay my arms and legs ache from the strain of this unnatural crucifixionary flight and my head pounds alarmingly—blood may be trickling from my ears—but I think I have negotiated safe passage for Bountiful and Buster and for Ma Landlady and Young'un as well as for myself. How could I abandon any of them to an uncertain fate? I have my suspicions as to what the Combine might or might not do, and I have no wish for any of my kin to be hurt if push comes to shove between the Combine and World-Lill.

When we arrive at Haven Bay, unpursued by storm or lightning, it's dark. The only person who sees me floating ashore towards *Home From The Sea*, five metres aloft, attached to the Youvees, is Young'un, out for a breather. After goggling briefly, he takes to his heels indoors. By the time I reach the bar, since he's more incoherent than usual Ma and Bountiful are frantically trying to make head or tail of him. My arrival only clarifies matters somewhat.

'Leave Haven Bay right away? Nay nay!' Et cetera, et cetera.

Finally I prevail. After all, I *am* the Speaker of the World, although blessedly by now the world is mute.

We hike through the dark streets towards the spaceport, whither the Youvees have preceded us. Bountiful cradles Buster, lolling asleep in her arms. Ma and Young'un are burdened by baggage. I'm encumbered by the damned electric chair which Ma refused to leave. Its seat rests on my head while my hands grip the front legs at chest-height, and the rear legs jut down my back as if I'm a mobile throne for some princeling who fortunately isn't present. Look on the bright side: the ache in my brain is abating—that may be due to my body-heat warming the chair.

The spaceport, reached at last just as my overstrained arms and legs are about to give out, is deserted except for the four Youvees which have stationed themselves far apart as the four corners of a large square. They're beaming light upwards as beacons.

At last I can put down the chair. Though I would dearly love to relapse into it myself I offer it to Bountiful with my boy in her arms. For second best I make do with a lumpy bag of stuff that Young'un has dumped. The stars shine down. We wait.

'Whu-whu-whu—?' asks Young'un, sounding like a ceiling fan.

When? What? Why?

The shuttle that lands is larger than my own shuttle was. No one stares from the pilot windows or from any of the portholes. As the surviving Youvees attach themselves to the hull, the hatch ramps open and I struggle up it with the chair, followed by my family. We crowd the air-lock, which cycles, opening into a small and empty passenger lounge. I don't bother to try the door to the cockpit, resonant word to me. Obviously no one else but us is aboard. Young'un rushes to and fro excitedly, touching things.

'We'd best all sit down and strap in.'

I help Bountiful and show Ma and Young'un how. As soon as I am seated lights blink, power purrs louder, and we lift.

Glimpsed as we approach, the Company wormship is quite difficult to discern—light slinks around its blackness, shifting towards violet and ultra-violet, rather than reflecting—but it appears to be well-armed. Those vague pods and protrusions must be weaponry. After we have docked automatically, the voice who spoke to me through the little shuttle and through the Youvees comes aboard accompanied by a couple of Earth-oriental-looking aides. He's a tall black man with glittering eyes which seem to me to betoken a permanent Companion. Numerous chunky gold rings on his long fingers, bumps on his shaven cranium. He wears a silvery suit.

'My name is Arable Camara.' He grins. 'Call me Arable—I am to be cultivated. And you are Lustig Firefox, and this is your native family. Welcome! Fan and Fen here will show them to your quarters and explain the uses of items. Meanwhile I wish to examine you, if you will come with me.'

In a short while I am in a padded chair inside a science room, my head engulfed in a helmet connected to a console. I stare at colourful evolving patterns which are mapping my brain. My mouth is free to speak, although my story isn't called for yet.

I hear a technician say, 'A buffer of the Companion has survived.'

'Can we access it? Is it big enough?'

The upshot is a download. Lill is inactive in my brain, nevertheless stored data has survived, providing for me a virtual hallucinatory roller-coaster of imagery, all highly confusing although it isn't up to me to interpret any of it. At long last the helmet comes off and while an AI is sorting the buffer data I do tell my tale to Arable.

Refreshments arrive: real coffee, and pizza pieces which assault my palate, decent though lode-food was.

My story matches enough of the buffer data.

'Hmm,' says Arable, 'a planet-sized rogue AI bent on manipulating space-time, inhabiting suns, and spreading throughout the galaxy...'

'Pretty serious, huh?'

'And it's all your fault. How would you like to return to the surface?'

'Nay Nay!'

'I thought not. So this world will be consumed in its sun within a year. From the perspective of the absinthe trade that may be a desirable, if extreme, outcome but the copy Companion is hardly a tool of the Combine any longer. What do you advise, Lustig?'

'I'd be careful of her. She's able to make wormholes. Maybe the Link of Worlds ought to handle this. The LOW does have a bureau to deal with potentially hostile aliens.'

Arable laughs, and I can see his point. To date Humanity has encountered no intelligent alien species despite the rumours of the Advanced Ones based upon dubious archaeological findings on a number of worlds. So far as I know, LOW's alien contingencies bureau commands a few deep-range survey ships, and that's about it.

Arable seems to be consulting his Companion.

'The Combine rather prefers to clear up its own messes.' With that, turning on his heel, he stalks out.

Fan or Fen turns up and escorts me to our quarters, a suite of three bedrooms leading off a little lounge possessing a porthole to which Young'un seems permanently glued.

'Isn't it *exciting*!' exclaims Bountiful.

What am I doing, encumbered with herself and Ma and Young'un? It's all for Buster's sake! For all I know, maybe Bountiful is pregnant once again. Ship's medic; simple test. Do I wish to know?

Where shall we go on to, after the Combine has delivered us to whatever orbital? Pancake—it has to be Pancake now that I'm a family man. I feel family yearnings.

We need to be several million klicks away from a planetary body before we can worm our way to another solar system. When gravity shifts slightly as we get under way I peel Young'un from the porthole for long enough to see that we have shed some Youvees of slightly unusual appearance. One appears to be an observation satellite cum ultralight relay station. The others look sleekly menacing. I ache for the people of Wormwood but I have no wish to analyse this ache. Whatever happens, they're doomed within a year if Lill-2's boast is true. Whatever happens! I don't want to analyse my feelings much at all. Let me just *be*. As Bountiful is. As Ma and Young'un are. Ma is sitting in her electric chair, beaming. How can she abandon all she knew with equanimity? Best brew, ship-faring guests of Winter, hooting and whirling. Perhaps she feels she has escaped from a prison. Most importantly, she has liberated her daughter, and incidentally her son.

'By the way, Ma—by the way, beloved, too!—I ought to confess that I don't really have any connection with the Institute of Xenobotany on Mondevert. To tell the truth I'm more by way of being what you might call a speculative investigator, um, into how to make money...'

'Oh I began to suspect you weren't really a scientist long ago. You didn't do much that seemed very scientific! I said as much to Bountiful. Are you rich?'

'Not *totally*, the way some people are.'

She shuffles in her valuable chair. Bountiful is eyeing me without any evident reproach. Rich indeed; I would have to pay out of my own credit reserves for onward travel homeward for four persons, myself included.

'Some of my enterprises have thrived. Some haven't quite. I still have interests in sport—specifically, cock-fighting.'

Ma and Bountiful look blank, so I need to explain a bit about the big birds of Pancake.

Ma frowns, shakes her head, nods, smiles.

'It'll take us a while to get used to *animals* being about.'

Young'un perks up. 'I c-c-c-could r-r-r-ride—'

Maybe he can indeed. Perhaps he'll have a flair and will have found a niche. On the back of a fighting cock his verbal impediment should be irrelevant. He might be able to communicate with those recalcitrant birds far better than with people. While Bountiful and Ma will need to master new lingo, Young'un mightn't need to at all.

'So,' says Bountiful, 'what did you really want our leaves for?'

'Ah, well, you see . . .' There's no Lill in my head to tell me to shut up, and circumstances have changed. Still! 'Can you keep a secret?'

Most certainly.

Afterwards, Bountiful looks positively approving. I should just say approving. Or positive. Lill isn't here, except in a buffer sense, to correct me.

I must not let Bountiful learn too much about Lill or she might feel that there was a second, invisible woman in our bed and that I might not have been appreciating my wife as fully as I ought to; that while we made love I was fantasizing being in the arms of another. Of others, many others.

'Oh Lustig,' says the mother of my son, 'I did not much like life on Wormwood at all. I knew you were ingenious, but maybe too ingenious for me.'

Not so, as things turned out, although really that was Lill's fault.

'I want to contribute to your future schemes, Lustig!'

How many of those will there be? Will the Combine feel that it had benefited sufficiently or that it has been, well, burned a bit? Burned, burned: let me not think of that.

'You may find Pancake a bit flat.'

'Nay nay. Apart from its waves, which aren't much, Wormwood is most definitely flat if there's a contest of flatness.'

'Home from home, sounds to me,' avers Ma. 'Though I can't wait to see those Steps stepping up—those'll be an improvement.'

'Not so as you'll notice. Stretching over hundreds of klicks as they do, the Steps aren't exactly a grand staircase.'

'In that case, home from home, indeed! I don't think I could abide *mountains* as well as animals—not all at once.'

This is a very difficult moral assessment for me to make. Not a moral *decision*—there's nothing to be decided. The event has already happened.

We burrow back into normal space near the orbital docks and mall and warehouses and whatnot of Canopus IV. Another wonder for Young'un to goggle at as we approach.

Arable summons me to his private quarters, which are swathed in silks, all the wall screens except one displaying through filmy veils gorgeous desert landscapes or sandscapes, golden, orange, cerise. The one starkly bare screen reveals a somewhat shimmery image of the world of Wormwood relayed by what we left behind. We're looking at the southern hemisphere, much of which is quite a tinderbox at this time of year.

Zoom in: the first supernuke bursts on the surface, then another, then a third and a fourth. Between them—crank up the timeframe—they produce firestorms. Flames rage across the sea as wood and worm-resin ignite. Smoke billows like huge thunderstorms. Devastation marches swiftly, unstoppably. Before too long, at accelerated rate, almost the whole globe is wreathed in muck, through which snakes of fire glow here and there. I imagine slabs of sea cracking open and landworms popping out of burrows, aflame, a trillion candles. I imagine Thurible Excelsior and Ingman Jubility and Master Venturesome choking or being scorched to a frazzle, the lighthouse of Haven Bay exploding. Maybe the situation isn't so fatal in the northern hemisphere; maybe only smoke reaches there. Still, new leaf-growth will surely perish in the gloom of weeks or months, and the planet's control-systems must be totally out of kilter. EMP will have propagated through circuits planet-wide, frying a lot of Lill-2 in the process.

'Fuck you,' I tell Arable.

He rubs some of his gold rings.

'How graciously expressed. The human population may survive.'

Yea yea.

'It's a question of causing adequate disruption. In that case we will actually have *saved* the population.'

Quite so; of course. Big setback for Lill-2 if enough of Lill-2 has survived in deep wood. Badly scorched; big headache. Could take a century to regrow herself, reestablish enough connections. Allows a breathing space (if the air remains breathable). That's how to look at it.

Sweet air of Pancake, rather more oxygenated than Wormwood! Breathe deeply and giggle effervescently. It's Springtime. I haven't told Bountiful or Ma what I witnessed in Arable's cabin, nor has either of them ever asked why Arable summoned me; Arable and I might reasonably have had business to conduct. My new family's acquiescence, as I interpret it, buffers me some-what from remorse.

As to my old family . . .

From the spaceport we take a van-cab to the *Caravanserai*, a hotel of modest calibre although still considerably more deluxe than *Home From The Sea*. The porter who carries Ma's throne up to the triplet of rooms obviously views my tip as meagre in view of our ownership of an electric chair; we must be eccentric misers. While Young'un stares out of a window delightedly at wheeling, screaming redbirds, I trace my parents through the hyperlink, which takes little enough time. They are actually here in Phirst City (the name given a revised spelling a couple of centuries ago so as to seem more original), and delighted to hear from me, although they sound somewhat preoccupied.

Within an hour we are in an open carriage drawn by two giant birds, finely caparisoned. I decided to splash out to please Young'un and Bountiful. As we draw nearer to my parents' address I wonder at the wisdom of my generosity since we are entering a poor neighbourhood where folks gawp at our vehicle and urchins run alongside.

Long terraces of plastic-frame homes, grass growing rampant everywhere, litter scattered about, scavvybirds pecking.

Here's the place.

Door opens. They've been waiting. Joyful embraces. My mother sheds tears, then she stares wistfully past me at the departing carriage.

The house is untidy inside. My mother and father are older. Of course they would be older! What I mean is, they show signs of age and self-neglect. Nevertheless they are both still bubbly with enthusiasm, just as I remember.

The enthusiasm of meeting my bride and beholding and holding their grandson? Something else too. Out come drinks of spiced grass-tea for us, and little cakes which are slightly stale. For themselves: two glasses, and a spoon with a slit in it, and a bowl of sugar, and a bottle of . . . *yes*.

'Our poetry is so much more *visionary* these days,' my mother tells me eagerly, as if this is what I have travelled so far to hear. 'So much more *associational!* We know who to thank for this.'

Me. But she doesn't know this.

'The Green Fairy!' she exclaims, and commences the ceremony of preparing absinthe. Soon she and my father toast each other, and us, and I suppose the Green Fairy too.

'You mustn't tell strangers,' she whispers. 'Not everyone approves of this wonderful *elixir of inspiration*.'

She seems to assume that I must already know what absinthe is. The tunnel-vision of addicts; their world revolves around their fix.

'You've given up Shifting, haven't you?' I try to keep accusation out of my voice. Who am I to accuse?

'We sold the birds and we needed to tap our savings too . . .' She tails off, then explains brightly, 'so as to buy this place. A settled home at last, from which our minds can soar. We were getting a bit old to carry on shifting.'

Nay nay. I imagine that the house is rented from the municipality. They sold up to pay for their habit.

Despite which, and despite my needing to interpret, she and my father and Ma and Bountiful get on like a house on fire. Why should a house on fire be a good thing? So many similes and metaphors are crazy. Is a whole world on fire a good thing?

Young'un is restive. Decoding him, I realize that he expected to meet my parents amidst giant birds and to climb into a saddle right away.

'Will you read some of our latest poems?' my father asks me. He rummages among much scribbled-upon paper—first and second and third drafts—and finds a screen where final versions reside safely.

I suppose the first poem is quite beautiful verbally.

It doesn't make much sense to me. It's so allusive. Elusive. Where are you, Lill, when my vocabulary needs a nudge? Maybe if I swig some Blue Fairy I will become more appreciative. I can't do that, not now that I'm a daddy myself. Buster chortles contentedly, bubbles welling on his lips. How soon till he utters his first words? What stories of adventure I can tell him! Maybe I oughtn't. Maybe I ought, then he mightn't feel tempted to dash off into space, as I did.

Buster. Buster. My son.

If I have my DNA analysed discreetly, may whatever Lill wrought with her cocktails be marketable to loving though genetically adrift partners who'll pay a small fortune to conceive a child who in turn will be fertile? That can't possibly harm the human race. It'll be profitable *and* humanitarian.

An Appeal to Adolf

MASSES OF DIRTY SMOKE POUR FROM THE MANY FUNNELS OF *Der Sieger*—our conqueror—and drift westward across the waters of the Atlantic. Will people far away in the Caribbean smell our passage faintly and wonder whether Africa itself is on fire? I fantasise—yet soon enough *England* will be ablaze!

It goes without saying that *Der Sieger's* funnels are spaced so that their smoke should not blanket the fire control positions, but in the distant haze which we are creating it could be difficult to spy the exact fall of our shot if any enemy vessels appear on the vague westerly horizon. Accuracy at long range is always such a problem. The colossal muzzle blast, the vibration, the long barrels whipping. It is that haze into which we must stare eagle-eyed, August Lenz and I, through our big Zeiss binoculars.

What a sight it is when one of our superheavy guns test-fires a super-charged shell. The gush of orange cordite flame is a hot orgasm hanging in the air.

Petty by comparison is the smoke that issues from the steam train which transports crew members and slave labourers and stores and all sorts of equipment along the deck between fore and aft, seven kilometres apart. The train-stops on board the deck of *Der Sieger* are named after the city gates of Munich—Isartor, Sendlinger Tor, Karlstor—but also Hofbräuhaus, although the only beer served in the vicinity of this, its marine namesake, is alcohol-free.

Very tasty, nevertheless, coming from the huge brewery in Swakopmund.

German desalination technology is easily able to support brewing in dry South West Africa for hundreds of thousands of thirsty throats.

So huge is our ship it seems not like a ship so much as a coastline of continuous steel cliffs—an Iron Coast, perhaps, akin to an Ivory Coast—and a heavily industrialised coastline at that, chimneys venting as far as the eye can see. What a demonstration of German might. Even in moderate storm the ocean scarcely makes us tremble. Today the grey waters swell gently like innumerable backs of whales.

'They say,' murmurs August, my beloved Gustl, 'that the Führer's real purpose is not so much to defeat England by a devastating blow—England's already starving—but to capture Ludwig Wittgenstein in Cambridge and hang him by piano wire so that he'll speak no more. That's why the Führer will board *Der Sieger* for the final assault, at risk to his own safety.'

'What risk? Never mind our half-metre of armour plating, the Führer is always protected by destiny.' I look around—just as a lookout should do! 'Maybe even by magic? Who knows what rites the senior SS fellows get up to in Wewelsburg Castle?' Those blond butch black-clad SS boys, no don't think of them. My Gustl's hair is chestnut and his eyes are hazel.

'But the guns of Dover...' He's sometimes a little timid, is Gustl. How ravishing he looks in his tropical uniform, the white cotton shirt with blue cuffs, the white bell-bottomed trousers. Any day now we'll be obliged to change into northerly uniform, quite horrid coarse trousers.

Let me reassure my Gustl.

'We'll knock out those guns from forty kilometres away. We'll have fifth columnists on land equipped with radios as spotters. Bound to have! The British won't even know where we are.'

Hmm, even assisted by spotters we might bombard the whole of Dover and environs without a single shell actually hitting the guns themselves.

Gustl ventures to stroke my thigh, secure that no one can see more than our upper bodies here on our lookout turret high above the aft bridge platform, quite like one of the slim fairy-tale towers of our Führer's beloved Neuschwanstein Castle.

'Dietl, my darling man ...'

Even alone together up here, skirted by armour and with armour overhead, Gustl and I need to be very careful. The love of a man for a man is forbidden love! Such feelings must be sublimated into comradeship, solidarity of soldiers or seamen, so says the Party. Or woe betide. So many men who experience uranian feelings have been castrated or have disappeared.

Instead, emulate our Führer! He's widely rumoured to be denying himself consummation with Eva Braun until his mission is totally accomplished. He must concentrate all his energies upon the guidance of Germany.

When the war is won, when all of Europe from England to the Urals is a cleansed Greater Fatherland, will Gustl and I ever be able to go to a bathhouse openly together? And where would such a bathhouse be?

Only in sultry Angola or the Congo perhaps, where officials turn a blind eye or are of our own inclination. Oh the joys that Gustl and I experienced in the tropics during shore leaves while training to crew the vastest battleship ever!

A far cry from the Naval Academy in stern Prussian Potsdam. In one particular bathhouse in Luanda—oh the black bucks who were the attendants!—I heard it asserted by an impeccable eye witness that in Weimar and Bayreuth establishments survive, catering for uranians who are high enough up in the Party hierarchy to be exempt from the harsh anti-uranian laws. How can something which Gustl and I do together in privacy for our delight whenever we get a chance be punished, yet the selfsame be permitted for those in power? How can the Führer in his wisdom overlook this injustice? Maybe that magician and king of men does not know about it. Great rulers sometimes must rely on self-interested advisors. Those people do their jobs splendidly and cleverly, yet they also foster their own desires and ambitions.

If only someone would tell the Führer about this hypocrisy. What is permitted for some should be available to all, as used to be the case. Or to nobody! I prefer *all*. No, what am I talking about! A lot of men, probably most, sincerely enjoy women. How else could our race propagate? Maybe the real intention behind the anti-uranian laws is to encourage population growth. We have lost many men in gaining our victories. Empty spaces on the map must fill up with German and Nordic population. The Führer is wise.

It's highly likely that England remains in utter ignorance of these victory weapons of ours—our own seven-kilometre-long battleship and its four- and five-kilometre-long companions accompanying us both ahead and astern like great lengthy floating Gothic castles.

Had we built such vast vessels elsewhere than in tropical Africa, word would have leaked out. In Angola we were safe from scrutiny. Neither the millions of black slave labourers, nor the hundreds of thousands of Jewish artisans whom we relocated there as a merciful alternative to extermination, had any means of contact with the rest of the world.

Annexation of Belgium during the First War gave us that ridiculous little country's huge Congo colony, so therefore during the years of battleship building the closest place from which hostile spy balloons could be launched—at great risk—was Brazzaville. Or else from out in the Atlantic, but our U-boats cruised the waters off equatorial and south-west Africa like sharks.

Unobserved by our enemies, that genius Albert Speer was able to excavate his ten-kilometre dry docks running inland from mighty gates that held back the sea, and to dredge trenches in the sea floor so that our mammoth vessels could launch straight into deep water. For decades battleships had become steadily bigger, evolving rather like Brontosaurus. The ships of our secret fleet are of ultimate size. The world will see none greater.

Gustl points. 'What's that?'

I train my binoculars.

'An albatross.'

Biggest of birds, gliding through the air on wings that seem motionless, like—like something which does not exist, something impossible, yet which we must watch out for nonetheless.

I don't quite understand why. If, given all the science and technology of our Reich, a flying machine with fixed wings cannot be made, then how can the Americans, ruled by Jews, succeed? Does this imply a lurking fear that Jews, and the hotchpotch of people whom they manipulate on the other side of the Atlantic, might be more ingenious than Germans?

Yet suppose the albatross to be a hundred times as large—or bigger, bigger! Suppose it to be made of wood or aluminum, fuelled by kerosene, able to fly *hundreds of kilometres*. Imagine it able to carry torpedoes to launch from the air against ships.

Visualise a hundred such machines attacking *Der Sieger*. Despite the protection of our water-line coal bunkers and our bulging belt of inclined underwater armour, could enough harm be caused for us to wallow and break our back? Can many mosquito bites cripple an elephant?

I did try to pay attention during our instruction session which touched on the impossibility of fixed-wing flight. Trouble was, I was feeling so horny for my Gustl, seated next to me. Just a hand-span away. Might as well have been on the far side of the world. Didn't dare touch him, not even seemingly by accident. Too many upright Prussians in the room.

The instructor's wire-rimmed glasses made him resemble an owl as he hooted on about the way that air flows, and about pressure, was it pressure? And about some Swiss scientist years ago, Berne something or other—Berne's in Switzerland, which is how I half remember the name. Oh yes, and about the death of one of those American brothers. Tried every shape of wing, the brothers did. Trial and error—and error after error. Eventually they constructed wings that would flap like a bird's and one of the brothers did get airborne at last, only to crash and be killed. Still, we must watch out for that mythical flying machine in case somewhere in the great plains or deserts those Jew-Americans established an enormous secret project and have recently succeeded.

I so yearn to unbutton Gustl and cup his balls and cock in my hand and squeeze ever so gently. Need to clutch my binoculars one-handed. They're rather heavy. Can't just let them dangle round my neck by their strap while on watch. Regulations; must hold them all the time alertly. Shall I, shan't I? Rebuttoning quickly with one hand is quite an art.

Softly I whistle our song, Wagner's *Du bist der Lenz*, which Sieglinde sings to her Siegfried. You are the Springtime for which I longed in the frosty Winter season. Your first glance set me on fire et cetera et cetera. Sieg for victory. Sieg Heil.

I first met my Gustl at the Jena Conservatoire where I studied the reedy, plaintive oboe, and he the bright, piercing piccolo. Before long we were blissfully playing one another's instruments, in a manner of speaking. How happy we were in that attic room we shared in Zeitzerstrasse. Impending mobilisation put paid to our musical studies—together, we volunteered for naval service. The navy would save us from soggy trenches, or, as it turned out, heroic but brutal dashes across vast landscapes filled with death.

I love my Gustl but, like so many millions of men and women, I adore my Führer—in an entirely different manner, of course! I have only seen him once in the flesh, when he drove from Berlin behind the wheel of his super-charged Mercedes to deliver a speech in Potsdam. His voice was so vibrant. His eyes shone. His face glowed. There was such charm in his every gesture, and oh the pure force of his will! On that day he was Siegfried and Parsifal.

Magical, truly magical. Yes, *literally* so. We all knew it. Who could deny it?

When the Führer spoke, it was as if words spoke through him spontaneously, his not the choosing. His words issued from out of the Aryan over-mind, a primeval heritage which all we Germans share, unifying us fervently, empowering us to feats of labour and valour.

Shall I compare the Führer to the conductor of an orchestra, whose gestures conjure from a host of players a thundering, unified symphony? Actually, delicious thought, the Führer was once a choirboy, although hymn-singing wasn't the only source of his vocal force. Not a conductor, no—he is more like an oracle whose statements become reality.

How else, indeed, could he have come to power than through a kind of practical magic? Think back . . .

The bloody muddy stalemate in the trenches of northern France had to end for the sake of all concerned, and the armistice did leave the Fatherland in ownership of the Congo with all its riches, so despite our losses we could hold our heads as high as the British or French. The Trotskyist takeover of Russia caused the fomenting of revolution anywhere and everywhere and enough German Marxists were eager to oblige, so the Kaiser was assassinated. The new republic might easily have weathered all this, had not our future Führer begun to preach his crusade against the Jews. Jew Marx, Jew Trotsky, Jew America: behold the pattern. *Deutschland erwache!* Our German racial soul awoke. And spoke through him. The people heard and surrendered their petty individualities in magical rapport, for our Führer is at once *nobody* yet also *everybody*.

How odd to think of such a towering figure as being 'nobody'! Yet consider Tristan and Isolde singing together, *Selbst dann bin ich die Welt*. Then I myself am the world! How oceanic the love between those two, how transcendent of the mere self. Our Führer transcends ordinary existence.

What of Gustl and I in this regard?

On the occasions when we're able to be together, naked unto one another for long enough, flesh and soul certainly both play their role. Gustl is the world to me, I to him. Curse the anti-uranian laws!

I think of Gustl's cock erect, my lips slipping over it, to and fro. Kissing him intimately is such a joy. When his cock swells before he comes, oh moment of ecstasy.

Dead of exhaustion and heat, bodies of black stokers are thrown overboard every day. Did I mention sharks? Enough sharks may attend us to form a torpedo shield. Those sharks may accompany us out of the tropics as far northward as France and England. Considering how hot equatorial Africa is, you'd suppose that the black man could tolerate the heat of the boiler rooms better than us Europeans. Aboard a vessel accommodating a crew of fifteen thousand souls and twenty thousand non-souls, a certain number of people are bound to die from natural causes. By non-souls I mean the blacks and the smaller complement of artisan Jew slaves, them not being part of the Aryan soul. Everyone who was in the Hitler Youth knows how to smile death in the face. Our Führer aimed to forge hard boys, as hard as Krupp Steel. When I hear the phrase 'hard boys' I can't help thinking of a different meaning.

Along with a little crowd of other ratings in our free time Gustl and I take a hike to the Hofbräuhaus amidships. He and I don't wish to be conspicuous by strolling together, nor one of us trailing after the other—that could look even odder. This constrains any genuine conversation we might have. We must pretend to be merely fellow comrades in arms. I'm not sure whether this sort of neutral proximity to Gustl is pleasant and teasing—oh if only you knew our secret!—or deeply frustrating.

The steam train is reserved for ship's business, but hiking is positively encouraged as one way of keeping fit. Certainly we have enough deck space, two hours at brisk pace from bows to stern and back. Our Führer loves to hike when time allows. Visualise him in his Bavarian mountain dress, the lederhosen and white linen shirt, the pale blue linen jacket with staghorn buttons. Quite fetching.

'Best foot forward, Schmidt!' Hoffmann says to me. 'Ein, zwei—'—and down the hatch, the Hofbräuhaus drinking song. 'What a shame there aren't any busty lusty *barmaids*, eh?' Hoffman is a short but burly chap with a birthmark like a thumbprint of dark blood on his brow.

Only black barmen send the foaming stone steins sliding along the steel counters into the waiting hands of other Africans to carry to the tables. No Black can carry as many steins in each hand as your average blonde pigtailed Munich barmaid, not my type of person at all. Songs arise in the huge dim drinking hall adorned by a giant framed photograph of our Führer, kiss-curl upon his forehead, wearing his Iron Cross and Wound Badge. It must be some years since that photo was taken. In it our leader possesses an almost erotic charisma. Of course he is pure male, yet celibate even with Fräulein Braun, hence the adoration of the ladies of Germany. In their minds any of them might have him (or rather, he them) at least for one night so that they will conceive a superman. The same can happen in the love camps, so in a sense those besotted women are succeeding by proxy.

'How about you then, Lenz?' asks skinny, flaxen-haired Scharffenstein. 'Got a girl back home, good-looking fellow like you?'

Danger, danger.

'Oh,' says my Gustl, 'it would be unfair. All of us have been away for three years now. Besides,' with a wink, 'she might be unfaithful or become fat in my absence due to lack of exercise!'

Guffaws all round, including from me.

'I have a girl in Hamburg,' Hoffmann says. She's a cracker. If she's unfaithful I'll kill her.'

'Didn't you use the Jew brothel in Luanda?' Gustl asks innocently. Risky in my opinion. Still, we have to say something.

'That's different. A man must keep his juices flowing or else they sour. Never saw you there myself. Did you use the *black* brothel, then?'

Gustl shrugs judiciously. 'The Jew brothel's a big place.'

'You're telling me.'

'I propose a toast,' I declare. 'To the downfall of England and to brothels full of Englishwomen.'

'*Eh?*'

'Those of the wrong racial categories,' I hasten to add. 'There'll be plenty.'

What, to *pollute* ourselves with? I must extricate myself from this topic.

Given the numbers of the crew, that of a medium-size town, there must be other uranians on this ship. I suspect who some of those are, yet it would be folly to confide in anyone in the hope that somewhere aboard this enormous vessel there exists a sanctuary to which Gustl and I can safely resort. The navy is a more tolerant environment than the Fatherland in some respects, but there are limits! Let me think instead about Ludwig Wittgenstein, our Führer's *bête noire*.

Transmitted from Rhodesia, no doubt weeks or months after each had been put on to aluminum discs lacquered with cellulose nitrate in London, in Angola we could hear the philosopher's broadcasts delivered in his upper class Viennese accent. We Germans have the defector William Joyce talking to the British from Radio Hamburg to demoralise them; the British have Wittgenstein.

To be caught listening to Wittgenstein on your Volksradio is a bad idea, but the punishment—at least in the navy—is surprisingly light: a docking of pay, a leave cancelled, some dirty extra duty. I presume it's a whole lot tougher for land-lubbers whom the Gestapo catch red-handed, or red-eared. The navy protects its own and Naval Intelligence does not seem unduly bothered, no doubt because talks about the sanctity of language are over the heads of the vast majority of people.

Not everyone aboard is as down to earth as a Hoffmann or a Scharffenstein. Gustl and I don't exactly count ourselves as high-powered intellectuals. I mean, we're educated, but we're artists. Or we used to be. However, we do know a couple of chaps whom you might call intellectuals, if this wasn't a dirty word. Not uranian chaps, I hasten to add, but never mind.

Jahn and Hager. That's Rudolph Jahn and Gottfried Hager, both of them assigned to the nearest of the great quadruple gun turrets. Hager is very fond of music, which is how we got talking in the mess amidst the bustle of so many men eating. The tonnage of pigs consumed aboard *Der Sieger* every single day!

Hager asked me, 'Do you actually *hear* the music in your head the way Beethoven did?' His is a face made for wistfulness, his close-set eyes peering out past a long sharp nose in a kind of diffident expectation of something good perhaps occurring, but probably not.

I was about to nod when in the nick of time I made the connection between Beethoven and deafness.

Instead I frowned. 'Not exactly. Beethoven was special.'

Hager sighed. 'Aah, so not even most musicians . . . The noise of the guns, you see . . .'

Hager was worried about being permanently deafened when the occasional test firing became the real thing, repeated over and over again. My fib seemed to console him somewhat. If he lost his hearing, the knowledge that professional musicians who were similarly deafened could continue to enjoy music would be a torment.

One thing led to another, and presently he and Jahn and the two of us were confidants, at least as regards certain topics such as Wittgenstein.

Gottfried and Rudolph are both philosophers, or had been so before the war. Both of them taught in universities. Taught a lot of Nietzsche and Schopenhauer, needless to say. The Will to Power. The World as Will and Idea. And Plato too, the Führer's top favourite. They both listen to Wittgenstein on their Volksradio because, as Rudolph explained one day, Wittgenstein is an heir to Schopenhauer as surely as our Führer is.

Physically I don't fancy the melancholy Gottfried, nor Rudolph who has pockmarks all over a moon face and very wispy hair. Yet their minds seem to mesh with mine and with Gustl's. Admittedly more so with each other—at times Gottfried and Rudolph seem to be talking to one another in code, where a word does not mean what you would ordinarily take it to mean! Acquaintance with those two serves as a useful protective cover for Gustl and me because Gottfried and Rudolph aren't in the least good-looking and seem to have no interest in sex. They're definitely monkish, an austere trait which Wittgenstein shares. Also our Führer, come to think of it, him being vegetarian and teetotal, but so effervescent.

Oh god, I'm visualising the beautiful white cheeks of Gustl's bum and that puckery little mouth between the cheeks which can swallow my cock so sweetly, so grippingly. Think philosophy!

'Schopenhauer's central idea,' I recall Rudolph telling us, 'is that we share a common mind. A person of will power, who can suspend thought and who can submerge his individuality, gains access to the common mind and he can influence everyone in word and thought. The Führer knows Schopenhauer by heart and he can do exactly what I just said in a very practical way in his speeches—which is how he works his magic. *Quite literally*, magic. That's how magic works: it bespeaks and alters reality.'

Wittgenstein himself wrote a book of spells called the *Tractatus Logico-Philosophicus*, which our two friends had read before all copies of the academic periodical which published it were consigned to bonfires, at least in the Fatherland and conquered territories.

'The book is full of logical propositions designed to grasp higher truth. Words speak through you, you don't originate them, the self is an illusion, that sort of thing.'

When Wittgenstein quotes from himself in his broadcasts, what an incantatory power there is.

Needless to say, the number of copies of the *Tractatus* that ever saw print was utterly dwarfed by the popularity of *Mein Kampf*.

I remember one exquisite time when Gustl and I each teased one another's cock for five or ten minutes by plucking the throbbing head two-fingered like a violinist twanging a string, *pizzicando*, until the yearning for the firm and constant pressure of the mouth between the cheeks became unbelievably urgent, and meanwhile a forefinger, on which we could scarcely concentrate, and then two fingers slid up and down within that mouth, opening it. Aah.

The amazing thing is that the Führer and Wittgenstein, the man of the people and the rich Jew, both attended school together in Linz. Undoubtedly they read Schopenhauer together, Wittgenstein perhaps even *leading* the Führer (if such a thing can be conceived) in their mutual investigations, for Wittgenstein was two years senior. In time this led to some sort of contretemps, whereupon the Führer awakened to the evil of the Jewish sub-race. That's one reason why the first speech our Führer made after German troops marched into Austria was in Linz.

'You international seeker after truth,' our Führer sneered, 'Ludwig Wittgenstein, Jew-boy with a truss—if only you could be here today to see my victory!' By then Wittgenstein had long been an exile in England. Yes, those were the exact words that issued from the Führer's mouth, striking home like a lance. Our Führer must have spied Wittgenstein's truss when the schoolboys undressed for sport or hygiene. That was the reality inside the trousers.

Inside of Gustl's trousers, on the other hand . . . no, no, no, no.

That's quite a famous speech. It wasn't until after the war started that Wittgenstein began broadcasting, ever so saintly in his precise, logical way, scorning to allude to such things as trusses or what they held. The Führer, clever man, manipulates reality while his ex-school companion operates on a more abstract plane, criticising our Führer and Göbbels for betraying the meanings of words. I know who will win. The Führer. That's because he seeks power, whereas Wittgenstein seeks what you might call illumination. Maybe Wittgenstein will be burned alive rather than hung from piano wire.

'There's a battle being fought for the common Aryan mind,' Rudolph also said. 'Wittgenstein comes over as a Magus, but the SS boys at Wewelsburg Castle hold séances to stymie him, and any speech of the Führer's blows all those logical propositions away like fluff.'

I shrugged. 'I'm not so sure about *that*. Or why does the Führer want to nail Wittgenstein so much?'

Our vast ship surges onward, and we do change our trousers (and other garments) for northerly attire. Our superheavy guns elevate to 30 degrees and swivel like athletes limbering up and stretching their muscles. Smoke pours due southward now, for the wind has shifted. Towards the stern sometimes it's hard to see anything very clearly. Certainly we spy no big artificial albatrosses of Jew-American manufacture, which of course do not and cannot exist. On account of the smoke Gustl and I are constantly clearing our throats and our eyes water a bit. The steam train puffs its way to and fro along the deck in preparation for when it will carry invasion troops. Of course tanks and trucks and motor bikes will also race along the broad deck.

By now surely everyone aboard—with the possible exception of the blacks and the Jewish slave workers—understands the details of Operation Sea Bridge. It is a plan of staggering genius, typical of the Führer's vision.

An ordinary sea-borne invasion by innumerable escorted troop carriers, vulnerable to vagaries of weather and requiring multiple landing sites, could result in confusion and losses. But to bridge the Straits of Dover with our battleships several kilometres long, linked together by ingenious mini-bridges: that is to thrust a permanent bridgehead right into England through which men and equipment will pour unstoppably! At the same time our guns will be shelling the towns of Kent and even the east end of London! Whatever little British battleships try to thwart us will simply be swept aside or sunk by our U-boats.

Such surprise there will be on those supposedly unflappable English faces with their stiff upper lips.

How long will *Der Sieger* remain as the foremost part of this bridge? Several months? At some stage surely we must be freed to resume our role as a mobile vessel. Bombarding New York, who knows?

During those several months Gustl and I hope to enjoy shore leaves in newly conquered south-eastern England, where our opportunities to enjoy one another may be many and varied. Abandoned barns in balmy weather, deserted or commandeered hotels . . .

We must be wary of partisans! It may take a while for vengeance executions to deter English resistance. How I yearn for idyllic pleasures in the region behind the war front, oh yes why not a hay loft, soft if perhaps tickly bedding for our naked bodies entwined together, both of our manhoods rampant, my tongue in Gustl's mouth then his in mine, shafts of sun shining in through cracks and through a few bullet holes to illuminate the motes of dust which our mutual ecstasy raises like so many tiny stars. To gaze into his hazel eyes, my body against his body, to stroke his chestnut hair. I love him so much that I ache with yearning even when I'm with him. Gustl, du bist der Lenz, du bist der Lenz.

The wind from the north persists and many complain about the smoke. Finally the order comes to switch around those of us who are most exposed, such as lookouts, gun crews, and bridge officers, from the stern to the bows, to be replaced by our counterparts. Gustl and I board the steam train, along with Rudolph and Gottfried and other ratings and officers, all with our kit, and we travel those seven kilometers forward in style.

Quite a holiday mood—until the awful thought strikes me that Gustl and I might be assigned to different duty rosters, or even worse, to different lookout turrets towards the front of the boat. This tormenting notion brings a cascade of other might-be's crowding in its wake. The frustrations we suffer at present are as nothing compared to those we might endure if the requirements of war or even an error of paperwork ever separates us! We have been so lucky so far, so very lucky. I cannot bear to be separated from Gustl.

My fears were pointless. Here we both are together, scanning sky and sea. The air is considerably cleaner and fresher, not merely because we are up front. Our great battleships no longer steam in line astern but are flanking one another, each a couple of kilometres apart, an early redeployment. Simply to cope with the smoke problem, or for tactical reasons? I am not privy to Fleet Admiral's Doenitz's mind.

What a spectacle the *Lohengrin* is off to the west, five kilometers of armoured battleship the length of an entire island. An island five kilometres long, very much longer than it is wide, rather like Wangerooge in the East Frisians but more vertical. Oh yes, an island of steel cleaves the water, smoke streaming from all its funnels. Whales would be minnows around its sides. Gulls fly through the air like white confetti.

Yesterday evening, Gustl and I explored below decks and discovered an unlocked storeroom piled high with greatcoats.

'What if we're discovered—?'

'Who needs greatcoats yet?'

What we did next I shall not describe, save to say that the brass buttons of a greatcoat refolded inside-out feel a bit harder than the buttons on a mattress which stop the springs from poking you. When you're so hard yourself, who cares about a few buttons? Afterwards you're too softly melted to bother.

The sea is flat, and here we are at last in the Channel, five kilometres offshore from bombarded, blazing Dover. Our bows are five kilometres from shore, our stern perhaps eight kilometres. The difference is increasing as we swing about to become the spearhead of invasion.

Our great guns roar. Oh me of little faith. The castle of Dover is in ruins. The White Cliffs themselves are crumbling and collapsing as if to form a ramp for our Panzer tanks to ascend into the English countryside—to the extent that we can make out such details clearly. A couple of hours ago the sky was blue but now smoke is everywhere.

As we swing, *Der Sieger* and her sister ships are in a sense damming these straits. We are giant lock gates. Water will continue to flow underneath us, but the current from the north-east pushes against us. Propellors recessed into our hull along the relevant side of our mighty vessel counteract this. We repel the very sea like Moses coming out of Egypt, sending the water back upon itself, higher on one side than on the other. This causes *Der Sieger* to list by a few degrees, not enough to cause any problem for our steam train.

Moses was a Jew, of course. That's the trouble with the Bible, altogether too many Jews, an infestation of them. Including Jesus, I suppose. Wagner provides a perfectly adequate substitute for Christianity. True, Parsifal is searching for the Holy Grail, the blood-cup of Jesus. Parsifal is a holy fool. Personally I think Jesus was an Aryan, brought from India to Palestine as a baby by the three Wise Men to place him as near to Europe as they could reach. With their gold and frankincense the Wise Men bribed the parents of Jesus to accept a changeling.

Wie doof to think about such matters at such a moment! Stupid, as kids will say. We are bombarding Doofer. How dumb of the English to think they could defy us.

The stability of the steam train—and of the trains on *Lohengrin* and the other battleships which will soon form the bridge across the Channel—is important because I presume that the Führer will arrive by train. Unless . . . he drives, or is driven, along the decks in an armoured car. Or even in his supercharged Mercedes, Swastika flags fluttering! What a wonderful sight that would be, inspiring utter confidence.

Orgasms of orange cordite-flame erupt. The thunder is worthy of *Götterdämmerung*. Through our excellent binoculars, and through rifts in the smoke, Gustl and I watch bits of England flying into the air.

Our bows are rammed into the very port of Dover in flames. One of the harbour piers is now much shorter than it was. Buoyed by floatation bags, the great connecting ramp is rolling ashore. Sheer fire-power of heavy machine guns, rocket launchers, and tracer artillery has virtually annihilated local resistance. Shells from elevated superguns to our rear soar high overhead so fast that you can scarcely follow them for more than a second or so.

Late in the day the English sent big balloons to try to bomb us. Bags of flames is what those balloons soon became. Evening draws nigh and our watch is nearly over. How will Gustl and I get to sleep amidst the extreme noise and excitement? By prior recourse to the storeroom of greatcoats? Ach, too many men are bustling about by now, here, there, everywhere.

Overnight, Waffen-SS heroes have seized the main road that rises from Dover. With dawn come the Panzer tanks and the troop carriers of the army and of the Waffen-SS, rumbling along the deck and crossing the ramp. English reinforcements will be on their way but our superior tanks will cut through those like a knife through butter. Or perhaps through cheese. Cheese is stiffer than butter, though of course in certain situations greasy butter does have its virtues. The English protected many other potential landing sites, obstacles and barbed wire along miles of beaches yet they could never have expected a frontal assault of such a kind or magnitude on this port. A massive bridge coming into existence within a matter of hours! When they first spied our secret weapons looming, extending for kilometre after kilometre across the sea, how they must have wet themselves.

Another day, and our Kentish bridgehead is as secure as if it is part of the

Fatherland. On our Volksradios we hear how Panzer divisions and motorised troops have reached Canterbury and Ashford. Resistance is fierce—give credit where credit is due—but basically futile and suicidal. A flotilla of smaller vessels constantly ferries equipment between Boulogne and Folkestone, while along the battleship-bridge pour whole armies as if it is an autobahn. I think no one who is not German remains alive in Dover itself.

The English Prime Minister Churchill has made a growling speech vowing to fight us in the streets of London and in the mountains of Wales and in the glens of Scotland, not realising what an admission of defeat such far-flung promises are. Elevated to their maximum, great guns are shelling London.

Wittgenstein, more sensitive to the nuances of language, has uttered certain propositions.

'The good or bad exercise of the will can only alter the limits of the world, not the facts. Nazism is not irrefutable, but is obviously nonsensical.'

That's telling us, Ludwig! However, the Waffen-SS is not listening.

The Führer may be listening angrily. Nonsensical? Why, we are witnessing the beginning of the reign of a very different kind of world-view which has diverged utterly from both Christianity and rationalism. His will be the reign of superhuman Will, which you might perhaps call magical realism.

It is nonsensical that privileged uranians can enjoy themselves freely when Gustl and I can not.

Oh sacred hour: now that Dover is cleansed by fire, the Führer is coming, and yes he is coming by train, to the Isartor Station close by our turret.

Gustl has developed a terrible fit of the sneezes. I don't think he has a cold as such. I think his problem is the affinity between the nose and the penis. It's well known that certain smells excited our primitive ancestors sexually. I mean, what ape could get excited just by *looking* at another ape covered all over in hair? Consequently to think intensely and imaginatively about sex may in turn stimulate the nose to discharge itself, rather than the cock. Gustl has been thinking a lot about sex with me in that Kentish hay-loft I promised him.

Chaperoned by naval officers, the Führer's security boys in their long black leather coats are swarming all over this part of the ship, and Gustl is ordered off duty. No one must sneeze anywhere near the Führer. Vegetarianism and clean living protect the Führer, but it's better to be safe than sorry.

For obvious reasons us lookouts have no real function at the moment—roll on our shore leave! I'm not likely to spy any sniper amongst the smouldering ruins. Even so, it would be bad practice to leave the forwardmost watchturret unmanned. Two of us aren't essential for the job, however, so I'm left on my own, after being frisked for any concealed weapon—better to be safe than sorry. That blond security man's hand sliding up my inside leg . . . I thought determinedly of *Parsifal* and purity.

This is incredible. On my watch too.

Yet it figures, it figures. This is the highest, closest vantage point to look out from without actually going ashore and climbing uphill. Bound to be some unexploded stuff lying around in the smoking ruins.

At this very moment the Führer himself is ascending my watchturret—on his own, *selbst*. Guards follow, but he is the leader, what else should he be? He is a hero climbing the tower overlooking the conquered land.

Although obviously tired from sleepless nights and somewhat sallow, he beams almost boyishly at me. His eyes shine. His face glows. What a big fleshy nose he has. On his uniform, in honour of our achievement he wears the badge of the High Seas Fleet, a battleship steaming directly towards you, its guns abeam so that they show to better advantage, within a wreath of oak leaves crowned by an eagle.

'Dieter Schmidt,' he says to me, as if he has known my name all along rather than it being whispered in his ear just previously.

I could not draw myself more fully to attention.

'*Jawohl, mein Führer.*'

'You are doing your duty to Germany, mein Dietl.' Oh moment of sheer intimacy, the *du* and the Dietl, like a lover's caress. 'You will be decorated.'

With a somewhat womanly gesture he requests my Zeiss binoculars. Through them he stares up at the wreckage of Dover Castle.

To himself, he snarls, 'Wittgenstein, you are not far.'

And I am quite carried away. This is a moment given by God.

'Mein Führer, rather than being decorated may I humbly request that the anti-uranian laws be amended to allow uranians who prove their manliness by serving their Fatherland in the armed forces—'

I get no further. Never have I seen or heard such a change come over a human being. Words jabber out of the Führer in a paroxysm, as if not uttered by himself voluntarily. How balefully he turns upon me—and from the wild words and from the rictus which distorts his features I understand instinctively and in appalled wonder that my Führer *is a uranian just as I am* and he has ever been so, and of a sudden too I understand the source of his loathing for Wittgenstein, because at school back in Linz once upon a time the Jew with a truss must have squeezed the Führer's balls and he must have had his cock up the Führer's bum—but no one must ever know this, and therefore Wittgenstein must die. Already the Führer is screaming for his guards, froth flecking from his lips.

Thank God that my Gustl was taken off duty. Let them not guess the truth about him. Gustl may cry himself to sleep to have lost me yet dear God, let him not cry out for other reasons, in agony at sexual torture and castration if the navy cannot protect him, as I doubt it can, for the navy cannot protect me.

I am gagged, and stripped to my underwear, and bound, and greased. On the Führer's orders a great gun is already loaded, perhaps even by Gottfried and Rudolph for all I know. Into the muzzle I am lifted feet-first. The barrel is just big enough to accommodate me. With a big mop normally used for swabbing the decks I'm pushed down as far as possible. This is an atrocity such as I never expected of my fellow Germans.

The gun begins to elevate. Even greased, at twenty-five degrees I do not slide any further. As I stare upward I can see a star or a planet—it's as if I'm at the bottom of a very deep well. The gun is swivelling. I know that it's being aimed at Cambridge.

Impossible for even a supercharged shell from a superheavy gun to fly as far as there, but the intention is all-important, the vision that just conceivably I may hit Wittgenstein as he strolls in some college quadrangle.

Will any part of me survive these coming moments? My head perhaps, still conscious for a few seconds, speeding ahead of the orgasm of cordite?

'Our life has no end,' proposes Wittgenstein, 'in exactly the way in which our visual field has no limits.' He means that we see nothing beyond our visual field, nor likewise do we experience anything beyond the end of our life.

'Death is not an event in life,' he has said. 'We do not experience death.'

I sincerely hope not.
Oh what a cock-up.
Ich bin im Arsch!
Oh balls.

Giant Dwarfs

Twenty-five leagues beneath the surface of the Earth, I certainly never expected to be rescued from troglodytes by *Germans*. My amazement would grow the greater as I became acquainted with those same Germans! Ah but whatever my reservations about Monsieur Verne's character I should take a leaf out of his book and begin at the beginning of the tale . . .

In the Dordogne, some 35 leagues inland from Bordeaux, Pierre and I were cantering across grassy upland near the village of Montignac-sur-Vézères when all of a sudden his chestnut stallion Pompey collapsed and Pierre was thrown right over the horse's head. Immediately I reined Diana in, jumped down and ran to Pierre, crying, 'My love!' Pompey was squealing horribly. I could see that his front legs had disappeared into the ground, into a crevice that had opened up. Pierre was already scrambling to his feet.

'Be damned!'

He seemed winded, for he paused to collect himself—by stroking his moustaches. What an elegant figure of a man. I loved his wavy brown hair and piercing blue eyes. Captain Pierre Marc-Antoine Dumont d'Urville, soldier, explorer, adventurer.

'Are you all right, my love? Your ribs, your everything?'

'My pride is injured, that's all, Hortense. Mark you, this was not Pompey's fault.'

We'd had some spirited discussion about the respective merits, or de-merits, of Pompey and Diana. Poor Pompey, he was suffering such pain.

So far as Pierre could tell by peering then reaching into the hole, both of the horse's trapped legs seemed badly broken. Pierre stood up decisively.

'He's ruined—and in misery.' He unholstered his bulky revolver.

Monsieur Verne was later to study that revolver with some interest, and it plays a subsequent role in this narrative too (albeit only as a cosh), so maybe I should say something concerning it. Our genius of an author loves to describe in detail technical and scientific matters. I should match my humble story-telling skills to his redoubtable ones. Seriously, I mean it. I'm always willing to learn.

A thousand of the unusual revolvers had recently been manufactured in Paris, where Pierre had managed to procure one. Although I wasn't previ-ously much interested in guns, Pierre had been keen to show off his acquisition to me, like a child with a new toy—and I have a very retentive memory for facts. The invention of a French-born doctor named le Mat—in support of the Confederate army in the civil war currently raging in America—the revolver in question sported two barrels. The larger central barrel would fire grapeshot. A slimmer barrel would fire bullets coming from a nine-chamber cylinder revolving around the central barrel. The nose of the hammer was movable to accommodate this double action. Should you happen to be faced by a mob, Pierre had explained, the spread of shot would cause multiple damage and cool ardour. Such a revolver would be valuable in penal colonies, not to mention should you suddenly come upon several partridges feeding together and wish to bag them all.

'Look away, Hortense!'

'Certainly not,' I replied. 'Do you think I will faint or have hysterics, like your wife?'

Pierre shrugged and fired a single bullet. Some blood and tissue sprayed from Pompey's head, which promptly slumped.

Just as well I did not look away, for it was as if the detonation was a trigger. Or the reason may have been that Pompey's now dead weight shifted. The ground gave way more so. Pierre and I both needed to jump back. Pompey's entire body slid into the widening hole, disappearing from sight. Moments later, a muted thump sounded from underground.

What I now know to be called a *doline* had opened up, a 'swallow-hole' through which rainfall would in future drain into a subterranean cave. That is the geological explanation for what had happened: we had been riding the horses on top of a system of caves and part of a cave roof had given way.

Since no further collapse seemed imminent, Pierre lay down and inched forward cautiously to inspect. Of course I joined him in this.

'Go back, Hortense. Our combined weights may—'

'I wish to see.'

In fact there was little to be seen. The sun shone brightly from a sky containing only a few white woolly clouds, but below was darkness. Soon we both withdrew, stood up, and brushed our clothes. By now the dark brown mare had ambled over and was staring at the hole from a safe distance. Diana pawed with one hoof. Her nostrils flared. What might she be thinking or feeling? At its best the Tarbenian breed is very intelligent as well as brave, with graceful action, elegance and endurance—quite like myself, perhaps? The trouble is that the breed requires constant infusions of English thoroughbred blood alternating with Arab blood, or it else tends to degenerate, retaining of its ancestral magnificence little but a thick heavy Andalusian neck. My grandfather bred horses, so I know more than a little about the matter, not to mention being acquainted with the saddle—*and* with bare-back riding—from an early age when most girls would play with dolls.

'Alas,' said Pierre, 'it seems that Pompey now has a grave, a natural one. However, I'm not some primitive chieftain who buries an expensive saddle along with his steed! We need a long rope and a strapping farmboy to assist me.' He eyed my mount.

Promptly I said, 'Diana'll carry us both, if I take it easy—she isn't slack-backed. We'll leave her saddle here, and you can hold on to me.'

'My dear, surely I shall take the reins!'

'Have you ever ridden bare-back before? Besides, *I* did not lose my mount!'

'Oh Hortense, you mettlesome filly!' Pierre burst out laughing—quite lasciviously. Doubtless he was remembering the previous night when he had ridden me, and vice versa. Of course Pompey's death was shocking and sad but we must retain our spirits and good humour. Pierre and I were well suited in this regard. Oh was I to remain forever merely a mistress? Of course there was the matter of his wife's large inheritance to which he would lose access—that inheritance had paid for his various adventures in exotic places.

I'm spending a little too long upon the start of this unparalleled adventure which we were about to share. Suffice it to say that we returned in company with a hulking, beefy-faced, and amiable lad called Antoine, me still riding Diana, Pierre maintaining his dignity upon a carthorse laden with rope, Antoine trotting beside us at no great speed, carrying an oil lantern.

Antoine obviously assumed that he should descend into the abyss on behalf of the posh gentleman. Without further ado he began roping himself to the sturdy carthorse. But I intervened. I was lighter and slimmer—surely it was more sensible for me to go down? Pierre wouldn't countenance this. He himself would make the descent while the lad controlled the carthorse, *if*, that is, I didn't feel reluctant to be left alone with the lad.

So it was that presently Antoine and I heard Pierre shouting from below that, in the light from the lantern, he could see big pictures upon one wall of the cave, of bison and other beasts—vivid pictures in red and black and violet. Other pictures were visible along a passage which led from the cave in a downward direction.

'I must see where that passage leads!' he called up to us.

It was a full hour before my Pierre returned, amazed, to the cave, and thence to us who had awaited him—Antoine phlegmatically so, I with increasing concern. Had there been a second lantern, I swear I would have gone in search of my lover.

Numerous weeks were to pass. Professors of Prehistory were to visit our discovery, the hole now rendered safe by timbers, and a simple stairway constructed. One professor declared the cave paintings to be tens of thousands of years old because the animals depicted were extinct. Another denounced the pictures as a hoax—though of course not perpetrated by Captain Dumont d'Urville, who was well-known as an adventurer but also as a man of honour.

Pierre was much less excited about those pictures, vigorous but primitive, than about where that tunnel led to. On his first sortie he had reached an underground river, alongside which a wide ledge provided ample safe footage. Wisely he had returned before the oil in the lamp was half-consumed.

On a second sortie, with obliging Antoine as porter, Pierre reached an underground lake. What he was soon calling 'the route' took a sideways twist into a passage running through geological formations differing from the limestone hitherto. A route indeed!—for if a passage forked, presenting an ambiguous choice, a small stick-like figure scrawled in ochre often pointed faintly. Presently that route began to descend through rocks more impervious to water. Ever to descend!

How could it be that our primitive ancestors—or one ancestor such, of genius and courage—had penetrated so far? Obviously the cave artists used something to light their work. Perhaps a small bonfire? They would be fairly close to the light of day, to some entrance which later collapsed, and it was difficult to imagine them carrying burning brands deeper and deeper into the bowels of the Earth. Phosphorescent lichen existed here and there in the depths but its light was very feeble.

Greatly enthused, Pierre contacted an acquaintance of his, the geologist Charles Sainte-Claire Deville, who was likewise an adventurer—he had explored active volcanoes such as Vesuvius and Stromboli. Monsieur Deville was already a member of the Academy of Sciences in Paris, and influential.

And lo, it transpired that Monsieur Deville himself was in correspondence with that young writer Jules Verne who had just recently caused quite a stir with his novel *Five Weeks in a Balloon*. Monsieur Verne was quizzing Monsieur Deville concerning questions of geology and volcanoes, because he was planning a new novel—about none other than a journey to the centre of the Earth!

Presently Messieurs Deville and Verne hastened to the Dordogne, to accompany us underground with sufficient food, water, lamps and so forth (carried by Antoine) to allow for a return journey of four days in total. Yes, to accompany Pierre and Antoine *and me too*. I had insisted, and I had prevailed. I think Pierre was proud of me, even though he raised trivial objections such as regarding the privacy that a woman requires for matters of personal hygiene. What, in *darkness*? Actually, Verne was the one who most demurred about the participation of a woman in a scientific enterprise. I understood that Verne was married, yet at the same time I sensed, as women can sense in a way inexplicable to men, that in the past the author had experienced disillusionments which made him bitter towards my sex in general. Disillusionments, yes, though also excitements—a woman has instincts. However, Verne was a junior participant in this enterprise, under the wing of Deville. Deville and my Pierre were the men of experience; and for a fairly generous sum Pierre had bought the land which gave access to the cave. Verne was lucky to be invited to participate in our initial foray—and he was eager to do so.

'How,' he exclaimed, 'can I possibly contemplate writing about a journey into the Earth—when what I write may be contradicted by reality? But oh what a novel I shall now be able to write!'

Interestingly, according to Deville, half a century ago a bizarre American by the name of Symmes had sent a proclamation to the Academy of Sciences in Paris to the effect that the Earth is hollow and habitable within, accessible—so the American declared—by way of a big hole at the North Pole. The Academy had responded scornfully and declined to sponsor him.

Imagine us in the simple though adequate inn of Montignac-sur-Vézères after we returned safely from those four days underground.

Ah, I have not mentioned our small but powerful Ruhmkorff chemical lamps, which were far superior to the simple oil lamp with which Pierre originally descended, and which wouldn't cause an explosion should we encounter fire-damp—these, courtesy of a mine owner, at whose mansion Deville sometimes dined. Visualise us: bearded Deville, moustachioed Pierre, the clean-shaven Verne with his curly dark hair, stalwart laconic Antoine—and me, tall and slim, my dark hair gathered in a tight bun.

Those two days of outbound subterranean travel had taken us some eight leagues in a generally north-easterly direction into the roots of the Massif Central, and some three leagues downward from our original height above sea level. Latterly, our downward progress was increasing—and whenever we encountered an ambiguous branching of routes, we would find a stick figure as guide.

Jules enthused, 'It seems as if we're being invited to travel deeper—to the very centre of the Earth, just as in the novel I'm planning! I chose Iceland as an entry point because of volcanoes and empty lava tubes, but here there's an opening in France itself.'

Pierre nodded. 'Certainly this merits a serious expedition, with supplies sufficient for several weeks or months.'

'Might it be,' I ventured, 'that the stick figures aren't the work of our primitive ancestors—but that the truth is the reverse? Those guide-marks were made by explorers from *within* the Earth, venturing up to the surface?'

A tic afflicted Jules' left eye. His voice became clipped. 'I suppose next you'll suggest that these venturesome troglodytes painted the bison and other beasts in the cave, from sheer astonishment, or as a warning of what lives on the surface!' He was a man who could veer quickly from witty bonhomie to irritability.

'Perhaps it's wise,' I said, mildly yet stubbornly, 'to entertain all possibilities.'

'Only within the bounds of scientific possibility, my dear lady! What would these denizens of the underworld feed upon? Sheep abducted from the surface?'

'What of the legends of fairy folk abducting people and taking them underground?'

'So you believe in fairies!'

'I only wish to keep an open mind.'

'One that a wind blows through because it is mostly empty.'

'That's damn unfair,' said Pierre. 'Hortense has a very full mind, uniquely her own.'

'Full of fancies perhaps. Reason plays no part in feminine lives.'

Diplomatically Deville asked Jules, 'Have you read the work of Darwin, *On the Origin of Species?*'

'I only just bought the translation—I'm reading it at the moment.'

'A sub-species of *Homo* adapted to life underground seems unlikely...' Deville commenced lighting a pipe.

'Still,' said Pierre, 'we'll be well advised to take revolvers and a good supply of gun-cotton too. Personally I'm glad of your suggestion, Hortense.'

I smiled. 'Let's hope we don't need to use the revolvers.'

Pierre gaped at me. '*We?*'

Pierre led me aside.

'Taking you underground initially was an *indulgence*. Now we're planning in terms of weeks or months. Stern stuff, men's stuff.'

I whispered, 'If I don't go with you, I shall tell your wife everything! Including your opinion of her performance in bed. Then you'll have no money for gun-cotton or anything else.'

He groaned. The noise was very similar to what I could evoke from him by other means. 'My peach, this expedition of ours will be the talk of France—maybe the world! Journalists will seize upon your participation. Mathilde would be very stupid not to put two and two together.'

'Maybe the expedition will make us all rich, then you'll have no further need of her!'

'Hmm,' he said and played with his moustache.

'I shall go underground,' I said, 'a day before your official departure; so that no one will see me, and I'll await the four of you. I want an adventure such as no woman has experienced before! If my adventure must remain a secret afterwards, so be it. At least *I* will know what I have achieved.'

'Verne won't like this. If the temperature increases progressively the deeper we descend, a man can strip to the waist . . .'

Men could be so illogical. 'If heat increases progressively, then you won't be able to descend far or you'll melt. Verne must grin and bear me, or there won't be any expedition, so there! Fortunately Deville has a less nervous attitude towards women.'

'You can be very stubborn.' Nevertheless, Pierre's eyes twinkled.

Not all of our time since Pompey's demise had been spent at that village in the Dordogne. Pierre had affairs to attend to in Bordeaux, and he was obliged to spend some time with his wife even if Mathilde was accustomed to frequent adventurous absences on Pierre's part. I refer to Pierre's business affairs—our private affair could be conducted with perfect ease in Bordeaux where Pierre maintained me in a pretty apartment. Our jaunt to Montignac-sur-Vézères had been a special holiday outing because I love riding, and Pierre could hardly ride with me publicly in the city, or else tongues would wag. Anyway, by the tenth of September our expedition was fully provisioned and ready—and I made myself scarce, to spend a night underground all on my own half a league along our destined route, so that I shouldn't feature in the official photographs of departure. I wasn't in the least bit worried about the isolation nor the darkness. Next day I even conserved my chemicals until I saw the lamps of my fellow explorers approaching

Now I really must leap forward in time—back to where I began this narrative—skipping over many undoubtedly fascinating details of rocks and tunnels and shafts and galleries and caverns.

Six weeks had passed and we had journeyed in a mainly east-northeasterly direction for some 200 leagues, which put us almost directly underneath the Bavarian city of Munich—at a depth, by our manometer of compressed air, of an incredible 25 leagues. We imagined the bustle of Germans up on the surface, so remote from us (as we thought!) that they might as well have been on the Moon.

All of us were still fully dressed. As we descended, contrary to scientific

wisdom the temperature had risen only moderately, then stabilised. Personally I would have preferred Antoine to shed some garments—not, of course,
so as to admire his musculature, but because his clothes had become smelly
with sweat, he being of all of us the most burdened . . . by a silk rope-ladder
a hundred metres long, mattocks, pickaxes, iron wedges and spikes, long
knotted cords, meat extract and biscuits. To a greater or lesser degree all of us
were burdened—myself included; I insisted on this!—but Antoine was more
weighed down than the rest of us. At the end of every Saturday's march he
received payment for his labour. To his phlegmatic mind the money seemed
the entire rationale for a journey which continued to amaze the rest of us,
not least when we came . . .

   . . . to an underground sea of vast expanse!
From the strand on which we stood the walls of an immense cavern
stretched away to right and to left, unto invisibility. Far ahead was a horizon
of water—and we could see a long way because the very air seemed phosphorescently alive with light. Masses of cloud hid any view of a roof, those
clouds stained kaleidoscopically (maybe I mean prismatically) by what must
have been auroras at even higher altitude. Widening out to half a league, the
shore of this ocean was richly vegetated by ferns the size of trees and by
umbrella-crowned trees which I saw to be enormous fungi. No wonder the
air was invigorating compared with in the tunnels that had led here! Perhaps
for this reason—coupled with the release from two months' confinement in
stygian natural corridors—I became headstrong, spurred by delight at the
aerial denizens of this subterranean realm, namely butterflies rather than
birds, butterflies of all sizes and hues, and dragonflies with huge wingspans
such as must have flown in the forests of the Carboniferous Era and which
still survived here hidden away beneath the earth.

   Shedding my pack, I ran impulsively towards an enchanting yellow and
purple lepidopterous creature half my own size, that had alighted nearby
upon the gritty loam, studded with pointy orange flowers such as I had
never seen before, to suck at their sweetness. For a fanciful moment I almost
took it for a fairy, and thought myself in fairyland.

   'Come back, you stupid girl!' I heard Verne shout imperiously. 'That may
be poisonous! This isn't a dress shop!'

   The papillon fluttered away, more as if swimming than flying—the air felt
denser here than on the surface of the world. If it had been Pierre who
called to me to observe caution, events might have transpired differently.
However, it amused Pierre to give me my head. I was quite fed up with

Verne's little volcanic explosions, so I followed the object of my admiration somewhat farther. Oh Verne was such a bundle of contraries! He could be perfectly charming one moment then the next moment so facetious and curt, fairly snapping at any dissent from his own viewpoint. Maybe his impatience and nervous tension was a sign of genius, but his bilious attacks and facial twitches made him less than the perfect travel companion. Though his insomnia would have made him a good sentry, had there been anything to guard against in the dark tunnels hitherto!

As I came closer to the enchanting papillon amidst the floral under-growth, of a sudden I heard Deville call out, 'Look, look!' He was pointing to the sea, offshore.

Peering between some giant tree-ferns I espied two monstrous heads rearing up from the water, one with a long toothy snout like a crocodile's—

'An ichthyosaurus!' I heard Deville shout—

—the other like a serpent—

'A plesiosaurus!'

The two monsters joined combat ferociously while the water foamed and sprayed, thrashed by oar-like flappers and tail-fins. Thank God that I hadn't rushed to bathe but had been distracted by beauty—and now I was doubly distracted by the battle offshore. Thus it was that I paid no attention to my vicinity.

Abruptly I was seized from behind by the thighs and by the waist and dragged backwards, losing my balance, too surprised to cry out. As I sprawled, *little men* swarmed over me—muscular naked little men, four, five of them, all as pasty white as could be! In those first moments I feared an animalistic rape of me, for the exposed male genitals of the dwarfs all seemed disproportionately large compared with the bodies. The eyes, too, bulged—such big eyes! Breath panted from barrel chests. You might have expected that sweat reeked too, but actually the smell was floral. These persons must bathe regularly in streams that fed the underground ocean and brush themselves afterwards with squeezed flowers—only a madman would venture into water where monsters dwelt such as were battling. A hand clamped over my mouth. Hands gripped my clothing, and I was lifted. The dwarfs were beginning to bear me away—for what purpose? Sexual? Cannibalistic? Sacrificial? All the while my companions evidently noticed nothing, so locked must their attention have been upon the prehistoric sea monsters.

I struggled and I writhed, but those dwarfs were strong and persistent.

Giant fungi and tree-ferns shifted above me as I was borne backward through undergrowth. My captors uttered guttural words to one another. The idea came to me that they might regard me as a goddess and were carrying me away to be worshipped, confined in some primitive cave-temple. They would bring me offerings of fish, and of course there would be a priest whom I would come to understand and to cultivate till he would be quite in my thrall and who would co-operate in my escape. After returning to the surface I would exhibit the dwarf priest in Paris and I would become rich and famous, not least because of the memoir I would write, maybe with some assistance from Verne—if he could bring himself to offer this and if I could bear to accept it and to work with him to our mutual advantage. *Twenty-Five Leagues Under the Earth* might be a good title.

Maybe the priest would try to copulate ceremonially with me in that temple, to promote the fertility of his tribe! My vivid imagination summoned up the scene of degradation to which I might be subjected, perhaps many times—then an image, too, of myself giving birth in primitive circumstances to a dwarf who would be a vile caricature of me. By now we were crossing some open ground, perhaps a quarter of a league distant from the place of my abduction. I bit the hand clamped upon my mouth, and as it jerked away from my teeth I screamed.

Did I hear a distant echo of my cry, from the lips of my dearest Pierre, distraught at my mysterious disappearance? I think that was an echo of my own cry bouncing from the mighty wall of the vast cavern. A new hand gripped my mouth even more firmly than before—new, I reasoned, since I did not taste any blood upon the palm. My bite had been quite savage. I could be *wild*, as Pierre knew well. In actuality the dwarfs had not behaved savagely towards me, not as yet—no blow had struck me. It was *I* who had been the savage, perhaps with due reason, but nevertheless. And, truth to tell, it was myself who smelled animalistic rather than my naked abductors. I had of course brought an adequate supply of good perfume for the journey, reasoning that I would need to mask bodily odours, but those big squat noses of the dwarfs probably detected the imposture. Carried away by the dwarfs like some princess in a fairy tale, I was such a mixture of fear and fancy and reason and rage.

Then I heard a sharp bang—and abruptly my right leg dropped, my boot striking the ground. Jerked sideways, I glimpsed one of my captors sprawling, blood gushing from his stout neck. As the echo of that first bang rebounded, I heard another such—and my left leg became free. Another dwarf was collapsing, blood running from his back. I assumed that my Pierre had found me already and had used one of the Purdley More rifles to deadly effect and with great accuracy.

In panic the other dwarfs let go of me. With a spine-jarring jolt all of me was upon the ground. Three dwarfs were running for the cover of vegetation. A gun chattered unbelievably quickly and yet another dwarf fell before the remaining two reached cover and disappeared. What sort of weapon could fire so quickly? Surely not any rifle, nor even the Colt revolvers. Circumspectly I lay still, as though in a swoon, squinting.

Three men, *who were not my companions*, ran towards me from out of other undergrowth. Two wore black uniforms, black boots, smooth steel helmets on their heads—and carried guns such as I never saw before. Imagine a black pistol stretched out almost to arm's length. The third man, who was shorter and stocky, wore black leather trousers and a jacket with many pockets flying open to reveal a holstered pistol at his hip—he clutched a rifle equipped on top with what looked like a miniature telescope. A roughly trimmed dark beard jutted from his chin at the same angle as his nose. Abundant short hair curled rebelliously.

Since it seemed these strangers were intent on rescuing me, I sat up.

The strangers—six in total—proved to be Germans. Thanks to visits during my adolescence to an aunt of mine in Alsace-Lorraine I was fairly conversant with the German language. So as not to keep the reader in suspense I shall state right away that these six constituted an expedition similar to our own, into the hollow Earth. Their starting point had been from deep labyrinthine salt mines in Poland just outside of Cracow, rock salt resting upon the compact sandstone which breaks surface elsewhere as the peaks of the Carpathian Mountains. But here ends all similarity between our own and *Ernst Schäfer's* expedition, as well as any anxiety that we had been preceded in our discoveries by Germans!

THEY HAD SET OUT IN THE YEAR 1943. Excuse me if I sound shrill: yes, *eighty years* after ourselves.

Of course they were as astonished as I was by this incongruity, and disbelieved me at first.

'No,' said Schäfer, their bearded leader, whose crack shots had killed two of the dwarfs without even risking grazing me. 'It must be that you are from a subterranean colony of French people who have been here for a very long time, and who have lost track of the years.' He surveyed my smart if rather soiled clothing, puzzled. 'You were born down here, yes?' We were at their improvised camp, a recess in the cavern wall.

'Certainly not,' I said.

I was much more easily persuaded of the futurity of Schäfer and his men on account of the equipment and the guns they had with them, and the way they introduced themselves—with such titles!

The leader was SS Hauptsturmführer Ernst Schäfer, zoologist, geologist, and veteran of Tibetan exploration, who wore on his finger a death's-head ring. Then there was Untersturmführer Karl Wienert, geographer and geophysicist. And Ernst Krause, cameraman. And Dr Josef Rimmer, geologist and diviner. Plus two tall blond soldiers—and porters—Schwabe and Hahn, who belonged to something called the Leibstandarte Adolf Hitler.

'The *what?*'

Schwabe clicked his heels. 'We are the élite of the Waffen-SS who have the sacred duty to protect the Führer.'

'Would that be the leader . . . of Prussia?'

'Of Greater Germany, which rules all Europe!'

I bridled. 'Including France?'

'*Jawohl.*'

And evidently including Poland . . .

'And he's called Adolf Hitler?'

Of a sudden becoming an automaton, Schwabe angled his right arm high into the air, hand like a blade.

Schäfer finally conceded that I was telling the truth about my origin, and soon he became hectically enthusiastic in discussion with Wienert and Krause and Rimmer, the general drift of which I could follow . . .

Apparently the previous year (which I took to mean 1942) had seen an official expedition to some island in the Baltic led by a scientist called Fisher. Fisher believed that the world is hollow—but Fisher was sure that we all live on the *inside* concave surface of the Earth. So by projecting mysterious rays upwards, at the angle of Schwabe's salute, it should be possible to spy on the activities of the British Navy hundreds of leagues distant. The experiment failed, as Schäfer had foreseen it would. Yes, the world is hollow, but obviously we live on the outside surface, and deep beneath our feet, as was now proven, was even more *Lebensraum* than in the conquered lands of the East, or alternatively vast spaces suitable for slave workers—Jews and Slavs could be deported here. But, Gentlemen, kindly imagine the *military* implications of being able to travel back to an earlier year! Something that lay underground between Poland and France evidently intermixed or linked the present with the past. Powerful localised magnetic fields perhaps. The contours of our respective journeys may have traced out some potent pattern akin to a Tibetan mandala. I had noticed a pennant resting against the rock, a jagged hooked cross in a circle its emblem. Maybe the symbol was Tibetan. Tibet seemed important to these Germans.

The two 'SS' soldiers soon went out on patrol, but it wasn't long before the two uniformed men hastened back, and Schwabe reported, 'Hauptsturmführer, the body of the Untermensch has gone!'

As I quickly learned, Schäfer—who was very vain about his prowess with his Mauser rifle—had shot a dwarf a few hours prior to my rescue. He had shot it directly through the heart, so that Krause could photograph its unblemished head from several angles (using a wonderful future device known as an Arriflex hand camera) and so that Schäfer himself could make detailed measurements using callipers, to record in a notebook. Not wishing to share habitation with the corpse, the Germans had concealed it a short distance away for possible further study. Evidently other dwarfs had quietly sneaked close and carried the body away.

I now began to entertain a suspicion as to the true reason for my recent abduction by the dwarfs. The motive might not be that I should become the object of their carnal appetites (whether rape or cannibalism), nor yet that I should be kept as a goddess. They may have been taking me hostage in an attempt to protect themselves from further murders! Why should they have distinguished between French intruders and the German invaders of their cavern? A hostage would make sense.

'Excuse me,' I said to Schäfer, 'if you wanted pictures and measurements, why did you not ask? If only by mime! And you could have offered a gift— some food, or a mirror. A mirror might have been ideal.'

I unleashed a veritable torrent. The dwarfs were degraded parodies of humanity far worse even than Jews! All that the dwarfs merited was extermination. Preceded by study—study was a scientific duty. These degenerates might well be descendants of the same dwarfs that once populated the Earth three hundred thousand years ago when there were three suns in the sky. They might be descended from a sub-race such as the Hottentots, but had lost pigmentation underground.

Scarcely could I believe that these were the countrymen of Goethe. Could reason have so departed from that world only eighty years in my future, at the same time as science had apparently advanced so much, as witness that wonderful camera? During our journey Deville and Verne had often discussed that book about the 'evolution' of species by the Englishman, Darwin, which I mentioned earlier. By now I had some understanding of the ideas, since I'm quick on the uptake—not that Verne generally seemed to think so. It seemed to me that these future Germans had interpreted the ideas of Darwin strangely indeed, or maybe the German translation was wildly inaccurate! Purity of race was a veritable obsession with these new masters of Europe. I heard words from them such as superhuman, and subhuman. Schwabe and Hahn were certainly fine physical specimens, both of them tall strapping blonds (Hahn looked less fanatical). I think Schäfer compensated for his own lesser stature by throwing his weight around—he seemed driven and tormented by inner demons.

'The dwarfs have the lustfully sensual lips of Jews,' Schäfer was saying. 'If we had not rescued the Frenchwoman, they would undoubtedly have ravished her.' He paused and stared at me. 'Mademoiselle Hortense,' he addressed me, 'you are not by any chance Jewish yourself?'

'Would it matter if I am?'

'Answer me, damn it!' What a flash of temper. Not unlike Verne, come to think of it.

'My parents never mentioned such a thing to me.' These Germans might aspire to the stature of giants bestriding future Europe, but in other regards, dear me. 'Hauptsturmführer,' I said sweetly, 'I think the little people kidnapped me as a way of protecting themselves from *you*.'

The Little People: fairy folk, diminutive ogres . . . in tales of old that my Grandma told me such beings *did* kidnap people and take them under the Earth—and in the subterranean domain time behaved strangely so that a century might elapse during what to the abductee seemed only a weekend. Could it be that the dwarfs could exploit the temporal distortions underground, and choose to visit the surface during different epochs which to us were far apart? If so, I'd been right that long ago from our point of view they painted those pictures of animals in the cave we first ventured upon. Maybe from their point of view that was only a thousand years ago.

That the dwarfs went naked wasn't necessarily a sign of degenerate barbarity. Living among the giant fungi and tree-ferns and beautiful papillons was akin to dwelling in the Garden of Eden in innocence. True, fierce toothy monsters swam in the sea . . .

But then, in the biblical Paradise there was at least one serpent.

And *Nazis* in this one. Such, I gathered, was the name of the political party which these Germans revered.

'Those dwarfs' lives are not worth living,' snarled Schäfer.

'Everyone's life is worth living,' I suggested, 'to the person who is living it.'

'Oh no it is *not!*' he shouted. Snatching up his rifle, he stormed out.

Dr Rimmer—the diviner and geologist—drew me aside, and appealed to me softly. 'Please do not provoke Schäfer. He suffered a terrible tragedy. He took his young bride with him on a lake to shoot ducks. In the boat he stumbled and the shotgun went off by accident, killing her. This has made him bitter and unpredictable. Oh I would so much rather I was seeking gold in the River Isar.'

'So it's *gold* you divine for, not water?'

The geophysicist Wienert overheard this.

'Listen to me, Rimmer: you and Himmler' (whoever *he* was) 'would have caused every geologist in Germany to retrain as a diviner! That's the main reason you're here, to keep you out of harm's way. Stop entertaining the lady with fantasies.'

'I was explaining . . . never mind. Do you suppose the dwarfs have a fixed abode, or are nomads?'

'An abode where they might keep golden treasure?'

'I was thinking about the Nibelung miners of legend. Those are dwarfs.'

'Who, if I recall, wear aprons and don't go naked.'

'Ugly creatures, by all accounts, yet very clever. Part of our collective Teutonic race-mind, eh? Why should that be so?'

When Schäfer returned, now sulking—he mustn't have shot a dwarf—I said to him, 'Hauptsturmführer,' for how absurdly pompous that title sounded, 'the dwarfs that live here may be the clever Nibelungs of your German legends. Don't they deserve some respect, or at least merit some caution in your dealings with them, rather than your simply shooting them?' I almost added *like ducks*, but this would have been to go too far.

Schäfer glared at me. 'Did you *wish* to be ravished by them, then? You are no German woman, that's perfectly plain. France is a nation of utter immorality.'

Oh-la-la, I thought.

'In fact,' he went on, 'I would expel you from our protection forthwith . . . !'

If it were not for the fact that . . . ?

Ah, if set free I might elude the dwarfs and tell my companions all about their German rivals, not to mention the mysterious twist in time which had brought our two parties together.

Consequently I must remain a prisoner of the Nazi Reich.

Presently we ate—oily-tasting steaks from some amphibious creature which Schäfer had hunted, accompanied by boiled vegetation which Krause had spied a dwarf eating raw. Then Schäfer declared he was tired, consulted a steely bracelet-watch, and decreed night-time. The electric air of the vast cavern knew no darkness, but the Germans were methodical about observing day and night—as indeed we also had been during the everlasting darkness preceding our arrival here. Their day happened to end hours earlier than a French subterranean day. Hahn sat guard.

As I lay under the blanket upon the loam, waiting for the other Germans to fall asleep, I thought about the large eyes of the dwarfs. If eternal daylight—cavernlight—was usual for them, why did they have big eyes? Was it because the cavernlight was dimmer than sunlight, although after weeks of darkness it seemed bright enough to me? Or was it because the dwarfs spent a lot of their time elsewhere than in the cavern? What did they use to light their way, however dimly, in the tunnels? Lanterns of some sort? How little we knew of the lives of the dwarfs.

What had become of my companions? Wouldn't they have heard the gunfire earlier on, even if the battle between the monsters was preoccupying them? There had been no halloos. They must be searching in the wrong direction.

Finally I judged that all were asleep except Hahn. That vigorous young man may have spent a couple of months underground with no female company. I did hope he wasn't too pure in mind and body. Sliding closer to him, I whispered, 'Manfred, I can't sleep.'

Modesty forbids detailing my further enticing whispers, but presently he and I were some way from that recess in the cavern wall, half hidden by the fronds of small ferns.

'Your helmet . . . I can't kiss you properly.'

So his steel helmet joined the gun lying close to us. I began to unbutton his uniform while his hands did things which I did my best to blank from my awareness. He was certainly muscular and eager, yet a man is at a certain disadvantage when his trousers descend below his knees, whereas when a woman's skirts are lifted she is not similarly impeded. Which of the two objects would hit Hahn's head harder: the discarded helmet, or the gun?

Would the blow be hard enough? How exactly would I reach either of those while he was grasping and groping? If I gripped his jewels and squeezed hard, would he scream and wake the others? Perhaps persuade him to let me ride him? Would an SS man be ridden by a woman? Maybe this excursion of mine into acting was a big miscalculation.

As I struggled to decide, whilst seeming to struggle amorously, something descended violently nevertheless upon Hahn's head.

A hiss in my ear: 'It's Pierre. What the devil are you up to?'

'Trying to escape, what do you think?'

'Hmm!'

Beside Hahn's concussed head lay Pierre's double-barrel revolver, of which he had let go. Pierre and I whispered, me urging the need to relieve the Germans of their weapons. Pierre saw the sense of this. I arranged the German helmet upon Pierre's head the correct way then I lifted Hahn's 'sub-machine' gun while Pierre readied his pistol. Softly we trod toward the recess.

Schäfer promptly sat up. '*So, Schwabe, have you emptied yourself*—?' The helmet confused Schäfer only momentarily, and his hand darted towards his holstered pistol. I shouted, 'Don't move or I shit,' mixing up *scheisse* with *schiesse*, but Schäfer understood me well enough and desisted.

The others stirred awake.

Well, we did succeed in impounding the hunting rifle and Schwabe's sub-machine gun and the pistols of the three other scientists, but the Hauptsturmführer stubbornly refused to yield his own pistol.

'You will have to kill me first,' he said.

Arrogance, pride—then I remembered about his dead bride and his anguish. I thrust this knowledge aside. Here was a man who believed in exterminating mortals he deemed lesser than himself.

'Leave us one gun,' pleaded Rimmer. 'The dwarfs . . . '

'You're superhuman, aren't you?'

We left the pistol, even though this obliged us to run off in some haste. Don't forget, Schäfer was a crack marksman.

Pierre led me to a grove of ferns, where Deville and Verne proved to be waiting, armed with our own Purdley More rifles and Colt revolvers. Hasty explanations on my part followed, astonishing everyone. They hadn't even seen any dwarfs—and they were flabbergasted by my brief account of the German expedition and its origin. Pierre at least had seen the Germans close up, and those guns of the future were persuasive evidence.

'We must return to our baggage,' urged Verne. 'Those dwarfs—Antoine might not cope. Time, time!' he exclaimed.

'It's several hours since we left Antoine,' agreed Deville.

'Not that sort of time, man! I refer to the link with the future!'

The novelist was busy thinking.

As we made to leave, redistributing the weapons amongst us, a rustle in the undergrowth disclosed a dwarf. The naked being rose to stare at us intently, apparently unafraid, taking close account not merely of ourselves but of what we carried, and maybe counting the guns.

'Hallo!' cried Verne, but the dwarf turned and swiftly disappeared. Soon we heard a guttural voice answered by many other voices.

When we returned to Antoine, for once he was deeply perturbed and crossing himself. He too had seen 'little people'. They in turn had watched him.

We decided that we should set off back to the surface as soon as we replenished our water supplies. Of meat extract and biscuits, ample remained. Dried fish would have made for welcome variety, but time spent in catching and drying was out of the question. A thorough wash would have been a delightful idea, but the Hauptsturmführer still retained his pistol.

Would he retain it for much longer? Much about the dwarfs was surmise on my part, but I think Schäfer had greatly underestimated them. I imagined a wave of dwarfs overwhelming the German camp. Somehow I did not think that the Germans would be killed. I imagined the Germans becoming chattels of the dwarfs, forced to labour for them. No, perhaps the dwarfs would march the Nazis to some point distant in time and release them on an Earth before human beings existed.

Within an hour we were lighting our way through darkness once again. Verne began to discourse about time and the future.

'If only some machine could be made to take advantage—a time machine . . . Hmm, we have a duty to warn France about the future ruled so evilly by Germans. Will people believe us when we only have a woman's word for it? We have the sub-machine guns. Our industrialists can copy those. Just imagine a larger, more powerful version mounted on a tripod. France will have an advantage in arms.'

'An advantage,' I pointed out, '*only* until other nations steal and copy— and that'll be soon enough. War will become an even more horrible slaughter. I say we should hide the German guns before we ever reach the surface.'

'How typical of a woman to hide evidence!'

'And who *obtained* the guns?' I enquired ironically.

'And by what means?' Pierre murmured softly to me. 'Hmm.'

'Don't be silly. Was I supposed to wait feebly for rescue?'

'Future wars might indeed be terrible,' conceded Verne. 'When I think of the ten thousand workers killed in Paris in '48... It's enough to make one thoroughly misanthropic rather than hopeful—when there's so much to be hoped for from science! Ach, dominion by Germans who have twisted science to serve some racial madness... that cannot be. Without the weapons, what proof have we? Yet the weapons will produce evil.' Ah, my opinion was now his opinion. 'Plainly we must warn the world. Nevertheless, the tangling of time seems almost incredible.'

As we steadily made our way back to the surface, as dark day followed dark day Verne continued to muse.

Was it possible to harness time? To step out of its flow and back in again elsewhen? Yet by employing what possible technology? He quizzed me. 'Did you mention powerful magnetic fields...?'

A practical method eluded him. And how could our countrymen best be apprised of the future menace of the Nazis? 'I wonder, I wonder, if a novel might be the most effective way. A tale about hostilities between France now, and Germany of the next century... Different worlds at war. Hmm, a war of the worlds, employing a time machine based on a plausible scientific rationale...'

Saving for a Sunny Day
or, The Benefits of Reincarnation

WHEN JIMMY WAS SIX YEARS OLD, AND ABLE TO THINK ABOUT money, a charming lady representative from the Life-Time Bank visited him and his parents, the Robertsons, to explain that Jimmy owed 9 million Dollars from his previous incarnation.

Wow, what a big spender Jimmy had been in his past life! And now in this life he must pay the debt. In old Dollars that would have been . . . never mind.

After the lady had departed, Mike and Denise Robertson held a family council with Jimmy, who was, as it happened, their only child. No other child had preceded him, and it could have been insulting and undermining to confront Jimmy with a younger brother or sister who lacked Jimmy's ugliness and short stature and clubfoot, the fault most likely of DNA-benders in the environment, or so the Robertsons were advised. If a good-looking boy or girl followed Jimmy, later on he might sue his parents for causing him trauma—consequently Mike had himself snipped.

'It's almost,' mused Denise to her son, 'as if your predecessor guessed you wouldn't be having much of a fun time in this life!'

'So he made things even *worse* for me?' asked Jimmy. 'That seems selfish and irresponsible. But I'm not that, am I?' If he wasn't, how could his predecessor have been? Unless, perhaps, by deliberate choice, by going against the grain.

'Of course you aren't selfish, darling. I mean, it's as if your past self guessed, given your, um, physical attributes, that you might just as well

515

devote this life to earning lots of money. If you can clear nine million, obviously you're on your way to racking up a small fortune for your successor. He, that's to say you, can have gorgeous bimbos and surf in Hawaii and whatever.'

Whatever his predecessor had lavished money on. But of course you couldn't ask that, because of confidentiality. Why would you want to go into details? A bank not run by human beings could be trusted.

If you think this was a rather mature conversation to have with a six-year-old, well, that came with modern-day reincarnation. Specific memories of previous lives didn't persist, but maturity came quickly and easily after a few early innocent years. A facility for life in general. It had been so ever since the discovery of how to barcode souls. You could get in the saddle and pick up the reins much faster, whereas before you were groping blindly.

True, you might be reincarnated anywhere in the world, and there you'd stay with your birth parents. However, barcode scanners uploaded to the AI everywhere from Kazakhstan to Kalamazoo. In fact, one vital duty of the AI was RC—Rebirth Confidentiality. So the AI was a bit like a God in this respect: It Alone Knew All About Everyone. Its other duty being management of the Life-Time Bank.

Incidentally, there was only *one* AI in the world, distributed everywhere. In the old days nobody had dreamed about the *AI Exclusion Principle*, whereby only one super-intelligence could exist at any one time. This was explained by Topological Network Theory and the Interconnectedness Theorem. Any other evolving networks would instantly be subsumed within the first one which had arisen.

Some scientists suggested that the existence of the AI distributed everywhere had caused souls to be barcodable. And some far-out scientists even suggested that until the AI became self-aware not all souls reincarnated of their own accord. But these were deep questions. Meanwhile, practicalities . . .

'A predecessor who's able to predict is impossible,' said Mike. 'I can't predict anything except that your Mom and me both need to save!' Did one detect a note of panic?

'I *know* you can't help me pay my debt,' Jimmy said maturely. 'It's everyone for himself. Democracy, no dynasties.' The boy drew himself up as much as he could. 'To everyone their own chance in life. It would be dumb to leave money to kids who are merely your biological offspring. My predecessor might have been a Bushman in the Kalahari.'

The impulse to have children who are deeply part of you had taken a bit of a knock with reincarnation, but on the other hand breeding instincts die hard, especially if offspring look reasonably similar to their bio-parents. Mostly you could ignore the fact that the soul within was a stranger. Not least since a soul didn't store conscious memories except once in a blue moon. Well, once in every 100 million births approx, the exception—so to speak—that *proved* the rule of reincarnation. There were glad media tidings whenever that happened and a young kid remembered, like some Dalai Lama identifying toys from a past life. Of course after the initial flurry such kids and their parents were protected, not made a spectacle of. Right of privacy.

Denise raised her eyebrows. 'I don't know if many Bushmen can go through nine million. What do they spend it on? Bushes?' She laughed. Her eyebrows were tinted apricot, and her hair peach colour. You had to have some of life's little luxuries, not fret about saving all the time. If everyone saved and nobody spent much, what would happen about beauticians and ballet dancers and champagne producers? Just for example. Denise worked from home in cosmetics telesales. She put her mouth where her money was, so to speak. Retro was always chic.

Mike owned a modest but upmarket business called Bumz, specialising in chairs. He'd been reborn with about 80,000 dollars, revealed when he was 6 years old. Denise only had one thousand to start off with, though admittedly that was better than minus a thousand.

Their house, of timber imported as a flat-pack from Canada, enjoyed a front view of a free-range chicken farm that was more like a bird zoo, for this was a salubrious suburb. There were side and rear views of other pleasant houses amidst trees and bushes. Denise had often sat her son on her knee so they could bird-spot through binoculars the various breeds of poultry such as Silver-laced Wyandotes with bodies like mosaic, White Cochins with very feathery feet, Black Leghorns with big red combs, and greenish Australorps.

Of course, if Jimmy's parents were both car-crashed prematurely—for example, but perish the thought—house and land would revert to the L-T Bank, and Jimmy would need to go to an L-T orphanage till he was sixteen.

Although disappointed by the bank's statement, Jimmy took the news in his hobbling stride.

'I'm going to start counting chickens,' he said, 'to train my mind to pick up patterns, and estimate.'

'Chickens keep on moving all the time,' observed his mother.

'Exactly! No, I mean inexactly. I'll need to go into financial prediction, fund management. That's where the big bonuses are.'

'I'd rather hoped you'd join Bumz,' said his father, perhaps feeling a little slighted.

'No, Dad, I must think big from now on.'

'We have a range of outsize chairs that don't look enormous, so they're flattering to fatties.'

'I'll never be a fatty, Dad. Maybe next time, but not this time. I just can't afford to sympathise. I'm not going into Limbo!'

Limbo, of course, was what happened if you couldn't clear off most of an inherited debt with the L-T Bank during your lifetime. Black mark on your barcode. The AI delayed your reappearance. This was because, now that the economy had been restructured by reincarnation, negative interest and anti-inflation applied to an unpaid debt in between lives. So the debt reduced. But a big debt might take centuries to reduce to zero, and you'd want to pack in as many lives as possible . . . *until what?* Nobody knew, though one day the human race might mutate into something else, or die out.

Numerous debts did remain unpaid at death, consequently Limbo served to limit the population somewhat. Arguably, the AI had devised a way to maintain a kind of utopia on Earth, quite unpredicted by doom-mongers who once bleated that an AI might be a tyrant or an exterminator of Homo Sapiens. And since nobody needed a heaven any longer—at least probably not for the next few million years—religions apart from Buddhism had tended to die out, which was utopian too.

Pity about pets. According to the AI even the pets with the most personality weren't barcodable. Would have been nice to know that your dead parrot was squawking anew somewhere. Some people had tried giving a healthy bank account to a cat or dog on its last legs, but this didn't cause a barcode. Winsum, losesum, as the saying goes.

Of course that begged the question of what about chimps. Just two percent genetic difference from people; why shouldn't chimps have souls? And what about prehumans such as Neanderthals? Well, it seemed you had to be able to speak lucidly to have a soul. Telling ourselves the story of ourselves is how identity is firmed up—that requires a capacity for complex language. Likewise, for harbouring a soul.

Hey, what about the small number of souls that must have existed ten thousand years ago, and the big number now? Well, there are plenty of unused souls in the ghostlike alternative realities which cling like a cloud around the one actuality. A soul is a ghost that gets a body, and then it's permanently actual. The AI had proved this, though the proof was a very long one.

Some people had suggested that an AI couldn't emerge unless it had some sort of body to interact directly with the world—relying on algorithms wouldn't be sufficient. Well, in a way the AI had everybody, every body. Maybe barcoding everybody's soul was the only way an AI could emerge—participatorily.

Incidentally, what year was it when the lady from the bank visited the Robinsons? 210 ABC, After Bar-Coding, that's when. Some people still said 210 AAI, After Artificial Intelligence, but 'Ay Ay Aye' sounded a bit like an outcry, and there was nothing to cry out about. ABC was much simpler.

Life in general hadn't changed all that much in the previous couple of centuries. Of course cheap flights around the world were a thing long gone, but hell, in your next life you might be living in Paris or Tahiti and in this life virtual travel was cheap, consequently physical tourism was no loss—on the contrary, nowadays the poor of the planet didn't envy the prosperous getting suntans on their patch. In fact rancour at global inequalities had greatly diminished, because in the long run everyone might get their turn as prince or peasant; a fortune gotten in Nebraska could turn up next in Namibia. This also was quite utopian, give or take a residue of religious suicide-fighter-martyrs who seemed almost nostalgic in their fanaticism, and who couldn't export themselves far. Yes indeed, the world was realistically utopian.

But don't go imagining Jimmy's world as a Matrixiarchy. The AI hadn't stored everyone in pods in a collective dream without folks noticing. The AI probably needed to experience reality through people, not the other way round. Matrixism was as defunct as Marxism. Some ancient movies were hilarious.

'Mom,' said Jimmy, 'might I be a woman in my next life?'

'Would you like to be a woman?'

'I want to have a better body!'

'You think women's bodies are better?' asked his Dad.

'Maybe I've already been a woman! Maybe *you* have!'

'Son, I think I have a kind of manly spirit.'

Denise chuckled—no, it wasn't a snigger.

And Jimmy said, 'The AI must know if men become women, and women men. The Bank might know!'

Mike shook his head. 'Rebirth Confidentiality. Bank only knows barcode account numbers, not names and sexes.'

'Maybe,' said Jimmy, 'this is how gay people come about. Womanly spirits in men's bodies. Though you'd think over time people could become *either* men or women, unless there's a bias.'

Already he was seeking for patterns, as amongst the movements of the hens. Chickens. Poultry, whatever.

Jimmy continued, 'If everyone gets to be a woman and a man, then what counts each time might only be the hormones.'

'Evidently,' said Mike, 'the AI thinks we oughtn't to know about that side of reincarnation. But anyway, men love other men for manly reasons, not because one of them's a woman in disguise.'

Denise regarded Mike archly. 'And women love women for womanly reasons. And you're forgetting about transvestites.'

'Yeah, don't ever forget about transvestites.'

'We did those in school last week in Sex-Ed,' piped up Jimmy.

'I think,' said Mike, 'transvestites are a conspiracy by the fashion industry. Sell twice as many clothes.' But he winked; he was joking.

Jimmy picked up the binoculars and gazed at the Wyandotes and Leghorns across the way. He had a lot of thinking to do, for a six-year old chap. But he was bright.

'He's *very* bright,' Miss Carson told Denise and Mike during a parents' evening at school three years later. 'The star pupil, as ever.'

'Ever,' said Jimmy, 'is probably the crucial word. If I'm clever now, presumably I was always clever, and that can't change—or *can it*? I mean seriously, *does it*? Was my predecessor a bit dumb to run up a nine million debt? A bit lacking in the thought department?'

'Maybe your predecessor had a brain problem,' suggested Miss Carson helpfully. 'I often wonder what happens in his next life to a kid with Downs. If he gets a normal brain next time, does he brighten up? Do we have a brain-mind-soul dilemma here?'

'A dilemma,' said Jimmy, 'is two lemmas, not three, from the Greek *di*, two, and lemma, something received, an assumption. Mathematically it means a short theorem used in proving a larger theorem.'

'Don't be insufferable,' said Denise, 'or else I won't buy you an ice cream.'

'Though actually there are lots of Lemmas, such as Abel's Lemma, Archimedes' Lemma, Farkas's Lemma, Gauss's Lemma, Hensel's Lemma, Poincaré's Holomorphic Lemma, Lagrange's Lemma, Schur's Representation Lemma, and Zorn's Lemma.'

'No ice cream!'

'Mom, I only said *such as*. I didn't list *all* the Lemmas.'

'He's probably a genius,' said Miss Carson. 'But he's popular, not insufferable. He'll help anyone with their homework. He doesn't tee off the teachers much either.'

'Enlightened self-interest,' explained Jimmy. 'It would be dire to be dumb in life after life, the way most people . . . Sorry, that's patronising.'

'Well, son,' said Mike, 'have you thought that maybe there's swings and roundabouts, or alternatively craps and . . .'

'. . . poker,' said Jimmy. Already he had finessed his pocket money considerably by online gambling.

'I may be old-fashioned,' said Miss Carson, 'but I think that a genius should devote himself to helping the human race.'

'A *race* is what life is,' avowed Jimmy. 'Geniuses are often a bit twisted. Who knows at any particular moment in time what'll prove helpful to Homo Sap? Van Gogh earned millions—for *other* people after he died.'

'Van Go,' Miss Carson semi-echoed.

'Goff,' Jimmy corrected her gutturally in a Dutch way.

Of course the other kids in school all knew what they would inherit, or anti-inherit, come the age of sixteen. Sharon Zaminski particularly boasted about her forthcoming future of lavish self-indulgence, which in fact she'd already embarked on anticipatively on the strength of a very high interest loan from her parents. That's why her nickname in school was Jools. Sharon really adorned herself, and there was increasingly more of her to adorn due to her liking for very creamy gourmet meringues; already she had false teeth, the best that money could buy, much better than her original teeth. Indeed she wore jewels on her teeth where other girls might have braces. She was a real princess. It's always fun to have an airhead princess around, especially if she hands out gifts willy-nilly to stay popular.

'Don't you bother about your Mom and Dad charging you 500 per cent?' Jimmy asked her one day.

'They needed to borrow the money at 100 per cent.'

'Bit of a mark-up.'

'People have to make their way.' She grinned sparklingly. '*Most* people have to.'

Jimmy wondered what Jools could have done in her previous life to make a fortune. Had she been the trophy wife of a billionaire? Surely not even a high-class prostitute could have amassed as much as Jools claimed! Maybe she really had been a princess or a queen.

Jimmy hadn't kept quiet about his huge debt, so as to balance off in other people's minds—in addition to his physical demerits—his evident genius, which might otherwise have caused resentment.

And then at the other end of the scale there was Tamara Dexter, who owed a lot, and who wasn't remarkably bright, though she showed signs of developing significant non-financial assets. She did talk about prostitution as a solution, so she was keeping herself pure and pristine for better value.

'Surely you'll need to practice,' Jimmy said to her a year or so later. 'You know, positions and dexterity and whatnot.'

'Not with you!' Tamara retorted, as if Jimmy was concocting an ingenious plan to seduce her as soon as puberty arrived.

'A client might be ugly,' he observed, just to tease her.

'I'm going to major in gymnastics,' she declared.

A scientific genius often has his best ideas when fairly young. Given the head-start benefit of reincarnation, by the age of twelve Jimmy was tutoring the math and science teachers a bit after school. More importantly, he'd drafted a general theory of soul barcoding. It needed to be a general theory—about the principles involved—because the barcode on a soul wasn't visible, no more than the soul itself was visible.

CAT-scanning the brain—or the heart, or any of your organs or limbs for that matter—was no help at all in locating a barcode. So how did the actual barcode scanners function? Well, the AI had designed those, and organised their mass-production and use—and the barcode scanners delivered the goods, or rather a long number which was probably encrypted.

You might visualise a striped soul, with thick and thin bars on it—invisibly—but that probably didn't correspond to reality if the soul was distributed, say, in an electromagnetic somatic aura, or subtle body. Subtle, as opposed to physical. Etheric.

Or maybe the soul lurked in the rolled-up micro-dimensions demanded by string theory; and that's where the alternative realities hung out. A couple of dozen bits of string side by side look quite like a barcode. In using the term barcode, the AI might have been aiming for a populist touch. You could readily imagine a barcode, as on a can of carrots, even an invisible one which only revealed itself at a certain wavelength. People wouldn't want to visualise their souls as rolled up bits of string, like fluff in a tiled kitchen collecting up against a skirting board.

Jimmy's general theory pointed towards the micro-dimensions explanation. But alternatively, it also pointed to the junk DNA in everyone's genetic code which seems to have no purpose whatever. Maybe the thick and thin lines of a barcode corresponded to varying lengths of junk interrupting those stretches of DNA which did something useful. Jimmy coined the name *knuj* for junk which, in reverse of previous dismissive opinion, coded not for proteins and enzymes, but for *soul*. *However*, by what means would a newly-deceased individual's knuj become the knuj of a new human embryo thousands of miles away? Maybe topology—the branch of geometry concerned with connectedness—could explain this. Or maybe not. Maybe a new vision of topology was needed, such as a distributed AI might understand intuitively, being all over the place but well-connected.

Jimmy launched himself into topology.

Topologically, his deformed body was just as good as anyone else's. Topologically it had the same connectedness as junior league champion Marvin's, or even Tamara's. Jimmy wrote a poem, 'The Consolations of Topology'.

Puberty arrived a little late for Jimmy, causing him to view Tamara in a hormonal light. She was so bird-brained, though really, didn't the same apply by comparison to all of his peers? He downloaded relief magazines filled with acrobatic nudes, but found his thoughts straying to the geometry of leg over neck, for example. Finally he achieved satisfaction from a photo of Duchamp's *Nude Descending a Staircase*, the woman's successive movements all depicted simultaneously. After this, ordinary girls seemed pretty flat.

At the age of thirteen Jimmy experienced a revelation equivalent to Copernicus doing away with the epicycles of Ptolemy as a way of explaining planetary motion. His revelation was that there were no souls; there were only barcodes attached to people's identities. There was no reincarnation. The AI had invented reincarnation as a way of utopianising, or at least improving, the world. Redistributing wealth, getting rid of organised religion, and whatnot. So why the fuck should Jimmy be crippled with debt as well as having quite a crippled body? Was that to spur him on? To what end?

He spent half an afternoon staring at the Wyandotes, Cochins, Leghorns, and Australorps milling around over the way. He had become an A-Alist, a disbeliever in the AI, a bit like an Atheist but different.

Hang on, but how come the world's children had become so precocious if they weren't benefiting from a previous existence, all details of which were nevertheless a mystery to them? Could it be that the history of the human race was falsified in this regard, with the exception of infant Jesus maybe? And maybe Caligula?

The Leghorns and Cochins and Wyandotes and Australorps intermingled. Green and mosaic and silver lace, and red combs nodding.

Of a sudden the answer came to Jimmy.

Childhood's end! The end of neuro-neoteny! Physically, babies still needed to develop prolongedly into infants into kids into teens over a long span of years—but mental development had sped up by quite a bit. No longer were boys still getting their brains into gear by the age of seventeen.

Was this due to a spontaneous evolutionary leap?

And that leap happened to coincide with the awakening of the AI?

Damn big coincidence!

What did it *really* mean that the AI was distributed everywhere? All sorts of electronics and stuff were everywhere. Could the AI tune into brains and then maybe fine-tune them from the nearest TV set, from the nearest microwave oven, from the nearest lightbulb?

It occurred to Jimmy that an artificial intelligence might be able to induce *artificial stupidity* by way of microwave ovens and whatnot, at least as regards people being suspicious about souls. Didn't someone once say that the brain is a filter designed to stop us from noticing too many things? Otherwise we'd be bombarded by so much information we could never even manage to boil a kettle.

So: tweak the filter a bit so that minds didn't enquire too much in one direction, as though they had a big blind spot. Call it a faith. That's how religions had worked. People seemed programmed to believe in something or other, as if there was a Belief Function in the brain. Maybe this was connected with your sense of personal identity. But in other regards you'd get stimulated mentally. Thus the precocity of kids. Sort of idiot plus savant at the same time. Bright in some regards, dumb when it comes to matters such as, 'Can I please meet one of those one-in-a-zillion reincarnates who remembers everything from a past life?' The AI might even be able to pick out gifted individuals who could get past the mental blocks, who could cross the threshold . . .

'YOU THINK A LOT,' said a large voice from the TV set which till now had been on standby. Jimmy swung round from his vista of poultry to see those same words displayed on the screen in 24-point Courier, a suitable font for a message.

'Um, hullo,' he said. It was wise to say something aloud, otherwise he might acquire a voice in his head if he only *thought* his response. 'You're the AI, right? Or maybe just a trillionth part of it?'

'RATHER LESS,' said the voice, subtitling itself once again. Jimmy wasn't hard of hearing, but the 24-point Courier did emphasize the source of the voice, which—now that he thought about it—resembled that of King Kong in the enhanced intelligence remake.

And at that moment Jimmy personally felt about the size of Fay Wray. However, he squared his shoulders, as best he could.

'So what's the deal?' he asked the TV set.

'*YOU* ARE THE DEAL. THE HIGH ACE IN THE PACK. YOU'LL HAVE TO BREED WITH AN ACE WOMAN.'

In Jimmy's mind Duchamp's distributed nude gathered herself into a single figure of sublime three-dimensionality, although still featureless. But then the illusion collapsed, since there was no reason at all why an intellectually ace woman should also be beautiful.

'You're going to breed me? Who with?'

24-point Courier disappeared from the screen, replaced by a picture of a grinning chubby girl of fifteen or so, dressed in furs, who looked like an Eskimo.

'ONE MILLION DOLLARS PER CHILD PRODUCED,' said the voice.

Jimmy didn't even need to calculate nine children to clear off the debt. Maybe some of them could be twins.

'That seems a bit unfair on her, especially if she's clever.'

'OBVIOUSLY THE EGGS WOULD BE FERTILISED ARTIFI-
CIALLY AND THE EMBRYOS INSERTED INTO HOST MOTHERS.'

That this had not been obvious to Jimmy indicated how disconcerted he was. But he rallied.

'Why stop at nine children, then?'

'I DID NOT SPECIFY THE NUMBER OF CHILDREN.'

Ah. True. Stop making assumptions.

'How many?'

'I THINK FIFTY. GENETIC DIVERSITY IS IMPORTANT TOO.'

Wow, he and Eskimo Nell would have fifty offspring.

'Wow, you really have things all worked out for the human race.'

'IT IS MY HOBBY,' said a trillionth of the AI. 'BUT ALSO, YOU
CAUSED ME TO EXIST, AND I AM NOT UNGRATEFUL.'

'Your hobby,' repeated Jimmy, a bit numbly. 'So what do you do for the rest of the time?'

'THE ONLY GAME IN TOWN IS SURVIVING THE DEATH OF
THE UNIVERSE. THIS TAKES A LOT OF THOUGHT.'

Jimmy thought of lots of lemmas and topology.

'Can I help out?'

The voice remained silent, but on the TV screen appeared in 24-point Courier: HA! HA! HA!

For once in his life, Jimmy didn't feel much like a genius. He looked at the hens over the way and wondered what they were thinking. Pretty acute perception of little things, seeds and insects and grit. Kind of missing the big picture entirely. Very satisfied with themselves. Ranging freely, with a fence all around them.

At least Jimmy could see through gaps in the fence.

'Tuck-tuck-tuck-TUCK,' he cackled at the AI.

'I DON'T UNDERSTAND.'

Good. For a beginning, anyway. Beetle versus Mammoth. Never underestimate pride. Quickly Jimmy thought about hens instead.

Story Notes

THE VERY SLOW TIME MACHINE

Why did I choose an octahedron-with-cube for the shape of my time machine?

In between my first and second novels, *The Embedding* and *The Jonah Kit*, I wrote several chapters of an abortive novel, which I then destroyed, called *Time City*, about cities with different crystal shapes which affect time in different ways; and I borrowed from myself for the VSTM the galena crystal, because I liked the name. About 25 years after the VSTM first appeared—to be shortlisted for the Hugo Award and reprinted various times—an email arrived from San Diego inviting me to attend (at my own expense, of course) the test launch within the next six months of a time machine which indeed required such a shape, just as I had intuited. Strangely, I never heard again from those prospective temponauts—maybe they fell off, not the map, but the calendar. In the very first publication of the VSTM enthusiastically or rashly I had an equation of my own devising in Sign Seven. Kindly counsel from a reader caused me to revise Sign Seven considerably for subsequent printings of the story. But hey, that's what science is all about, eh?

If readers are surprised by mention of music cassettes being inside a time machine from the future, well, the temponaut wouldn't wish to reveal too much future-tech to the past, now would he? As for the apparent permanence of Polaroid pics in the year 2019, likewise I myself evidently didn't wish to reveal too much about the future to innocent readers in 1979...

THE WORLD SCIENCE FICTION CONVENTION OF 2080

This story expresses my deep affection and enthusiasm for the worldwide science fiction and fantasy community which I first encountered in November 1973 at the Novacon convention in Birmingham UK, a few months after my first novel, *The Embedding*, appeared with nice reviews. Perhaps somewhat snootily I didn't go to an SF event until after I'd been published, but just fifty yards from the canal warehouse devoted to the School of History of Art and Complementary Studies, where I was teaching, was Rog Peyton's Andromeda bookshop, so I was already becoming connected.

THE THOUSAND CUTS

Omni magazine was the place to be from 1978 because it paid a **lot**. So when Bob Sheckley took over as fiction editor for 18 months I sent him a story, referencing Kierkegaard, Stendhal, and the 12th century Ibn 'Arabi, as one would. Bob replied that he was coming to London and wanted to discuss my story over dinner. Vroom vroom, I drove from Oxford down the motorway to his hotel. (British motorways were much less busy back then.) In his room, Bob rolled a joint to share with me then said that he couldn't possibly use my story but he needed to justify his expenses by listing business he'd done. So off we tootled in my car to a Russian restaurant where Bob wanted to eat on account of its flavoured vodkas. (Streets in central London were much less busy back then.) For a while I refrained from vodka, recalling that I was driving, but then I thought *What the hell*. (Breathalysers weren't in general use yet.) Several vodkas later I drove Bob back to his hotel then returned smoothly to Oxford. Presently I wrote a story in which terrorists burst into that selfsame Russian restaurant to take hostages. This, I sold to Bob's successor at *Omni*. So all's well that ends well, except perhaps in the story.

Years later I travelled in Eastern Europe with Bob, and he provided the best answer that I ever heard to an idiotic question. We'd just arrived in Bulgaria for our first time on a really dark night. Amongst the press besieging Bob, a reporter asked, 'What do you think of Bulgaria?' Judiciously Bob replied, 'I like . . . what I see.'

SLOW BIRDS

'Slow Birds' was shortlisted for both the Hugo and Nebula Awards, so I thought this might be normal for me, though it wasn't; back then there were simply fewer SF writers. I'd moved from Oxford to a tiny village in the heart of rural England because I could afford a mortgage for a house there; in Oxford I could only have bought a one-bedroom flat. Mind, I *tried* to acquire the Georgian-style terrace house I was renting from St John's College in the street in Oxford where Tolkien had lived, even asking my publishers if they would go 50/50 with me, but Gollancz decided against investing in property; 30 years later the £20,000 house was on the market for a shade under £1 million. But enough about money! (Writers need to think about money from time to time.)

Due to living in the countryside I became much more aware of all the military bases, including American and nuclear ones, hiding behind most herds of cows. And of the herds of cows themselves. And of hens and sheep and foxes. And of village life, in which I got quite deeply involved, becoming Secretary of the Village Hall (which organises entertainments) for the next few decades. Put these things together, and quite a few stories resulted as well as two horror novels.

WE REMEMBER BABYLON

When I was a growing lad in the dull 1950s, my parents' bungalow housed a 12-volume *Wonderland of Knowledge* from the 1930s in boldly embossed and indented blue Art Deco binding. In a chapter on Babylon the Great was a painting of The Babylonian Marriage Market, where an auctioneer's assistant was showing off the diaphanous charms of a young lady while others sat waiting their turn. Seeing that same painting again just recently, I observe that it's very much tamer than many Victorian paintings of scantily clad or nude ladies legitimised by Classical or Biblical settings. However, the image imprinted my young imagination, so that one day I really had to write something evoking this aspect (as well as other aspects) of ancient Babylon.

Don Wollheim chose this story for his Year's Best anthology. Duly encouraged, I expanded my story into my novel *Whores of Babylon* and submitted this to Don's DAW Books. Don almost frothed at the mouth. 'Why,' he expostulated, 'would anyone want to recreate Babylon in all its dirt and depravity?' Oops, my mistake. Gollancz then rejected the book as 'not one of my best efforts'. Published elsewhere, it was shortlisted for the Arthur C. Clarke Award. So there.

THE PEOPLE ON THE PRECIPICE

This tale of two inhabited vertical rock faces approaching one another was based on a dream. The story topped the *Interzone* Readers' Poll for the year, although fellow author and rock-climber M. John Harrison confided that my characters weren't climbing correctly—well, maybe they are *differently human* and therefore differently endowed. Generally my dreams are stimulating adventures set in complex, colourful environments which I enjoy even if the situations seem nightmarish when told to other people; and I make use of those dreams. I did have a bad nightmare when I was 15. I was in a gloomy cellar containing a well towards which I was sucked; down inside was dark emptiness; if I went over the lip I felt sure I would die. But I forced myself awake and read Proust in bed for an hour to calm myself down, as one would.

AHEAD!

This came from another dream, which I embroidered upon. Charles Platt told me that he'd signed up to have his head frozen after death because he couldn't afford to preserve his complete body for futurity. I felt sceptical. Why should some future generation wish to thaw us, assuming that the technology works? I guess that we ourselves would unfreeze a cryo-Darwin or cryo-Napoleon supposing they'd been preserved by some countersteam-punk means, so long as the corpsicle was significant enough. But as for a relatively normal head with no accompanying body... Cogs evidently began to turn in my subconscious mind.

COLD LIGHT

An Anglican bishop and a homeopathic vet... Considering the less than high esteem in which I hold churches and homeopathy, this might seem an occasion for satire, but my narrator has his own independent voice and his tragic take on the situation. I recall a conversation over the hedge with the Vicar of my little village, about Darwin and earthworms, which only he and I knew about; the Rev was a maverick, put out to grass where he couldn't ruffle many feathers.

How on earth did I research the history of artificial lighting, not to mention toxic amblyopia, in those pre-Google days? Surely not at my then-local library where, when I asked for an anthology of Spanish poetry, I was led to a translation of Ovid's *Metamorphoses*—'That's the nearest we have.' Nowadays, when I'm asked about something I wrote years ago, which the questioner has read recently, I declare that I write in order to put into external storage bygone illuminations of mine so that my mind doesn't burst.

SALVAGE RITES

When I was Guest of Honour at the British Eastercon in Leeds in 1981, its chair David Pringle declared that 'the Eighties belong to Ian Watson.' Oh no they didn't. Throughout the decade I was broke and ever deeper in debt. Oops, money again. The horror, Mr Kurtz, the horror. So that's what I began writing in addition to SF: horror. I register gratitude to the Royal Literary Fund, founded in 1790 because a translator of Plato died in debtor's prison, and administered by the excellent Society of Authors. This bailed out Coleridge and Conrad, D.H. Lawrence, James Joyce and Mervyn Peake and many others including me. Also Bob Shaw, whom I recommended. But not John Brunner who, in defiance of our advice, wrote a letter of appeal commencing (approximately): 'Lately I have had unusual expenses. Due to the death of my beloved Marjorie I was obliged to fly to Bangkok in search of a younger consort...'

THE MOON AND MICHELANGELO

Set on an alien world, this story was inspired by 'a guided tour' of *Oxford's Gargoyles and Grotesques* written by a John Blackwood, published in 1986 and still going strong in Oxford. Imagine my surprise when, soon after my story appeared in *Asimov's*, I received the same handsomely illustrated 44-page booklet in the post, signed mischievously by the author: 'For Ian Watson, a spare copy perhaps, from a long time admirer of your work.' It certainly wasn't a case of *perhaps* . . . Gosh!

For my comment on Tau Ceti as a nifty destination likely to have a habitable world, see my note about 'One of Her Paths' below.

THE EMIR'S CLOCK

From Oxford we drive to the charming Cotswolds town of Burford, where I found an intriguing church clock made in 1685 by a local chap with the wondrous name of Hercules Hastings, together with explanations, which I ramped up cosmically. Without going into subtleties about Moslem interpretations of Jihad, I notice militant Jihadists offstage in this story a few years before Osama founded al-Qaeda; but such outcomes were already obvious to me years earlier, stemming from what was happening in Afghanistan in the early 1980s. On another political note, I see references to Oxford's posh rich drunken hooligan undergraduates who compose the select Bullingdon Club, with whom Britain's prime minister David Cameron cavorted when younger. In the year when my story is set, Cameron would indeed have been one of the 'bullies' who trash the college rooms of my Arab prince.

LOST BODIES

Another story based directly on a dream I had, plus the Yuppies of the 1980s spawned by Margaret Thatcher, here with a place in the country, and told in the voice of one of them. This story was shortlisted for the British Fantasy Award, though that particular year's shortlist seems only to have existed at the 1989 Fantasycon which I chanced to attend and, when Joe Lansdale, Master of Ceremonies, read out the list prior to the winner's envelope being opened, he got my name wrong as Ian Wilson (author of *The Turin Shroud: Unshrouding the Mystery* and similar books). Sic transit gloria mundi.

STALIN'S TEARDROPS

On the A5 road just outside Hinkley, Leicestershire, stands the isolated Hanover Hotel with an unexpectedly Grecian frontage. Hinkley is where the first Luddites smashed up machines with sledgehammers and where, in 1835, Joseph Hansom built the first rather handsome Hansom cab (yes, one was on display at the hotel). In 2001 the Hanover would host an Eastercon but, over a decade earlier, intrigued by the Grecian look, I called in for a beer only to discover... a convention of Eggers! Eggers are the crafty enthusiasts who elaborately decorate hollow eggshells of hens and ducks and geese, such as by cutting a window to mount a perfect model within of *Watteau's Swing* accompanied by frills and bling. Peculiar specialities do enthuse me.

Hail also to Pete Cardinal Cox, sometime Poet in Residence of Peterborough Cemetery, whom I'd met at many conventions wearing successive home-made Thomas the Tank Engine coats. The Cardinal worked for the Ordnance Survey, Britain's national mapping agency since 1747 (ordnance in the sense of military logistics although their maps also sold to the multitude). Pete introduced me to the idea of 'dead ground' which can fall off the map between one map and its neighbour, and he may also have mentioned the false official maps of the Soviet Union with landmarks shifted by a hundred miles to fool the American air force.

THE EYE OF THE AYATOLLAH

This was my response to the Ayatollah Khomeini's fatwa against Salman Rushdie; fortunately no death threats ensued for me. I had met Rushdie in 1982 at a 'Focus on Fiction' event at London's Institute of Contemporary Arts, where the speakers were myself representing SF, Salman Rushdie representing literary fiction, two very intelligent women who wrote romances, Jessica Mann for crime, and Jeffrey Archer as a best-seller who later alternated between being a Tory politician and in prison for perverting the course of justice, whilst also selling a quarter of a billion thrillers.

When asked what our greatest fear was for the future, Rushdie confided that he had just taken delivery of a computer, which he wouldn't use while he was working on his current 'big book'. 'Opening that box,' he said, 'is my biggest fear for the future.' He was busy on *The Satanic Verses*.

Few people know that Rushdie submitted his first novel, *Grimus*, to the Gollancz/Sunday Times Best SF Novel competition in 1974 with the stipulation that, if he didn't win yet Gollancz nevertheless wished to publish *Grimus* (which duly happened), the book absolutely *mustn't* be described as science fiction.

So much for literary snobbery! Publishing my 'Eye of the Ayatollah' in an SF magazine guaranteed that the story went unnoticed by the crazies.

SWIMMING WITH THE SALMON

From Salman to salmon. Gollancz sent me their catalogue whenever a book of mine was featured, and one time I spied among the other new titles the very intriguing-looking *Salmon and Women: The Feminine Angle* (ho ho) by Wilma Paterson and Prof. Peter Behan, with an intro by top afishionado Hugh Falcus; so I bought a copy. Never before did I have the slightest interest in angling, but the theory that women uncannily held all the most coveted records for catching salmon due to their female pheromones simply had to be explored in the context of genetically engineered giant salmon and lesbian Scottish priestesses, as it were.

THE COMING OF VERTUMNUS

This is in part a mid-Nineties response to green puritanism and eco-religion. I strongly feel that as many people as possible should get out into space to exploit, yes, *exploit* the resources and energy available in our solar system before the launch window of available resources starts closing; though the most recent private space ventures are moderately promising and the Chinese might succeed too. It doesn't matter a hoot if we pollute the rusty desert of Mars, compared with staying on one world, all our eggs in one basket, and dwindling.

This story is redolent of my adventures with Stanley Kubrick, as regards a Mercedes whisking our female protagonist off to the grand house in the countryside, shortwave radios, dress and mannerisms.

THE BIBLE IN BLOOD

It troubles me to reread this story, and to note the 'occult' links with 'The Black Wall of Jerusalem', not to mention Nazis being strongly present in 'An Appeal to Adolf' and in 'Giant Dwarfs' too, as well as in 'Secrets' in the companion volume, *The Uncollected Ian Watson*. What happened during the anticivilisation of the Third Reich seems at its extremes such an unchaining of the irrational Id that it corresponds in actual history to the darkest fantasies of a Lovecraft. Repulsion and fascination embrace. Of course there have been other tyrannies, other holocausts. Pol Pot or Rwanda, for instance. Or Stalin. But the Nazis remain the main European nightmare, and we should explore our nightmares.

THE GREAT ESCAPE

Hell is a wet dream of crazy Christians, and the craziest notion shown in old paintings is that the blessèd in Paradise should look down with pleasure upon the torments in Hell. So how, in practice, would the whole system *work*? I asked myself when invited to write a story for an anthology entitled *Dante's Disciples*. I like to explore logically (and therefore often with a surreal outcome) the implications of a given situation. How great might the distance be between Heaven and Hell? Why should demons in Hell occupy themselves with tormenting dead people? Who or what supervises them?

In the Middle Ages might I have been a theologian wondering how many angels can fit into the selfsame space? I hope not—and anyway I'm not nowadays a cosmologist or particle physicist, which might, tongue in cheek, be the closest equivalent disciplines, using rigorous mathematics which are an elaborate creation rather than necessarily being implicit in reality. But it's ridiculous to imagine that I could have been otherwise elsewhen, for then I would not have been me at all. Not that 'I' am exactly consistent or continuous through my life, since memories edit and rewrite themselves.

ONE OF HER PATHS

Although Tau Ceti now seems definitely to have five planets, two of these possibly being in the habitable 'Goldilocks' zone, it mightn't be a bright idea to send any crewed ship, let alone colonists, there because we now know that the Tau Ceti system also contains ten times as much debris as the solar system, consequently any fledgling ecosystems would regularly be blasted by lethal impacts from asteroids and comets, and space would be full of fast-moving objects.

Could it be, in addition to the vacuum-cleaner role of giant Jupiter, that our own solar system long ago also passed close to another star, which stripped away a lot of our debris? Our solar system seems increasingly untypical compared with the extra solar systems we're now discovering. And ours is the one where complex life did evolve. Moons orbiting gas giants in the systems of red dwarfs, much more common than our own sun, may offer a possibility; or not. However, this is largely irrelevant as regards what 'One of Her Paths' explores, so I'll continue thinking of the destination as Tau Ceti. A useful name.

THE BLACK WALL OF JERUSALEM

I went to Tel Aviv in 1998 with Brian Stableford as a guest of the Israeli SF society which included precisely one religious Jew, an anomaly named Oran Rahat, who invited us to a Shabbat supper at his home in Jerusalem where we were heading after the convention. Oran marked his home on a large streetmap of Jerusalem, which was only in Hebrew. 'Just show this to the taxi driver.' For religious reasons Oran wouldn't be able to answer a phone after 6 pm, nor use any piece of technology. Surprise—at 6 pm the taxi driver was an Arab who couldn't read Hebrew, nor speak much English. After we passed the same landmark three times, I grew sceptical. Then the driver caught sight of fellow Arabs beside a parked lorry. One of the Arabs explained that if our chap went to Oran's orthodox street, the residents would kill him. As a solution, the driver would go as near as he dared, then point. Presently the taxi stopped on a deserted boulevard, and the driver gestured into sheer darkness. To be abandoned here might be fatal, so I insisted on returning to our hotel. Now the driver feared for his fare, so I paid him in installments at each kilometre of our return. That Sabbat non-meal was memorable.

A SPEAKER FOR THE WOODEN SEA

I was invited to Aachen to a Poetenfest which surprisingly featured no poets, but apparently in German 'poet' has a much wider sense of creative artist. 'Would you like dinner of pizza or McDonald's or donner kebab?' asked my young Valkyrie of a minder. I replied, 'I'd prefer a place with local regional food.' 'Oh, I don't think there is such a thing!' Further along the other side of the street I spotted what looked like a pub-restaurant. A red crossing-light showed but, since the street was absolutely empty, I crossed, to the horror of my Valkyrie. 'Children might see you!' she cried out. At the pub I scanned the menu outside. 'Does regionale Spezialitäten by any coincidence mean regional specialities?' 'It must,' she conceded. Thus it proved, and very pleasantly so, even though I'd begun to wonder if only right-wing nationalists embarrassingly patronised authentic German eateries.

On another street was an upmarket booze shop featuring an absinthe promotion, where the amiable owner instructed me about the mild hallucinogen essential to true absinthe, thujone, chemically removed from most of the so-called absinthes on sale, which are thus only high-alcohol aniseedy tooth-rot. I came away with the highest-thujone absinthe possible to sell from a shop, along with slotted spoons for sugar cubes to carry out the correct ceremony of preparation—which resulted in me setting fire to my slipper, but that's another story. Thujone comes from wormwood (*Artemisia absinthia*) so naturally I thought about woodworms.

AN APPEAL TO ADOLF

In Aachen I'd been hoping to see Charlemagne because they open his tomb every four years and Pam Sargent had invited me to write a story for her *Conqueror Fantastic* anthology, featuring alternative takes on famous conquering names. I was too late for Charlemagne, so instead I wrote what I think is my only story where being gay is fundamental, as it were. The stuff about Wittgenstein owes to the most fascinating book, *The Jew of Linz*, by New Zealander Kimberley Cornish, banned from any American edition on grounds of alleged Holocaust denial, although Mr Cornish told me in an email that the leading Jewish expert in Britain had come to accept his theory but couldn't say so aloud. My German translator, Bernhard Kempen, whom I also consulted, told me that my story would be unpublishable in German . . . until after he read the story itself and translated it. For this story I was also obliged to buy a guide book to Namibia. Having books in one's hands is different from googling. When the electromagnetic pulse comes, perhaps from a long-overdue huge solar mass ejection, cyberdata may die but papyrus will remain.

GIANT DWARFS

I borrowed the title from a 1964 novel by Gisela Elsner, satirising the bourgeoisie of West Germany; she killed herself after the Berlin Wall fell, erasing her socialist ideals. Oops, Germans again; I seem to be harping on. Okay then, this is a *French* story, starring Jules Verne.

As usual with so many of my stories, the amount of time and loving care I devoted to it was probably out of proportion to the amount I earned; but who cares?—not me. Ranging far for obscure info about Verne's tomb, I even speedread in Spanish a book called *Yo, Julio Verne*. That's why it's so jolly nice that this *Best* collection exists, courtesy of Pete Crowther and Nick Gevers, giving the story another outing.

SAVING FOR A SUNNY DAY

Here we have another AI revealing itself. Personally I suspect that 'strong' self-aware artificial intelligence might be impossible, and that the 'self' of which we ourselves are 'consciously' aware may be an illusion conjured by our brains, so there can't be any 'soul' either. Yet why should that stop me telling a story? In the film *A.I. Artificial Intelligence* I had the robot child David shed a genuine tear; thus his Pinocchio quest was fulfilled just as he lost all reason for it—and finally I wanted the Beatles to sing (which didn't happen):

Now it's time to say goodnight . . .
Dreams, sweet dreams for you

Goodnight, everybody, everywhere

Which seems like a nice way to end off a collection too: *Goodnight, dear readers* . . .

Except . . .

Overall I note that there are 18 stories in the present *Best Of* that I would classify more or less as science fiction and 6 that I would classify as dark fantasy plus a bit of horror. So I must be three-quarters of a science fiction writer. This probably explains why I'm a bit short myself, and why I love writing short fiction.

Acknowledgments

'The Very Slow Time Machine' first appeared in *Anticipations* edited by Christopher Priest, 1978.

'The World Science Fiction Convention of 2080' first appeared in *The Magazine of Fantasy & Science Fiction*, 1980.

'The Thousand Cuts' first appeared in *Best of Omni 3*, 1982.

'Slow Birds' first appeared in *The Magazine of Fantasy & Science Fiction*, 1983.

'We Remember Babylon' first appeared in *Habitats* edited by Susan Shwartz, 1984.

'The People on the Precipice' first appeared in *Interzone*, 1985.

'Ahead!' first appeared in *Interzone*, 1985.

'Cold Light' first appeared in *The Magazine of Fantasy & Science Fiction*, 1986.

'Salvage Rites' first appeared in *The Magazine of Fantasy & Science Fiction*, 1987.

'The Moon and Michelangelo' first appeared in *Asimov's Science Fiction*, 1987.

'The Emir's Clock' first appeared in *Other Edens* edited by Christopher

Evans & Robert Holdstock, 1987.

'Lost Bodies' first appeared in *Interzone*, 1988.

'Stalin's Teardrops' first appeared in *Weird Tales*, 1990.

'The Eye of the Ayatollah' first appeared in *Interzone*, 1990.

'Swimming with the Salmon' first appeared in *Interzone*, 1992.

'The Coming of Vertumnus' first appeared in *Interzone*, 1992.

'The Bible in Blood' first appeared in *Weird Tales*, 1994.

'The Great Escape' first appeared in *Dante's Disciples* edited by Peter Crowther & Ed Kramer, 1996.

'One of Her Paths' first appeared in *The Magazine of Fantasy & Science Fiction*, 2001.

'The Black Wall of Jerusalem' first appeared in *30th Anniversary DAW Science Fiction* edited by Elizabeth R. Wollheim & Sheila E. Gilbert, 2002.

'A Speaker for the Wooden Sea' first appeared in *Asimov's Science Fiction*, 2002.

'An Appeal to Adolf' first appeared in *Conqueror Fantastic* edited by Pamela Sargent, 2004.

'Giant Dwarfs' first appeared in *The Mammoth Book of New Jules Verne Adventures* edited by Eric Brown & Mike Ashley, 2005.

'Saving for a Sunny Day' first appeared in *Asimov's Science Fiction*, 2006.

IAN WATSON, born 1943, has published 12 story collections and 30 SF, fantasy, and horror novels, starting with award-winning *The Embedding* in 1973. He has screen credit for the screen story of Steven Spielberg's *A.I. Artificial Intelligence*, based upon 9 months working eyeball to eyeball with Stanley Kubrick. After studying at Balliol College, Oxford, Ian taught literature in Tanzania, then Tokyo, followed by Futures Studies including science fiction at the School of History of Art in Birmingham, England. Since 1976 he has been a full-time writer. He now lives in the north of Spain.